The Editors

NELLIE Y. MCKAY is Evjue-Bascom Professor of American and African-American Literature at the University of Wisconsin, Madison. She is the author of *Jean Toomer—the Artist: A Study of His Literary Life and Work, 1894–1936*; editor of *Critical Essays on Toni Morrison*; and associate editor of the *African American Review*. She is a co–general editor of *The Norton Anthology of African American Literature*.

FRANCES SMITH FOSTER is Charles Howard Candler Professor of English and Women's Studies at Emory University. Her books include *Written by Herself: Literary Production by African American Women, 1746–1892*; *Minnie's Sacrifice: Sowing and Reaping*; *Trial and Triumph: Three Rediscovered Novels by Frances Ellen Watkins Harper*; and *Witnessing Slavery: The Development of the Antebellum Slave Narrative*. She is an editor of *The Norton Anthology of African American Literature* and coeditor of the *Oxford Companion to African American Literature*.

A NORTON CRITICAL EDITION

Harriet Jacobs

INCIDENTS IN THE LIFE OF A SLAVE GIRL

CONTEXTS

CRITICISM

Edited by

NELLIE Y. McKAY

UNIVERSITY OF WISCONSIN, MADISON

FRANCES SMITH FOSTER

EMORY UNIVERSITY

W • W • NORTON & COMPANY • *New York* • *London*

The text of this book is composed in Electra
with the display set in Bernhard Modern.
Composition by Publishing Synthesis Ltd., New York.
Manufacturing by Maple-Vail Book Group.
Book design by Antonina Krass.

Library of Congress Cataloging-in-Publication Data

Jacobs, Harriet A. (Harriet Ann), 1813–1897.
Incidents in the life of a slave girl : contexts, criticism / Harriet Jacobs; edited
by Nellie Y. McKay, Frances Smith Foster.
p. cm.—(A Norton critical edition)
Includes bibliographical references.

ISBN 0-393-97637-8 (pbk.)

1. Jacobs, Harriet A. (Harriet Ann), 1813–1897. 2. Slaves—United States—
Biography. 3. Women slaves—United States—Biography. 4. Slaves—United
States—Social conditions. I. McKay, Nellie Y. II. Foster, Frances Smith. III.
Title.

E444.J17 2000
305.5'67'092—dc21

[B]   00-056877

W. W. Norton & Company, Inc., 500 Fifth Avenue, New York, N.Y. 10110
www.wwnorton.com

W. W. Norton & Company Ltd., Castle House, 75/76 Wells Street,
London W1T 3QT
5 6 7 8 9 0

Contents

Criticism

Introduction

American literary history is rife with stories of writers who achieved prominence only long after their time. No less illustrious figures than Herman Melville, Henry James, Edgar Allan Poe, Emily Dickinson, and Margaret Fuller experienced that fate. These writers, overlooked by their generations, gained laudable recognition from writers and critics who came after them. Not surprisingly then, the reputations of a large number of earlier African American writers, who in their time, like all others in their group, were marginalized in American society as a whole, followed a similar path. While changing literary trends and tastes were largely responsible for the recuperation of the careers of many white writers previously ignored by the literary world, it took massive social changes in this country, beginning in the 1960s, and the direct action of a black community outraged at the historical white treatment of African Americans in America to set in motion the recovery of many lost or forgotten black writers of the eighteenth through the mid-twentieth century. This recovery, combined with the efforts of a cross-racial group of scholars and critics, led to a complete reconstruction of the landscape of American literary history by the end of the twentieth century.[1] Harriet Jacobs, a former slave who published *Incidents in the Life of a Slave Girl, Written by Herself* in 1861 under the pseudonym Linda Brent, is one such African American author whose long-neglected text's coming to light in the 1970s has contributed significantly to the new history.

Jacobs was born in Edenton, North Carolina, in 1813, to slave parents Delilah and Daniel Jacobs; Daniel was a skilled and highly valued carpenter. The couple had different but benevolent owners, who respected their union. As a result they were able to provide a family situation for Harriet and her brother, John (William),[2] who was two years younger than his sister. In addition, the children were also fortunate in having a supportive extended family in their maternal grandmother, Molly Horniblow (Aunt Martha); her older son, Mark Ramsey (Uncle Phillip); her daughter, Betty (Aunt Nancy); and her younger son, Joseph (Uncle

---

1. Although the reference here is specific to African American literature, the reconstruction of American literary history that began in the 1960s incorporates the literatures of America's many previously marginalized ethnic and cultural groups. African Americanists, however, were the first group of scholars to speak out for their inclusion in the canon.
2. Names in parentheses in the introduction are the fictive names that narrator Linda Brent uses to conceal the identities of the people whose lives touched Harriet Jacobs's through the early 1860s.

Benjamin). As a consequence of these favorable circumstances, unlike the majority of slave children, Harriet was oblivious to her status as a slave during the first six years of her life. The sudden deaths of both her parents, her mother's in 1819 and her father's in 1826, changed her world. At first, she lived in the home of her mother's owner, Margaret Horniblow, where although Harriet was aware of her social position, her material circumstances did not change. Her mistress even taught her to read and gave her moral instructions. But in 1825 Margaret Horniblow died, and in her will she left the twelve-year-old slave girl to her three-year-old niece, Mary Matilda Norcom (Emily Flint, later Mrs. Dodge). Then Harriet and her brother were placed under the guardianship of their new owner's father, Dr. James Norcom (Dr. Flint), who was a well-known and well-respected physician in the community but whose lecherous behavior toward Harriet soon provided the catalyst that "ended her happy days" by awakening the pubescent girl to the realities of slave women's lives.

Incidents in the Life of a Slave Girl, the first full-length narrative written by a former slave woman in America, is a record of events and experiences of slavery seen through the eyes of the young Harriet during the years she lived in captivity in Edenton, through her escape, when she becomes a fugitive in the North at age twenty-nine, and concluding soon after a northern white friend buys her freedom in 1852. A large part of the drama in the book focuses on the time between Jacobs's mid-teen years and her late twenties, when she was the object of James Norcom's unrelenting sexual pursuit. Using her body as the source of her literary authority, she demonstrated the nature of one of the most egregious evils of the peculiar institution by recording her account movingly and with the passion of a human being who understood slavery as a moral wrong perpetuated against one group of powerless people by another group made more powerful by dint of the ideology of racial inferiority and superiority.

Incidents addressed an implied audience of northern white women with lives bound by codes of the cult of true womanhood. This is not to suggest that African Americans, especially women, did not buy and read books like Jacobs's for their own instruction, only that in her text, Jacobs appealed directly to a group of other women from whom she hoped for a compassionate hearing and for an understanding of the far-reaching effects of slavery, especially of how it linked together the sexual defilement of slave women and the violation of the natural laws of mother/child relationships. She had no illusions that this was anything other than a difficult group for a fugitive slave like her to convince, for as a woman who had never been married and who chose motherhood voluntarily, her life was outside of the frame that automatically claimed sympathetic responses from them. She understood the risk involved in revealing her sexual transgressions in her narrative and in defending her deliberate choice to sacrifice female virtue to the conviction that the result of her decision would deliver a significant blow to the slave master's will to control the mind and body of his female slave. For we believe, as Jacobs must have, that her struggle with Norcom had less to do with sex than with her refusal to submit to his will. Thus, Jacobs fought her struggles for black freedom on different territory from that chosen by other black women. While slave men used graphic images in their writings to expose the revolting nature of the sexual harassment and brutality that slave owners visited upon slave women, in general, women writing about their lives in slavery avoided the topic as much as possible. Instead, in their oral and written self-representations, women foregrounded their strengths, achievements, and the support they received from family and community members as the sources of their survival. Jacobs's strategy, recorded through a manipulation of the conventions of the popular sentimental fiction of her day, focused on her working behind the scenes with the help of a cross-racial, cross-gendered, cross-generational community that protected her interests to thwart Norcom's designs on her and to outwit him by securing her freedom and her children's safety from him. The success of her efforts offers a compelling case for the effectiveness of literally facing down a great evil in the system.

When she published *Incidents* in 1861 Harriet Jacobs was already forty-eight years old and had been out of the South for nineteen years. She had lived in New York and Massachusetts periodically and traveled to England twice during the pre–Civil War years. Her first visit was in 1845, the same year that Frederick Douglass made his first trip there. Although a fugitive slave too, Douglass was already a prominent voice in the abolitionist movement. Both Douglass and Jacobs, who seem not to have been aware of each other then, took these trips out of the fear of capture and of being remanded to slavery. Jacobs returned to England in 1858 in a futile attempt to find a publisher for her book and made a third visit there in 1868 to raise funds for two of her postwar projects. In the years before the war, and especially before 1852, when she became legally free, Jacobs supported herself and her children through domestic employment and did very little to attract attention to herself. However, by the late 1840s, she was well known to such prominent abolitionist figures as Amy and Isaac Post, in whose Rochester, New York, home she lived for almost a year between 1849 and 1850, when she was fleeing Norcom's persistent attempts to retrieve her as his property. There she worked in the Anti-Slavery Office and Reading Room set up by her brother, John. In New York, with her employers, Nathaniel Parker Willis (Mr. Bruce), a journalist and writer; his first wife, Mary Stace Willis (Mrs. Bruce), who died in 1845; and later Cornelia Grinnel Willis (the second Mrs. Bruce), Jacobs was reticent about discussing her slave condition because although both women were sympathetic to her situation, she suspected that Mr. Willis was unsympathetic to the plight of fugitives.

Nevertheless, it was Cornelia Grinnel Willis who paid the purchase price for Jacobs's freedom in 1852. Persistent to the last that no one should have to "buy" Jacobs's freedom, because her human status entitled her to it, Cornelia Grinnel assured Jacobs that she had no claim to ownership of Jacobs and that her action was taken only to release Jacobs from her harassers. Although almost a decade had passed between the time of Grinnel Willis's "purchase" of her and the completion of her book, Jacobs, in recalling her sentiments at the time, still seemed unreconciled to the exchange of money made for her freedom. Although she understood Mrs. Willis's generous intentions, as the recipient of such largess, Jacobs considered herself bound to her former employer by the compulsory bonds of "[l]ove, duty, [and] gratitude."

Although she knew that Jacobs was sensitive about revealing the events of her southern past to the public, between 1852 and 1853, Amy Post, a former Quaker, believing that such an account would be useful to the abolition movement and other fugitives, suggested to Jacobs that she write the story of her life in slavery. Jacobs, not anxious to expose her past in this way, held back for a while, but eventually, encouraged by Post, she agreed to do so. Cornelia Willis suggested the effort was more likely to succeed if the services of an accomplished writer such as Harriet Beecher Stowe, to whom Jacobs could dictate her narrative, were enlisted to do it. Unfortunately, Stowe had no interest in serving as Jacobs's scribe and condescendingly offered instead to use some of the material as part of another text she was working hard to complete: *The Key to Uncle Tom's Cabin*. Correspondences between Mrs. Willis, Amy Post, Harriet Beecher Stowe, and Jacobs did not resolve the issue to Jacobs's satisfaction, and by 1853 she decided to write her story herself. In preparation for such a bold venture, that summer, identifying herself only as "A Fugitive Slave," she wrote three letters giving personal accounts of the cruelties of slave life in the South and published them in the *New York Tribune*. Meanwhile, although she had heavy responsibilities in the Willis household, she wrote *Incidents*. However, as a result of her distrust of Nathaniel Willis, she did her writing surreptitiously. The secrecy made it difficult for her to find adequate time for the project, but she persisted. In a letter to Amy Post, probably written in March 1854, she spoke of the book as a "chrysalis" that she despaired would ever become a butterfly, and wished she would fall into a Rip Van Winkle sleep to awaken as "Witch Topsy."[3] In spite of the difficulties, she completed the manuscript by 1858 and began a search to arrange for its publication. This also proved difficult to accomplish when her trip to England in 1858 "to sell the book" failed and two American publishers with interests in handling it suffered bankruptcy shortly after agreeing to

3. Quoted from *Incidents in the Life of a Slave Girl*, ed. Jean Fagan Yellin (Cambridge: Harvard UP, 1987) 238.

take on the project. Finally, in 1861, she bought the stereotyped plates of the manuscript and found a printer who enabled her to publish it that year. An English edition, *The Deeper Wrong*, appeared the following year.

After 1862, in Washington, D.C.; Alexandria, Virginia; and Savannah, Georgia, Jacobs, joined by her daughter, Louisa Matilda, turned her efforts toward work that benefited the recently freed slaves and their children. The work included distributing clothing to the needy, providing health care, establishing schools, and teaching. In 1865 and 1867 she visited Edenton (James Norcom had died in 1850 and her grandmother, in 1858), where she continued her good works. In 1868 she traveled to England for the last time, to raise funds for an orphanage and a home for the aged in Savannah. In 1870 she lived in Cambridge, Massachusetts, but returned to Washington by 1885 and died there in 1897. Jacobs, her brother, John, and her daughter are buried in Mount Auburn Cemetery, in Cambridge.

When the 1973 edition of *Incidents* appeared, and for several years after, it generated a controversial debate among scholars who disputed the validity of its authorship and its authenticity as a slave narrative. Jean Fagan Yellin's work was the first to break through the debate and conclusively prove not only that Linda Brent was Harriet Jacobs, but also that she wrote her own text, and that feminist writer Lydia Maria Child was only the editor who arranged parts of it. Through painstaking archival research in North Carolina; Washington, D.C.; New York City; Rochester, New York; Boston, Massachusetts; and Ann Arbor, Michigan, Yellen uncovered personal and published correspondences between Jacobs and her friends, articles in newspapers about her work and her book, and various other documents that verified claims of her ownership of the text. The editors of this edition of *Incidents*, like scholars and readers everywhere, are indebted to Yellin's meticulous work and her patience, which made possible the first scholarly edition of this text, published in 1987.

In addition to the introductory materials and a copy of the 1861 text of the narrative, this edition of *Incidents* includes two additional sections: "Contexts" and "Criticism." The editors divide "Contexts" into three parts. The first contains responses to *Incidents* at the time of its original publication, the second, selections from Jacob's other writings, and the third, a small mixed sample of documents that offer additional insights into Harriet Jacobs's world. Among the "Contemporary Responses" we have included two letters that endorsed the book: one, written by the black abolitionist William C. Nell, appeared in the *Liberator* (21 January 1861), the journal published by the white abolitionist William Lloyd Garrison; the other is by Lydia Maria Child (4 April 1861), addressed to the New England poet and abolitionist John Greenleaf Whittier. Three announcements/advertisements for it appeared in the *Anti-Slavery Bugle* (unsigned, 9 February 1861), the *Liberator* (William C. Nell, 18 February 1861), and the *Christian Recorder* (unsigned, 11 January 1862).

In including "Selections from Jacobs's Other Writings," the editors hope to provide additional evidence of Jacobs as a *writer*, not only the narrator of an edited self-history. The selections demonstrate her ongoing commitment to the antislavery movement even when she was no longer at risk for capture and reenslavement and to her self-appointed mission to educate and do whatever she could for the former slaves and their children. These writings include two of the three letters she published in the *New York Tribune* in 1853; two 1853 letters and another from sometime in the 1860s to her close friend Amy Post; a letter she wrote to William Lloyd Garrison that appeared in the *Liberator* in 1862; an 1863 letter to the Reverend Sella Martin, published in the *Black Abolitionist Papers*; an 1864 letter to Lydia Maria Child that appeared in the *National Anti-Slavery Standard* while she was in Alexandria, Virginia, where she and Louisa Matilda were teaching; a short report she made on the progress of her school in Alexandria, printed in the *Freedmen's Record*; another on the same topic written from Savannah; and her "Appeal" to the English for funds to establish a home for orphans in that city. Jacobs's 1853 letters to the *New York Tribune* bore the signature "A Fugitive Slave." We were unable to locate the third *Tribune* letter, and to our knowledge no one else has either. In the first, Jacobs rebuts the assertions of the former first lady Julia Tyler, who a few days before, on June 19, had published an article in the *Tribune* on the positive effects of slavery on the black family. Her second letter is also a rebuttal aimed at an opinion circulating in the news media that slaves were treated fairly in North Carolina. Her oppositional eyewitness account describes the brutal murder of a runaway slave, which was not an unusual event in that state.

The seven items in "Jacobs's World" include two letters from Lydia Maria Child to Harriet Jacobs concerning the preparation of *Incidents* for publication; published information on the progress of her school in Alexandria; her eulogy prepared and delivered by the renowned Reverend Francis J. Grimke of the Fifteenth Street Presbyterian Church in Washington, D.C.; and a chapter from Nathaniel Willis's *The Convalescent* (1859), the first selection in the section. Jacobs distrusted Willis's sentiments toward slavery, and his public "Letter" on "Negro Happiness In Virginia" indicates that he gave her good reason for her feelings. "Negro Happiness" is a picturesque description of slave life in the Old Dominion, a precursor to what later became the popular Plantation Tradition in southern literature. Here Willis suggested that in general, by freeing them from "the monster and nightmare" of the responsibility to make a living for themselves, slavery had positive effects on the dispositions of slaves. As evidence of this hypothesis he writes that on a trip to Virginia he had an opportunity to observe slaves in their cabins as well as to see a group of them during their transport from Virginia to Arkansas. Across age groups, he found them to be consistently "ingeniously" courteous, polite, good-humored, and possessing "the look of easy, care-for-nothing happiness" missing among the white working classes. Seemingly neither overworked nor physically abused, in the evenings on the plantations, they had ample food, made their own music, and devised their own entertainments. With no beds in the cabins, when tired, they stretched themselves out on the ground in their clothes and went to sleep. They were a happy group. In three days of travel in the region, the only sad situation among black people that Willis encountered was in a remote cabin where the widow of a free negro [sic] lived in dire poverty with her children, her husband having only recently been hanged for murder. Yet, even surrounded by squalor and poverty, hunger, illness, emaciated bodies and nakedness, the child "bundled in rags" to whom he handed the few coins he felt moved to give to the group rewarded him with a "more beautiful smile than . . . ever was born in a palace."

The world that *Incidents in the Life of a Slave Girl* entered in 1973 was very different from the world that it will be a part of in the 2000s.[4] In 1981, when Jean Fagan Yellin published "Written by Herself: Harriet Jacobs' Slave Narrative," which qualifies her as the founding mother of modern criticism on Jacobs's text and which leads off the "Criticism" section in this edition, literary interpreters and historians were still arguing over the proper discipline for autobiography, while many of today's most insightful scholars writing on *Incidents* were just getting ready to enter college. In the 1980s and early 1990s, the immediate followers of Yellin's lead, seeking to make Jacobs's achievement widely known, were also burdened with creating the new fields of intellectual inquiry in African American and women's literature and history. They turned their attention mainly to defining and making known the major themes in Jacobs's text. Nevertheless, they produced a significant body of work on which many others have been building for more than a decade. In this time, increased interest in *Incidents* has led to a broad proliferation of significant criticism on this work. Notably, scholars from a variety of disciplinary areas with wide-ranging critical curiosities now engage this text within the provinces of their individual fields. The editors of this edition seek to give readers a small sample of the range of these approaches to, and the differences in perspectives on, *Incidents* that are now part of the

---

4. *Incidents* entered the academic world with the publication of the Harcourt Brace Jovanovich edition in 1973 and was widely adopted in African American and women's studies classes. Editors of that volume could not have known then that later in the decade there would be an energetic sprouting of scholarship on Jacobs and *Incidents*. Their printing was quickly superceded by the Harvard University Press scholarly edition published in 1987. Since then, readership and critical interest in this text, already a classic in black literature, have continued to grow rapidly.

current discourse. To do this, the final section of this edition, "Criticism," contains eleven essays by a number of literary scholars, as well as a philosopher, two historians, and a scholar in religious studies. Among the authors of these essays, even in the same field of inquiry, critical modes differ and new interpretations expand the boundaries of traditional literary studies.

Almost before anyone else did, historian Jean Fagan Yellin believed that *Incidents in the Life of a Slave Girl* was a bona fide autobiographical text written by its subject. Yellin's "Written by Herself: Harriet Jacobs' Slave Narrative" (1981) was one of the first publications to state unequivocally that Harriet Jacobs, a slave woman in the South who escaped to the North before the Civil War, was the author of *Incidents*, and that the narrative was not fiction. Yellin thus opened up the conversation that has made Jacobs a serious figure in African American literature. In this essay, Yellin outlines the nature of her search for the truth of the genesis of the text in order to dispel further debate on that aspect of its existence. Much of the evidence she uses comes from letters between Jacobs and the activist Amy Post and from antislavery newspapers and other documents in archival holdings. Yellin's essay also includes the story behind Jacob's brief mediated exchange with Harriet Beecher Stowe, whose attitude toward the former fugitive slave angered Jacobs very much. "Written by Herself" set in motion the full recovery of Harriet Jacobs and her writings into history and literature in the twentieth century.

In "Spiritual Purity and Sexual Shame: Religious Themes in the Writings of Harriet Jacobs," published in 1987, Professor of Church History Ann Taves explores the former slave's narrative for insights into the religious life of its author. Taves points out that although Jacobs often comes to this subject indirectly, mainly through her focus on shame, remorse, and purity, she is one of a small number of former slaves who address their religious lives in their texts. Jacobs more overtly shares her observations of the religious activities of other slaves and her criticisms of the southern white church with her readers than she reveals her own beliefs in this area. Yet, she appears to have accepted Christianity, if critically: she refused to join the southern church because of its double standard of treatment toward black and white women.

Taves suggests that in the textual unfolding of her relationships with her mother, grandmother, and first mistress, Jacobs makes a connection, as did many in her time, between purity and spirituality. The question for Taves is whether, given the complicated literary conventions of the narrative (its slave narrative and sentimental novel traditions), Jacobs's many protestations of shame and her consistent affirmation of the virtues of purity were associated with her personal spiritual dilemma or appeared in her narrative for conventional convenience. Drawing on the work of Erik Erikson and Helen Lynd, among others, Taves critiques

Jacobs's language of sin and confession as the outcome of the shame she feels for having violated the sexual and religious ideals of her grand-mother, her mother, and her kind mistress. Taves concludes that Jacobs never overcame her need for the forgiveness her grandmother withheld from her for the difficult choices she made and that her narrative con-stitutes a public confession in her ongoing search for self-esteem.

Literary critic Valerie Smith's "Form and Ideology in Three Slave Narratives," also published in 1987, engages the Jacobs narrative along with two male slave narratives: Frederick Douglass's *Narrative of the Life of Frederick Douglass, An American Slave, Written by Himself* and *The Interesting Narrative of the Life of Olaudah Equiano, Written by Himself*. Smith examines these narratives against a background of external inter-ventions, such as the active presence of the influences of authenticating documents, amanuenses, and editors in the preparation of the published stories of slaves. Such mediation, she asserts, made their productions seem to express the viewpoints of others rather than those of slaves. For even when a narrative, as does each of those she studies, announces it was written by a slave, that slave's claim to authorship was questionable. In addition, the hybrid structure of the form, a mixture of history, autobiog-raphy, and fiction, raises unique questions of interpretation.

Smith holds that, for all of these disadvantages, Jacobs and those with whom Smith associates her, tested the limits of the prescribed slave nar-rative formula and succeeded to a large degree in transforming its con-ventions to create images that enabled them to leave their peculiar imprints on their individual stories. Jacobs, even more constrained than her male counterparts because of her gender, manipulated the senti-mental tradition to find her own voice in speaking of her particular vul-nerability: that of sexual oppression. With great ingenuity, she made use of the current tradition in women's writings to exploit the reality of the small spaces she was forced to occupy. In her control of narrative, she punctuated the literal and figurative structures of that form to seize valu-able advantages from it. Smith observes that Jacobs's final escape from slavery was achieved through a progression of movements from one small space to another, and if her influences in each were minimal, they nevertheless gave her incremental degrees of control.

Smith shows in her critique both the weaknesses in how Jacobs made use of the sentimental tradition and, conversely, how it helped her to get her message across. Jacobs knew she was more unlike the white heroines in those stories than like them, as she often implied in her address to them, and expresses that sentiment at the end of *Incidents* when she dis-misses marriage as the ultimate goal of her life. While Jacobs may have gained by superimposing the slave narrative tradition onto the form of sentimental novel, our understanding of her as a black woman who embraced that identity comes through our ability to read the ironies, silences, and spaces she leaves in her book.

In the 1990s, with Jacobs's place firmly established in history, scholarship on *Incidents* moved in a number of interesting directions. In 1991, in "The Girls Who Became the Women: Childhood Memories in the Autobiographies of Harriet Jacobs, Mary Church Terrell, and Anne Moody," literary critic Nellie Y. McKay included Jacobs in a brief examination of the lives of three African American women from the South who were born in different historical times, experienced different hardships because of who and where they were, but who eventually transcended the destinies that might have been predicted for them. Harriet Jacobs, who was born in 1813 in North Carolina, lived with the problems of slavery and sexual exploitation in her early life; Mary Church Terrell, born in 1863 in Memphis, Tennessee, although materially the best situated of the three women, endured a forced separation from her parents from the time she was six years old; and Anne Moody, born in Mississippi in 1940, lived through the nightmares of a dysfunctional family mired in poverty until she became an adult. Then she separated herself from their company, went to college, and became an activist in the civil rights movement. She was strongly discouraged by her mother from engaging in any of these activities—an unusual, and therefore notable, circumstance. The backgrounds and times of these women were different, yet each went on to distinguish herself in adult life, breaking through boundaries that others expected would restrain her. Although each wrote an autobiography that provides information on some of her thoughts, none can fully explain her motivations toward the goals she achieved. However, each identifies a strong urge in early life to resist social prescriptions. These women refused to conform to family pressures that would have circumscribed limits of race and gender within their lives. At the center of each of their autobiographical texts is a rebel with a moral cause that joins the author to previous generations of women who were also not defeated by the difficulties they faced on their way to finding themselves.

A year later, "Runaway Tongues: Resistant Orality in *Uncle Tom's Cabin, Our Nig, Incidents in the Life of a Slave Girl*, and *Beloved*," by literary scholar Harryette Mullen, broadened considerably the discussion of Jacobs's text. For although Mullen focuses mainly on these four texts, she references many others that reinforce her argument on the presence of a resistant orality in many African American women's writings. This tradition, she states, responds to two dominant traditions in nineteenth-century white women's and black men's literature, respectively: the sentimental novel, associated with white women, domesticity, and a submission to culturally defined roles, represented by Harriet Beecher Stowe's *Uncle Tom's Cabin*, and the slave narrative, associated with black men who linked literacy to freedom and the flight from oppression, a view that Frederick Douglass's *Narrative of the Life* espouses. However, being neither white women nor black men, and having differ-

ent experiences from both, black women turned toward another direction and by grafting literacy onto orality discovered, in black women's
writings, a resistant orality inclusive of both the literate and the illiterate
traditions that represented their lives. Resistant orality is verbal self-
defense manifest in speech acts often interpreted in the nineteenth century as sassiness, impudence, impertinence, and insolence on the part of
women slaves who "did not know their place."

Mullen's essay demonstrates that since the nineteenth century, black
women writers have continuously appropriated and refigured the ideologies of the sentimental novel and slave narrative traditions to incorporate
both the oral and written traditions into meaningful dialogue. Rejecting
silence as a mechanism for dealing with their social oppression, and insisting on the significance of the black oral tradition, writers like Jacobs and
the others discussed in this essay make use of writing practices that integrate orality into the currency of the literate traditions they also use. As a
result, they speak out and write a mother tongue of resistance.

Literary critic Michelle Burnham's "Loopholes of Resistance: Harriet
Jacobs' Slave Narrative and the Critique of Agency in Foucault" (1993)
strikes out on a different path. She explores "the tactical operation of the
loophole" in Jacobs's narrative and in Foucault's work. She focuses on
the possibilities in concepts of concealment and openness that the narrative suggests, while simultaneously reconfiguring agency in the face of
powerlessness. Burnham observes that the chapter called "The
Loophole of Retreat" in *Incidents* appears in the center of the book, a
position that gives it special prominence in the text, although that is not
automatically obvious to the reader. Similarly, the location of Jacobs's
body in the chapter, concealed in a space where she can watch the life
of Edenton without revealing her presence, gives her the advantage of
being hidden in plain sight. Burnham argues that this level of concealment occurs throughout the text in situations in which Jacobs takes both
offensive and defensive measures against her oppressors. Thus, in her
struggle against slavery and patriarchy, the person Jacobs and the text
Incidents engage in successful camouflage.

This is clear in Jacobs's uses of the conventions of sentimentality.
While this is the predominant language in the narrative, the disjunctions
between the lives that slave women led and those of her white readers
enabled her to manipulate these conventions and to reject and condemn them even while using them to her advantage. Thus, Burnham
claims, the movement of sentimentality in *Incidents* resembles that of
the loopholes she uncovers in her situation, through which she can
simultaneously inscribe and transgress the status quo. This political
ambiguity in her world permits a play between concealing and revealing
secrets that serve Harriet Jacobs well in her search for personal freedom.

Historian Nell Irvin Painter's "Three Southern Women and Freud: A
Non-Exceptionalist Approach to Race, Class, and Gender in the Slave

South" (1994) links southern history to literature and European history, which accounts for the term "non-exceptionalist" in the title. The essay brings together three nineteenth-century women: black gentile fugitive slave Harriet Jacobs, white gentile fictional protagonist Lily Vere, and Jewish Dora, the central figure in one of Sigmund Freud's best-known case studies. They come from two continents, two religious traditions, and both sides of the color line. Although the genres that present them to the public are different, these three women's experiences teach the same lessons, and their fortunes illustrate Jacobs's insights in *Incidents in the Life of a Slave Girl*. Painter argues that Jacobs realized that all women in society belong to the same emotional economy—that when men have access to women of varying statuses, all women compete with each other no matter how oppressed or privileged their racial or class standings. Jacobs also embodied—in the extreme—the common quandry of nineteenth-century young girls of all races, whom men regarded as little more than prey. As an author, Jacobs linked gender hierarchy with racial hierarchy and called slavery "that cage of obscene birds" for its sacrifice of white as well as black women to men's unlimited power. This essay shows that she realized a system of racial domination cannot be contained within one dimension: race, class, or gender.

In "Resisting *Incidents*" (1996), literary historian Frances Smith Foster, examines some of the ways and reasons that Harriet Jacobs resisted writing her narrative, and some of the ways and reasons that readers have resisted believing what Jacobs wrote. Using elements of reader-response theory, Foster first discusses a series of general examples of reader resistance stemming from habitual attitudes about gender, race, and class. Turning to *Incidents*, she notes that among the reasons Jacobs was reluctant to write were her wishes to protect her privacy, to spare her friends and relatives embarrassment and harassment, and to avoid contributing to negative stereotypes of African American morality. In reviewing the responses of critics and readers, Foster suggests that Jacobs had good reason to be concerned, for despite her rhetorical and literary strategies used to focus attention upon the antislavery activism that motivated her writing, critics have continued to question Jacobs's authority and the authenticity of her statements about what she did, and what she did not, think and do. Since much of Foster's discussion focuses upon contested readings of contemporary critics and scholars, this essay helps us to identify and perhaps understand the moments in which we, too, might need to examine our reception and interpretation of this text.

In "Reading and Redemption in *Incidents in the Life of a Slave Girl*," also published in 1996, literary critic Sandra Gunning demonstrates that over time African American women have resisted white attempts to invalidate them by separating their voices from their bodies and by appropriating their voices and attempting to interpret their experiences for them. She cites the occasion on which activist abolitionist Sojourner

Truth brilliantly undermined such an attempt when in 1858 she refused to have her body and her voice separated: she dramatically disrobed in public before a large gathering of white women and men and, through her words, presented her body as a tangible representation of the crime of American slavery.

Gunning sees Harriet Jacobs's character Linda Brent, her alter ego in her narrative, facing a similar situation. *Incidents* critiques black powerlessness in the face of white reading practices that separate the black voice from the black body. When Jacobs entered the political arena by agreeing to write her story, she was well aware that many in her audience would ignore her voice and construct her as a body contaminated by the moral decadence of slavery. To offset this, she chose to reveal her story through the language of domesticity, which was highly valued by white women at the time. Yet, Gunning points out, even Jacobs's friends Lydia Maria Child and Amy Post, in considering the sentiments of the book's audience in their framing of the text, with an introduction and an appendix, silenced Linda Brent. However, in her author's preface to the volume, Brent recovers her place and sets the stage for a narrative that enables her to break out of that silence. Reuniting her voice and her body, she becomes the survivor whose experiences *she* can best interpret. By unveiling what Child and Post rendered invisible in their frame to her text, Jacobs, like Truth, uses the exploitation of her body to critique, by calling into question, the distance that separates northern and southern white female bodies from black female bodies. Hers is the voice of reform that white women should heed in order to achieve moral salvation.

In "The Heady Political Life of Compassion" (1997), philosopher Elizabeth Spelman explores the political dimensions of compassion in *Incidents.* Jacobs makes clear to her readers that one motivation to write the book was that it would engender compassion among free women for the plight of slave women and move them to speak out against the conditions of that plight. But, Spelman insists, Jacobs was also aware that her pleas for compassion were complicated and problematic. On one hand, she was the supplicant; on the other, she knew that she had to be the "active agent" who controlled her audience's understanding of the meaning of her suffering to prevent their misreadings and misunderstandings of the slave women's dilemma. So throughout her text, Jacobs attempts to shape and control what she means by compassion.

Spelman suggests that this effort on Jacobs's part proves that she understood the risk she took in making a plea for and being the object of compassion. She believes, too, that *Incidents* teaches lessons in asserting the self as a moral agent in control of defining one's experiences, even while informing others of those experiences. Jacobs, she says, is less interested in gaining friendships than in being taken seriously. For example, in speaking to her readers about her relationship with her white lover, Samuel Tredwell Sawyer (Mr. Sands), on one hand, she does not flinch from taking responsibility for "the painful and humiliating memory" of her sexual actions, while on the other, she excuses herself from blame by suggesting that the standards by which she should be judged should perhaps be different from those by which free women are judged. By revealing to readers the various ways in which she and other slave women suffered, and in seeking compassion from her listeners, Jacobs shows that she understood that those who heard her would have different reactions to her behavior. But her task remained one of instructing her readers on how to feel toward her while she presented herself as a moral agent and, as Spelman points out, a social critic.

In the final essay in this collection, "'The laws were laid down to me anew': Harriet Jacobs and the Reframing of Legal Fictions" (1998), Christina Accomando, a literary scholar, examines nineteenth-century statutes, particularly *An Inquiry into the Law of Negro Slavery in the United States of America: To Which is Prefixed, An Historical Sketch of Slavery*, an 1858 legal treatise by Thomas Cobb, a Georgian lawyer, alongside Jacobs's oppositional critique of slave law, to discover the contradictions in white discourses on slavery that make them legal fictions. Jacobs's argument against slavery, she claims, "reframes and rearticulates . . . [the existing] legal and cultural discourses of slavery and womanhood." Cobb, one framer of the Confederate Constitution, was highly regarded by his white admirers for seeking "truth" by pursuing legal objectivity.

Against Cobb's defense of southern laws that erase and silence African Americans, especially women, Accomando shows how *Incidents* reframes the laws and redefines womanhood. Unlike Cobb, Jacobs challenges the laws and suggests that readers be alert to their sources and origins. Jacobs's narrative highlights evidence of the fictions such laws perpetuate in oppressing black people. In terms of womanhood, Jacobs rebutts claims of black women's inborn immorality when slave laws make black women sexual victims and protect and shelter the virtue of white women. Accomando points out that Cobb's concerns are for the "honor" of the law while Jacobs proves the law dishonorable. His attempts to defend slavery on the grounds of the neutrality of legal rationality fall short compared to her ability to show, through her experiences, the criminality of such laws that give her the right to claim allegiance to a higher law not made by white men.

Incidents in the Life of a Slave Girl was and continues to be a groundbreaking text. When it was published in 1861, most likely its proximity to the Civil War and the Emancipation deprived it of the public attention it might otherwise have received. At the same time, it was the first full-length slave narrative by a woman and the first to challenge the dominance of the male slave narrative as the voice of all slaves. For while male slave narrators often spoke to the oppression that women suffered, in most cases, even when they noted women who defied their owners, they had little to say about the ways in which these women were other than helpless victims of white slave owners. Harriet Jacobs's *Incidents* changed that by unveiling the horror of the situation as well as the hard-earned triumph of one woman.

At the same time, it is not difficult to understand why freed former slave women generally turned away from making their sexual experiences during slavery central to their stories and instead spoke to their subversions of a system meant to demean them in every way, and to their strategies for survival. Harriet Jacobs demonstrated great courage when she decided to confront the sexual exploitation she experienced as the central issue in her text. Before her, the voices of women like Maria Stewart, Jarena Lee, and Mary Ann Shadd Cary, among others, in different life situations from hers, established their own records of black women's history and experiences. But Jacobs's voice was peculiar and especially significant because of the space out of which it came, and as many of her modern critics point out, because of her ability, beginning at a very early age and continuing throughout her life, to maintain her integrity as a moral human being in the face of seemingly insurmountable odds. She was not the first woman of African descent in America to produce a book, but hers is indeed another story, to borrow a phrase from Toni Morrison, not to pass on.

NELLIE Y. MCKAY
FRANCES SMITH FOSTER

Acknowledgments

We acknowledge the work of the many scholars (known and unknown to us) whose efforts over the past two decades enrich this edition of Harriet Jacobs's narrative. Most directly, we know that we could not have accomplished our task as thoroughly as we have without the existence of Jean Fagan Yellin's 1987 edition of this text, and we recognize our debt to her. The richness of literary traditions comes from the continuing work of those who follow after and who add their voices and insights to those of their forerunners. Following in that tradition, we hope that this edition will be worthy of its heritage.

For assisting us in preparing this volume we wish to thank many colleagues who offered their encouragement; our graduate students who are excited about it; and especially Dee McGraw, Connie Munson, Lynn Jennings, Yolanda Gilmore, and Nancy Calamari of Emory University and the University of Wisconsin, Madison, who did most of the library and other necessary behind-the-scenes work involved in the process. We are deeply grateful to William McHugh, reference librarian at Northwestern University, who located and provided us with the copy of Nathaniel P. Willis's "Letter" on his observations of slaves in Virginia, included in this book.

Finally, we thank our editor at W. W. Norton, Carol Bemis, for her patience and the good work that brought the project to its conclusion.

The Text of
INCIDENTS IN THE LIFE
OF A SLAVE GIRL

INCIDENTS

IN THE

LIFE OF A SLAVE GIRL.

WRITTEN BY HERSELF.

"Northerners know nothing at all about Slavery. They think it is perpetual bondage only. They have no conception of the depth of *degradation* involved in that word, SLAVERY; if they had, they would never cease their efforts until so horrible a system was overthrown."   A WOMAN OF NORTH CAROLINA.

"Rise up, ye women that are at ease! Hear my voice, ye careless daughters! Give ear unto my speech."   ISAIAH xxxii. 9.

EDITED BY L. MARIA CHILD.

BOSTON:
PUBLISHED FOR THE AUTHOR.
1861.

Self depricating

Preface by the Author

Reader, be assured this narrative is no fiction. I am aware that some of my adventures may seem incredible; but they are, nevertheless, strictly true. I have not exaggerated the wrongs inflicted by Slavery; on the contrary, my descriptions fall far short of the facts. I have concealed the names of places, and given persons fictitious names. I had no motive for secrecy on my own account, but I deemed it kind and considerate towards others to pursue this course.

I wish I were more competent to the task I have undertaken. But I trust my readers will excuse deficiencies in consideration of circumstances. I was born and reared in Slavery; and I remained in a Slave State twenty-seven years. Since I have been at the North, it has been necessary for me to work diligently for my own support, and the education of my children. This has not left me much leisure to make up for the loss of early opportunities to improve myself; and it has compelled me to write these pages at irregular intervals, whenever I could snatch an hour from household duties.

When I first arrived in Philadelphia, Bishop Paine[1] advised me to publish a sketch of my life, but I told him I was altogether incompetent to such an undertaking. Though I have improved my mind somewhat since that time, I still remain of the same opinion; but I trust my motives will excuse what might otherwise seem presumptuous. I have not written my experiences in order to attract attention to myself; on the contrary, it would have been more pleasant to me to have been silent about my own history. Neither do I care to excite sympathy for my own sufferings. But I do earnestly desire to arouse the women of the North to a realizing sense of the condition of two millions of women at the South, still in bondage, suffering what I suffered, and most of them far worse. I want to add my testimony to that of abler pens to convince the people of the Free States what Slavery really is. Only by experience can any one realize how deep, and dark, and foul is that pit of abominations. May the blessing of God rest on this imperfect effort in behalf of my persecuted people!

LINDA BRENT

Introduction by the Editor

The author of the following autobiography is personally known to me, and her conversation and manners inspire me with confidence. During the last seventeen years, she has lived the greater part of the time with a

---

1. Daniel A. Payne (1811–1893), a bishop of the African Methodist Episcopal Church and later president of Wilberforce University.

distinguished family in New York, and has so deported herself as to be highly esteemed by them. This fact is sufficient, without further credentials of her character. I believe those who know her will not be disposed to doubt her veracity, though some incidents in her story are more romantic than fiction.

At her request, I have revised her manuscript; but such changes as I have made have been mainly for purposes of condensation and orderly arrangement. I have not added any thing to the incidents, or changed the import of her very pertinent remarks. With trifling exceptions, both the ideas and the language are her own. I pruned excrescences a little, but otherwise I had no reason for changing her lively and dramatic way of telling her own story. The names of both persons and places are known to me; but for good reasons I suppress them.

It will naturally excite surprise that a woman reared in Slavery should be able to write so well. But circumstances will explain this. In the first place, nature endowed her with quick perceptions. Secondly, the mistress, with whom she lived till she was twelve years old, was a kind, considerate friend, who taught her to read and spell. Thirdly, she was placed in favorable circumstances after she came to the North; having frequent intercourse with intelligent persons, who felt a friendly interest in her welfare, and were disposed to give her opportunities for self-improvement.

I am well aware that many will accuse me of indecorum for presenting these pages to the public; for the experiences of this intelligent and much-injured woman belong to a class which some call delicate subjects, and others indelicate. This peculiar phase of Slavery has generally been kept veiled; but the public ought to be made acquainted with its monstrous features, and I willingly take the responsibility of presenting them with the veil withdrawn. I do this for the sake of my sisters in bondage, who are suffering wrongs so foul, that our ears are too delicate to listen to them. I do it with the hope of arousing conscientious and reflecting women at the North to a sense of their duty in the exertion of moral influence on the question of Slavery, on all possible occasions. I do it with the hope that every man who reads this narrative will swear solemnly before God that, so far as he has power to prevent it, no fugitive from Slavery shall ever be sent back to suffer in that loathsome den of corruption and cruelty.

L. MARIA CHILD[2]

---

2. Lydia Maria Child (1802–1880), novelist, journalist, activist. Child's abolitionist credentials had been established earlier by her editorship of the *National Anti-Slavery Standard* and public support of John Brown.

Contents

Incidents in the Life of a Slave Girl, Seven Years Concealed

I. Childhood

I was born a slave; but I never knew it till six years of happy childhood had passed away. My father was a carpenter, and considered so intelligent and skilful in his trade, that, when buildings out of the common line were to be erected, he was sent for from long distances, to be head workman. On condition of paying his mistress two hundred dollars a year, and supporting himself, he was allowed to work at his trade, and manage his own affairs. His strongest wish was to purchase his children; but, though he several times offered his hard earnings for that purpose, he never succeeded. In complexion my parents were a light shade of brownish yellow, and were termed mulattoes. They lived together in a comfortable home; and, though we were all slaves, I was so fondly shielded that I never dreamed I was a piece of merchandise, trusted to them for safe keeping, and liable to be demanded of them at any moment. I had one brother, William, who was two years younger than myself—a bright, affectionate child. I had also a great treasure in my maternal grandmother, who was a remarkable woman in many respects. She was the daughter of a planter in South Carolina, who, at his death, left her mother and his three children free, with money to go to St. Augustine,[3] where they had relatives. It was during the Revolutionary War; and they were captured on their passage, carried back, and sold to different purchasers. Such was the story my grandmother used to tell me; but I do not remember all the particulars. She was a little girl when she was captured and sold to the keeper of a large hotel. I have often heard her tell how hard she fared during childhood. But as she grew older she evinced so much intelligence, and was so faithful, that her master and mistress could not help seeing it was for their interest to take care of such a valuable piece of property. She became an indispensable personage in the household, officiating in all capacities, from cook and wet nurse to seamstress. She was much praised for her cooking; and her nice crackers became so famous in the neighborhood that many people were desirous of obtaining them. In conse-

parents don't own them their are entrusted to the parents

---

3. St. Augustine (in present-day Florida) was a British port during the Revolutionary War.

quence of numerous requests of this kind, she asked permission of her mistress to bake crackers at night, after all the household work was done; and she obtained leave to do it, provided she would clothe herself and her children from the profits. Upon these terms, after working hard all day for her mistress, she began her midnight bakings, assisted by her two oldest children. The business proved profitable; and each year she laid by a little, which was saved for a fund to purchase her children. Her master died, and the property was divided among his heirs. The widow had her dower[4] in the hotel, which she continued to keep open. My grandmother remained in her service as a slave; but her children were divided among her master's children. As she had five, Benjamin, the youngest one, was sold, in order that each heir might have an equal portion of dollars and cents. There was so little difference in our ages that he seemed more like my brother than my uncle. He was a bright, handsome lad, nearly white; for he inherited the complexion my grandmother had derived from Anglo-Saxon ancestors. Though only ten years old, seven hundred and twenty dollars were paid for him. His sale was a terrible blow to my grandmother; but she was naturally hopeful, and she went to work with renewed energy, trusting in time to be able to purchase some of her children. She had laid up three hundred dollars, which her mistress one day begged as a loan, promising to pay her soon. The reader probably knows that no promise or writing given to a slave is legally binding; for, according to Southern laws, a slave, *being* property, can *hold* no property. When my grandmother lent her hard earnings to her mistress, she trusted solely to her honor. The honor of a slaveholder to a slave!

To this good grandmother I was indebted for many comforts. My brother Willie and I often received portions of the crackers, cakes, and preserves, she made to sell; and after we ceased to be children we were indebted to her for many more important services.

Such were the unusually fortunate circumstances of my early childhood. When I was six years old, my mother died; and then, for the first time, I learned, by the talk around me, that I was a slave. My mother's mistress was the daughter of my grandmother's mistress. She was the foster sister of my mother; they were both nourished at my grandmother's breast. In fact, my mother had been weaned at three months old, that the babe of the mistress might obtain sufficient food. They played together as children; and, when they became women, my mother was a most faithful servant to her whiter foster sister. On her death-bed her mistress promised that her children should never suffer for any thing; and during her lifetime she kept her word. They all spoke kindly of my dead mother, who had been a slave merely in name, but in nature was noble and womanly. I grieved for her, and my young mind was troubled with the thought

---

4. The portion of her deceased husband's estate allowed to a widow during her lifetime.

who would now take care of me and my little brother. I was told that my home was now to be with her mistress; and I found it a happy one. No toilsome or disagreeable duties were imposed upon me. My mistress was so kind to me that I was always glad to do her bidding, and proud to labor for her as much as my young years would permit. I would sit by her side for hours, sewing diligently, with a heart as free from care as that of any free-born white child. When she thought I was tired, she would send me out to run and jump; and away I bounded, to gather berries or flowers to decorate her room. Those were happy days—too happy to last. The slave child had no thought for the morrow; but there came that blight, which too surely waits on every human being born to be a chattel.

When I was nearly twelve years old, my kind mistress sickened and died. As I saw the cheek grow paler, and the eye more glassy, how earnestly I prayed in my heart that she might live! I loved her; for she had been almost like a mother to me. My prayers were not answered. She died, and they buried her in the little churchyard, where, day after day, my tears fell upon her grave.

I was sent to spend a week with my grandmother. I was now old enough to begin to think of the future; and again and again I asked myself what they would do with me. I felt sure I should never find another mistress so kind as the one who was gone. She had promised my dying mother that her children should never suffer for any thing; and when I remembered that, and recalled her many proofs of attachment to me, I could not help having some hopes that she had left me free. My friends were almost certain it would be so. They thought she would be sure to do it, on account of my mother's love and faithful service. But, alas! we all know that the memory of a faithful slave does not avail much to save her children from the auction block.

After a brief period of suspense, the will of my mistress was read, and we learned that she had bequeathed me to her sister's daughter, a child of five years old. So vanished our hopes. My mistress had taught me the precepts of God's Word: "Thou shalt love thy neighbor as thyself." "Whatsoever ye would that men should do unto you, do ye even so unto them."[5] But I was her slave, and I suppose she did not recognize me as her neighbor. I would give much to blot out from my memory that one great wrong. As a child, I loved my mistress; and, looking back on the happy days I spent with her, I try to think with less bitterness of this act of injustice. While I was with her, she taught me to read and spell; and for this privilege, which so rarely falls to the lot of a slave, I bless her memory.

She possessed but few slaves; and at her death those were all distributed among her relatives. Five of them were my grandmother's children,

---

5. First quote: Mark 12.31. Many Christians consider this the "second greatest commandment." Second quote: Matthew 7.12. Many Christians believe this declaration summarizes "the law and the prophets."

and had shared the same milk that nourished her mother's children. Notwithstanding my grandmother's long and faithful service to her owners, not one of her children escaped the auction block. These God-breathing machines are no more, in the sight of their masters, than the cotton they plant, or the horses they tend.

II. The New Master and Mistress

Dr. Flint, a physician in the neighborhood, had married the sister of my mistress, and I was now the property of their little daughter. It was not without murmuring that I prepared for my new home; and what added to my unhappiness, was the fact that my brother William was purchased by the same family. My father, by his nature, as well as by the habit of transacting business as a skilful mechanic, had more of the feelings of a freeman than is common among slaves. My brother was a spirited boy; and being brought up under such influences, he early detested the name of master and mistress. One day, when his father and his mistress both happened to call him at the same time, he hesitated between the two; being perplexed to know which had the strongest claim upon his obedience. He finally concluded to go to his mistress. When my father reproved him for it, he said, "You both called me, and I didn't know which I ought to go to first."

"You are _my_ child," replied our father, "and when I call you, you should come immediately, if you have to pass through fire and water."

Poor Willie! He was now to learn his first lesson of obedience to a master. Grandmother tried to cheer us with hopeful words, and they found an echo in the credulous hearts of youth.

When we entered our new home we encountered cold looks, cold words, and cold treatment. We were glad when the night came. On my narrow bed I moaned and wept, I felt so desolate and alone.

I had been there nearly a year, when a dear little friend of mine was buried. I heard her mother sob, as the clods fell on the coffin of her only child, and I turned away from the grave, feeling thankful that I still had something left to love. I met my grandmother, who said, "Come with me, Linda;" and from her tone I knew that something sad had happened. She led me apart from the people, and then said, "My child, your father is dead." Dead! How could I believe it? He had died so suddenly I had not even heard that he was sick. I went home with my grandmother. My heart rebelled against God, who had taken from me mother, father, mistress, and friend. The good grandmother tried to comfort me. "Who knows the ways of God?" said she. "Perhaps they have been kindly taken from the evil days to come." Years afterwards I often thought of this. She promised to be a mother to her grandchildren, so far as she might be permitted to do so; and strengthened by her love, I returned to my master's. I thought

I should be allowed to go to my father's house the next morning; but I was ordered to go for flowers, that my mistress's house might be decorated for an evening party. I spent the day gathering flowers and weaving them into festoons, while the dead body of my father was lying within a mile of me. What cared my owners for that? he was merely a piece of property. Moreover, they thought he had spoiled his children, by teaching them to feel that they were human beings. This was blasphemous doctrine for a slave to teach; presumptuous in him, and dangerous to the masters.

The next day I followed his remains to a humble grave beside that of my dear mother. There were those who knew my father's worth, and respected his memory.

My home now seemed more dreary than ever. The laugh of the little slave-children sounded harsh and cruel. It was selfish to feel so about the joy of others. My brother moved about with a very grave face. I tried to comfort him, by saying, "Take courage, Willie; brighter days will come by and by."

"You don't know any thing about it, Linda," he replied. "We shall have to stay here all our days; we shall never be free."

I argued that we were growing older and stronger, and that perhaps we might, before long, be allowed to hire our own time, and then we could earn money to buy our freedom. William declared this was much easier to say than to do; moreover, he did not intend to *buy* his freedom. We held daily controversies upon this subject.

Little attention was paid to the slaves' meals in Dr. Flint's house. If they could catch a bit of food while it was going, well and good. I gave myself no trouble on that score, for on my various errands I passed my grandmother's house, where there was always something to spare for me. I was frequently threatened with punishment if I stopped there; and my grandmother, to avoid detaining me, often stood at the gate with something for my breakfast or dinner. I was indebted to *her* for all my comforts, spiritual or temporal. It was *her* labor that supplied my scanty wardrobe. I have a vivid recollection of the linsey-woolsey[6] dress given me every winter by Mrs. Flint. How I hated it! It was one of the badges of slavery.

While my grandmother was thus helping to support me from her hard earnings, the three hundred dollars she had lent her mistress were never repaid. When her mistress died, her son-in-law, Dr. Flint, was appointed executor. When grandmother applied to him for payment, he said the estate was insolvent, and the law prohibited payment. It did not, however, prohibit him from retaining the silver candelabra, which had been purchased with that money. I presume they will be handed down in the family, from generation to generation.

My grandmother's mistress had always promised her that, at her death, she should be free; and it was said that in her will she made good the

---

6. Cheap coarse cloth made of crude linen or cotton fibers mixed with wool.

promise. But when the estate was settled, Dr. Flint told the faithful old servant that, under existing circumstances, it was necessary she should be sold.

On the appointed day, the customary advertisement was posted up, proclaiming that there would be a "public sale of negroes, horses, &c." Dr. Flint called to tell my grandmother that he was unwilling to wound her feelings by putting her up at auction, and that he would prefer to dispose of her at private sale. My grandmother saw through his hypocrisy; she understood very well that he was ashamed of the job. She was a very spirited woman, and if he was base enough to sell her, when her mistress intended she should be free, she was determined the public should know it. She had for a long time supplied many families with crackers and preserves; consequently, "Aunt Marthy," as she was called, was generally known, and every body who knew her respected her intelligence and good character. Her long and faithful service in the family was also well known, and the intention of her mistress to leave her free. When the day of sale came, she took her place among the chattels, and at the first call she sprang upon the auction-block. Many voices called out, "Shame! Shame! Who is going to sell *you*, aunt Marthy? Don't stand there! That is no place for *you*." Without saying a word, she quietly awaited her fate. No one bid for her. At last, a feeble voice said, "Fifty dollars." It came from a maiden lady, seventy years old, the sister of my grandmother's deceased mistress. She had lived forty years under the same roof with my grandmother; she knew how faithfully she had served her owners, and how cruelly she had been defrauded of her rights; and she resolved to protect her. The auctioneer waited for a higher bid; but her wishes were respected; no one bid above her. She could neither read nor write; and when the bill of sale was made out, she signed it with a cross. But what consequence was that, when she had a big heart overflowing with human kindness? She gave the old servant her freedom.

At that time, my grandmother was just fifty years old. Laborious years had passed since then; and now my brother and I were slaves to the man who had defrauded her of her money, and tried to defraud her of her freedom. One of my mother's sisters, called Aunt Nancy, was also a slave in his family. She was a kind, good aunt to me; and supplied the place of both housekeeper and waiting maid to her mistress. She was, in fact, at the beginning and end of every thing.

Mrs. Flint, like many southern women, was totally deficient in energy. She had not strength to superintend her household affairs; but her nerves were so strong, that she could sit in her easy chair and see a woman whipped, till the blood trickled from every stroke of the lash. She was a member of the church; but partaking of the Lord's supper did not seem to put her in a Christian frame of mind. If dinner was not served at the exact time on that particular Sunday, she would station herself in the kitchen, and wait till it was dished, and then spit in all the kettles and pans

that had been used for cooking. She did this to prevent the cook and her children from eking out their meagre fare with the remains of the gravy and other scrapings. The slaves could get nothing to eat except what she chose to give them. Provisions were weighed out by the pound and ounce, three times a day. I can assure you she gave them no chance to eat wheat bread from her flour barrel. She knew how many biscuits a quart of flour would make, and exactly what size they ought to be.

Dr. Flint was an epicure.[7] The cook never sent a dinner to his table without fear and trembling; for if there happened to be a dish not to his liking, he would either order her to be whipped, or compel her to eat every mouthful of it in his presence. The poor, hungry creature might not have objected to eating it; but she did object to having her master cram it down her throat till she choked.

They had a pet dog, that was a nuisance in the house. The cook was ordered to make some Indian mush[8] for him. He refused to eat, and when his head was held over it, the froth flowed from his mouth into the basin. He died a few minutes after. When Dr. Flint came in, he said the mush had not been well cooked, and that was the reason the animal would not eat it. He sent for the cook, and compelled her to eat it. He thought that the woman's stomach was stronger than the dog's; but her sufferings afterwards proved that he was mistaken. This poor woman endured many cruelties from her master and mistress; sometimes she was locked up, away from her nursing baby, for a whole day and night.

When I had been in the family a few weeks, one of the plantation slaves was brought to town, by order of his master. It was near night when he arrived, and Dr. Flint ordered him to be taken to the work house, and tied up to the joist, so that his feet would just escape the ground. In that situation he was to wait till the doctor had taken his tea. I shall never forget that night. Never before, in my life, had I heard hundreds of blows fall, in succession, on a human being. His piteous groans, and his "O, pray don't, massa," rang in my ear for months afterwards. There were many conjectures as to the cause of this terrible punishment. Some said master accused him of stealing corn; others said the slave had quarrelled with his wife, in presence of the overseer, and had accused his master of being the father of her child. They were both black, and the child was very fair.

I went into the work house next morning, and saw the cowhide still wet with blood, and the boards all covered with gore. The poor man lived, and continued to quarrel with his wife. A few months afterwards Dr. Flint handed them both over to a slave-trader. The guilty man put their value into his pocket, and had the satisfaction of knowing that they were out of sight and hearing. When the mother was delivered into the trader's hands, she said, "You *promised* to treat me well." To which he replied,

7. A person who enjoys fine food; a gourmet.
8. A corn porridge.

"You have let your tongue run too far; damn you!" She had forgotten that it was a crime for a slave to tell who was the father of her child.

From others than the master persecution also comes in such cases. I once saw a young slave girl dying soon after the birth of a child nearly white. In her agony she cried out, "O Lord, come and take me!" Her mistress stood by, and mocked at her like an incarnate fiend. "You suffer, do you?" she exclaimed. "I am glad of it. You deserve it all, and more too."

The girl's mother said, "The baby is dead, thank God; and I hope my poor child will soon be in heaven, too."

"Heaven!" retorted the mistress. "There is no such place for the like of her and her bastard."

The poor mother turned away, sobbing. Her dying daughter called her, feebly, and as she bent over her, I heard her say, "Don't grieve so, mother; God knows all about it; and HE will have mercy upon me."

Her sufferings, afterwards, became so intense, that her mistress felt unable to stay; but when she left the room, the scornful smile was still on her lips. Seven children called her mother. The poor black woman had but the one child, whose eyes she saw closing in death, while she thanked God for taking her away from the greater bitterness of life.

III. The Slaves' New Year's Day

Dr. Flint owned a fine residence in town, several farms, and about fifty slaves, besides hiring a number by the year.

Hiring-day at the south takes place on the 1st of January. On the 2d, the slaves are expected to go to their new masters. On a farm, they work until the corn and cotton are laid. They then have two holidays. Some masters give them a good dinner under the trees. This over, they work until Christmas eve. If no heavy charges are meantime brought against them, they are given four or five holidays, whichever the master or overseer may think proper. Then comes New Year's eve; and they gather together their little alls, or more properly speaking, their little nothings, and wait anxiously for the dawning of day. At the appointed hour the grounds are thronged with men, women, and children, waiting, like criminals, to hear their doom pronounced. The slave is sure to know who is the most humane, or cruel master, within forty miles of him.

It is easy to find out, on that day, who clothes and feeds his slaves well; for he is surrounded by a crowd, begging, "Please, massa, hire me this year. I will work *very* hard, massa."

If a slave is unwilling to go with his new master, he is whipped, or locked up in jail, until he consents to go, and promises not to run away during the year. Should he chance to change his mind, thinking it justifiable to violate an extorted promise, woe unto him if he is caught! The

whip is used till the blood flows at his feet; and his stiffened limbs are put in chains, to be dragged in the field for days and days!

If he lives until the next year, perhaps the same man will hire him again, without even giving him an opportunity of going to the hiring-ground. After those for hire are disposed of, those for sale are called up.

O, you happy free women, contrast *your* New Year's day with that of the poor bond-woman! With you it is a pleasant season, and the light of the day is blessed. Friendly wishes meet you every where, and gifts are showered upon you. Even hearts that have been estranged from you soften at this season, and lips that have been silent echo back, "I wish you a happy New Year." Children bring their little offerings, and raise their rosy lips for a caress. They are your own, and no hand but that of death can take them from you.

But to the slave mother New Year's day comes laden with peculiar sorrows. She sits on her cold cabin floor, watching the children who may all be torn from her the next morning; and often does she wish that she and they might die before the day dawns. She may be an ignorant creature, degraded by the system that has brutalized her from childhood; but she has a mother's instincts, and is capable of feeling a mother's agonies.

On one of these sale days, I saw a mother lead seven children to the auction-block. She knew that *some* of them would be taken from her; but they took *all*. The children were sold to a slave-trader, and their mother was bought by a man in her own town. Before night her children were all far away. She begged the trader to tell her where he intended to take them; this he refused to do. How *could* he, when he knew he would sell them, one by one, wherever he could command the highest price? I met that mother in the street, and her wild, haggard face lives to-day in my mind. She wrung her hands in anguish, and exclaimed, "Gone! All gone! Why *dont* God kill me?" I had no words wherewith to comfort her. Instances of this kind are of daily, yea, of hourly occurrence.

Slaveholders have a method, peculiar to their institution, of getting rid of *old* slaves, whose lives have been worn out in their service. I knew an old woman, who for seventy years faithfully served her master. She had become almost helpless, from hard labor and disease. Her owners moved to Alabama, and the old black woman was left to be sold to any body who would give twenty dollars for her.

IV. The Slave Who Dared to Feel like a Man

Two years had passed since I entered Dr. Flint's family, and those years had brought much of the knowledge that comes from experience, though they had afforded little opportunity for any other kinds of knowledge.

My grandmother had, as much as possible, been a mother to her orphan grandchildren. By perseverance and unwearied industry, she was now mistress of a snug little home, surrounded with the necessaries of life. She would have been happy could her children have shared them with her. There remained but three children and two grandchildren, all slaves. Most earnestly did she strive to make us feel that it was the will of God: that He had seen fit to place us under such circumstances; and though it seemed hard, we ought to pray for contentment.

It was a beautiful faith, coming from a mother who could not call her children her own. But I, and Benjamin, her youngest boy, condemned it. We reasoned that it was much more the will of God that we should be situated as she was. We longed for a home like hers. There we always found sweet balsam[9] for our troubles. She was so loving, so sympathizing! She always met us with a smile, and listened with patience to all our sorrows. She spoke so hopefully, that unconsciously the clouds gave place to sunshine. There was a grand big oven there, too, that baked bread and nice things for the town, and we knew there was always a choice bit in store for us.

But, alas! even the charms of the old oven failed to reconcile us to our hard lot. Benjamin was now a tall, handsome lad, strongly and gracefully made, and with a spirit too bold and daring for a slave. My brother William, now twelve years old, had the same aversion to the word master that he had when he was an urchin of seven years. I was his confidant. He came to me with all his troubles. I remember one instance in particular. It was on a lovely spring morning, and when I marked the sunlight dancing here and there, its beauty seemed to mock my sadness. For my master, whose restless, craving, vicious nature roved about day and night, seeking whom to devour, had just left me, with stinging, scorching words; words that scathed ear and brain like fire. O, how I despised him! I thought how glad I should be, if some day when he walked the earth, it would open and swallow him up, and disencumber the world of a plague.

When he told me that I was made for his use, made to obey his command in *every* thing; that I was nothing but a slave, whose will must and should surrender to his, never before had my puny arm felt half so strong.

So deeply was I absorbed in painful reflections afterwards, that I neither saw nor heard the entrance of any one, till the voice of William sounded close beside me. "Linda," said he, "what makes you look so sad? I love you. O, Linda, isn't this a bad world? Every body seems so cross and unhappy. I wish I had died when poor father did."

I told him that every body was *not* cross, or unhappy; that those who had pleasant homes, and kind friends, and who were not afraid to love them, were happy. But we, who were slave-children, without father or mother, could not expect to be happy. We must be good; perhaps that would bring us contentment.

---

9. A healing plant resin, balm.

"Yes," he said, "I try to be good; but what's the use? They are all the time troubling me." Then he proceeded to relate his afternoon's difficulty with young master Nicholas. It seemed that the brother of master Nicholas had pleased himself with making up stories about William. Master Nicholas said he should be flogged, and he would do it. Whereupon he went to work; but William fought bravely, and the young master, finding he was getting the better of him, undertook to tie his hands behind him. He failed in that likewise. By dint of kicking and fisting, William came out of the skirmish none the worse for a few scratches.

He continued to discourse on his young master's *meanness*; how he whipped the *little* boys, but was a perfect coward when a tussle ensued between him and white boys of his own size. On such occasions he always took to his legs. William had other charges to make against him. One was his rubbing up pennies with quicksilver, and passing them off for quarters of a dollar on an old man who kept a fruit stall. William was often sent to buy fruit, and he earnestly inquired of me what he ought to do under such circumstances. I told him it was certainly wrong to deceive the old man, and that it was his duty to tell him of the impositions practised by his young master. I assured him the old man would not be slow to comprehend the whole, and there the matter would end. William thought it might with the old man, but not with *him*. He said he did not mind the smart of the whip, but he did not like the *idea* of being whipped.

While I advised him to be good and forgiving I was not unconscious of the beam in my own eye.[1] It was the very knowledge of my own short-comings that urged me to retain, if possible, some sparks of my brother's God-given nature. I had not lived fourteen years in slavery for nothing. I had felt, seen, and heard enough, to read the characters, and question the motives, of those around me. The war of my life had begun; and though one of God's most powerless creatures, I resolved never to be conquered. Alas, for me!

If there was one pure, sunny spot for me, I believed it to be in Benjamin's heart, and in another's, whom I loved with all the ardor of a girl's first love. My owner knew of it, and sought in every way to render me miserable. He did not resort to corporal punishment, but to all the petty, tyrannical ways that human ingenuity could devise.

I remember the first time I was punished. It was in the month of February. My grandmother had taken my old shoes, and replaced them with a new pair. I needed them; for several inches of snow had fallen, and it still continued to fall. When I walked through Mrs. Flint's room, their creaking grated harshly on her refined nerves. She called me to her, and asked what I had about me that made such a horrid noise. I told her it was my new shoes. "Take them off," said she; "and if you put them on again, I'll throw them into the fire."

---

1. Reference to Matthew 7.3–5 and Luke 6.41–42.

I took them off, and my stockings also. She then sent me a long distance, on an errand. As I went through the snow, my bare feet tingled. That night I was very hoarse; and I went to bed thinking the next day would find me sick, perhaps dead. What was my grief on waking to find myself quite well!

I had imagined if I died, or was laid up for some time, that my mistress would feel a twinge of remorse that she had so hated "the little imp," as she styled me. It was my ignorance of that mistress that gave rise to such extravagant imaginings.

Dr. Flint occasionally had high prices offered for me; but he always said, "She don't belong to me. She is my daughter's property, and I have no right to sell her." Good, honest man! My young mistress was still a child, and I could look for no protection from her. I loved her, and she returned my affection. I once heard her father allude to her attachment to me; and his wife promptly replied that it proceeded from fear. This put unpleasant doubts into my mind. Did the child feign what she did not feel? or was her mother jealous of the mite of love she bestowed on me? I concluded it must be the latter. I said to myself, "Surely, little children are true."

One afternoon I sat at my sewing, feeling unusual depression of spirits. My mistress had been accusing me of an offence, of which I assured her I was perfectly innocent; but I saw, by the contemptuous curl of her lip, that she believed I was telling a lie.

I wondered for what wise purpose God was leading me through such thorny paths, and whether still darker days were in store for me. As I sat musing thus, the door opened softly, and William came in. "Well, brother," said I, "what is the matter this time?"

"O Linda, Ben and his master have had a dreadful time!" said he.

My first thought was that Benjamin was killed. "Don't be frightened, Linda," said William; "I will tell you all about it."

It appeared that Benjamin's master had sent for him, and he did not immediately obey the summons. When he did, his master was angry, and began to whip him. He resisted. Master and slave fought, and finally the master was thrown. Benjamin had cause to tremble; for he had thrown to the ground his master—one of the richest men in town. I anxiously awaited the result.

That night I stole to my grandmother's house, and Benjamin also stole thither from his master's. My grandmother had gone to spend a day or two with an old friend living in the country.

"I have come," said Benjamin, "to tell you good by. I am going away."

I inquired where.

"To the north," he replied.

I looked at him to see whether he was in earnest. I saw it all in his firm, set mouth. I implored him not to go, but he paid no heed to my words. He said he was no longer a boy, and every day made his yoke more galling. He had raised his hand against his master, and was to be publicly whipped for the offence. I reminded him of the poverty and hardships he must encounter among strangers. I told him he might be caught and brought back; and that was terrible to think of.

He grew vexed, and asked if poverty and hardships with freedom, were not preferable to our treatment in slavery. "Linda," he continued, "we are dogs here; foot-balls, cattle, every thing that's mean. No, I will not stay. Let them bring me back. We don't die but once."

He was right; but it was hard to give him up. "Go," said I, "and break your mother's heart."

I repented of my words ere they were out.

"Linda," said he, speaking as I had not heard him speak that evening, "how *could* you say that? Poor mother! be kind to her, Linda; and you, too, cousin Fanny."

Cousin Fanny was a friend who had lived some years with us.

Farewells were exchanged, and the bright, kind boy, endeared to us by so many acts of love, vanished from our sight.

It is not necessary to state how he made his escape. Suffice it to say, he was on his way to New York when a violent storm overtook the vessel. The captain said he must put into the nearest port. This alarmed Benjamin, who was aware that he would be advertised in every port near his own town. His embarrassment was noticed by the captain. To port they went. There the advertisement met the captain's eye. Benjamin so exactly answered its description, that the captain laid hold on him, and bound him in chains. The storm passed, and they proceeded to New York. Before reaching that port Benjamin managed to get off his chains and throw them overboard. He escaped from the vessel, but was pursued, captured, and carried back to his master.

When my grandmother returned home and found her youngest child had fled, great was her sorrow; but, with characteristic piety, she said, "God's will be done." Each morning, she inquired if any news had been heard from her boy. Yes, news *was* heard. The master was rejoicing over a letter, announcing the capture of his human chattel.

That day seems but as yesterday, so well do I remember it. I saw him led through the streets in chains, to jail. His face was ghastly pale, yet full of determination. He had begged one of the sailors to go to his mother's house and ask her not to meet him. He said the sight of her distress would take from him all self-control. She yearned to see him, and she went; but she screened herself in the crowd, that it might be as her child had said.

We were not allowed to visit him; but we had known the jailer for years, and he was a kind-hearted man. At midnight he opened the jail door for my grandmother and myself to enter, in disguise. When we entered the cell not a sound broke the stillness. "Benjamin, Benjamin!" whispered my grandmother. No answer. "Benjamin!" she again faltered. There was a jingle of chains. The moon had just risen, and cast an uncertain light through the bars of the window. We knelt down and took Benjamin's cold hands in ours. We did not speak. Sobs were heard, and Benjamin's lips were unsealed; for his mother was weeping on his neck. How vividly does memory bring back that sad night! Mother and son talked together. He asked her pardon for the suffering he had caused her. She said she had nothing to forgive; she could not blame his desire for freedom. He told her that when he was captured, he broke away, and was about casting himself into the river, when thoughts of *her* came over him, and he desisted. She asked if he did not also think of God. I fancied I saw his face grow fierce in the moonlight. He answered, "No, I did not think of him. When a man is hunted like a wild beast he forgets there is a God, a heaven. He forgets every thing in his struggle to get beyond the reach of the bloodhounds."

"Don't talk so, Benjamin," said she. "Put your trust in God. Be humble, my child, and your master will forgive you."

"Forgive me for *what*, mother? For not letting him treat me like a dog? No! I will never humble myself to him. I have worked for him for nothing all my life, and I am repaid with stripes and imprisonment. Here I will stay till I die, or till he sells me."

The poor mother shuddered at his words. I think he felt it; for when he next spoke, his voice was calmer. "Don't fret about me, mother. I ain't worth it," said he. "I wish I had some of your goodness. You bear every thing patiently, just as though you thought it was all right. I wish I could."

She told him she had not always been so; once, she was like him; but when sore troubles came upon her, and she had no arm to lean upon, she learned to call on God, and he lightened her burdens. She besought him to do likewise.

We overstaid our time, and were obliged to hurry from the jail.

Benjamin had been imprisoned three weeks, when my grandmother went to intercede for him with his master. He was immovable. He said Benjamin should serve as an example to the rest of his slaves; he should be kept in jail till he was subdued, or be sold if he got but one dollar for him. However, he afterwards relented in some degree. The chains were taken off, and we were allowed to visit him.

As his food was of the coarsest kind, we carried him as often as possible a warm supper, accompanied with some little luxury for the jailer.

Three months elapsed, and there was no prospect of release or of a purchaser. One day he was heard to sing and laugh. This piece of indecorum was told to his master, and the overseer was ordered to re-chain him. He was now confined in an apartment with other prisoners, who were covered with filthy rags. Benjamin was chained near them, and was soon covered with vermin. He worked at his chains till he succeeded in getting out of them. He passed them through the bars of the window, with a request that they should be taken to his master, and he should be informed that he was covered with vermin.

This audacity was punished with heavier chains, and prohibition of our visits.

My grandmother continued to send him fresh changes of clothes. The old ones were burned up. The last night we saw him in jail his mother still begged him to send for his master, and beg his pardon. Neither persuasion nor argument could turn him from his purpose. He calmly answered, "I am waiting his time."

Those chains were mournful to hear.

Another three months passed, and Benjamin left his prison walls. We that loved him waited to bid him a long and last farewell. A slave trader had bought him. You remember, I told you what price he brought when ten years of age. Now he was more than twenty years old, and sold for three hundred dollars. The master had been blind to his own interest. Long confinement had made his face too pale, his form too thin; moreover, the trader had heard something of his character, and it did not strike him as suitable for a slave. He said he would give any price if the handsome lad was a girl. We thanked God that he was not.

Could you have seen that mother clinging to her child, when they fastened the irons upon his wrists; could you have heard her heart-rending groans, and seen her bloodshot eyes wander wildly from face to face, vainly pleading for mercy; could you have witnessed that scene as I saw it, you would exclaim, *Slavery is damnable!*

Benjamin, her youngest, her pet, was forever gone! She could not realize it. She had had an interview with the trader for the purpose of ascertaining if Benjamin could be purchased. She was told it was impossible, as he had given bonds not to sell him till he was out of the state. He promised that he would not sell him till he reached New Orleans.

With a strong arm and unvaried trust, my grandmother began her work of love. Benjamin must be free. If she succeeded, she knew they would still be separated; but the sacrifice was not too great. Day and night she labored. The trader's price would treble that he gave; but she was not discouraged.

She employed a lawyer to write to a gentleman, whom she knew, in New Orleans. She begged him to interest himself for Benjamin, and he willingly favored her request. When he saw Benjamin, and stated his business, he thanked him; but said he preferred to wait a while before making the trader an offer. He knew he had tried to obtain a high price for him, and had invariably failed. This encouraged him to make another effort for freedom. So one morning, long before day, Benjamin was missing. He was riding over the blue billows, bound for Baltimore.

For once his white face did him a kindly service. They had no suspicion that it belonged to a slave; otherwise, the law would have been followed out to the letter, and the *thing* rendered back to slavery. The brightest skies are often overshadowed by the darkest clouds. Benjamin was taken sick, and compelled to remain in Baltimore three weeks. His strength was slow in returning; and his desire to continue his journey seemed to retard his recovery. How could he get strength without air and exercise? He resolved to venture on a short walk. A by-street was selected, where he thought himself secure of not being met by any one that knew him; but a voice called out, "Halloo, Ben, my boy! what are you doing *here*?"

His first impulse was to run; but his legs trembled so that he could not stir. He turned to confront his antagonist, and behold, there stood his old master's next door neighbor! He thought it was all over with him now; but it proved otherwise. That man was a miracle. He possessed a goodly number of slaves, and yet was not quite deaf to that mystic clock, whose ticking is rarely heard in the slaveholder's breast.

"Ben, you are sick," said he. "Why, you look like a ghost. I guess I gave you something of a start. Never mind, Ben, I am not going to touch you. You had a pretty tough time of it, and you may go on your way rejoicing for all me. But I would advise you to get out of this place plaguy quick,[2] for there are several gentlemen here from our town." He described the nearest and safest route to New York, and added, "I shall be glad to tell your mother I have seen you. Good by, Ben."

Benjamin turned away, filled with gratitude, and surprised that the town he hated contained such a gem—a gem worthy of a purer setting.

This gentleman was a Northerner by birth, and had married a southern lady. On his return, he told my grandmother that he had seen her son, and of the service he had rendered him.

Benjamin reached New York safely, and concluded to stop there until he had gained strength enough to proceed further. It happened that my grandmother's only remaining son had sailed for the same city on business for his mistress. Through God's providence, the brothers met. You may be sure it was a happy meeting. "O Phil," exclaimed Benjamin, "I am here at last." Then he told him how near he came to dying, almost in sight of free land, and how he prayed that he might live to get one breath of free air. He said life was worth something now, and it would be hard to die. In the old jail he had not valued it; once, he was tempted to destroy it; but something, he did not know what, had prevented him; perhaps it was fear. He had heard those who profess to be religious declare there was no heaven for self-murderers; and as his life had been pretty hot here, he did not desire a continuation of the same in another world. "If I die now," he exclaimed, "thank God, I shall die a freeman!"

He begged my uncle Phillip not to return south; but stay and work with him, till they earned enough to buy those at home. His brother told him it would kill their mother if he deserted her in her trouble. She had pledged her house, and with difficulty had raised money to buy him. Would he be bought?

"No, never!" he replied. "Do you suppose, Phil, when I have got so far out of their clutches, I will give them one red cent? No! And do you sup-

---

2. That is, awfully quick, very quick.

pose I would turn mother out of her home in her old age? That I would
let her pay all those hard-earned dollars for me, and never to see me? For
you know she will stay south as long as her other children are slaves. What
a good mother! Tell her to buy *you*, Phil. You have been a comfort to her,
and I have been a trouble. And Linda, poor Linda; what'll become of her?
Phil, you don't know what a life they lead her. She has told me something
about it, and I wish old Flint was dead, or a better man. When I was in
jail, he asked her if she didn't want *him* to ask my master to forgive me,
and take me home again. She told him, No; that I didn't want to go back.
He got mad, and said we were all alike. I never despised my own master
half as much as I do that man. There is many a worse slaveholder than
my master; but for all that I would not be his slave."

While Benjamin was sick, he had parted with nearly all his clothes to
pay necessary expenses. But he did not part with a little pin I fastened in
his bosom when we parted. It was the most valuable thing I owned, and
I thought none more worthy to wear it. He had it still.

His brother furnished him with clothes, and gave him what money he
had.

They parted with moistened eyes; and as Benjamin turned away, he
said, "Phil, I part with all my kindred." And so it proved. We never heard
from him again.

Uncle Phillip came home; and the first words he uttered when he entered the house were, "Mother, Ben is free! I have seen him in New York."
She stood looking at him with a bewildered air. "Mother, don't you believe it?" he said, laying his hand softly upon her shoulder. She raised her
hands, and exclaimed, "God be praised! Let us thank him." She dropped
on her knees, and poured forth her heart in prayer. Then Phillip must sit
down and repeat to her every word Benjamin had said. He told her all;
only he forbore to mention how sick and pale her darling looked. Why
should he distress her when she could do him no good?

The brave old woman still toiled on, hoping to rescue some of her
other children. After a while she succeeded in buying Phillip. She paid
eight hundred dollars, and came home with the precious document that
secured his freedom. The happy mother and son sat together by the old
hearthstone that night, telling how proud they were of each other, and
how they would prove to the world that they could take care of themselves, as they had long taken care of others. We all concluded by saying,
"He that is *willing* to be a slave, let him be a slave."

V. The Trials of Girlhood

During the first years of my service in Dr. Flint's family, I was accustomed to share some indulgences with the children of my mistress.

Though this seemed to me no more than right, I was grateful for it, and tried to merit the kindness by the faithful discharge of my duties. But I now entered on my fifteenth year—a sad epoch in the life of a slave girl. My master began to whisper foul words in my ear. Young as I was, I could not remain ignorant of their import. I tried to treat them with indifference or contempt. The master's age, my extreme youth, and the fear that his conduct would be reported to my grandmother, made him bear this treatment for many months. He was a crafty man, and resorted to many means to accomplish his purposes. Sometimes he had stormy, terrific ways, that made his victims tremble; sometimes he assumed a gentleness that he thought must surely subdue. Of the two, I preferred his stormy moods, although they left me trembling. He tried his utmost to corrupt the pure principles my grandmother had instilled. He peopled my young mind with unclean images, such as only a vile monster could think of. I turned from him with disgust and hatred. But he was my master. I was compelled to live under the same roof with him—where I saw a man forty years my senior daily violating the most sacred commandments of nature. He told me I was his property; that I must be subject to his will in all things. My soul revolted against the mean tyranny. But where could I turn for protection? No matter whether the slave girl be as black as ebony or as fair as her mistress. In either case, there is no shadow of law to protect her from insult, from violence, or even from death; all these are inflicted by fiends who bear the shape of men. The mistress, who ought to protect the helpless victim, has no other feelings towards her but those of jealousy and rage. The degradation, the wrongs, the vices, that grow out of slavery, are more than I can describe. They are greater than you would willingly believe. Surely, if you credited one half the truths that are told you concerning the helpless millions suffering in this cruel bondage, you at the north would not help to tighten the yoke. You surely would refuse to do for the master, on your own soil, the mean and cruel work which trained bloodhounds and the lowest class of whites do for him at the south. *Fugitive Slave Law—*

Every where the years bring to all enough of sin and sorrow; but in slavery the very dawn of life is darkened by these shadows. Even the little child, who is accustomed to wait on her mistress and her children, will learn, before she is twelve years old, why it is that her mistress hates such and such a one among the slaves. Perhaps the child's own mother is among those hated ones. She listens to violent outbreaks of jealous passion, and cannot help understanding what is the cause. She will become prematurely knowing in evil things. Soon she will learn to tremble when she hears her master's footfall. She will be compelled to realize that she is no longer a child. If God has bestowed beauty upon her, it will prove her greatest curse. That which commands admiration in the white woman only hastens the degradation of the female slave. I know that some are too much brutalized by slavery to feel the humiliation of their position; but many slaves feel it most acutely, and shrink from the memory of it. I cannot tell how much I suffered in the presence of these wrongs, nor how I am still pained by the retrospect. My master met me at every turn, reminding me that I belonged to him, and swearing by heaven and earth that he would compel me to submit to him. If I went out for a breath of fresh air, after a day of unwearied toil, his footsteps dogged me. If I knelt by my mother's grave, his dark shadow fell on me even there. The light heart which nature had given me became heavy with sad forebodings. The other slaves in my master's house noticed the change. Many of them pitied me; but none dared to ask the cause. They had no need to inquire. They knew too well the guilty practices under that roof; and they were aware that to speak of them was an offence that never went unpunished.

I longed for some one to confide in. I would have given the world to have laid my head on my grandmother's faithful bosom, and told her all my troubles. But Dr. Flint swore he would kill me, if I was not as silent as the grave. Then, although my grandmother was all in all to me, I feared her as well as loved her. I had been accustomed to look up to her with a respect bordering upon awe. I was very young, and felt shamefaced about telling her such impure things, especially as I knew her to be very strict on such subjects. Moreover, she was a woman of a high spirit. She was usually very quiet in her demeanor; but if her indignation was once roused, it was not very easily quelled. I had been told that she once chased a white gentleman with a loaded pistol, because he insulted one of her daughters. I dreaded the consequences of a violent outbreak; and both pride and fear kept me silent. But though I did not confide in my grandmother, and even evaded her vigilant watchfulness and inquiry, her presence in the neighborhood was some protection to me. Though she had been a slave, Dr. Flint was afraid of her. He dreaded her scorching rebukes. Moreover, she was known and patronized by many people; and he did not wish to have his villany made public. It was lucky for me that I did not live on a distant plantation, but in a town not so large that the inhabitants were ignorant of each other's affairs. Bad as are the laws and customs in a slaveholding community, the doctor, as a professional man, deemed it prudent to keep up some outward show of decency.

O, what days and nights of fear and sorrow that man caused me! Reader, it is not to awaken sympathy for myself that I am telling you truthfully what I suffered in slavery. I do it to kindle a flame of compassion in your hearts for my sisters who are still in bondage, suffering as I once suffered.

I once saw two beautiful children playing together. One was a fair white child; the other was her slave, and also her sister. When I saw them embracing each other, and heard their joyous laughter, I turned sadly away from the lovely sight. I foresaw the inevitable blight that would fall on the little slave's heart. I knew how soon her laughter would be changed to sighs. The fair child grew up to be a still fairer woman. From childhood to womanhood her pathway was blooming with flowers, and overarched by a sunny sky. Scarcely one day of her life had been clouded when the sun rose on her happy bridal morning.

How had those years dealt with her slave sister, the little playmate of her childhood? She, also, was very beautiful; but the flowers and sunshine of love were not for her. She drank the cup of sin, and shame, and misery, whereof her persecuted race are compelled to drink.

In view of these things, why are ye silent, ye free men and women of the north? Why do your tongues falter in maintenance of the right? Would that I had more ability! But my heart is so full, and my pen is so weak! There are noble men and women who plead for us, striving to help those who cannot help themselves. God bless them! God give them strength and courage to go on! God bless those, every where, who are laboring to advance the cause of humanity!

VI. The Jealous Mistress

I would ten thousand times rather that my children should be the half-starved paupers of Ireland[3] than to be the most pampered among the slaves of America. I would rather drudge out my life on a cotton plantation, till the grave opened to give me rest, than to live with an unprincipled master and a jealous mistress. The felon's home in a penitentiary is preferable. He may repent, and turn from the error of his ways, and so find peace; but it is not so with a favorite slave. She is not allowed to have any pride of character. It is deemed a crime in her to wish to be virtuous.

Mrs. Flint possessed the key to her husband's character before I was born. She might have used this knowledge to counsel and to screen the young and the innocent among her slaves; but for them she had no sympathy. They were the objects of her constant suspicion and malevolence. She watched her husband with unceasing vigilance; but he was well practised in means to evade it. What he could not find opportunity to say in words he manifested in signs. He invented more than were ever thought of in a deaf and dumb asylum. I let them pass, as if I did not understand what he meant; and many were the curses and threats bestowed on me for my stupidity. One day he caught me teaching myself to write. He frowned, as if he was not well pleased; but I suppose he came to the conclusion that such an accomplishment might help to advance his favorite scheme. Before long, notes were often slipped into my hand. I would return them, saying, "I can't read them, sir." "Can't you?" he replied; "then

---

3. Abolitionists frequently compared the situation of American slaves to the Irish sufferings during the potato famine of 1845–49.

I must read them to you." He always finished the reading by asking, "Do you understand?" Sometimes he would complain of the heat of the tea room, and order his supper to be placed on a small table in the piazza. He would seat himself there with a well-satisfied smile, and tell me to stand by and brush away the flies. He would eat very slowly, pausing between the mouthfuls. These intervals were employed in describing the happiness I was so foolishly throwing away, and in threatening me with the penalty that finally awaited my stubborn disobedience. He boasted much of the forbearance he had exercised towards me, and reminded me that there was a limit to his patience. When I succeeded in avoiding opportunities for him to talk to me at home, I was ordered to come to his office, to do some errand. When there, I was obliged to stand and listen to such language as he saw fit to address to me. Sometimes I so openly expressed my contempt for him that he would become violently enraged, and I wondered why he did not strike me. Circumstanced as he was, he probably thought it was better policy to be forbearing. But the state of things grew worse and worse daily. In desperation I told him that I must and would apply to my grandmother for protection. He threatened me with death, and worse than death, if I made any complaint to her. Strange to say, I did not despair. I was naturally of a buoyant disposition, and always I had a hope of somehow getting out of his clutches. Like many a poor, simple slave before me, I trusted that some threads of joy would yet be woven into my dark destiny.

I had entered my sixteenth year, and every day it became more apparent that my presence was intolerable to Mrs. Flint. Angry words frequently passed between her and her husband. He had never punished me himself, and he would not allow any body else to punish me. In that respect, she was never satisfied; but, in her angry moods, no terms were too vile for her to bestow upon me. Yet I, whom she detested so bitterly, had far more pity for her than he had, whose duty it was to make her life happy. I never wronged her, or wished to wrong her; and one word of kindness from her would have brought me to her feet.

After repeated quarrels between the doctor and his wife, he announced his intention to take his youngest daughter, then four years old, to sleep in his apartment. It was necessary that a servant should sleep in the same room, to be on hand if the child stirred. I was selected for that office, and informed for what purpose that arrangement had been made. By managing to keep within sight of people, as much as possible, during the day time, I had hitherto succeeded in eluding my master, though a razor was often held to my throat to force me to change this line of policy. At night I slept by the side of my great aunt, where I felt safe. He was too prudent to come into her room. She was an old woman, and had been in the family many years. Moreover, as a married man, and a professional man, he deemed it necessary to save appearances in some degree. But he resolved to remove the obstacle in the way of his scheme; and he thought he had planned it so that he should evade suspicion. He was well aware how much I prized my refuge by the side of my old aunt, and he determined to dispossess me of it. The first night the doctor had the little child in his room alone. The next morning, I was ordered to take my station as nurse the following night. A kind Providence interposed in my favor. During the day Mrs. Flint heard of this new arrangement, and a storm followed. I rejoiced to hear it rage.

After a while my mistress sent for me to come to her room. Her first question was, "Did you know you were to sleep in the doctor's room?"

"Yes, ma'am."

"Who told you?"

"My master."

"Will you answer truly all the questions I ask?"

"Yes, ma'am."

"Tell me, then, as you hope to be forgiven, are you innocent of what I have accused you?"

"I am."

She handed me a Bible, and said, "Lay your hand on your heart, kiss this holy book, and swear before God that you tell me the truth."

I took the oath she required, and I did it with a clear conscience.

"You have taken God's holy word to testify your innocence," said she. "If you have deceived me, beware! Now take this stool, sit down, look me directly in the face, and tell me all that has passed between your master and you."

I did as she ordered. As I went on with my account her color changed frequently, she wept, and sometimes groaned. She spoke in tones so sad, that I was touched by her grief. The tears came to my eyes; but I was soon convinced that her emotions arose from anger and wounded pride. She felt that her marriage vows were desecrated, her dignity insulted; but she had no compassion for the poor victim of her husband's perfidy. She pitied herself as a martyr; but she was incapable of feeling for the condition of shame and misery in which her unfortunate, helpless slave was placed.

Yet perhaps she had some touch of feeling for me; for when the conference was ended, she spoke kindly, and promised to protect me. I should have been much comforted by this assurance if I could have had confidence in it; but my experiences in slavery had filled me with distrust. She was not a very refined woman, and had not much control over her passions. I was an object of her jealousy, and, consequently, of her hatred; and I knew I could not expect kindness or confidence from her under the circumstances in which I was placed. I could not blame her. Slaveholders' wives feel as other women would under similar circumstances. The fire of her temper kindled from small sparks, and now the flame became so intense that the doctor was obliged to give up his intended arrangement.

I knew I had ignited the torch, and I expected to suffer for it afterwards; but I felt too thankful to my mistress for the timely aid she rendered me to care much about that. She now took me to sleep in a room adjoining her own. There I was an object of her especial care, though not of her especial comfort, for she spent many a sleepless night to watch over me. Sometimes I woke up, and found her bending over me. At other times she whispered in my ear, as though it was her husband who was speaking to me, and listened to hear what I would answer. If she startled me, on such occasions, she would glide stealthily away; and the next morning she would tell me I had been talking in my sleep, and ask who I was talking to. At last, I began to be fearful for my life. It had been often threatened; and you can imagine, better than I can describe, what an unpleasant sensation it must produce to wake up in the dead of night and find a jealous woman bending over you. Terrible as this experience was, I had fears that it would give place to one more terrible.

My mistress grew weary of her vigils; they did not prove satisfactory. She changed her tactics. She now tried the trick of accusing my master of crime, in my presence, and gave my name as the author of the accusation. To my utter astonishment, he replied, "I don't believe it; but if she did acknowledge it, you tortured her into exposing me." Tortured into exposing him! Truly, Satan had no difficulty in distinguishing the color of his soul! I understood his object in making this false representation. It was to show me that I gained nothing by seeking the protection of my mistress; that the power was still all in his own hands. I pitied Mrs. Flint. She was a second wife, many years the junior of her husband; and the hoary-headed miscreant was enough to try the patience of a wiser and better woman. She was completely foiled, and knew not how to proceed. She would gladly have had me flogged for my supposed false oath; but, as I have already stated, the doctor never allowed any one to whip me. The old sinner was politic. The application of the lash might have led to remarks that would have exposed him in the eyes of his children and grandchildren. How often did I rejoice that I lived in a town where all the inhabitants knew each other! If I had been on a remote plantation, or lost among the multitude of a crowded city, I should not be a living woman at this day.

The secrets of slavery are concealed like those of the Inquisition. My master was, to my knowledge, the father of eleven slaves. But did the mothers dare to tell who was the father of their children? Did the other slaves dare to allude to it, except in whispers among themselves? No, indeed! They knew too well the terrible consequences.

My grandmother could not avoid seeing things which excited her suspicions. She was uneasy about me, and tried various ways to buy me; but the never-changing answer was always repeated: "Linda does not belong to *me*. She is my daughter's property, and I have no legal right to sell her." The conscientious man! He was too scrupulous to *sell* me; but he had no scruples whatever about committing a much greater wrong against the helpless young girl placed under his guardianship, as his daughter's property. Sometimes my persecutor would ask me whether I would like to be sold. I told him I would rather be sold to any body than to lead such a life as I did. On such occasions he would assume the air of a very injured individual, and reproach me for my ingratitude. "Did I not take you into the house, and make you the companion of my own children?" he would say. "Have I ever treated you like a negro? I have never allowed you to be punished, not even to please your mistress. And this is the recompense I get, you ungrateful girl!" I answered that he had reasons of his own for screening me from punishment, and that the course he pursued made my mistress hate me and persecute me. If I wept, he would say, "Poor child! Don't cry! don't cry! I will make peace for you with your mistress. Only let me arrange matters in my own way. Poor, foolish girl! you don't know what is for your own good. I would cherish you. I would make a lady of you. Now go, and think of all I have promised you."

I did think of it.

Reader, I draw no imaginary pictures of southern homes. I am telling you the plain truth. Yet when victims make their escape from this wild beast of Slavery, northerners consent to act the part of bloodhounds, and hunt the poor fugitive back into his den, "full of dead men's bones, and all uncleanness."[4] Nay, more, they are not only willing, but proud, to give their daughters in marriage to slaveholders. The poor girls have romantic notions of a sunny clime, and of the flowering vines that all the year round shade a happy home. To what disappointments are they destined! The young wife soon learns that the husband in whose hands she has placed her happiness pays no regard to his marriage vows. Children of every shade of complexion play with her own fair babies, and too well she knows that they are born unto him of his own household. Jealousy and hatred enter the flowery home, and it is ravaged of its loveliness.

Southern women often marry a man knowing that he is the father of many little slaves. They do not trouble themselves about it. They regard such children as property, as marketable as the pigs on the plantation; and it is seldom that they do not make them aware of this by passing them into the slave-trader's hands as soon as possible, and thus getting them out of their sight. I am glad to say there are some honorable exceptions.

I have myself known two southern wives who exhorted their husbands to free those slaves towards whom they stood in a "parental relation;" and their request was granted. These husbands blushed before the superior nobleness of their wives' natures. Though they had only counselled them to do that which it was their duty to do, it commanded their respect, and

---

4. Matthew 23.27. Bloodhounds are a breed of hunting dogs that were frequently used to track slaves.

rendered their conduct more exemplary. Concealment was at an end, and confidence took the place of distrust.

Though this bad institution deadens the moral sense, even in white women, to a fearful extent, it is not altogether extinct. I have heard southern ladies say of Mr. Such a one, "He not only thinks it no disgrace to be the father of those little niggers, but he is not ashamed to call himself their master. I declare, such things ought not to be tolerated in any decent society!"

TREAT PEOPLE UNTO OTHERS ., ^ ^ ·

VII. The Lover

Why does the slave ever love? Why allow the tendrils of the heart to twine around objects which may at any moment be wrenched away by the hand of violence? When separations come by the hand of death, the pious soul can bow in resignation, and say, "Not my will, but thine be done, O Lord!" But when the ruthless hand of man strikes the blow, regardless of the misery he causes, it is hard to be submissive. I did not reason thus when I was a young girl. Youth will be youth. I loved, and I indulged the hope that the dark clouds around me would turn out a bright lining. I forgot that in the land of my birth the shadows are too dense for light to penetrate. A land

> "Where laughter is not mirth; nor thought the mind;
> Nor words a language; nor e'en men mankind.
> Where cries reply to curses, shrieks to blows,
> And each is tortured in his separate hell."[5]

There was in the neighborhood a young colored carpenter; a free born man. We had been well acquainted in childhood, and frequently met together afterwards. We became mutually attached, and he proposed to marry me. I loved him with all the ardor of a young girl's first love. But when I reflected that I was a slave, and that the laws gave no sanction to the marriage of such, my heart sank within me. My lover wanted to buy me; but I knew that Dr. Flint was too wilful and arbitrary a man to consent to that arrangement. From him, I was sure of experiencing all sorts of opposition, and I had nothing to hope from my mistress. She would have been delighted to have got rid of me, but not in that way. It would have relieved her mind of a burden if she could have seen me sold to some distant state, but if I was married near home I should be just as much in her husband's power as I had previously been, — for the husband of a slave has no power to protect her. Moreover, my mistress, like many others, seemed to think that slaves had no right to any family ties of their

5. Lord Byron, "The Lament of Tasso."

own; that they were created merely to wait upon the family of the mistress. I once heard her abuse a young slave girl, who told her that a colored man wanted to make her his wife. "I will have you peeled and pickled, my lady," said she, "if I ever hear you mention that subject again. Do you suppose that I will have you tending *my* children with the children of that nigger?" The girl to whom she said this had a mulatto child, of course not acknowledged by its father. The poor black man who loved her would have been proud to acknowledge his helpless offspring.

Many and anxious were the thoughts I revolved in my mind. I was at a loss what to do. Above all things, I was desirous to spare my lover the insults that had cut so deeply into my own soul. I talked with my grandmother about it, and partly told her my fears. I did not dare to tell her the worst. She had long suspected all was not right, and if I confirmed her suspicious I knew a storm would rise that would prove the overthrow of all my hopes.

This love-dream had been my support through many trials: and I could not bear to run the risk of having it suddenly dissipated. There was a lady in the neighborhood, a particular friend of Dr. Flint's, who often visited the house. I had a great respect for her, and she had always manifested a friendly interest in me. Grandmother thought she would have great influence with the doctor. I went to this lady, and told her my story. I told her I was aware that my lover's being a free-born man would prove a great objection; but he wanted to buy me; and if Dr. Flint would consent to that arrangement, I felt sure he would be willing to pay any reasonable price. She knew that Mrs. Flint disliked me; therefore, I ventured to suggest that perhaps my mistress would approve of my being sold, as that would rid her of me. The lady listened with kindly sympathy, and promised to do her utmost to promote my wishes. She had an interview with the doctor, and I believe she pleaded my cause earnestly; but it was all to no purpose.

How I dreaded my master now! Every minute I expected to be summoned to his presence; but the day passed, and I heard nothing from him. The next morning, a message was brought to me: "Master wants you in his study." I found the door ajar, and I stood a moment gazing at the hateful man who claimed a right to rule me, body and soul. I entered, and tried to appear calm. I did not want him to know how my heart was bleeding. He looked fixedly at me, with an expression which seemed to say, "I have half a mind to kill you on the spot." At last he broke the silence, and that was a relief to both of us.

"So you want to be married, do you?" said he, "and to a free nigger."

"Yes, sir."

"Well, I'll soon convince you whether I am your master, or the nigger fellow you honor so highly. If you *must* have a husband, you may take up with one of my slaves."

What a situation I should be in, as the wife of one of *his* slaves, even if my heart had been interested!

I replied, "Don't you suppose, sir, that a slave can have some preference about marrying? Do you suppose that all men are alike to her?"

"Do you love this nigger?" said he, abruptly.

"Yes, sir."

"How dare you tell me so!" he exclaimed, in great wrath. After a slight
pause, he added, "I supposed you thought more of yourself; that you felt
above the insults of such puppies."

"I replied, "If he is a puppy I am a puppy, for we are both of the negro
race. It is right and honorable for us to love each other. The man you call
a puppy never insulted me, sir: and he would not love me if he did not
believe me to be a virtuous woman."

He sprang upon me like a tiger, and gave me a stunning blow. It was
the first time he had ever struck me; and fear did not enable me to control my anger. When I had recovered a little from the effects, I exclaimed,
"You have struck me for answering you honestly. How I despise you!"

There was silence for some minutes. Perhaps he was deciding what
should be my punishment; or, perhaps, he wanted to give me time to reflect on what I had said, and to whom I had said it. Finally, he asked, "Do
you know what you have said?"

"Yes, sir; but your treatment drove me to it."

"Do you know that I have a right to do as I like with you,—that I can
kill you, if I please?"

"You have tried to kill me, and I wish you had; but you have no right
to do as you like with me."

"Silence!" he exclaimed, in a thundering voice. "By heavens, girl, you
forget yourself too far! Are you mad? If you are, I will soon bring you to
your senses. Do you think any other master would bear what I have borne
from you this morning? Many masters would have killed you on the spot.
How would you like to be sent to jail for your insolence?"

"I know I have been disrespectful, sir," I replied; "but you drove me to
it; I couldn't help it. As for the jail, there would be more peace for me
there than there is here."

"You deserve to go there," said he, "and to be under such treatment,
that you would forget the meaning of the word *peace*. It would do you
good. It would take some of your high notions out of you. But I am not
ready to send you there yet, notwithstanding your ingratitude for all my
kindness and forbearance. You have been the plague of my life. I have
wanted to make you happy, and I have been repaid with the basest ingratitude; but though you have proved yourself incapable of appreciating
my kindness, I will be lenient towards you, Linda. I will give you one
more chance to redeem your character. If you behave yourself and do as
I require, I will forgive you and treat you as I always have done; but if you
disobey me, I will punish you as I would the meanest slave on my plantation. Never let me hear that fellow's name mentioned again. If I ever
know of your speaking to him, I will cowhide you both; and if I catch him

lurking about my premises, I will shoot him as soon as I would a dog. Do you hear what I say? I'll teach you a lesson about marriage and free niggers! Now go, and let this be the last time I have occasion to speak to you on this subject."

Reader, did you ever hate? I hope not. I never did but once; and I trust I never shall again. Somebody has called it "the atmosphere of hell;" and I believe it is so.

For a fortnight the doctor did not speak to me. He thought to mortify me; to make me feel that I had disgraced myself by receiving the honorable addresses of a respectable colored man, in preference to the base proposals of a white man. But though his lips disdained to address me, his eyes were very loquacious. No animal ever watched its prey more narrowly than he watched me. He knew that I could write, though he had failed to make me read his letters; and he was now troubled lest I should exchange letters with another man. After a while he became weary of silence; and I was sorry for it. One morning, as he passed through the hall, to leave the house, he contrived to thrust a note into my hand. I thought I had better read it, and spare myself the vexation of having him read it to me. It expressed regret for the blow he had given me, and reminded me that I myself was wholly to blame for it. He hoped I had become convinced of the injury I was doing myself by incurring his displeasure. He wrote that he had made up his mind to go to Louisiana; that he should take several slaves with him, and intended I should be one of the number. My mistress would remain where she was; therefore I should have nothing to fear from that quarter. If I merited kindness from him, he assured me that it would be lavishly bestowed. He begged me to think over the matter, and answer the following day.

The next morning I was called to carry a pair of scissors to his room. I laid them on the table, with the letter beside them. He thought it was my answer, and did not call me back. I went as usual to attend my young mistress to and from school. He met me in the street, and ordered me to stop at his office on my way back. When I entered, he showed me his letter, and asked me why I had not answered it. I replied, "I am your daughter's property, and it is in your power to send me, or take me, wherever you please." He said he was very glad to find me so willing to go, and that we should start early in the autumn. He had a large practice in the town, and I rather thought he had made up the story merely to frighten me. However that might be, I was determined that I would never go to Louisiana with him.

Summer passed away, and early in the autumn Dr. Flint's eldest son was sent to Louisiana to examine the country, with a view to emigrating. That news did not disturb me. I knew very well that I should not be sent with *him*. That I had not been taken to the plantation before this time, was owing to the fact that his son was there. He was jealous of his son; and jealousy of the overseer had kept him from punishing me by sending me into the fields to work. Is it strange that I was not proud of these protectors? As for the overseer, he was a man for whom I had less respect than I had for a bloodhound.

Young Mr. Flint did not bring back a favorable report of Louisiana, and I heard no more of that scheme. Soon after this, my lover met me at the corner of the street, and I stopped to speak to him. Looking up, I saw my master watching us from his window. I hurried home, trembling with fear. I was sent for, immediately, to go to his room. He met me with a blow. "When is mistress to be married?" said he, in a sneering tone. A shower of oaths and imprecations followed. How thankful I was that my lover was a free man! that my tyrant had no power to flog him for speaking to me in the street!

Again and again I revolved in my mind how all this would end. There was no hope that the doctor would consent to sell me on any terms. He had an iron will, and was determined to keep me, and to conquer me. My lover was an intelligent and religious man. Even if he could have obtained permission to marry me while I was a slave, the marriage would give him no power to protect me from my master. It would have made him miserable to witness the insults I should have been subjected to. And then, if we had children, I knew they must "follow the condition of the mother."[6] What a terrible blight that would be on the heart of a free, intelligent father! For *his* sake, I felt that I ought not to link his fate with my own unhappy destiny. He was going to Savannah to see about a little property left him by an uncle; and hard as it was to bring my feelings to it, I earnestly entreated him not to come back. I advised him to go to the Free States, where his tongue would not be tied, and where his intelligence would be of more avail to him. He left me, still hoping the day would come when I could be bought. With me the lamp of hope had gone out. The dream of my girlhood was over. I felt lonely and desolate.

Still I was not stripped of all. I still had my good grandmother, and my affectionate brother. When he put his arms round my neck, and looked into my eyes, as if to read there the troubles I dared not tell, I felt that I still had something to love. But even that pleasant emotion was chilled by the reflection that he might be torn from me at any moment, by some sudden freak of my master. If he had known how we loved each other, I think he would have exulted in separating us. We often planned together how we could get to the north. But, as William remarked, such things are easier said than done. My movements were very closely watched, and we had no means of getting any money to defray our expenses. As for grandmother, she was strongly opposed to her children's undertaking any such project. She had not forgotten poor Benjamin's sufferings, and she was afraid that if another child tried to escape, he would have a similar or a worse fate. To me,

---

6. Whether a child was free or enslaved was determined by the legal status of his or her mother.

nothing seemed more dreadful than my present life. I said to myself, "William *must* be free. He shall go to the north, and I will follow him." Many a slave sister has formed the same plans.

VIII. What Slaves Are Taught to Think of the North

Slaveholders pride themselves upon being honorable men; but if you were to hear the enormous lies they tell their slaves, you would have small respect for their veracity. I have spoken plain English. Pardon me. I cannot use a milder term. When they visit the north, and return home, they tell their slaves of the runaways they have seen, and describe them to be in the most deplorable condition. A slaveholder once told me that he had seen a runaway friend of mine in New York, and that she besought him to take her back to her master, for she was literally dying of starvation; that many days she had only one cold potato to eat, and at other times could get nothing at all. He said he refused to take her, because he knew her master would not thank him for bringing such a miserable wretch to his house. He ended by saying to me, "This is the punishment she brought on herself for running away from a kind master."

This whole story was false. I afterwards staid with that friend in New York, and found her in comfortable circumstances. She had never thought of such a thing as wishing to go back to slavery. Many of the slaves believe such stories, and think it is not worth while to exchange slavery for such a hard kind of freedom. It is difficult to persuade such that freedom could make them useful men, and enable them to protect their wives and children. If those heathen in our Christian land had as much teaching as some Hindoos, they would think otherwise. They would know that liberty is more valuable than life. They would begin to understand their own capabilities, and exert themselves to become men and women.

But while the Free States sustain a law which hurls fugitives back into slavery, how can the slaves resolve to become men? There are some who strive to protect wives and daughters from the insults of their masters; but those who have such sentiments have had advantages above the general mass of slaves. They have been partially civilized and Christianized by favorable circumstances. Some are bold enough to *utter* such sentiments to their masters. O, that there were more of them!

Some poor creatures have been so brutalized by the lash that they will sneak out of the way to give their masters free access to their wives and daughters. Do you think this proves the black man to belong to an inferior order of beings? What would *you* be, if you had been born and brought up a slave, with generations of slaves for ancestors? I admit that the black man *is* inferior. But what is it that makes him so? It is the ignorance in which white men compel him to live; it is the torturing whip that lashes manhood out of him; it is the fierce bloodhounds of the South, and the scarcely less cruel human bloodhounds of the north, who enforce the Fugitive Slave Law. *They* do the work.

Southern gentlemen indulge in the most contemptuous expressions about the Yankees, while they, on their part, consent to do the vilest work for them, such as the ferocious bloodhounds and the despised negro-hunters are employed to do at home. When southerners go to the north, they are proud to do them honor; but the northern man is not welcome south of Mason and Dixon's line, unless he suppresses every thought and feeling at variance with their "peculiar institution." Nor is it enough to be silent. The masters are not pleased, unless they obtain a greater degree of subservience than that; and they are generally accomodated. Do they respect the northerner for this? I trow[7] not. Even the slaves despise "a northern man with southern principles;" and that is the class they generally see. When northerners go to the south to reside, they prove very apt scholars. They soon imbibe the sentiments and disposition of their neighbors, and generally go beyond their teachers. Of the two, they are proverbially the hardest masters.

They seem to satisfy their consciences with the doctrine that God created the Africans to be slaves. What a libel upon the heavenly Father, who "made of one blood all nations of men!" And then who *are* Africans? Who can measure the amount of Anglo-Saxon blood coursing in the veins of American slaves?

I have spoken of the pains slaveholders take to give their slaves a bad opinion of the north; but, notwithstanding this, intelligent slaves are aware that they have many friends in the Free States. Even the most ignorant have some confused notions about it. They knew that I could read; and I was often asked if I had seen any thing in the newspapers about white folks over in the big north, who were trying to get their freedom for them. Some believe that the abolitionists have already made them free, and that it is established by law, but that their masters prevent the law from going into effect. One woman begged me to get a newspaper and read it over. She said her husband told her that the black people had sent word to the queen of 'Merica that they were all slaves; that she didn't believe it, and went to Washington city to see the president about it. They quarrelled; she drew her sword upon him, and swore that he should help her to make them all free.

That poor, ignorant woman thought that America was governed by a Queen, to whom the President was subordinate. I wish the President was subordinate to Queen Justice.

7. Know.

IX. Sketches of Neighboring Slaveholders

There was a planter in the country, not far from us, whom I will call Mr. Litch. He was an ill-bred, uneducated man, but very wealthy. He had six hundred slaves, many of whom he did not know by sight. His extensive plantation was managed by well-paid overseers. There was a jail and a whipping post on his grounds; and whatever cruelties were perpetrated there, they passed without comment. He was so effectually screened by his great wealth that he was called to no account for his crimes, not even for murder.

Various were the punishements resorted to. A favorite one was to tie a rope round a man's body, and suspend him from the ground. A fire was kindled over him, from which was suspended a piece of fat pork. As this cooked, the scalding drops of fat continually fell on the bare flesh. On his own plantation, he required very strict obedience to the eight commandment.[8] But depredations on the neighbors were allowable, provided the culprit managed to evade detection or suspicion. If a neighbor brought a charge of theft against any of his slaves, he was browbeaten by the master, who assured him that his slaves had enough of every thing at home, and had no inducement to steal. No sooner was the neighbor's back turned, than the accused was sought out, and whipped for his lack of discretion. If a slave stole from him even a pound of meat or a peck of corn, if detection followed, he was put in chains and imprisoned, and so kept till his form was attenuated by hunger and suffering.

A freshet[9] once bore his wine cellar and meat house miles away from the plantation. Some slaves followed, and secured bits of meat and bottles of wine. Two were detected; a ham and some liquor being found in their huts. They were summoned by their master. No words were used, but a club felled them to the ground. A rough box was their coffin, and their interment was a dog's burial. Nothing was said.

Murder was so common on his plantation that he feared to be alone after nightfall. He might have believed in ghosts.

His brother, if not equal in wealth, was at least equal in cruelty. His bloodhounds were well trained. Their pen was spacious, and a terror to the slaves. They were let loose ón a runaway, and if they tracked him, they literally tore the flesh from his bones. When this slaveholder died, his shrieks and groans were so frightful that they appalled his own friends. His last words were, "I am going to hell; bury my money with me."

After death his eyes remained open. To press the lids down, silver dollars were laid on them. These were buried with him. From this circumstance, a rumor went abroad that his coffin was filled with money. Three times his grave was opened, and his coffin taken out. The last time, his

---

8. Exodus 20.15, "Thou Shalt not Steal."
9. Freshwater stream that empties into a sea.

body was found on the ground, and a flock of buzzards were pecking at it. He was again interred, and a sentinel set over his grave. The perpetrators were never discovered.

Cruelty is contagious in uncivilized communities. Mr. Conant, a neighbor of Mr. Litch, returned from town one evening in a partial state of intoxication. His body servant gave him some offence. He was divested of his clothes, except his skirt, whipped, and tied to a large tree in front of the house. It was a stormy night in winter. The wind blew bitterly cold, and the boughs of the old tree crackled under falling sleet. A member of the family, fearing he would freeze to death, begged that he might be taken down; but the master would not relent. He remained there three hours; and, when he was cut down, he was more dead than alive. Another slave, who stole a pig from this master, to appease his hunger, was terribly flogged. In desperation, he tried to run away. But at the end of two miles, he was so faint with loss of blood, he thought he was dying. He had a wife, and he longed to see her once more. Too sick to walk, he crept back that long distance on his hands and knees. When he reached his master's, it was night. He had not strength to rise and open the gate. He moaned, and tried to call for help. I had a friend living in the same family. At last his cry reached her. She went out and found the prostate man at the gate. She ran back to the house for assistance, and two men returned with her. They carried him in, and laid him on the floor. The back of his shirt was one clot of blood. By means of lard, my friend loosened it from the raw flesh. She bandaged him, gave him cool drink, and left him to rest. The master said he deserved a hundred more lashes. When his own labor was stolen from him, he had stolen food to appease his hunger. This was his crime.

Another neighbor was a Mrs. Wade. At no hour of the day was there cessation of the lash on her premises. Her labors began with the dawn, and did not cease till long after nightfall. The barn was her particular place of torture. There she lashed the slaves with the might of a man. An old slave of hers once said to me, "It is hell in missis's house. 'Pears I can never get out. Day and night I prays to die."

The mistress died before the old woman, and, when dying, entreated her husband not to permit any one of her slaves to look on her after death. A slave who had nursed her children, and had still a child in her care, watched her chance, and stole with it in her arms to the room where lay her dead mistress. She gazed a while on her, then raised her hand and dealt two blows on her face, saying, as she did so, "The devil is got you *now!*" She forgot that the child was looking on. She had just begun to talk; and she said to her father, "I did see ma, and mammy did strike ma, so," striking her own face with her little hand. The master was startled. He could not imagine how the nurse could obtain access to the room where the corpse lay; for he kept the door locked. He questioned her. She confessed that what the child had said was true, and told how she had procured the key. She was sold to Georgia.

In my childhood I knew a valuable slave, named Charity, and loved her, as all children did. Her young mistress married, and took her to Louisiana. Her little boy, James, was sold to a good sort of master. He became involved in debt, and James was sold again to a wealthy slaveholder, noted for his cruelty. With this man he grew up to manhood, receiving the treatment of a dog. After a severe whipping, to save himself from further infliction of the lash, with which he was threatened, he took to the woods. He was in a most miserable condition—cut by the cowskin, half naked, half starved, and without the means of procuring a crust of bread.

Some weeks after his escape, he was captured, tied, and carried back to his master's plantation. This man considered punishment in his jail, on bread and water, after receiving hundreds of lashes, too mild for the poor slave's offence. Therefore he decided, after the overseer should have whipped him to his satisfaction, to have him placed between the screws of the cotton gin, to stay as long as he had been in the woods. This wretched creature was cut with the whip from his head to his feet, then washed with strong brine, to prevent the flesh from mortifying, and make it heal sooner than it otherwise would. He was then put into the cotton gin, which was screwed down, only allowing him room to turn on his side when he could not lie on his back. Every morning a slave was sent with a piece of bread and bowl of water, which were placed within reach of the poor fellow. The slave was charged, under penalty of severe punishment, not to speak to him.

Four days passed, and the slave continued to carry the bread and water. On the second morning, he found the bread gone, but the water untouched. When he had been in the press four days and five nights, the slave informed his master that the water had not been used for four mornings, and that a horrible stench came from the gin house. The overseer was sent to examine into it. When the press was unscrewed, the dead body was found partly eaten by rats and vermin. Perhaps the rats that devoured his bread had gnawed him before life was extinct. Poor Charity! Grandmother and I often asked each other how her affectionate heart would bear the news, if she should ever hear of the murder of her son. We had known her husband, and knew that James was like him in manliness and intelligence. These were the qualities that made it so hard for him to be a plantation slave. They put him into a rough box, and buried him with less feeling that would have been manifested for an old house dog. Nobody asked any questions. He was a slave; and the feeling was that the master had a right to do what he pleased with his own property. And what did *he* care for the value of a slave? He had hundreds of them. When they had finished their daily toil, they must hurry to eat their little morsels, and be ready to extinguish their pine knots before nine o'clock, when the overseer went his patrol rounds. He entered every cabin, to see that men and their wives had gone to bed together, lest the men, from over-fatigue, should fall asleep in the chimney corner, and remain there till the morning horn called them to their daily task. Women are considered of no value, unless they continually increase their owner's stock. They are put on a par with animals. This same master shot a woman through the head, who had run away and been brought back to him. No one called him to account for it. If a slave resisted being whipped, the bloodhounds were unpacked, and set upon him, to tear his flesh from his bones. The master who did these things was highly educated, and styled a perfect gentleman. He also boasted the name and standing of a Christian, though Satan never had a truer follower.

I could tell of more slaveholders as cruel as those I have described. They are not exceptions to the general rule. I do not say there are no humane slaveholders. Such characters do exist, notwithstanding the hardening influences around them. But they are "like angels' visits—few and far between."[1]

I knew a young lady who was one of these rare specimens. She was an orphan, and inherited as slaves a woman and her six children. Their father was a free man. They had a comfortable home of their own, parents and children living together. The mother and eldest daughter served their mistress during the day, and at night returned to their dwelling, which was on the premises. The young lady was very pious, and there was some reality in her religion. She taught her slaves to lead pure lives, and wished them to enjoy the fruit of their own industry. *Her* religion was not a garb put on for Sunday, and laid aside till Sunday returned again. The eldest daughter of the slave mother was promised in marriage to a free man; and the day before the wedding this good mistress emancipated her, in order that her marriage might have the sanction of *law*.

Report said that this young lady cherished an unrequited affection for a man who had resolved to marry for wealth. In the course of time a rich uncle of hers died. He left six thousand dollars to his two sons by a colored woman, and the remainder of his property to this orphan niece. The metal soon attracted the magnet. The lady and her weighty purse became his. She offered to manumit her slaves—telling them that her marriage might make unexpected changes in their destiny, and she wished to insure their happiness. They refused to take their freedom, saying that she had always been their best friend, and they could not be so happy any where as with her. I was not surprised. I had often seen them in their comfortable home, and thought that the whole town did not contain a happier family. They had never felt slavery; and, when it was too late, they were convinced of its reality.

When the new master claimed this family as his property, the father became furious, and went to his mistress for protection. "I can do nothing for you now, Harry," said she. "I no longer have the power I had a

---

1. John Norris, *The Parting* (1678): "Like angels' visits, short and bright"; Robert Blair, *The Grave* (1743): "Like those of angels, short and far between."

week ago. I have succeeded in obtaining the freedom of your wife; but I cannot obtain it for your children." The unhappy father swore that nobody should take his children from him. He concealed them in the woods for some days; but they were discovered and taken. The father was put in jail, and the two oldest boys sold to Georgia. One little girl, too young to be of service to her master, was left with the wretched mother. The other three were carried to their master's plantation. The eldest soon became a mother; and, when the slaveholder's wife looked at the babe, she wept bitterly. She knew that her own husband had violated the purity she had so carefully inculcated. She had a second child by her master, and then he sold her and his offspring to his brother. She bore two children to the brother, and was sold again. The next sister went crazy. The life she was compelled to lead drove her mad. The third one became the mother of five daughters. Before the birth of the fourth the pious mistress died. To the last, she rendered every kindness to the slaves that her unfortunate circumstances permitted. She passed away peacefully, glad to close her eyes on a life which had been made so wretched by the man she loved.

This man squandered the fortune he had received, and sought to retrieve his affairs by a second marriage; but, having retired after a night of drunken debauch, he was found dead in the morning. He was called a good master; for he fed and clothed his slaves better than most masters, and the lash was not heard on his plantation so frequently as on many others. Had it not been for slavery, he would have been a better man, and his wife a happier woman.

No pen can give an adequate description of the all-pervading corruption produced by slavery. The slave girl is reared in an atmosphere of licentiousness and fear. The lash and the foul talk of her master and his sons are her teachers. When she is fourteen or fifteen, her owner, or his sons, or the overseer, or perhaps all of them, begin to bribe her with presents. If these fail to accomplish their purpose, she is whipped or starved into submission to their will. She may have had religious principles inculcated by some pious mother or grandmother, or some good mistress; she may have a lover, whose good opinion and peace of mind are dear to her heart; or the profligate men who have power over her may be exceedingly odious to her. But resistance is hopeless.

> "The poor worm
> Shall prove her contest vain. Life's little day
> Shall pass, and she is gone!"

The slaveholder's sons are, of course, vitiated, even while boys, by the unclean influences every where around them. Nor do the master's daughters always escape. Severe retributions sometimes come upon him for the wrongs he does to the daughters of the slaves. The white daughters early hear their parents quarrelling about some female slave. Their curiosity is excited, and they soon learn the cause. They are attended by the young slave girls whom their father has corrupted; and they hear such talk as should never meet youthful ears, or any other ears. They know that the women slaves are subject to their father's authority in all things; and in some cases they exercise the same authority over the men slaves. I have myself seen the master of such a household whose head was bowed down in shame; for it was known in the neighborhood that his daughter had selected one of the meanest slaves on his plantation to be the father of his first grandchild. She did not make her advances to her equals, nor even to her father's more intelligent servants. She selected the most brutalized, over whom her authority could be exercised with less fear of exposure. Her father, half frantic with rage, sought to revenge himself on the offending black man; but his daughter, foreseeing the storm that would arise, had given him free papers, and sent him out of the state.

In such cases the infant is smothered, or sent where it is never seen by any who know its history. But if the white parent is the *father*, instead of the mother, the offspring are unblushingly reared for the market. If they are girls, I have indicated plainly enough what will be their inevitable destiny.

You may believe what I say; for I write only that whereof I know. I was twenty-one years in that cage of obscene birds. I can testify, from my own experience and observation, that slavery is a curse to the whites as well as to the blacks. It makes the white fathers cruel and sensual; the sons violent and licentious; it contaminates the daughters, and makes the wives wretched. And as for the colored race, it needs an abler pen than mine to describe the extremity of their sufferings, the depth of their degradation.

Yet few slaveholders seem to be aware of the widespread moral ruin occasioned by this wicked system. Their talk is of blighted cotton crops—not of the blight on their children's souls.

If you want to be fully convinced of the abominations of slavery, go on a southern plantation, and call yourself a negro trader. Then there will be no concealment; and you will see and hear things that will seem to you impossible among human beings with immortal souls.

X. A Perilous Passage in the Slave Girl's Life

After my lover went away, Dr. Flint contrived a new plan. He seemed to have an idea that my fear of my mistress was his greatest obstacle. In the blandest tones, he told me that he was going to build a small house for me, in a secluded place, four miles away from the town. I shuddered; but I was constrained to listen, while he talked of his intention to give me a home of my own, and to make a lady of me. Hitherto, I had escaped my dreaded fate, by being in the midst of people. My grandmother had already had high words with my master about me. She had told him pretty plainly what she thought of his character, and there was considerable gossip in the neighborhood about our affairs, to which the open-mouthed jealousy of Mrs. Flint contributed not a little. When my master said he was going to build a house for me, and that he could do it with little trouble and expense, I was in hopes something would happen to frustrate his scheme; but I soon heard that the house was actually begun. I vowed before my Maker that I would never enter it. I had rather toil on the plantation from dawn till dark; I had rather live and die in jail, than drag on, from day to day, through such a living death. I was determined that the master, whom I so hated and loathed, who had blighted the prospects of my youth, and made my life a desert, should not, after my long struggle with him, succeed at last in trampling his victim under his feet. I would do any thing, every thing, for the sake of defeating him. What *could* I do? I thought and thought, till I became desperate, and made a plunge into the abyss.

And now, reader, I come to a period in my unhappy life, which I would gladly forget if I could. The remembrance fills me with sorrow and shame. It pains me to tell you of it; but I have promised to tell you the truth, and I will do it honestly, let it cost me what it may. I will not try to screen myself behind the plea of compulsion from a master; for it was not so. Neither can I plead ignorance or thoughtlessness. For years, my master had done his utmost to pollute my mind with foul images, and to destroy the pure principles inculcated by my grandmother, and the good mistress of my childhood. The influences of slavery had had the same effect on me that they had on other young girls; they had made me prematurely knowing, concerning the evil ways of the world. I knew what I did, and I did it with deliberate calculation.

But, O, ye happy women, whose purity has been sheltered from childhood, who have been free to choose the objects of your affection, whose homes are protected by law, do not judge the poor desolate slave girl too severely! If slavery had been abolished, I, also, could have married the man of my choice; I could have had a home shielded by the laws; and I should have been spared the painful task of confessing what I am now about to relate; but all my prospects had been blighted by slavery. I wanted to keep myself pure; and, under the most adverse circumstances, I tried hard to preserve my self-respect; but I was struggling alone in the powerful grasp of the demon Slavery; and the monster proved too strong for me. I felt as if I was forsaken by God and man; as if all my efforts must be frustrated; and I became reckless in my despair.

I have told you that Dr. Flint's persecutions and his wife's jealousy had given rise to some gossip in the neighborhood. Among others, it chanced that a white unmarried gentleman had obtained some knowledge of the circumstances in which I was placed. He knew my grandmother, and often spoke to me in the street. He became interested for me, and asked questions about my master, which I answered in part. He expressed a great deal of sympathy, and a wish to aid me. He constantly sought opportunities to see me, and wrote to me frequently. I was a poor slave girl, only fifteen years old.

So much attention from a superior person was, of course, flattering; for human nature is the same in all. I also felt grateful for his sympathy, and encouraged by his kind words. It seemed to me a great thing to have such a friend. By degrees, a more tender feeling crept into my heart. He was an educated and eloquent gentleman; too eloquent, alas, for the poor slave girl who trusted in him. Of course I saw whither all this was tending. I knew the impassable gulf between us; but to be an object of interest to a man who is not married, and who is not her master, is agreeable to the pride and feelings of a slave, if her miserable situation has left her any pride or sentiment. It seems less degrading to give one's self, than to submit to compulsion. There is something akin to freedom in having a lover who has no control over you, except that which he gains by kindness and attachment. A master may treat you as rudely as he pleases, and you dare not speak; moreover, the wrong does not seem so great with an unmarried man, as with one who has a wife to be made unhappy. There may be sophistry in all this; but the condition of a slave confuses all principles of morality, and, in fact, renders the practice of them impossible.

When I found that my master had actually begun to build the lonely cottage, other feelings mixed with those I have described. Revenge, and calculations of interest, were added to flattered vanity and sincere gratitude for kindness. I knew nothing would enrage Dr. Flint so much as to know that I favored another; and it was something to triumph over my tyrant even in that small way. I thought he would revenge himself by selling me, and I was sure my friend, Mr. Sands, would buy me. He was a man of more generosity and feeling than my master, and I thought my freedom could be easily obtained from him. The crisis of my fate now came so near that I was desperate. I shuddered to think of being the mother of children that should be owned by my old tyrant. I knew that as soon as a new fancy took him, his victims were sold far off to get rid of them; especially if they had children. I had seen several women sold, with his babies at the breast. He never allowed his offspring by slaves to remain long in sight of himself and his wife. Of a man who was not my master I could ask to have my children well supported; and in this case, I felt confident I should obtain the boon.[2] I also felt quite sure that they would be made free. With all these thoughts revolving in my mind, and seeing no other way of escaping the doom I so much dreaded, I made a headlong plunge. Pity me, and pardon me, O virtuous reader! You never knew what it is to be a slave; to be entirely unprotected by law or custom; to have the laws reduce you to the condition of a chattel, entirely subject to the will

2. Request, or favor.

of another. You never exhausted your ingenuity in avoiding the snares, and eluding the power of a hated tyrant; you never shuddered at the sound of his footsteps, and trembled within hearing of his voice. I know I did wrong. No one can feel it more sensibly than I do. The painful and humiliating memory will haunt me to my dying day. Still, in looking back, calmly, on the events of my life, I feel that the slave woman ought not to be judged by the same standard as others.

The months passed on. I had many unhappy hours. I secretly mourned over the sorrow I was bringing on my grandmother, who had so tried to shield me from harm. I knew that I was the greatest comfort of her old age, and that it was a source of pride to her that I had not degraded myself, like most of the slaves. I wanted to confess to her that I was no longer worthy of her love; but I could not utter the dreaded words.

As for Dr. Flint, I had a feeling of satisfaction and triumph in the thought of telling *him*. From time to time he told me of his intended arrangements, and I was silent. At last, he came and told me the cottage was completed, and ordered me to go to it. I told him I would never enter it. He said, "I have heard enough of such talk as that. You shall go, if you are carried by force; and you shall remain there."

I replied, "I will never go there. In a few months I shall be a mother."

He stood and looked at me in dumb amazement, and left the house without a word. I thought I should be happy in my triumph over him. But now that the truth was out, and my relatives would hear of it, I felt wretched. Humble as were their circumstances, they had pride in my good character. Now, how could I look them in the face? My self-respect was gone! I had resolved that I would be virtuous, though I was a slave. I had said, "Let the storm beat! I will brave it till I die." And now, how humiliated I felt!

I went to my grandmother. My lips moved to make confession, but the words stuck in my throat. I sat down in the shade of a tree at her door and began to sew. I think she saw something unusual was the matter with me. The mother of slaves is very watchful. She knows there is no security for her children. After they have entered their teens she lives in daily expectation of trouble. This leads to many questions. If the girl is of a sensitive nature, timidity keeps her from answering truthfully, and this well-meant course has a tendency to drive her from maternal counsels. Presently, in came my mistress, like a mad woman, and accused me concerning her husband. My grandmother, whose suspicions had been previously awakened, believed what she said. She exclaimed, "O Linda! has it come to this? I had rather see you dead than to see you as you now are. You are a disgrace to your dead mother." She tore from my fingers my mother's wedding ring and her silver thimble. "Go away!" she exclaimed, "and never come to my house, again." Her reproaches fell so hot and heavy, that they left me no chance to answer. Bitter tears, such as the eyes never shed but once, were my only answer. I rose from my seat, but fell back

again, sobbing. She did not speak to me; but the tears were running down
her furrowed cheeks, and they scorched me like fire. She had always been
so kind to me! So kind! How I longed to throw myself at her feet, and tell
her all the truth! But she had ordered me to go, and never to come there
again. After a few minutes, I mustered strength, and started to obey her.
With what feelings did I now close that little gate, which I used to open
with such an eager hand in my childhood! It closed upon me with a
sound I never heard before.

Where could I go? I was afraid to return to my master's. I walked on
recklessly, not caring where I went, or what would become of me. When
I had gone four or five miles, fatigue compelled me to stop. I sat down on
the stump of an old tree. The stars were shining through the boughs
above me. How they mocked me, with their bright, calm light! The hours
passed by, and as I sat there alone a chilliness and deadly sickness came
over me. I sank on the ground. My mind was full of horrid thoughts. I
prayed to die; but the prayer was not answered. At last, with great effort I
roused myself, and walked some distance further, to the house of a
woman who had been a friend of my mother. When I told her why I was
there, she spoke soothingly to me; but I could not be comforted. I thought
I could bear my shame if I could only be reconciled to my grandmother.
I longed to open my heart to her. I thought if she could know the real
state of the case, and all I had been bearing for years, she would perhaps
judge me less harshly. My friend advised me to send for her. I did so; but
days of agonizing suspense passed before she came. Had she utterly forsaken me? No. She came at last. I knelt before her, and told her the things
that had poisoned my life; how long I had been persecuted; that I saw no
way of escape; and in an hour of extremity I had become desperate. She
listened in silence. I told her I would bear any thing and do any thing, if
in time I had hopes of obtaining her forgiveness. I begged of her to pity
me, for my dead mother's sake. And she did pity me. She did not say, "I
forgive you;" but she looked at me lovingly, with her eyes full of tears. She
laid her old hand gently on my head, and murmured, "Poor child! Poor
child!"

XI. The New Tie to Life

I returned to my good grandmother's house. She had an interview with
Mr. Sands. When she asked him why he could not have left her one ewe
lamb,[3]—whether there were not plenty of slaves who did not care about
character,—he made no answer; but he spoke kind and encouraging

---

3. I.e., one girl child unsullied. Perhaps a reference to the Old Testament practice of sacrifice, in
which the sacrificial animal was generally male.

words. He promised to care for my child, and to buy me, be the conditions what they might.

I had not seen Dr. Flint for five days. I had never seen him since I made the avowal to him. He talked of the disgrace I had brought on myself; how I had sinned against my master, and mortified my old grandmother. He intimated that if I had accepted his proposals, he, as a physician, could have saved me from exposure. He even condescended to pity me. Could he have offered wormwood[4] more bitter? He, whose persecutions had been the cause of my sin!

"Linda," said he, "though you have been criminal towards me, I feel for you, and I can pardon you if you obey my wishes. Tell me whether the fellow you wanted to marry is the father of your child. If you deceive me, you shall feel the fires of hell."

I did not feel as proud as I had done. My strongest weapon with him was gone. I was lowered in my own estimation, and had resolved to bear his abuse in silence. But when he spoke contemptuously of the lover who had always treated me honorably; when I remembered that but for *him* I might have been a virtuous, free, and happy wife, I lost my patience. "I have sinned against God and myself," I replied; "but not against you."

He clinched his teeth, and muttered, "Curse you!" He came towards me, with ill-suppressed rage, and exclaimed, "You obstinate girl! I could grind your bones to powder! You have thrown yourself away on some worthless rascal. You are weak-minded, and have been easily persuaded by those who don't care a straw for you. The future will settle accounts between us. You are blinded now; but hereafter you will be convinced that your master was your best friend. My lenity towards you is a proof of it. I might have punished you in many ways. I might have had you whipped till you fell dead under the lash. But I wanted you to live; I would have bettered your condition. Others cannot do it. You are my slave. Your mistress, disgusted by your conduct, forbids you to return to the house; therefore I leave you here for the present; but I shall see you often. I will call tomorrow."

He came with frowning brows, that showed a dissatisfied state of mind. After asking about my health, he inquired whether my board was paid, and who visited me. He then went on to say that he had neglected his duty; that as a physician there were certain things that he ought to have explained to me. Then followed talk such as would have made the most shameless blush. He ordered me to stand up before him. I obeyed. "I command you," said he, "to tell me whether the father of your child is white or black." I hesitated. "Answer me this instant!" he exclaimed. I did answer. He sprang upon me like a wolf, and grabbed my arm as if he would have broken it. "Do you love him?" said he, in a hissing tone.

"I am thankful that I do not despise him," I replied.

4. Bitter plant used as a tonic.

He raised his hand to strike me; but it fell again. I don't know what arrested the blow. He sat down, with lips tightly compressed. At last he spoke. "I came here," said he, "to make you a friendly proposition; but your ingratitude chafes me beyond endurance. You turn aside all my good intentions towards you. I don't know what it is that keeps me from killing you." Again he rose, as if he had a mind to strike me.

But he resumed. "On one condition I will forgive your insolence and crime. You must henceforth have no communication of any kind with the father of your child. You must not ask any thing from him, or receive any thing from him. I will take care of you and your child. You had better promise this at once, and not wait till you are deserted by him. This is the last act of mercy I shall show towards you."

I said something about being unwilling to have my child supported by a man who had cursed it and me also. He rejoined, that a woman who had sunk to my level had no right to expect any thing else. He asked, for the last time, would I accept his kindness? I answered that I would not.

"Very well," said he; "then take the consequences of your wayward course. Never look to me for help. You are my slave, and shall always be my slave. I will never sell you, that you may depend upon."

Hope died away in my heart as he closed the door after him. I had calculated that in his rage he would sell me to a slave-trader; and I knew the father of my child was on the watch to buy me.

About this time my uncle Phillip was expected to return from a voyage. The day before his departure I had officiated as bridesmaid to a young friend. My heart was then ill at ease, but my smiling countenance did not betray it. Only a year had passed; but what fearful changes it had wrought! My heart had grown gray in misery. Lives that flash in sunshine, and lives that are born in tears, receive their hue from circumstances. None of us know what a year may bring forth.

I felt no joy when they told me my uncle had come. He wanted to see me, though he knew what had happened. I shrank from him at first; but at last consented that he should come to my room. He received me as he always had done. O, how my heart smote me when I felt his tears on my burning cheeks! The words of my grandmother came to my mind, — "Perhaps your mother and father are taken from the evil days to come." My disappointed heart could now praise God that it was so. But why, thought I, did my relatives ever cherish hopes for me? What was there to save me from the usual fate of slave girls? Many more beautiful and more intelligent than I had experienced a similar fate, or a far worse one. How could they hope that I should escape?

My uncle's stay was short, and I was not sorry for it. I was too ill in mind and body to enjoy my friends as I had done. For some weeks I was unable to leave my bed. I could not have any doctor but my master, and I would not have him sent for. At last, alarmed by my increasing illness, they sent for him. I was very weak and nervous; and as soon as he entered the room,

I began to scream. They told him my state was very critical. He had no wish to hasten me out of the world, and he withdrew.

When my babe was born, they said it was premature. It weighed only four pounds; but God let it live. I heard the doctor say I could not survive till morning. I had often prayed for death; but now I did not want to die, unless my child could die too. Many weeks passed before I was able to leave my bed. I was a mere wreck of my former self. For a year there was scarcely a day when I was free from chills and fever. My babe also was sickly. His little limbs were often racked with pain. Dr. Flint continued his visits, to look after my health; and he did not fail to remind me that my child was an addition to his stock of slaves.

I felt too feeble to dispute with him, and listened to his remarks in silence. His visits were less frequent; but his busy spirit could not remain quiet. He employed my brother in his office, and he was made the medium of frequent notes and messages to me. William was a bright lad, and of much use to the doctor. He had learned to put up medicines, to leech, cup, and bleed.[5] He had taught himself to read and spell. I was proud of my brother; and the old doctor suspected as much. One day, when I had not seen him for several weeks, I heard his steps approaching the door. I dreaded the encounter, and hid myself. He inquired for me, of course; but I was nowhere to be found. He went to his office, and despatched William with a note. The color mounted to my brother's face when he gave it to me; and he said, "Don't you hate me, Linda, for bringing you these things?" I told him I could not blame him; he was a slave, and obliged to obey his master's will. The note ordered me to come to his office. I went. He demanded to know where I was when he called. I told him I was at home. He flew into a passion, and said he knew better. Then he launched out upon his usual themes,—my crimes against him, and my ingratitude for his forbearance. The laws were laid down to me anew, and I was dismissed. I felt humiliated that my brother should stand by, and listen to such language as would be addressed only to a slave. Poor boy! He was powerless to defend me; but I saw the tears, which he vainly strove to keep back. This manifestation of feeling irritated the doctor. William could do nothing to please him. One morning he did not arrive at the office so early as usual; and that circumstance afforded his master an opportunity to vent his spleen.[6] He was put in jail. The next day my brother sent a trader to the doctor, with a request to be sold. His master was greatly incensed at what he called his insolence. He said he had put him there to reflect upon his bad conduct, and he certainly was not giving any evidence of repentance. For two days he harassed himself to find somebody to do his office work; but every thing went wrong without

---

5. Leech: to apply leeches, as a bloodletting agent, for medicinal purposes; cup: to apply heated cups to the skin as a counter-irritant; bleed: bloodletting was thought to be the best way to cure many illnesses.
6. The spleen was once considered the seat of the emotions in the body, later associated with rage.

William. He was released, and ordered to take his old stand, with many threats, if he was not careful about his future behavior.

As the months passed on, my boy improved in health. When he was a year old, they called him beautiful. The little vine was taking deep root in my existence, though its clinging fondness excited a mixture of love and pain. When I was most sorely oppressed I found a solace in his smiles. I loved to watch his infant slumbers; but always there was a dark cloud over my enjoyment. I could never forget that he was a slave. Sometimes I wished that he might die in infancy. God tried me. My darling became very ill. The bright eyes grew dull, and the little feet and hands were so icy cold that I thought death had already touched them. I had prayed for his death, but never so earnestly as I now prayed for his life; and my prayer was heard. Alas, what mockery it is for a slave mother to try to pray back her dying child to life! Death is better than slavery. It was a sad thought that I had no name to give my child. His father caressed him and treated him kindly, whenever he had a chance to see him. He was not unwilling that he should bear his name; but he had no legal claim to it; and if I had bestowed it upon him, my master would have regarded it as a new crime, a new piece of insolence, and would, perhaps, revenge it on the boy. O, the serpent of Slavery has many and poisonous fangs!

XII. Fear of Insurrection

Not far from this time Nat Turner's[7] insurrection broke out; and the news threw our town into great commotion. Strange that they should be alarmed, when their slaves were so "contented and happy"! But so it was.

It was always the custom to have a muster[8] every year. On that occasion every white man shouldered his musket. The citizens and the so-called country gentlemen wore military uniforms. The poor whites took their places in the ranks in every-day dress, some without shoes, some without hats. This grand occasion had already passed; and when the slaves were told there was to be another muster, they were surprised and rejoiced. Poor creatures! They thought it was going to be a holiday. I was informed of the true state of affairs, and imparted it to the few I could trust. Most gladly would I have proclaimed it to every slave; but I dared not. All could not be relied on. Mighty is the power of the torturing lash.

By sunrise, people were pouring in from every quarter within twenty miles of the town. I knew the houses were to be searched; and I expected

---

9. Nat Turner was the leader of an 1831 insurrection in Southampton County, Virginia, during which several whites were killed. In the aftermath, Turner and his allies were tried and executed, and in a flood of punitive violence all across the South, dozens, maybe hundreds, of black people were killed.

8. A gathering for display, inspection, drill, or service.

it would be done by country bullies and the poor whites. I knew nothing annoyed them so much as to see colored people living in comfort and respectability; so I made arrangements for them with especial care. I arranged every thing in my grandmother's house as neatly as possible. I put white quilts on the beds, and decorated some of the rooms with flowers. When all was arranged, I sat down at the window to watch. Far as my eye could reach, it rested on a motley crowd of soldiers. Drums and fifes were discoursing martial music. The men were divided into companies of sixteen, each headed by a captain. Orders were given, and the wild scouts rushed in every direction, wherever a colored face was to be found.

It was a grand opportunity for the low whites, who had no negroes of their own to scourge. They exulted in such a chance to exercise a little brief authority, and show their subserviency to the slaveholders; not reflecting that the power which trampled on the colored people also kept themselves in poverty, ignorance, and moral degradation. Those who never witnessed such scenes can hardly believe what I know was inflicted at this time on innocent men, women, and children, against whom there was not the slightest ground for suspicion. Colored people and slaves who lived in remote parts of the town suffered in an especial manner. In some cases the searchers scattered powder and shot among their clothes, and then sent other parties to find them, and bring them forward as proof that they were plotting insurrection. Every where men, women, and children were whipped till the blood stood in puddles at their feet. Some received five hundred lashes; others were tied hands and feet, and tortured with a bucking paddle, which blisters the skin terribly. The dwellings of the colored people, unless they happened to be protected by some influential white person, who was nigh at hand, were robbed of clothing and every thing else the marauders thought worth carrying away. All day long these unfeeling wretches went round, like a troop of demons, terrifying and tormenting the helpless. At night, they formed themselves into patrol bands, and went wherever they chose among the colored people, acting out their brutal will. Many women hid themselves in woods and swamps, to keep out of their way. If any of the husbands or fathers told of these outrages, they were tied up to the public whipping post, and cruelly scourged for telling lies about white men. The consternation was universal. No two people that had the slightest tinge of color in their faces dared to be seen talking together.

I entertained no positive fears about our household, because we were in the midst of white families who would protect us. We were ready to receive the soldiers whenever they came. It was not long before we heard the tramp of feet and the sound of voices. The door was rudely pushed open; and in they tumbled, like a pack of hungry wolves. They snatched at every thing within their reach. Every box, trunk, closet, and corner underwent a thorough examination. A box in one of the drawers containing some silver change was eagerly pounced upon. When I stepped forward to take it from them, one of the soldiers turned and said angrily, "What d'ye foller us fur? D'ye s'pose white folks is come to steal?"

I replied, "You have come to search; but you have searched that box, and I will take it, if you please."

At that moment I saw a white gentleman who was friendly to us; and I called to him, and asked him to have the goodness to come in and stay till the search was over. He readily complied. His entrance into the house brought in the captain of the company, whose business it was to guard the outside of the house, and see that none of the inmates left it. This officer was Mr. Litch, the wealthy slaveholder whom I mentioned, in the account of neighboring planters, as being notorious for his cruelty. He felt above soiling his hands with the search. He merely gave orders; and, if a bit of writing was discovered, it was carried to him by his ignorant followers, who were unable to read.

My grandmother had a large trunk of bedding and table cloths. When that was opened, there was a great shout of surprise; and one exclaimed, "Where'd the damned niggers git all dis sheet an' table clarf?"

My grandmother, emboldened by the presence of our white protector, said, "You may be sure we didn't pilfer 'em from *your* houses."

"Look here, mammy," said a grim-looking fellow without any coat, "you seem to feel mighty gran' 'cause you got all them 'ere fixens. White folks oughter have 'em all."

His remarks were interrupted by a chorus of voices shouting, "We's got 'em! We's got 'em! Dis 'ere yaller gal's got letters!"

There was a general rush for the supposed letter, which, upon examination, proved to be some verses written to me by a friend. In packing away my things, I had overlooked them. When their captain informed them of their contents, they seemed much disappointed. He inquired of me who wrote them. I told him it was one of my friends. "Can you read them?" he asked. When I told him I could, he swore, and raved, and tore the paper into bits. "Bring me all your letters!" said he, in a commanding tone. I told him I had none. "Don't be afraid," he continued, in an insinuating way. "Bring them all to me. Nobody shall do you any harm." Seeing I did not move to obey him, his pleasant tone changed to oaths and threats. "Who writes to you? half free niggers?" inquired he. I replied, "O, no; most of my letters are from white people. Some request me to burn them after they are read, and some I destroy without reading."

An exclamation of surprise from some of the company put a stop to our conversation. Some silver spoons which ornamented an old-fashioned buffet had just been discovered. My grandmother was in the habit of preserving fruit for many ladies in the town, and of preparing suppers for parties; consequently she had many jars of preserves. The closet that contained these was next invaded, and the contents tasted. One of them, who was helping himself freely, tapped his neighbor on the shoulder, and said, "Wal done! Don't wonder de niggers want to kill all de white folks, when dey live on 'sarves" [meaning preserves]. I stretched out my hand to take the jar, saying, "You were not sent here to search for sweetmeats."[9]

"And what *were* we sent for?" said the captain, bristling up to me. I evaded the question.

The search of the house was completed, and nothing found to condemn us. They next proceeded to the garden, and knocked about every bush and vine, with no better success. The captain called his men together, and, after a short consultation, the order to march was given. As they passed out of the gate, the captain turned back, and pronounced a malediction on the house. He said it ought to be burned to the ground, and each of its inmates receive thirty-nine lashes. We came out of this affair very fortunately; not losing any thing except some wearing apparel.

Towards evening the turbulence increased. The soldiers, stimulated by drink, committed still greater cruelties. Shrieks and shouts continually rent the air. Not daring to go to the door, I peeped under the window curtain. I saw a mob dragging along a number of colored people, each white man, with his musket upraised, threatening instant death if they did not stop their shrieks. Among the prisoners was a respectable old colored minister. They had found a few parcels of shot in his house, which his wife had for years used to balance her scales. For this they were going to shoot him on Court House Green. What a spectacle was that for a civilized country! A rabble, staggering under intoxication, assuming to be the administrators of justice!

The better class of the community exerted their influence to save the innocent, persecuted people; and in several instances they succeeded, by keeping them shut up in jail till the excitement abated. At last the white citizens found that their own property was not safe from the lawless rabble they had summoned to protect them. They rallied the drunken swarm, drove them back into the country, and set a guard over the town.

The next day, the town patrols were commissioned to search colored people that lived out of the city; and the most shocking outrages were committed with perfect impunity. Every day for a fortnight, if I looked out, I saw horsemen with some poor panting negro tied to their saddles, and compelled by the lash to keep up with their speed, till they arrived at the jail yard. Those who had been whipped too unmercifully to walk were washed with brine, tossed into a cart, and carried to jail. One black man, who had not fortitude to endure scourging, promised to give information about the conspiracy. But it turned out that he knew nothing at all. He had not even heard the name of Nat Turner. The poor fellow had, however, made up a story, which augmented his own sufferings and those of the colored people.

The day patrol continued for some weeks, and at sundown a night guard was substituted. Nothing at all was proved against the colored peo-

9. Confections rich in sugar, such as the preserves.

ple, bond or free. The wrath of the slaveholders was somewhat appeased by the capture of Nat Turner. The imprisoned were released. The slaves were sent to their masters, and the free were permitted to return to their ravaged homes. Visiting was strictly forbidden on the plantations. The slaves begged the privilege of again meeting at their little church in the woods, with their burying ground around it. It was built by the colored people, and they had no higher happiness than to meet there and sing hymns together, and pour out their hearts in spontaneous prayer. Their request was denied, and the church was demolished. They were permitted to attend the white churches, a certain portion of the galleries being appropriated to their use. There, when every body else had partaken of the communion, and the benediction had been pronounced, the minister said, "Come down, now, my colored friends." They obeyed the summons, and partook of the bread and wine, in commemoration of the meek and lowly Jesus, who said, "God is your Father, and all ye are brethren."

XIII. The Church and Slavery

After the alarm caused by Nat Turner's insurrection had subsided, the slaveholders came to the conclusion that it would be well to give the slaves enough of religious instruction to keep them from murdering their masters. The Episcopal clergyman offered to hold a separate service on Sundays for their benefit. His colored members were very few, and also very respectable—a fact which I presume had some weight with him. The difficulty was to decide on a suitable place for them to worship. The Methodist and Baptist churches admitted them in the afternoon; but their carpets and cushions were not so costly as those at the Episcopal church. It was at last decided that they should meet at the house of a free colored man, who was a member.

I was invited to attend, because I could read. Sunday evening came, and, trusting to the cover of night, I ventured out. I rarely ventured out by daylight, for I always went with fear, expecting at every turn to encounter Dr. Flint, who was sure to turn me back, or order me to his office to inquire where I got my bonnet, or some other article of dress. When the Rev. Mr. Pike came, there were some twenty persons present. The reverend gentleman knelt in prayer, then seated himself, and requested all present, who could read, to open their books, while he gave out the portions he wished them to repeat or respond to.

His text was, "Servants, be obedient to them that are your masters according to the flesh, with fear and trembling, in singleness of your heart, as unto Christ."

Pious Mr. Pike brushed up his hair till it stood upright, and, in deep, solemn tones, began: "Hearken, ye servants! Give strict heed unto my words. You are rebellious sinners. Your hearts are filled with all manner of evil. 'Tis the devil who tempts you. God is angry with you, and will surely punish you, if you don't forsake your wicked ways. You that live in town are eye-servants behind your master's back. Instead of serving your masters faithfully, which is pleasing in the sight of your heavenly Master, you are idle, and shirk your work. God sees you. You tell lies. God hears you. Instead of being engaged in worshipping him, you are hidden away somewhere, feasting on your master's substance; tossing coffee-grounds with some wicked fortuneteller, or cutting cards with another old hag. Your masters may not find you out, but God sees you, and will punish you. O, the depravity of your hearts! When your master's work is done, are you quietly together, thinking of the goodness of God to such sinful creatures? No; you are quarrelling, and tying up little bags of roots to bury under the door-steps to poison each other with. God sees you. You men steal away to every grog[1] shop to sell your master's corn, that you may buy rum to drink. God sees you. You sneak into the back streets, or among the bushes, to pitch coppers. Although your masters may not find you out, God sees you; and he will punish you. You must forsake your sinful ways, and be faithful servants. Obey your old master and your young master— your old mistress and your young mistress. If you disobey your earthly master, you offend your heavenly Master. You must obey God's commandments. When you go from here, don't stop at the corners of the streets to talk, but go directly home, and let your master and mistress see that you have come."

The benediction was pronounced. We went home, highly amused at brother Pike's gospel teaching, and we determined to hear him again. I went the next Sabbath evening, and heard pretty much a repetition of the last discourse. At the close of the meeting, Mr. Pike informed us that he found it very inconvenient to meet at the friend's house, and he should be glad to see us, every Sunday evening, at his own kitchen.

I went home with the feeling that I had heard the Reverend Mr. Pike for the last time. Some of his members repaired to his house, and found that the kitchen sported two tallow candles; the first time, I am sure, since its present occupant owned it, for the servants never had any thing but pine knots. It was so long before the reverend gentleman descended from his comfortable parlor that the slaves left, and went to enjoy a Methodist shout. They never seem so happy as when shouting and singing at religious meetings. Many of them are sincere, and nearer to the gate of heaven than sanctimonious Mr. Pike, and other long-faced Christians, who see wounded Samaritans, and pass by on the other side.

The slaves generally compose their own songs and hymns; and they do not trouble their heads much about the measure. They often sing the following verses:

---

1. Home-brewed alcohol.

"Old Satan is one busy ole man;
  He rolls dem blocks all in my way;
 But Jesus is my bosom friend;
  He rolls dem blocks away.

"If I had died when I was young,
  Den how my stam'ring tongue would have sung;
 But I am ole, and now I stand
  A narrow chance for to tread dat heavenly land."

I well remember one occasion when I attended a Methodist class meeting.[2] I went with a burdened spirit, and happened to sit next a poor, bereaved mother, whose heart was still heavier than mine. The class leader was the town constable—a man who bought and sold slaves, who whipped his brethren and sisters of the church at the public whipping post, in jail or out of jail. He was ready to perform that Christian office any where for fifty cents. This white-faced, black-hearted brother came near us, and said to the stricken woman, "Sister, can't you tell us how the Lord deals with your soul? Do you love him as you did formerly?"

She rose to her feet, and said, in piteous tones, "My Lord and Master, help me! My load is more than I can bear. God has hid himself from me, and I am left in darkness and misery." Then, striking her breast, she continued, "I can't tell you what is in here! They've got all my children. Last week they took the last one. God only knows where they've sold her. They let me have her sixteen years, and then— O! O! Pray for her brothers and sisters! I've got nothing to live for now. God make my time short!"

She sat down, quivering in every limb. I saw that constable class leader become crimson in the face with suppressed laughter, while he held up his handkerchief, that those who were weeping for the poor woman's calamity might not see his merriment. Then, with assumed gravity, he said to the bereaved mother, "Sister, pray to the Lord that every dispensation of his divine will may be sanctified to the good of your poor needy soul!"

The congregation struck up a hymn, and sung as though they were as free as the birds that warbled round us,—

"Ole Satan thought he had a mighty aim;
  He missed my soul, and caught my sins.
  Cry Amen, cry Amen, cry Amen to God!

"He took my sins upon his back;
  Went muttering and grumbling down to hell.
  Cry Amen, cry Amen, cry Amen to God!

2. In some denominations, members were assigned to small groups called "classes," with whom they studied, socialized, and practiced various religious activities.

> "Ole Satan's church is here below.
> Up to God's free church I hope to go.
> Cry Amen, cry Amen, cry Amen to God!"

Precious are such moments to the poor slaves. If you were to hear them at such times, you might think they were happy. But can that hour of singing and shouting sustain them through the dreary week, toiling without wages, under constant dread of the lash?

The Episcopal clergyman, who, ever since my earliest recollection, had been a sort of god among the slaveholders, concluded, as his family was large, that he must go where money was more abundant. A very different clergyman took his place. The change was very agreeable to the colored people, who said, "God has sent us a good man this time." They loved him, and their children followed him for a smile or a kind word. Even the slaveholders felt his influence. He brought to the rectory five slaves. His wife taught them to read and write, and to be useful to her and themselves. As soon as he was settled, he turned his attention to the needy slaves around him. He urged upon his parishioners the duty of having a meeting expressly for them every Sunday, with a sermon adapted to their comprehension. After much argument and importunity, it was finally agreed that they might occupy the gallery of the church on Sunday evenings. Many colored people, hitherto unaccustomed to attend church, now gladly went to hear the gospel preached. The sermons were simple, and they understood them. Moreover, it was the first time they had ever been addressed as human beings. It was not long before his white parishioners began to be dissatisfied. He was accused of preaching better sermons to the negroes than he did to them. He honestly confessed that he bestowed more pains upon those sermons than upon any others; for the slaves were reared in such ignorance that it was a difficult task to adapt himself to their comprehension. Dissensions arose in the parish. Some wanted he should preach to them in the evening, and to the slaves in the afternoon. In the midst of these disputings his wife died, after a very short illness. Her slaves gathered round her dying bed in great sorrow. She said, "I have tried to do you good and promote your happiness; and if I have failed, it has not been for want of interest in your welfare. Do not weep for me; but prepare for the new duties that lie before you. I leave you all free. May we meet in a better world." Her liberated slaves were sent away, with funds to establish them comfortably. The colored people will long bless the memory of that truly Christian woman. Soon after her death her husband preached his farewell sermon, and many tears were shed at his departure.

Several years after, he passed through our town and preached to his former congregation. In his afternoon sermon he addressed the colored people. "My friends," said he, "it affords me great happiness to have an opportunity of speaking to you again. For two years I have been striving to do something for the colored people of my own parish; but nothing is yet accomplished. I have not even preached a sermon to them. Try to live according to the word of God, my friends. Your skin is darker than mine; but God judges men by their hearts, not by the color of their skins." This was strange doctrine from a southern pulpit. It was very offensive to slave-holders. They said he and his wife had made fools of their slaves, and that he preached like a fool to the negroes.

I knew an old black man, whose piety and childlike trust in God were beautiful to witness. At fifty-three years old he joined the Baptist church. He had a most earnest desire to learn to read. He thought he should know how to serve God better if he could only read the Bible. He came to me, and begged me to teach him. He said he could not pay me, for he had no money; but he would bring me nice fruit when the season for it came. I asked him if he didn't know it was contrary to law; and that slaves were whipped and imprisoned for teaching each other to read. This brought the tears into his eyes. "Don't be troubled, uncle Fred,"[3] said I. "I have no thoughts of refusing to teach you. I only told you of the law, that you might know the danger, and be on your guard." He thought he could plan to come three times a week without its being suspected. I selected a quiet nook, where no intruder was likely to penetrate, and there I taught him his A, B, C. Considering his age, his progress was astonishing. As soon as he could spell in two syllables he wanted to spell out words in the Bible. The happy smile that illuminated his face put joy into my heart. After spelling out a few words, he paused, and said, "Honey, it 'pears when I can read dis good book I shall be nearer to God. White man is got all de sense. He can larn easy. It ain't easy for ole black man like me. I only wants to read dis book, dat I may know how to live; den I hab no fear 'bout dying."

I tried to encourage him by speaking of the rapid progress he had made. "Hab patience, child," he replied. "I larns slow."

I had no need of patience. His gratitude, and the happiness I imparted, were more than a recompense for all my trouble.

At the end of six months he had read through the New Testament, and could find any text in it. One day, when he had recited unusually well, I said, "Uncle Fred, how do you manage to get your lessons so well?"

"Lord bress you, chile," he replied. "You nebber gibs me a lesson dat I don't pray to God to help me to understan' what I spells and what I reads. And he *does* help me, chile. Bress his holy name!"

There are thousands, who, like good uncle Fred, are thirsting for the water of life; but the law forbids it, and the churches withhold it. They send the Bible to heathen abroad, and neglect the heathen at home. I am glad that missionaries go out to the dark corners of the earth; but I ask them not to overlook the dark corners at home. Talk to American slave-

3. "Uncle" (and "aunt") were often used as titles of respect.

holders as you talk to savages in Africa. Tell *them* it is wrong to traffic in men. Tell them it is sinful to sell their own children, and atrocious to violate their own daughters. Tell them that all men are brethren, and that man has no right to shut out the light of knowledge from his brother. Tell them they are answerable to God for sealing up the Fountain of Life from souls that are thirsting for it.

There are men who would gladly undertake such missionary work as this; but, alas! their number is small. They are hated by the south, and would be driven from its soil, or dragged to prison to die, as others have been before them. The field is ripe for the harvest, and awaits the reapers. Perhaps the great grandchildren of uncle Fred may have freely imparted to them the divine treasures, which he sought by stealth, at the risk of the prison and the scourge.

Are doctors of divinity blind, or are they hypocrites? I suppose some are the one, and some the other; but I think if they felt the interest in the poor and the lowly, that they ought to feel, they would not be so *easily* blinded. A clergyman who goes to the south, for the first time, has usually some feeling, however vague, that slavery is wrong. The slaveholder suspects this, and plays his game accordingly. He makes himself as agreeable as possible; talks on theology, and other kindred topics. The reverend gentleman is asked to invoke a blessing on a table loaded with luxuries. After dinner he walks round the premises, and sees the beautiful groves and flowering vines, and the comfortable huts of favored household slaves. The southerner invites him to talk with these slaves. He asks them if they want to be free, and they say, "O, no, massa." This is sufficient to satisfy him. He comes home to publish a "South-Side View of Slavery,"[4] and to complain of the exaggerations of abolitionists. He assures people that he has been to the south, and seen slavery for himself; that it is a beautiful "patriarchal institution;" that the slaves don't want their freedom; that they have hallelujah meetings, and other religious privileges.

What does *he* know of the half-starved wretches toiling from dawn till dark on the plantations? of mothers shrieking for their children, torn from their arms by slave traders? of young girls dragged down into moral filth? of pools of blood around the whipping post? of hounds trained to tear human flesh? of men screwed into cotton gins to die? The slaveholder showed him none of these things, and the slaves dared not tell of them if he had asked them.

There is a great difference between Christianity and religion at the south. If a man goes to the communion table, and pays money into the treasury of the church, no matter if it be the price of blood, he is called religious. If a pastor has offspring by a woman not his wife, the church

---

4. After touring the South in 1854, the Reverend Nehemiah Adams of Boston wrote A *South-Side View of Slavery*.

dismiss him, if she is a white woman; but if she is colored, it does not hinder his continuing to be their good shepherd.

When I was told that Dr. Flint had joined the Episcopal church, I was much surprised. I supposed that religion had a purifying effect on the character of men; but the worst persecutions I endured from him were after he was a communicant. The conversation of the doctor, the day after he had been confirmed, certainly gave *me* no indication that he had "renounced the devil and all his works." In answer to some of his usual talk, I reminded him that he had just joined the church. "Yes, Linda," said he. "It was proper for me to do so. I am getting in years, and my position in society requires it, and it puts an end to all the damned slang.[5] You would do well to join the church, too, Linda."

"There are sinners enough in it already," rejoined I. "If I could be allowed to live like a Christian, I should be glad."

"You can do what I require; and if you are faithful to me, you will be as virtuous as my wife," he replied.

I answered that the Bible didn't say so.

His voice became hoarse with rage. "How dare you preach to me about your infernal Bible!" he exclaimed. "What right have you, who are my negro, to talk to me about what you would like, and what you wouldn't like? I am your master, and you shall obey me."

No wonder the slaves sing, —

> "Ole Satan's church is here below;
> Up to God's free church I hope to go."

XIV. Another Link to Life

I had not returned to my master's house since the birth of my child. The old man raved to have me thus removed from his immediate power; but his wife vowed, by all that was good and great, she would kill me if I came back; and he did not doubt her word. Sometimes he would stay away for a season. Then he would come and renew the old threadbare discourse about his forbearance and my ingratitude. He labored, most unnecessarily, to convince me that I had lowered myself. The venomous old reprobate had no need of descanting[6] on that theme. I felt humiliated enough. My unconscious babe was the ever-present witness of my shame. I listened with silent contempt when he talked about my having forfeited *his* good opinion; but I shed bitter tears that I was no longer worthy of being respected by the good and pure. Alas! slavery still held me in its poi-

5. Vulgar abuse.
6. Elaborating or commenting at great length upon a topic.

sonous grasp. There was no chance for me to be respectable. There was no prospect of being able to lead a better life.

Sometimes, when my master found that I still refused to accept what he called his kind offers, he would threaten to sell my child. "Perhaps that will humble you," said he.

Humble *me!* Was I not already in the dust? But his threat lacerated my heart. I knew the law gave him power to fulfil it; for slaveholders have been cunning enough to enact that "the child shall follow the condition of the *mother*," not of the *father*; thus taking care that licentiousness shall not interfere with avarice. This reflection made me clasp my innocent babe all the more firmly to my heart. Horrid visions passed through my mind when I thought of his liability to fall into the slave trader's hands. I wept over him, and said, "O my child! perhaps they will leave you in some cold cabin to die, and then throw you into a hole, as if you were a dog."

When Dr. Flint learned that I was again to be a mother, he was exasperated beyond measure. He rushed from the house, and returned with a pair of shears. I had a fine head of hair; and he often railed about my pride of arranging it nicely. He cut every hair close to my head, storming and swearing all the time. I replied to some of his abuse, and he struck me. Some months before, he had pitched me down stairs in a fit of passion; and the injury I received was so serious that I was unable to turn myself in bed for many days. He then said, "Linda, I swear by God I will never raise my hand against you again;" but I knew that he would forget his promise.

After he discovered my situation, he was like a restless spirit from the pit. He came every day; and I was subjected to such insults as no pen can describe. I would not describe them if I could; they were too low, too revolting. I tried to keep them from my grandmother's knowledge as much as I could. I knew she had enough to sadden her life, without having my troubles to bear. When she saw the doctor treat me with violence, and heard him utter oaths terrible enough to palsy a man's tongue, she could not always hold her peace. It was natural and motherlike that she should try to defend me; but it only made matters worse.

When they told me my new-born babe was a girl, my heart was heavier than it had ever been before. Slavery is terrible for men; but it is far more terrible for women. Superadded to the burden common to all, *they* have wrongs, and sufferings, and mortifications peculiarly their own.

Dr. Flint had sworn that he would make me suffer, to my last day, for this new crime against *him*, as he called it; and as long as he had me in his power he kept his word. On the fourth day after the birth of my babe, he entered my room suddenly, and commanded me to rise and bring my baby to him. The nurse who took care of me had gone out of the room to prepare some nourishment, and I was alone. There was no alternative. I rose, took up my babe, and crossed the room to where he sat. "Now stand there," said he, "till I tell you to go back!" My child bore a strong resemblance to her father, and to the deceased Mrs. Sands, her grandmother. He noticed this; and while I stood before him, trembling with weakness, he heaped upon me and my little one every vile epithet he could think of. Even the grandmother in her grave did not escape his curses. In the midst of his vituperations[7] I fainted at his feet. This recalled him to his senses. He took the baby from my arms, laid it on the bed, dashed cold water in my face, took me up, and shook me violently, to restore my consciousness before any one entered the room. Just then my grandmother came in, and he hurried out of the house. I suffered in consequence of this treatment; but I begged my friends to let me die, rather than send for the doctor. There was nothing I dreaded so much as his presence. My life was spared; and I was glad for the sake of my little ones. Had it not been for these ties to life, I should have been glad to be released by death, though I had lived only nineteen years.

Always it gave me a pang that my children had no lawful claim to a name. Their father offered his; but, if I had wished to accept the offer, I dared not while my master lived. Moreover, I knew it would not be accepted at their baptism. A Christian name they were at least entitled to; and we resolved to call my boy for our dear good Benjamin, who had gone far away from us.

My grandmother belonged to the church; and she was very desirous of having the children christened. I knew Dr. Flint would forbid it, and I did not venture to attempt it. But chance favored me. He was called to visit a patient out of town, and was obliged to be absent during Sunday. "Now is the time," said my grandmother; "we will take the children to church, and have them christened."

When I entered the church, recollections of my mother came over me, and I felt subdued in spirit. There she had presented me for baptism, without any reason to feel ashamed. She had been married, and had such legal rights as slavery allows to a slave. The vows had at least been sacred to *her*, and she had never violated them. I was glad she was not alive, to know under what different circumstances her grandchildren were presented for baptism. Why had my lot been so different from my mother's? *Her* master had died when she was a child; and she remained with her mistress till she married. She was never in the power of any master; and thus she escaped one class of the evils that generally fall upon slaves.

When my baby was about to be christened, the former mistress of my father stepped up to me, and proposed to give it her Christian name. To this I added the surname of my father, who had himself no legal right to it; for my grandfather on the paternal side was a white gentleman. What tangled skeins[8] are the genealogies of slavery! I loved my father; but it mortified me to be obliged to bestow his name on my children.

7. Cursing and swearing.
8. Webs.

When we left the church, my father's old mistress invited me to go home with her. She clasped a gold chain round my baby's neck. I thanked her for this kindness; but I did not like the emblem. I wanted no chain to be fastened on my daughter, not even if its links were of gold. How earnestly I prayed that she might never feel the weight of slavery's chain, whose iron entereth into the soul!

XV. Continued Persecutions

My children grew finely; and Dr. Flint would often say to me, with an exulting smile, "These brats will bring me a handsome sum of money one of these days."

I thought to myself that, God being my helper, they should never pass into his hands. It seemed to me I would rather see them killed than have them given up to his power. The money for the freedom of myself and my children could be obtained; but I derived no advantage from that circumstance. Dr. Flint loved money, but he loved power more. After much discussion, my friends resolved on making another trial. There was a slaveholder about to leave for Texas, and he was commissioned to buy me. He was to begin with nine hundred dollars, and go up to twelve. My master refused his offers. "Sir," said he, "she don't belong to me. She is my daughter's property, and I have no right to sell her. I mistrust that you come from her paramour. If so, you may tell him that he cannot buy her for any money; neither can he buy her children."

The doctor came to see me the next day, and my heart beat quicker as he entered. I never had seen the old man tread with so majestic a step. He seated himself and looked at me with withering scorn. My children had learned to be afraid of him. The little one would shut her eyes and hide her face on my shoulder whenever she saw him; and Benny, who was now nearly five years old, often inquired, "What makes that bad man come here so many times? Does he want to hurt us?" I would clasp the dear boy in my arms, trusting that he would be free before he was old enough to solve the problem. And now, as the doctor sat there so grim and silent, the child left his play and came and nestled up by me. At last my tormentor spoke. "So you are left in disgust, are you?" said he. "It is no more than I expected. You remember I told you years ago that you would be treated so. So he is tired of you? Ha! ha! ha! The virtuous madam don't like to hear about it, does she? Ha! ha! ha!" There was a sting in his calling me virtuous madam. I no longer had the power of answering him as I had formerly done. He continued: "So it seems you are trying to get up another intrigue. Your new paramour came to me, and offered to buy you; but you may be assured you will not succeed. You are mine; and you shall be mine for life. There lives no human being that can take you out of slavery. I would have done it; but you rejected my kind offer."

I told him I did not wish to get up any intrigue; that I had never seen the man who offered to buy me.

"Do you tell me I lie?" exclaimed he, dragging me from my chair. "Will you say again that you never saw that man?"

I answered, "I do say so."

He clinched my arm with a volley of oaths. Ben began to scream, and I told him to go to his grandmother.

"Don't you stir a step, you little wretch!" said he. The child drew nearer to me, and put his arms round me, as if he wanted to protect me. This was too much for my enraged master. He caught him up and hurled him across the room. I thought he was dead, and rushed towards him to take him up.

"Not yet!" exclaimed the doctor. "Let him lie there till he comes to."

"Let me go! Let me go!" I screamed, "or I will raise the whole house." I struggled and got away; but he clinched me again. Somebody opened the door, and he released me. I picked up my insensible child, and when I turned my tormentor was gone. Anxiously I bent over the little form, so pale and still; and when the brown eyes at last opened, I don't know whether I was very happy.

All the doctor's former persecutions were renewed. He came morning, noon, and night. No jealous lover ever watched a rival more closely than he watched me and the unknown slaveholder, with whom he accused me of wishing to get up an intrigue. When my grandmother was out of the way he searched every room to find him.

In one of his visits, he happened to find a young girl, whom he had sold to a trader a few days previous. His statement was, that he sold her because she had been too familiar with the overseer. She had had a bitter life with him, and was glad to be sold. She had no mother, and no near ties. She had been torn from all her family years before. A few friends had entered into bonds for her safety, if the trader would allow her to spend with them the time that intervened between her sale and the gathering up of his human stock. Such a favor was rarely granted. It saved the trader the expense of board and jail fees, and though the amount was small, it was a weighty consideration in a slave-trader's mind.

Dr. Flint always had an aversion to meeting slaves after he had sold them. He ordered Rose out of the house; but he was no longer her master, and she took no notice of him. For once the crushed Rose was the conqueror. His gray eyes flashed angrily upon her; but that was the extent of his power. "How came this girl here?" he exclaimed. "What right had you to allow it, when you knew I had sold her?"

I answered "This is my grandmother's house, and Rose came to see her. I have no right to turn any body out of doors, that comes here for honest purposes."

He gave me the blow that would have fallen upon Rose if she had still been his slave. My grandmother's attention had been attracted by loud voices, and she entered in time to see a second blow dealt. She was not a woman to let such an outrage, in her own house, go unrebuked. The doctor undertook to explain that I had been insolent. Her indignant feelings rose higher and higher, and finally boiled over in words. "Get out of my house!"she exclaimed. "Go home, and take care of your wife and children, and you will have enough to do, without watching my family."

He threw the birth of my children in her face, and accused her of sanctioning the life I was leading. She told him I was living with her by compulsion of his wife; that he needn't accuse her, for he was the one to blame; he was the one who had caused all the trouble. She grew more and more excited as she went on. "I tell you what, Dr. Flint," said she, "you ain't got many more years to live, and you'd better be saying your prayers. It will take 'em all, and more too, to wash the dirt off your soul."

"Do you know whom you are talking to?" he exclaimed.

She replied, "Yes, I know very well who I am talking to."

He left the house in a great rage. I looked at my grandmother. Our eyes met. Their angry expression had passed away, but she looked sorrowful and weary—weary of incessant strife. I wondered that it did not lessen her love for me; but if it did she never showed it. She was always kind, always ready to sympathize with my troubles. There might have been peace and contentment in that humble home if it had not been for the demon Slavery.

The winter passed undisturbed by the doctor. The beautiful spring came; and when Nature resumes her loveliness, the human soul is apt to revive also. My drooping hopes came to life again with the flowers. I was dreaming of freedom again; more for my children's sake than my own. I planned and I planned. Obstacles hit against plans. There seemed no way of overcoming them; and yet I hoped.

Back came the wily doctor. I was not at home when he called. A friend had invited me to a small party, and to gratify her I went. To my great consternation, a messenger came in haste to say that Dr. Flint was at my grandmother's, and insisted on seeing me. They did not tell him where I was, or he would have come and raised a disturbance in my friend's house. They sent me a dark wrapper; I threw it on and hurried home. My speed did not save me; the doctor had gone away in anger. I dreaded the morning, but I could not delay it; it came, warm and bright. At an early hour the doctor came and asked me where I had been last night. I told him. He did not believe me, and sent to my friend's house to ascertain the facts. He came in the afternoon to assure me he was satisfied that I had spoken the truth. He seemed to be in a facetious mood, and I expected some jeers were coming. "I suppose you need some recreation," said he, "but I am surprised at your being there, among those negroes. It was not the place for *you*. Are you *allowed* to visit such people?"

I understood this covert fling at the white gentleman who was my friend; but I merely replied, "I went to visit my friends, and any company they keep is good enough for me."

He went on to say, "I have seen very little of you of late, but my interest in you is unchanged. When I said I would have no more mercy on you I was rash. I recall my words. Linda, you desire freedom for yourself and your children, and you can obtain it only through me. If you agree to what I am about to propose, you and they shall be free. There must be no communication of any kind between you and their father. I will procure a cottage, where you and the children can live together. Your labor shall be light, such as sewing for my family. Think what is offered you, Linda—a home and freedom! Let the past be forgotten. If I have been harsh with you at times, your wilfulness drove me to it. You know I exact obedience from my own children, and I consider you as yet a child."

He paused for an answer, but I remained silent.

"Why don't you speak?" said he. "What more do you wait for?"

"Nothing, sir."

"Then you accept my offer?"

"No, sir."

His anger was ready to break loose; but he succeeded in curbing it, and replied. "You have answered without thought. But I must let you know there are two sides to my proposition; if you reject the bright side, you will be obliged to take the dark one. You must either accept my offer, or you and your children shall be sent to your young master's plantation, there to remain till your young mistress is married; and your children shall fare like the rest of the negro children. I give you a week to consider of it."

He was shrewd; but I knew he was not to be trusted. I told him I was ready to give my answer now.

"I will not receive it now," he replied. "You act too much from impulse. Remember that you and your children can be free a week from to-day if you choose."

On what a monstrous chance hung the destiny of my children! I knew that my master's offer was a snare, and that if I entered it escape would be impossible. As for his promise, I knew him so well that I was sure if he gave me free papers, they would be so managed as to have no legal value. The alternative was inevitable. I resolved to go to the plantation. But then I thought how completely I should be in his power, and the prospect was apalling. Even if I should kneel before him, and implore him to spare me, for the sake of my children, I knew he would spurn me with his foot, and my weakness would be his triumph.

Before the week expired, I heard that young Mr. Flint was about to be married to a lady of his own stamp. I foresaw the position I should occupy in his establishment. I had once been sent to the plantation for punishment, and fear of the son had induced the father to recall me very soon. My mind was made up; I was resolved that I would foil my master and save my children, or I would perish in the attempt. I kept my plans to my-self; I knew that friends would try to dissuade me from them, and I would not wound their feelings by rejecting their advice.

On the decisive day the doctor came, and said he hoped I had made a wise choice.

"I am ready to go to the plantation, sir," I replied.

"Have you thought how important your decision is to your children?" said he.

I told him I had.

"Very well. Go to the plantation, and my curse go with you," he replied. "Your boy shall be put to work, and he shall soon be sold; and your girl shall be raised for the purpose of selling well. Go your own ways!" He left the room with curses, not to be repeated.

As I stood rooted to the spot, my grandmother came and said, "Linda, child, what did you tell him?"

I answered that I was going to the plantation.

"*Must* you go?" said she. "Can't something be done to stop it?"

I told her it was useless to try; but she begged me not to give up. She said she would go to the doctor, and remind him how long and how faith-fully she had served in the family, and how she had taken her own baby from her breast to nourish his wife. She would tell him I had been out of the family so long they would not miss me; that she would pay them for my time, and the money would procure a woman who had more strength for the situation than I had. I begged her not to go; but she persisted in saying, "He will listen to *me*, Linda." She went, and was treated as I ex-pected. He coolly listened to what she said, but denied her request. He told her that what he did was for my good, that my feelings were entirely above my situation, and that on the plantation I would receive treatment that was suitable to my behavior.

My grandmother was much cast down. I had my secret hopes; but I must fight my battle alone. I had a woman's pride, and a mother's love for my children; and I resolved that out of the darkness of this hour a brighter dawn should rise for them. My master had power and law on his side; I had a determined will. There is might in each.

XVI. Scenes at the Plantation

Early the next morning I left my grandmother's with my youngest child. My boy was ill, and I left him behind. I had many sad thoughts as the old wagon jolted on. Hitherto, I had suffered alone; now, my little one was to be treated as a slave. As we drew near the great house, I thought of the time when I was formerly sent there out of revenge. I wondered for what purpose I was now sent. I could not tell. I resolved to obey orders so far as duty required; but within myself, I determined to make my stay as short as possible. Mr. Flint was waiting to receive us, and told me to follow him up stairs to receive orders for the day. My little Ellen was left below in the kitchen. It was a change for her, who had always been so carefully tended. My young master said she might amuse herself in the yard. This was kind of him, since the child was hateful to his sight. My task was to fit up the house for the reception of the bride. In the midst of sheets, tablecloths, towels, drapery, and carpeting, my head was as busy planning, as were my fingers with the needle. At noon I was allowed to go to Ellen. She had sobbed herself to sleep. I heard Mr. Flint say to a neighbor, "I've got her down here, and I'll soon take the town notions out of her head. My father is partly to blame for her nonsense. He ought to have broke her in long ago." The remark was made within my hearing, and it would have been quite as manly to have made it to my face. He *had* said things to my face which might, or might not, have surprised his neighbor if he had known of them. He was "a chip of the old block."

I resolved to give him no cause to accuse me of being too much of a lady, so far as work was concerned. I worked day and night, with wretchedness before me. When I lay down beside my child, I felt how much easier it would be to see her die than to see her master beat her about, as I daily saw him beat other little ones. The spirit of the mothers was so crushed by the lash, that they stood by, without courage to remonstrate. How much more must I suffer, before I should be "broke in" to that degree?

I wished to appear as contented as possible. Sometimes I had an opportunity to send a few lines home; and this brought up recollections that made it difficult, for a time, to seem calm and indifferent to my lot. Notwithstanding my efforts, I saw that Mr. Flint regarded me with a suspicious eye. Ellen broke down under the trials of her new life. Separated from me, with no one to look after her, she wandered about, and in a few days cried herself sick. One day, she sat under the window where I was at work, crying that weary cry which makes a mother's heart bleed. I was obliged to steel myself to bear it. After a while it ceased. I looked out, and she was gone. As it was near noon, I ventured to go down in search of her. The great house was raised two feet above the ground. I looked under it, and saw her about midway, fast asleep. I crept under and drew her out. As I held her in my arms, I thought how well it would be for her if she never waked up; and I uttered my thought aloud. I was startled to hear some one say, "Did you speak to me?" I looked up, and saw Mr. Flint standing beside me. He said nothing further, but turned, frowning, away. That night he sent Ellen a biscuit and a cup of sweetened milk. This generosity surprised me. I learned afterwards, that in the afternoon he had killed a large snake, which crept from under the house; and I supposed that incident had prompted his unusual kindness.

The next morning the old cart was loaded with shingles for town. I put

Ellen into it, and sent her to her grandmother. Mr. Flint said I ought to have asked his permission. I told him the child was sick, and required attention which I had no time to give. He let it pass; for he was aware that I had accomplished much work in a little time.

I had been three weeks on the plantation, when I planned a visit home. It must be at night, after every body was in bed. I was six miles from town, and the road was very dreary. I was to go with a young man, who, I knew, often stole to town to see his mother. One night, when all was quiet, we started. Fear gave speed to our steps, and we were not long in performing the journey. I arrived at my grandmother's. Her bed room was on the first floor, and the window was open, the weather being warm. I spoke to her and she awoke. She let me in and closed the window, lest some late passer-by should see me. A light was brought, and the whole household gathered round me, some smiling and some crying. I went to look at my children, and thanked God for their happy sleep. The tears fell as I leaned over them. As I moved to leave, Benny stirred. I turned back, and whispered, "Mother is here." After digging at his eyes with his little fist, they opened, and he sat up in bed, looking at me curiously. Having satisfied himself that it was I, he exclaimed, "O mother! you ain't dead, are you? They didn't cut off your head at the plantation, did they?"

My time was up too soon, and my guide was waiting for me. I laid Benny back in his bed, and dried his tears by a promise to come again soon. Rapidly we retraced our steps back to the plantation. About half way we were met by a company of four patrols.[9] Luckily we heard their horse's hoofs before they came in sight, and we had time to hide behind a large tree. They passed, hallooing and shouting in a manner that indicated a recent carousal. How thankful we were that they had not their dogs with them! We hastened our footsteps, and when we arrived on the plantation we heard the sound of the hand-mill. The slaves were grinding their corn. We were safely in the house before the horn summoned them to their labor. I divided my little parcel of food with my guide, knowing that he had lost the chance of grinding his corn, and must toil all day in the field.

Mr. Flint often took an inspection of the house, to see that no one was idle. The entire management of the work was trusted to me, because he knew nothing about it; and rather than hire a superintendent he contented himself with my arrangements. He had often urged upon his father the necessity of having me at the plantation to take charge of his affairs, and make clothes for the slaves; but the old man knew him too well to consent to that arrangement.

When I had been working a month at the plantation, the great aunt of Mr. Flint came to make him a visit. This was the good old lady who paid fifty dollars for my grandmother, for the purpose of making her free, when

---

9. Volunteer guards who patrolled the area seeking any slave who was away from his or her owner without written permission.

she stood on the auction block. My grandmother loved this old lady, whom we all called Miss Fanny. She often came to take tea with us. On such occasions the table was spread with a snow-white cloth, and the china cups and silver spoons were taken from the old-fashioned buffet. There were hot muffins, tea rusks,[1] and delicious sweetmeats. My grandmother kept two cows, and the fresh cream was Miss Fanny's delight. She invariably declared that it was the best in town. The old ladies had cosey times together. They would work and chat, and sometimes, while talking over old times, their spectacles would get dim with tears, and would have to be taken off and wiped. When Miss Fanny bade us good by, her bag was filled with grandmother's best cakes, and she was urged to come again soon.

There had been a time when Dr. Flint's wife came to take tea with us, and when her children were also sent to have a feast of "Aunt Marthy's" nice cooking. But after I became an object of her jealousy and spite, she was angry with grandmother for giving a shelter to me and my children. She would not even speak to her in the street. This wounded my grandmother's feelings, for she could not retain ill will against the woman whom she had nourished with her milk when a babe. The doctor's wife would gladly have prevented our intercourse[2] with Miss Fanny if she could have done it, but fortunately she was not dependent on the bounty of the Flints. She had enough to be independent; and that is more than can ever be gained from charity, however lavish it may be.

Miss Fanny was endeared to me by many recollections, and I was rejoiced to see her at the plantation. The warmth of her large, loyal heart made the house seem pleasanter while she was in it. She staid a week, and I had many talks with her. She said her principal object in coming was to see how I was treated, and whether any thing could be done for me. She inquired whether she could help me in any way. I told her I believed not. She condoled with me in her own peculiar way; saying she wished that I and all my grandmother's family were at rest in our graves, for not until then should she feel any peace about us. The good old soul did not dream that I was planning to bestow peace upon her, with regard to myself and my children; not by death, but by securing our freedom.

Again and again I had traversed those dreary twelve miles, to and from the town; and all the way, I was meditating upon some means of escape for myself and my children. My friends had made every effort that ingenuity could devise to effect our purchase, but all their plans had proved abortive. Dr. Flint was suspicious, and determined not to loosen his grasp upon us. I could have made my escape alone; but it was more for my helpless children than for myself that I longed for freedom. Though the boon would have been precious to me, above all price, I would not have taken

1. A delicate, twice-baked biscuit.
2. Contact or conversation.

it at the expense of leaving them in slavery. Every trial I endured, every sacrifice I made for their sakes, drew them closer to my heart, and gave me fresh courage to beat back the dark waves that rolled and rolled over me in a seemingly endless night of storms.

The six weeks were nearly completed, when Mr. Flint's bride was expected to take possession of her new home. The arrangements were all completed, and Mr. Flint said I had done well. He expected to leave home on Saturday, and return with his bride the following Wednesday. After receiving various orders from him, I ventured to ask permission to spend Sunday in town. It was granted; for which favor I was thankful. It was the first I had ever asked of him, and I intended it should be the last. It needed more than one night to accomplish the project I had in view; but the whole of Sunday would give me an opportunity. I spent the Sabbath with my grandmother. A calmer, more beautiful day never came down out of heaven. To me it was a day of conflicting emotions. Perhaps it was the last day I should ever spend under that dear, old sheltering roof! Perhaps these were the last talks I should ever have with the faithful old friend of my whole life! Perhaps it was the last time I and my children should be together! Well, better so, I thought, than that they should be slaves. I knew the doom that awaited my fair baby in slavery, and I determined to save her from it, or perish in the attempt. I went to make this vow at the graves of my poor parents, in the burying-ground of the slaves. "There the wicked cease from troubling, and there the weary be at rest. There the prisoners rest together; they hear not the voice of the oppressor; the servant is free from his master." I knelt by the graves of my parents, and thanked God, as I had often done before, that they had not lived to witness my trials, or to mourn over my sins. I had received my mother's blessing when she died; and in many an hour of tribulation I had seemed to hear her voice, sometimes chiding me, sometimes whispering loving words into my wounded heart. I have shed many and bitter tears, to think that when I am gone from my children they cannot remember me with such entire satisfaction as I remembered my mother.

The graveyard was in the woods, and twilight was coming on. Nothing broke the death-like stillness except the occasional twitter of a bird. My spirit was overawed by the solemnity of the scene. For more than ten years I had frequented this spot, but never had it seemed to me so sacred as now. A black stump, at the head of my mother's grave, was all that remained of a tree my father had planted. His grave was marked by a small wooden board, bearing his name, the letters of which were nearly obliterated. I knelt down and kissed them, and poured forth a prayer to God for guidance and support in the perilous step I was about to take. As I passed the wreck of the old meeting house, where, before Nat Turner's time, the slaves had been allowed to meet for worship, I seemed to hear my father's voice come from it, bidding me not to tarry till I reached freedom or the grave. I rushed on with renovated hopes. My trust in God had been strengthened by that prayer among the graves.

My plan was to conceal myself at the house of a friend, and remain there a few weeks till the search was over. My hope was that the doctor would get discouraged, and, for fear of losing my value, and also of subsequently finding my children among the missing, he would consent to sell us; and I knew somebody would buy us. I had done all in my power to make my children comfortable during the time I expected to be separated from them. I was packing my things, when grandmother came into the room, and asked what I was doing. "I am putting my things in order," I replied. I tried to look and speak cheerfully; but her watchful eye detected something beneath the surface. She drew me towards her, and asked me to sit down. She looked earnestly at me, and said, "Linda, do you want to kill your old grandmother? Do you mean to leave your little, helpless children? I am old now, and cannot do for your babies as I once did for you."

I replied, that if I went away, perhaps their father would be able to secure their freedom.

"Ah, my child," said she, "don't trust too much to him. Stand by your own children, and suffer with them till death. Nobody respects a mother who forsakes her children; and if you leave them, you will never have a happy moment. If you go, you will make me miserable the short time I have to live. You would be taken and brought back, and your sufferings would be dreadful. Remember poor Benjamin. Do give it up, Linda. Try to bear a little longer. Things may turn out better than we expect."

My courage failed me, in view of the sorrow I should bring on that faithful, loving old heart. I promised that I would try longer, and that I would take nothing out of her house without her knowledge.

Whenever the children climbed on my knee, or laid their heads on my lap, she would say, "Poor little souls! what would you do without a mother? She don't love you as I do." And she would hug them to her own bosom, as if to reproach me for my want of affection; but she knew all the while that I loved them better than my life. I slept with her that night, and it was the last time. The memory of it haunted me for many a year.

On Monday I returned to the plantation, and busied myself with preparations for the important day. Wednesday came. It was a beautiful day, and the faces of the slaves were as bright as the sunshine. The poor creatures were merry. They were expecting little presents from the bride, and hoping for better times under her administration. I had no such hopes for them. I knew that the young wives of slaveholders often thought their authority and importance would be best established and maintained by cruelty; and what I had heard of young Mrs. Flint gave me no reason to expect that her rule over them would be less severe than that of the master and overseer. Truly, the colored race are the most cheerful and forgiving people on the face of the earth. That their masters sleep in safety is owing to their superabundance of heart; and yet they look upon their sufferings with less pity than they would bestow on those of a horse or a dog.

I stood at the door with others to receive the bridegroom and bride. She was a handsome, delicate-looking girl, and her face flushed with emotion at sight of her new home. I thought it likely that visions of a happy future were rising before her. It made me sad; for I knew how soon clouds would come over her sunshine. She examined every part of the house, and told me she was delighted with the arrangements I had made. I was afraid old Mrs. Flint had tried to prejudice her against me, and I did my best to please her.

All passed off smoothly for me until dinner time arrived. I did not mind the embarrassment of waiting on a dinner party, for the first time in my life, half so much as I did the meeting with Dr. Flint and his wife, who would be among the guests. It was a mystery to me why Mrs. Flint had not made her appearance at the plantation during all the time I was putting the house in order. I had not met her, face to face, for five years, and I had no wish to see her now. She was a praying woman, and, doubtless, considered my present position a special answer to her prayers. Nothing could please her better than to see me humbled and trampled upon. I was just where she would have me—in the power of a hard, unprincipled master. She did not speak to me when she took her seat at table; but her satisfied, triumphant smile, when I handed her plate, was more eloquent than words. The old doctor was not so quiet in his demonstrations. He ordered me here and there, and spoke with peculiar emphasis when he said "your *mistress*." I was drilled like a disgraced soldier. When all was over, and the last key turned, I sought my pillow, thankful that God had appointed a season of rest for the weary.

The next day my new mistress began her housekeeping. I was not exactly appointed maid of all work; but I was to do whatever I was told. Monday evening came. It was always a busy time. On that night the slaves received their weekly allowance of food. Three pounds of meat, a peck of corn, and perhaps a dozen herring were allowed to each man. Women received a pound and half of meat, a peck of corn, and the same number of herring. Children over twelve years old had half the allowance of the women. The meat was cut and weighed by the foreman of the field hands, and piled on planks before the meat house. Then the second foreman went behind the building, and when the first foreman called out, "Who takes this piece of meat?" he answered by calling somebody's name. This method was resorted to as a means of preventing partiality in distributing the meat. The young mistress came out to see how things were done on her plantation, and she soon gave a specimen of her character. Among those in waiting for their allowance was a very old slave, who had faithfully served the Flint family through three generations. When he hobbled up to get his bit of meat, the mistress said he was too old to have any allowance; that when niggers were too old to work, they ought to be fed on grass. Poor old man! He suffered much before he found rest in the grave.

My mistress and I got along very well together. At the end of a week, old Mrs. Flint made us another visit, and was closeted a long time with her daughter-in-law. I had my suspicions what was the subject of the conference. The old doctor's wife had been informed that I could leave the plantation on one condition, and she was very desirous to keep me there. If she had trusted me, as I deserved to be trusted by her, she would have had no fears of my accepting that condition. When she entered her carriage to return home, she said to young Mrs. Flint, "Don't neglect to send for them as quick as possible." My heart was on the watch all the time, and I at once concluded that she spoke of my children. The doctor came the next day, and as I entered the room to spread the tea table, I heard him say, "Don't wait any longer. Send for them to-morrow." I saw through the plan. They thought my children's being there would fetter me to the spot, and that it was a good place to break us all in to abject submission to our lot as slaves. After the doctor left, a gentleman called, who had always manifested friendly feelings towards my grandmother and her family. Mr. Flint carried him over the plantation to show him the results of labor performed by men and women who were unpaid, miserably clothed, and half famished. The cotton crop was all they thought of. It was duly admired, and the gentleman returned with specimens to show his friends. I was ordered to carry water to wash his hands. As I did so, he said, "Linda, how do you like your new home?" I told him I liked it as well as I expected. He replied, "They don't think you are contented, and to-morrow they are going to bring your children to be with you. I am sorry for you, Linda. I hope they will treat you kindly." I hurried from the room, unable to thank him. My suspicions were correct. My children were to be brought to the plantation to be "broke in."

To this day I feel grateful to the gentleman who gave me this timely information. It nerved me to immediate action.

XVII. The Flight

Mr. Flint was hard pushed for house servants, and rather than lose me he had restrained his malice. I did my work faithfully, though not, of course, with a willing mind. They were evidently afraid I should leave them. Mr. Flint wished that I should sleep in the great house instead of the servants' quarters. His wife agreed to the proposition, but said I mustn't bring my bed into the house, because it would scatter feathers on her carpet. I knew when I went there that they would never think of such a thing as furnishing a bed of any kind for me and my little one. I therefore carried my own bed, and now I was forbidden to use it. I did as I was ordered.

But now that I was certain my children were to be put in their power, in order to give them a stronger hold on me, I resolved to leave them that night. I remembered the grief this step would bring upon my dear old grandmother; and nothing less than the freedom of my children would have induced me to disregard her advice. I went about my evening work with trembling steps. Mr. Flint twice called from his chamber door to inquire why the house was not locked up. I replied that I had not done my work. "You have had time enough to do it," said he. "Take care how you answer me!"

I shut all the windows, locked all the doors, and went up to the third story, to wait till midnight. How long those hours seemed, and how fervently I prayed that God would not forsake me in this hour of utmost need! I was about to risk every thing on the throw of a die; and if I failed, O what would become of me and my poor children? They would be made to suffer for my fault.

At half past twelve I stole softly down stairs. I stopped on the second floor, thinking I heard a noise. I felt my way down into the parlor, and looked out of the window. The night was so intensely dark that I could see nothing. I raised the window very softly and jumped out. Large drops of rain were falling, and the darkness bewildered me. I dropped on my knees, and breathed a short prayer to God for guidance and protection. I groped my way to the road, and rushed towards the town with almost lightning speed. I arrived at my grandmother's house, but dared not see her. She would say, "Linda, you are killing me;" and I knew that would unnerve me. I tapped softly at the window of a room, occupied by a woman, who had lived in the house several years. I knew she was a faithful friend, and could be trusted with my secret. I tapped several times before she heard me. At last she raised the window, and I whispered, "Sally, I have run away. Let me in, quick." She opened the door softly, and said in low tones, "For God's sake, don't. Your grandmother is trying to buy you and de chillern. Mr. Sands was here last week. He tole her he was going away on business, but he wanted her to go ahead about buying you and de chillern, and he would help her all he could. Don't run away, Linda. Your grandmother is all bowed down wid trouble now."

I replied, "Sally, they are going to carry my children to the plantation to-morrow; and they will never sell them to any body so long as they have me in their power. Now, would you advise me to go back?"

"No, chile, no," answered she. "When dey finds you is gone, dey won't want de plague ob de chillern; but where is you going to hide? Dey knows ebery inch ob dis house."

I told her I had a hiding-place, and that was all it was best for her to know. I asked her to go into my room as soon as it was light, and take all my clothes out of my trunk, and pack them in hers; for I knew Mr. Flint and the constable would be there early to search my room. I feared the sight of my children would be too much for my full heart; but I could not go out into the uncertain future without one last look. I bent over the bed where lay my little Benny and baby Ellen. Poor little ones! fatherless and motherless! Memories of their father came over me. He wanted to be kind to them; but they were not all to him, as they were to my womanly heart. I knelt and prayed for the innocent little sleepers. I kissed them lightly, and turned away.

As I was about to open the street door, Sally laid her hand on my shoulder, and said, "Linda, is you gwine all alone? Let me call your uncle."

"No, Sally," I replied, "I want no one to be brought into trouble on my account."

I went forth into the darkness and rain. I ran on till I came to the house of the friend who was to conceal me.

Early the next morning Mr. Flint was at my grandmother's inquiring for me. She told him she had not seen me, and supposed I was at the plantation. He watched her face narrowly, and said, "Don't you know any thing about her running off?" She assured him that she did not. He went on to say, "Last night she ran off without the least provocation. We had treated her very kindly. My wife liked her. She will soon be found and brought back. Are her children with you?" When told that they were, he said, "I am very glad to hear that. If they are here, she cannot be far off. If I find out that any of my niggers have had any thing to do with this damned business, I'll give 'em five hundred lashes." As he started to go to his father's, he turned round and added, persuasively, "Let her be brought back, and she shall have her children to live with her."

The tidings made the old doctor rave and storm at a furious rate. It was a busy day for them. My grandmother's house was searched from top to bottom. As my trunk was empty, they concluded I had taken my clothes with me. Before ten o'clock every vessel northward bound was thoroughly examined, and the law against harboring fugitives was read to all on board. At night a watch was set over the town. Knowing how distressed my grandmother would be, I wanted to send her a message; but it could not be done. Every one who went in or out of her house was closely watched. The doctor said he would take my children, unless she became responsible for them; which of course she willingly did. The next day was spent in searching. Before night, the following advertisement was posted at every corner, and in every public place for miles round:—

"$300 Reward! Ran away from the subscriber, an intelligent, bright, mulatto girl, named Linda, 21 years of age. Five feet four inches high. Dark eyes, and black hair inclined to curl; but it can be made straight. Has a decayed spot on a front tooth. She can read and write, and in all probability will try to get to the Free States. All persons are forbidden, under penalty of the law, to harbor or employ said slave. $150 will be given to whoever takes her in the state, and $300 if taken out of the state and delivered to me, or lodged in jail.

Dr. Flint."

XVIII. Months of Peril

The search for me was kept up with more perseverance than I had anticipated. I began to think that escape was impossible. I was in great anxiety lest I should implicate the friend who harbored me. I knew the consequences would be frightful; and much as I dreaded being caught, even that seemed better than causing an innocent person to suffer for kindness to me. A week had passed in terrible suspense, when my pursuers came into such close vicinity that I concluded they had tracked me to my hiding-place. I flew out of the house, and concealed myself in a thicket of bushes. There I remained in an agony of fear for two hours. Suddenly, a reptile of some kind seized my leg. In my fright, I struck a blow which loosened its hold, but I could not tell whether I had killed it; it was so dark, I could not see what it was; I only knew it was something cold and slimy. The pain I felt soon indicated that the bite was poisonous. I was compelled to leave my place of concealment, and I groped my way back into the house. The pain had become intense, and my friend was startled by my look of anguish. I asked her to prepare a poultice of warm ashes and vinegar, and I applied it to my leg, which was already much swollen. The application gave me some relief, but the swelling did not abate. The dread of being disabled was greater than the physical pain I endured. My friend asked an old woman, who doctored among the slaves, what was good for the bite of a snake or a lizard. She told her to steep a dozen coppers in vinegar, over night, and apply the cankered vinegar to the inflamed part.[3]

I had succeeded in cautiously conveying some messages to my relatives. They were harshly threatened, and despairing of my having a chance to escape, they advised me to return to my master, ask his forgiveness, and let him make an example of me. But such counsel had no influence with me. When I started upon this hazardous undertaking, I had resolved that, come what would, there should be no turning back. "Give me liberty, or give me death," was my motto. When my friend contrived to make known to my relatives the painful situation I had been in for twenty-four hours, they said no more about my going back to my master. Something must be done, and that speedily; but where to turn for help, they knew not. God in his mercy raised up "a friend in need."

Among the ladies who were acquainted with my grandmother, was one who had known her from childhood, and always been very friendly to her. She had also known my mother and her children, and felt interested for them. At this crisis of affairs she called to see my grandmother, as she not unfrequently did. She observed the sad and troubled expression of her

---

3. The poison of a snake is a powerful acid, and is counteracted by powerful alkalies, such as potash, ammonia, &c. The Indians are accustomed to apply wet ashes, or plunge the limb into strong lie. White men, employed to lay out railroads in snaky places, often carry ammonia with them as an antidote. —Editor [Child's note].

face, and asked if she knew where Linda was, and whether she was safe. My grandmother shook her head, without answering. "Come, Aunt Martha," said the kind lady, "tell me all about it. Perhaps I can do something to help you." The husband of this lady held many slaves, and bought and sold slaves. She also held a number in her own name; but she treated them kindly, and would never allow any of them to be sold. She was unlike the majority of slaveholders' wives. My grandmother looked earnestly at her. Something in the expression of her face said "Trust me!" and she did trust her. She listened attentively to the details of my story, and sat thinking for a while. At last she said, "Aunt Martha, I pity you both. If you think there is any chance of Linda's getting to the Free States, I will conceal her for a time. But first you must solemnly promise that my name shall never be mentioned. If such a thing should become known, it would ruin me and my family. No one in my house must know of it, except the cook. She is so faithful that I would trust my own life with her; and I know she likes Linda. It is a great risk; but I trust no harm will come of it. Get word to Linda to be ready as soon as it is dark, before the patrols are out. I will send the housemaids on errands, and Betty shall go to meet Linda." The place where we were to meet was designated and agreed upon. My grandmother was unable to thank the lady for this noble deed; overcome by her emotions, she sank on her knees and sobbed like a child.

I received a message to leave my friend's house at such an hour, and go to a certain place where a friend would be waiting for me. As a matter of prudence no names were mentioned. I had no means of conjecturing who I was to meet, or where I was going. I did not like to move thus blindfolded, but I had no choice. It would not do for me to remain where I was. I disguised myself, summoned up courage to meet the worst, and went to the appointed place. My friend Betty was there; she was the last person I expected to see. We hurried along in silence. The pain in my leg was so intense that it seemed as if I should drop; but fear gave me strength. We reached the house and entered unobserved. Her first words were: "Honey, now you is safe. Dem devils ain't coming to search *dis* house. When I get you into missis' safe place, I will bring some nice hot supper. I specs you need it after all dis skeering." Betty's vocation led her to think eating the most important thing in life. She did not realize that my heart was too full for me to care much about supper.

The mistress came to meet us, and led me up stairs to a small room over her own sleeping apartment. "You will be safe here, Linda," said she; "I keep this room to store away things that are out of use. The girls are not accustomed to be sent to it, and they will not suspect any thing unless they hear some noise. I always keep it locked, and Betty shall take care of the key. But you must be very careful, for my sake as well as your own; and you must never tell my secret; for it would ruin me and my family. I will keep the girls busy in the morning, that Betty may have a chance to bring your breakfast; but it will not do for her to come to you again till night. I will come to see you sometimes. Keep up your courage. I hope this state of things will not last long." Betty came with the "nice hot supper," and the mistress hastened down stairs to keep things straight till she returned. How my heart overflowed with gratitude! Words choked in my throat; but I could have kissed the feet of my benefactress. For that deed of Christian womanhood, may God forever bless her!

I went to sleep that night with the feeling that I was for the present the most fortunate slave in town. Morning came and filled my little cell with light. I thanked the heavenly Father for this safe retreat. Opposite my window was a pile of feather beds. On the top of these I could lie perfectly concealed, and command a view of the street through which Dr. Flint passed to his office. Anxious as I was, I felt a gleam of satisfaction when I saw him. Thus far I had outwitted him, and I triumphed over it. Who can blame slaves for being cunning? They are constantly compelled to resort to it. It is the only weapon of the weak and oppressed against the strength of their tyrants.

I was daily hoping to hear that my master had sold my children; for I knew who was on the watch to buy them. But Dr. Flint cared even more for revenge than he did for money. My brother William, and the good aunt who had served in his family twenty years, and my little Benny, and Ellen, who was a little over two years old, were thrust into jail, as a means of compelling my relatives to give some information about me. He swore my grandmother should never see one of them again till I was brought back. They kept these facts from me for several days. When I heard that my little ones were in a loathsome jail, my first impulse was to go to them. I was encountering dangers for the sake of freeing them, and must I be the cause of their death? The thought was agonizing. My benefactress tried to soothe me by telling me that my aunt would take good care of the children while they remained in jail. But it added to my pain to think that the good old aunt, who had always been so kind to her sister's orphan children, should be shut up in prison for no other crime than loving them. I suppose my friends feared a reckless movement on my part, knowing, as they did, that my life was bound up in my children. I received a note from my brother William. It was scarcely legible, and ran thus: "Wherever you are, dear sister, I beg of you not to come here. We are all much better off than you are. If you come, you will ruin us all. They would force you to tell where you had been, or they would kill you. Take the advice of your friends; if not for the sake of me and your children, at least for the sake of those you would ruin."

Poor William! He also must suffer for being my brother. I took his advice and kept quiet. My aunt was taken out of jail at the end of a month, because Mrs. Flint could not spare her any longer. She was tired of being her own housekeeper. It was quite too fatiguing to order her dinner and eat it too. My children remained in jail, where brother William did all he could for their comfort. Betty went to see them sometimes, and brought me tidings. She was not permitted to enter the jail; but William would hold them up to the grated window while she chatted with them. When she repeated their prattle, and told me how they wanted to see their ma, my tears would flow. Old Betty would exclaim, "Lors, chile! what's you crying 'bout? Dem young uns vil kill you dead. Don't be so chick'n hearted! If you does, you vil nebber git thro' dis world."

Good old soul! She had gone through the world childless. She had never had little ones to clasp their arms around her neck; she had never seen their soft eyes looking into hers; no sweet little voices had called her mother; she had never pressed her own infants to her heart, with the feeling that even in fetters there was something to live for. How could she realize my feelings? Betty's husband loved children dearly, and wondered why God had denied them to him. He expressed great sorrow when he came to Betty with the tidings that Ellen had been taken out of jail and carried to Dr. Flint's. She had the measles a short time before they carried her to jail, and the disease had left her eyes affected. The doctor had taken her home to attend to them. My children had always been afraid of the doctor and his wife. They had never been inside of their house. Poor little Ellen cried all day to be carried back to prison. The instincts of childhood are true. She knew she was loved in the jail. Her screams and sobs annoyed Mrs. Flint. Before night she called one of the slaves, and said, "Here, Bill, carry this brat back to the jail. I can't stand her noise. If she would be quiet I should like to keep the little minx. She would make a handy waiting-maid for my daughter by and by. But if she staid here, with her white face, I suppose I should either kill her or spoil her. I hope the doctor will sell them as far as wind and water can carry them. As for their mother, her ladyship will find out yet what she gets by running away. She hasn't so much feeling for her children as a cow has for its calf. If she had, she would have come back long ago, to get them out of jail, and save all this expense and trouble. The good-for-nothing hussy! When she is caught, she shall stay in jail, in irons, for one six months, and then be sold to a sugar plantation. I shall see her broke in yet. What do you stand there for, Bill? Why don't you go off with the brat? Mind, now, that you don't let any of the niggers speak to her in the street!"

When these remarks were reported to me, I smiled at Mrs. Flint's saying that she should either kill my child or spoil her. I thought to myself there was very little danger of the latter. I have always considered it as one of God's special providences that Ellen screamed till she was carried back to jail.

That same night Dr. Flint was called to a patient, and did not return till near morning. Passing my grandmother's, he saw a light in the house, and thought to himself, "Perhaps this has something to do with Linda." He knocked, and the door was opened. "What calls you up so early?" said he. "I saw your light, and I thought I would just stop and tell you that I have found out where Linda is. I know where to put my hands on her, and I shall have her before twelve o'clock." When he had turned away, my grandmother and my uncle looked anxiously at each other. They did not know whether or not it was merely one of the doctor's tricks to frighten them. In their uncertainty, they thought it was best to have a message conveyed to my friend Betty. Unwilling to alarm her mistress, Betty resolved to dispose of me herself. She came to me, and told me to rise and dress quickly. We hurried down stairs, and across the yard, into the kitchen. She locked the door, and lifted up a plank in the floor. A buffalo skin and a bit of carpet were spread for me to lie on, and a quilt thrown over me. "Stay dar," said she, "till I sees if dey know 'bout you. Dey say dey vil put thar hans on you afore twelve o'clock. If dey *did* know whar you are, dey won't know *now*. Dey'll be disapinted dis time. Dat's all I got to say. If dey comes rummagin 'mong *my* tings, dey'll get one bressed sarssin from dis 'ere nigger." In my shallow bed I had but just room enough to bring my hands to my face to keep the dust out of my eyes; for Betty walked over me twenty times in an hour, passing from the dresser to the fireplace. When she was alone, I could hear her pronouncing anathemas over Dr. Flint and all his tribe, every now and then saying, with a chuckling laugh, "Dis nigger's too cute for 'em dis time." When the housemaids were about, she had sly ways of drawing them out, that I might hear what they would say. She would repeat stories she had heard about my being in this, or that, or the other place. To which they would answer, that I was not fool enough to be staying round there; that I was in Philadelphia or New York before this time. When all were abed and asleep, Betty raised the plank, and said, "Come out, chile; come out. Dey don't know nottin 'bout you. 'Twas only white folks' lies, to skeer de niggers."

Some days after this adventure I had a much worse fright. As I sat very still in my retreat above stairs, cheerful visions floated through my mind. I thought Dr. Flint would soon get discouraged, and would be willing to sell my children, when he lost all hopes of making them the means of my discovery. I knew who was ready to buy them. Suddenly I heard a voice that chilled my blood. The sound was too familiar to me, it had been too dreadful, for me not to recognize at once my old master. He was in the house, and I at once concluded he had come to seize me. I looked round in terror. There was no way of escape. The voice receded. I supposed the constable was with him, and they were searching the house. In my alarm I did not forget the trouble I was bringing on my generous benefactress. It seemed as if I were born to bring sorrow on all who befriended me, and that was the bitterest drop in the bitter cup of my life. After a while I heard approaching footsteps; the key was turned in my door. I braced myself against the wall to keep from falling. I ventured to look up, and there stood my kind benefactress alone. I was too much overcome to speak, and sunk down upon the floor.

"I thought you would hear your master's voice," she said; "and knowing you would be terrified, I came to tell you there is nothing to fear. You may even indulge in a laugh at the old gentleman's expense. He is so sure you are in New York, that he came to borrow five hundred dollars to go in pursuit of you. My sister had some money to loan on interest. He has obtained it, and proposes to start for New York to-night. So, for the present, you see you are safe. The doctor will merely lighten his pocket hunting after the bird he has left behind."

XIX. The Children Sold

The doctor came back from New York, of course without accomplishing his purpose. He had expended considerable money, and was rather disheartened. My brother and the children had now been in jail two months, and that also was some expense. My friends thought it was a favorable time to work on his discouraged feelings. Mr. Sands sent a speculator to offer him nine hundred dollars for my brother William, and eight hundred for the two children. These were high prices, as slaves were then selling; but the offer was rejected. If it had been merely a question of money, the doctor would have sold any boy of Benny's age for two hundred dollars; but he could not bear to give up the power of revenge. But he was hard pressed for money, and he revolved the matter in his mind. He knew that if he could keep Ellen till she was fifteen, he could sell her for a high price; but I presume he reflected that she might die, or might be stolen away. At all events, he came to the conclusion that he had better accept the slave-trader's offer. Meeting him in the street, he inquired when he would leave town. "To-day, at ten o'clock," he replied. "Ah, do you go so soon?" said the doctor; "I have been reflecting upon your proposition, and I have concluded to let you have the three negroes if you will say nineteen hundred dollars." After some parley, the trader agreed to his terms. He wanted the bill of sale drawn up and signed immediately, as he had a great deal to attend to during the short time he remained in town. The doctor went to the jail and told William he would take him back into his service if he would promise to behave himself; but he replied that he would rather be sold. "And you *shall* be sold, you ungrateful rascal!" exclaimed the doctor. In less than an hour the money was paid, the papers were signed, sealed, and delivered, and my brother and children were in the hands of the trader.

It was a hurried transaction; and after it was over, the doctor's characteristic caution returned. He went back to the speculator, and said, "Sir, I have come to lay you under obligations of a thousand dollars not to sell any of those negroes in this state." "You come too late," replied the trader; "our bargain is closed." He had, in fact, already sold them to Mr. Sands, but he did not mention it. The doctor required him to put irons on "that rascal, Bill," and to pass through the back streets when he took his gang out of town. The trader was privately instructed to concede to his wishes. My good old aunt went to the jail to bid the children good by, supposing them to be the speculator's property, and that she should never see them again. As she held Benny in her lap, he said, "Aunt Nancy, I want to show you something." He led her to the door and showed her a long row of marks, saying, "Uncle Will taught me to count. I have made a mark for every day I have been here, and it is sixty days. It is a long time; and the speculator is going to take me and Ellen away. He's a bad man. It's wrong for him to take grandmother's children. I want to go to my mother."

My grandmother was told that the children would be restored to her, but she was requested to act as if they were really to be sent away. Accordingly, she made up a bundle of clothes and went to the jail. When she arrived, she found William handcuffed among the gang, and the children in the trader's cart. The scene seemed too much like reality. She was afraid there might have been some deception or mistake. She fainted, and was carried home.

When the wagon stopped at the hotel, several gentlemen came out and proposed to purchase William, but the trader refused their offers, without stating that he was already sold. And now came the trying hour for that drove of human beings, driven away like cattle, to be sold they knew not where. Husbands were torn from wives, parents from children, never to look upon each other again this side the grave. There was wringing of hands and cries of despair.

Dr. Flint had the supreme satisfaction of seeing the wagon leave town, and Mrs. Flint had the gratification of supposing that my children were going "as far as wind and water would carry them." According to agreement, my uncle followed the wagon some miles, until they came to an old farm house. There the trader took the irons from William, and as he did so, he said, "You are a damned clever fellow. I should like to own you myself. Them gentlemen that wanted to buy you said you was a bright, honest chap, and I must git you a good home. I guess your old master will swear to-morrow, and call himself an old fool for selling the children. I reckon he'll never git their mammy back agin. I expect she's made tracks for the north. Good by, old boy. Remember, I have done you a good turn. You must thank me by coaxing all the pretty gals to go with me next fall. That's going to be my last trip. This trading in niggers is a bad business for a fellow that's got any heart. Move on, you fellows!" And the gang went on, God alone knows where.

Much as I despise and detest the class of slave-traders, whom I regard as the vilest wretches on earth, I must do this man the justice to say that he seemed to have some feeling. He took a fancy to William in the jail, and wanted to buy him. When he heard the story of my children, he was willing to aid them in getting out of Dr. Flint's power, even without charging the customary fee.

My uncle procured a wagon and carried William and the children back to town. Great was the joy in my grandmother's house! The curtains were closed, and the candles lighted. The happy grandmother cuddled the little ones to her bosom. They hugged her, and kissed her, and clapped their hands, and shouted. She knelt down and poured forth one of her heartfelt prayers of thanksgiving to God. The father was present for a while; and though such a "parental relation" as existed between him and my children takes slight hold of the hearts or consciences of slaveholders, it must be that he experienced some moments of pure joy in witnessing the happiness he had imparted.

I had no share in the rejoicings of that evening. The events of the day had not come to my knowledge. And now I will tell you something that happened to me; though you will, perhaps, think it illustrates the superstition of slaves. I sat in my usual place on the floor near the window, where I could hear much that was said in the street without being seen. The family had retired for the night, and all was still. I sat there thinking of my children, when I heard a low strain of music. A band of serenaders were under the window, playing "Home, sweet home." I listened till the sounds did not seem like music, but like the moaning of children. It seemed as if my heart would burst. I rose from my sitting posture, and knelt. A streak of moonlight was on the floor before me, and in the midst of it appeared the forms of my two children. They vanished; but I had seen them distinctly. Some will call it a dream, others a vision. I know not how to account for it, but it made a strong impression on my mind, and I felt certain something had happened to my little ones.

I had not seen Betty since morning. Now I heard her softly turning the key. As soon as she entered, I clung to her, and begged her to let me know whether my children were dead, or whether they were sold; for I had seen their spirits in my room, and I was sure something had happened to them. "Lor, chile," said she, putting her arms round me, "you's got de highsterics. I'll sleep wid you to-night, 'cause you'll make a noise, and ruin missis. Something has stirred you up mightily. When you is done cryin, I'll talk wid you. De chillern is well, and mighty happy. I seed 'em myself. Does dat satisfy you? Dar, chile, be still! Somebody will hear you." I tried to obey her. She lay down, and was soon sound asleep; but no sleep would come to my eyelids.

At dawn, Betty was up and off to the kitchen. The hours passed on, and the vision of the night kept constantly recurring to my thoughts. After a while I heard the voices of two women in the entry. In one of them I recognized the housemaid. The other said to her, "Did you know Linda Brent's children was sold to the speculator yesterday. They say ole massa Flint was mighty glad to see 'em drove out of town; but they say they've come back agin. I 'spect it's all their daddy's doings. They say he's bought William too. Lor! how it will take hold of ole massa Flint! I'm going roun' to aunt Marthy's to see 'bout it."

I bit my lips till the blood came to keep from crying out. Were my children with their grandmother, or had the speculator carried them off? The suspense was dreadful. Would Betty *never* come, and tell me the truth about it? At last she came, and I eagerly repeated what I had overheard. Her face was one broad, bright smile. "Lor, you foolish ting!" said she. "I'se gwine to tell you all 'bout it. De gals is eating thar breakfast, and missus tole me to let her tell you; but, poor creeter! t'aint right to keep you waitin', and I'se gwine to tell you. Brudder, chillern, all is bought by de daddy! I'se laugh more dan nuff, tinking 'bout ole massa Flint. Lor, how he *vill* swar! He's got ketched dis time, any how; but I must be getting out o' dis, or dem gals vill come and ketch *me*."

Betty went off laughing; and I said to myself, "Can it be true that my children are free? I have not suffered for them in vain. Thank God!"

Great surprise was expressed when it was known that my children had returned to their grandmother's. The news spread through the town, and many a kind word was bestowed on the little ones.

Dr. Flint went to my grandmother's to ascertain who was the owner of my children, and she informed him. "I expected as much," said he. "I am glad to hear it. I have had news from Linda lately, and I shall soon have her. You need never expect to see *her* free. She shall be my slave as long as I live, and when I am dead she shall be the slave of my children. If I ever find out that you or Phillip had any thing to do with her running off I'll kill him. And if I meet William in the street, and he presumes to look at me, I'll flog him within an inch of his life. Keep those brats out of my sight!"

As he turned to leave, my grandmother said something to remind him of his own doings. He looked back upon her, as if he would have been glad to strike her to the ground.

I had my season of joy and thanksgiving. It was the first time since my childhood that I had experienced any real happiness. I heard of the old doctor's threats, but they no longer had the same power to trouble me. The darkest cloud that hung over my life had rolled away. Whatever slavery might do to me, it could not shackle my children. If I fell a sacrifice, my little ones were saved. It was well for me that my simple heart believed all that had been promised for their welfare. It is always better to trust than to doubt.

XX. New Perils

The doctor, more exasperated than ever, again tried to revenge himself on my relatives. He arrested uncle Phillip on the charge of having aided my flight. He was carried before a court, and swore truly that he knew nothing of my intention to escape, and that he had not seen me since I left my master's plantation. The doctor then demanded that he should give bail for five hundred dollars that he would have nothing to do with me. Several gentlemen offered to be security for him; but Mr. Sands told him he had better go back to jail, and he would see that he came out without giving bail.

The news of his arrest was carried to my grandmother, who conveyed it to Betty. In the kindness of her heart, she again stowed me away under the floor; and as she walked back and forth, in the performance of her culinary duties, she talked apparently to herself, but with the intention that I should hear what was going on. I hoped that my uncle's imprisonment would last but few days; still I was anxious. I thought it likely Dr. Flint would do his utmost to taunt and insult him, and I was afraid my uncle might lose control of himself, and retort in some way that would be construed into a punishable offence; and I was well aware that in court his word would not be taken against any white man's. The search for me was renewed. Something had excited suspicions that I was in the vicinity. They searched the house I was in. I heard their steps and their voices. At night, when all were asleep, Betty came to release me from my place of confinement. The fright I had undergone, the constrained posture, and the dampness of the ground, made me ill for several days. My uncle was soon after taken out of prison; but the movements of all my relatives, and of all our friends, were very closely watched.

We all saw that I could not remain where I was much longer. I had already staid longer than was intended, and I knew my presence must be a source of perpetual anxiety to my kind benefactress. During this time, my friends had laid many plans for my escape, but the extreme vigilance of my persecutors made it impossible to carry them into effect.

One morning I was much startled by hearing somebody trying to get into my room. Several keys were tried, but none fitted. I instantly conjectured it was one of the housemaids; and I concluded she must either have heard some noise in the room, or have noticed the entrance of Betty. When my friend came, at her usual time, I told her what had happened. "I knows who it was," said she. "'Pend upon it, 'twas dat Jenny. Dat nigger allers got de debble in her." I suggested that she might have seen or heard something that excited her curiosity.

"Tut! tut! chile!" exclaimed Betty, "she ain't seen notin', nor hearn notin'. She only 'spects something. Dat's all. She wants to fine out who hab cut and make my gownd. But she won't nebber know. Dat's sartin. I'll git missis to fix her."

I reflected a moment, and said, "Betty, I must leave here to-night."

"Do as you tink best, poor chile," she replied. "I'se mighty 'fraid dat 'ere nigger vill pop on you some time."

She reported the incident to her mistress, and received orders to keep Jenny busy in the kitchen till she could see my uncle Phillip. He told her he would send a friend for me that very evening. She told him she hoped I was going to the north, for it was very dangerous for me to remain any where in the vicinity. Alas, it was not an easy thing, for one in my situation, to go to the north. In order to leave the coast quite clear for me, she went into the country to spend the day with her brother, and took Jenny with her. She was afraid to come and bid me good by, but she left a kind message with Betty. I heard her carriage roll from the door, and I never again saw her who had so generously befriended the poor, trembling fugitive! Though she was a slaveholder, to this day my heart blesses her!

I had not the slightest idea where I was going. Betty brought me a suit of sailor's clothes,—jacket, trowsers, and tarpaulin hat. She gave me a small bundle, saying I might need it where I was going. In cheery tones, she exclaimed, "I'se *so* glad you is gwine to free parts! Don't forget ole Betty. P'raps I'll come 'long by and by."

I tried to tell her how grateful I felt for all her kindness, but she interrupted me. "I don't want no tanks, honey. I'se glad I could help you, and I hope de good Lord vill open de path for you. I'se gwine wid you to de lower gate. Put your hands in your pockets, and walk rickety, like de sailors."

I performed to her satisfaction. At the gate I found Peter, a young colored man, waiting for me. I had known him for years. He had been an apprentice to my father, and had always borne a good character. I was not afraid to trust to him. Betty bade me a hurried good by, and we walked off. "Take courage, Linda," said my friend Peter. "I've got a dagger, and no man shall take you from me, unless he passes over my dead body."

It was a long time since I had taken a walk out of doors, and the fresh air revived me. It was also pleasant to hear a human voice speaking to me above a whisper. I passed several people whom I knew, but they did not recognize me in my disguise. I prayed internally that, for Peter's sake, as well as my own, nothing might occur to bring out his dagger. We walked on till we came to the wharf. My aunt Nancy's husband was a seafaring man, and it had been deemed necessary to let him into our secret. He took me into his boat, rowed out to a vessel not far distant, and hoisted me on board. We three were the only occupants of the vessel. I now ventured to ask what they proposed to do with me. They said I was to remain on board till near dawn, and then they would hide me in Snaky Swamp, till my uncle Phillip had prepared a place of concealment for me. If the vessel had been bound north, it would have been of no avail to me, for it would certainly have been searched. About four o'clock, we were again seated in the boat, and rowed three miles to the swamp. My fear of snakes had been increased by the venomous bite I had received, and I dreaded to enter this hiding-place. But I was in no situation to choose, and I gratefully accepted the best that my poor, persecuted friends could do for me.

Peter landed first, and with a large knife cut a path through bamboos and briers of all descriptions. He came back, took me in his arms, and carried me to a seat made among the bamboos. Before we reached it, we were covered with hundreds of mosquitos. In an hour's time they had so poisoned my flesh that I was a pitiful sight to behold. As the light increased, I saw snake after snake crawling round us. I had been accustomed to the sight of snakes all my life, but these were larger than any I had ever seen. To this day I shudder when I remember that morning. As evening approached, the number of snakes increased so much that we were continually obliged to thrash them with sticks to keep them from crawling over us. The bamboos were so high and so thick that it was impossible to see beyond a very short distance. Just before it became dark we procured a seat nearer to the entrance of the swamp, being fearful of losing our way back to the boat. It was not long before we heard the paddle of oars, and the low whistle, which had been agreed upon as a signal. We made haste to enter the boat, and were rowed back to the vessel. I passed a wretched night; for the heat of the swamp, the mosquitos, and the constant terror of snakes, had brought on a burning fever. I had just dropped asleep, when they came and told me it was time to go back to that horrid swamp. I could scarcely summon courage to rise. But even those large, venomous snakes were less dreadful to my imagination than the white men in that community called civilized. This time Peter took a quantity of tobacco to burn, to keep off the mosquitos. It produced the desired effect on them, but gave me nausea and severe headache. At dark we returned to the vessel. I had been so sick during the day, that Peter declared I should go home that night, if the devil himself was on patrol. They told me a place of concealment had been provided for me at my grandmother's. I could not imagine how it was possible to hide me in her house, every nook and corner of which was known to the Flint family. They told me to wait and see. We were rowed ashore, and went boldly through the streets, to my grandmother's. I wore my sailor's clothes, and had blackened my face with charcoal. I passed several people whom I knew. The father of my children came so near that I brushed against his arm; but he had no idea who it was.

"You must make the most of this walk," said my friend Peter, "for you may not have another very soon."

I thought his voice sounded sad. It was kind of him to conceal from me what a dismal hole was to be my home for a long, long time.

XXI. The Loophole of Retreat

A small shed had been added to my grandmother's house years ago. Some boards were laid across the joists at the top, and between these boards and the roof was a very small garret, never occupied by any thing but rats and mice. It was a pent roof, covered with nothing but shingles, according to the southern custom for such buildings. The garret was only nine feet long and seven wide. The highest part was three feet high, and sloped down abruptly to the loose board floor. There was no admission for either light or air. My uncle Philip, who was a carpenter, had very skilfully made a concealed trap-door, which communicated with the storeroom. He had been doing this while I was waiting in the swamp. The storeroom opened upon a piazza.[4] To this hole I was conveyed as soon as I entered the house. The air was stifling; the darkness total. A bed had been spread on the floor. I could sleep quite comfortably on one side; but the slope was so sudden that I could not turn on the other without hitting the roof. The rats and mice ran over my bed; but I was weary, and I slept such sleep as the wretched may, when a tempest has passed over them. Morning came. I knew it only by the noises I heard; for in my small den day and night were all the same. I suffered for air even more than for light. But I was not comfortless. I heard the voices of my children. There was joy and there was sadness in the sound. It made my tears flow. How I longed to speak to them! I was eager to look on their faces; but there was no hole, no crack, through which I could peep. This continued darkness was oppressive. It seemed horrible to sit or lie in a cramped position day after day, without one gleam of light. Yet I would have chosen this, rather than my lot as a slave, though white people considered it an easy one; and it was so compared with the fate of others. I was never cruelly overworked; I was never lacerated with the whip from head to foot; I was never so beaten and bruised that I could not turn from one side to the other; I never had my heel-strings cut to prevent my running away; I was never chained to a log and forced to drag it about, while I toiled in the fields from morning till night; I was never branded with hot iron, or torn by bloodhounds. On the contrary, I had always been kindly treated, and tenderly cared for, until I came into the hands of Dr. Flint. I had never wished for freedom till then. But though my life in slavery was comparatively devoid of hardships, God pity the woman who is compelled to lead such a life!

My food was passed up to me through the trap-door my uncle had contrived; and my grandmother, my uncle Phillip, and aunt Nancy would seize such opportunities as they could, to mount up there and chat with me at the opening. But of course this was not safe in the daytime. It must all be done in darkness. It was impossible for me to move in an erect position, but I crawled about my den for exercise. One day I hit my head against something, and found it was a gimlet. My uncle had left it sticking there when he made the trap-door. I was as rejoiced as Robinson Crusoe could have been at finding such a treasure. It put a lucky thought into my head. I said to myself, "Now I will have some light. Now I will see my children." I did not dare to begin my work during the daytime, for fear of attracting attention. But I groped round; and having found the side next the street, where I could frequently see my children, I stuck the gimlet in

4. An open patio or courtyard.

and waited for evening. I bored three rows of holes, one above another; then I bored out the interstices between. I thus succeeded in making one hole about an inch long and an inch broad. I sat by it till late into the night, to enjoy the little whiff of air that floated in. In the morning I watched for my children. The first person I saw in the street was Dr. Flint. I had a shuddering, superstitious feeling that it was a bad omen. Several familiar faces passed by. At last I heard the merry laugh of children, and presently two sweet little faces were looking up at me, as though they knew I was there, and were conscious of the joy they imparted. How I longed to *tell* them I was there!

My condition was now a little improved. But for weeks I was tormented by hundreds of little red insects, fine as a needle's point, that pierced through my skin, and produced an intolerable burning. The good grandmother gave me herb teas and cooling medicines, and finally I got rid of them. The heat of my den was intense, for nothing but thin shingles protected me from the scorching summer's sun. But I had my consolations. Through my peeping-hole I could watch the children, and when they were near enough, I could hear their talk. Aunt Nancy brought me all the news she could hear at Dr. Flint's. From her I learned that the doctor had written to New York to a colored woman, who had been born and raised in our neighborhood, and had breathed his contaminating atmosphere. He offered her a reward if she could find out any thing about me. I know not what was the nature of her reply; but he soon after started for New York in haste, saying to his family that he had business of importance to transact. I peeped at him as he passed on his way to the steamboat. It was a satisfaction to have miles of land and water between us, even for a little while; and it was a still greater satisfaction to know that he believed me to be in the Free States. My little den seemed less dreary than it had done. He returned, as he did from his former journey to New York, without obtaining any satisfactory information. When he passed our house next morning, Benny was standing at the gate. He had heard them say that he had gone to find me, and he called out, "Dr. Flint, did you bring my mother home? I want to see her." The doctor stamped his foot at him in a rage, and exclaimed, "Get out of the way, you little damned rascal! If you don't, I'll cut off your head."

Benny ran terrified into the house, saying, "You can't put me in jail again. I don't belong to you now." It was well that the wind carried the words away from the doctor's ear. I told my grandmother of it, when we had our next conference at the trap-door; and begged of her not to allow the children to be impertinent to the irascible old man.

Autumn came, with a pleasant abatement of heat. My eyes had become accustomed to the dim light, and by holding my book or work in a certain position near the aperture I contrived to read and sew. That was a great relief to the tedious monotony of my life. But when winter came, the cold penetrated through the thin shingle roof, and I was dreadfully

chilled. The winters there are not so long, or so severe, as in northern lat-
itudes; but the houses are not built to shelter from cold, and my little den
was peculiarly comfortless. The kind grandmother brought me bed-
clothes and warm drinks. Often I was obliged to lie in bed all day to keep
comfortable; but with all my precautions, my shoulders and feet were
frostbitten. O, those long, gloomy days, with no object for my eye to rest
upon, and no thoughts to occupy my mind, except the dreary past and
the uncertain future! I was thankful when there came a day sufficiently
mild for me to wrap myself up and sit at the loophole to watch the passers
by. Southerners have the habit of stopping and talking in the streets, and
I heard many conversations not intended to meet my ears. I heard slave-
hunters planning how to catch some poor fugitive. Several times I heard
allusions to Dr. Flint, myself, and the history of my children, who, perhaps, were playing near the gate. One would say, "I wouldn't move my
little finger to catch her, as old Flint's property." Another would say, "I'll
catch *any* nigger for the reward. A man ought to have what belongs to
him, if he *is* a damned brute." The opinion was often expressed that I was
in the Free States. Very rarely did any one suggest that I might be in the
vicinity. Had the least suspicion rested on my grandmother's house, it
would have been burned to the ground. But it was the last place they
thought of. Yet there was no place, where slavery existed, that could have
afforded me so good a place of concealment.

Dr. Flint and his family repeatedly tried to coax and bribe my children
to tell something they had heard said about me. One day the doctor took
them into a shop, and offered them some bright little silver pieces and
gay handkerchiefs if they would tell where their mother was. Ellen shrank
away from him, and would not speak; but Benny spoke up, and said, "Dr.
Flint, I don't know where my mother is. I guess she's in New York; and
when you go there again, I wish you'd ask her to come home, for I want
to see her; but if you put her in jail, or tell her you'll cut her head off, I'll
tell her to go right back."

XXII. Christmas Festivities

Christmas was approaching. Grandmother brought me materials, and
I busied myself making some new garments and little playthings for my
children. Were it not that hiring day is near at hand, and many families
are fearfully looking forward to the probability of separation in a few days,
Christmas might be a happy season for the poor slaves. Even slave mothers try to gladden the hearts of their little ones on that occasion. Benny
and Ellen had their Christmas stockings filled. Their imprisoned mother
could not have the privilege of witnessing their surprise and joy. But I had
the pleasure of peeping at them as they went into the street with their new

suits on. I heard Benny ask a little playmate whether Santa Claus brought him any thing. "Yes," replied the boy; "but Santa Claus ain't a real man. It's the children's mothers that put things into the stockings." "No, that can't be," replied Benny, "for Santa Claus brought Ellen and me these new clothes, and my mother has been gone this long time."

How I longed to tell him that his mother made those garments, and that many a tear fell on them while she worked!

Every child rises early on Christmas morning to see the Johnkannaus.[5] Without them, Christmas would be shorn of its greatest attraction. They consist of companies of slaves from the plantations, generally of the lower class. Two athletic men, in calico wrappers, have a net thrown over them, covered with all manner of bright-colored stripes. Cows' tails are fastened to their backs, and their heads are decorated with horns. A box, covered with sheepskin, is called the gumbo box. A dozen beat on this, while others strike triangles and jawbones, to which bands of dancers keep time. For a month previous they are composing songs, which are sung on this occasion. These companies, of a hundred each, turn out early in the morning, and are allowed to go round till twelve o'clock, begging for contributions. Not a door is left unvisited where there is the least chance of obtaining a penny or a glass of rum. They do not drink while they are out, but carry the rum home in jugs, to have a carousal. These Christmas donations frequently amount to twenty or thirty dollars. It is seldom that any white man or child refuses to give them a trifle. If he does, they regale his ears with the following song: —

> "Poor massa, so dey say;
> Down in de heel, so dey say;
> Got no money, so dey say;
> Not one shillin, so dey say;
> God A'mighty bress you, so dey say."

Christmas is a day of feasting, both with white and colored people. Slaves, who are lucky enough to have a few shillings, are sure to spend them for good eating; and many a turkey and pig is captured, without saying, "By your leave, sir." Those who cannot obtain these, cook a 'possum, or a raccoon, from which savory dishes can be made. My grandmother raised poultry and pigs for sale; and it was her established custom to have both a turkey and a pig roasted for Christmas dinner.

On this occasion, I was warned to keep extremely quiet, because two guests had been invited. One was the town constable, and the other was a free colored man, who tried to pass himself off for white, and who was always ready to do any mean work for the sake of currying favor with white people. My grandmother had a motive for inviting them. She managed to take them all over the house. All the rooms on the lower floor were

5. Also "junkanoos." A celebration featuring costumes and masks originating in African culture.

thrown open for them to pass in and out; and after dinner, they were invited up stairs to look at a fine mocking bird my uncle had just brought home. There, too, the rooms were all thrown open, that they might look in. When I heard them talking on the piazza, my heart almost stood still. I knew this colored man had spent many nights hunting for me. Every body knew he had the blood of a slave father in his veins; but for the sake of passing himself off for white, he was ready to kiss the slaveholders' feet. How I despised him! As for the constable, he wore no false colors. The duties of his office were despicable, but he was superior to his companion, inasmuch as he did not pretend to be what he was not. Any white man, who could raise money enough to buy a slave, would have considered himself degraded by being a constable; but the office enabled its possessor to exercise authority. If he found any slave out after nine o'clock, he could whip him as much as he liked; and that was a privilege to be coveted. When the guests were ready to depart, my grandmother gave each of them some of her nice pudding, as a present for their wives. Through my peep-hole I saw them go out of the gate, and I was glad when it closed after them. So passed the first Christmas in my den.

XXIII. Still in Prison

When spring returned, and I took in the little patch of green the aperture commanded, I asked myself how many more summers and winters I must be condemned to spend thus. I longed to draw in a plentiful draught of fresh air, to stretch my cramped limbs, to have room to stand erect, to feel the earth under my feet again. My relatives were constantly on the lookout for a chance of escape; but none offered that seemed practicable, and even tolerably safe. The hot summer came again, and made the turpentine drop from the thin roof over my head.

During the long nights I was restless for want of air, and I had no room to toss and turn. There was but one compensation; the atmosphere was so stifled that even mosquitos would not condescend to buzz in it. With all my detestation of Dr. Flint, I could hardly wish him a worse punishment, either in this world or that which is to come, than to suffer what I suffered in one single summer. Yet the laws allowed *him* to be out in the free air, while I, guiltless of crime, was pent up here, as the only means of avoiding the cruelties the laws allowed him to inflict upon me! I don't know what kept life within me. Again and again, I thought I should die before long; but I saw the leaves of another autumn whirl through the air, and felt the touch of another winter. In summer the most terrible thunder storms were acceptable, for the rain came through the roof, and I rolled up my bed that it might cool the hot boards under it. Later in the season, storms sometimes wet my clothes through and through, and that was not comfortable when the air grew chilly. Moderate storms I could keep out by filling the chinks with oakum.[6]

But uncomfortable as my situation was, I had glimpses of things out of doors, which made me thankful for my wretched hiding-place. One day I saw a slave pass our gate, muttering, "It's his own, and he can kill it if he will." My grandmother told me that woman's history. Her mistress had that day seen her baby for the first time, and in the lineaments of its fair face she saw a likeness to her husband. She turned the bondwoman and her child out of doors, and forbade her ever to return. The slave went to her master, and told him what had happened. He promised to talk with her mistress, and make it all right. The next day she and her baby were sold to a Georgia trader.

Another time I saw a woman rush wildly by, pursued by two men. She was a slave, the wet nurse of her mistress's children. For some trifling offence her mistress ordered her to be stripped and whipped. To escape the degradation and the torture, she rushed to the river, jumped in, and ended her wrongs in death.

Senator Brown,[7] of Mississippi, could not be ignorant of many such facts as these, for they are of frequent occurrence in every Southern State. Yet he stood up in the Congress of the United States, and declared that slavery was "a great moral, social, and political blessing; a blessing to the master, and a blessing to the slave!"

I suffered much more during the second winter than I did during the first. My limbs were benumbed by inaction, and the cold filled them with cramp. I had a very painful sensation of coldness in my head; even my face and tongue stiffened, and I lost the power of speech. Of course it was impossible, under the circumstances, to summon any physician. My brother William came and did all he could for me. Uncle Phillip also watched tenderly over me; and poor grandmother crept up and down to inquire whether there were any signs of returning life. I was restored to consciousness by the dashing of cold water in my face, and found myself leaning against my brother's arm, while he bent over me with streaming eyes. He afterwards told me he thought I was dying, for I had been in an unconscious state sixteen hours. I next became delirious, and was in great danger of betraying myself and my friends. To prevent this, they stupefied me with drugs. I remained in bed six weeks, weary in body and sick at heart. How to get medical advice was the question. William finally went to a Thompsonian doctor,[8] and described himself as having all my pains and aches. He returned with herbs, roots, and ointment. He was especially charged to rub on the ointment by a fire; but how could a fire be made in my little den? Charcoal in a furnace was tried, but there was no

---

6. Loose fiber picked from rope and used to caulk ships or fill holes.
7. Albert G. Brown (1830–1880), a Mississippi senator.
8. Samuel Thomson (1763–1843) treated illnesses by hyperthermia, or raising the patient's body temperature.

outlet for the gas, and it nearly cost me my life. Afterwards coals, already kindled, were brought up in an iron pan, and placed on bricks. I was so weak, and it was so long since I had enjoyed the warmth of a fire, that those few coals actually made me weep. I think the medicines did me some good; but my recovery was very slow. Dark thoughts passed through my mind as I lay there day after day. I tried to be thankful for my little cell, dismal as it was, and even to love it, as part of the price I had paid for the redemption of my children. Sometimes I thought God was a compassionate Father, who would forgive my sins for the sake of my sufferings. At other times, it seemed to me there was no justice or mercy in the divine government. I asked why the curse of slavery was permitted to exist, and why I had been so persecuted and wronged from youth upward. These things took the shape of mystery, which is to this day not so clear to my soul as I trust it will be hereafter.

In the midst of my illness, grandmother broke down under the weight of anxiety and toil. The idea of losing her, who had always been my best friend and a mother to my children, was the sorest trial I had yet had. O, how earnestly I prayed that she might recover! How hard it seemed, that I could not tend upon her, who had so long and so tenderly watched over me!

One day the screams of a child nerved me with strength to crawl to my peeping-hole, and I saw my son covered with blood. A fierce dog, usually kept chained, had seized and bitten him. A doctor was sent for, and I heard the groans and screams of my child while the wounds were being sewed up. O, what torture to a mother's heart, to listen to this and be unable to go to him!

But childhood is like a day in spring, alternately shower and sunshine. Before night Benny was bright and lively, threatening the destruction of the dog; and great was his delight when the doctor told him the next day that the dog had bitten another boy and been shot. Benny recovered from his wounds; but it was long before he could walk.

When my grandmother's illness became known, many ladies, who were her customers, called to bring her some little comforts, and to inquire whether she had every thing she wanted. Aunt Nancy one night asked permission to watch with her sick mother, and Mrs. Flint replied, "I don't see any need of your going. I can't spare you." But when she found other ladies in the neighborhood were so attentive, not wishing to be outdone in Christian charity, she also sallied forth, in magnificent condescension, and stood by the bedside of her who had loved her in her infancy, and who had been repaid by such grievous wrongs. She seemed surprised to find her so ill, and scolded uncle Phillip for not sending for Dr. Flint. She herself sent for him immediately, and he came. Secure as I was in my retreat, I should have been terrified if I had known he was so near me. He pronounced my grandmother in a very critical situation, and said if her attending physician wished it, he would visit her. Nobody wished to have him coming to the house at all hours, and we were not disposed to give him a chance to make out a long bill.

As Mrs. Flint went out, Sally told her the reason Benny was lame was, that a dog had bitten him. "I'm glad of it," replied she. "I wish he had killed him. It would be good news to send to his mother. *Her* day will come. The dogs will grab *her* yet." With these Christian words she and her husband departed, and, to my great satisfaction, returned no more.

I heard from uncle Phillip, with feelings of unspeakable joy and gratitude, that the crisis was passed and grandmother would live. I could now say from my heart, "God is merciful. He has spared me the anguish of feeling that I caused her death."

XXIV. The Candidate for Congress

The summer had nearly ended, when Dr. Flint made a third visit to New York, in search of me. Two candidates were running for Congress, and he returned in season to vote. The father of my children was the Whig candidate. The doctor had hitherto been a stanch Whig; but now he exerted all his energies for the defeat of Mr. Sands. He invited large parties of men to dine in the shade of his trees, and supplied them with plenty of rum and brandy. If any poor fellow drowned his wits in the bowl, and, in the openness of his convivial heart, proclaimed that he did not mean to vote the Democratic ticket, he was shoved into the street without ceremony.

The doctor expended his liquor in vain. Mr. Sands was elected; an event which occasioned me some anxious thoughts. He had not emancipated my children, and if he should die they would be at the mercy of his heirs. Two little voices, that frequently met my ear, seemed to plead with me not to let their father depart without striving to make their freedom secure. Years had passed since I had spoken to him. I had not even seen him since the night I passed him, unrecognized, in my disguise of a sailor. I supposed he would call before he left, to say something to my grandmother concerning the children, and I resolved what course to take.

The day before his departure for Washington I made arrangements, towards evening, to get from my hiding-place into the storeroom below. I found myself so stiff and clumsy that it was with great difficulty I could hitch from one resting place to another. When I reached the storeroom my ankles gave way under me, and I sank exhausted on the floor. It seemed as if I could never use my limbs again. But the purpose I had in view roused all the strength I had. I crawled on my hands and knees to the window, and, screened behind a barrel, I waited for his coming. The clock struck nine, and I knew the steamboat would leave between ten and eleven. My hopes were failing. But presently I heard his voice, saying to some one, "Wait for me a moment. I wish to see aunt Martha." When he came out, as he passed the window, I said, "Stop one moment, and let me speak for my children." He started, hesitated, and then passed on, and went out of the gate. I closed the shutter I had partially opened, and sank down behind the barrel. I had suffered much; but seldom had I experienced a keener pang than I then felt. Had my children, then, become of so little consequence to him? And had he so little feeling for their wretched mother that he would not listen a moment while she pleaded for them? Painful memories were so busy within me, that I forgot I had not hooked the shutter, till I heard some one opening it. I looked up. He had come back. "Who called me?" said he, in a low tone. "I did," I replied. "Oh, Linda," said he, "I knew your voice; but I was afraid to answer, lest my friend should hear me. Why do you come here? Is it possible you risk yourself in this house? They are mad to allow it. I shall expect to hear that you are all ruined." I did not wish to implicate him, by letting him know my place of concealment; so I merely said, "I thought you would come to bid grandmother good by, and so I came here to speak a few words to you about emancipating my children. Many changes may take place during the six months you are gone to Washington, and it does not seem right for you to expose them to the risk of such changes. I want nothing for myself; all I ask is, that you will free my children, or authorize some friend to do it, before you go."

He promised he would do it, and also expressed a readiness to make any arrangements whereby I could be purchased.

I heard footsteps approaching, and closed the shutter hastily. I wanted to crawl back to my den, without letting the family know what I had done; for I knew they would deem it very imprudent. But he stepped back into the house, to tell my grandmother that he had spoken with me at the storeroom window, and to beg of her not to allow me to remain in the house over night. He said it was the height of madness for me to be there; that we should certainly all be ruined. Luckily, he was in too much of a hurry to wait for a reply, or the dear old woman would surely have told him all.

I tried to go back to my den, but found it more difficult to go up than I had to come down. Now that my mission was fulfilled, the little strength that had supported me through it was gone, and I sank helpless on the floor. My grandmother, alarmed at the risk I had run, came into the storeroom in the dark, and locked the door behind her. "Linda," she whispered, "where are you?"

"I am here by the window," I replied. "I *couldn't* have him go away without emancipating the children. Who knows what may happen?"

"Come, come, child," said she, "it won't do for you to stay here another minute. You've done wrong; but I can't blame you, poor thing!"

I told her I could not return without assistance, and she must call my uncle. Uncle Phillip came, and pity prevented him from scolding me. He carried me back to my dungeon, laid me tenderly on the bed, gave me some medicine, and asked me if there was any thing more he could do. Then he went away, and I was left with my own thoughts—starless as the midnight darkness around me.

My friends feared I should become a cripple for life; and I was so weary of my long imprisonment that, had it not been for the hope of serving my children, I should have been thankful to die; but, for their sakes, I was willing to bear on.

XXV. Competition in Cunning

Dr. Flint had not given me up. Every now and then he would say to my grandmother that I would yet come back, and voluntarily surrender myself; and that when I did, I could be purchased by my relatives, or any one who wished to buy me. I knew his cunning nature too well not to percieve that this was a trap laid for me; and so all my friends understood it. I resolved to match my cunning against his cunning. In order to make him believe that I was in New York, I resolved to write him a letter dated from that place. I sent for my friend Peter, and asked him if he knew any trustworthy seafaring person, who would carry such a letter to New York, and put it in the post office there. He said he knew one that he would trust with his own life to the ends of the world. I reminded him that it was a hazardous thing for him to undertake. He said he knew it, but he was willing to do any thing to help me. I expressed a wish for a New York paper, to ascertain the names of some of the streets. He run his hand into his pocket, and said, "Here is half a one, that was round a cap I bought of a pedler yesterday." I told him the letter would be ready the next evening. He bade me good by, adding, "Keep up your spirits, Linda; brighter days will come by and by."

My uncle Phillip kept watch over the gate until our brief interview was over. Early the next morning, I seated myself near the little aperture to examine the newspaper. It was a piece of the New York Herald;[9] and, for once, the paper that systematically abuses the colored people, was made to render them a service. Having obtained what information I wanted concerning streets and numbers, I wrote two letters, one to my grandmother, the other to Dr. Flint. I reminded him how he, a gray-headed man, had treated a helpless child, who had been placed in his power, and what years of misery he had brought upon her. To my grandmother, I expressed a wish to have my children sent to me at the north, where I could teach them to respect themselves, and set them a virtuous example;

9. One of the first papers in the penny-press movement and generally considered to be proslavery.

which a slave mother was not allowed to do at the south. I asked her to direct her answer to a certain street in Boston, as I did not live in New York, though I went there sometimes. I dated these letters ahead, to allow for the time it would take to carry them, and sent a memorandum of the date to the messenger. When my friend came for the letters, I said, "God bless and reward you, Peter, for this disinterested kindness. Pray be careful. If you are detected, both you and I will have to suffer dreadfully. I have not a relative who would dare to do it for me." He replied, "You may trust to me, Linda. I don't forget that your father was my best friend, and I will be a friend to his children so long as God lets me live."

It was necessary to tell my grandmother what I had done, in order that she might be ready for the letter, and prepared to hear what Dr. Flint might say about my being at the north. She was sadly troubled. She felt sure mischief would come of it. I also told my plan to aunt Nancy, in order that she might report to us what was said at Dr. Flint's house. I whispered it to her through a crack, and she whispered back, "I hope it will succeed. I shan't mind being a slave all *my* life, if I can only see you and the children free."

I had directed that my letters should be put into the New York post office on the 20th of the month. On the evening of the 24th my aunt came to say that Dr. Flint and his wife had been talking in a low voice about a letter he had received, and that when he went to his office he promised to bring it when he came to tea. So I concluded I should hear my letter read the next morning. I told my grandmother Dr. Flint would be sure to come, and asked her to have him sit near a certain door, and leave it open, that I might hear what he said. The next morning I took my station within sound of that door, and remained motionless as a statue. It was not long before I heard the gate slam, and the well-known footsteps enter the house. He seated himself in the chair that was placed for him, and said, "Well, Martha, I've brought you a letter from Linda. She has sent me a letter, also. I know exactly where to find her; but I don't choose to go to Boston for her. I had rather she would come back of her own accord, in a respectable manner. Her uncle Phillip is the best person to go for her. With *him*, she would feel perfectly free to act. I am willing to pay his expenses going and returning. She shall be sold to her friends. Her children are free; at least I suppose they are; and when you obtain her freedom, you'll make a happy family. I suppose, Martha, you have no objection to my reading to you the letter Linda has written to you."

He broke the seal, and I heard him read it. The old villain! He had suppressed the letter I wrote to grandmother, and prepared a substitute of his own, the purport of which was as follows:—

"Dear Grandmother: I have long wanted to write to you; but the disgraceful manner in which I left you and my children made me ashamed to do it. If you knew how much I have suffered since I ran away, you would pity and forgive me. I have purchased freedom at a dear rate. If any arrangement could be made for me to return to the south without being a slave, I would gladly come. If not, I beg of you to send my children to the north. I cannot live any longer without them. Let me know in time, and I will meet them in New York or Philadelphia, whichever place best suits my uncle's convenience. Write as soon as possible to your unhappy daughter,

Linda."

"It is very much as I expected it would be," said the old hypocrite, rising to go. "You see the foolish girl has repented of her rashness, and wants to return. We must help her to do it, Martha. Talk with Phillip about it. If he will go for her, she will trust to him, and come back. I should like an answer tomorrow. Good morning, Martha."

As he stepped out on the piazza, he stumbled over my little girl. "Ah, Ellen, is that you?" he said, in his most gracious manner. "I didn't see you. How do you do?"

"Pretty well, sir," she replied. "I heard you tell grandmother that my mother is coming home. I want to see her."

"Yes, Ellen, I am going to bring her home very soon," rejoined he; "and you shall see her as much as you like, you little curly-headed nigger."

This was as good as a comedy to me, who had heard it all; but grandmother was frightened and distressed, because the doctor wanted my uncle to go for me.

The next evening Dr. Flint called to talk the matter over. My uncle told him that from what he had heard of Massachusetts, he judged he should be mobbed if he went there after a runaway slave. "All stuff and nonsense, Phillip!" replied the doctor. "Do you suppose I want you to kick up a row in Boston? The business can all be done quietly. Linda writes that she wants to come back. You are her relative, and she would trust *you*. The case would be different if I went. She might object to coming with *me*; and the damned abolitionists, if they knew I was her master, would not believe me, if I told them she had begged to go back. They would get up a row; and I should not like to see Linda dragged through the streets like a common negro. She has been very ungrateful to me for all my kindness; but I forgive her, and want to act the part of a friend towards her. I have no wish to hold her as my slave. Her friends can buy her as soon as she arrives here."

Finding that his arguments failed to convince my uncle, the doctor "let the cat out of the bag," by saying that he had written to the mayor of Boston, to ascertain whether there was a person of my description at the street and number from which my letter was dated. He had omitted this date in the letter he had made up to read to my grandmother. If I had dated from New York, the old man would probably have made another journey to that city. But even in that dark region, where knowledge is so

carefully excluded from the slave, I had heard enough about Massachusetts to come to the conclusion that slaveholders did not consider it a
comfortable place to go to in search of a runaway. That was before the
Fugitive Slave Law was passed; before Massachusetts had consented to
become a "nigger hunter" for the south.

My grandmother, who had become skittish by seeing her family always
in danger, came to me with a very distressed countenance, and said,
"What will you do if the mayor of Boston sends him word that you haven't
been there? Then he will suspect the letter was a trick; and maybe he'll
find out something about it, and we shall all get into trouble. O Linda, I
wish you had never sent the letters."

"Don't worry yourself, grandmother," said I. "The mayor of Boston
won't trouble himself to hunt niggers for Dr. Flint. The letters will do
good in the end. I shall get out of this dark hole some time or other."

"I hope you will, child," replied the good, patient old friend. "You have
been here a long time; almost five years; but whenever you do go, it will
break your old grandmother's heart. I should be expecting every day to
hear that you were brought back in irons and put in jail God help you,
poor child! Let us be thankful that some time or other we shall go "where
the wicked cease from troubling, and the weary are at rest." My heart responded, Amen.

The fact that Dr. Flint had written to the mayor of Boston convinced
me that he believed my letter to be genuine, and of course that he had
no suspicion of my being any where in the vicinity. It was a great object
to keep up this delusion, for it made me and my friends feel less anxious,
and it would be very convenient whenever there was a chance to escape.
I resolved, therefore, to continue to write letters from the north from time
to time.

Two or three weeks passed, and as no news came from the mayor of
Boston, grandmother began to listen to my entreaty to be allowed to leave
my cell, sometimes, and exercise my limbs to prevent my becoming a
cripple. I was allowed to slip down into the small storeroom, early in the
morning, and remain there a little while. The room was all filled up with
barrels, except a small open space under my trap-door. This faced the
door, the upper part of which was of glass, and purposely left uncur-
tained, that the curious might look in. The air of this place was close; but
it was so much better than the atmosphere of my cell, that I dreaded
to return. I came down as soon as it was light, and remained till eight
o'clock, when people began to be about, and there was danger that some
one might come on the piazza. I had tried various applications to bring
warmth and feeling into my limbs, but without avail. They were so numb
and stiff that it was a painful effort to move; and had my enemies come
upon me during the first mornings I tried to exercise them a little in the
small unoccupied space of the storeroom, it would have been impossible
for me to have escaped.

XXVI. Important Era in My Brother's Life

I missed the company and kind attentions of my brother William, who had gone to Washington with his master, Mr. Sands. We received several letters from him, written without any allusion to me, but expressed in such a manner that I knew he did not forget me. I disguised my hand, and wrote to him in the same manner. It was a long session; and when it closed, William wrote to inform us that Mr. Sands was going to the north, to be gone some time, and that he was to accompany him. I knew that his master had promised to give him his freedom, but no time had been specified. Would William trust to a slave's chances? I remembered how we used to talk together, in our young days, about obtaining our freedom, and I thought it very doubtful whether he would come back to us.

Grandmother received a letter from Mr. Sands, saying the William had proved a most faithful servant, and he would also say a valued friend; that no mother had ever trained a better boy. He said he had travelled through the Northern States and Canada; and though the abolitionists had tried to decoy him away, they had never succeeded. He ended by saying they should be at home shortly.

We expected letters from William, describing the novelties of his journey, but none came. In time, it was reported that Mr. Sands would return late in the autumn, accompanied by a bride. Still no letters from William. I felt almost sure I should never see him again on southern soil; but had he no word of comfort to send to his friends at home? to the poor captive in her dungeon? My thoughts wandered through the dark past, and over the uncertain future. Alone in my cell, where no eye but God's could see me, I wept bitter tears. How earnestly I prayed to him to restore me to my children, and enable me to be a useful woman and a good mother!

At last the day arrived for the return of the travellers. Grandmother had made loving preparations to welcome her absent boy back to the old hearthstone. When the dinner table was laid, William's plate occupied its old place. The stage coach went by empty. My grandmother waited dinner. She thought perhaps he was necessarily detained by his master. In my prison I listened anxiously, expecting every moment to hear my dear brother's voice and step. In the course of the afternoon a lad was sent by Mr. Sands to tell grandmother that William did not return with him; that the abolitionists had decoyed him away. But he begged her not to feel troubled about it, for he felt confident she would see William in a few days. As soon as he had time to reflect he would come back, for he could never expect to be so well off at the north as he had been with him.

If you had seen the tears, and heard the sobs, you would have thought the messenger had brought tidings of death instead of freedom. Poor old grandmother felt that she should never see her darling boy again. And I was selfish. I thought more of what I had lost, than of what my brother had gained. A new anxiety began to trouble me. Mr. Sands had expended a good deal of money, and would naturally feel irritated by the loss he had incurred. I greatly feared this might injure the prospects of my children, who were now becoming valuable property. I longed to have their emancipation made certain. The more so, because their master and father was now married. I was too familiar with slavery not to know that promises made to slaves, though with kind intentions, and sincere at the time, depend upon many contingencies for their fulfilment.

Much as I wished William to be free, the step he had taken made me sad and anxious. The following Sabbath was calm and clear; so beautiful that it seemed like a Sabbath in the eternal world. My grandmother brought the children out on the piazza, that I might hear their voices. She thought it would comfort me in my despondency; and it did. They chatted merrily, as only children can. Benny said, "Grandmother, do you think uncle Will has gone for good? Won't he ever come back again? May be he'll find mother. If he does, *won't* she be glad to see him! Why don't you and uncle Phillip, and all of us, go and live where mother is? I should like it; wouldn't you, Ellen?"

"Yes, I should like it," replied Ellen; "but how could we find her? Do you know the place, grandmother? I don't remember how mother looked—do you, Benny?"

Benny was just beginning to describe me when they were interrupted by an old slave woman, a near neighbor, named Aggie. This poor creature had witnessed the sale of her children, and seen them carried off to parts unknown, without any hopes of ever hearing from them again. She saw that my grandmother had been weeping, and she said, in a sympathizing tone, "What's the matter, aunt Marthy?"

"O Aggie," she replied, "it seems as if I shouldn't have any of my children or grandchildren left to hand me a drink when I'm dying, and lay my old body in the ground. My boy didn't come back with Mr. Sands. He staid at the north."

Poor old Aggie clapped her hands for joy. "Is *dat* what you's crying fur?" she exclaimed. "Git down on your knees and bress de Lord! I don't know whar my poor chillern is, and I nebber 'spect to know. You don't know whar poor Linda's gone to; but you *do* know whar her brudder is. He's in free parts; and dat's de right place. Don't murmur at de Lord's doings, but git down on your knees and tank him for his goodness."

My selfishness was rebuked by what poor Aggie said. She rejoiced over the escape of one who was merely her fellow-bondman, while his own sister was only thinking what his good fortune might cost her children. I knelt and prayed God to forgive me; and I thanked him from my heart, that one of my family was saved from the grasp of slavery.

It was not long before we received a letter from William. He wrote that Mr. Sands had always treated him kindly, and that he had tried to do his duty to him faithfully. But ever since he was a boy, he had longed to be free; and he had already gone through enough to convince him he had better not lose the chance that offered. He concluded by saying, "Don't worry about me, dear grandmother. I shall think of you always; and it will spur me on to work hard and try to do right. When I have earned money enough to give you a home, perhaps you will come to the north, and we can all live happy together."

Mr. Sands told my uncle Phillip the particulars about William's leaving him. He said, "I trusted him as if he were my own brother, and treated him as kindly. The abolitionists talked to him in several places; but I had no idea they could tempt him. However, I don't blame William. He's young and inconsiderate, and those Northern rascals decoyed him. I must confess the scamp was very bold about it. I met him coming down the steps of the Astor House with his trunk on his shoulder, and I asked him where he was going. He said he was going to change his old trunk. I told him it was rather shabby, and asked if he didn't need some money. He said, No, thanked me, and went off. He did not return so soon as I expected; but I waited patiently. At last I went to see if our trunks were packed, ready for our journey. I found them locked, and a sealed note on the table informed me where I could find the keys. The fellow even tried to be religious. He wrote that he hoped God would always bless me, and reward me for my kindness; that he was not unwilling to serve me; but he wanted to be a free man; and that if I thought he did wrong, he hoped I would forgive him. I intended to give him his freedom in five years. He might have trusted me. He has shown himself ungrateful; but I shall not go for him, or send for him. I feel confident that he will soon return to me."

I afterwards heard an account of the affair from William himself. He had not been urged away by abolitionists. He needed no information they could give him about slavery to stimulate his desire for freedom. He looked at his hands, and remembered that they were once in irons. What security had he that they would not be so again? Mr. Sands was kind to him; but he might indefinitely postpone the promise he had made to give him his freedom. He might come under pecuniary embarrassments, and his property be seized by creditors; or he might die, without making any arrangements in his favor. He had too often known such accidents to happen to slaves who had kind masters, and he wisely resolved to make sure of the present opportunity to own himself. He was scrupulous about taking any money from his master on false pretences; so he sold his best clothes to pay for his passage to Boston. The slaveholders pronounced him a base, ungrateful wretch, for thus requiting his master's indulgence. What would *they* have done under similar circumstances?

When Dr. Flint's family heard that William had deserted Mr. Sands, they chuckled greatly over the news. Mrs. Flint made her usual manifestations of Christian feeling, by saying, "I'm glad of it. I hope he'll never get him again. I like to see people paid back in their own coin. I reckon

Linda's children will have to pay for it. I should be glad to see them in the speculator's hands again, for I'm tired of seeing those little niggers march about the streets."

XXVII. New Destination for the Children

Mrs. Flint proclaimed her intention of informing Mrs. Sands who was the father of my children. She likewise proposed to tell her what an artful devil I was; that I had made a great deal of trouble in her family; that when Mr. Sands was at the north, she didn't doubt I had followed him in disguise, and persuaded William to run away. She had some reason to entertain such an idea; for I had written from the north, from time to time, and I dated my letters from various places. Many of them fell into Dr. Flint's hands, as I expected they would; and he must have come to the conclusion that I travelled about a good deal. He kept a close watch over my children, thinking they would eventually lead to my detection.

A new and unexpected trial was in store for me. One day, when Mr. Sands and his wife were walking in the street, they met Benny. The lady took a fancy to him, and exclaimed, "What a pretty little negro! Whom does he belong to?"

Benny did not hear the answer; but he came home very indignant with the stranger lady, because she had called him a negro. A few days afterwards, Mr. Sands called on my grandmother, and told her he wanted her to take the children to his house. He said he had informed his wife of his relation to them, and told her they were motherless; and she wanted to see them.

When he had gone, my grandmother came and asked what I would do. The question seemed a mockery. What *could* I do? They were Mr. Sands's slaves, and their mother was a slave, whom he had represented to be dead. Perhaps he thought I was. I was too much pained and puzzled to come to any decision; and the children were carried without my knowledge.

Mrs. Sands had a sister from Illinois staying with her. This lady, who had no children of her own, was so much pleased with Ellen, that she offered to adopt her, and bring her up as she would a daughter. Mrs. Sands wanted to take Benjamin. When grandmother reported this to me, I was tried almost beyond endurance. Was this all I was to gain by what I had suffered for the sake of having my children free? True, the prospect *seemed* fair; but I knew too well how lightly slaveholders held such "parental relations." If pecuniary troubles should come, or if the new wife required more money than could conveniently be spared, my children might be thought of as a convenient means of raising funds. I had no trust in thee, O Slavery! Never should I know peace till my children were emancipated with all due formalities of law.

I was too proud to ask Mr. Sands to do any thing for my own benefit; but I could bring myself to become a supplicant for my children. I resolved to remind him of the promise he had made me, and to throw myself upon his honor for the performance of it. I persuaded my grandmother to go to him, and tell him I was not dead, and that I earnestly entreated him to keep the promise he had made me; that I had heard of the recent proposals concerning my children, and did not feel easy to accept them; that he had promised to emancipate them, and it was time for him to redeem his pledge. I knew there was some risk in thus betraying that I was in the vicinity; but what will not a mother do for her children? He received the message with surprise, and said, "The children are free. I have never intended to claim them as slaves. Linda may decide their fate. In my opinion, they had better be sent to the north. I don't think they are quite safe here. Dr. Flint boasts that they are still in his power. He says they were his daughter's property, and as she was not of age when they were sold, the contract is not legally binding."

So, then, after all I had endured for their sakes, my poor children were between two fires; between my old master and their new master! And I was powerless. There was no protecting arm of the law for me to invoke. Mr. Sands proposed that Ellen should go, for the present, to some of his relatives, who had removed to Brooklyn, Long Island. It was promised that she should be well taken care of, and sent to school. I consented to it, as the best arrangement I could make for her. My grandmother, of course, negotiated it all; and Mrs. Sands knew of no other person in the transaction. She proposed that they should take Ellen with them to Washington, and keep her till they had a good chance of sending her, with friends, to Brooklyn. She had an infant daughter. I had had a glimpse of it, as the nurse passed with it in her arms. It was not a pleasant thought to me, that the bondwoman's child should tend her free-born sister; but there was no alternative. Ellen was made ready for the journey. O, how it tried my heart to send her away, so young, alone, among strangers! Without a mother's love to shelter her from the storms of life; almost without memory of a mother! I doubted whether she and Benny would have for me the natural affection that children feel for a parent. I thought to myself that I might perhaps never see my daughter again, and I had a great desire that she should look upon me, before she went, that she might take my image with her in her memory. It seemed to me cruel to have her brought to my dungeon. It was sorrow enough for her young heart to know that her mother was a victim of slavery, without seeing the wretched hiding-place to which it had driven her. I begged permission to pass the last night in one of the open chambers, with my little girl. They thought I was crazy to think of trusting such a young child with my perilous secret. I told them I had watched her character, and I felt sure she would not betray me; that I was determined to have an interview, and if they would not facilitate it, I would take my own way to obtain it. They remonstrated against the rashness of such a proceeding; but finding they could not change my purpose, they yielded. I slipped through the trapdoor into the storeroom, and my uncle kept watch at the gate, while I passed into the piazza and went up stairs, to the room I used to occupy. It was more than five years since I had seen it; and how the memories crowded on me! There I had taken shelter when my mistress drove me from her house; there came my old tyrant, to mock, insult, and curse me; there my children were first laid in my arms; there I had watched over them, each day with a deeper and sadder love; there I had knelt to God, in anguish of heart, to forgive the wrong I had done. How vividly it all came back! And after this long, gloomy interval, I stood there such a wreck!

In the midst of these meditations, I heard footsteps on the stairs. The door opened, and my uncle Phillip came in, leading Ellen by the hand. I put my arms round her, and said, "Ellen, my dear child, I am your mother." She drew back a little, and looked at me; then, with sweet confidence, she laid her cheek against mine, and I folded her to the heart that had been so long desolated. She was the first to speak. Raising her head, she said, inquiringly, "You really *are* my mother?" I told her I really was; that during all the long time she had not seen me, I had loved her most tenderly; and that now she was going away, I wanted to see her and talk with her, that she might remember me. With a sob in her voice, she said, "I'm glad you've come to see me; but why didn't you ever come before? Benny and I have wanted so much to see you! He remembers you, and sometimes he tells me about you. Why didn't you come home when Dr. Flint went to bring you?"

I answered, "I couldn't come before, dear. But now that I am with you, tell me whether you like to go away." "I don't know," said she, crying. "Grandmother says I ought not to cry; that I am going to a good place, where I can learn to read and write, and that by and by I can write her a letter. But I shan't have Benny, or grandmother, or uncle Phillip, or any body to love me. Can't you go with me? O, *do* go, dear mother!"

I told her I couldn't go now; but sometime I would come to her, and then she and Benny and I would live together, and have happy times. She wanted to run and bring Benny to see me now. I told her he was going to the north, before long, with uncle Phillip, and then I would come to see him before he went away. I asked if she would like to have me stay all night and sleep with her. "O, yes," she replied. Then, turning to her uncle, she said, pleadingly, "*May* I stay? Please, uncle! She is my own mother." He laid his hand on her head, and said, solemnly, "Ellen, this is the secret you have promised grandmother never to tell. If you ever speak of it to any body, they will never let you see your grandmother again, and your mother can never come to Brooklyn." "Uncle," she replied, "I will never tell." He told her she might stay with me; and when he had gone, I took her in my arms and told her I was a slave, and that was the reason she must never say she had seen me. I exhorted her to be a good child, to try to please the people where she was going, and that God would raise her up friends. I told her to say her prayers, and remember always to pray for her poor mother, and that God would permit us to meet again. She wept, and I did not check her tears. Perhaps she would never again have a chance to pour her tears into a mother's bosom. All night she nestled in my arms, and I had no inclination to slumber. The moments were too precious to lose any of them. Once, when I thought she was asleep, I kissed her forehead softly, and she said, "I am not asleep, dear mother."

Before dawn they came to take me back to my den. I drew aside the window curtain, to take a last look of my child. The moonlight shone on her face, and I bent over her, as I had done years before, that wretched night when I ran away. I hugged her close to my throbbing heart; and tears, too sad for such young eyes to shed, flowed down her cheeks, as she gave her last kiss, and whispered in my ear, "Mother, I will never tell." And she never did.

When I got back to my den, I threw myself on the bed and wept there alone in the darkness. It seemed as if my heart would burst. When the time for Ellen's departure drew nigh, I could hear neighbors and friends saying to her, "Good by, Ellen. I hope your poor mother will find you out. Won't you be glad to see her!" She replied, "Yes, ma'am;" and they little dreamed of the weighty secret that weighed down her young heart. She was an affectionate child, but naturally very reserved, except with those she loved, and I felt secure that my secret would be safe with her. I heard the gate close after her, with such feelings as only a slave mother can experience. During the day my meditations were very sad. Sometimes I feared I had been very selfish not to give up all claim to her, and let her go to Illinois, to be adopted by Mrs. Sands's sister. It was my experience of slavery that decided me against it. I feared that circumstances might arise that would cause her to be sent back. I felt confident that I should go to New York myself; and then I should be able to watch over her, and in some degree protect her.

Dr. Flint's family knew nothing of the proposed arrangement till after Ellen was gone, and the news displeased them greatly. Mrs. Flint called on Mrs. Sands's sister to inquire into the matter. She expressed her opinion very freely as to the respect Mr. Sands showed for his wife, and for his own character, in acknowledging those "young niggers." And as for sending Ellen away, she pronounced it to be just as much stealing as it would be for him to come and take a piece of furniture out of her parlor. She said her daughter was not of age to sign the bill of sale, and the children were her property; and when she became of age, or was married, she could take them, wherever she could lay hands on them.

Miss Emily Flint, the little girl to whom I had been bequeathed, was now in her sixteenth year. Her mother considered it all right and honorable for her, or her future husband, to steal my children; but she did not understand how any body could hold up their heads in respectable society, after they had purchased their own children, as Mr. Sands had done. Dr. Flint said very little. Perhaps he thought that Benny would be less likely to be sent away if he kept quiet. One of my letters, that fell into his hands, was dated from Canada; and he seldom spoke of me now. This state of things enabled me to slip down into the storeroom more frequently, where I could stand upright, and move my limbs more freely.

Days, weeks, and months passed, and there came no news of Ellen. I sent a letter to Brooklyn, written in my grandmother's name, to inquire whether she had arrived there. Answer was returned that she had not. I wrote to her in Washington; but no notice was taken of it. There was one person there, who ought to have had some sympathy with the anxiety of the child's friends at home; but the links of such relations as he had formed with me, are easily broken and cast away as rubbish. Yet how protectingly and persuasively he once talked to the poor, helpless slave girl! And how entirely I trusted him! But now suspicions darkened my mind. Was my child dead, or had they deceived me, and sold her?

If the secret memoirs of many members of Congress should be published, curious details would be unfolded. I once saw a letter from a member of Congress to a slave, who was the mother of six of his children. He wrote to request that she would send her children away from the great house before his return, as he expected to be accompanied by friends. The woman could not read, and was obliged to employ another to read the letter. The existence of the colored children did not trouble this gentleman, it was only the fear that friends might recognize in their features a resemblance to him.

At the end of six months, a letter came to my grandmother, from Brooklyn. It was written by a young lady in the family, and announced that Ellen had just arrived. It contained the following message from her: "I do try to do just as you told me to, and I pray for you every night and morning." I understood that these words were meant for me; and they were a balsam to my heart. The writer closed her letter by saying, "Ellen is a nice little girl, and we shall like to have her with us. My cousin, Mr. Sands, has given her to me, to be my little waiting maid. I shall send her to school, and I hope some day she will write to you herself." This letter perplexed and troubled me. Had my child's father merely placed her there till she was old enough to support herself? Or had he given her to his cousin, as a piece of property? If the last idea was correct, his cousin might return to the south at any time, and hold Ellen as a slave. I tried to put away from me the painful thought that such a foul wrong could have been done to us. I said to myself, "Surely there must be *some* justice in man;" then I remembered, with a sigh, how slavery perverted all the natural feelings of the human heart. It gave me a pang to look on my light-hearted boy. He believed himself free; and to have him brought under the yoke of slavery, would be more than I could bear. How I longed to have him safely out of the reach of its power!

XXVIII. Aunt Nancy

I have mentioned my great-aunt, who was a slave in Dr. Flint's family, and who had been my refuge during the shameful persecutions I suffered from him. This aunt had been married at twenty years of age; that is, as far as slaves *can* marry. She had the consent of her master and mistress, and a clergyman performed the ceremony. But it was a mere form, without any legal value. Her master or mistress could annul it any day they pleased. She had always slept on the floor in the entry, near Mrs. Flint's chamber door, that she might be within call. When she was married, she was told she might have the use of a small room in an out-house. Her mother and her husband furnished it. He was a seafaring man, and was allowed to sleep there when he was at home. But on the wedding evening, the bride was ordered to her old post on the entry floor.

Mrs. Flint, at that time, had no children; but she was expecting to be a mother, and if she should want a drink of water in the night, what could she do without her slave to bring it? So my aunt was compelled to lie at her door, until one midnight she was forced to leave, to give premature birth to a child. In a fortnight, she was required to resume her place on the entry floor, because Mrs. Flint's babe needed her attentions. She kept her station there through summer and winter, until she had given premature birth to six children; and all the while she was employed as night-nurse to Mrs. Flint's children. Finally, toiling all day, and being deprived of rest at night, completely broke down her constitution, and Dr. Flint declared it was impossible she could ever become the mother of a living child. The fear of losing so valuable a servant by death, now induced them to allow her to sleep in her little room in the out-house, except when there was sickness in the family. She afterwards had two feeble babes, one of whom died in a few days, and the other in four weeks. I well remember her patient sorrow as she held the last dead baby in her arms. "I wish it could have lived," she said; "it is not the will of God that any of my children should live. But I will try to be fit to meet their little spirits in heaven."

Aunt Nancy was housekeeper and waiting-maid in Dr. Flint's family. Indeed, she was the *factotum* of the household. Nothing went on well without her. She was my mother's twin sister, and, as far as was in her power, she supplied a mother's place to us orphans. I slept with her all the time I lived in my old master's house, and the bond between us was very strong. When my friends tried to discourage me from running away, she always encouraged me. When they thought I had better return and ask my master's pardon, because there was no possibility of escape, she sent me word never to yield. She said if I persevered I might, perhaps, gain the freedom of my children; and even if I perished in doing it, that was better than to leave them to groan under the same persecutions that had blighted my own life. After I was shut up in my dark cell, she stole away, whenever she could, to bring me the news and say something cheering. How often did I kneel down to listen to her words of consolation, whispered through a crack! "I am old, and have not long to live," she used to say; "and I could die happy if I could only see you and the children free. You must pray to God, Linda, as I do for you, that he will lead you out of this darkness." I would beg her not to worry herself on my account; that there was an end of all suffering sooner or later, and that whether I lived in chains or in freedom, I should always remember her as the good friend who had been the comfort of my life. A word from her always strengthened me; and not me only. The whole family relied upon her judgment, and were guided by her advice.

I had been in my cell six years when my grandmother was summoned to the bedside of this, her last remaining daughter. She was very ill, and they said she would die. Grandmother had not entered Dr. Flint's house for several years. They had treated her cruelly, but she thought nothing of that now. She was grateful for permission to watch by the death-bed of her child. They had always been devoted to each other; and now they sat looking into each other's eyes, longing to speak of the secret that had weighed so much on the hearts of both. My aunt had been stricken with paralysis. She lived but two days, and the last day she was speechless. Before she lost the power of utterance, she told her mother not to grieve if she could not speak to her; that she would try to hold up her hand, to let her know that all was well with her. Even the hard-hearted doctor was a little softened when he saw the dying woman try to smile on the aged mother, who was kneeling by her side. His eyes moistened for a moment, as he said she had always been a faithful servant, and they should never be able to supply her place. Mrs. Flint took to her bed, quite overcome by the shock. While my grandmother sat alone with the dead, the doctor came in, leading his youngest son, who had always been a great pet with aunt Nancy, and was much attached to her. "Martha," said he, "aunt Nancy loved this child, and when he comes where you are, I hope you will be kind to him, for her sake." She replied, "Your wife was my foster-child, Dr. Flint, the foster-sister of my poor Nancy, and you little know me if you think I can feel any thing but good will for her children."

"I wish the past could be forgotten, and that we might never think of it," said he; "and that Linda would come to supply her aunt's place. She would be worth more to us than all the money that could be paid for her. I wish it for your sake also, Martha. Now that Nancy is taken away from you, she would be a great comfort to your old age."

He knew he was touching a tender chord. Almost choking with grief, my grandmother replied, "It was not I that drove Linda away. My grandchildren are gone; and of my nine children only one is left. God help me!"

To me, the death of this kind relative was an inexpressible sorrow. I knew that she had been slowly murdered; and I felt that my troubles had helped to finish the work. After I heard of her illness, I listened constantly to hear what news was brought from the great house; and the thought that I could not go to her made me utterly miserable. At last, as uncle Phillip came into the house, I heard some one inquire, "How is she?" and he answered, "She is dead." My little cell seemed whirling round, and I knew nothing more till I opened my eyes and found uncle Phillip bending over me. I had no need to ask any questions. He whispered, "Linda, she died happy." I could not weep. My fixed gaze troubled him. "Don't look *so,*" he said. "Don't add to my poor mother's trouble. Remember how much she has to bear, and that we ought to do all we can to comfort her." Ah, yes, that blessed old grandmother, who for seventy-three years had borne the pelting storms of a slave-mother's life. She did indeed need consolation!

Mrs. Flint had rendered her poor foster-sister childless, apparently without any compunction; and with cruel selfishness had ruined her health by years of incessant, unrequited toil, and broken rest. But now she became very sentimental. I suppose she thought it would be a beautiful illustration of the attachment existing between slaveholder and slave, if the body of her old worn-out servant was buried at her feet. She sent for the clergyman and asked if he had any objection to burying aunt Nancy in the doctor's family burial-place. No colored person had ever been allowed interment in the white people's burying-ground, and the minister knew that all the deceased of our family reposed together in the old graveyard of the slaves. He therefore replied, "I have no objection to complying with your wish; but perhaps aunt Nancy's *mother* may have some choice as to where her remains shall be deposited."

It had never occurred to Mrs. Flint that slaves could have any feelings. When my grandmother was consulted, she at once said she wanted Nancy to lie with all the rest of her family, and where her own old body would be buried. Mrs. Flint graciously complied with her wish, though she said it was painful to her to have Nancy buried away from *her.* She might have added with touching pathos, "I was so long *used* to sleep with her lying near me, on the entry floor."

My uncle Phillip asked permission to bury his sister at his own expense; and slaveholders are always ready to grant *such* favors to slaves and their relatives. The arrangements were very plain, but perfectly respectable. She was buried on the Sabbath, and Mrs. Flint's minister read the funeral service. There was a large concourse of colored people, bond and free, and a few white persons who had always been friendly to our family. Dr. Flint's carriage was in the procession; and when the body was deposited in its humble resting place, the mistress dropped a tear, and returned to her carriage, probably thinking she had performed her duty nobly.

It was talked of by the slaves as a mighty grand funeral. Northern travellers, passing through the place, might have described this tribute of respect to the humble dead as a beautiful feature in the "patriarchal institution;" a touching proof of the attachment between slaveholders and their servants; and tender-hearted Mrs. Flint would have confirmed this impression, with handkerchief at her eyes. We could have told them a different story. We could have given them a chapter of wrongs and sufferings, that would have touched their hearts, if they *had* any hearts to feel for the colored people. We could have told them how the poor old slave-mother had toiled, year after year, to earn eight hundred dollars to buy her son Phillip's right to his own earnings; and how that same Phillip paid the expense of the funeral, which they regarded as doing so much credit to the master. We could also have told them of a poor, blighted young creature, shut up in a living grave for years, to avoid the tortures that would be inflicted on her, if she ventured to come out and look on the face of her departed friend.

All this, and much more, I thought of, as I sat at my loophole, waiting for the family to return from the grave; sometimes weeping, sometimes falling asleep, dreaming strange dreams of the dead and the living.

It was sad to witness the grief of my bereaved grandmother. She had always been strong to bear, and now, as ever, religious faith supported her. But her dark life had become still darker, and age and trouble were leaving deep traces on her withered face. She had four places to knock for me to come to the trap-door, and each place had a different meaning. She now came oftener than she had done, and talked to me of her dead daughter, while tears trickled slowly down her furrowed cheeks. I said all I could to comfort her; but it was a sad reflection, that instead of being able to help her, I was a constant source of anxiety and trouble. The poor old back was fitted to its burden. It bent under it, but did not break.

XXIX. Preparations for Escape

I hardly expect that the reader will credit me, when I affirm that I lived in that little dismal hole, almost deprived of light and air, and with no space to move my limbs, for nearly seven years. But it is a fact; and to me a sad one, even now; for my body still suffers from the effects of that long imprisonment, to say nothing of my soul. Members of my family, now living in New York and Boston, can testify to the truth of what I say.

Countless were the nights that I sat late at the little loophole scarcely large enough to give me a glimpse of one twinkling star. There, I heard the patrols and slave-hunters conferring together about the capture of runaways, well knowing how rejoiced they would be to catch me.

Season after season, year after year, I peeped at my children's faces, and heard their sweet voices, with a heart yearning all the while to say, "Your mother is here." Sometimes it appeared to me as if ages had rolled away since I entered upon that gloomy, monotonous existence. At times, I was stupefied and listless; at other times I became very impatient to know when these dark years would end, and I should again be allowed to feel the sunshine, and breathe the pure air.

After Ellen left us, this feeling increased. Mr. Sands had agreed that Benny might go to the north whenever his uncle Phillip could go with him; and I was anxious to be there also, to watch over my children, and protect them so far as I was able. Moreover, I was likely to be drowned out of my den, if I remained much longer; for the slight roof was getting badly out of repair, and uncle Phillip was afraid to remove the shingles, lest some one should get a glimpse of me. When storms occurred in the night, they spread mats and bits of carpet, which in the morning appeared to have been laid out to dry; but to cover the roof in the daytime might have attracted attention. Consequently, my clothes and bedding were often drenched; a process by which the pains and aches in my cramped and stiffened limbs were greatly increased. I revolved various plans of escape in my mind, which I sometimes imparted to my grandmother, when she came to whisper with me at the trap-door. The kind-hearted old woman had an intense sympathy for runaways. She had known too much of the cruelties inflicted on those who were captured. Her memory always flew back at once to the sufferings of her bright and handsome son, Benjamin, the youngest and dearest of her flock. So, whenever I alluded to the subject, she would groan out, "O, don't think of it, child. You'll break my heart." I had no good old aunt Nancy now to encourage me; but my brother William and my children were continually beckoning me to the north.

And now I must go back a few months in my story. I have stated that the first of January was the time for selling slaves, or leasing them out to new masters. If time were counted by heart-throbs, the poor slaves might reckon years of suffering during that festival so joyous to the free. On the New Year's day preceding my aunt's death, one of my friends, named Fanny, was to be sold at auction, to pay her master's debts. My thoughts were with her during all the day, and at night I anxiously inquired what had been her fate. I was told that she had been sold to one master, and her four little girls to another master, far distant; that she had escaped from her purchaser, and was not to be found. Her mother was the old Aggie I have spoken of. She lived in a small tenement belonging to my grandmother, and built on the same lot with her own house. Her dwelling was searched and watched, and that brought the patrols so near me that I was obliged to keep very close in my den. The hunters were somehow eluded; and not long afterwards Benny accidentally caught sight of Fanny in her mother's hut. He told his grandmother, who charged him never to speak of it, explaining to him the frightful consequences; and he never betrayed the trust. Aggie little dreamed that my grandmother knew where her daughter was concealed, and that the stooping form of her old neighbor was bending under a similar burden of anxiety and fear; but these dangerous secrets deepened the sympathy between the two old persecuted mothers.

My friend Fanny and I remained many weeks hidden within call of each other; but she was unconscious of the fact. I longed to have her share my den, which seemed a more secure retreat than her own; but I had brought so much trouble on my grandmother, that it seemed wrong to ask her to incur greater risks. My restlessness increased. I had lived too long in bodily pain and anguish of spirit. Always I was in dread that by some accident, or some contrivance, slavery would succeed in snatching my children from me. This thought drove me nearly frantic, and I determined to steer for the North Star at all hazards. At this crisis, Providence opened an unexpected way for me to escape. My friend Peter came one evening, and asked to speak with me. "Your day has come, Linda," said he. "I have found a chance for you to go to the Free States. You have a fortnight to decide." The news seemed too good to be true; but Peter explained his arrangements, and told me all that was necessary was for me to say I would go. I was going to answer him with a joyful yes, when the thought of Benny came to my mind. I told him the temptation was exceedingly strong, but I was terribly afraid of Dr. Flint's alleged power over my child, and that I could not go and leave him behind. Peter remonstrated earnestly. He said such a good chance might never occur again; that Benny was free, and could be sent to me; and that for the sake of my children's welfare I ought not to hesitate a moment. I told him I would consult with uncle Phillip. My uncle rejoiced in the plan, and bade me go by all means. He promised, if his life was spared, that he would either bring or send my son to me as soon as I reached a place of safety. I resolved to go, but thought nothing had better be said to my grandmother till very near the time of departure. But my uncle thought she would feel it more keenly if I left her so suddenly. "I will reason with her," said he, "and convince her how necessary it is, not only for your sake, but for hers also. You cannot be blind to the fact that she is sinking under her burdens." I was not blind to it. I knew that my concealment was an ever-present source of anxiety, and that the older she grew the more nervously fearful she was of discovery. My uncle talked with her, and finally succeeded in persuading her that it was absolutely necessary for me to seize the chance so unexpectedly offered.

The anticipation of being a free woman proved almost too much for my weak frame. The excitement stimulated me, and at the same time bewildered me. I made busy preparations for my journey, and for my son to follow me. I resolved to have an interview with him before I went, that I might give him cautions and advice, and tell him how anxiously I should be waiting for him at the north. Grandmother stole up to me as often as possible to whisper words of counsel. She insisted upon my writing to Dr. Flint, as soon as I arrived in the Free States, and asking him to sell me to her. She said she would sacrifice her house, and all she had in the world, for the sake of having me safe with my children in any part of the world. If she could only live to know *that* she could die in peace. I promised the dear old faithful friend that I would write to her as soon as I arrived, and put the letter in a safe way to reach her; but in my own mind I resolved that not another cent of her hard earnings should be spent to pay rapacious slaveholders for what they called their property. And even if I had not been unwilling to buy what I had already a right to possess, common humanity would have prevented me from accepting the generous offer, at the expense of turning my aged relative out of house and home, when she was trembling on the brink of the grave.

I was to escape in a vessel; but I forbear to mention any further paticulars. I was in readiness, but the vessel was unexpectedly detained several days. Meantime, news came to town of a most horrible murder committed on a fugitive slave, named James. Charity, the mother of this unfortunate young man, had been an old acquaintance of ours. I have told the shocking particulars of his death, in my description of some of the neighboring slaveholders. My grandmother, always nervously sensitive about runaways, was terribly frightened. She felt sure that a similar fate awaited me, if I did not desist from my enterprise. She sobbed, and groaned, and entreated me not to go. Her excessive fear was somewhat contagious, and my heart was not proof against her extreme agony. I was grievously disappointed, but I promised to relinquish my project.

When my friend Peter was apprised of this, he was both disappointed and vexed. He said, that judging from our past experience, it would be a long time before I had such another chance to throw away. I told him it need not be thrown away; that I had a friend concealed near by, who would be glad enough to take the place that had been provided for me. I told him about poor Fanny, and the kind-hearted, noble fellow, who never turned his back upon any body in distress, white or black, expressed his readiness to help her. Aggie was much surprised when she found that we knew her secret. She was rejoiced to hear of such a chance for Fanny, and arrangements were made for her to go on board the vessel the next night. They both supposed that I had long been at the north, therefore my name was not mentioned in the transaction. Fanny was carried on board at the appointed time, and stowed away in a very small cabin. This accommodation had been purchased at a price that would pay for a voyage to England. But when one proposes to go to fine old England, they stop to calculate whether they can afford the cost of the pleasure; while in making a bargain to escape from slavery, the trembling victim is ready to say, "Take all I have, only don't betray me!"

The next morning I peeped through my loophole, and saw that it was dark and cloudy. At night I received news that the wind was ahead, and the vessel had not sailed. I was exceedingly anxious about Fanny, and Peter too, who was running a tremendous risk at my instigation. Next day the wind and weather remained the same. Poor Fanny had been half dead with fright when they carried her on board, and I could readily imagine how she must be suffering now. Grandmother came often to my den, to say how thankful she was I did not go. On the third morning she rapped for me to come down to the storeroom. The poor old sufferer was breaking down under her weight of trouble. She was easily flurried now. I found her in a nervous, excited state, but I was not aware that she had forgotten to lock the door behind her, as usual. She was exceedingly worried about the detention of the vessel. She was afraid all would be discovered, and then Fanny, and Peter, and I, would all be tortured to death, and Phillip would be utterly ruined, and her house would be torn down. Poor Peter! If he should die such a horrible death as the poor slave James had lately done, and all for his kindness in trying to help me, how dreadful it would be for us all! Alas, the thought was familiar to me, and had sent many a sharp pang through my heart. I tried to suppress my own anxiety, and speak soothingly to her. She brought in some allusion to aunt Nancy, the dear daughter she had recently buried, and then she lost all control of herself. As she stood there, trembling and sobbing, a voice from the piazza called out, "Whar is you, aunt Marthy?" Grandmother was startled, and in her agitation opened the door, without thinking of me. In stepped Jenny, the mischievous housemaid, who had tried to enter my room, when I was concealed in the house of my white benefactress. "I's bin huntin ebery whar for you, aunt Marthy," said she. "My missis wants you to send her some crackers." I had slunk down behind a barrel, which entirely screened me, but I imagined that Jenny was looking directly at the spot, and my heart beat violently. My grandmother immediately thought what she had done, and went out quickly with Jenny to count the crackers locking the door after her. She returned to me, in a few minutes, the perfect picture of despair. "Poor child!" she exclaimed, "my carelessness has ruined you. The boat ain't gone yet. Get ready immediately, and go with Fanny. I ain't got another word to say against it now; for there's no telling what may happen this day."

Uncle Phillip was sent for, and he agreed with his mother in thinking that Jenny would inform Dr. Flint in less than twenty-four hours. He advised getting me on board the boat, if possible; if not, I had better keep very still in my den, where they could not find me without tearing the house down. He said it would not do for him to move in the matter, because suspicion would be immediately excited; but he promised to communicate with Peter. I felt reluctant to apply to him again, having implicated him too much already; but there seemed to be no alternative. Vexed as Peter had been by my indecision, he was true to his generous nature, and said at once that he would do his best to help me, trusting I should show myself a stronger woman this time.

He immediately proceeded to the wharf, and found that the wind had shifted, and the vessel was slowly beating down stream. On some pretext of urgent necessity, he offered two boatmen a dollar apiece to catch up with her. He was of lighter complexion than the boatmen he hired, and when the captain saw them coming so rapidly, he thought officers were pursuing his vessel in search of the runaway slave he had on board. They hoisted sails, but the boat gained upon them, and the indefatigable Peter sprang on board.

The captain at once recognized him. Peter asked him to go below, to speak about a bad bill he had given him. When he told his errand, the captain replied, "Why, the woman's here already; and I've put her where you or the devil would have a tough job to find her."

"But it is another woman I want to bring," said Peter. "*She* is in great distress, too, and you shall be paid any thing within reason, if you'll stop and take her."

"What's her name?" inquired the captain.

"Linda," he replied.

"That's the name of the woman already here," rejoined the captain. "By George! I believe you mean to betray me."

"O!" exclaimed Peter, "God knows I wouldn't harm a hair of your head. I am too grateful to you. But there really *is* another woman in great danger. Do have the humanity to stop and take her!"

After a while they came to an understanding. Fanny, not dreaming I was any where about in that region, had assumed my name, though she called herself Johnson. "Linda is a common name," said Peter, "and the woman I want to bring is Linda Brent."

The captain agreed to wait at a certain place till evening, being handsomely paid for his detention.

Of course, the day was an anxious one for us all. But we concluded that if Jenny had seen me, she would be too wise to let her mistress know of it; and that she probably would not get a chance to see Dr. Flint's family till evening, for I knew very well what were the rules in that household. I afterwards believed that she did not see me; for nothing ever came of it, and she was one of those base characters that would have jumped to betray a suffering fellow being for the sake of thirty pieces of silver.

I made all my arrangements to go on board as soon as it was dusk. The intervening time I resolved to spend with my son. I had not spoken to him for seven years, though I had been under the same roof, and seen him every day, when I was well enough to sit at the loophole. I did not dare to venture beyond the storeroom; so they brought him there, and locked us up together, in a place concealed from the piazza door. It was an agitating interview for both of us. After we had talked and wept together for a little while, he said, "Mother, I'm glad you're going away. I wish I could go with you. I knew you was here; and I have been so afraid they would come and catch you!"

I was greatly surprised, and asked him how he had found it out.

He replied, "I was standing under the eaves, one day, before Ellen went away, and I heard somebody cough up over the wood shed. I don't know what made me think it was you, but I did think so. I missed Ellen, the night before she went away; and grandmother brought her back into the room in the night; and I thought maybe she'd been to see *you*, before she went, for I heard grandmother whisper to her, 'Now go to sleep; and remember never to tell.'"

I asked him if he ever mentioned his suspicions to his sister. He said he never did; but after he heard the cough, if he saw her playing with other children on that side of the house, he always tried to coax her round to the other side, for fear they would hear me cough, too. He said he had kept a close lookout for Dr. Flint, and if he saw him speak to a constable, or a patrol, he always told grandmother. I now recollected that I had seen him manifest uneasiness, when people were on that side of the house, and I had at the time been puzzled to conjecture a motive for his actions. Such prudence may seem extraordinary in a boy of twelve years, but slaves, being surrounded by mysteries, deceptions, and dangers, early learn to be suspicious and watchful, and prematurely cautious and cunning. He had never asked a question of grandmother, or uncle Phillip, and I had often heard him chime in with other children, when they spoke of my being at the north.

I told him I was now really going to the Free States, and if he was a good, honest boy, and a loving child to his dear old grandmother, the Lord would bless him, and bring him to me, and we and Ellen would live together. He began to tell me that grandmother had not eaten any thing all day. While he was speaking, the door was unlocked, and she came in with a small bag of money, which she wanted me to take. I begged her to keep a part of it, at least, to pay for Benny's being sent to the north; but she insisted, while her tears were falling fast, that I should take the whole. "You may be sick among strangers," she said, "and they would send you to the poorhouse to die." Ah, that good grandmother!

For the last time I went up to my nook. Its desolate appearance no longer chilled me, for the light of hope had risen in my soul. Yet, even with the blessed prospect of freedom before me, I felt very sad at leaving forever that old homestead, where I had been sheltered so long by the dear old grandmother; where I had dreamed my first young dream of love; and where, after that had faded away, my children came to twine themselves so closely round my desolate heart. As the hour approached for me to leave, I again descended to the storeroom. My grandmother and Benny were there. She took me by the hand, and said, "Linda, let us pray." We knelt down together, with my child pressed to my heart, and my other arm round the faithful, loving old friend I was about to leave forever. On no other occasion has it ever been my lot to listen to so fervent a supplication for mercy and protection. It thrilled through my heart, and inspired me with trust in God.

Peter was waiting for me in the street. I was soon by his side, faint in body, but strong of purpose. I did not look back upon the old place, though I felt that I should never see it again.

XXX. Northward Bound

I never could tell how we reached the wharf. My brain was all of a whirl, and my limbs tottered under me. At an appointed place we met my uncle Phillip, who had started before us on a different route, that he might reach the wharf first, and give us timely warning if there was any danger. A row-boat was in readiness. As I was about to step in, I felt something pull me gently, and turning round I saw Benny, looking pale and anxious. He whispered in my ear, "I've been peeping into the doctor's window, and he's at home. Good by, mother. Don't cry; I'll come." He hastened away. I clasped the hand of my good uncle, to whom I owed so much, and of Peter, the brave, generous friend who had volunteered to run such terrible risks to secure my safety. To this day I remember how his bright face beamed with joy, when he told me he had discovered a safe method for me to escape. Yet that intelligent, enterprising, noble-hearted man was a chattel! liable, by the laws of a country that calls itself civilized, to be sold with horses and pigs! We parted in silence. Our hearts were all too full for words!

Swiftly the boat glided over the water. After a while, one of the sailors said, "Don't be down-hearted, madam. We will take you safely to your husband, in———." At first I could not imagine what he meant; but I had presence of mind to think that it probably referred to something the captain had told him; so I thanked him, and said I hoped we should have pleasant weather.

When I entered the vessel the captain came forward to meet me. He was an elderly man, with a pleasant countenance. He showed me to a little box of a cabin, where sat my friend Fanny. She started as if she had seen a spectre. She gazed on me in utter astonishment, and exclaimed, "Linda, can this be *you*? or is it your ghost?" When we were locked in each other's arms, my overwrought feelings could no longer be restrained. My sobs reached the ears of the captain, who came and very kindly reminded us, that for his safety, as well as our own, it would be prudent for us not to attract any attention. He said that when there was a sail in sight he wished us to keep below; but at other times, he had no objection to our being on deck. He assured us that he would keep a good lookout, and if we acted prudently, he thought we should be in no danger. He had represented us as women going to meet our husbands in——. We thanked him, and promised to observe carefully all the directions he gave us.

Fanny and I now talked by ourselves, low and quietly, in our little cabin. She told me of the sufferings she had gone through in making her escape, and of her terrors while she was concealed in her mother's house. Above all, she dwelt on the agony of separation from all her children on that dreadful auction day. She could scarcely credit me, when I told her of the place where I had passed nearly seven years. "We have the same sorrows," said I. "No," replied she, "you are going to see your children soon, there is no hope that I shall ever even hear from mine."

The vessel was soon under way, but we made slow progress. The wind was against us. I should not have cared for this, if we had been out of sight of the town; but until there were miles of water between us and our enemies, we were filled with constant apprehensions that the constables would come on board. Neither could I feel quite at ease with the captain and his men. I was an entire stranger to that class of people, and I had heard that sailors were rough, and sometimes cruel. We were so completely in their power, that if they were bad men, our situation would be dreadful. Now that the captain was paid for our passage, might he not be tempted to make more money by giving us up to those who claimed us as property? I was naturally of a confiding disposition, but slavery had made me suspicious of every body. Fanny did not share my distrust of the captain or his men. She said she was afraid at first, but she had been on board three days while the vessel lay in the dock, and nobody had betrayed her, or treated her otherwise than kindly.

The captain soon came to advise us to go on deck for fresh air. His friendly and respectful manner, combined with Fanny's testimony, reassured me, and we went with him. He placed us in a comfortable seat, and occasionally entered into conversation. He told us he was a Southerner by birth, and had spent the greater part of his life in the Slave States, and that he had recently lost a brother who traded in slaves. "But," said he, "it is a pitiable and degrading business, and I always felt ashamed to acknowledge my brother in connection with it." As we passed Snaky Swamp, he pointed to it, and said, "There is a slave territory that defies all the laws." I thought of the terrible days I had spent there, and though it was not called Dismal Swamp, it made me feel very dismal as I looked at it.

I shall never forget that night. The balmy air of spring was so refreshing! And how shall I describe my sensations when we were fairly sailing on Chesapeake Bay? O, the beautiful sunshine! the exhilarating breeze! and I could enjoy them without fear or restraint. I had never realized what grand things air and sunlight are till I had been deprived of them.

Ten days after we left land we were approaching Philadelphia. The captain said we should arrive there in the night, but he thought we had better wait till morning, and go on shore in broad daylight, as the best way to avoid suspicion.

I replied, "You know best. But will you stay on board and protect us?"

He saw that I was suspicious, and he said he was sorry, now that he had brought us to the end of our voyage, to find I had so little confidence in him. Ah, if he had ever been a slave he would have known how difficult it was to trust a white man. He assured us that we might sleep through the night without fear; that he would take care we were not left unprotected. Be it said to the honor of this captain, Southerner as he was, that if Fanny and I had been white ladies, and our passage lawfully engaged, he could not have treated us more respectfully. My intelligent friend, Peter, had rightly estimated the character of the man to whose honor he had intrusted us.

The next morning I was on deck as soon as the day dawned. I called Fanny to see the sun rise, for the first time in our lives, on free soil; for such I *then* believed it to be. We watched the reddening sky, and saw the great orb come up slowly out of the water, as it seemed. Soon the waves began to sparkle, and every thing caught the beautiful glow. Before us lay the city of strangers. We looked at each other, and the eyes of both were moistened with tears. We had escaped from slavery, and we supposed ourselves to be safe from the hunters. But we were alone in the world, and we had left dear ties behind us; ties cruelly sundered by the demon Slavery.

XXXI. Incidents in Philadelphia

I had heard that the poor slave had many friends at the north. I trusted we should find some of them. Meantime, we would take it for granted that all were friends, till they proved to the contrary. I sought out the kind captain, thanked him for his attentions, and told him I should never cease to be grateful for the service he had rendered us. I gave him a message to the friends I had left at home, and he promised to deliver it. We were placed in a row-boat, and in about fifteen minutes were landed on a wood wharf in Philadelphia. As I stood looking round, the friendly captain touched me on the shoulder, and said, "There is a respectable-looking colored man behind you. I will speak to him about the New York trains, and tell him you wish to go directly on." I thanked him, and asked him to direct me to some shops where I could buy gloves and veils. He did so, and said he would talk with the colored man till I returned. I made what haste I could. Constant exercise on board the vessel, and frequent rubbing with salt water, had nearly restored the use of my limbs. The noise of the great city confused me, but I found the shops, and bought some double veils and gloves for Fanny and myself. The shopman told me they were so many levies.[1] I had never heard the word before, but I did not tell him so. I thought if he knew I was a stranger he might ask me where I came from. I gave him a gold piece, and when he returned the change, I counted it, and found out how much a levy was. I made my way back to the wharf, where the captain introduced me to the colored man, as the Rev. Jeremiah Durham, minister of Bethel church. He took me by the hand, as if I had been an old friend. He told us we were too late for the morning cars to New York, and must wait until the evening, or the next morning. He invited me to go home with him, assuring me that his wife would give me a cordial welcome; and for my friend he would provide a home with one of his neighbors. I thanked him for so much kindness to strangers, and told him if I must be detained, I should like to hunt up some people who formerly went from our part of the country. Mr. Durham insisted that I should dine with him, and then he would assist me in finding my friends. The sailors came to bid us good by. I shook their hardy hands, with tears in my eyes. They had all been kind to us, and they had rendered us a greater service than they could possibly conceive of.

I had never seen so large a city, or been in contact with so many people in the streets. It seemed as if those who passed looked at us with an expression of curiosity. My face was so blistered and peeled, by sitting on deck, in wind and sunshine, that I thought they could not easily decide to what nation I belonged.

Mrs. Durham met me with a kindly welcome, without asking any questions. I was tired, and her friendly manner was a sweet refreshment. God bless her! I was sure that she had comforted other weary hearts, before I received her sympathy. She was surrounded by her husband and children, in a home made sacred by protecting laws. I thought of my own children, and sighed.

After dinner Mr. Durham went with me in quest of the friends I had spoken of. They went from my native town, and I anticipated much pleasure in looking on familiar faces. They were not at home, and we retraced our steps through streets delightfully clean. On the way, Mr. Durham observed that I had spoken to him of a daughter I expected to meet; that he was surprised, for I looked so young he had taken me for a single woman. He was approaching a subject on which I was extremely sensitive. He would ask about my husband next, I thought, and if I answered him truly, what would he think of me? I told him I had two children, one in New York the other at the south. He asked some further questions, and I frankly told him some of the most important events of my life. It was painful for me to do it; but I would not deceive him. If he was desirous of

---

1. Short for "eleven-penny bit," a levy was a coin used in Pennsylvania, Maryland, and Virginia worth between eleven and twelve and a half cents.

being my friend, I thought he ought to know how far I was worthy of it. "Excuse me, if I have tried your feelings," said he. "I did not question you from idle curiosity. I wanted to understand your situation, in order to know whether I could be of any service to you, or your little girl. Your straight-forward answers do you credit; but don't answer every body so openly. It might give some heartless people a pretext for treating you with contempt."

That word *contempt* burned me like coals of fire. I replied, "God alone knows how I have suffered; and He, I trust, will forgive me. If I am permitted to have my children, I intend to be a good mother, and to live in such a manner that people cannot treat me with contempt."

"I respect your sentiments," said he. "Place your trust in God, and be governed by good principles, and you will not fail to find friends."

When we reached home, I went to my room, glad to shut out the world for a while. The words he had spoken made an indelible impression upon me. They brought up great shadows from the mournful past. In the midst of my meditations I was startled by a knock at the door. Mrs. Durham entered, her face all beaming with kindness, to say that there was an anti-slavery friend down stairs, who would like to see me. I overcame my dread of encountering strangers, and went with her. Many questions were asked concerning my experiences, and my escape from slavery; but I observed how careful they all were not to say any thing that might wound my feelings. How gratifying this was, can be fully understood only by those who have been accustomed to be treated as if they were not included within the pale of human beings. The anti-slavery friend had come to inquire into my plans, and to offer assistance, if needed. Fanny was comfortably established, for the present, with a friend of Mr. Durham. The Anti-Slavery Society agreed to pay her expenses to New York. The same was offered to me, but I declined to accept it; telling them that my grandmother had given me sufficient to pay my expenses to the end of my journey. We were urged to remain in Philadelphia a few days, until some suitable escort could be found for us. I gladly accepted the proposition, for I had a dread of meeting slaveholders, and some dread also of railroads. I had never entered a railroad car in my life, and it seemed to me quite an important event.

That night I sought my pillow with feelings I had never carried to it before. I verily believed myself to be a free woman. I was wakeful for a long time, and I had no sooner fallen asleep, than I was roused by fire-bells. I jumped up, and hurried on my clothes. Where I came from, every body hastened to dress themselves on such occasions. The white people thought a great fire might be used as a good opportunity for insurrection, and that it was best to be in readiness; and the colored people were ordered out to labor in extinguishing the flames. There was but one engine in our town, and colored women and children were often required to drag it to the river's edge and fill it. Mrs. Durham's daughter slept in the same room with me, and seeing that she slept through all the din, I thought it was my duty to wake her. "What's the matter?" said she, rubbing her eyes.

"They're screaming fire in the streets, and the bells are ringing," I replied.

"What of that?" said she, drowsily. "We are used to it. We never get up, without the fire is very near. What good would it do?"

I was quite surprised that it was not necessary for us to go and help fill the engine. I was an ignorant child, just beginning to learn how things went on in great cities.

At daylight, I heard women crying fresh fish, berries, radishes, and various other things. All this was new to me. I dressed myself at an early hour, and sat at the window to watch that unknown tide of life. Philadelphia seemed to me a wonderfully great place. At the breakfast table, my idea of going out to drag the engine was laughed over, and I joined in the mirth.

I went to see Fanny, and found her so well contented among her new friends that she was in no haste to leave. I was also very happy with my kind hostess. She had had advantages for education, and was vastly my superior. Every day, almost every hour, I was adding to my little stock of knowledge. She took me out to see the city as much as she deemed prudent. One day she took me to an artist's room, and showed me the portraits of some of her children. I had never seen any paintings of colored people before, and they seemed to me beautiful.

At the end of five days, one of Mrs. Durham's friends offered to accompany us to New York the following morning. As I held the hand of my good hostess in a parting clasp, I longed to know whether her husband had repeated to her what I had told him. I supposed he had, but she never made any allusion to it. I presume it was the delicate silence of womanly sympathy.

When Mr. Durham handed us our tickets, he said, "I am afraid you will have a disagreeable ride; but I could not procure tickets for the first class cars."

Supposing I had not given him money enough, I offered more. "O, no," said he, "they could not be had for any money. They don't allow colored people to go in the first-class cars."

This was the first chill to my enthusiasm about the Free States. Colored people were allowed to ride in a filthy box, behind white people, at the south, but there they were not required to pay for the privilege. It made me sad to find how the north aped the customs of slavery.

We were stowed away in a large, rough car, with windows on each side, too high for us to look out without standing up. It was crowded with people, apparently of all nations. There were plenty of beds and cradles, containing screaming and kicking babies. Every other man had a cigar or pipe in his mouth, and jugs of whiskey were handed round freely. The fumes of the whiskey and the dense tobacco smoke were sickening to my senses, and my mind was equally nauseated by the coarse jokes and ribald songs around me. It was a very disagreeable ride. Since that time there has been some improvement in these matters.

XXXII. The Meeting of Mother and Daughter

When we arrived in New York, I was half crazed by the crowd of coachmen calling out, "Carriage, ma'am?" We bargained with one to take us to Sullivan Street for twelve shillings. A burly Irishman stepped up and said, "I'll tak' ye for sax shillings." The reduction of half the price was an object to us, and we asked if he could take us right away. "Troth an I will, ladies," he replied. I noticed that the hackmen smiled at each other, and I inquired whether his conveyance was decent. "Yes, it's dacent it is, marm. Devil a bit would I be after takin' ladies in a cab that was not dacent." We gave him our checks. He went for the baggage, and soon reappeared, saying, "This way, if you plase, ladies." We followed, and found our trunks on a truck,[2] and we were invited to take our seats on them. We told him that was not what we bargained for, and he must take the trunks off. He swore they should not be touched till we had paid him six shillings. In our situation it was not prudent to attract attention, and I was about to pay him what he required, when a man near by shook his head for me not to do it. After a great ado we got rid of the Irishman, and had our trunks fastened on a hack. We had been recommended to a boarding-house in Sullivan Street, and thither we drove. There Fanny and I separated. The Anti-Slavery Society provided a home for her, and I afterwards heard of her in prosperous circumstances. I sent for an old friend from my part of the country, who had for some time been doing business in New York. He came immediately. I told him I wanted to go to my daughter, and asked him to aid me in procuring an interview.

I cautioned him not to let it be known to the family that I had just arrived from the south, because they supposed I had been at the north seven years. He told me there was a colored woman in Brooklyn who came from the same town I did, and I had better go to her house, and have my daughter meet me there. I accepted the proposition thankfully, and he agreed to escort me to Brooklyn. We crossed Fulton ferry, went up Myrtle Avenue, and stopped at the house he designated. I was just about to enter, when two girls passed. My friend called my attention to them. I turned, and recognized in the eldest, Sarah, the daughter of a woman who used to live with my grandmother, but who had left the south years

2. An open cart meant for hauling heavy cargo.

ago. Surprised and rejoiced at this unexpected meeting, I threw my arms round her, and inquired concerning her mother.

"You take no notice of the other girl," said my friend. I turned, and there stood my Ellen! I pressed her to my heart, then held her away from me to take a look at her. She had changed a good deal in the two years since I parted from her. Signs of neglect could be discerned by eyes less observing than a mother's. My friend invited us all to go into the house; but Ellen said she had been sent of an errand, which she would do as quickly as possible, and go home and ask Mrs. Hobbs to let her come and see me. It was agreed that I should send for her the next day. Her companion, Sarah, hastened to tell her mother of my arrival. When I entered the house, I found the mistress of it absent, and I waited for her return. Before I saw her, I heard her saying, "Where is Linda Brent? I used to know her father and mother." Soon Sarah came with her mother. So there was quite a company of us, all from my grandmother's neighborhood. These friends gathered round me and questioned me eagerly. They laughed, they cried, and they shouted. They thanked God that I had got away from my persecutors and was safe on Long Island. It was a day of great excitement. How different from the silent days I had passed in my dreary den!

The next morning was Sunday. My first waking thoughts were occupied with the note I was to send to Mrs. Hobbs, the lady with whom Ellen lived. That I had recently come into that vicinity was evident; otherwise I should have sooner inquired for my daughter. It would not do to let them know I had just arrived from the south, for that would involve the suspicion of my having been harbored there, and might bring trouble, if not ruin, on several people.

I like a straightforward course, and am always reluctant to resort to subterfuges. So far as my ways have been crooked, I charge them all upon slavery. It was that system of violence and wrong which now left me no alternative but to enact a falsehood. I began my note by stating that I had recently arrived from Canada, and was very desirous to have my daughter come to see me. She came and brought a message from Mrs. Hobbs, inviting me to her house, and assuring me that I need not have any fears. The conversation I had with my child did not leave my mind at ease. When I asked if she was well treated, she answered yes; but there was no heartiness in the tone, and it seemed to me that she said it from an unwillingness to have me troubled on her account. Before she left me, she asked very earnestly, "Mother, when will you take me to live with you?" It made me sad to think that I could not give her a home till I went to work and earned the means; and that might take me a long time. When she was placed with Mrs. Hobbs, the agreement was that she should be sent to school. She had been there two years, and was now nine years old, and she scarcely knew her letters. There was no excuse for this, for there were good public schools in Brooklyn, to which she could have been sent without expense.

She staid with me till dark, and I went home with her. I was received in a friendly manner by the family, and all agreed in saying that Ellen was a useful, good girl. Mrs. Hobbs looked me coolly in the face, and said, "I suppose you know that my cousin, Mr. Sands, has *given* her to my eldest daughter. She will make a nice waiting-maid for her when she grows up." I did not answer a word. How *could* she, who knew by experience the strength of a mother's love, and who was perfectly aware of the relation Mr. Sands bore to my children,—how *could* she look me in the face, while she thrust such a dagger into my heart?

I was no longer surprised that they had kept her in such a state of ignorance. Mr. Hobbs had formerly been wealthy, but he had failed, and afterwards obtained a subordinate situation in the Custom House. Perhaps they expected to return to the south some day; and Ellen's knowledge was quite sufficient for a slave's condition. I was impatient to go to work and earn money, that I might change the uncertain position of my children. Mr. Sands had not kept his promise to emancipate them. I had also been deceived about Ellen. What security had I with regard to Benjamin? I felt that I had none.

I returned to my friend's house in an uneasy state of mind. In order to protect my children, it was necessary that I should own myself. I called myself free, and sometimes felt so; but I knew I was insecure. I sat down that night and wrote a civil letter to Dr. Flint, asking him to state the lowest terms on which he would sell me; and as I belonged by law to his daughter, I wrote to her also, making a similar request.

Since my arrival at the north I had not been unmindful of my dear brother William. I had made diligent inquiries for him, and having heard of him in Boston, I went thither. When I arrived there, I found he had gone to New Bedford. I wrote to that place, and was informed he had gone on a whaling voyage, and would not return for some months. I went back to New York to get employment near Ellen. I received an answer from Dr. Flint, which gave me no encouragement. He advised me to return and submit myself to my rightful owners, and then any request I might make would be granted. I lent this letter to a friend, who lost it; otherwise I would present a copy to my readers.

XXXIII. A Home Found

My greatest anxiety now was to obtain employment. My health was greatly improved, though my limbs continued to trouble me with swelling whenever I walked much. The greatest difficulty in my way was, that those who employed strangers required a recommendation; and in my peculiar position, I could, of course, obtain no certificates from the families I had so faithfully served.

One day an acquaintance told me of a lady who wanted a nurse for her babe, and I immediately applied for the situation. The lady told me she preferred to have one who had been a mother, and accustomed to the care of infants. I told her I had nursed two babes of my own. She asked me many questions, but, to my great relief, did not require a recommendation from my former employers. She told me she was an English woman, and that was a pleasant circumstance to me, because I had heard they had less prejudice against color than Americans entertained. It was agreed that we should try each other for a week. The trial proved satisfactory to both parties, and I was engaged for a month.

The heavenly Father had been most merciful to me in leading me to this place. Mrs. Bruce was a kind and gentle lady, and proved a true and sympathizing friend. Before the stipulated month expired, the necessity of passing up and down stairs frequently, caused my limbs to swell so painfully, that I became unable to perform my duties. Many ladies would have thoughtlessly discharged me; but Mrs. Bruce made arrangements to save me steps, and employed a physician to attend upon me. I had not yet told her that I was a fugitive slave. She noticed that I was often sad, and kindly inquired the cause. I spoke of being separated from my children, and from relatives who were dear to me; but I did not mention the constant feeling of insecurity which oppressed my spirits. I longed for some one to confide in; but I had been so deceived by white people, that I had lost all confidence in them. If they spoke kind words to me, I thought it was for some selfish purpose. I had entered this family with the distrustful feelings I had brought with me out of slavery; but ere six months had passed, I found that the gentle deportment of Mrs. Bruce and the smiles of her lovely babe were thawing my chilled heart. My narrow mind also began to expand under the influences of her intelligent conversation, and the opportunities for reading, which were gladly allowed me whenever I had leisure from my duties. I gradually became more energetic and more cheerful.

The old feeling of insecurity, especially with regard to my children, often threw its dark shadow across my sunshine. Mrs. Bruce offered me a home for Ellen; but pleasant as it would have been, I did not dare to accept it, for fear of offending the Hobbs family. Their knowledge of my precarious situation placed me in their power; and I felt that it was important for me to keep on the right side of them, till, by dint of labor and economy, I could make a home for my children. I was far from feeling satisfied with Ellen's situation. She was not well cared for. She sometimes came to New York to visit me; but she generally brought a request from Mrs. Hobbs that I would buy her a pair of shoes, or some article of clothing. This was accompanied by a promise of payment when Mr. Hobbs's salary at the Custom House became due; but some how or other the pay-day never came. Thus many dollars of my earnings were expended to keep my child comfortably clothed. That, however, was a slight trouble, compared with the fear that their pecuniary embarrassments might induce them to sell my precious young daughter. I knew they were in constant communication with Southerners, and had frequent opportunities to do it. I have stated that when Dr. Flint put Ellen in jail, at two years old, she had an inflammation of the eyes, occasioned by measles. This disease still troubled her; and kind Mrs. Bruce proposed that she should come to New York for a while, to be under the care of Dr. Elliott, a well known oculist. It did not occur to me that there was any thing improper in a mother's making such a request; but Mrs. Hobbs was very angry, and refused to let her go. Situated as I was, it was not politic to insist upon it. I made no complaint, but I longed to be entirely free to act a mother's part towards my children. The next time I went over to Brooklyn, Mrs. Hobbs, as if to apologize for her anger, told me she had employed her own physician to attend to Ellen's eyes, and that she had refused my request because she did not consider it safe to trust her in New York. I accepted the explanation in silence; but she had told me that my child *belonged* to her daughter, and I suspected that her real motive was a fear of my conveying her property away from her. Perhaps I did her injustice; but my knowledge of Southerners made it difficult for me to feel otherwise.

Sweet and bitter were mixed in the cup of my life, and I was thankful that it had ceased to be entirely bitter. I loved Mrs. Bruce's babe. When it laughed and crowed in my face, and twined its little tender arms confidingly about my neck, it made me think of the time when Benny and Ellen were babies, and my wounded heart was soothed. One bright morning, as I stood at the window, tossing baby in my arms, my attention was attracted by a young man in sailor's dress, who was closely observing every house as he passed. I looked at him earnestly. Could it be my brother William? It *must* be he — and yet, how changed! I placed the baby safely, flew down stairs, opened the front door, beckoned to the sailor, and in less than a minute I was clasped in my brother's arms. How much we had to tell each other! How we laughed, and how we cried, over each other's adventures! I took him to Brooklyn, and again saw him with Ellen, the dear child whom he had loved and tended so carefully, while I was shut up in my miserable den. He staid in New York a week. His old feelings of affection for me and Ellen were as lively as ever. There are no bonds so strong as those which are formed by suffering together.

XXXIV. The Old Enemy Again

My young mistress, Miss Emily Flint, did not return any answer to my letter requesting her to consent to my being sold. But after a while, I received a reply, which purported to be written by her younger brother. In order rightly to enjoy the contents of this letter, the reader must bear in mind that the Flint family supposed I had been at the north many years. They had no idea that I knew of the doctor's three excursions to New York in search of me; that I had heard his voice, when he came to borrow five hundred dollars for that purpose; and that I had seen him pass on his way to the steamboat. Neither were they aware that all the particulars of aunt Nancy's death and burial were conveyed to me at the time they occurred. I have kept the letter, of which I herewith subjoin a copy:—

"Your letter to sister was received a few days ago. I gather from it that you are desirous of returning to your native place, among your friends and relatives. We were all gratified with the contents of your letter; and let me assure you that if any members of the family have had any feeling of resentment towards you, they feel it no longer. We all sympathize with you in your unfortunate condition, and are ready to do all in our power to make you contented and happy. It is difficult for you to return home as a free person. If you were purchased by your grandmother, it is doubtful whether you would be permitted to remain, although it would be lawful for you to do so. If a servant should be allowed to purchase herself, after absenting herself so long from her owners, and return free, it would have an injurious effect. From your letter, I think your situation must be hard and uncomfortable. Come home. You have it in your power to be reinstated in our affections. We would receive you with open arms and tears of joy. You need not apprehend any unkind treatment, as we have not put ourselves to any trouble or expense to get you. Had we done so, perhaps we should feel otherwise. You know my sister was always attached to you, and that you were never treated as a slave. You were never put to hard work, nor exposed to field labor. On the contrary, you were taken into the house, and treated as one of us, and almost as free; and we, at least, felt that you were above disgracing yourself by running away. Believing you may be induced to come home voluntarily has induced me to write for my sister. The family will be rejoiced to see you; and your poor old grandmother expressed a great desire to have you come, when she heard your letter read. In her old age she needs the consolation of having her children round her. Doubtless you have heard of the death of your aunt. She was a faithful servant, and a faithful member of the Episcopal church. In her Christian life she taught us how to live—and, O, too high the price of knowledge, she taught us how to die! Could you have seen us round her death bed, with her mother, all mingling our tears in one common stream, you would have thought the same heartfelt tie existed between a master and his servant, as between a mother and her child. But this subject is too painful to dwell upon. I must bring my letter to a close. If you are contented to stay away from your old grandmother, your child, and the friends who love you, stay where you are. We shall never trouble ourselves to apprehend you. But should you prefer to come home, we will do all that we can to make you happy. If you do not wish to remain in the family, I know that father, by our persuasion, will be induced to let you be purchased by any person you may choose in our community. You will please answer this as soon as possible, and let us know your decision. Sister sends much love to you. In the mean time believe me your sincere friend and well wisher."

This letter was signed by Emily's brother, who was as yet a mere lad. I knew, by the style, that it was not written by a person of his age, and though the writing was disguised, I had been made too unhappy by it, in former years, not to recognize at once the hand of Dr. Flint. O, the hypocrisy of slaveholders! Did the old fox suppose I was goose enough to go into such a trap? Verily, he relied too much on "the stupidity of the African race." I did not return the family of Flints any thanks for their cordial invitation—a remissness for which I was, no doubt, charged with base ingratitude.

Not long afterwards I received a letter from one of my friends at the south, informing me that Dr. Flint was about to visit the north. The letter had been delayed, and I supposed he might be already on the way. Mrs. Bruce did not know I was a fugitive. I told her that important business called me to Boston, where my brother then was, and asked permission to bring a friend to supply my place as nurse, for a fortnight. I started on my journey immediately; and as soon as I arrived, I wrote to my grandmother that if Benny came, he must be sent to Boston. I knew she was only waiting for a good chance to send him north, and, fortunately, she had the legal power to do so, without asking leave of any body. She was a free woman; and when my children were purchased, Mr. Sands preferred to have the bill of sale drawn up in her name. It was conjectured that he advanced the money, but it was not known. At the south, a gentleman may have a shoal of colored children without any disgrace; but if he is known to purchase them, with the view of setting them free, the example is thought to be dangerous to their "peculiar institution," and he becomes unpopular.

There was a good opportunity to send Benny in a vessel coming directly to New York. He was put on board with a letter to a friend, who was requested to see him off to Boston. Early one morning, there was a loud rap at my door, and in rushed Benjamin, all out of breath. "O mother!" he exclaimed, "here I am! I run all the way; and I come all alone. How d'you do?"

O reader, can you imagine my joy? No, you cannot, unless you have been a slave mother. Benjamin rattled away as fast as his tongue could go. "Mother, why don't you bring Ellen here? I went over to Brooklyn to see her, and she felt very bad when I bid her good by. She said, 'O Ben, I wish I was going too.' I thought she'd know ever so much; but she don't know so much as I do; for I can read, and she can't. And, mother, I lost all my clothes coming. What can I do to get some more? I 'spose free boys can get along here at the north as well as white boys."

I did not like to tell the sanguine, happy little fellow how much he was mistaken. I took him to a tailor, and procured a change of clothes. The rest of the day was spent in mutual asking and answering of questions, with the wish constantly repeated that the good old grandmother was with us, and frequent injunctions from Benny to write to her immediately, and be sure to tell her every thing about his voyage, and his journey to Boston.

Dr. Flint made his visit to New York, and made every exertion to call upon me, and invite me to return with him; but not being able to ascertain where I was, his hospitable intentions were frustrated, and the affectionate family, who were waiting for me with "open arms," were doomed to disappointment.

As soon as I knew he was safely at home, I placed Benjamin in the care of my brother William, and returned to Mrs. Bruce. There I remained through the winter and spring, endeavoring to perform my duties faithfully, and finding a good degree of happiness in the attractions of baby Mary, the considerate kindness of her excellent mother, and occasional interviews with my darling daughter.

But when summer came, the old feeling of insecurity haunted me. It was necessary for me to take little Mary out daily, for exercise and fresh air, and the city was swarming with Southerners, some of whom might recognize me. Hot weather brings out snakes and slaveholders, and I like one class of the venomous creatures as little as I do the other. What a comfort it is, to be free to *say* so!

XXXV. Prejudice against Color

It was a relief to my mind to see preparations for leaving the city. We went to Albany in the steamboat Knickerbocker. When the gong sounded for tea, Mrs. Bruce said, "Linda, it is late, and you and baby had better come to the table with me." I replied, "I know it is time baby had her supper, but I had rather not go with you, if you please. I am afraid of being insulted." "O no, not if you are with *me*," she said. I saw several white nurses go with their ladies, and I ventured to do the same. We were at the extreme end of the table. I was no sooner seated, than a gruff voice said, "Get up! You know you are not allowed to sit here." I looked up, and, to my astonishment and indignation, saw that the speaker was a colored man. If his office required him to enforce the by-laws of the boat, he might, at least, have done it politely. I replied, "I shall not get up, unless the captain comes and takes me up." No cup of tea was offered me, but Mrs. Bruce handed me hers and called for another. I looked to see whether the other nurses were treated in a similar manner. They were all properly waited on.

Next morning, when we stopped at Troy for breakfast, every body was making a rush for the table. Mrs. Bruce said, "Take my arm, Linda, and we'll go in together." The landlord heard her, and said, "Madam, will you allow your nurse and baby to take breakfast with my family?" I knew this was to be attributed to my complexion; but he spoke courteously, and therefore I did not mind it.

At Saratoga we found the United States Hotel crowded, and Mr. Bruce took one of the cottages belonging to the hotel. I had thought, with gladness, of going to the quiet of the country, where I should meet few people, but here I found myself in the midst of a swarm of Southerners. I looked round me with fear and trembling, dreading to see some one who would recognize me. I was rejoiced to find that we were to stay but a short time.

We soon returned to New York, to make arrangements for spending the remainder of the summer at Rockaway. While the laundress was putting the clothes in order, I took an opportunity to go over to Brooklyn to see Ellen. I met her going to a grocery store, and the first words she said, were, "O, mother, don't go to Mrs. Hobbs's. Her brother, Mr. Thorne, has come from the south, and may be he'll tell where you are." I accepted the warning. I told her I was going away with Mrs. Bruce the next day, and would try to see her when I came back.

Being in servitude to the Anglo-Saxon race, I was not put into a "Jim Crow car," on our way to Rockaway, neither was I invited to ride through the streets on the top of trunks in a truck; but every where I found the same manifestations of that cruel prejudice, which so discourages the feelings, and represses the energies of the colored people. We reached Rockaway before dark, and put up at the Pavilion—a large hotel, beautifully situated by the sea-side—a great resort of the fashionable world. Thirty or forty nurses were there, of a great variety of nations. Some of the ladies had colored waiting-maids and coachmen, but I was the only nurse tinged with the blood of Africa. When the tea bell rang, I took little Mary and followed the other nurses. Supper was served in a long hall. A young man, who had the ordering of things, took the circuit of the table two or three times, and finally pointed me to a seat at the lower end of it. As there was but one chair, I sat down and took the child in my lap. Whereupon the young man came to me and said, in the blandest manner possible, "Will you please to seat the little girl in the chair, and stand behind it and feed her? After they have done, you will be shown to the kitchen, where you will have a good supper."

This was the climax! I found it hard to preserve my self-control, when I looked round, and saw women who were nurses, as I was, and only one shade lighter in complexion, eyeing me with a defiant look, as if my presence were a contamination. However, I said nothing. I quietly took the child in my arms, went to our room, and refused to go to the table again. Mr. Bruce ordered meals to be sent to the room for little Mary and I. This answered for a few days; but the waiters of the establishment were white, and they soon began to complain, saying they were not hired to wait on negroes. The landlord requested Mr. Bruce to send me down to my meals, because his servants rebelled against bringing them up, and the colored servants of other boarders were dissatisfied because all were not treated alike.

My answer was that the colored servants ought to be dissatisfied with *themselves*, for not having too much self-respect to submit to such treatment; that there was no difference in the price of board for colored and white servants, and there was no justification for difference of treatment. I said a month after this, and finding I was resolved to stand up for my rights, they concluded to treat me well. Let every colored man and woman do this, and eventually we shall cease to be trampled under foot by our oppressors.

XXXVI. The Hairbreadth Escape

After we returned to New York, I took the earliest opportunity to go and see Ellen. I asked to have her called down stairs; for I supposed Mrs. Hobb's southern brother might still be there, and I was desirous to avoid seeing him, if possible. But Mrs. Hobbs came to the kitchen, and insisted on my going up stairs. "My brother wants to see you," said she, "and he is sorry you seem to shun him. He knows you are living in New York. He told me to say to you that he owes thanks to good old aunt Martha for too many little acts of kindness for him to be base enough to betray her grandchild."

This Mr. Thorne had become poor and reckless long before he left the south, and such persons had much rather go to one of the faithful old slaves to borrow a dollar, or get a good dinner, than to go to one whom they consider an equal. It was such acts of kindness as these for which he professed to feel grateful to my grandmother. I wished he had kept at a distance, but as he was here, and knew where I was, I concluded there was nothing to be gained by trying to avoid him; on the contrary, it might be the means of exciting his ill will. I followed his sister up stairs. He met me in a very friendly manner, congratulated me on my escape from slavery, and hoped I had a good place, where I felt happy.

I continued to visit Ellen as often as I could. She, good thoughtful child, never forgot my hazardous situation, but always kept a vigilant lookout for my safety. She never made any complaint about her own inconveniences and troubles; but a mother's observing eye easily perceived that she was not happy. On the occasion of one of my visits I found her unusually serious. When I asked her what was the matter, she said nothing was the matter. But I insisted upon knowing what made her look so very grave. Finally, I ascertained that she felt troubled about the dissipation that was continually going on in the house. She was sent to the store very often for rum and brandy, and she felt ashamed to ask for it so often; and Mr. Hobbs and Mr. Thorne drank a great deal, and their hands trembled so that they had to call her to pour out the liquor for them. "But for all that," said she, "Mr. Hobbs is good to me, and I can't help liking him. I feel sorry for him." I tried to comfort her, by telling her that I had laid up a hundred dollars, and that before long I hoped to be able to give her and Benjamin a home, and send them to school. She was always desirous not to add to my troubles more than she could help, and I did not discover till years afterwards that Mr. Thorne's intemperance was not the only annoyance she suffered from him. Though he professed too much gratitude to my grandmother to injure any of her descendants, he had poured vile language into the ears of her innocent great-grandchild.

I usually went to Brooklyn to spend Sunday afternoon. One Sunday, I found Ellen anxiously waiting for me near the house. "O, mother," said she, "I've been waiting for you this long time. I'm afraid Mr. Thorne has written to tell Dr. Flint where you are. Make haste and come in. Mrs. Hobbs will tell you all about it!"

The story was soon told. While the children were playing in the grape-vine arbor, the day before, Mr. Thorne came out with a letter in his hand, which he tore up and scattered about. Ellen was sweeping the yard at the time, and having her mind full of suspicions of him, she picked up the pieces and carried them to the children, saying, "I wonder who Mr. Thorne has been writing to."

"I'm sure I don't know, and don't care," replied the oldest of the children; "and I don't see how it concerns you."

"But it does concern me," replied Ellen; "for I'm afraid he's been writing to the south about my mother."

They laughed at her, and called her a silly thing, but good-naturedly put the fragments of writing together, in order to read them to her. They were no sooner arranged, than the little girl exclaimed, "I declare, Ellen, I believe you are right."

The contents of Mr. Thorne's letter, as nearly as I can remember, were as follows: "I have seen your slave, Linda, and conversed with her. She can be taken very easily, if you manage prudently. There are enough of us here to swear to her identity as your property. I am a patriot, a lover of my country, and I do this as an act of justice to the laws." He concluded by informing the doctor of the street and number where I lived. The children carried the pieces to Mrs. Hobbs, who immediately went to her brother's room for an explanation. He was not to be found. The servants said they saw him go out with a letter in his hand, and they supposed he had gone to the post office. The natural inference was, that he had sent to Dr. Flint a copy of those fragments. When he returned, his sister accused him of it, and he did not deny the charge. He went immediately to his room, and the next morning he was missing. He had gone over to New York, before any of the family were astir.

It was evident that I had no time to lose; and I hastened back to the city with a heavy heart. Again I was to be torn from a comfortable home, and all my plans for the welfare of my children were to be frustrated by that demon Slavery! I now regretted that I never told Mrs. Bruce my story. I had not concealed it merely on account of being a fugitive; that would have made her anxious, but it would have excited sympathy in her kind heart. I valued her good opinion, and I was afraid of losing it, if I told her all the particulars of my sad story. But now I felt that it was necessary for her to know how I was situated. I had once left her abruptly, without explaining the reason, and it would not be proper to do it again. I went home resolved to tell her in the morning. But the sadness of my face attracted her attention, and, in answer to her kind inquiries, I poured out my full heart to her, before bed time. She listened with true womanly sympathy, and told me she would do all she could to protect me. How my heart blessed her!

Early the next morning, Judge Vanderpool and Lawyer Hopper were consulted. They said I had better leave the city at once, as the risk would be great if the case came to trial. Mrs. Bruce took me in a carriage to the house of one of her friends, where she assured me I should be safe until my brother could arrive, which would be in a few days. In the interval my thoughts were much occupied with Ellen. She was mine by birth, and she was also mine by Southern law, since my grandmother held the bill of sale that made her so. I did not feel that she was safe unless I had her with me. Mrs. Hobbs, who felt badly about her brother's treachery, yielded to my entreaties, on condition that she should return in ten days. I avoided making any promise. She came to me clad in very thin garments, all outgrown, and with a school satchel on her arm, containing a few articles. It was late in October, and I knew the child must suffer; and not daring to go out in the streets to purchase any thing, I took off my own flannel skirt and converted it into one for her. Kind Mrs. Bruce came to bid me good by, and when she saw that I had taken off my clothing for my child, the tears came to her eyes. She said, "Wait for me, Linda," and went out. She soon returned with a nice warm shawl and hood for Ellen. Truly, of such souls as hers are the kingdom of heaven.

My brother reached New York on Wednesday. Lawyer Hopper advised us to go to Boston by the Stonington route, as there was less Southern travel in that direction. Mrs. Bruce directed her servants to tell all inquirers that I formerly lived there, but had gone from the city.

We reached the steamboat Rhode Island in safety. That boat employed colored hands, but I knew that colored passengers were not admitted to the cabin. I was very desirous for the seclusion of the cabin, not only on account of exposure to the night air, but also to avoid observation. Lawyer Hopper was waiting on board for us. He spoke to the stewardess, and asked, as a particular favor, that she would treat us well. He said to me, "Go and speak to the captain yourself by and by. Take your little girl with you, and I am sure that he will not let her sleep on deck." With these kind words and a shake of the hand he departed.

The boat was soon on her way, bearing me rapidly from the friendly home where I had hoped to find security and rest. My brother had left me to purchase the tickets, thinking that I might have better success than he would. When the stewardess came to me, I paid what she asked, and she gave me three tickets with clipped corners. In the most unsophisticated manner I said, "You have made a mistake; I asked you for cabin tickets. I cannot possibly consent to sleep on deck with my little daughter." She assured me there was no mistake. She said on some of the routes colored people were allowed to sleep in the cabin, but not on this route, which was much travelled by the wealthy. I asked her to show me to the captain's office, and she said she would after tea. When the time came, I took Ellen by the hand and went to the captain, politely requesting him to change our tickets, as we should be very uncomfortable on deck. He said it was contrary to their custom, but he would see that we had berths below; he would also try to obtain comfortable seats for us in the cars; of that he was not certain, but he would speak to the conductor about it, when the boat arrived. I thanked him, and returned to the ladies' cabin. He came afterwards and told me that the conductor of the cars was on board, that he had spoken to him, and he had promised to take care of us. I was very much surprised at receiving so much kindness. I don't know whether the pleasing face of my little girl had won his heart, or whether the stewardess inferred from Lawyer Hopper's manner that I was a fugitive, and had pleaded with him in my behalf.

When the boat arrived at Stonington, the conductor kept his promise, and showed us to seats in the first car, nearest the engine. He asked us to take seats next the door, but as he passed through, we ventured to move on toward the other end of the car. No incivility was offered us, and we reached Boston in safety.

The day after my arrival was one of the happiest of my life. I felt as if I was beyond the reach of the bloodhounds; and, for the first time during many years, I had both my children together with me. They greatly enjoyed their reunion, and laughed and chatted merrily. I watched them with a swelling heart. Their every motion delighted me.

I could not feel safe in New York, and I accepted the offer of a friend, that we should share expenses and keep house together. I represented to Mrs. Hobbs that Ellen must have some schooling, and must remain with me for that purpose. She felt ashamed of being unable to read or spell at her age, so instead of sending her to school with Benny, I instructed her myself till she was fitted to enter an intermediate school. The winter passed pleasantly, while I was busy with my needle, and my children with their books.

XXXVII. A Visit to England

In the spring, sad news came to me. Mrs. Bruce was dead. Never again, in this world, should I see her gentle face, or hear her sympathizing voice. I had lost an excellent friend, and little Mary had lost a tender mother. Mr. Bruce wished the child to visit some of her mother's relatives in England, and he was desirous that I should take charge of her. The little motherless one was accustomed to me, and attached to me, and I thought she would be happier in my care than in that of a stranger. I could also earn more in this way than I could by my needle. So I put Benny to a trade, and left Ellen to remain in the house with my friend and go to school.

We sailed from New York, and arrived in Liverpool after a pleasant voyage of twelve days. We proceeded directly to London, and took lodgings at the Adelaide Hotel. The supper seemed to me less luxurious than those I had seen in American hotels; but my situation was indescribably more pleasant. For the first time in my life I was in a place where I was treated according to my deportment, without reference to my complexion. I felt as if a great millstone had been lifted from my breast. Ensconced in a pleasant room, with my dear little charge, I laid my head on my pillow, for the first time, with the delightful consciousness of pure, unadulterated freedom.

As I had constant care of the child, I had little opportunity to see the wonders of that great city; but I watched the tide of life that flowed through the streets, and found it a strange contrast to the stagnation in our Southern towns. Mr. Bruce took his little daughter to spend some days with friends in Oxford Crescent, and of course it was necessary for me to accompany her. I had heard much of the systematic method of English education, and I was very desirous that my dear Mary should steer straight in the midst of so much propriety. I closely observed her little playmates and their nurses, being ready to take any lessons in the science of good management. The children were more rosy than American children, but I did not see that they differed materially in other respects. They were like all children—sometimes docile and sometimes wayward.

We next went to Steventon, in Berkshire. It was a small town, said to be the poorest in the county. I saw men working in the fields for six shillings, and seven shillings, a week, and women for sixpence, and sevenpence, a day, out of which they boarded themselves. Of course they lived in the most primitive manner; it could not be otherwise, where a woman's wages for an entire day were not sufficient to buy a pound of meat. They paid very low rents, and their clothes were made of the cheapest fabrics, though much better than could have been procured in the United States for the same money. I had heard much about the oppression of the poor in Europe. The people I saw around me were, many of them, among the poorest poor. But when I visited them in their little thatched cottages, I felt that the condition of even the meanest and most ignorant among them was vastly superior to the condition of the most favored slaves in America. They labored hard; but they were not ordered out to toil while the stars were in the sky, and driven and slashed by an overseer, through heat and cold, till the stars shone out again. Their homes were very humble; but they were protected by law. No insolent patrols could come, in the dead of night, and flog them at their pleasure. The father, when he closed his cottage door, felt safe with his family around him. No master or overseer could come and take from him his wife, or his daughter. They must separate to earn their living; but the parents knew where their children were going, and could communicate with them by letters. The relations of husband and wife, parent and child, were too sacred for the richest noble in the land to violate with impunity. Much was being done to enlighten these poor people. Schools were established among them, and benevolent societies were active in efforts to ameliorate their condition. There was no law forbidding them to learn to read and write; and if they helped each other in spelling out the Bible, they were in no danger of thirty-nine lashes, as was the case with myself and poor, pious, old uncle Fred. I repeat that the most ignorant and the most destitute of these peasants was a thousand fold better off than the most pampered American slave.

I do not deny that the poor are oppressed in Europe. I am not disposed to paint their condition so rose-colored as the Hon. Miss Murray[3] paints the condition of the slaves in the United States. A small portion of *my* experience would enable her to read her own pages with anointed eyes. If she were to lay aside her title, and, instead of visiting among the fashionable, become domesticated, as a poor governess, on some plantation in Louisiana or Alabama, she would see and hear things that would make her tell quite a different story.

My visit to England is a memorable event in my life, from the fact of my having there received strong religious impressions. The contemptuous manner in which the communion had been administered to colored people, in my native place; the church membership of Dr. Flint, and others like him; and the buying and selling of slaves, by professed ministers of the gospel, had given me a prejudice against the Episcopal church. The whole service seemed to me a mockery and a sham. But my home in Steventon was in the family of a clergyman, who was a true disciple of Jesus. The beauty of his daily life inspired me with faith in the genuineness of Christian professions. Grace entered my heart, and I knelt at the communion table, I trust, in true humility of soul.

I remained abroad ten months, which was much longer than I had an-

---

3. Amelia Matilda Murray (1795–1884), British author, portrayed slavery positively in her writings about her travels to the United States.

ticipated. During all that time, I never saw the slightest symptom of prejudice against color. Indeed, I entirely forgot it, till the time came for us to return to America.

XXXVIII. Renewed Invitations to Go South

We had a tedious winter passage, and from the distance spectres seemed to rise up on the shores of the United States. It is a sad feeling to be afraid of one's native country. We arrived in New York safely, and I hastened to Boston to look after my children. I found Ellen well, and improving at her school; but Benny was not there to welcome me. He had been left at a good place to learn a trade, and for several months every thing worked well. He was liked by the master, and was a favorite with his fellow-apprentices; but one day they accidentally discovered a fact they had never before suspected—that he was colored! This at once transformed him into a different being. Some of the apprentices were Americans, others American-born Irish; and it was offensive to their dignity to have a "nigger" among them, after they had been told that he *was* a "nigger." They began by treating him with silent scorn, and finding that he returned the same, they resorted to insults and abuse. He was too spirited a boy to stand that, and he went off. Being desirous to do something to support himself, and having no one to advise him, he shipped for a whaling voyage. When I received these tidings I shed many tears, and bitterly reproached myself for having left him so long. But I had done it for the best, and now all I could do was to pray to the heavenly Father to guide and protect him.

Not long after my return, I received the following letter from Miss Emily Flint, now Mrs. Dodge:—

"In this you will recognized the hand of your friend and mistress. Having heard that you had gone with a family to Europe, I have waited to hear of your return to write to you. I should have answered the letter you wrote to me long since, but as I could not then act independently of my father, I knew there could be nothing done satisfactory to you. There were persons here who were willing to buy you and run the risk of getting you. To this I would not consent. I have always been attached to you, and would not like to see you the slave of another, or have unkind treatment. I am married now, and can protect you. My husband expects to move to Virginia this spring, where we think of settling. I am very anxious that you should come and live with me. If you are not willing to come, you may purchase yourself; but I should prefer having you live with me. If you come, you may, if you like, spend a month with your grandmother and friends, then come to me in Norfolk, Virginia. Think this over, and write as soon as possible, and let me know the conclusion. Hoping that your children are well, I remain you friend and mistress."

Of course I did not write to return thanks for this cordial invitation. I felt insulted to be thought stupid enough to be caught by such professions.

> " 'Come up into my parlor,' said the spider to the fly;
> "Tis the prettiest little parlor that ever you did spy.' "[4]

It was plain that Dr. Flint's family were apprised of my movements, since they knew of my voyage to Europe. I expected to have further trouble from them; but having eluded them thus far, I hoped to be as successful in future. The money I had earned, I was desirous to devote to the education of my children, and to secure a home for them. It seemed not only hard, but unjust, to pay for myself. I could not possibly regard myself as a piece of property. Moreover, I had worked many years without wages, and during that time had been obliged to depend on my grandmother for many comforts in food and clothing. My children certainly belonged to me; but though Dr. Flint had incurred no expense for their support, he had received a large sum of money for them. I knew the law would decide that I was his property, and would probably still give his daughter a claim to my children; but I regarded such laws as the regulations of robbers, who had no rights that I was bound to respect.

The Fugitive Slave Law had not then passed. The judges of Massachusetts had not then stooped under chains to enter her courts of justice, so called. I knew my old master was rather skittish of Massachusetts. I relied on her love of freedom, and felt safe on her soil. I am now aware that I honored the old Commonwealth beyond her deserts.

XXXIX. The Confession

For two years my daughter and I supported ourselves comfortably in Boston. At the end of that time, my brother William offered to send Ellen to a boarding school. It required a great effort for me to consent to part with her, for I had few near ties, and it was her presence that made my two little rooms seem home-like. But my judgment prevailed over my selfish feelings. I made preparations for her departure. During the two years we had lived together I had often resolved to tell her something about her father; but I had never been able to muster sufficient courage. I had a shrinking dread of diminishing my child's love. I knew she must

---

4. Reference to Mary Howitt's poem *The Spider and the Fly* (1844), which ends with the following lesson: "And now, dear little children, who may this story read, / To idle, silly flattering words I pray you ne'er give heed; / Unto an evil counselor close heart and ear and eye, / And take a lesson from this tale of the spider and the fly."

have curiosity on the subject, but she had never asked a question. She was always very careful not to say any thing to remind me of my troubles. Now that she was going from me, I thought if I should die before she returned, she might hear my story from some one who did not understand the palliating circumstances; and that if she were entirely ignorant on the subject, her sensitive nature might receive a rude shock.

When we retired for the night, she said, "Mother, it is very hard to leave you alone. I am almost sorry I am going, though I do want to improve myself. But you will write to me often; won't you, mother?"

I did not throw my arms round her. I did not answer her. But in a calm, solemn way, for it cost me great effort, I said, "Listen to me, Ellen; I have something to tell you!" I recounted my early sufferings in slavery, and told her how nearly they had crushed me. I began to tell her how they had driven me into a great sin, when she clasped me in her arms, and exclaimed, "O, don't, mother! Please don't tell me any more."

I said, "But, my child, I want you to know about your father."

"I know all about it, mother," she replied; "I am nothing to my father, and he is nothing to me. All my love is for you. I was with him five months in Washington, and he never cared for me. He never spoke to me as he did to his little Fanny. I knew all the time he was my father, for Fanny's nurse told me so; but she said I must never tell any body, and I never did. I used to wish he would take me in his arms and kiss me, as he did Fanny; or that he would sometimes smile at me, as he did at her. I thought if he was my own father, he ought to love me. I was a little girl then, and didn't know any better. But now I never think any thing about my father. All my love is for you." She hugged me closer as she spoke, and I thanked God that the knowledge I had so much dreaded to impart had not diminished the affection of my child. I had not the slightest idea she knew that portion of my history. If I had, I should have spoken to her long before; for my pent-up feelings had often longed to pour themselves out to some one I could trust. But I loved the dear girl better for the delicacy she had manifested towards her unfortunate mother.

The next morning, she and her uncle started on their journey to the village in New York, where she was to be placed at school. It seemed as if all the sunshine had gone away. My little room was dreadfully lonely. I was thankful when a message came from a lady, accustomed to employ me, requesting me to come and sew in her family for several weeks. On my return, I found a letter from brother William. He thought of opening an anti-slavery reading room in Rochester, and combining with it the sale of some books and stationery; and he wanted me to unite with him. We tried it, but it was not successful. We found warm anti-slavery friends there, but the feeling was not general enough to support such an establishment. I passed nearly a year in the family of Isaac and Amy Post,[5] prac-

---

5. Amy Post (1802–1889), Quaker abolitionist and women's rights activist.

tical believers in the Christian doctrine of human brotherhood. They measured a man's worth by his character, not by his complexion. The memory of those beloved and honored friends will remain with me to my latest hour.

XL. The Fugitive Slave Law[6]

My brother, being disappointed in his project, concluded to go to California; and it was agreed that Benjamin should go with him. Ellen liked her school, and was a great favorite there. They did not know her history, and she did not tell it, because she had no desire to make capital out of their sympathy. But when it was accidentally discovered that her mother was a fugitive slave, every method was used to increase her advantages and diminish her expenses.

I was alone again. It was necessary for me to be earning money, and I preferred that it should be among those who knew me. On my return from Rochester, I called at the house of Mr. Bruce, to see Mary, the darling little babe that had thawed my heart, when it was freezing into a cheerless distrust of all my fellow-beings. She was growing a tall girl now, but I loved her always. Mr. Bruce had married again, and it was proposed that I should become nurse to a new infant. I had but one hesitation, and that was my feeling of insecurity in New York, now greatly increased by the passage of the Fugitive Slave Law. However, I resolved to try the experiment. I was again fortunate in my employer. The new Mrs. Bruce was an American, brought up under aristocratic influences; and still living in the midst of them; but if she had any prejudice against color, I was never made aware of it; and as for the system of slavery, she had a most hearty dislike of it. No sophistry of Southerners could blind her to its enormity. She was a person of excellent principles and a noble heart. To me, from that hour to the present, she has been a true and sympathizing friend. Blessings be with her and hers!

About the time that I reëntered the Bruce family an event occurred of disastrous import to the colored people. The slave Hamlin,[7] the first fugitive that came under the new law, was given up by the bloodhounds of the north to the bloodhounds of the south. It was the beginning of a reign of terror to the colored population. The great city rushed on in its whirl of excitement, taking no note of the "short and simple annals of the poor."[8] But while fashionables were listening to

---

6. Part of the set of laws known as the "Compromise of 1850," this law made it a federal crime to help fugitive slaves.
7. James Hamelt was purportedly the first person recaptured in New York under the provisions of the Fugitive Slave Act.
8. From Thomas Gray's "Elegy Written in a Country Churchyard."

the thrilling voice of Jenny Lind[9] in Metropolitan Hall, the thrilling voices of poor hunted colored people went up, in an agony of supplication, to the Lord, from Zion's church. Many families, who had lived in the city for twenty years, fled from it now. Many a poor washerwoman, who, by hard labor, had made herself a comfortable home, was obliged to sacrifice her furniture, bid a hurried farewell to friends, and seek her fortune among strangers in Canada. Many a wife discovered a secret she had never known before—that her husband was a fugitive, and must leave her to insure his own safety. Worse still, many a husband discovered that his wife had fled from slavery years ago, and as "the child follows the condition of its mother," the children of his love were liable to be seized and carried into slavery. Every where, in those humble homes, there was consternation and anguish. But what cared the legislators of the "dominant race" for the blood they were crushing out of trampled hearts?

When my brother William spent his last evening with me, before he went to California, we talked nearly all the time of the distress brought on our oppressed people by the passage of this iniquitous law; and never had I seen him manifest such bitterness of spirit, such stern hostility to our oppressors. He was himself free from the operation of the law; for he did not run from any Slaveholding State, being brought into the Free States by his master. But I was subject to it; and so were hundreds of intelligent and industrious people all around us. I seldom ventured into the streets; and when it was necessary to do an errand for Mrs. Bruce, or any of the family, I went as much as possible through back streets and by-ways. What a disgrace to a city calling itself free, that inhabitants, guiltless of offence, and seeking to perform their duties conscientiously, should be condemned to live in such incessant fear, and have nowhere to turn for protection! This state of things, of course, gave rise to many impromptu vigilance committees. Every colored person, and every friend of their persecuted race, kept their eyes wide open. Every evening I examined the newspapers carefully, to see what Southerners had put up at the hotels. I did this for my own sake, thinking my young mistress and her husband might be among the list; I wished also to give information to others, if necessary; for if many were "running to and fro," I resolved that "knowledge should be increased."[1]

This brings up one of my Southern reminiscences, which I will here briefly relate. I was somewhat acquainted with a slave named Luke, who belonged to a wealthy man in our vicinity. His master died, leaving a son and daughter heirs to his large fortune. In the division of the slaves, Luke was included in the son's portion. This young man became a prey to the vices growing out of the "patriarchal institution,"

9. Popular entertainer known as "The Swedish Soprano."
1. Daniel 12.4. The prophet describes the situation at the time of Israel's deliverance.

and when he went to the north, to complete his education, he carried his vices with him. He was brought home, deprived of the use of his limbs, by excessive dissipation. Luke was appointed to wait upon his bed-ridden master, whose despotic habits were greatly increased by exasperation at his own helplessness. He kept a cowhide beside him, and, for the most trivial occurrence, he would order his attendant to bare his back, and kneel beside the couch, while he whipped him till his strength was exhausted. Some days he was not allowed to wear any thing but his shirt, in order to be in readiness to be flogged. A day seldom passed without his receiving more or less blows. If the slightest resistance was offered, the town constable was sent for to execute the punishment, and Luke learned from experience how much more the constable's strong arm was to be dreaded than the comparatively feeble one of his master. The arm of his tyrant grew weaker, and was finally palsied; and then the constable's services were in constant requisition. The fact that he was entirely dependent on Luke's care, and was obliged to be tended like an infant, instead of inspiring any gratitude or compassion towards his poor slave, seemed only to increase his irritability and cruelty. As he lay there on his bed, a mere degraded wreck of manhood, he took into his head the strangest freaks of despotism; and if Luke hesitated to submit to his orders, the constable was immediately sent for. Some of these freaks were of a nature too filthy to be repeated. When I fled from the house of bondage, I left poor Luke still chained to the bedside of this cruel and disgusting wretch.

One day, when I had been requested to do an errand for Mrs. Bruce, I was hurrying through back streets, as usual, when I saw a young man approaching, whose face was familiar to me. As he came nearer, I recognized Luke. I always rejoiced to see or hear of any one who had escaped from the black pit; but, remembering this poor fellow's extreme hardships, I was peculiarly glad to see him on Northern soil, though I no longer called it *free* soil. I well remembered what a desolate feeling it was to be alone among strangers, and I went up to him and greeted him cordially. At first, he did not know me; but when I mentioned my name, he remembered all about me. I told him of the Fugitive Slave Law, and asked him if he did not know that New York was a city of kidnappers.

He replied, "De risk ain't so bad for me, as 'tis fur you. 'Cause I runned away from de speculator, and you runned away from de massa. Dem speculators vont spen dar money to come here fur a runaway, if dey ain't sartin sure to put dar hans right on him. An I tell you I's tuk good car 'bout dat. I had too hard times down dar, to let 'em ketch dis nigger."

He then told me of the advice he had received, and the plans he had laid. I asked if he had money enough to take him to Canada. "'Pend upon it, I hab," he replied. "I tuk car fur dat. I'd bin workin all my days fur dem cussed whites, an got no pay but kicks and cuffs. So I tought dis nigger had a right to money nuff to bring him to de Free States. Massa Henry he lib till ebery body vish him dead; an ven he did die, I knowed de debbil would hab him, an vouldn't vant him to bring his money 'long too. So I tuk some of his bills, and put 'em in de pocket of his ole trousers. An ven he was buried, dis nigger ask fur dem ole trousers, an dey gub 'em to me." With a low, chuckling laugh, he added, "You see I didn't *steal* it; dey *gub* it to me. I tell you, I had mighty hard time to keep de speculator from findin it; but he didn't git it."

This is a fair specimen of how the moral sense is educated by slavery. When a man has his wages stolen from him, year after year, and the laws sanction and enforce the theft, how can he be expected to have more regard to honesty than has the man who robs him? I have become somewhat enlightened, but I confess that I agree with poor, ignorant, much-abused Luke, in thinking he had a *right* to that money, as a portion of his unpaid wages. He went to Canada forthwith, and I have not since heard from him.

All that winter I lived in a state of anxiety. When I took the children out to breathe the air, I closely observed the countenances of all I met. I dreaded the approach of summer, when snakes and slaveholders make their appearance. I was, in fact, a slave in New York, as subject to slave laws as I had been in a Slave State. Strange incongruity in a State called free!

Spring returned, and I received warning from the south that Dr. Flint knew of my return to my old place, and was making preparations to have me caught. I learned afterwards that my dress, and that of Mrs. Bruce's children, had been described to him by some of the Northern tools, which slaveholders employ for their base purposes, and then indulge in sneers at their cupidity and mean servility.

I immediately informed Mrs. Bruce of my danger, and she took prompt measures for my safety. My place as nurse could not be supplied immediately, and this generous, sympathizing lady proposed that I should carry her baby away. It was a comfort to me to have the child with me; for the heart is reluctant to be torn away from every object it loves. But how few mothers would have consented to have one of their own babes become a fugitive, for the sake of a poor, hunted nurse, on whom the legislators of the country had let loose the bloodhounds! When I spoke of the sacrifice she was making, in depriving herself of her dear baby, she replied, "It is better for you to have baby with you, Linda; for if they get on your track, they will be obliged to bring the child to me; and then, if there is a possibility of saving you, you shall be saved."

This lady had a very wealthy relative, a benevolent gentleman in many respects, but aristocratic and proslavery. He remonstrated with her for harboring a fugitive slave; told her she was violating the laws of her country; and asked her if she was aware of the penalty. She replied, "I am very well aware of it. It is imprisonment and one thousand dollars fine. Shame on my country that it *is* so! I am ready to incur the penalty. I will go to the state's prison, rather than have any poor victim torn from *my* house, to be carried back to slavery."

The noble heart! The brave heart! The tears are in my eyes while I write of her. May the God of the helpless reward her for her sympathy with my persecuted people!

I was sent into New England, where I was sheltered by the wife of a senator, whom I shall always hold in grateful remembrance. This honorable gentleman would not have voted for the Fugitive Slave Law, as did the senator in "Uncle Tom's Cabin;" on the contrary, he was strongly opposed to it; but he was enough under its influence to be afraid of having me remain in his house many hours. So I was sent into the country, where I remained a month with the baby. When it was supposed that Dr. Flint's emissaries had lost track of me, and given up the pursuit for the present, I returned to New York.

XLI. Free at Last

Mrs. Bruce, and every member of her family, were exceedingly kind to me. I was thankful for the blessings of my lot, yet I could not always wear a cheerful countenance. I was doing harm to no one; on the contrary, I was doing all the good I could in my small way; yet I could never go out to breathe God's free air without trepidation at my heart. This seemed hard; and I could not think it was a right state of things in any civilized country.

From time to time I received news from my good old grandmother. She could not write; but she employed others to write for her. The following is an extract from one of her last letters:—

"Dear Daughter: I cannot hope to see you again on earth; but I pray to God to unite us above, where pain will no more rack this feeble body of mine; where sorrow and parting from my children will be no more. God has promised these things if we are faithful unto the end. My age and feeble health deprive me of going to church now; but God is with me here at home. Thank your brother for his kindness. Give much love to him, and tell him to remember the Creator in the days of his youth, and strive to meet me in the Father's kingdom. Love to Ellen and Benjamin. Don't neglect him. Tell him for me, to be a good boy. Strive, my child, to train them for God's children. May he protect and provide for you, is the prayer of your loving old mother."

These letters both cheered and saddened me. I was always glad to have tidings from the kind, faithful old friend of my unhappy youth; but her messages of love made my heart yearn to see her before she died, and I mourned over the fact that it was impossible. Some months after I returned from my flight to New England, I received a letter from her, in which she wrote, "Dr. Flint is dead. He has left a distressed family. Poor old man! I hope he made his peace with God."

I remembered how he had defrauded my grandmother of the hard earnings she had loaned; how he had tried to cheat her out of the freedom her mistress had promised her, and how he had persecuted her children; and I thought to myself that she was a better Christian than I was, if she could entirely forgive him. I cannot say, with truth, that the news of my old master's death softened my feelings towards him. There are wrongs which even the grave does not bury. The man was odious to me while he lived, and his memory is odious now.

His departure from this world did not diminish my danger. He had threatened my grandmother that his heirs should hold me in slavery after he was gone; that I never should be free so long as a child of his survived. As for Mrs. Flint, I had seen her in deeper afflictions than I supposed the loss of her husband would be, for she had buried several children; yet I never saw any signs of softening in her heart. The doctor had died in embarrassed circumstances, and had little to will to his heirs, except such property as he was unable to grasp. I was well aware what I had to expect from the family of Flints; and my fears were confirmed by a letter from the south, warning me to be on my guard, because Mrs. Flint openly declared that her daughter could not afford to lose so valuable a slave as I was.

I kept close watch of the newspapers for arrivals; but one Saturday night, being much occupied, I forgot to examine the Evening Express as usual. I went down into the parlor for it, early in the morning, and found the boy about to kindle a fire with it. I took it from him and examined the list of arrivals. Reader, if you have never been a slave, you cannot imagine the acute sensation of suffering at my heart, when I read the names of Mr. and Mrs. Dodge, at a hotel in Courtland Street. It was a third-rate hotel, and that circumstance convinced me of the truth of what I had heard, that they were short of funds and had need of my value, as *they* valued me; and that was by dollars and cents. I hastened with the paper to Mrs. Bruce. Her heart and hand were always open to every one in distress, and she always warmly sympathized with mine. It was impossible to tell how near the enemy was. He might have passed and repassed the house while we were sleeping. He might at that moment be waiting to pounce upon me if I ventured out of doors. I had never seen the husband of my young mistress, and therefore I could not distinguish him from any other stranger. A carriage was hastily ordered; and, closely veiled, I followed Mrs. Bruce, taking the baby again with me into exile. After various turnings and crossings, and returnings, the carriage stopped at the house of one of Mrs. Bruce's friends, where I was kindly received. Mrs. Bruce returned immediately, to instruct the domestics what to say if any one came to inquire for me.

It was lucky for me that the evening paper was not burned up before I had a chance to examine the list of arrivals. It was not long after Mrs.

Bruce's return to her house, before several people came to inquire for me. One inquired for me, another asked for my daughter Ellen, and another said he had a letter from my grandmother, which he was requested to deliver in person.

They were told, "She *has* lived here, but she has left."

"How long ago?"

"I don't know, sir."

"Do you know where she went?"

"I do not, sir." And the door was closed.

This Mr. Dodge, who claimed me as his property, was originally a Yankee pedler in the south; then he became a merchant, and finally a slaveholder. He managed to get introduced into what was called the first society, and married Miss Emily Flint. A quarrel arose between him and her brother, and the brother cowhided him. This led to a family feud, and he proposed to remove to Virginia. Dr. Flint left him no property, and his own means had become circumscribed, while a wife and children depended upon him for support. Under these circumstances, it was very natural that he should make an effort to put me into his pocket.

I had a colored friend, a man from my native place, in whom I had the most implicit confidence. I sent for him, and told him that Mr. and Mrs. Dodge had arrived in New York. I proposed that he should call upon them to make inquiries about his friends at the south, with whom Dr. Flint's family were well acquainted. He thought there was no impropriety in his doing so, and he consented. He went to the hotel, and knocked at the door of Mr. Dodge's room, which was opened by the gentleman himself, who gruffly inquired, "What brought you here? How came you to know I was in the city?"

"Your arrival was published in the evening papers, sir; and I called to ask Mrs. Dodge about my friends at home. I didn't suppose it would give any offence."

"Where's that negro girl, that belongs to my wife?"

"What girl, sir?"

"You know well enough. I mean Linda, that ran away from Dr. Flint's plantation, some years ago. I dare say you've seen her, and know where she is."

"Yes, sir, I've seen her, and know where she is. She is out of your reach, sir."

"Tell me where she is, or bring her to me, and I will give her a chance to buy her freedom."

"I don't think it would be of any use, sir. I have heard her say she would go to the ends of the earth, rather than pay any man or woman for her freedom, because she thinks she has a right to it. Besides, she couldn't do it, if she would, for she has spent her earnings to educate her children."

This made Mr. Dodge very angry, and some high words passed between them. My friend was afraid to come where I was; but in the course of the day I received a note from him. I supposed they had not come from the south, in the winter, for a pleasure excursion; and now the nature of their business was very plain.

Mrs. Bruce came to me and entreated me to leave the city the next morning. She said her house was watched, and it was possible that some clew to me might be obtained. I refused to take her advice. She pleaded with an earnest tenderness, that ought to have moved me; but I was in a bitter, disheartened mood. I was weary of flying from pillar to post. I had been chased during half my life, and it seemed as if the chase was never to end. There I sat, in that great city, guiltless of crime, yet not daring to worship God in any of the churches. I heard the bells ringing for afternoon service, and, with contemptuous sarcasm, I said, "Will the preachers take for their text, 'Proclaim liberty to the captive, and the opening of prison doors to them that are bound'? or will they preach from the text, 'Do unto others as ye would they should do unto you'?"[2] Oppressed Poles and Hungarians could find a safe refuge in that city; John Mitchell[3] was free to proclaim in the City Hall his desire for "a plantation well stocked with slaves;" but there I sat, an oppressed American, not daring to show my face. God forgive the black and bitter thoughts I indulged on that Sabbath day! The Scripture says, "Oppression makes even a wise man mad;"[4] and I was not wise.

I had been told that Mr. Dodge said his wife had never signed away her right to my children, and if he could not get me, he would take them. This it was, more than any thing else, that roused such a tempest in my soul. Benjamin was with his uncle William in California, but my innocent young daughter had come to spend a vacation with me. I thought of what I had suffered in slavery at her age, and my heart was like a tiger's when a hunter tries to seize her young.

Dear Mrs. Bruce! I seem to see the expression of her face, as she turned away discouraged by my obstinate mood. Finding her expostulations unavailing, she sent Ellen to entreat me. When ten o'clock in the evening arrived and Ellen had not returned, this watchful and unwearied friend became anxious. She came to us in a carriage, bringing a well-filled trunk for my journey—trusting that by this time I would listen to reason. I yielded to her, as I ought to have done before.

The next day, baby and I set out in a heavy snow storm, bound for New England again. I received letters from the City of Iniquity, addressed to me under an assumed name. In a few days one came from Mrs. Bruce, informing me that my new master was still searching for me, and that she intended to put an end to this persecution by buying my freedom. I felt grateful for the kindness that prompted this offer, but the idea was not so pleasant to me as might have been expected. The more my mind had be-

2. Isaiah 61.1, Matthew 7.12.
3. Irish activist.
4. Ecclesiastes 7.7.

come enlightened, the more difficult it was for me to consider myself an article of property; and to pay money to those who had so grievously oppressed me seemed like taking from my sufferings the glory of triumph. I wrote to Mrs. Bruce, thanking her, but saying that being sold from one owner to another seemed too much like slavery; that such a great obligation could not be easily cancelled; and that I preferred to go to my brother in California.

Without my knowledge, Mrs. Bruce employed a gentleman in New York to enter into negotiations with Mr. Dodge. He proposed to pay three hundred dollars down, if Mr. Dodge would sell me, and enter into obligations to relinquish all claim to me or my children forever after. He who called himself my master said he scorned so small an offer for such a valuable servant. The gentleman replied, "You can do as you choose, sir. If you reject this offer you will never get any thing; for the woman has friends who will convey her and her children out of the country."

Mr. Dodge concluded that "half a loaf was better than no bread," and he agreed to the proffered terms. By the next mail I received this brief letter from Mrs. Bruce: "I am rejoiced to tell you that the money for your freedom has been paid to Mr. Dodge. Come home to-morrow. I long to see you and my sweet babe."

My brain reeled as I read these lines. A gentleman near me said, "It's true; I have seen the bill of sale." "The bill of sale!" Those words struck me like a blow. So I was *sold* at last! A human being *sold* in the free city of New York! The bill of sale is on record, and future generations will learn from it that women were articles of traffic in New York, late in the nineteenth century of the Christian religion. It may hereafter prove a useful document to antiquaries, who are seeking to measure the progress of civilization in the United States. I well know the value of that bit of paper; but much as I love freedom, I do not like to look upon it. I am deeply grateful to the generous friend who procured it, but I despise the miscreant who demanded payment for what never rightfully belonged to him or his.

I had objected to having my freedom bought, yet I must confess that when it was done I felt as if a heavy load had been lifted from my weary shoulders. When I rode home in the cars I was no longer afraid to unveil my face and look at people as they passed. I should have been glad to have met Daniel Dodge himself; to have had him seen me and known me, that he might have mourned over the untoward circumstances which compelled him to sell me for three hundred dollars.

When I reached home, the arms of my benefactress were thrown round me, and our tears mingled. As soon as she could speak, she said, "O Linda, I'm so glad it's all over! You wrote to me as if you thought you were going to be transferred from one owner to another. But I did not buy you for your services. I should have done just the same, if you had been going to sail for California to-morrow. I should, at least, have the satisfaction of knowing that you left me a free woman."

My heart was exceedingly full. I remembered how my poor father had tried to buy me, when I was a small child, and how he had been disappointed. I hoped his spirit was rejoicing over me now. I remembered how my good old grandmother had laid up her earnings to purchase me in later years, and how often her plans had been frustrated. How that faithful, loving old heart would leap for joy, if she could look on me and my children now that we were free! My relatives had been foiled in all their efforts, but God had raised me up a friend among strangers, who had bestowed on me the precious, long-desired boon. Friend! It is a common word, often lightly used. Like other good and beautiful things, it may be tarnished by careless handling; but when I speak of Mrs. Bruce as my friend, the word is sacred.

My grandmother lived to rejoice in my freedom; but not long after, a letter came with a black seal. She had gone "where the wicked cease from troubling, and the weary are at rest."[5]

Time passed on, and a paper came to me from the south, containing an obituary notice of my uncle Phillip. It was the only case I ever knew of such an honor conferred upon a colored person. It was written by one of his friends, and contained these words: "Now that death has laid him low, they call him a good man and a useful citizen; but what are eulogies to the black man, when the world has faded from his vision? It does not require man's praise to obtain rest in God's kingdom." So they called a colored man a *citizen!* Strange words to be uttered in that region!

Reader, my story ends with freedom; not in the usual way, with marriage. I and my children are now free! We are as free from the power of slaveholders as are the white people of the north; and though that, according to my ideas, is not saying a great deal, it is a vast improvement in *my* condition. The dream of my life is not yet realized. I do not sit with my children in a home of my own. I still long for a hearthstone of my own, however humble. I wish it for my children's sake far more than for my own. But God so orders circumstances as to keep me with my friend Mrs. Bruce. Love, duty, gratitude, also bind me to her side. It is a privilege to serve her who pities my oppressed people, and who has bestowed the inestimable boon of freedom on me and my children.

It has been painful to me, in many ways, to recall the dreary years I passed in bondage. I would gladly forget them if I could. Yet the retrospection is not altogether without solace; for with those gloomy recollections come tender memories of my good old grandmother, like light, fleecy clouds floating over a dark and troubled sea.

5. Job 3.17.

Appendix

The following statement is from Amy Post, a member of the Society of Friends in the State of New York, well known and highly respected by friends of the poor and the oppressed. As has been already stated, in the preceding pages, the author of this volume spent some time under her hospitable roof.   L. M. C.

"The author of this book is my highly-esteemed friend. If its readers knew her as I know her, they could not fail to be deeply interested in her story. She was a beloved inmate of our family nearly the whole of the year 1849. She was introduced to us by her affectionate and conscientious brother, who had previously related to us some of the almost incredible events in his sister's life. I immediately became much interested in Linda; for her appearance was prepossessing, and her deportment indicated remarkable delicacy of feeling and purity of thought.

"As we became acquainted, she related to me, from time to time some of the incidents in her bitter experiences as a slave-woman. Though impelled by a natural craving for human sympathy, she passed through a baptism of suffering, even in recounting her trials to me, in private confidential conversations. The burden of these memories lay heavily upon her spirit—naturally virtuous and refined. I repeatedly urged her to consent to the publication of her narrative; for I felt that it would arouse people to a more earnest work for the disinthralment of millions still remaining in that soul-crushing condition, which was so unendurable to her. But her sensitive spirit shrank from publicity. She said, 'You know a woman can whisper her cruel wrongs in the ear of a dear friend much easier than she can record them for the world to read.' Even in talking with me, she wept so much, and seemed to suffer such mental agony, that I felt her story was too sacred to be drawn from her by inquisitive questions, and I left her free to tell as much, or as little, as she chose. Still, I urged upon her the duty of publishing her experience, for the sake of the good it might do; and, at last, she undertook the task.

"Having been a slave so large a portion of her life, she is unlearned; she is obliged to earn her living by her own labor, and she has worked untiringly to procure education for her children; several times she has been obliged to leave her employments, in order to fly from the man-hunters and woman-hunters of our land; but she pressed through all these obstacles and overcame them. After the labors of the day were over, she traced secretly and wearily, by the midnight lamp, a truthful record of her eventful life.

"This Empire State is a shabby place of refuge for the oppressed; but here, through anxiety, turmoil, and despair, the freedom of Linda and her children was finally secured, by the exertions of a generous friend. She was grateful for the boon; but the idea of having been *bought* was always galling to a spirit that could never acknowledge itself to be a chattel. She wrote to us thus, soon after the event: 'I thank you for your kind expressions in regard to my freedom; but the freedom I had before the money was paid was dearer to me. God gave me *that* freedom; but man put God's image in the scales with the paltry sum of three hundred dollars. I served for my liberty as faithfully as Jacob served for Rachel. At the end, he had large possessions; but I was robbed of my victory; I was obliged to resign my crown, to rid myself of a tyrant.'

"Her story, as written by herself, cannot fail to interest the reader. It is a sad illustration of the condition of this country, which boasts of its civilization, while it sanctions laws and customs which make the experiences of the present more strange than any fictions of the past.

AMY POST.

"ROCHESTER, N. Y., Oct. 30th, 1859."

The following testimonial is from a man who is now a highly respectable colored citizen of Boston.   L. M.

"This narrative contains some incidents so extraordinary, that, doubtless, many persons, under whose eyes it may chance to fall will be ready to believe that it is colored highly, to serve as special purpose. But, however it may be regarded by the incredulous, I know that it is full of living truths. I have been well acquainted with the author from my boyhood. The circumstances recounted in her history are perfectly familiar to me. I knew of her treatment from her master; of the imprisonment of her children; of their sale and redemption; of her seven years' concealment; and of her subsequent escape to the North. I am now a resident of Boston, and am a living witness to the truth of this interesting narrative.

GEORGE W. LOWTHER"[6]

---

6. George W. Lowther (1822–1898), a free black man, was raised in Jacobs's hometown of Edenton, North Carolina. In 1878, he was elected from Massachusetts to the House of Representatives.

CONTEXTS

Contemporary Responses

WILLIAM C. NELL

Linda, the Slave Girl[†]

Boston, January 21, 1861.

Dear Mr. Garrison:

Crowded though I know the *Liberator* columns to be just now, I am constrained to solicit space for a word in announcement of a book just issued from the press, entitled "LINDA: *Incidents in the Life of a Slave Girl, seven years concealed in Slavery.*" It is a handsome volume of 306 pages, and is on sale at the Anti-Slavery Office, price $1.00. I feel confident that its circulation at this crisis in our country's history will render a signal and most acceptable service.

The lamented Mrs. Follen, in her admirable tract addressed to Mothers in the Free States, and with which that indefatigable colporteur,[1] Miss Putnam, is doing so much good in her visits to families, seems to have anticipated just such a contribution to anti-slavery literature as this book, "Linda." It presents features more attractive than many of its predecessors purporting to be histories of slave life in America, because, in contrast with their mingling of fiction with fact, this record of complicated experience in the life of a young woman, a doomed victim to America's peculiar institution—her seven years' concealment in slavery—continued persecutions—hopes, often deferred, but which at length culminated in her freedom—surely need not the charms that any pen of fiction, however gifted and graceful, could lend. They shine by the lustre of their own truthfulness—a rhetoric which always commends itself to the wise head and honest heart. In furtherance of the object of its author, LYDIA MARIA CHILD has furnished a graceful introduction, and AMY POST a well-written letter; and wherever the names of these two devoted friends of humanity are known, no higher credentials can be required or given. My own acquaintance, too, with the author and her relatives, of whom special mention is made in the book, warrants an expression of the hope that it will find its way into every family, where all, especially mothers and

† *Liberator*, 21 January 1861.
1. An itinerant bookseller [*Editor*].

daughters, may learn yet more of the barbarism of American slavery and the character of its victims.

Yours, for breaking every yoke,

WM. C. NELL.

UNSIGNED ANNOUNCEMENT

From the *Anti-Slavery Bugle*[†]

INCIDENTS IN THE LIFE OF A SLAVE GIRL; the narrative of Linda Brent—
We have read this unpretending work with much pleasure. It is a veritable history of the trials and sufferings to which a slave girl was subjected, but who finally triumphed over all discouragements, and obtained freedom for herself and her two children. The manuscript was revised by Mrs. Child, who is acquainted with the author, and who assures the reader that she "has not added anything to the incidents, or changed the import of her very pertinent remarks," the revision being merely for condensation and orderly arrangement. The style is simple and attractive—you feel less as though you were reading a book, than talking with the woman herself. Her revelations of the *domestic* character of the domestic institution unfolds a fearful sum of infamy, that demands the active opposition of every wife and mother in our land.

The work, which forms a handsome volume of over 300 pages, is published for the benefit of the author, and those who desire to benefit themselves as well as the writer, can procure a copy for $1, at the Anti-Slavery office, 221 Washingon St. Boston.

WILLIAM C. NELL[‡]

Linda

INCIDENTS IN THE LIFE OF A SLAVE GIRL, Seven Years concealed in Slavery; narrated by herself; with an Introduction by LYDIA MARIA CHILD, and a Letter by AMY POST. A handsome book of 306 pages, just issued, which is receiving highly commendatory notices from the press. Price, $1.00. Orders for mailing must include sixteen cents in postage stamps.

<table>
<tr><td>Address</td><td>WM. C. NELL,</td></tr>
<tr><td>F8 tf</td><td>221 Washington street.</td></tr>
</table>

---

† *Anti-Slavery Bugle*, 9 February 1861.
‡ *Liberator*, 18 February 1861.

LYDIA MARIA CHILD

Letter to John Greenleaf Whittier[†]

Medford, April 4'th 1861

Dear Friend Whittier,

I thank you for your friendly letter, and your gentle sister also for her kindly greeting.

I am glad you liked "Linda". I have taken a good deal of pains to publish it, and circulate it, because it seemed to me well calculated to take hold of many minds, that will not attend to *arguments* against slavery. The author is a quick-witted, intelligent woman, with great refinement and propriety of manner. Her daughter, now a young woman grown, is a stylish-looking, attractive young person, white as an Italian lady, and very much *like* an Italian of refined education. If she were the daughter of any of the Beacon St. gentry,[1] she would produce a sensation in the fashionable world. The Mrs. *Bruce*, with whom the mother is described as living in New York, is in fact Mrs. *Willis*; for in fact my protegée has for many years been the factotum in the family of N.P. Willis, the distinguished poet. He has mentioned her incidentally in "Letters from Idlewild," in the Home Journal, as "our intelligent housekeeper," our "household oracle," &c. He would not have *dared* to mention that she had ever been a fugitive slave. The Home Journal is not *violently* pro-slavery, but it is very *insidiously* and *systematically* so. The N.Y. Herald, the Day Book, and the Home Journal, are announced by the Jeff. Davis organs[2] to be the *only* Northern papers that the South can securely *trust*. Mr. Willis entertains many Southerners at Idlewild, and is a favorite with them; for that reason, the author of "Linda" did not ask *him* to help her about her M.S. though he has always been very friendly to her, and would have far more influence than I have. *Mrs.* Willis is decidedly *Anti* Slavery in her feelings. The advent of *any* truth into society is always a Messiah, which divides families, and brings "not peace, but a sword."[3] These things ought not to be mentioned in the *papers*. I use fictitious names in the book; first, lest the Southern family, who secreted Linda some months, should be brought into difficulty; secondly, lest some of her surviving relatives at the South should be persecuted; and thirdly, out of delicacy to Mrs. Willis, who would not like to have her name bandied about in the newspapers, perhaps to the injury of her husband's *interests*, and certainly to the injury of his *feelings*.

---

† From *Selected Letters, 1817–1880*, edited by Milton Meltzer and P. S. Holland (Amherst, 1982) 378–79.
1. Boston's Beacon Street was a fashionable, white neighborhood [*Editor*].
2. Pro-Confederacy periodicals [*Editor*].
3. Matthew 10.34 [*Editor*].

The publishers of "Linda," failed, before a copy had been sold. The author succeeded in buying the plates, paying half the money down. The Boston booksellers are dreadfully afraid of soiling their hands with an Anti-Slavery book; so we have a good deal of trouble in getting the book into the market. Do you think any bookseller, or other *responsible* person in Newburyport, would be answerable for a few? They sell here, at retail, $1 a volume. Whoever would take one or two dozen of them might have them at 68 cts per vol. If you think it worth while to send any to Newburyport or Amesbury, please inform me to whom to send.

With regard to the present crisis of affairs,[4] I think the *wisest* can hardly foresee what turn events will take; but *whatever* way they may develope, I have faith that the present agitation will shorten the existence of slavery; and we ought to be willing to suffer *any*thing to bring about *that* result. The ancient proverb declares that "whom the gods would destroy, they first make mad"; and surely the South are mad enough to secure destruction. My *own* soul utters but *one* prayer; and that is, that we may be effectually separated from *all* the Slave-States. My reasons are, first, that we can in no *other* way present to the world a fair experiment of a free Republic; second, that if the Border-States[5] remain with us, we shall be just as much bound to deliver up fugitives as we now are; third those Border-States will form a line of armed sentinels between us and the New Confederacy of "Slave-own-ia", (as Punch[6] wittily calls it) preventing the escape of slaves from the far south, just as they now do; lastly, we shall continue to be demoralized, politically and socially, by a *few* slave-states, as much as we should by *all* of them; they will always be demanding concessions of principle, and our politicians will always be finding reasons for compromise. There is no *health* for us, unless we can get *rid* of the accursed thing. My prayer is, "Deliver us, O Lord, from this body of Death!["][7]

This does not arise from any sectional or partisan feeling; but simply because my reason, my heart, and my conscience, *all* pronounce this Union to be *wicked*. The original compact is *wrong*; and the attempt to obey the laws of *man*, when they are in open conflict with the laws of *God*, must *inevitably* demoralize a nation, and ultimately undermine all true prosperity, even in a material point of view.

. . .

---

4. Though the Civil War had not yet officially begun, several states had already seceded from the Union and established themselves as the Confederate States of America [*Editor*].
5. Delaware, Kentucky, Maryland, and Missouri were slave states that had not yet decided whether to stay with the Union or join the Confederacy [*Editor*].
6. A British periodical famous for satiric humor [*Editor*].
7. Reference to Romans 7.24: "Who shall deliver me from the body of this death?"

UNSIGNED ANNOUNCEMENT

Linda[†]

This is the title of a new work put into our hands by the author, Mrs. Jacobs, of New York, a colored lady, who was born a slave in North Carolina, but managed so as to wend her way to the so-called Free States. It is a work of more than three hundred pages, giving a history of her life in slavedom, and the various transactions which came under her notice. We most cheerfully commend the work as worthy of perusal. She is in this city for a few days, and those who wish the book can procure it of her, at No. 107 North Fifth St.

[†] *Christian Recorder*, 11 January 1862.

Selections from Jacobs's Other Writings

HARRIET JACOBS

Letter from a Fugitive Slave[†]

Slaves Sold under Peculiar Circumstances.

[We publish the subjoined communication exactly as written by the author, with the exception of corrections in punctuation and spelling, and the omission of one or two passages — Ed.]

To the Editor of the N.Y. Tribune.

SIR: Having carefully read your paper for some months I became very much interested in some of the articles and comments written on Mrs. Tyler's Reply to the Ladies of England.[1] Being a slave myself, I could not have felt otherwise. Would that I could write an article worthy of notice in your columns. As I never enjoyed the advantages of an education, therefore I could not study the arts of reading and writing, yet poor as it may be, I had rather give it from my own hand, than have it said that I employed others to do it for me. The truth can never be told so well through the second and third person as from yourself. But I am straying from the question. In that Reply to the Ladies of England, Mrs. Tyler said that slaves were never sold only under very peculiar circumstances. As Mrs. Tyler and her friend Bhains were so far used up, that he could not explain what those peculiar circumstances were, let one whose peculiar suffering justifies her in explaining it for Mrs. Tyler.

I was born a slave, reared in the Southern hot-bed until I was the mother of two children, sold at the early age of two and four years old. I have been hunted through all of the Northern States, but no, I will not

† *New York Tribune*, 21 June 1853.
1. Julia G. Tyler, former first lady, had written a rebuttal to an abolitionist appeal for British women's support [*Editor*].

tell you of my own suffering—no, it would harrow up my soul, and defeat the object that I wish to pursue. Enough—the dregs of that bitter cup
have been my bounty for many years.

And as this is the first time that I ever took my pen in hand to make
such an attempt, you will not say that it is fiction, for had I the inclination, I have neither the brain or talent to write it. But to this very peculiar circumstance under which slaves are sold.

My mother was held as property by a maiden lady; when she married,
my younger sister was in her fourteenth year, whom they took into the
family. She was as gentle as she was beautiful. Innocent and guileless
child, the light of our desolate hearth! But oh, my heart bleeds to tell you
of the misery and degradation she was forced to suffer in slavery. The
monster who owned her had no humanity in his soul. The most sincere
affection that his heart was capable of, could not make him faithful to his
beautiful and wealthy bride the short time of three months, but every
stratagem was used to seduce my sister. Mortified and tormented beyond
endurance, this child came and threw herself on her mother's bosom, the
only place where she could seek refuge from her persecutor; and yet she
could not protect her child that she bore into the world. On that bosom
with *bitter tears* she told her troubles, and entreated her mother to save
her. And oh, Christian mothers! you that have daughters of your own, can
you think of your sable sisters without offering a prayer to that God who
created all in their behalf! My poor mother, naturally high-spirited,
smarting under what she considered as the wrongs and outrages which
her child had to bear, sought her master, entreating him to spare her
child. Nothing could exceed his rage at this what he called impertinence.
My mother was dragged to jail, there remained twenty-five days, with
negro traders to come in as they liked to examine her, as she was offered
for sale. My sister was told that she must yield, or never expect to see her
mother again. There were three younger children; on no other condition
could she be restored to them without the sacrifice of one. That child
gave herself up to her master's bidding, to save one that was dearer to her
than life itself. And can you, Christian, find it in your heart to despise her?
Ah, no! not even Mrs. Tyler; for though we believe that the vanity of a
name would lead her to bestow her hand where her heart could never go
with it, yet, with all her faults and follies, she is nothing more than
a *woman*. For if her domestic hearth is surrounded with slaves, ere long
before this she has opened her eyes to the evils of slavery, and that the
mistress as well as the slave must submit to the indignities and vices imposed on them by their lords of body and soul. But to one of those peculiar circumstances.

At fifteen, my sister held to her bosom an innocent offspring of her
guilt and misery. In this way she dragged a miserable existence of two
years, between the fires of her mistress's jealousy and her master's brutal
passion. At seventeen, she gave birth to another helpless infant, heir to all

the evils of slavery. Thus life and its sufferings were meted out to her until her twenty-first year. Sorrow and suffering had made its ravages upon her—she was less the object to be desired by the fiend who had crushed her to the earth; and as her children grew, they bore too strong a resemblance to him who desired to give them no other inheritance save Chains and Handcuffs, and in the dead hour of the night, when this young, deserted mother lay with her little ones clinging around her, little dreaming of the dark and inhuman plot that would be carried into execution before another dawn, and when the sun rose on God's beautiful earth, that broken-hearted mother was far on her way to the capitol of Virginia. That day should have refused her light to so disgraceful and inhuman an act in your boasted country of Liberty. Yet, reader, it is true, those two helpless children were the *sons* of one of your sainted Members in Congress; that agonized mother, his victim and slave. And where she now is God only knows, who has kept a record on high of all that she has suffered on earth.

And, you would exclaim, Could not the master have been more merciful to his children? God is merciful to all of his children, but it is seldom that a slaveholder has any mercy for his slave child. And you will believe it when I tell you that mother and her children were sold to make room for another sister, who was now the age of that mother when she entered the family. And this selling appeased the mistress's wrath, and satisfied her desire for *revenge,* and made the path more smooth for her young rival at first. For there is a strong rivalry between a handsome mulatto girl and a jealous and *faded* mistress, and her liege lord sadly neglects those little attentions for a while that once made her happy. For the master will either neglect his wife or double his attentions, to save him from being suspected by his wife. Would you not think that Southern women had cause to despise that Slavery which forces them to bear so much deception practiced by their *husbands?* Yet all this is true, for a slaveholder seldom takes a white mistress, for she is an expensive commodity, not submissive as he would like to have her, but more apt to be tyrannical; and when his passion seeks another object, he must leave her in quiet possession of all the gewgaws that she has sold herself for. But not so with his poor *slave victim,* that he has robbed of everything that could make life desirable; she must be torn from the little that is left to bind her to life, and sold by her *seducer* and *master,* caring not where, so that it puts him in possession of enough to purchase another victim. And such are the peculiar circumstances of American Slavery—of all the evils in God's sight the most to be abhorred.

Perhaps while I am writing this, you too, dear Emily, may be on your way to the Mississippi River, for those peculiar circumstances occur every day in the midst of my poor oppressed fellow-creatures in bondage. And oh ye Christians, while your arms are extended to receive the oppressed of all nations, while you exert every power of your soul to assist them to raise funds, put weapons in their hands, tell them to return to their own country to slay every foe until they break the accursed yoke from off their necks, not buying and selling; this they never do under any circumstances. But while Americans do all this, they forget the millions of slaves they have at home, bought and sold under very peculiar circumstances.

And because one friend of the slave has dared to tell of their wrongs you would annihilate her. But in Uncle Tom's Cabin she has not told the half. Would that I had one spark from her storehouse of genius and talent, I would tell you of my own sufferings—I would tell you of wrongs that Hungary has never inflicted, nor England ever dreamed of in this free country where all nations fly for liberty, equal rights and protection under your stripes and stars. It should be stripes and scars, for they go along with Mrs. Tyler's peculiar circumstances, of which I have told you only one.

A FUGITIVE SLAVE.

HARRIET JACOBS

Letter to Amy Post[†]

Cornwall, [New York] June 25th, [1853]

My Dearest Amy,

I stop in the midst of all kind of care and perplexities to scratch you a line and commit to you a breach of trust which I have never breathed to anyone therefore I cannot ask the favor of any one else without appearing very ludicrous in their opinion. I love you and can bear your severest criticism because you know what my advantages have been and what they have not been. When I was in New York last week I picked up a paper with a piece alluding to the buying and selling of slaves mixed up with some of Mrs. Tylers views. I felt so indignant. With the impulse of the moment I determined to reply to it.[1] Were to leave next day. I had no time for thought but as soon as every body was safe in bed I began to look back that I might tell the truth. And every word was true accept my Mother and sisters. It was one whom I dearly loved. It was my first attempt and when morning found me I had not time to correct it or copy it. I must send it or leave it to some future time. The spelling I believe was every word correct. Punctuation I did not attempt for I never studied grammar therefore I know nothing about it. But I have taken the hint and will com-

† From the manuscripts found in the Post Papers of the Rochester Library and reprinted in the microfilms of the *Black Abolitionist Papers*, edited by C. Peter Ripley. For clarity and convenience we have silently edited certain mechanical or grammatical inconsistencies.

1. Jacobs refers here to her letter published in the *New York Tribune* on June 21, 1853, and reprinted in this text as "Letter from a Fugitive Slave" [*Editor*].

mence that one study with all my soul. This letter I wrote in reply I sent it to the Tribune. I left the same morning. The second day it was in the paper. It came here while Mr W[2] was at dinner. I glanced at it. After dinner he took the paper with him. It is headed Slaves Sold under Peculiar Circumstances. It was Tuesday 21st. I thought perhaps it might be copied in the North Star.[3] If so will you get two and cut the articles out and enclose them to me? I have another but I can not offer it before I can read over the first to see more of its imperfections. Please answer this dear Amy as soon as possible. I want to write you a long letter but I am working very hard preparing the new house. Mrs W cant give me any assistance. She is so feeble. Give a great deal of love to all my much loved friends. Kiss dear Willie for Dah[?] and a heart full of warmest and happiest congratulations to Dear Sarah and [I] beg you to give them for me.[4] I must stop. God bless is my prayer.

Harriet

HARRIET JACOBS

Cruelty to Slaves[†]

To the Editor of The N. Y. Tribune.

SIR: Having seen an article, a few days ago, that was going the rounds in some of the daily papers, denying the truth of an advertisement wherein Slaves were outlawed in North Carolina. I wish to reply to it through your columns. I was born in that good old State, and less than 20 years since I left it, and it is not that length of time since I witnessed there a sight which I can never forget. It was a slave that been a runaway from his master twelvemonths. After that time a white man is justified in shooting a slave as he is considered an outlaw. This slave man was brought to the wharf, placed in a small boat, by two white men, early in the morning, with his *head* severed from his body, and remained there in an August sun until noon, before an inquest was held. Then he was buried, and not a word of murder or of arrest was heard. He was a negro and runaway slave, and it was all right. It mattered not who murdered him—if he was a white man he was sure of the reward, and the name of being a brave fellow, truly. The writer of that article has said, the people of North Carolina have hearts and souls like our own. Surely, many of

---

2. Nathaniel P. Willis, her employer [*Editor*].
3. A newspaper edited by Frederick Douglass [*Editor*].
4. Willett ("Willie") Post was Amy's son. Sarah Kirby was Amy's sister and was also active in the abolition movement [*Editor*].
† *New York Tribune*, 25 July 1853.

them have. The poor slave, however, who had his head severed from his body was owned by a merchant in New York.

A FUGITIVE

HARRIET JACOBS

Letter to Amy Post[†]

Oct. 9th [1853?]

My Dear Friend,

I was more than glad to receive your welcome letter for I must acknowledge that your long silence had troubled me much. I should have written before this but we have had a little member added to the family and I have had little time for anything besides the extras. It makes my heart sad to tell you that I have not heard from my brother and Joseph.[1] And, dear Amy, I have lost that dear old grandmother that I so dearly loved. Oh, her life has been one of sorrow and trial but he in whom she trusted has never forsaken her. Her death was beautiful. May my last end be like hers. Louisa is with me.[2] I don't know how long she will remain. I shall try and keep her all winter as I want to try and make arrangements to have some of my time.

Mrs. Stowe never answered any of my letters after I refused to have my history in her key.[3] Perhaps, it's for the best. At least I will try and think so. Have you seen any more of my scribbling? They were marked "fugitive."[4] William Nell[5] told Louisa about the piece and sent her a copy. I was careful to keep it from her and no one here never suspected me. I would not have Mrs. W.[6] to know it before I had undertaken my history for I must write just what I have lived and witnessed myself. Don't expect much of me, Dear Amy. You shall have truth but not talent. God did not give me that gift, but he gave me a soul that burned for freedom and a heart nerved with determination to suffer even unto death in pursuit of that liberty which without makes life an intolerable burden. But, dear A, I fear that I am burdening you. The request in your letter—I told you it

---

[†] From the manuscripts found in the Post Papers of the Rochester Library and reprinted in the microfilms of the *Black Abolitionist Papers,* edited by C. Peter Ripley. We have silently edited certain mechanical or grammatical inconsistencies.
1. Her brother, John S. Jacobs, and her son, Joseph [*Editor*].
2. Louisa was Jacobs's daughter [*Editor*].
3. Originally Jacobs had wanted Harriet Beecher Stowe to help write her narrative. Stowe, however, wanted to incorporate Jacobs's story into Stowe's *A Key to Uncle Tom's Cabin.* Jacobs refused [*Editor*].
4. Jacobs refers here to the letters published in the *New York Tribune.* They are reprinted in this volume [*Editor*].
5. William C. Nell (1816–1874), African American writer and abolitionist who had assisted Jacobs in her attempts to find a publisher [*Editor*].
6. Cornelia Willis, Jacobs's employer [*Editor*].

was true in all its statements except its being my mother and sister. But we grew up together. The answer to the slave's being outlawed in North Carolina [is] I was home when the poor outlawed was brought in town with his head severed from his body. The piece on Colonisation was just what my poor little indignant heart felt towards the society. And now, my dear friend, don't flatter me. I am aware of my many mistakes and willing to be told of them. Only let me come before the world as I have been, an uneducated oppressed slave. But I must stop. Love to all. God bless you. Excuse the hasty scrawl.

Yours,
Harriet

1 o'clock

HARRIET JACOBS

Letter to Amy Post†

New York
June 18th [1861]

My Dear Friends,

I have just received a letter from my brother[1] and one enclosed to his friend Mr. Post. As it was not under cover, I read it myself. I then read mine which was only a few scolding lines—because I had not sent my book to different people in England. In the first place it costs too much to send them while in debt, and in the next I did not care to give it a circulation then before I tried to turn it to some account. So I have taken it very patiently—but I don't give up as I used to. The trouble is I begin to find out we poor women have always been too meek. When I hear a man call a woman an Angel when she is out of sight—I begin to think about poor Leah of the Bible, not Leah of the Spirits. I told our spirit friend it was better to be born lucky than rich—but to my letter. I read mine and a part of yours to Oliver Jackson.[2] He wanted me to take some notes from it. With your permission, may I give them for the *Liberator* and the *Standard*?[3] What my brother says about me is true, in his letter. I am going to Statten Island tomorrow for the first time. I shall register my brother's letter. There is fifteen pounds enclosed in it. I meant to write you a long let-

---

† From the manuscripts found in the Post Papers of the Rochester Library and reprinted in the microfilms of the *Black Abolitionist Papers*, edited by C. Peter Ripley. We have silently edited certain mechanical or grammatical inconsistencies.

1. Harriet's brother, John Jacobs, was living in England at the time [*Editor*].
2. Oliver Jackson (1809–89), an editor of the *Liberator*, an antislavery newspaper [*Editor*].
3. The *National Anti-Slavery Standard* had once been edited by L. Maria Child [*Editor*].

ter but they are waiting for me. I am so tired. I long to see you. Kindest remembrance to my friends.
With much love,

Harriet

HARRIET JACOBS

Life among the Contrabands[†]

DEAR MR. GARRISON:

I thank you for the request of a line on the condition of the contra-bands,[1] and what I have seen while among them. When we parted at that pleasant gathering of the Progressive Friends at Longwood, you to return to the Old Bay State,[2] to battle for freedom and justice to the slave, I to go to the District of Columbia, where the shackles had just fallen,[3] I hoped that the glorious echo from the blow had aroused the spirit of freedom, if a spark slumbered in its bosom. Having purchased my ticket through to Washington at the Philadelphia station, I reached the capital without molestation. Next morning, I went to Duff Green's Row, Government head-quarters for the contrabands here. I found men, women and children all huddled together, without any distinction or regard to age or sex. Some of them were in the most pitiable condition. Many were sick with measles, diptheria, scarlet and typhoid fever. Some had a few filthy rags to lie on; others had nothing but the bare floor for a couch. There seemed to be no established rules among them; they were coming in at all hours, often through the night, in large numbers, and the Superintendent had enough to occupy his time in taking the names of those who came in, and of those who were sent out. His office was thronged through the day by persons who came to hire these poor creatures, who they say will not work and take care of themselves. Single women hire at four dollars a month; a woman with one child, two and a half or three dollars a month. Men's wages are ten dollars per month. Many of them, accustomed as they have been to field labor, and to living almost entirely out of doors, suffer much from the confinement in this crowded building. The little children pine like prison birds for their native element. It is almost impossible to keep the building in a healthy condition. Each day brings its fresh additions of the hungry, naked and sick. In the early part of June, there were, some days, as many as ten deaths reported at this place in twenty-four hours. At this time, there was no matron in the house, and nothing at hand to

---

† *Liberator,* 5 September 1862.
1. A term applied to slaves liberated from Confederates during the Civil War [*Editor*].
2. Massachusetts [*Editor*].
3. Slavery had been declared illegal in the District of Columbia on April 16, 1862 [*Editor*].

administer to the comfort of the sick and dying. I felt that their sufferings must be unknown to the people. I did not meet kindly, sympathizing people, trying to soothe the last agonies of death. Those tearful eyes often looked up to me with the language. "Is this freedom?"

A new Superintendent was engaged, Mr. Nichol, who seemed to understand what these people most needed. He laid down rules, went to work in earnest pulling down partitions to enlarge the rooms, that he might establish two hospitals, one for the men and another for the women. This accomplished, cots and matresses were needed. There is a small society in Washington—the Freedman's Association—who are doing all they can; but remember, Washington is not New England. I often met Rev. W. H. Channing,[4] whose hands and heart are earnestly in the cause of the enslaved of his country. This gentleman was always ready to act in their behalf. Through these friends, an order was obtained from Gen. Wadsworth for cots for the contraband hospitals.

At this time, I met in Duff Green Row, Miss Hannah Stevenson, of Boston, and Miss Kendall. The names of these ladies need no comment. They were the first white females whom I had seen among these poor creatures, except those who had come in to hire them. These noble ladies had come to work, and their names will be lisped in prayer by many a dying slave. Hoping to help a little in the good work they had begun, I wrote to a lady in New York, a true and tried friend of the slave, who from the first moment had responded to every call of humanity. This letter was to ask for such articles as would make comfortable the sick and dying in the hospital. On the Saturday following, the cots were put up. A few hours after, an immense box was received from New York. Before the sun went down, those ladies who have labored so hard for the comfort of those people had the satisfaction of seeing every man, woman and child with clean garments, lying in a clean bed. What a contrast! They seemed different beings. Every countenance beamed with gratitude and satisfied rest. To me, it was a picture of holy peace within. The next day was the first Christian Sabbath they had ever known. One mother passed away as the setting sun threw its last rays across her dying bed, and as I looked upon her, I could not but say—"One day of freedom, and gone to her God." Before the dawn, others were laid beside her. It was a comfort to know that some effort had been made to soothe their dying pillows. Still, there were other places in which I felt, if possible, more interest, where the poor creatures seemed so far removed from the immediate sympathy of those who would help them. These were the contrabands in Alexandria. This place is strongly secesh;[5] the inhabitants are kept quiet only at the point of Northern bayonets. In this place, the contrabands are distributed more over the city. In visiting those places, I had the assistance of two kind friends,

4. William Henry Channing (1810–1884), Unitarian clergyman and abolitionist [*Editor*].
5. A term applied to those who seceded from the Union and joined the Confederacy [*Editor*].

women. True at heart, they felt the wrongs and degradation of their race. These ladies were always ready to aid me, as far as lay in their power. To Mrs. Brown, of 3d street, Washington, and Mrs. Dagans, of Alexandria, the contrabands owe much gratitude for the kindly aid they gave me in serving them. In this place, the men live in an old foundry, which does not afford protection from the weather. The sick lay on boards on the ground floor; some, through the kindness of the soldiers, have an old blanket. I did not hear a complaint among them. They said it was much better than it had been. All expressed a willingness to work, and were anxious to know what was to be done with them after the work was done. All of them said they had not received pay for their work, and some wanted to know if I thought it would be paid to their masters. One old man said, "I don't kere if dey don't pay, so dey give me freedom. I bin working for ole mass all de time; he nebber gib me five cent. I like de Unions fuss rate. If de Yankee Unions didn't come long, I'd be working tu de ole place now." All said they had plenty to eat, but no clothing, and no money to buy any.

Another place, the old school-house in Alexandria, is the Government head-quarters for the women. This I thought the most wretched of all the places. Any one who can find an apology for slavery should visit this place, and learn its curse. Here you see them from infancy up to a hundred years old. What but the love of freedom could bring these old people hither! One old man, who told me he was a hundred, said he had come to be free with his children. The journey proved too much for him. Each visit, I found him sitting in the same spot, under a shady tree, suffering from rheumatism. Unpacking a barrel, I found a large coat, which I thought would be so nice for the old man, that I carried it to him. I found him sitting in the same spot, with his head on his bosom. I stooped down to speak to him. Raising his head, I found him dying. I called his wife. The old woman, who seems in her second childhood, looked on as quietly as though we were placing him for a night's rest. In this house are scores of women and children, with nothing to do, and nothing to do with. Their husbands are at work for the Government. Here they have food and shelter, but they cannot get work. The slaves who come into Washington from Maryland are sent here to protect them from the Fugitive Slave Law. These people are indebted to Mr. Rufus Leighton, formerly of Boston, for many comforts. But for their Northern friends, God pity them in their wretched and destitute condition! The Superintendent, Mr. Clarke, a Pennsylvanian, seems to feel much interest in them, and is certainly very kind. They told me they had confidence in him as a friend. That is much for a slave to say.

From this place, I went to Birch's slave-pen, in Alexandria. This place forms a singular contrast with what it was two years ago. The habitable part of the building is filled with contrabands; the old jail is filled with secesh prisoners—all within speaking distance of each other. Many a compliment is passed between them on the change in their positions. There is another house on Cameron street, which is filled with very destitute people. To these places I distributed large supplies of clothing, given me by the ladies of New York, New Bedford, and Boston. They have made many a desolate heart glad. They have clothed the naked, fed the hungry. To them, God's promise is sufficient.

Let me tell you of another place, to which I always planned my last visit for the day. There was something about this house to make you forget that you came to it with a heavy heart. The little children you meet at this door bring up pleasant memories when you leave it; from the older ones you carry pleasant recollections. These were what the people call the more favored slaves, and would boast of having lived in the first families in Virginia. They certainly had reaped some advantage from the contact. It seemed by a miracle that they had all fallen together. They were intelligent, and some of the young women and children beautiful. One young girl, whose beauty I cannot describe, although its magnetism often drew me to her side, I loved to talk with, and look upon her sweet face, covered with blushes; besides, I wanted to learn her true position, but her gentle shyness I had to respect. One day, while trying to draw her out, a fine-looking woman, with all the pride of a mother, stepped forward, and said— "Madam, this young woman is my son's wife." It was a relief. I thanked God that this young creature had an arm to lean upon for protection. Here I looked upon slavery, and felt the curse of their heritage was what is considered the best blood of Virginia. On one of my visits here, I met a mother who had just arrived from Virginia, bringing with her four daughters. Of course, they belonged to one of the first families. This man's strong attachment to this woman and her children caused her, with her children, to be locked up one month. She made her escape one day while her master had gone to learn the news from the Union army. She fled to the Northern army for freedom and protection. These people had earned for themselves many little comforts. Their houses had an inviting aspect. The clean floors, the clean white spreads on their cots, and the general tidiness throughout the building, convinced me they had done as well as any other race could have done, under the same circumstances.

Let me tell you of another place—Arlington Heights. Every lady has heard of Gen. Lee's beautiful residence, which has been so faithfully guarded by our Northern army. It looks as though the master had given his orders every morning. Not a tree around that house has fallen. About the forts and camps they have been compelled to use the axe. At the quarters, there are many contrabands. The men are employed, and most of the women. Here they have plenty of exercise in the open air, and seem very happy. Many of the regiments are stationed here. It is a delightful place for both the soldier and the contraband. Looking around this place, and remembering what I had heard of the character of the man who owned it before it passed into the hands of its present owner, I was much inclined to say, Although the wicked prosper for a season, the way of the transgressor is hard.

When in Washington for the day, my morning visit would be up at Duff Green's Row. My first business would be to look into a small room on the ground floor. This room was covered with lime. Here I would learn how many deaths had occurred in the last twenty-four hours. Men, women and children lie here together, without a shadow of those rites which we give to our poorest dead. There they lie, in the filthy rags they wore from the plantation. Nobody seems to give it a thought. It is an every-day occurrence, and the scenes have become familiar. One morning, as I looked in, I saw lying there five children. By the side of them lay a young man. He escaped, was taken back to Virginia, whipped nearly to death, escaped again the next night, dragged his body to Washington, and died, literally cut to pieces. Around his feet I saw a rope; I could not see that put into the grave with him. Other cases similar to this came to my knowledge, but this I saw.

Amid all this sadness, we sometimes would hear a shout of joy. Some mother had come in, and found her long-lost child; some husband his wife. Brothers and sisters meet. Some, without knowing it, had lived years within twenty miles of each other.

A word about the schools. It is pleasant to see that eager group of old and young, striving to learn their A, B, C, and Scripture sentences. Their great desire is to learn to read. While in the school-room, I could not but feel how much these young women and children needed female teachers who could do something more than teach them their A, B, C. They need to be taught the right habits of living and the true principles of life.

My last visit intended for Alexandria was on Saturday. I spent the day with them, and received showers of thanks for myself and the good ladies who had sent me; for I had been careful to impress upon them that these kind friends sent me, and that all that was given by me was from them. Just as I was on the point of leaving, I found a young woman, with an infant, who had just been brought in. She lay in a dying condition, with nothing but a piece of an old soldier coat under her head. Must I leave her in this condition? I could not beg in Alexandria. It was time for the last boat to leave for Washington, and I promised to return in the morning. The Superintendent said he would meet me at the landing. Early next morning, Mrs. Brown and myself went on a begging expedition, and some old quilts were given us. Mr. Clarke met us, and offered the use of his large Government wagon, with the horses and driver, for the day, and said he would accompany us, if agreeable. I was delighted, and felt I should spend a happy Sabbath in exploring Dixie, while the large bundles that I carried with me would help make others happy. After attending to the sick mother and child, we started for Fairfax Seminary. They send many of the convalescent soldiers to this place. The houses are large, and the location is healthy. Many of the contrabands are here. Their condition is much better than that of those kept in the city. They soon gathered around Mr.

Clarke, and begged him to come back and be their boss. He said, "Boys, I want you all to go to Hayti." They said, "You gwine wid us, Mr. Clarke!" "No, I must stay here, and take care of the rest of the boys." "Den, if you aint gwine, de Lord knows I aint a gwine." Some of them will tell Uncle Abe[6] the same thing. Mr. Clarke said they would do anything for him — seldom gave him any trouble. They spoke kindly of Mr. Thomas, who is constantly employed in supplying their wants, as far as he can. To the very old people at this place, I gave some clothing, returned to Alexandria, and bade all good bye. Begging me to come back they promised to do all they could to help themselves. One old woman said — "Honey tink, when all get still, I kin go an fine de old place? Tink de Union 'stroy it? You can't get nothin on dis place. Down on de ole place, you can raise ebery ting. I ain't seen bacca since I bin here. Neber git a libin here, where de peoples eben buy pasly." This poor old woman thought it was nice to live where tobacco grew, but it was dreadful to be compelled to buy a bunch of parsley. Here they have preaching once every Sabbath. They must have a season to sing and pray, and we need true faith in Christ to go among them and do our duty. How beautiful it is to find it among themselves! Do not say the slaves take no interest in each other. Like other people, some of them are designedly selfish, some are ignorantly selfish. With the light and instruction you give them, you will see this selfishness disappear. Trust them, make them free, and give them the responsibility of caring for themselves, and they will soon learn to help each other. Some of them have been so degraded by slavery that they do not know the usages of civilized life: they know little else than the overseer's lash. Have patience with them. You have helped to make them what they are: teach them civilization. You owe it to them, and you will find them as apt to learn as any other people that come to you stupid from oppression. The negroes' strong attachment no one doubts; the only difficulty is, they have cherished it too strongly. Let me tell you of an instance among the contrabands. One day, while in the hospital, a woman came in to ask that she might take a little orphan child. The mother had just died, leaving two children, the eldest three years old. This woman had five children in the house with her. In a few days, the number would be six. I said to this mother, "What can you do with this child, shut up here with your own? They are as many as you can attend to." She looked up with tears in her eyes, and said — "The child's mother was a stranger; none of her friends cum wid her from de ole place. I took one boy down on de plantation; he is a big boy now, working mong de Unions. De Lord help me to bring up dat boy, and he will help me to take care dis child. My husband work for de Unions when dey pay him. I can make home for all. Dis child shall hab part ob de crust." How few white mothers, living in luxury, with six children, could find room in her heart for a seventh, and that child a stranger!

<hr />

6. President Abraham Lincoln [Editor].

In this house there are scores of children, too young to help themselves, from eight years old down to the little one-day freeman, born at railroad speed, while the young mother was flying from Virginia to save her babe from breathing its tainted air.

I left the contrabands, feeling that the people were becoming more interested in their behalf, and much had been done to make their condition more comfortable. On my way home, I stopped a few days in Philadelphia. I called on a lady who had sent a large supply to the hospital, and told her of the many little orphans who needed a home. This lady advised me to call and see the Lady Managers of an institution for orphan children supported by those ladies. I did so, and they agreed to take the little orphans. They employed a gentleman to investigate the matter, and it was found impossible to bring them through Baltimore. This gentleman went to the captains of the propellers in Philadelphia, and asked if those orphan children could have a passage on their boats. Oh no, it could not be; it would make an unpleasant feeling among the people! Some of those orphans have died since I left, but the number is constantly increasing. Many mothers, on leaving the plantations, pick up the little orphans, and bring them with their own children; but they cannot provide for them; they come very destitute themselves.

To the ladies who have so nobly interested themselves in behalf of my much oppressed race, I feel the deepest debt of gratitude. Let me beg the reader's attention to these orphans. They are the innocent and helpless of God's poor. If you cannot take one, you can do much by contributing your mite to the institution that will open its doors to receive them.

LINDA.

HARRIET JACOBS

Letter from Mrs. Jacobs[†]

The following letter from Mrs. Jacobs—the "Linda" of the "Deeper Wrong"—to the Rev. Sella Martin,[1] is just received. We think she will not blame us for its publication when she knows how useful it will be.

"*Alexandria, April* 13*th.*

"My Esteemed Friend,

"Accept my sincere thanks for the very kind manner in which you spoke of me before the anti-slavery friends in England. The memory of

---

[†] *Black Abolitionist Papers*, 13 April 1863.

1. John Sella Martin (1832–?); as a former slave and abolitionist leader, Martin frequently traveled and lectured abroad [*Editor*].

the past in my early life, the cruel wrongs that a slave must suffer, has served to bind me more closely to those around me; whatever I have done or may do, is a christian duty I owe to my race—I owe it to God's suffering poor. When these grateful creatures gather around me, some looking so sad and desolate, while others with their faces beaming happiness, and their condition so much improved by the blessings of freedom, I can but feel within my heart the last chain is to be broken, the accursed blot wiped out. This lightens my labours, and if any sacrifices have been made, they are forgotten. I have often wished you were here,—the field is large, but the labourers are few. We have passed through a trying season;—may I never again behold the misery I have witnessed this winter. When I wrote to our little Society in Boston, the small pox raged fearfully—death met you at every turn. From the 20th of October to the 4th of March, 800 refugees were buried in this town by the Government, beside many private burials, that were not put in the list, but were refugees. The authorities really do not know the number of ex-slaves in this place. We have no superintendent appointed by the Government to look after them: this we need sadly in a place like this, where the citizens are so strongly secessionist—kept down only at the point of northern bayonets. You may imagine there is little sympathy among them for these poor creatures. I found them packed together in the most miserable quarters, dying without the commonest necessities of life; for most of the comforts they have had, we are indebted to the Society of Orthodox Friends in New York. They have indeed proved themselves friends to this poor neglected race.

"When I hear the many eloquent appeals made from the pulpit and the forum in behalf of the soldiers, stating our duty to them ought to be paramount to all others, I feel it is right: thank God! I am proud to know the coloured man is helping to fill up these ranks, and he, too, will be acknowledged a man.

"I am gratified to know we are remembered with sympathy by our friends across the water. England has been the coloured man's boast of freedom; we will still believe our English friends true to their declared principles.

"How I should like to talk with you! I have been ill here, and it has left my eyes so weak, I can use them but very little.

"I must say one word about our schools. We have 125 scholars; we have no paid teachers as yet, the children have been taught by convalescent soldiers, who kindly volunteer their services until called to join their regiment. We need female teachers: the little ones are apt; it is surprising to see what progress some of them make. I have a large sewing class of children and adults. I had a long battle about the marriage rites for the poor people, at length I carried my point. The first wedding took place in the school-house; the building was so densely crowded, the rafters above gave way; the excitement was intense for a few moments, the poor creatures thought the rebels were upon them."

HARRIET JACOBS

Letter from Teachers of the Freedmen[†]

FRIEND JOHNSON: I last night received letters from Mrs. Jacobs and her daughter, who you know are employed by the Society of Friends in New York to teach the emancipated slaves in the region of Alexandria, Virginia I send you extracts from their letters, because I am sure your readers will feel gratified, as I do, to see these two highly intelligent women laboring so zealously and faithfully for the good of their long-oppressed people; and also because the account they give of the conduct of the freedmen is so cheering to the friends, who are praying and laboring for their growth in knowledge, and virtue, and worldly comfort.

L. MARIA CHILD

ALEXANDRIA, March 26, 1864.

DEAR MRS. CHILD: When I went to the North, last Fall, the Freedmen here were building a school-house, and I expected it would have been finished by the time I returned. But when we arrived, we found it uncompleted. Their funds had got exhausted, and the work was at a standstill for several weeks. This was a disappointment; but the time did not hang idle on our hands, I assure you. We went round visiting the new homes of the Freedmen, which now dot the landscape, built with their first earnings as free laborers. Within the last eight months seven hundred little cabins have been built, containing from two to four rooms. The average cost was from one hundred to two hundred and fifty dollars. In building school-houses or shelters for the old and decrepid, they have received but little assistance. They have had to struggle along and help themselves as they could. But though this has been discouraging, at times, it teaches them self reliance; and that is good for them, as it is for everybody. We have over seven thousand colored refugees in this place, and, including the hospitals, less than four hundred rations are given out. This shows that they are willing to earn their own way, and generally capable of it. Indeed, when I look back on the condition in which I first found them, and compare it with their condition now, I am convinced they are not so far behind other races as some people represent them. The two rooms we occupy were given to me by the Military Governor, to be appropriated to the use of decrepid women, when we leave them.

When we went round visiting the homes of these people, we found much to commend them for. Many of them showed marks of industry, neatness, and natural refinement. In others, chaos reigned supreme. There was nothing about them to indicate the presence of a wifely wife, or a motherly mother. They bore abundant marks of the half-barbarous, miserable condition of Slavery, from which the inmates had lately come. It made me sad to see their shiftlessness and discomfort; but I was hopeful for the future. The consciousness of working for themselves, and of having a character to gain, will inspire them with energy and enterprise, and a higher civilization will gradually come.

Children abounded in these cabins. They peeped out from every nook and corner. Many of them were extremely pretty and bright-looking. Some had features and complexions purely Anglo-Saxon; showing plainly enough the slaveholder's horror of amalgamation. Some smiled upon us, and were very ready to be friends. Others regarded us with shy, suspicious looks, as is apt to be the case with children who have had a cramped childhood. But they all wanted to accept our invitation to go to school, and so did all the parents for them.

In the course of our rounds, we visited a settlement which had received no name. We suggested to the settlers that it would be proper to name if for some champion of Liberty. We told them of the Hon. Chas. Sumner,[1] whose large heart and great mind had for years been devoted to the cause of the poor slaves. We told how violent and cruel slaveholders had nearly murdered him for standing up so manfully in defense of Freedom. His claim to their gratitude was at once recognized, and the settlement was called Sumnerville.

Before we came here, a white lady, from Chelsea, Mass., was laboring as a missionary among the Refugees; and a white teacher, sent by the Educational Commission of Boston, accompanied us. One of the freedmen, whose cabin consisted of two rooms, gave it up to us for our school. We soon found that the clamor of little voices begging for admittance far exceeded the narrow limits of this establishment.

Friends at the North had given us some articles left from one of the Fairs. To these we added what we could, and got up a little Fair here, to help them in the completion of the school-house. By this means we raised one hundred and fifty dollars, and they were much gratified by the result. With the completion of the school-house our field of labor widened, and we were joyful over the prospect of extended usefulness. But some difficulties occurred, as there always do in the settlement of such affairs. A question arose whether the white teachers or the colored teachers should be superintendents. The freedmen had built the school-house for their children, and were Trustees of the school. So, after some discussion, it was decided that it would be best for them to hold a meeting, and settle the question for themselves. I wish you could have been at that meeting. Most of the people were slaves, until quite recently, but they talked sensibly, and I assure you that they put the question to vote in quite parliamentary style. The result was a decision that the colored

---

1. Charles Sumner (1811–1874), abolitionist senator from Massachusetts [*Editor*].

teachers should have charge of the school. We were gratified by this re-sult, because our sympathies are closely linked with our oppressed race. These people, born and bred in slavery, had always been so accustomed to look upon the white race as their natural superiors and masters, that we had some doubts whether they could easily throw off the habit; and the fact of their giving preference to colored teachers, as managers of the establishment, seemed to us to indicate that even their brief possession of freedom had begun to inspire them with respect for their race.

On the 11th of January we opened school in the new school-house, with seventy-five scholars. Now, we have two hundred and twenty-five. Slavery has not crushed out the animal spirits of these children. Fun lurks in the corners of their eyes, dimples their mouths, tingles at their fingers' ends, and is, like a torpedo, ready to explode at the slightest touch. The war-spirit has a powerful hold upon them. No one turns the other cheek for a second blow. But they evince a generous nature. They never allow an older and stronger scholar to impose upon a younger and weaker one; and when they happen to have any little delicacies, they are very ready to share them with others. The task of regulating them is by no means an easy one; but we put heart, mind, and strength freely into the work, and only regret that we have not more physical strength. Their ardent desire to learn is very encourag-ing, and the improvement they make consoles us for many trials. You would be astonished at the progress many of them have made in this short time. Many who less than three months ago scarcely knew the A. B. C. are now reading and spelling in words of two or three syllables. When I look at these bright little boys, I often wonder whether there is not some Frederick Dou-glass among them, destined to do honor to his race in the future. No one can predict, now-a-days, how rapidly the wheels of progress will move on.

There is also an evening-school here, chiefly consisting of adults and largely attended; but with that I am not connected.

On the 10th of this month, there was considerable excitement here. The bells were rung in honor of the vote to abolish slavery in Virginia. Many did not know what was the cause of such a demonstration. Some thought it was an alarm of fire; others supposed the rebels had made a raid, and were marching down King st. We were, at first, inclined to the latter opinion; for, looking up that street we saw a company of the most woe-begone looking horsemen. It was raining hard, and some of them had dismounted, leading their poor jaded skeletons of horses. We soon learned that they were a portion of Kilpatrick's cavalry, on their way to Culpepper. Poor fellows! they had had a weary tramp, and must still tramp on, through mad and rain, till they reached their journey's end. What hopeless despondency would take possession of our hearts, if we looked only on the suffering occasioned by this war, and not on the good already accomplished, and the still grander results shadowed forth in the future. The slowly-moving ambulance often passes by, with low beat of the drum, as the soldiers convey some comrade to his last resting-place.

Buried on strange soil, far away from mother, wife, and children! Poor fellows! !But they die the death of brave men in a noble cause. The Soldier's Burying Ground here is well cared for, and is a beautiful place.

How nobly are the colored soldiers fighting and dying in the cause of Freedom! Our hearts are proud of the manhood they evince, in spite of the indignities heaped upon them. They are kept constantly on fatigue duty, digging trenches, and unloading vessels. Look at the Massachusetts Fifty-Fourth! Every man of them a hero! marching so boldly and steadily to victory or death, for the freedom of their race, and the salvation of their country! *Their* country! It makes my blood run warm to think how that country treats her colored sons, even the bravest and the best. If merit deserves reward, surely the 54th regiment is worthy of shoulder-straps. I have lately heard, from a friend in Boston, that the rank of second-lieutenant has been conferred. I am thankful there is a beginning. I am full of hope for the future. A Power mightier than man is guiding this revolution; and though justice moves slowly, it will come at last. The American people will outlive this mean prejudice against complexion. Sooner or later, they will learn that "a man's a man for a' that."

We went to the wharf last Tuesday, to welcome the emigrants returned from Hayti. It was a bitter cold day, the snow was falling, and they were barefooted and bareheaded, with scarely rags enough to cover them. They were put in wagons and carried to Green Heights. We did what we could for them. I went to see them next day, and found that three had died during the night. I was grieved for their hard lot; but I comforted myself with the idea that this would put an end to colonization projects. They are eight miles from here, but I shall go to see them again to-morrow. I hope to obtain among them some recruits for the Massachusetts Cavalry. I am trying to help Mr. Downing and Mr. Remond; not for money, but because I want to do all I can to strengthen the hands of those who are battling for Freedom.

Thank you for your letter. I wish you could have seen the happy group of faces round me, at our little Fair, while I read it to them. The memory of the grateful hearts I have found among these freed men and women, will cheer me all my life.

Yours truly,   H. JACOBS AND L. JACOBS.

HARRIET JACOBS

Jacobs School[†]

ALEXANDRIA, Jan. 13. 1865.
I must say one word about our school. While we were fitting up the house, the scholars were very much scattered in other schools, particu-

---

† *Freedmen's Record*, March 1865.

larly the most advanced scholars. With the new year many of them have come back.

My daughter's health will not allow her to be confined to the school. She has charge of the Industrial Department, is teacher in the sabbath school, and assists me in my out-door work. We need another teacher.

The school is making progress under the charge of their teachers. It is the largest, and I am anxious it shall be the best. The New-York and Pennsylvania associations are establishing new schools in Alexandria. All seem to be well attended.

We have three large churches, beside the L'Ouverture hospital. At this hospital, they are erecting another large building.

The chaplain at the L'Ouverture has opened a school for the soldiers. It is well attended. They need a building for this purpose. Could you see the young men with one arm and leg, with their book and slate, crowded into a small room, I know you would suggest something better for these brave boys.

Yours truly,   H. JACOBS.

HARRIET JACOBS

From Savannah[†]

We arrived here on the 15th. Mr. Eberhart came on board the steamer, and advised us to go to Atlanta, as there was great suffering: both white and black men living with nothing but the bushes over their heads. He said there was no suffering in Savannah. They had nineteen schools, principally sustained by the colored people. I told Mr. E. that our Society wished me to look around in Savannah, and see what the condition of the freedmen was. I went on shore, and obtained board with a very nice colored family. My first visit was to the hospital for freedmen and refugees, in charge of Major Augustus, colored surgeon in the army. This hospital was the city poor-house. It is a large building, and will accommodate three hundred patients. The doctor is faithful in the discharge of his duties, but has very little to work with. The Bureau is poor. We have to depend on our friends to assist us in relieving the wants of these poor creatures. I brought clothing with me, and immediately set the convalescents to work, and soon had a change of clothing for all the women and children. With the doctor's permission, my daughter opened a school in the hospital on the 20th. She has a large room, with fifty-five pupils, white and colored. There are six schools in the city. Mr. Bradley is fitting up

---

† *Freedmen's Record*, 18 January 1866.

one of the slave-auction rooms to open the seventh. Col. Sickles has commenced the erection of an Orphan Asylum and Old Folks' Home. My daughter has applied for the situation of matron in the Asylum. I expect to take the Home.

The colored people in Georgia are mostly poor compared with those in South Carolina. The free colored citizens here were allowed to buy and sell slaves, but not allowed to own real estate.

We shall be badly off when the military protection is withdrawn.

HARRIET JACOBS.

HARRIET JACOBS

Savannah Freedmen's Orphan Asylum[†]

We have much pleasure in publishing the following Appeal. It is made by a well-known victim of Slavery, Linda Brent now Harriet Jacob, whose narrative, entitled "Linda," every one should read. We hope her appeal will be met with a generous response.

An Appeal.

"My object in visiting England is to solicit aid in the erection of an Orphan Asylum in connection with a home for the destitute among the aged freedmen of Savannah, Georgia. There are many thousand orphans in the Southern States. In a few of the States homes have been established through the benevolence of Northern friends; in others, no provision has been made except through the Freedmen's Bureau, which provides that the orphan be apprenticed till of age. It not unfrequently happens that the apprenticeship is to the former owner. As the spirit of Slavery is not exorcised yet, the child, in many instances, is cruelly treated. It is our earnest desire to do something for this class of children; to give them a shelter surrounded by some home influences, and instruction that shall fit them for usefulness, and, when apprenticed, the right of an oversight. I know of the degradation of Slavery—the blight it leaves; and, thus knowing, feel how strong the necessity is of throwing around the young, who, through God's mercy, have come out of it, the most salutary influences.

"The aged freedmen have likewise a claim upon us. Many of them are worn out with field-labour. Some served faithfully as domestic slaves, nursing their masters and masters' children. Infirm, penniless, homeless, they wander about dependent on charity for bread and shelter. Many of

† *Anti-Slavery Reporter* (London), 3 March 1868.

them suffer and die from want. Freedom is a priceless boon, but its value is enhanced when accompanied with some of life's comforts. The old freed man and the old freed woman have obtained their's after a long weary march through a desolate way. If some peace and light can be shed on the steps so near the grave, it were but human kindness and Christian love.

"I was sent as an agent to Savannah in 1865 by the Friends of New-York city. I there found that a number of coloured persons had organized a Society for the relief of freed orphans and aged freedmen. Their object was to found an asylum, and take the destitute of that class under their care. They asked my co-operation. I promised my assistance, with the understanding that they should raise among themselves the money to purchase the land. They are now working for that purpose. Their plan is to make the institution wholly, or in part, self-sustaining. It is proposed to cultivate the land (about fifteen acres) in vegetables and fruit. The institution will thereby be supplied, while a large surplus will remain for market sale. Poultry will also be raised for the market. This arrangement will afford a pleasant occupation to many of the old people, and a useful one to the older children out of school hours. I am deeply sensible of the interest taken and the aid rendered by the friends of Great Britain since the emancipation of Slavery. It is a noble evidence of their joy at the downfall of American Slavery and the advancement of human rights. I shall be grateful to any who shall respond to my efforts for the object in view. Every mite will tell in the balance.

"LINDA JACOBS.

"Contributions can be sent to

"STAFFORD ALLEN, ESQ., *Honorary Secretary*, 17, Church Street.

ROBERT ALSOP, ESQ., 36 Park Road, Stoke Newington, N.

MRS. PETER TAYLOR, Aubrey House, Notting Hill, W."

Jacobs's World

NATHANIEL WILLIS

From *The Convalescent*[†]

Letter IV.

Negro Happiness in Virginia—Persevering Politeness against Discouragement—Family's Slaves Moving West—Evening View of a Negro Cabin—Aunt Fanny, the Centenarian and the Black Baby—New kind of Negro Music—Pig-matins at Daylight—Chats with Negro Woodsmen—Virginia Supply of Black Walnut for Coffins—Adroit Negro Compliment—Family Graves on Plantation—Visit to the Hut of a Murderer's Widow.

IDLEWILD, *December.*

Did it ever occur to you to speculate upon the difference it would make, in the minds, moods and manners of the throngs in our streets, if that monster and nightmare of life, commonly understood by the phrase "care for a livelihood," were removed! I cannot explain in any, other way, the prompt and good-humored politeness, the ready wit, the really almost universal apparent gaiety and content, of the negroes of Virginia. We were all very much struck with this, in our few days' ramble through the Old Dominion.[1] The smile and service were so ready, the reply was so invariably and often so ingeniously courteous, the look of easy, care-for-nothing happiness was so habitual upon the countenances of all ages, that, for the first time, I realized what I had been always used to, as the contrary—how haunted are our working-classes at home by the spectre of responsibility in want. What a smile-killer it is! What a dampener of spontaneousness of tongue and brain! What a spoiler of the general sunshine of human faces is this care for a livelihood! Truly, the mere doing the work is the least part of earning a living.

The perseverance of the southern negro's politeness—however you may account for it—is a very agreeable difference between him and his brethren at the North. On board the different steamboats on the Potomac and Rappahannock, where many of the passengers were of the rougher

† From Nathaniel Parker Willis, *The Convalescent* (New York: Scribner, 1859).
1. Nickname for the state of Virginia [*Editor*].

classes of white men, we saw it very thoroughly tested. Nothing could well be more repelling than the early heave of the shoulder or the curt mono-syllable with which the best-phrased civilities of the waiters on table were oftenest received—yet it made no difference! Their ingenuity to suggest or invent a want, if there was none waiting to be supplied, was wholly in-defatigable. The smile was easy, and most submissively appealing. The manner and the words were well chosen and graceful. How is all this per-severed in, against so much discouragement!

On the forward deck of one of the boats ascending the Rappahannock was a bevy of some twenty slaves, whose master was taking them to his new residence in Arkansas. As they had come from an old Virginia plan-tation, in the interior, we watched them with some interest. They were of all ages, men, women and children, and a better conditioned or more contented company of working-people I never saw. I looked in vain for any sulkiness, or abstraction, or other sign of brooding over a hidden pain or sorrow. Whatever care any one of them might have had, personal or conditional, it seemed overbalanced by the blessed consciousness that the cares of the day were no business of his—he "was only a passenger."

At one of the plantations where we passed the night, the master of the house kindly assented to my wish for an inside view of one of the log-cabins. Somewhere about eight o'clock, in company with the young man whom he gave me for a guide, I crossed the courtyard to a low hut, from the cracks and crevices of which streamed the light of a bright fire within. It was the domicil of ten or twelve "haulers and steady cutters," who, after their work all day in the pine woods, came here to cook their supper and sleep. The scene as we opened the door was very picturesque. One whole side of the hut, according to the proportions of backwoods architecture, was fireplace; and, in front of a glowing heap of pine logs, sat the two who had charge of the cooking—a most tempting looking corn cake in one frying pan and a mess of pork in another. A boy of fourteen or fifteen years of age, sat with a jack-knife by a large heap of oysters, on one side; open-ing for the company; and around, in all possible attitudes, on the floor and up against the wall, lay the laborers, with their feet to the fire. I saw no beds. They seemed to lie down with their clothes on. One or two were asleep—probably to be waked up when supper should be ready. From one old fellow in the corner came the only approach to an uncivil speech which I heard while in Virginia. "Hullo, dar!" he roared out, very gruffly, to the boy who was sitting with his jack-knife by the heap of shells, "keep digging out dem oysters, and don't be looking roun' at noting at all!" Though perhaps this was intended as a correction of the lad's freedom in looking at the stranger.

On another plantation where we were most kindly entertained, there was a curiosity in the shape of a negro woman of great age; and, the little son of our host undertaking willingly to show me the way to "old Aunt Fanny's," we started for our visit after breakfast. There were several huts close together; and, at the half open door of one of them, the little fellow stood for a moment, calling to Aunt Fanny to make her appearance. And she came presently, with quite a lively step, a neatly-dressed little old mummy, as nearly dried up as skin and bones would any way permit, and most politely invited us in. It was a log-cabin, and the interior was exceedingly neat and comfortable. A bright fire burned on the hearth, the floor was cleanly swept, the bed in the corner with its patch-work quilt looked very inviting, and, on one side of the chimney, sat a handsome young woman of perhaps twenty-five years of age, rocking a cradle in which lay a black infant asleep. These were descendants of Aunt Fanny; and, with her they had lately fallen to their present master by inheritance—a comfortable home for the old woman, while she shall live, being thus provided by law. And to "the institution," it appeared also that the young mother was somewhat indebted, for the lad who was now her husband having fallen in love with her, his master had bought her from a neighboring planter and seen them happily married. In the ten minutes' conversation which I had with the old woman, she expressed herself very religiously, and seemed patiently "biding her time" to go to a better world. It was apparently as happy an old age as is often seen.

I was a little mystified, at one of our sleeping-places, with a new specimen of negro music. Just before day light, a sort of half melodious, half painful scream commenced making the circuit of the house—something which I, at first, took to be the incoherent wail of a madman, but which, by long repetition, grew at last into a concerted tune; aided also by a gradually strengthening accompaniment of something like the stamping of feet. Straining my eyes in all directions, I at last discovered a radiation, towards the house, of innumerable little black pigs, coming from every quarter across the fields and at all sorts of paces. The chanter of the pig-matin revolved presently around, a tall old negro with a slouched hat and his arms folded so as to get his hands out of the cold, and past him scampered his light-footed parish to their morning devorations—the song continuing vigorously, to make sure that they were all called in. It appeared that the little sinners have the run of the woods all day and night fed, in the morning only, at the trough; and it is this healthful exercise, probably, with perhaps some little flavor from their nut-eating and rooting, which gives the fame to the "Virginia ham." But the established music which summons them home is certainly a very penitential combination of notes, and, as the overture to a *peccavimus omnes,* to be chanted before daylight in Lent, is worthy of Catholic notice and analysis.

As much of the time of my companions was occupied in verifying the surveys of land where the felling of timber was going on, I had plenty of opportunity for chat with the negro wood-choppers; and I found them as amusing as they were universally good-humored and polite. The "stint" of work, I found, was but the cutting of one cord of pine wood a day—scarcely the half of what is "piled up" by any regular woodsman in our neighborhood. For this (where the slave is hired of his master), the wages are from ten to twelve dollars a month, besides food, lodging and clothing—somewhat more than a laborer gets for his winter work, with us. One very intelligent fellow, who handled his axe quite beautifully, inquired of me whether the *fashion for coffins* was likely to change at the North. I was a little puzzled with his question, till he explained that the present demand of *black-walnut*, for that final convenience, affected his class of chopping very considerably. The supply of the obituary staple from Virginia was new to me; and I could not tell him, of course, how soon the dead might return to their mahogany. Curious twin products for which to be indebted to the good old State—coffins and tobacco!

I was amused at the adroitness with which another young fellow contrived to turn a reply into a bantering compliment. He happened to have a remarkably handsome beard; and, in talking of the way coal was now superseding wood, so that the trees would soon be left to stand, not paying to cut and send away, I said: "So, this fine timber will be like that long beard of yours, very handsome where it grows, but not worth paying taxes upon, for want of a market." "Ah", said he, "massa! you and I too young to be berry anxious what dey'll tax us for our beards quite yet!" As the handsome rascal stood showing his teeth, and stroking down the silky black floss upon his chin, I wondered whether he knew how much of a courtier he was—coupling his own age and beard with those of a gentleman past fifty!

Our host, for one night, was but a temporary tenant occupying what was once the mansion-house of an old plantation. The graves of the family were in one corner of the garden, and those of the slaves in the field outside, separated only by the wooden paling. The last proprietor had sold out and moved to Alabama; but he had lately sent to know whether he could take the liberty to come and inclose the whole graveyard with a handsome paling, and plant it with evergreens, to be kept sacred. There seemed to me a very precious privacy in this old Virginia usage of burying within the limits of the home estate, and, if it were not for the uncertainty of tenure, how preferable it would always be to the kind of disowning that there is in the putting away of beloved remains to the common graveyard!

There was one home that we saw, upon our third day's tramp into the interior, of which I can scarce hope to describe to you the unutterable sadness. It was a log-cabin in the very heart of the wilderness, far removed from any other human dwelling; and here lived the widow and children of Tasco Adams, the free negro who, a few months ago, was hanged for murder. The mother was away—gone probably to some distant house to beg food for her children—and we went in to see what might be the refuge of the affrighted little ones who had fled from the door at our approach. Over the embers of a nearly extinct fire, stood shivering a little sickly girl of six or seven years, holding in her arms an infant of perhaps ten or twelve months, bundled in rags, while an almost naked child of two or three years clung to the tattered petticoat hanging in strings around her. A dog, as nearly starved as an animal could well be, crouched in behind the last brand in the chimney. There was no fuel around the entrance, and no sign of food within. The floor was of hardened mud, and a few rags in the corner were all that looked like a bed. For a picture of squalor and starvation, I had never seen the equal of that hovel's interior! And what a place to be left alone in, with such a memory! Yet a smile could be born, even here. As we gave the little wasted girl three pieces of money, one for each, she evidently remembered her mother, and looked up to me with a gleam over her dark face: "If you please, sir, one more!" she said. And a more beautiful smile than received that "one more" piece of money, never was born in a palace!

It were too long a step to pass from this entail of shame and want to the mention of the largest of human inheritances—the memory left behind by Washington—so, of our next day's approach to the childhood's home of the Father of his Country, I will reserve the description for another letter.

Yours always.

LYDIA MARIA CHILD

Letters to Harriet Jacobs

Wayland, Aug. 13th 1860

Dear Mrs. Jacobs,

I have been busy with your M.S. ever since I saw you; and have only done one third of it. I have very little occasion to alter the language, which is wonderfully good, for one whose opportunities for education have been so limited. The events are interesting, and well told; the remarks are also good, and to the purpose. But I am copying a great deal of it, for the purpose of transposing sentences and pages, so as to bring the story into continuous *order*, and the remarks into *appropriate* places. I think you will see that this renders the story much more clear and entertaining.

I should not take so much pains, if I did not consider the book unusually interesting, and likely to do much service to the Anti-Slavery cause. So you need not feel under great personal obligations. You know I would go through fire and water to help give a blow to Slavery. I suppose you will want to see the M.S. after I have exercised my bump of mental order upon it; and I will send it wherever you direct, a fortnight hence.

My object in writing at this time is to ask you to write what you can recollect of the outrages committed on the colored people, in Nat Turner's time.[1] You say the reader would not believe what you saw "inflicted on men, women, and children, without the slightest ground of suspicion against them." What *were* those inflictions? Were any tortured to make them confess? and how? Where [*sic*] any killed? Please write down some of the most striking particulars, and let me have them to insert.

I think the last Chapter, about John Brown,[2] had better be omitted. It does not naturally come into your story, and the M.S. is already too long. Nothing can be so appropriate to end with, as the death of your grandmother.

Mr. Child desires to be respectfully remembered to you.

> Very cordially your friend,
> L. Maria Child.

Wayland, Sep 27th, 1860

Dear Mrs. Jacobs,

I have signed and sealed the contract with Thayer & Eldridge, in my name and told them to take out the copyright in my name. Under the circumstances *your* name could not be used, you know. I inquired of other booksellers, and could find none that were willing to undertake it, except Thayer & Eldridge. I have never heard a word to the disparagement of either of them, and I do not think you could do better than to let them have it. They *ought* to have the monopoly of it for some time, if they *stereotype* it, because that process involves considerable expense, and if you changed publishers, their plates would be worth nothing to them. When I spoke of limiting them to an edition of 2000, I did not suppose they intended to stereotype it. They have agreed to pay you ten per cent on the retail price of all sold, and to let you have as many as you want, at the lowest wholesale price. On your part, I have agreed that they may publish it for five years on those terms, and that you will not print any abridgement, or altered copy, meanwhile.

I have no reason whatever to think that Thayer & Eldridge are likely to fail. I merely made the suggestion because they were *beginners*. However, several of the *oldest* bookselling firms have failed within the last three years; mine among the rest. We must run for luck in these matters.

I have promised to correct the proof-sheets, and I don't think it would be of any use to the book to have you here at this time. They say they shall get it out by the 1'st of Nov.

. . .

I want you to sign the following paper, and send it back to me. It will

---

1. Nat Turner (1800–1831) was the slave leader of a major rebellion in Southampton County, Virginia [*Editor*].
2. John Brown (1800–1859), white abolitionist who sought to end slavery by armed rebellion [*Editor*].

make Thayer and Eldridge safe about the contract in *my* name, and in case of my death, will prove that the book is *your* property, not *mine*.

Cordially your friend,

L. Maria Child.

. . .

FREEDMEN'S RECORD

Jacobs (Linda) School, Alexandria, VA.[†]

Many of our readers are familiar with a book called "Linda; or, the Autobiography of a Slave Girl." Perhaps few of them know that this slave girl is now one of the most zealous and efficient workers in the Freedmen's cause. Mrs. Harriet Jacobs was sent to Alexandria more than two years ago, by a society of Friends in New York, to look after the Freedmen who were gathered there. Her first winter's service was a very hard one. Smallpox and other diseases made fearful havoc among the people; and all her energies were exhausted in caring for their physical needs.

She has been unwearied in her labors, in providing orphan children with homes, in nursing the sick, in assisting the able-bodied to find work, and in encouraging all in habits of industry and self-reliance. They have established a school, and sent to the New-England Society for assistance in maintaining it. We offered them a teacher, and sent them Miss Virginia Lawton, a young colored woman of good education and great worth of character (the grand-daughter of one well known to the fashionable circles in Boston, as the administrator of good things at weddings, christenings, parties, and other merry-makings), who has taught there for a year. They have this autumn completed their school-house; and as the school was too large for Miss Lawton's care, we have sent them also Mr. Banfield, a finely educated young man from New Hampshire, who enters most heartily into the work. The most remarkable feature of Linda's slave life was this: to escape the persecution of a master not cruel, but *cruelly kind*, she hid in a small loft, under the roof of her grandmother's house, where light and air came only through the chinks in the boards, and where she lay concealed for seven years, within sound both of her children's voices and of her master's threats, before she succeeded in escaping altogether from the town.

No doubt, when she sank to sleep overwearied with the monotony of suffering, visions of hope and joy came through the golden gate of slumber, which snatched her away from her vile den, and gave her strength and courage to endure still longer. But was any dream of the night dearer and sweeter to her than the present reality?—her people freed, and the school-house, built mainly by her own exertions, named in her honor, and presided over by black and white teachers, working harmoniously together.

And yet, this woman, this lady,—who for years has been treated as a friend in the family of one of our celebrated literary men, and who has won the respect and love of all who have associated with her,—cannot ride in the street-cars at Washington, and is insulted even in a concert-room in Boston, on account of the slight tinge of color in her skin.

We have made great progress; but much yet remains to be done. We add extracts from letters of the teachers of this school.

FREEDMEN'S RECORD

School at Alexandria[†]

Mrs. Jacobs (Linda) has sent us an admirable photograph of the school in Alexandria which she aided in establishing, and which is so ably conducted by Mr. Banfield, and his assistants, the Misses Lawton. It is delightful to see this group of neatly dressed children, of all ages, and with faces of every variety of the African and mixed type, all intelligent, eager, and happy. Mrs. Jacobs's honest, beaming countenance irradiates the whole picture; and the good teacher stands in the background looking over his scholars with great complacency. It is a whole volume of answers to the sceptical and superficial questions often put as to the desire and capacity of the negro race for improvement.

The picture may be seen at our office by any friends wishing to know how a freedman's school looks.

FREEDMEN'S RECORD

A Milestone of Progress[‡]

We have before referred to Mrs. Harriet Jacobs, whose autobiography is well known under the title of "Linda." For the last three years she has been working among the freedmen of Alexandria, having established a school there whose teachers have been supplied by this society. The people at Alexandria are now so far advanced towards education and self-support,

† *Freedmen's Record*, September 1865.
‡ *Freedmen's Record*, December 1865.

that she feels justified in leaving them, that she may carry the blessings of her influence to those more in need. She has lately paid a visit to her early home in Edenton, N.C., where her years of slavery were passed. All was changed; only a few old people remembered "the chile who had been gone so long." But she looked up to her old prison-house, and thanked God for the deliverance vouchsafed her that she might lead her people, and felt that she would willingly bear seven years more of such misery, for such recompense. The son of her old master came to see her. He has lost all his property, and professes to have been all through the war a good Union man, and a great friend of the negro. He asks the influence of his former slave to procure him an office under the Freedmen's Bureau. We have seen a set of German pictures, called "The World Farned Upside Down." We think this incident would add another scene to the series.

Eulogy by Reverend Francis J. Grimke[1] (c. 1897)

It has been some years since I first made the acquaintance of Mrs. Jacobs. She was then living in Cambridge Mass. I took to her a letter of introduction from an intimate friend, who a few years afterwards passed into the silent land, into which she has now also entered. I remember as distinctly, as though it were yesterday, our first meeting. The cordiality with which she received me and made me welcome to her pleasant and hospitable home, I shall never forget. I soon felt, in her presence, as much at home as though I had known her all my life. And from that day to the present, as I came to know her more intimately, to get a clearer and fuller insight into the inner workings of her soul, the more strongly was I drawn towards her, and the more highly did I come to esteem her. Since her residence in this city I have seen much of her. I called frequently at her home; and it was always a pleasure to meet her, to get a glimpse of her kind, benevolent face; to feel the pressure of the warm grasp of her friendly hand; and to hear her speak of the stirring times before the war when the great struggle for freedom was going on, and of the events immediately after the war. She was thoroughly alive to all that was transforming, and had a most vivid recollection of the events and of the actors, the prominent men and women who figured on the stage of action at that time. She herself at the close of the war took an active interest in, and played a most important part in caring for the freedmen, in looking out for their physical needs, and in providing schools for the training of their children. My purpose however, is not to attempt a sketch of her life; that will be done at another time, and by other hands. All I desire to do, in the

---

1. Francis J. Grimke (1850–1937) was minister of the prominent and socially active Fifteenth Street Presbyterian Church in Washington, D.C. [*Editor*].

few moments that I shall occupy, is to state simply in a word, the impression she has left upon me, as I have come in contact with her during the years that I have known her.

She impressed me as a woman of marked individuality. There was never any danger of overlooking her, or of mistaking her for anybody else. Some people are mere nonentities, or, are merely negative quantities. They leave no very clear or marked impression upon those with whom they are associated. It was not so however, in her case. She was always a positive quantity, easily recognizable, and always sure to be felt wherever her lot was cast. She rose above the dead level of mediocrity, like the mountain peaks that shoot above the mountain range.

She was a woman of strong character. She possessed all the elements that go to make up such a character. She had great will power. She knew how to say, No, when it was necessary, and how to adhere to it. She was no reed shaken by the wind, vacillating, easily moved from a position. She did her own thinking; had opinions of her own, and held to them with great tenacity. Only when her judgment was convinced could she be moved.

With great strength of character, there was also combined in her a heart as tender as that of a little child. How wonderfully sympathetic she was; how readily did she enter into the sorrows, the heartaches of others; how natural it seemed for her to take up in the arms of her great love, all who needed to be soothed and comforted. The very Spirit of the Lord was upon her, that Spirit to which the prophet referred when he said: "The spirit of the Lord God is upon me, because he hath sent me to bind up the broken hearted; to comfort all that mourn; to give unto them beauty for ashes, the oil of joy for mourning, the garment of praise for the spirit of heaviness." How divinely beautiful was her sympathy, her tenderness.

She was also the very soul of generosity; she possessed in a remarkable degree, what we sometimes call the milk of human kindness. Especially did her sympathies go out towards the poor, the suffering, the destitute. She never hesitated to share what she had with others, to deny herself for the sake of helping a suffering fellow creature. There are hundreds, who if they had the opportunity to day, would rise up and call her blessed, to whom she has been a real sister of charity, a veritable Dorcas. As I think of her, I am reminded of that impressive scene which took place in the upper room at Joppa, so touchingly recounted in the Acts of the Apostles. How, as that noble woman lay in the icy embrace of death, those whom she had ministered to with her own hands came around and with tears in their eyes spoke of her kind, loving deeds. It is one of the most beautiful pictures presented in the whole word of God: and that which gives it its beauty, is the spirit of unselfish love which animated that noble woman while she lived,—beautiful because it is illumined with that divinest thing in the universe, unselfish love. And it is that love which made that life beautiful, and radiant, and divine, that is one of the crowning glories of this life which has just come to a close, and which has filled it with light and beauty. The estimate which the Master himself placed upon this quality may be seen in the summing up which he makes in the twenty fifth of Matthew, "Come ye blessed of my father, inherit the kingdom prepared for you from the foundation of the world: for I was an hungered and ye gave me meat: I was thirsty and ye gave me drink: I was naked and ye clothed me." And when they protested that they had no recollection of ever having thus ministering to him, his reply was, "In as much as ye have done it unto one of the least of these my brethren, ye have done it unto me." Surely this is what he will say to this departed friend. She ministered to such poor and suffering ones, as God gave her the ability.

I remember some years ago, — it was on Thanksgiving day, — how she gathered into her home a goodly company of old people, who were in destitute circumstances, and made a feast for them. Thus carrying out the Savior's [. . .] And I remember also how happy it made her to see the old people enjoy themselves. It was a real pleasure to her. How her face lighted up as she looked upon their bright, happy countenances. She seemed even happier than the old people themselves, though their hearts were overflowing with joy. And that is but a sample of what she was constantly doing. The alabaster box of precious ointment which Mary broke and poured out upon the head of Jesus, as an expression of her love, she was constantly breaking and pouring out, in his name, upon the poor, the suffering, the destitute. And like the odor of that precious ointment, the influence of her beautiful and unselfish life shall long continue to be felt amongst us.

As a friend, she was true to the heart's core. She could always be depended upon. She was absolutely loyal. There was not the slightest trace of insincerity about her. There was not a false note in all her make up. She grappled her friends to her soul with hooks of steel.

Religiously, she was a woman of real, genuine piety, of deep heart-felt spirituality. Hers was no mere empty profession: she lived the life of a Christian; hers was the faith that works by love, and that purifies the heart. She believed in God; she believed in Jesus Christ; she rested upon him as her only and all-sufficient Saviour. She desired to please him; to live to his glory; to be wholly conformed to his image; she was constantly reaching forth, ever pressing towards the mark, for the prize of the high calling of God, in Christ Jesus.

This is the life she lived; and with faith unshaken—the faith that looks death in the face and says, where is thy sting? grave, where is thy victory? she fell asleep on last Sabbath morning, in the beautiful realization of the fact that it was well with her soul.

> "Asleep in Jesus, blessed sleep
>   From which none ever wakes to weep,
>   A calm and undisturbed repose
>   Unbroken by the last of foes."

We say farewell to her, but it is only for a little time. We sorrow not like those without hope. Ours is the hope, not only of an inheritance that is incorruptible, undefiled and that fadeth not away; but also of a glorious reunion beyond, the smiling and the weeping.

> "We shall reach the summer-land,
>   Some sweet day, by and by;
> We shall press the golden strand,
>   Some sweet day, by and by;
> Oh, the loved ones watching there,
>   By the tree of life so fair;
> Till we come their joy to share,
>   Some sweet day, by and by.
>
> At the crystal river's brink,
>   Some sweet day, by and by;
> We shall find each broken link,
>   Some sweet day, by and by;
> Then the star which faded here,
>   Left our hearts and homes so drear,
> We shall see more bright and clear,
>   Some sweet day, by and by.

CRITICISM

JEAN FAGAN YELLIN

Written by Herself: Harriet Jacobs' Slave Narrative[†]

I

Your proposal to me has been thought over and over again, but not without some most painful remembrance. Dear Amy, if it was the life of a heroine with no degradation associated with it! Far better to have been one of the starving poor of Ireland whose bones had to bleach on the highways than to have been a slave with the curse of slavery stamped upon yourself and children. . . . I have tried for the last two years to conquer . . . [my stubborn pride] and I feel that God has helped me, or I never would consent to give my past life to anyone, for I would not do it without giving the whole truth. If it could help save another from my fate, it would be selfish and unChristian in me to keep it back.[1]

With these words, more than a century ago the newly emancipated fugitive slave Harriet Jacobs expressed conflicting responses to a friend's suggestion that she make her life story public. Although she finally succeeded in writing and publishing her sensational tale, its authenticity—long questioned—has recently been denied. Jacobs' *Incidents in the Life of a Slave Girl: Written By Herself* has just been transformed from a questionable slave narrative into a well-documented pseudonymous autobiography, however, by the discovery of a cache of her letters.[2]

This correspondence establishes Jacobs' authorship and clarifies the role of her editor. In doing so, it provides us with a new perspective on an unlikely grouping of nineteenth-century writers—Nathaniel P. Willis,

---

† From *American Literature* 53.3 (November 1981): 379–486. Copyright 1981, Duke University Press. All rights reserved. Reprinted with permission.

1. This passage comes from one of thirty letters from Harriet Jacobs to Amy Post in the Post Family Papers recently acquired by the University of Rochester Library. Labeled a.d. #84, it was probably written at the end of 1852 or the beginning of 1853. All of the letters cited from Jacobs to Post are in this collection. Most note only day and month; my attempts to supply missing dates may be in error. Editing Jacobs' letters, I have regularized paragraphing, capitalization, punctuation, and spelling, but not otherwise tampered with text.

I hasten to record my considerable debt to Dorothy Sterling who includes some of Jacobs' letters in *A Woman and Black* (Norton, in press) and with whom I am writing a book on Jacobs; to Karl Kabelac of the University of Rochester Library; and to Patricia G. Holland, co-editor of *The Collected Correspondence of Lydia Maria Child*, 1817–1880 (Millwood, N.Y.: K.T.O. Microform, 1979).

2. [Harriet Jacobs], *Incidents in the Life of a Slave Girl. Written by Herself.* Ed. L. Maria Child (Boston: For the Author, 1861). An English edition appeared the following year: [Harriet Jacobs], *The Deeper Wrong: Or, Incidents in the Life of a Slave Girl. Written by Herself.* Ed. L. Maria Child. (London: W. Tweedie, 1862).

Examining *Incidents* in a discussion of "fictional accounts . . . in which the major character may have been a real fugitive, but the narrative of his life is probably false," John Blassingame recently judged that "the work is not credible." See *The Slave Community* (New York: Oxford Univ. Press, 1972), pp. 233–34.

Harriet Beecher Stowe, William C. Nell, and L. Maria Child—and enriches our literary history by presenting us with a unique chronicle of the
efforts of an underclass black woman to write and publish her autobiography in antebellum America.

II

The appearance of Jacobs' letters has made it possible to trace her life.
She was born near Edenton, North Carolina, about 1815. In *Incidents*,
she writes that her parents died while she was a child, and that at the
death of her beloved mistress (who had taught her to read and spell) she
was sent to a licentious master. He subjected her to unrelenting sexual
harassment. In her teens she bore two children to another white man.
When her jealous master threatened her with concubinage, Jacobs ran
away. Aided by sympathetic black and white neighbors, she was sheltered
by her family and for years remained hidden in the home of her grandmother, a freed slave. During this time the father of her children, who
had bought them from her master, allowed them to live with her grandmother. Although later he took their little girl to a free state, he failed to
keep his promise to emancipate the children.

About 1842, Harriet Jacobs finally escaped North, contacted her
daughter, was joined by her son, and found work in New York City. Because the baby she was hired to tend was the daughter of litterateur N.P.
Willis, it has been possible to use Willis' materials to piece out—and to
corroborate—Jacobs' story.[3] In 1849 she moved to Rochester, New York,
where the Women's Rights Convention had recently met and where
Frederick Douglass' *North Star* was being published each week. With her
brother, a fugitive active in the abolitionist movement, she ran an anti-
slavery reading room and met other reformers. Jacobs made the
Rochester Quaker Amy Post, a feminist and abolitionist, her confidante;
her letters to Post date from this period. In September 1850 Jacobs returned to New York and resumed work in the Willis household. When
she was again hounded by her owner, she and her children were purchased and manumitted by Willis.

It was following this—between 1853 and 1858—that Jacobs acqui-
esced to Post's urgings; after a brush with Harriet Beecher Stowe, she
wrote out the story of her life by herself. With the help of black abolitionist writer William C. Nell and white abolitionist woman of letters L.
Maria Child (whose correspondence, too, corroborates Jacobs'), her narrative was finally published early in 1861.[4] As the national crisis deepened, Jacobs attempted to swell sentiment for Emancipation by

---

3. Willis referred to Jacobs directly—though not by name—in a *House and Home* column
   reprinted in *Outdoors at Idlewild* (New York: Scribner's, 1855), pp. 275–76.
4. Nell reviewed *Incidents* in *The Liberator*, 25 Jan. 1861. Other reviews include *The National Anti-
   Slavery Standard*, 23 Feb. 1861, and *The Weekly Anglo-African*, 13 April 1861. Relevant passages
   from Child's correspondence are cited below.

publicizing and circulating her book. During the Civil War she went to Washington, D.C., to nurse black troops; she later returned South to help the freedmen. Jacobs remained actively engaged for the next thirty years. She died at Washington, D.C., in 1897.

III

The primary literary importance of Harriet Jacobs' letters to Amy Post is that they establish her authorship of *Incidents* and define the role of her editor, L. Maria Child. They also yield a fascinating account of the experiences of this underclass black female autobiographer with several antebellum writers.

Jacobs' letters express her conviction that, unlike both his first and his second wife, Nathaniel P. Willis was "pro-slavery," and writings like his picturesque 1859 account of slave life entitled "Negro Happiness in Virginia" must have confirmed her judgment.[5] Because of this—although she repeatedly sought help to win the time and privacy to write, and even requested introductions to public figures in hope that they would effect the publication of her book—Jacobs consistently refused to ask for Willis' aid. She did not even want him to know that she was writing. For years, while living under his roof, she worked on her book secretly and at night.

Her brief involvement with Harriet Beecher Stowe was decisive in the genesis of *Incidents*. When Jacobs first agreed to a public account of her life, she did not plan to write it herself, but to enlist Stowe's aid in helping her produce a dictated narrative. To this end, Jacobs asked Post to approach Uncle Tom's creator with the suggestion that Jacobs be invited to Stowe's home so they could become acquainted. Then, reading in the papers of the author's plan to travel abroad, Jacobs persuaded Mrs. Willis to write suggesting that Stowe permit Jacobs' daughter Louisa to accompany her to England as a "representative southern slave."

Harriet Beecher Stowe evidently responded by writing to Mrs. Willis that she would not take Jacobs' daughter with her, by forwarding to Mrs. Willis Post's sketch of Jacobs' sensational life for verification, and by proposing that if it was true, she herself use Jacobs' story in *The Key to Uncle Tom's Cabin*, which she was rushing to complete. Reporting all of this to Post, Jacobs suggests that she felt denigrated as a mother, betrayed as a woman, and threatened as a writer by Stowe's action.

> [Mrs. Stowe] said it would be much care to her to take Louisa. As she went by invitation, it would not be right, and she was afraid that if . . . [Louisa's] situation as a slave should be known, it would subject her to much petting and patronizing, which would be more

---

5. For Jacobs on Willis, see Jacobs to Post, Cornwall, Orange County (late 1852–early 1853?) n.d. #84. Child commented on Jacobs' relationship with Willis in a letter to John G. Whittier dated 4 April 1861, now in the Child Papers, Manuscript Division, the Library of Congress. Willis' article was anthologized in *The Convalescent* (New York: Scribner's, 1859), pp. 410–16.

pleasing to a young girl than useful; and the English were very apt to do it, and . . . [Mrs. Stowe] was very much opposed to it with this class of people. . . .

I had never opened my life to Mrs. Willis concerning my children. . . . It embarrassed me at first, but I told her the truth; but we both thought it wrong in Mrs. Stowe to have sent your letter. She might have written to inquire if she liked.

Mrs. Willis wrote her a very kind letter begging that she would not use any of the facts in her *Key*, saying that I wished it to be a history of my life entirely by itself, which would do more good, and it needed no romance; but if she wanted some facts for her book, that I would be most happy to give her some. She never answered the letter. She [Mrs. Willis] wrote again, and I wrote twice, with no better success. . . .

I think she did not like my objection. I can't help it.[6]

Jacobs later expressed her racial outrage: "Think, dear Amy, that a visit to Stafford House would spoil me, as Mrs. Stowe thinks petting is more than my race can bear? Well, what a pity we poor blacks can't have the firmness and stability of character that you white people have!"[7]

Jacobs' distrust of Willis and disillusionment with Stowe contrast with her confidence in William C. Nell and L. Maria Child. After the Stowe episode, Jacobs decided to write her story herself. She spent years on the manuscript and, when it was finished, more years trying to get it published in England and America. Finally, in a letter spelling out the cost of her lack of an endorsement from Willis or Stowe, she reported to Post that Nell and Child were helping arrange for the publication of her autobiography.

Difficulties seemed to thicken, and I became discouraged. . . . My manuscript was read at Phillips and Sampson. They agreed to take it if I could get Mrs. Stowe or Mr. Willis to write a preface for it. The former I had the second clinch [?] from, and the latter I would not ask, and before anything was done, this establishment failed. So I gave up the effort until this autumn [when] I sent it to Thayer and Eldridge of Boston. They were willing to publish it if I could obtain a preface from Mrs. Child. . . .

I had never seen Mrs. Child. Past experience made me tremble at the thought of approaching another satellite of so great magnitude . . . [but] through W. C. Nell's ready kindness, I met Mrs. Child at the antislavery office. Mrs. C. is like yourself, a whole-souled

---

6. My discussion of Jacobs and Stowe is based on five letters from Jacobs to Post: Cornwall, Orange County (late 1852–early 1853?) n.d. #84; 14 Feb. (1853?); 4 April (1853?); New Bedford, Mass. (Spring, 1853?) n.d. #80; 31 July (1854?) n.d. #88. The lengthy quotation is from Jacobs to Post, 4 April (1853?). I have been unable to locate any letters to Stowe from Post, Cornelia Willis, or Jacobs, or from Stowe to Cornelia Willis.

7. Jacobs to Post, New Bedford, Mass. (Spring, 1853?) n.d. #80.

woman. We soon found the way to each other's heart. I will send you some of her letters. . . .[8]

Accompanying this correspondence are two letters from L. Maria Child to Harriet Jacobs. These, I believe, resolve the questions historians have repeatedly raised concerning the editing of Jacobs' manuscript. Child begins the first by describing her editorial procedures in much the same way she later discussed them in her Introduction to *Incidents.*

> I have been busy with your M.S. ever since I saw you; and have only done one-third of it. I have very little occasion to alter the language, which is wonderfully good, for one whose opportunities for education have been so limited. The events are interesting, and well told; the remarks are also good, and to the purpose. But I am copying a great deal of it, for the purpose of transposing sentences and pages, so as to bring the story into continuous *order*, and the remarks into *appropriate* places. I think you will see that this renders the story much more clear and entertaining.

Child's second letter is a detailed explanation of the publisher's contract.[9]

Jacobs' letters are also of value in providing a unique running account of the efforts of this newly emancipated Afro-American woman to produce her autobiography. After deciding to write the manuscript herself, she followed the long-standing practice of sending apprentice pieces to the newspapers. In style and in subject, her first public letter reflects her private correspondence and prefigures her book by using the language of polite letters to discuss the sexual exploitation of women in slavery. Jacobs begins with an announcement of her newly found determination to tell her tale by herself. Then—as in the letters and the book—she expresses the pain she feels as she recalls and writes about her life.

> Poor as it may be, I had rather give . . . [my story] from my own hand, than have it said that I employed others to do it for me. . . .
> I was born a slave, raised in the Southern hot-bed until I was the mother of two children, sold at the early age of two and four years old. I have been hunted through all of the Northern States—but no,

---

8. Jacobs to Post, 8 Oct. (1860?). I have not been able to document a second attempt to gain Stowe's backing. Jacobs discusses her efforts to publish her book abroad in letters to Post dated 21 June (1857?) n.d. #90; New Bedford, 9 August (1857?); 1 March (1858?); and Cambridge, 3 May (1858?) n.d. #87.
9. Child to Jacobs, Wayland, 13 August 1860; and Wayland, 27 Sept. 1860. Any remaining doubts concerning Child's role must, I think, rest on an undated plea for secrecy from Jacobs to Post: "Please let no one see these letters. I am pledged to Mrs. Child that I will tell no one what she has done, as she is beset by so many people, and it would affect the book. It must be the slave's own story—which it truly is." To my mind, this reflects an effort to shield Child from interruption while she edits the manuscript, not an attempt to hide editorial improprieties. Also see Child to Lucy [Searle], 4 Feb. 1861 in the Lydia Maria Child Papers, Anti-Slavery Collection of Cornell University Libraries.

I will not tell you of my own suffering—no, it would harrow up my soul. . . .[1]

Encouraged by the publication of this letter, Jacobs secretly composed others. Her correspondence during this period reveals that she was at once determined to write, apprehensive about her ability to do so, and fearful of being discovered: "No one here ever suspected me [of writing to the *Tribune*]. I would not have Mrs. W. to know it before I had undertaken my history, for I must write just what I have lived and witnessed myself. Don't expect much of me, dear Amy. You shall have truth, but not talent."[2]

The letters record other pressures. During the years Jacobs composed her extraordinary memoirs, Mr. and Mrs. Willis moved into an eighteen-room estate and added two more children to their family; Jacobs' work load increased accordingly. Writing to Post, she voiced the frustrations of a would-be writer who earned her living as a nursemaid: "Poor Hatty's name is so much in demand that I cannot accomplish much; if I could steal away and have two quiet months to myself, I would work night and day though it should all fall to the ground." She went on, however, to say that she preferred the endless interruptions to revealing her project to her employers: "To get this time I should have to explain myself, and no one here except Louisa knows that I have ever written anything to be put in print. I have not the courage to meet the criticism and ridicule of educated people."[3]

Her distress about the content of her book was even worse than her embarrassment about its formal flaws. As her manuscript neared completion, Jacobs asked Post to identify herself with the book in a letter expressing her concern about its sensational aspects and her need for the acceptance of another woman: "I have thought that I wanted some female friend to write a preface or some introductory remarks . . . yet believe me, dear friend, there are many painful things in . . . [my book] that make me shrink from asking the sacrifice from one so good and pure as yourself."[4]

IV

While *Incidents* embodies the general characteristics of the slave narrative, it has long been judged a peculiar example of this American genre. It is not, like most, the story of a life but, as its title announces, of incidents in a life. Like other narrators, Jacobs asserted her authorship in her subtitle, wrote in the first person, and addressed the subject of the op-

---

1. "Letter From a Fugitive Slave," New York *Tribune*, 21 June 1853. Jacobs' second letter appeared on 25 July 1853.
2. Jacobs to Post, 9 Oct. (1853?) n.d. #85. Also see Jacobs to Post, Cornwall, 25 June (1853?).
3. Jacobs to Post, Cornwall, 11 Jan. (1854?).
4. Jacobs to Post, 18 May and 8 June (1857?). Post's signed statement in the Appendix to *Incidents* was written in response to this request.

pression of chattel slavery and the struggle for freedom from the perspective of one who had been enslaved. But in her title she identified herself by gender, and in her text addressed a specific aspect of this subject.
Incidents is an account by a woman of her struggle against her oppression
in slavery as a sexual object and as a mother. Thus it presents a double
critique of our nineteenth-century ideas and institutions. It inevitably
challenges not only the institution of chattel slavery and its supporting
ideology of white racism; it also challenges traditional patriarchal institutions and ideas.

Publication of this book marked, I think, a unique moment in our literary history. *Incidents* defied the taboos prohibiting women from discussing their sexuality—much less their sexual exploitation—in print.
Within its pages, a well-known woman writer presented to the public the
writing of a pseudynomous "impure woman" on a "forbidden subject."
Here a black American woman, defying barriers of caste and class, defying rules of sexual propriety, was joined by a white American woman to
make her history known in an attempt to effect social change. It is ironic
that this narrative, which was painfully written in an effort to give "the
whole truth," has been branded false. Now that the discovery of Harriet
Jacobs' letters has established that her book was indeed *Written By Herself*, we can reexamine its place within women's writings, Afro-American
literature, and the body of our national letters.

ANN TAVES

Spiritual Purity and Sexual Shame: Religious Themes in the Writings of Harriet Jacobs[†]

In a review published in 1849, Ephraim Peabody observed that "America has the mournful honor of adding a new department to the literature
of civilization,—the autobiographies of escaped slaves."[1] As Peabody
went on to point out, "these narratives show how it [slavery] looks as seen
from the side of the slave. They contain the *victim's account* of the workings of this great institution."[2] As such, they have proved an invaluable re-
source for examining the religious life of Afro-Americans under slavery.
Yet despite the fact that Peabody and others recognized "the peculiar

---

† From *Church History* March 1987: 59–72. Reprinted with the permission of the American Society of Church History. Page references to this Norton Critical Edition are given in brackets following Taves's original citations. [I would like to thank David W. Wills, Albert Raboteau, and
the members of the Summer 1986 NEH Institute on Afro-American Religion for their help, both
direct and indirect, in revising this paper (Taves's acknowledgment).]
1. Ephraim Peabody, "Narratives of Fugitive Slaves," *Christian Examiner* 47 (1849): 61–93, quoted
in Charles T. Davis and Henry Louis Gates, Jr., *The Slave's Narrative* (Oxford, 1985), p. 19.
2. Ibid., p. 20.

hardships to which the female slave [was] subjected" during the nineteenth century, few recent studies of slavery have paid attention to differences in gender and none, to my knowledge, have explored the impact of gender differences on the religious life of slaves.[3]

Of the more than one hundred and thirty autobiographical narratives and slave narratives written by persons of African descent and published prior to 1865, only sixteen were written by women. Of these, a number with considerable religious interest are autobiographical works by free black women in the north.[4] Of the actual slave narratives, many focus almost entirely on their author's escape from the South and pay almost no attention to religious issues.[5] Harriet Jacobs's *Incidents in the Life of a Slave Girl*, published in 1861 under the pseudonym Linda Brent, is one of the few narratives which gives considerable, albeit often indirect, insight into the religious life of its author.[6] Although Jacobs, an unusually intelligent, literate, mulatto daughter of relatively independent slave parents, cannot be taken to represent the female slave experience, careful examination of her experience in its particularity promises to broaden our understanding of the diversity and complexity of the religious life of Afro-Americans under slavery.

Like many Afro-Americans, particularly those who were enslaved, Jacobs appropriated Christianity critically. Baptized as a child, her participation in the rituals of institutional church life appear to have been sporadic. After the Nat Turner revolt led slaveowners to intensify their missionary efforts "to keep [the slaves] from murdering their masters," Jacobs was invited to participate in a segregated, but still elitist, Episcopal service because she could read. She reports that she and the others in attendance were amused by the priest's sermons on the duty of servants to obey their masters.[7] Although she also apparently attended Methodist class meetings on occasion, she describes the enthusiastic style of worship (the "shouting and singing") of her fellow slaves in a detached, yet sym-

3. Ibid., p. 22; Lydia Maria Child, *An Appeal in Favor of that Class of Americans Called Africans* (New York, 1836; reprint ed., New York, 1968), p. 23; Deborah Gray White, *Ar'n't I a Woman?: Female Slaves in the Plantation South* (New York, 1985), is one of the few works to focus on the experience of women under slavery.

4. Davis and Gates, *The Slave's Narrative*, pp. 319–330; see, for example, Jarena Lee, *The Life and Religious Experiences of Jarena Lee, A Coloured Lady, Giving an Account of Her Call to Preach the Gospel* (Philadelphia, 1836); Maria W. Stewart, *Productions of Mrs. Maria Stewart* (Boston, 1835); Harriet E. Adams Wilson, *Our Nig; or, Sketches from the Life of a Free Black, in a Two-Story White House, North* (Boston, 1859); and Zipha Elaw, *Memoirs of the Life, Religious Experiences, Ministerial Travels and Labours* (London, 1846). The autobiographies of Lee, Elaw, and Julia Foote are reprinted in *Sisters of the Spirit: Three Black Women's Autobiographies of the Nineteenth Century*, ed. William L. Andrews (Bloomington, Ind., 1986).

5. See, for example, Frances Whipple Greene, *Memoirs of Eleanor Eldridge* (Providence, 1838); Sally Williams, *Aunt Sally; or The Cross the Way to Freedom* (Cincinnati, 1858); Jane Brown, *Narrative of the Life of Jane Brown* (Hartford, 1860); and William Craft, *Running a Thousand Miles for Freedom; or, the Escape of William and Ellen Craft from Slavery* (London, 1860).

6. Linda Brent [Harriet Jacobs], *Incidents in the Life of a Slave Girl*, ed. L. Maria Child (Boston, 1861; New York, 1973).

7. Ibid., pp. 69–70 [57–58].

pathetic, way.[8] She shows no signs of having had an evangelical conversion experience. In addition, her critical comments about southern white church life and her refusal to join a white church suggest that her attraction to Christianity was ambivalent and was grounded less in her admiration for whites, especially white males, than in her own intense, female-oriented family relationships. Specifically, I would suggest that the connection which Jacobs makes between sexual purity and spirituality, a connection which lies at the heart of her narrative and indeed was prevalent among Christians of her era, was grounded in her relationships with her mother, her grandmother, and her first mistress.

Jacobs's autobiography, like most of the slave narratives, was written to aid the abolitionist cause. It differs from the majority of slave narratives, though, not only in its female authorship, but also in its frank treatment of the issue of sexuality (and sexual abuse) between masters and female slaves. Briefly summarized, the plot of Jacobs's narrative runs as follows: Jacobs, who refers to herself as Linda Brent in the book, was born of slave parents in Edenton, North Carolina in 1818. Her father was a skilled carpenter who worked independently and paid his mistress two hundred dollars a year. Harriet lived with her parents and her younger brother, William (John Jacobs), in their own home.[9] Harriet's grandmother, who had managed to obtain her freedom late in life, also supported herself and had her own home in Edenton. When Harriet was six, her mother died, and she was sent to live with her mother's mistress. This woman, whom Harriet calls her "good mistress," taught her how to read and write.[1] She died when Harriet was twelve, bequeathing her to her niece, a five-year-old child. Harriet's father died shortly thereafter. Beginning when she was fifteen, however, Dr. Flint, the niece's father and now Jacob's master, began to threaten her sexually. At the point when she felt she could no longer evade his advances, she voluntarily entered into a sexual relationship with an unmarried slaveowner, Mr. Sands, in hope of so angering her master that he would sell her. She bore two children by Sands. When her master refused to sell her or her children, Jacobs hid in a small garret attached to her grandmother's house and eventually deceived her master into thinking she had escaped to the north. Her master finally sold her children, who were then bought by Sands with the promise that he would free them. After seven years in the garret, Jacobs did escape to the north. There she worked for a Mr. and Mrs. Bruce (ac-

8. Ibid., pp. 71–73 [58–60].
9. This situation was not unusual. According to James E. Newton and Ronald L. Lewis, "bondage in the United States actually took a variety of forms. [Because] American slavery is usually associated with the plantation regime, . . . we tend to forget that by 1860 a large percentage of the slave population lived in southern towns and cities laboring at a multitude of non-agricultural pursuits"; *The Other Slaves: Mechanics, Artisans and Craftsmen* (Boston, 1978), pp. xi–xii.
1. Most slaves who learned to read were, like Jacobs, taught by their owners out of religious motives. See Janet Cornelius, "'We Slipped and Learned to Read': Slave Accounts of the Literacy Process, 1830–1865," *Phylon* 44 (1983): 171–186.

tually Mr. and Mrs. N. P. Willis) in New York City, where she was reunited with her daughter, Ellen (Louisa Jacobs).

Published pseudonymously with the help of abolitionist Lydia Maria
Child and addressed to a northern female audience, the book's appropriation of the conventions of the sentimental novel, as well as of the slave
narrative, led many to assume that Child herself was the author.[2] Recently, Jean Fagan Yellin has established Jacob's authorship by means of
letters written by Jacobs to white abolitionist Amy Post during the time
she was writing the book and by letters written by Child to Jacobs which
describe Child's role as editor.[3]

Although the authorship puzzle has been solved, access to the text is
complicated by the literary conventions used by the author. Were her
protestations of shame and affirmations of the virtues of purity merely
conventional, or did they go to the heart of her own spiritual dilemma?
Conventional though her beliefs may appear, Jacobs's narrative roots her
struggles with issues of shame and purity in family relationships lived out
in the context of slavery. Her letters to Amy Post reveal that her inability
to conform to the conventional canons of nineteenth-century Protestant
morality in the context of slavery was both a powerful weapon in the
hands of the abolitionist movement and a continuing source of personal
shame.

Shame, according to Helen Lynd, "includes the subjective feeling of
the person and the objective nature of the act." Subjectively, it is experienced "as a wound to one's self-esteem, a painful feeling or sense of degradation excited by the consciousness of having done something unworthy
of one's previous idea of one's own excellence." Objectively, shame is the
result of an action which "incurs the scorn or contempt of others."[4]
Shame is thus a relational concept in which the individual's loss of self-
esteem is linked to the scornful or contemptuous response of others.

In his discussion of emotional development, Erik Erikson links shame
and autonomy.[5] Although typically, he argues, small children first wres-

---

2. Valerie Smith, "'Loopholes of Retreat': Architecture and Ideology in Harriet Jacob's *Incidents in
the Life of a Slave Girl*," Paper given at the biennial meeting of the American Studies Association, San Diego, Calif., November 1985.
3. Jean Fagin Yellin, "Text and Contexts of Harriet Jacobs's Incidents in the Life of a Slave Girl:
Written by Herself," in Davis and Gates, *The Slave's Narrative*, pp. 262–282. Excerpts from the
letters are contained in Yellin's article. Child's letters to Jacobs are published in *Lydia Maria
Child, Selected Letters, 1817–1880*, ed. Milton Meltzer and Patricia G. Holland (Amherst,
1982), pp. 357–359; two other letters also refer to Jacobs, pp. 374–375, 378–379. The original
copies of the letters by and to Jacobs are in the Isaac and Amy Post Family Papers at the University of Rochester.
4. Helen Merrill Lynd, *On Shame and the Search for Identity* (New York, 1958), pp. 23–24.
5. Ibid., pp. 206–210. Where feelings of shame presuppose a sense of relatedness, feelings of autonomy presuppose a sense of independence. In their most extreme form, feelings of shame suggest a need to conform oneself entirely to the expectations of others in order to avoid rejection
by them. Feelings of autonomy, when carried to an extreme, suggest a need to reject others entirely in order to avoid being overwhelmed by their needs and expectations. A balance between
the two requires a stable sense of self, such that the individual can experience the needs and expectations of others without necessarily meeting them and withstand the risk of rejection, should
that occur.

tle with the issues of autonomy and shame in relation to their parents, such issues often resurface later in life, particularly during adolescence.[6] It is to this developmental issue that Jacobs returned when confronted as an adolescent with her master's threats of sexual abuse. Her master threatened her autonomy; the thought of telling her grandmother, who she was sure would disapprove, brought feelings of shame. Her decision to have an affair with Mr. Sands in order to avoid being raped by her master led to the shame of sex outside marriage and to two illegitimate children.

Moreover, as Leon Wurmser has pointed out, an important phenomenological characteristic of shame is that it may result both from the "particular *content* that is exposed" and from "the *function* of self-exposure." The fear at the heart of the feeling of shame is "rejection with contempt" and thus isolation.[7] The problem of whom, if anyone, to tell was a continuous issue for Jacobs, both before and after her escape from the South. The fear of rejection as a result of her past, which recurs both in her narrative and in her letters to Amy Post, is indicative of her ongoing struggles with issues of autonomy and shame.

It was not until the late 1840s, when Louisa was in her early teens, that Jacobs first broached the subject of Mr. Sands with her daughter. In a short chapter entitled "The Confession," Jacobs explained to her daughter how her "early sufferings in slavery . . . had crushed [her] . . . [and] driven [her] into a great sin." Louisa revealed that she had been told who her father was by a nurse when she was a child but had been told not to tell anyone. Jacobs states: "I thanked God that the knowledge I had so much dreaded to impart had not diminished the affection of my child. I had not the slightest idea she knew that portion of my history. If I had, I should have spoken to her long before; for my pent-up feelings had often longed to pour themselves out to someone I could trust."[8] The religious language of sin and confession provided Jacobs with a way of conceptualizing her underlying need to pour out her pent-up feelings to someone she could trust, while at the same time revealing how difficult it was for her to describe her feelings to someone whose affection she needed so badly.

A year later Jacobs moved to Rochester, New York to run an antislavery reading room with her brother John. Although the reading room was not successful and her brother left for California accompanied by her son, Jacobs stayed on in Rochester for a year, living with and working for Isaac and Amy Post, white abolitionists whom she described as "practical

---

6. A number of feminist scholars, following Nancy Choderow and Dorothy Dinnerstein, have argued that assymetries in parenting responsibilities lead to differences in the ways that male and female children typically balance autonomy and relatedness. The traditional identification of masculinity with autonomy and femininity with relatedness suggests that feelings of shame may be more problematic for women, making it more difficult for women than men to transgress cultural norms.

7. Leon Wurmser, *The Mask of Shame* (Baltimore, 1981), pp. 56, 82–83.

8. Brent, *Incidents*, pp. 194–195 [146].

believers in the Christian doctrine of human brotherhood."[9] Jacobs became close friends with Amy Post, an ex-Hicksite Quaker turned spiritualist, who had aided a number of women who had been abused and abandoned by their husbands and sheltered numerous escaped slaves.[1] Jacobs was able to tell Post about her past and her letters to Amy during the 1850s and 1860s describe the feelings which Jacobs had to overcome in order to write her narrative.

It is clear from the letters that it was Post who encouraged Jacobs to write and publish her story and that Jacobs was very reluctant to do so. In a letter written to Post in late 1852 or early 1853, Jacobs states: "Your proposal to me [to write a book] has been thought over and over again but not without some most painful remembrances. Dear Amy, if it was the life of a heroine with no degradation associated with it. Far better to have been one of the starving poor of Ireland whose bones had to bleach on the highways than to have been a slave with the curse of slavery stamped upon yourself and children."[2]

Jacobs indicates that her initial decision had been to avoid speaking of her past. Although Post's "purity of heart and kindly sympathies [led her] at one time to speak of [her] children," those were, Jacobs says, "the only words that [had] passed [her] lips" on the subject since she left the South. "I had determined," she continues, "to let others think as they pleased but my lips would be sealed." As a result, Jacobs indicates that "when [she] first came North, [she] avoided the antislavery people as much as possible because [she] felt that [she] could not be honest and tell [them] the whole truth." She may have come to this conclusion as a result of her conversation with Reverend Durham of Bethel AME Church in Philadelphia. She records in the *Incidents* that upon arriving in Philadelphia from the South, she did risk telling Rev. Durham that she was an unmarried

---

9. Ibid., p. 194 [146–47]; Yellin, "Texts and Contexts," p. 264.
1. Nancy A. Hewitt, "Amy Kirby Post: 'Of whom it was said, 'being dead, yet speaketh,'" *The University of Rochester Library Bulletin* 37 (1984): 5–22; Ann D. Braude, "Spirit Defend the Rights of Women: Spiritualism and Changing Sex Roles in Nineteenth-Century America," in *Women, Religion, and Social Change,* ed. Yvonne Y. Haddad (Albany, 1985), pp. 419–431. Jacobs was introduced to spiritualism by the Posts and made several references to the spirits in her letters. In addition to several humorous references (Jacobs to Post, no. 91: "Ask him [Isaac Post] if he sends the spirits to look for me. I am afraid they would give a bad report"; Jacobs to Post, no. 80 [Written around the margin of the letter]: "What you can't read the spirits will. Heart full of love to all of you."), one of her letters suggests that she had asked the spirits to help her get in touch with her brother and son. In a letter written after they had left for California, she has "felt so anxious about son and brother not hearing anything from them. It makes me feel that she [Louisa] is all that is left to me in this world." (Jacobs to Post, no. 82, 27 Dec. 18—.) In another undated letter, she provides an update stating: "I will tell you some good news. I have had a letter from my brother and son just as the spirits told me it would be. Even the very language was in the letter." (Jacobs to Post, 7 Aug. 18—, no. 81.) This suggests that Jacobs attended a seance and asked the spirits for help in contacting her *living* relatives. Jacobs's request of the spirits was an unusual one; most spiritualists tried to contact *dead* people. Again, however, it indicates how important Jacobs's family ties were to her and her willingness to enlist the aid of the spiritual world in maintaining those relationships.
2. The date is based on notes made by Jean Fagan Yellin for the University of Rochester Archives. Quotation is from Jacobs to Post, n.d., no. 84.

mother. Durham's seemingly well-meant warning not to "answer everyone so openly" since it might give them "a pretext for treating [her] with
contempt" burned Harriet "like coals of fire."[3]

At some point, however, she did decide to talk over her feelings and
her decision to keep silent with her brother. In a letter to Post, she states:
"I [went] to my poor brother with my grieved and mortified spirits. He
would mingle his tears with mine, while he would advise me to do what
was right. My conscience approved of it but my stubborn pride would not
yield. I have tried for the past two years to conquer it and I feel that God
has helped me or I never would consent to give my past life to anyone,
for I would not do it without giving the whole truth. If it could help some
other from my fate, it would be selfish and unChristian in me to keep it
back."[4] Jacobs's references to her "painful and humiliating memory," her
"degradation," her "grieved and mortified spirits," and to burning "like
coals of fire" at the thought of being treated with contempt all suggest her
ongoing struggle with feelings of shame.

In constructing her narrative, Jacobs upheld the ideal of sexual and religious purity, while arguing that slave women should not be judged by
the same moral standards as free women. She advances this position with
some trepidation, still fearing the contempt of others. Writing to Amy
Post in June of 1857, she says: "I have left nothing out [of the manuscript]
but what I thought the world might believe that a slave woman was too
willing to pour out, that she might gain their sympathies. I ask nothing. I
have placed myself before you to be judged as a woman, whether I deserve your pity or contempt."[5] Although nervous about Amy's response to
her book, her confession, coupled with her affirmation of purity as a religious and sexual ideal, formed an effective basis for an abolitionist appeal to an audience of female readers. On a deeper level, however, it also
allowed her to reestablish or rework her connections with the most important figures of her childhood: her mother, her grandmother, and, to a
certain extent, her first mistress.

Issues of shame and secrecy first arise in her autobiography in con-
junction with Dr. Flint's sexual threats. Jacobs indicates that she "longed
for some one to confide in" at the time, but her master placed a high pre-
mium on secrecy and threatened to kill her if, in her words, "I was not as
silent as the grave."[6] Knowledge of Dr. Flint's abusive behavior was widespread among the house slaves but was only discussed among themselves.[7] According to Jacobs, the acknowledgement of sexual relations
between masters and female slaves was tabooed: "My master was, to my
knowledge, the father of eleven slaves. But did the mothers dare to tell

3. Ibid., p. 166.
4. Jacobs to Post, n.d., no. 84.
5. Jacobs to Post, 21 June [1857], no. 90; dated by Yellin.
6. Brent, *Incidents*, p. 28 [27].
7. Ibid., p. 27 [27].

who was the father of their children? Did the other slaves dare to allude to it, except in whispers among themselves? No, indeed. They knew too well the terrible consequences."[8] Secrets about sexual relations between white masters and the black women they owned thus lay at the heart of the slave system.

Fear of her master, however, was not the only reason Jacobs kept silent. Although she "would have given the world" to have "told her [grandmother] all [her] troubles," she was afraid of how her grandmother would respond. "I had been accustomed to look up to her with a respect bordering on awe. I was very young, and felt shamefaced telling her such impure things, especially as I knew her to be very strict on such subjects."[9] According to Jacobs, it was "[her] grandmother, and the good mistress of [her] childhood" who inculcated "the pure principles" which her master was attempting to destroy.[1] Although Jacobs was critical of both her grandmother's and her first mistress's willingness to consider slavery as the will of God, she appropriated their attitudes toward purity and impurity.[2]

Jacobs's own beliefs come out most clearly in her praise of a young white woman "who taught her slaves to lead pure lives, and wished them to enjoy the fruit of their own industry. *Her* religion was not a garb put on for Sunday, and laid aside till Sunday returned again. The eldest daughter of the slave mother was promised in marriage to a free man; and the day before the wedding this good mistress emancipated her, in order that her marriage might have the sanction of *law*."[3] Unlike the other whites described by Jacobs, this woman shared Jacobs's belief that true piety linked purity, freedom, and justice.[4] In this passage Jacobs implicitly defines purity in terms of sexuality; sex outside marriage, in her view, leads to impurity or defilement. As property, however, slaves could not contract a legal marriage. The power to say no to sexual overtures outside marriage and the legal sanction of sex within marriage were integral to maintaining one's purity. Without freedom, both were impossible.

Jacobs refused to join the church, at least in the South, because of its double standard with respect to black and white women. After Flint joined the church because his "position in society" required it, he urged Jacobs to join also. She responded that she would be glad to join "if [she] could be allowed to live like a Christian." Flint, rejecting her under-

8. Ibid., p. 34 [31].
9. Ibid., p. 28 [27].
1. Ibid., pp. 54–55 [46].
2. See ibid., pp. 10, 15, 6 [14, 18, 11–12].
3. Ibid., p. 50 [43].
4. This young woman's piety is similar to that of Anne Meade Page, an Episcopal woman whom Donald G. Mathews uses to illustrate evangelically oriented white southern religion at its best. According to Mathews, "she made her efforts for slaves the measure of her Christian commitment, as did many other southern women. She sternly condemned the sexual exploitation of black women and tried to prevent it whenever she could. She schooled her slave in order to erase their terrible ignorance, provided religious exercises to convert them from 'heathenish darkness,' and tried to persuade them to prepare for freedom in Africa." *Religion in the Old South* (Chicago, 1977), p. 117.

standing of Christianity, told her: "You can do what I require; and if you are faithful to me, you will be as virtuous as my wife." When Jacobs replied "that the Bible didn't say so," Flint, enraged by her outspoken independence, responded with a tirade on obedience.[5]

Jacobs's narrative reveals that in a context where women were literally the sexual property of their masters, her religious convictions about purity were a powerful, albeit ultimately limited, weapon in service of female autonomy. They were powerful in so far as they allowed Jacobs to define herself as a victim with the right to resist and, thus, to assert her autonomy in the face of Flint's demand for obedience. They were limited in that as a slave, and therefore without legal rights, Jacobs had nothing but psychological weapons with which to back her claims.

In the conflict between Jacobs and her master, Jacobs's ideas about purity allowed her to fight, but they did not allow her to win. As she put it, "I wanted to keep myself pure; and, under the most adverse circumstances, I tried hard to preserve my self-respect; but I was struggling alone in the powerful grasp of the demon Slavery; and the monster proved too strong for me. I felt as if I was forsaken by God and man; as if all my efforts must be frustrated; and I became reckless in my despair."[6]

Reflecting some twenty-five years later on her decision to turn to Sands for help, Jacobs states: "I know I did wrong. The painful and humiliating memory will haunt me to my dying day. Still, in looking back, calmly, on the events of my life, I feel that the slave woman ought not to be judged by the same standard as others."[7] In this passage Jacobs indicates two things: first, that the memory was still painful and humiliating; and second, that although she believed her action to have been "wrong," she did not in her calmer moments condemn herself for the decision she made. The logic of her ethical claim was relatively straightforward: women who were enslaved could not be held responsible for their actions in the same way as women who were free. Her acknowledgments that the memory was still painful and humiliating and that she could only refrain from judging herself in her calmer moments suggest that a more complex process was occurring at an emotional level.

Her emotional dilemma may have centered around unconscious feelings of ambivalence. As she indicates, she turned to Sands in desperation, at a point when she felt "forsaken by God and man." Although she may have felt forsaken by "man" in general, she had been forsaken in rather particular ways: by her first mistress, who had taught her about purity and yet died without freeing her; by her second mistress, who was unable to stop her husband's abusive behavior; and by her grandmother, who she felt was too "strict" about such matters to understand. While she could easily express her anger toward Dr. Flint and her white mistresses, it was

5. Brent, *Incidents*, p. 77 [62–63].
6. Ibid., pp. 54–55 [46].
7. Ibid., p. 56 [48].

much more difficult for her to express anger toward her grandmother for judging her by standards which she could not uphold; in relation to her grandmother, she simply felt ashamed.

Jacobs's feelings of shame did not surface, however, until after she told Flint that she was pregnant and she realized that her relatives would find out what she had done. "Humble as were their circumstances, they had pride in my good character. Now, how could I look them in the face? I had resolved that I would be virtuous, though I was a slave."[8] Humiliated and shamed, she went to her grandmother "to make confession." Her grandmother, having heard from Jacobs's mistress that Harriet was pregnant, declared her a "disgrace to [her] dead mother," took back Harriet's mother's wedding ring, and threw her out of the house.[9]

Harriet walked some distance to a friend's house, praying on the way that she might die. The friend "spoke soothingly" to her, but it did not comfort her. Jacobs states, "I thought I could bear my shame if I could only be reconciled to my grandmother. I longed to open my heart to her. I thought if she could know the real state of the case, and all I had been bearing for years, she would perhaps judge me less harshly."[1] She sent for her grandmother but had to wait days, wondering whether she had been "forsaken," before she came. Then, using the language of the confessional, Jacobs states:

> I knelt before her, and told her things that had poisoned my life; how long I had been persecuted; that I saw no way of escape; and in an hour of extremity I had become desperate. I told her I would bear any thing and do any thing, if in time I had hopes of obtaining her forgiveness. I begged of her to pity me, for my dead mother's sake. And she did pity me. She did not say, "I forgive you;" but she looked at me lovingly, with her eyes full of tears. She laid her old hand gently on my head, and murmured, "Poor child! Poor child!"[2]

It is significant to note, first, that Jacobs's feelings of shame were relationally specific. She felt shame in relation to her relatives, particularly her grandmother. When Dr. Flint told her that she had "sinned against [him] and mortified [her] old grandmother," she felt ashamed. Yet when Flint "spoke contemptuously of the lover who had always treated her honorably [Sands]," she lost her temper, saying, "I have sinned against God and myself . . . but not against you."[3] Second, dead relatives as well as living ones were dishonored by Jacobs's act. Harriet's grandmother declared her a "disgrace to her dead mother," while Harriet begged her grandmother's pity, "for [her] dead mother's sake." Third, as was later the

8. Ibid., p. 57 [48].
9. Ibid., p. 58 [48].
1. Ibid. [49].
2. Ibid., p. 58 [49].
3. Ibid., p. 59 [50].

case with her daughter, Jacobs couched her feelings of shame and her need for acceptance in religious language. Her first impulse was to confess. When her grandmother condemned her, she prayed to God that she might die. When her prayer was not answered, she turned again to her grandmother for forgiveness, stating that she thought she could bear her shame, if only she could be reconciled to her grandmother.

The shame resurfaced several years later when she entered a church to present her children for baptism. At that time, she recounts, "recollections of my mother came over me, and I felt subdued in spirit. There she had presented me for baptism, without any reason to feel ashamed. She had been married, and had such legal rights as slavery allows to a slave. The vows had at least been sacred to *her*, and she had never violated them. I was glad she was not alive, to know under what different circumstances her grandchildren were presented for baptism."[4]

Here again Jacobs's mother surfaces in relation to her feelings of shame. Moreover, the feelings of shame surface in a ritual context, where her desire for purity may have been heightened and where her children's illegitimacy would have been publicly apparent. Having her children baptized apparently had been important to Harriet's mother. In contrast to Harriet, she had been able to participate without shame. Reflecting on the differences in their lives, Harriet indicates that her mother had been able to maintain her vows because she was owned by a woman rather than by a man.[5] Thus the desire to remain pure is presented by Jacobs as a female desire, perpetuated by two generations of women in her own family and by some of the white women who had owned them. The family tradition was broken by Jacobs, and she felt this disgrace acutely at the point when her children (the next generation) were to be incorporated into the church.

It was Jacobs's fear of the effect which slavery would have on her daughter which finally led her to risk escape.[6] She made a vow to this effect at her parents' graves in the slave burial ground near the remains of the old slave church. There, in the place where "[slaves] hear not the voice of the oppressor," Jacobs knelt and kissed the markers on her parents' graves. She thanked God that her parents had not lived to witness her trials and prayed for God's help in escaping. She indicates in that context that "[she] had received [her] mother's blessing when she died; and in many an hour of tribulation [she] had seemed to hear her voice, sometimes chiding [her], sometimes whispering loving words into [her] wounded heart." Then as she left the graveyard, she "passed the wreck of the old [slave] meeting house . . . [and] seemed to hear [her] father's voice come from it, bidding [her] not to tarry till [she] reached freedom

---

4. Ibid., p. 80 [65].
5. Ibid. [65].
6. Ibid., p. 92 [74].

or the grave. [She] rushed on with renovated hopes. [Her] trust in God . . . strengthened by that prayer among the graves."[7]

Here at the slave burying-ground—at the graves of her parents—purity, freedom, and sacrality intersect in her vow to God to save her daughter or die in the attempt. "Nothing broke the death-like stillness except the occasional twitter of a bird. My spirit was overawed by the solemnity of the scene. For more than ten years I had frequented this spot, but never had it seemed to me so sacred as now."[8]

The slave burial ground and the nearby slave church were the two specifically Afro-American institutions in the community.[9] As the locus of black autonomy, the slave church was such a threat that whites destroyed it in the aftermath of the Turner revolt and began encouraging slaves to attend the white churches.[1] Jacobs had been frequenting the burial ground for the past ten years, since around the time of her mother's death. The church had been destroyed about five years prior to this particular visit. Although she did not indicate whether she or her family had attended the slave church, she heard her dead father's voice coming from it as she left the graveyard. Whatever her own family's involvement in the slave church, she clearly associated the church-graveyard complex with her parents and with freedom. The two came together as her father bid her not to tarry till she reached freedom or the grave.

Perhaps most significant is the fact that, for Jacobs, the graveyard where her parents were buried was a sacred place. Among the Kongo peoples of West Africa, from among whom a large percentage of the American slaves came, the ancestral spirits are intermediaries between the individual and "the one almighty god." The Bakongo communicate with the dead by means of charms called *minkisi*. Graves, in the words of anthropologist Elizabeth Fenn, "are the ultimate charm, providing a particularly effective medium for communicating with the dead." Moreover, according to Fenn, "in the Afro-American cemeteries of the South, often associated with Christian churches, Kongo decorative traditions remain strong."[2] Although Kongo-American graves are decorated most frequently with objects which belonged to the deceased, trees are sometimes planted on graves "as a sign of the spirit, on its way to the other world." According to Robert Thompson, such trees grace "countless Afro-American burials."[3] Jacobs's parents' gravemarkers were "a small wooded board" on the grave of her father and "a black stump, at the head of [her]

7. Ibid., pp. 92–93 [74–75].
8. Ibid. [74].
9. Albert J. Raboteau, *Slave Religion: The "Invisible Institution" in the Antebellum South* (New York, 1978).
1. Brent, *Incidents*, p. 69 [57].
2. Elizabeth A. Fenn, "Honoring the Ancestors: Kongo-American Graves in the American South," *Southern Exposure* 13 (Sept.–Oct. 1985): 43.
3. Robert Farris Thompson, *Flash of the Spirit: African and Afro-American Art and Philosophy* (New York, 1984), pp. 138–139.

mother's grave." The stump "was all that remained of a tree [her] father had planted."[4]

It is perhaps significant that the tree on her mother's grave was only a blackened stump. According to Thompson, the trees were identified with the dead person, and a flourishing tree meant that all was well with the departed spirit. It is possible that Jacobs associated the blackened stump with the disgrace which Jacobs believed she had brought upon her mother. Since Jacobs knew that she could not guard the purity of her own daughter any more effectively than she had been able to guard her own, her vow to rectify the situation by escaping might also have represented an attempt to mollify her mother's spirit.[5]

Although Jacobs may not have recognized, or simply may not have wanted to discuss, the African roots of her actions, her concern for her standing in the eyes of her dead parents, her sense of the sacrality of the graveyard, and her attention to their gravemarkers suggest that aspects of her African heritage were alive within a self-consciously Christian framework. Moreover, the presence of African-derived traditions within a self-consciously Christian narrative suggests that it may be fruitful to explore points of connection between West African and European beliefs about purity, rather than emphasizing presumed differences.

Although Jacobs's trust in God was strengthened by her prayers in the graveyard, her feelings about the God who had "forsaken" her in the face of her master's abuses and who seemed unable or perhaps unwilling to abolish slavery remained overtly ambivalent. These feelings came out forcefully while she was hidden in the garret: "Dark thoughts passed through my mind as I lay there day after day. . . . Sometimes I thought God was a compassionate Father, who would forgive my sins for the sake of my sufferings. At other times, it seemed to me there was no justice or mercy in the divine government. I asked why the curse of slavery was permitted to exist, and why I had been so persecuted and wronged from youth upward. These things took the shape of a mystery, which is to this day not so clear to my soul as I trust it will be hereafter."[6] As with her grandmother, Jacobs wanted God to be compassionate and forgive her sins because of what she had suffered. But she sometimes doubted whether God would do this; when she had begged her grandmother for forgiveness, she had received only pity. Although she never questioned her grandmother's expectations, she did allow herself to doubt God's justice. She was clearly angry with God for allowing slavery to exist.

Similar thoughts continued to plague her after her escape. As she wrote Amy Post in March of 1857: "When I see the evil that is spreading throughout the land my whole soul sickens. Oh my dear friend this poor heart that has bled in slavery is often wrung most bitterly to behold the

---

4. Brent, *Incidents*, p. 93 [74].
5. Thompson, *Flash of the Spirit*, p. 138.
6. Brent, *Incidents*, p. 126 [98].

injustice, the wrongs, the oppression, the cruel outrages inflicted on my race. Sometimes I am almost ready to exclaim—where dwells that just Father whom I love—and in whom must be might—and Strength—Liberty—and Death."[7]

Although she was ready at times to doubt the existence of the "just Father whom [she] love[d]," she still credited God with helping her to overcome her shame. Just as her mother "whispered loving words into her wounded heart" and her father's voice "bid her not to tarry," so too God enabled her to "conquer" the "stubborn pride" which prevented her from writing even though her conscience approved. In the end she decided that not to reveal the degradation she had suffered "would be selfish and unChristian . . . if it could help some other from my fate."[8] Just as she decided to escape in order to save her daughter, so she decided to write to save others. Yet in saving her daughter she freed herself, and in writing she began to integrate the shameful aspects of her past into her public presentation of herself.

If the goal of shame is secrecy and outward conformity to the expectations of others, then the movement toward autonomy requires the reintegration and ultimately the acceptance of that which has been deemed unacceptable. "Confession" as a mode of discourse locates the power to accept or forgive in the "other." It is thus a repetitive mode which must retest the other's power to forgive whenever the feelings of shame recur. To the extent that Jacobs expected her readers to decide whether she was, in her words to Amy, deserving of "pity or contempt," her narrative takes on the form of a public confession. Within a confessional mode, she remained dependent on others for her sense of self-esteem—in part, I would suggest, for conventional or stylistic reasons, and in part because she still found it difficult to accept the choices she had made while enslaved.

VALERIE SMITH

Form and Ideology in Three Slave Narratives[†]

The way in which the narratives of freed and fugitive slaves were produced has been largely responsible for their uncertain status as subjects of critical inquiry. In form they most closely resemble autobiographies.

7. Jacobs to Post, March [1857?], no. 86; dated by Yellin.
8. Jacobs to Post, n.d., no. 84.
† From *Self-Discovery and Authority in Afro-American Narrative* (Cambridge: Harvard UP, 1987) 9–43. Reprinted by permission of the publisher, Harvard University Press. Copyright © 1987 by the President and Fellows of Harvard College. Page references to this Norton Critical Edition are given in brackets following Smith's original citations.

But if we expect autobiographies to present us with rhetorical figures and thematic explorations that reveal the author's sense of what his or her life means, then these stories disappoint. In each stage of their history, the presence of an intermediary renders the majority of the narratives not artistic constructions of personal experience but illustrations of someone else's view of slavery.

In the earliest examples of the genre, as William L. Andrews has shown, the relationship between narrator and text was triangulated through the ordering intelligence of a white amanuensis or editor. Relying on a model of slavery as a fundamentally benevolent institution, the early narratives portray the slave as either an outlaw or a wayfarer in need of the protection that only white paternal authority could provide.[1] Most of the middle-period accounts, published from the 1830s through the 1860s, claim to be written by the narrators themselves, yet these cases too serve an outside interest: the stories are shaped according to the requirements of the abolitionists who published them and provided them with readers. And as Marion Wilson Starling and Dorothy Sterling have acknowledged, even the narratives transcribed in the twentieth century by the Federal Writers' Project of the Works Progress Administration (WPA) bear more than their share of the interviewers' influence.[2] As Sterling remarks:

> Few of the interviewers were linguists. They transcribed the ex-slaves' speech as they heard it, as they thought they heard it, or as they thought it should have been said—and sometimes, the whiter the interviewer's skin, the heavier the dialect and the more erratic the spelling. A number of the interviews also went through an editorial process in which dialect was cleaned up or exaggerated, depending on the editors' judgment. To attempt to make the language of the interviews consistent or to "translate" them into standard English would add still another change.[3]

It is not surprising that a scholarly tradition that values the achievements of the classically educated, middle-class white male has dismissed the transcriptions of former slaves' oral accounts. Nor is it surprising that even those narratives that purport to be written by slaves themselves have come into disrepute: when three popular narratives were exposed as inauthentic between 1836 and 1838, serious doubts arose about authorship

---

1. William L. Andrews, "The First Fifty Years of the Slave Narrative, 1760–1810," in *The Art of Slave Narrative: Original Essays in Criticism and Theory*, ed. John Sekora and Darwin T. Turner (Macomb, Ill.: Western Illinois University Press, 1982), p. 7.

2. Marion Wilson Starling, *The Slave Narrative: Its Place in American History* (Boston: G. K. Hall, 1981), pp. xvii–xviii; Dorothy Sterling, ed., *We Are Your Sisters: Black Women in the Nineteenth Century* (New York: W. W. Norton, 1984), pp. 3–4.

3. Sterling, *We Are Your Sisters*, p. 4. For a compelling discussion of ways in which the WPA narratives might be used, see Paul D. Escott, "The Art and Science of Reading WPA Slave Narratives," in *The Slave's Narrative*, ed. Charles T. Davis and Henry Louis Gates, Jr. (New York: Oxford University Press, 1985), pp. 40–48.

in the genre as a whole.[4] But the intrusive abolitionist influence has interfered with the critical reception of even those narratives that are demonstrably genuine. The former slaves may have seized upon the writing of their life stories as an opportunity to celebrate their escape and to reveal the coherence and meaning of their lives. These personal motives notwithstanding, the narratives were also (if not primarily) literary productions that documented the antislavery crusade. Their status as both popular art and propaganda imposed upon them a repetitiveness of structure, tone, and content that obscured individual achievements and artistic merit.[5]

As Henry Louis Gates, Jr., has shown, apologists and detractors alike have failed to attend to the formal dimensions of black texts:

> For all sorts of complex historical reasons, the very act of writing has been a "political" act for the black author. Even our most solipsistic texts, at least since the Enlightenment in Europe, have been treated as political evidence of one sort or another both implicitly and explicitly. And because our life in the West has been one struggle after another, our literature has been defined from without, and rather often from within, as primarily just one more polemic in those struggles.[6]

The formulaic and hybrid quality of the narratives has rendered their status as critical subjects even more elusive than that of other examples of Afro-American literary expression. Combining elements of history, autobiography, and fiction, they raise unique questions of interpretation. To study them as, for example, sustained images of an author's experience ignores the fact that they conform rather programmatically to a conventional pattern. Or to talk about the unity of an individual narrative is to ignore the fact that the texts as we read them contain numerous authenticating documents that create a panoply of other voices. Only by beginning from a clear sense of the narratives' generic properties does one capture the subtlety and achievement of the most compelling accounts.[7]

---

4. Starling, The Slave Narrative, pp. 226–232.
5. See James Olney's provocative discussion of this tension in "'I Was Born': The Slave Narratives, Their Status as Autobiography and as Literature," Callaloo, 20 (Winter 1984), 46–73.
6. Henry Louis Gates, Jr., "Criticism in the Jungle," in Black Literature and Literary Theory (New York: Methuen, 1984), p. 5.
7. The narratives first emerge as a subject in critical literature in the 1970s. The nature of the commentary bespeaks their troublesomeness as a literary category more precisely than does their omission from earlier studies. Two seminal books, Stephen Butterfield's Black Autobiography in America (Amherst: University of Massachusetts Press, 1974) and Sidonie Ann Smith's Where I'm Bound: Patterns of Slavery and Freedom in Black American Autobiography (Westport, Conn.: Greenwood Press, 1974) explore the connections between the narratives and modern black autobiography. Neither acknowledges the characteristics of the narratives that distinguish them from either history or autobiography; both present an image of the narratives as a monolithic body of work.

   More recent studies seek to establish the relationship of the accounts to the conditions out of which they arose. Frances Smith Foster's Witnessing Slavery (Westport, Conn.: Greenwood Press, 1979) and Starling's Slave Narrative: Its Place in American History contribute immeasur-

[Some] narratives, [however, like Harriet Jacobs's *Incidents in the Life of a Slave Girl* (1861),] elude the domination of received generic structures and conventions. * * * [Such] narratives * * * test the limits of the formula [and] tell us most about what those conventions signify. Furthermore, the narrators who transform the conventions into an image of what they believe their lives mean most closely resemble autobiographers; they leave the impress of their personal experience on the structure in which they tell their story. Perhaps most important, these narratives are of interest because in their variations on the formula they provide a figure for the author's liberation from slavery, the central act of the accounts themselves. In these places of difference, the narrators of these stories of freedom reveal their resistance even to the domination of their white allies.

* * *

* * * Harriet Jacobs's freedom to reconstruct her life was limited by a genre that suppressed subjective experience in favor of abolitionist polemics. But if slave narrators in general were restricted by the antislavery agenda, she was doubly bound by the form in which she wrote, for it contained a plot more compatible with received notions of masculinity than with those of womanhood. As Niemtzow has suggested, Jacobs incorporated the rhetoric of the sentimental novel into her account, at least in part because it provided her with a way of talking about her vulnerability to the constant threat of rape. This form imposed upon her restrictions of its own.[8] Yet she seized authority over her literary restraints in much the same way that she seized power in life. From within her ellipses and ironies—equivalents of the garret in which she concealed herself for seven years—she expresses the complexity of her experience as a black woman.

In *Incidents in the Life of a Slave Girl*, the account of her life as a slave and her escape to freedom, Harriet Jacobs refers to the crawl space in which she concealed herself for seven years as a "loophole of retreat."[9] The phrase calls attention both to the closeness of her hiding place—

ably to our understanding of the narratives in their political, cultural, and literary contexts. Both provide detailed summaries of the themes and plots of the narratives, but neither discusses the common rhetorical structures that bind the texts as a genre.

   H. Bruce Franklin in *The Victim as Criminal and Artist: Literature from the American Prison* (New York: Oxford University Press, 1978) and Houston A. Baker, Jr., in *The Journey Back: Issues in Black Literature and Criticism* (Chicago: University of Chicago Press, 1980), in contrast, demonstrate ways in which the texts respond to the ideological context in which they were produced. By analyzing the resonance and textual strategies of the Douglass and Jacobs narratives in the one case and of the Equiano and Douglass narratives in the other, they offer the most persuasive evidence of their literariness. To borrow Franklin's formulation (p. 7), by using methods that ordinarily illuminate our readings of classic texts, they make a strong argument for the narratives' subtlety and complexity.

8. Niemtzow, "The Problematic of Self," pp. 105–108.

9. Linda Brent [Harriet Jacobs], *Incidents in the Life of a Slave Girl* (New York: Harcourt Brace Jovanovich, 1973), p. 117 [91]. Subsequent references will be given in the text.

three feet high, nine feet long, and seven feet wide—and the passivity that even voluntary confinement imposes. For if the combined weight of racism and sexism have already placed inexorable restrictions upon her as a black female slave in the antebellum South, her options seem even narrower after she conceals herself in the garret, where just to speak to her loved ones jeopardizes her own and her family's welfare.

And yet Jacobs's phrase "the loophole of retreat" possesses an ambiguity of meaning that extends to the literal loophole as well. For if a loophole signifies for Jacobs a place of withdrawal, it signifies in common parlance an avenue of escape. Likewise, and perhaps more important, the garret, a place of confinement, also renders the narrator spiritually independent of her master, and makes possible her ultimate escape to freedom. It is thus hardly surprising that Jacobs finds her imprisonment, however uncomfortable, an improvement over her "lot as a slave" (p. 117) [92]. As her statement implies, she dates her emancipation from the time she entered her loophole, even though she did not cross into the free states until seven years later. Given the constraints that framed her life, even the act of choosing her own mode of confinement constitutes an exercise of will, an indirect assault against her master's domination.[1]

The plot of Jacobs's narrative, her journey from slavery to freedom, is punctuated by a series of similar structures of confinement, both literal and figurative. Not only does she spend much of her time in tiny rooms (her grandmother's garret, closets in the homes of two friends), but she seems as well to have been penned in by the importunities of Dr. Flint, her master: "My master met me at every turn, reminding me that I belonged to him, and swearing by heaven and earth that he would compel me to submit to him. If I went out for a breath of fresh air after a day of unwearied toil, his footsteps dogged me. If I knelt by my mother's grave, his dark shadow fell on me even there" (p. 27) [27]. Repeatedly she escapes overwhelming persecutions only by choosing her own space of confinement: the stigma of unwed motherhood over sexual submission to her master; concealment in one friend's home, another friend's closet, and her grandmother's garret over her own and her children's enslavement on a plantation; Jim Crowism and the threat of the Fugitive Slave Law in the North over institutionalized slavery at home. Yet each moment of apparent enclosure actually empowers Jacobs to redirect her own and her children's destiny. To borrow Elaine Showalter's formulation, she inscribes a subversive plot of empowerment beneath the more orthodox, public plot of weakness and vulnerability.[2]

It is not surprising that both literal and figurative enclosures prolifer-

---

1. As I completed revisions of this discussion, I read Houston A. Baker, Jr.'s, *Blues, Ideology, and Afro-American Literature: A Vernacular Theory* (Chicago: University of Chicago Press, 1984). He too considers the significance of this image to Jacobs's account, but he focuses on Jacobs's ability to transform the economics of her oppression, whereas I concentrate on her use of received literary conventions.
2. Elaine Showalter, "Review Essay," *Signs*, I (1975), 435.

ate in Jacobs's narrative. As a nineteenth-century black woman, former slave, and writer, she labored under myriad social and literary restrictions that shaped the art she produced.[3] Feminist scholarship has shown that, in general, women's writing in the nineteenth and twentieth centuries has been strongly marked by imagery of confinement, a pattern of imagery that reflects the limited cultural options available to the authors because of their gender and chosen profession. Sandra Gilbert and Susan Gubar, for instance, describe the prodigious restraints historically imposed upon women that led to the recurrence of structures of concealment and evasion in their literature.[4] Not only were they denied access to the professions, civic responsibilities, and higher education, but also their secular and religious instruction encouraged them from childhood to adopt the "feminine," passive virtues of "submissiveness, modesty, selflessness."[5] Taken to its extreme, such an idealization of female weakness and self-effacement contributed to what Ann Douglas has called a "domestication of death," characterized by the prevalence in literature of a hagiography of dying women and children, and the predilection in life for dietary, sartorial, and medical practices that led to actual or illusory weakness and illness.[6]

Literary women confronted additional restraints, given the widespread cultural identification of creativity with maleness. As Gubar argues elsewhere, our "culture is steeped in . . . myths of male primacy in theological, artistic, and scientific creativity," myths that present women as art objects, perhaps, but never as creators.[7] These ideological restraints, made concrete by inhospitable editors, publishers, and reviewers and disapproving relatives and friends have, as Gilbert and Gubar demonstrate, traditionally invaded women's literary undertakings with all manner of tensions. The most obvious sign of nineteenth-century women writers' anxiety about their vocation (but one that might also be attributed to the demands of the literary marketplace) is the frequency with which they published either anonymously or under a male pseudonym. Their sense of engaging in an improper enterprise is evidenced as well by their tendency both to disparage their own accomplishments in autobiographical remarks and to inscribe deprecations of women's creativity within their fictions. Moreover, they found themselves in a curious relation to the im-

3. Only recently have scholars accepted the authenticity of Jacobs's account, thanks largely to Jean Fagan Yellin's meticulous and illuminating documentation of Jacobs's life and writing. See her essay "Texts and Contexts of Harriet Jacobs's *Incidents in the Life of a Slave Girl: Written by Herself*," in Davis and Gates, *The Slave's Narrative*, pp. 262–282. See also Yellin's edition of this text (Cambridge, Mass.: Harvard University Press, 1987).

4. Sandra M. Gilbert and Susan Gubar, *The Madwoman in the Attic* (New Haven: Yale University Press, 1979), pp. 3–104 passim.

5. Ibid., p. 23.

6. Ann Douglas, *The Feminization of American Culture* (New York: Avon Books, 1977), pp. 240–273 passim.

7. Susan Gubar, "'The Blank Page' and the Issues of Female Creativity," in *Writing and Sexual Difference*, ed. Elizabeth Abel (Chicago: University of Chicago Press, 1982), p. 74.

plements of their own craft. The literary conventions they received from genres dominated by male authors perpetuated reductive, destructive images of women that cried out to be revised. Yet the nature of women writer's socialization precluded their confronting problematic stereotypes directly. Instead, as Patricia Meyer Spacks, Carolyn Heilbrun, and Catherine Stimpson, as well as Showalter and Gilbert and Gubar have shown, the most significant women writers secreted revisions of received plots and assumptions either within or behind the more accessible content of their work.[8]

Jacobs's *Incidents* reveals just such a tension between the manifest and the concealed plot. Jacobs explicitly describes her escape as a progression from one small space to another. As if to underscore her helplessness and vulnerability, she indicates that although she ran alone to her first friend's home, she left each of her hiding places only with the aid of someone else. In fact, when she goes to her second and third hiding places, she is entirely at the mercy of her companion, for she is kept ignorant of her destination. Yet each closet, while at one level a prison, may be seen as well as a station on her journey to freedom. Moreover, from the garret of her seven-year imprisonment she uses to her advantage all the power of the voyeur—the person who sees but remains herself unseen. When she learns that Sands, her white lover and the father of her children, is about to leave town, she descends from her hiding place and, partly because she catches him unawares, is able to secure his promise to help free her children. In addition, she prevents her own capture not merely by remaining concealed but, more important, by embroiling her master, Dr. Flint, in an elaborate plot that deflects his attention. Fearing that he suspects her whereabouts, she writes him letters that she then has postmarked in Boston and New York to send him off in hot pursuit in the wrong direction. Despite her grandmother's trepidation. Jacobs clearly delights in exerting some influence over the man who has tried to control her.

Indeed, if the architectural close places are at once prisons and exits, then her relationship to Sands is both as well. She suggests that when she decides to take him as her lover, she is caught between Scylla and Charybdis. Forbidden to marry the free black man she loves, she knows that by becoming Sands's mistress she will compromise her virtue and reputation. But, she remarks, since her alternative is to yield to the master she loathes, she has no choice but to have sexual relations with Sands. As she writes: "It seems less degrading to give one's self, than to submit to compulsion. There is something akin to freedom in having a lover who has no control over you, except that which he gains by kindness and attachment" (p. 55)[47].

8. See Showalter, "Review Essay," and Gilbert and Gubar, *The Madwoman in the Attic.* See also Patricia Meyer Spacks, *The Female Imagination* (New York: Knopf, 1975), p. 317, and Carolyn Heilbrun and Catharine Stimpson, "Theories of Feminist Criticism: A Dialogue," in *Feminist Literary Criticism*, ed. Josephine Donovan (Lexington, Ky.: University Press of Kentucky, 1975), p. 62.

One might argue that Jacobs's dilemma encapsulates the slave woman's sexual victimization and vulnerability. I do not mean to impugn that reading, but I would suggest that her relationship with Sands provides her with a measure of power. Out of his consideration for her, he purchases her children and her brother from Flint. William, her brother, eventually escapes from slavery on his own, but Sands frees the children in accordance with their mother's wishes. In a system that allowed the buying and selling of people as if they were animals, Jacobs's influence was clearly minimal. Yet even at the moments when she seems most vulnerable, she exercises some degree of control.

* * *

* * * [Still,] Jacobs's tale is not the classic story of the triumph of the individual will; rather it is more a story of a triumphant self-in-relation.[9] With the notable exception of the narrative of William and Ellen Craft, most of the narratives by men represent the life in slavery and the escape as essentially solitary journeys. This is not to suggest that male slaves were more isolated than their female counterparts, but it does suggest that they were attempting to prove their equality, their manhood, in terms acceptable to their white, middle-class readers.

Under different, equally restrictive injunctions, Jacobs readily acknowledges the support and assistance she received, as the description of her escape makes clear. Not only does she diminish her own role in her escape, but she is also quick to recognize the care and generosity of her family in the South and her friends in the North. The opening chapter of her account focuses not on the solitary "I" of so many narratives but on Jacobs's relatives. And she associates her desire for freedom with her desire to provide opportunities for her children.

By mythologizing rugged individuality, physical strength, and geographical mobility, the narratives enshrine cultural definitions of masculinity.[1] The plot of the standard narrative may thus be seen as not only the journey from slavery to freedom but also the journey from slavehood to manhood. Indeed, that rhetoric explicitly informs some of the best-known and most influential narratives. In the key scene in William Wells Brown's account, for example, a Quaker friend and supporter renames the protagonist, saying, "Since thee has got out of slavery, thee has become a man, and men always have two names."[2] Douglass also explicitly

9. I draw here on the vocabulary of recent feminist psychoanalytic theory, which revises traditional accounts of female psychosexual development. See Jean Baker Miller, *Toward a New Psychology of Women* (Boston: Beacon Press, 1976); Nancy Chodorow, *The Reproduction of Mothering: Psychoanalysis and the Sociology of Gender* (Berkeley: University of California Press, 1978); and Carol Gilligan, *In a Different Voice* (Cambridge, Mass.: Harvard University Press, 1982).
1. I acknowledge here my gratitude to Mary Helen Washington for pointing out to me this characteristic of the narratives.
2. William Wells Brown, *Narrative of William W. Brown* (Boston: The Anti-Slavery Office, 1847; rpt. New York: Arno Press, 1968), p. 105.

contrasts slavehood with manhood, for he argues that learning to read made him a man but being beaten made him a slave. Only by overpowering his overseer was he able to become a man—thus free—again.

Simply by underscoring her reliance on other people, Jacobs reveals another way in which the story of slavery and escape might be written. But in at least one place in the narrative she makes obvious her problematic relation to the rhetoric she uses. The fourth chapter, "The Slave Who Dared to Feel Like a Man," bears a title reminiscent of one of the most familiar lines from Douglass's 1845 *Narrative*. Here Jacobs links three anecdotes that illustrate the fact that independence of mind is incompatible with the demands of life as a slave. She begins with a scene in which her grandmother urges her family to content themselves with their lot as slaves; her son and grandchildren, however, cannot help resenting her admonitions. The chapter then centers on the story of her Uncle Ben, a slave who retaliates when his master tries to beat him and eventually escapes to the North.

The chapter title thus refers explicitly to Ben, the slave who, by defending himself, dares to feel like a man. And yet it might also refer to the other two stories included in the chapter. In the first, Jacobs's brother, William, refuses to capitulate to his master's authority. In the second, Jacobs describes her own earliest resolution to resist her master's advances. Although the situation does not yet require her to fight back, she does say that her young arm never felt half so strong. Like her uncle and brother, she determines to remain unconquered.

The chapter focuses on Ben's story, then, but it indicates also that his niece and nephew can resist authority. Its title might therefore refer to either of them as well. As Jacobs suggests by indirection, as long as the rhetoric of the genre identifies freedom and independence of thought with manhood, it lacks a category for describing the achievements of the tenacious black woman.

As L. Maria Child's introduction, Jacobs's own preface, and the numerous asides in the narrative make clear, Jacobs was writing for an audience of northern white women, a readership that by midcentury had grown increasingly leisured, middle class, and accustomed to the conventions of the novel of domestic sentiment. Under the auspices of Child, herself an editor and writer of sentimental fiction, Jacobs constructed the story of her life in terms that her reader would find familiar. Certainly Jacobs's *Incidents* contains conventional apostrophes that call attention to the interests she shares with her readers. But as an additional strategy for enlisting their sympathy, she couches her story in the rhetoric and structures of popular fiction.

The details of the narrator's life that made her experience as a slave more comfortable than most are precisely those that render her story particularly amenable to the conventions and assumptions of the sentimental novel. Like Douglass's, slave narratives often begin with an absence, the narrator announcing from the first that he has no idea where or when he was born or who his parents were. But Jacobs was fortunate enough to have been born into a stable family at once nuclear and extended. Although both of her parents died young, she nurtured vivid, pleasant memories of them. Moreover, she remained close to her grandmother, an emancipated, self-supporting, property-owning black woman, and to her uncles and aunts, until she escaped to the North.

Jacobs's class affiliation, and the fact that she was subjected to relatively minor forms of abuse as a slave, enabled her to locate a point of identification both with her readers and with the protagonists of sentimental fiction. Like them, she aspired to chastity and piety as consummate feminine virtues and hoped that marriage and family would be her earthly reward. Her master, for some reason reluctant to force her to submit sexually, harassed her, pleaded with her, and tried to bribe her into capitulating in the manner of an importunate suitor like Richardson's seducer. He tells her, for example, that he would be within his rights to kill her or have her imprisoned for resisting his advances, but he wishes to make her happy and thus will be lenient toward her. She likens his behavior to that of a jealous lover on one occasion when he becomes violent with her son. And he repeatedly offers to make a lady of her if she will grant him her favors, volunteering to set her up in a cottage of her own where she can raise her children.

By pointing up the similarities between her own story and those plots with which her readers would have been familiar, Jacobs could thus expect her readers to identify with her suffering. Moreover, this technique would enable them to appreciate the ways in which slavery converts into liabilities the very qualities of virtue and beauty that women were taught to cultivate. This tactic has serious limitations, however. As is always the case when one attempts to universalize a specific political point, Jacobs here trivializes the complexity of her situation when she likens it to a familiar paradigm. Like Richardson's Pamela, Jacobs is her pursuer's servant. But Pamela is free to escape, if she chooses, to the refuge of her parents' home, while as Dr. Flint's property, Jacobs has severely limited options. Moreover, Mr. B., in the terms the novel constructs, can redeem his importunities by marrying Pamela and elevating her and their progeny to his position. No such possibility exists for Jacobs and her master. Indeed, the system of slavery, conflating as it does the categories of property and sexual relationships, ensures that her posterity will become his material possessions.

For other reasons as well, the genre seems inappropriate for Jacobs's purposes. As the prefatory documents imply, Jacobs's readers were accustomed to a certain degree of propriety and circumlocution in fiction. In keeping with cultural injunctions against women's assertiveness and directness in speech, the literature they wrote and read tended to be "exercises in euphemism" that excluded certain subjects from the purview of fiction.[3] But Jacobs's purpose was to celebrate her freedom to express what she had undergone, and to engender additional abolitionist support. Child and Jacobs both recognized that Jacobs's story might well violate the rules of decorum in the genre. Their opening statements express the tension between the content of the narrative and the form in which it appears.

Child's introduction performs the function conventional to the slave narrative of establishing the narrator's veracity and the reliability of the account. What is unusual about her introduction, however, is the basis of her authenticating statement: she establishes her faith in Jacobs's story on the correctness and delicacy of the author's manner.

> The author of the following autobiography is personally known to me, and her conversation and manners inspire me with confidence. During the last seventeen years, she has lived the greater part of the time with a distinguished family in New York, and has so deported herself as to be highly esteemed by them. This fact is sufficient, without further credentials of her character. I believe those who know her will not be disposed to doubt her veracity, though some incidents in her story are more romantic than fiction.   (p. xi) [5–6]

This paragraph attempts to equate contradictory notions; Child implies not only that Jacobs is both truthful and a model of decorous behavior but also that her propriety ensures her veracity. Child's assumption is troublesome, since ordinarily decorousness connotes the opposite of candor: one equates propriety not with openness but with concealment in the interest of taste.

Indeed, later in her introduction Child seems to recognize that an explicit political imperative may well be completely incompatible with bourgeois notions of propriety. While in the first paragraph she suggests that Jacobs's manner guarantees her veracity, by the last she has begun to ask if questions of delicacy have any place at all in discussions of human injustice. In the last paragraph, for example, she writes, "I am well aware that many will accuse me of indecorum for presenting these pages to the public." Here, rather than equating truthfulness with propriety, she acknowledges somewhat apologetically that candor about her chosen subject may well violate common rules of decorum. From this point she proceeds tactfully but firmly to dismantle the usefulness of delicacy as a category where subjects of urgency are concerned. She remarks, for instance, that "the experiences of this intelligent and much-injured woman belong to a class which some call delicate subjects, and others indelicate." By pointing to the fact that one might identify Jacobs's story as either delicate or its opposite, she acknowledges the superfluity of this particular label.

3. Niemtzow, "The Problematic of Self," pp. 105–106.

In the third and fourth sentences of this paragraph Child offers her most substantive critique of delicacy, for she suggests that it allows the reader an excuse for insensitivity and self-involvement. The third sentence reads as follows: "This peculiar phase of slavery has generally been kept veiled; but the public ought to be made acquainted with its monstrous features, and I willingly take the responsibility of presenting them with the veil withdrawn." Here she invokes and reverses the traditional symbol of feminine modesty. A veil (read: euphemism) is ordinarily understood to protect the wearer (read: reader) from the ravages of a threatening world. Child suggests, however, that a veil (or euphemism) may also work the other way, concealing the hideous counternance of truth from those who choose ignorance above discomfort.

In the fourth sentence she pursues further the implication that considerations of decorum may well excuse the reader's self-involvement. She writes, "I do this for the sake of my sisters in bondage, who are suffering wrongs so foul, that our ears are too delicate to listen to them." The structure of this sentence is especially revealing, for it provides a figure for the narcissism of which she implicity accuses the reader. A sentence that begins, as Child's does, "I do this for the sake of my sisters in bondage, who are suffering wrongs so foul that . . ." would ordinarily conclude with some reference to the "sisters" or the wrongs they endure. We would thus expect the sentence to read something like: "I do this for the sake of my sisters in bondage, who are suffering wrongs so foul that they must soon take up arms against their master," or "that they no longer believe in a moral order." Instead, Child's sentence rather awkwardly imposes the reader in the precise grammatical location where the slave woman ought to be. This usurpation of linguistic space parallels the potential for narcissism of which Child suggests her reader is guilty.

Child, the editor, the voice of form and convention in the narrative—the one who revised, condensed, and ordered the manuscript and "pruned [its] excrescences" (p. xi) [6]—thus prepares the reader for its straightforwardness. Jacobs, whose life provides the narrative subject, in apparent contradiction to Child calls attention in her preface to her book's silences. Rather conventionally she admits to concealing the names of places and people to protect those who aided in her escape. And, one might again be tempted to say conventionally, she apologizes for the inadequacy of her literary skills. But in fact, when Jacobs asserts that her narrative is no fiction, that her adventures may seem incredible but are nevertheless true, and that only experience can reveal the abomination of slavery, she underscores the inability of her form adequately to capture her experience.

Although Child and Jacobs are aware of the limitations of genre, the account often rings false. Characters speak like figures out of a romance. Moreover, the form allows Jacobs to talk about her sexual experiences only when they are the result of her victimization. She becomes curiously silent about the fact that her relationship with Sands continued even after Flint no longer seemed a threat.

Its ideological assumptions are the most serious problem the form presents. Jacobs invokes a plot initiated by Richardson's *Pamela*, and recapitulated in nineteenth-century American sentimental novels, in which a persistent male of elevated social rank seeks to seduce a woman of a lower class. Through her resistance and piety, she educates her would-be seducer into an awareness of his own depravity and his capacity for true, honorable love. In the manner of Pamela's Mr. B, the reformed villain rewards the heroine's virtue by marrying her.

As is true with popular literature generally, this paradigm affirms the dominant ideology, in this instance (as in Douglass's case) the power of patriarchy.[4] As Tania Modleski and Janice Radway have shown, the seduction plot typically represents pursuit or harassment as love, allowing the protagonist and reader alike to interpret the male's abusiveness as a sign of his inability to express his profound love for the heroine.[5] The problem is one that Ann Douglas attributes to sentimentalism as a mode of discourse, in that it never challenges fundamental assumptions and structures: "Sentimentalism is a complex phenomenon. It asserts that the values a society's activity denies are precisely the ones it cherishes; it attempts to deal with the phenomenon of cultural bifurcation by the manipulation of nostalgia. Sentimentalism provides a way to protest a power to which one has already in part capitulated."[6] Like Douglass, Jacobs does not intend to capitulate, especially since patriarchy is for her synonymous with slavocracy. But to invoke that plot is to invoke the clusters of associations and assumptions that surround it.

As Jacobs exercises authority over the limits of the male narrative, however, she triumphs as well over the limits of the sentimental novel, a genre more suited to the experience of her white, middle-class reader than to her own. From at least three narrative spaces, analogs to the garret in which she concealed herself, she displays her power over the forms at her disposal.

In a much-quoted line from the last paragraph of her account she writes: "Reader, my story ends with freedom, not in the usual way, with marriage" (p. 207) [156]. In this sentence she calls attention to the space between the traditional happy ending of the novel of domestic sentiment and the ending of her story. She acknowledges that however much her story may resemble superficially the story of the sentimental heroine, as a black woman she plays for different stakes; marriage is not the ultimate reward she seeks.

---

4. See Douglas, *The Feminization of American Culture*, p. 72.
5. See Tania Modleski, *Loving with a Vengeance: Mass-Produced Fantasies for Women* (New York: Archon Books, 1982), p. 17, and Janice Radway, *Reading the Romance: Women, Patriarchy, and Popular Literature* (Chapel Hill: University of North Carolina Press, 1984), p. 75.
6. See Douglas, *The Feminization of American Culture*, p. 12.

Another gap occurs at the point where she announces her second pregnancy. She describes her initial involvement with Sands as a conundrum. The brutality of neighboring masters, the indifference of the legal system, and her own master's harassment have forced her to take a white man as her lover. Both in the way she leads up to this revelation and in the apostrophes to the reader, she presents it as a situation in which she had no choice. Her explanation for taking Sands as her lover is accompanied by expressions of the appropriate regret and chagrin and then followed by two general chapters about slave religion and the local response to the Nat Turner rebellion. When we return to Jacobs's story, she remarks that Flint's harassment has persisted, and she announces her second pregnancy by saying simply, "When Dr. Flint learned that I was again to be a mother, he was exasperated beyond measure" (p. 79) [64]. Her continued relationship with Sands and her own response to her second pregnancy are submerged in the subtext of the two previous chapters and in the space between paragraphs. By consigning to the narrative silences those aspects of her own sexuality for which the genre does not allow, Jacobs points to an inadequacy in the form.

The third such gap occurs a bit later, just before she leaves the plantation. Her master's great aunt, Miss Fanny, a kind-hearted elderly woman who is a great favorite with Jacobs's grandmother, comes to visit. Jacobs is clearly fond of this woman, but as she tells the story, she admits that she resents Miss Fanny's attempts to sentimentalize her situation. As Jacobs tells it, Miss Fanny remarks at one point that she "wished that I and all my grandmother's family were at rest in our graves, for not until then should she feel any peace about us" (p. 91) [73]. Jacobs then reflects privately that "the good old soul did not dream that I was planning to bestow peace upon her, with regard to myself and my children; not by death, but by securing our freedom." Here, Jacobs resists becoming the object of someone else's sentimentality and calls attention to the inappropriateness of this response. Although she certainly draws on the conventions of sentimentalism when they suit her purposes, she is also capable of replacing the self-indulgent mythicization of death with the more practical solution of freedom.

The complex experience of the black woman has eluded analyses and theories that focus on any one of the variables of race, class, and gender alone. As Barbara Smith has remarked, the effect of the multiple oppression of race, class, and gender is not merely arithmetic.[7] That is, one cannot say only that in addition to racism, black women have had to confront

---

7. See Barbara Smith, "Notes for Yet Another Paper on Black Feminism, or Will the Real Enemy Please Stand Up," *Conditions: Five*, 3 (October 1978), 123–132. For further discussion of this issue see Paula Giddings, *When and Where I Enter: The Impact of Black Women on Race and Sex in America* (New York: William Morrow, 1984); Angela Davis, *Women, Race, and Class* (New York: Vintage Books, 1983); and Elizabeth V. Spelman, "Theories of Race and Gender: The Erasure of Black Women," *Quest*, 5 (1979), 36–62.

the problem of sexism. Rather, issues of class and race alter one's experience of gender, just as gender alters the experience of class and race. Whatever the limitations of her narrative, Jacobs anticipates recent developments in class, race, and gender analysis. Her account indicates that this story of a black woman does not emerge from the superimposition of a slave narrative on a sentimental novel. Rather, in the ironies and silences and spaces of her book, she makes not quite adequate forms more truly her own.

NELLIE Y. McKAY

The Girls Who Became the Women: Childhood Memories in the Autobiographies of Harriet Jacobs, Mary Church Terrell, and Anne Moody[†]

> "You a woman and a colored woman at that. . . . You can't act like a man . . . all independent like." . . . "You say I'm a woman and colored. Ain't that the same as being a man?"
>
> —Toni Morrison, *Sula*

In an essay entitled "Self-Concept Formation and the Afro-American Woman," Vernaline Watson observes that "the role of the individual as an active participant in his [*sic*] development has been neglected or minimized in most social psychological perspectives on the self-concept" (p. 83). Watson believes that this neglect stems from a widespread uncritical acceptance of the findings of prestigious white social scientists whose categorical research denies the experiences of people outside of their group. From a position of privilege, and without giving consideration to the full meaning of the heterogeneity of our society, they promote the idea that human socialization takes place in an atmosphere in which the self is valued and communal institutions and traditions shape the individual personality to conform to the values of the larger group. Clearly, such a perspective takes no account of the effects of those influences on the socialization of minority-group people, including black women, who come to selfhood in racist, sexist white America and whom the traditions and institutions of the dominant culture do not nourish. Yet, as Watson and others who study black women's experiences note, many in the group develop positive selves, live fulfilling lives, and attain major achievements

† From *Tradition and the Talents of Women*, ed. Florence Howe (Urbana and Chicago: U of Illinois P, 1991) 106–24. Reprinted with the permission of the University of Illinois Press. Page references to this Norton Critical Edition are given in brackets following McKay's original citations, with the exception of references to extratextual material included in the Yellin edition.

even in extremely hostile environments.[1] This phenomenon challenges the stereotype that the damage that racism causes to the identities of all black children results in total black self-rejection. Further, it affirms the idea that black people succeed in part by actively participating in the process of their psychological development, rejecting the status quo and opposing the values that demean their humanity.[2] Many black women's autobiographies vividly illustrate this rejection of conventional social norms and their authors' efforts to create a healthy sense of self.

In spite of differences among individual Afro-Americans in skin color, class background, and political and philosophical beliefs, which have particular impact on each separate life, the search for individual and group freedom is central to the black autobiographical enterprise. As Stephen Butterfield points out in *Black Autobiography*, beginning with the slave narratives (exemplars of the basic search for human freedom), black autobiography has been the assertion of a radical "other" in relationship to the white American self (pp. 1–7). Pre-1863 texts inscribe the ideology in accounts of the lives of fugitives from servitude who addressed it in outcries against the inhumanity of physical bondage. Post-1865 narratives focus on making the black self the subject of its own discourse in the face of racial discrimination and oppression.[3] To further complicate the issue for women, the black female self shares psychological space within the experiences of black men and white women, and, like other groups, is overshadowed by the dominance of patriarchy. Differences internal to black women's experiences, and others between black women's and men's, and white and black women's experiences, give the autobiographies of black women an especially complex infrastructure that mitigates a unified group identity.[4] Yet, within this complicated network of

---

1. Vernaline Watson, "Self-Concept Formation and the Afro-American Woman," in *Perspectives on Afro-American Women*, ed. Willa D. Johnson and Thomas L. Green (Washington, D.C.: ECCA Publications, 1975), p. 83. The writings of such well-known social scientists as Erik H. Erikson, who discuss stages of human development, address issues of identity formation from this exclusionary perspective. Conversely, American life had always been oppressive for black women and men, for whom the supportive institutions of the larger society are usually roadblocks to positive self-development. For some recent historical studies on the situation for black women in slavery and beyond, see Deborah Gray White, *Ar'n't I a Woman? Female Slaves in the Plantation South* (New York: W. W. Norton, 1985); Jacqueline Jones, *Labor of Love, Labor of Sorrow: Black Women, Work and the Family from Slavery to Present* (New York: Random House, 1985); and Angela Davis, *Women, Race and Class* (New York: Random House, 1981). Also see Watson, "Self-Concept Formation," p. 88.
2. See Kenneth B. Clark, *Prejudice and Your Child* (Boston: Beacon Press, 1963); Abram Kardiner and Lionel Ovesey, *The Mark of Oppression: Explorations in the Personality of the American Negro* (New York: W. W. Norton, 1951).
3. Stephen Butterfield, *Black Autobiography* (Amherst: University of Massachusetts Press, 1974), pp. 1–7. All critical studies of black autobiography make this point. For other book-length discussions of this claim see William Andrews, *To Tell a Free Story: The First One Hundred Years of Afro-American Autobiography* (Urbana: University of Illinois Press, 1986); Frances Foster, *Witnessing Slavery: The Development of Ante-Bellum Slave Narratives* (Westport: Greenwood Press, 1979); and Sidonie A. Smith, *Where I'm Bound: Patterns of Slavery and Freedom in Black American Autobiography* (Westport: Greenwood Press, 1974).
4. See Hazel Carby, *Reconstructing Womanhood: The Emergence of the Afro-American Woman Novelist* (New York: Oxford University Press, 1987), and Deborah McDowell, "'The Self and

interrelationships, large numbers of black women are joined in a common (though individual) search for freedom and autonomy as they resist any identity, conferred by a white- and male-dominated society, that designates them inferior to others.

Childhood remembrances, recorded in autobiography, provide an excellent source for examining how these women understood their own development toward such radical stances. Psychologists agree that children develop their basic cognitive and conceptual maps of the world at an early age, and while these may be modified later, they do not disappear. In his book on young radicals against the Vietnam War, Kenneth Keniston explains it this way: "childhood creates in each of us psychological configurations that summarize the tensions and joys of our early lives. These configurations are, in one way or another, interwoven into our adult political commitments. . . . Just as the foundation of a building limits, but does not determine, what can be built upon the site, so the legacy of childhood sets outer limits and establishes enduring sensitivities for later development, but does not dictate it" (p. 76). In this essay, we need to recognize that for many Afro-Americans (and some members of other minority groups), the definition, perimeters, and activities of childhood (especially in respect to chronological age) are largely different from those within dominant middle-class society. For the purposes of this essay I define childhood in autobiography as the period from earliest recall to late adolescence, as we generally understand the latter in relationship to chronological age, even though, psychologically, the childhood of these subjects may have ended years earlier.

Sociologists and psychologists (supporters and detractors) of the black experience agree that large numbers of black youngsters do not have traditional childhoods. One of the characters in Claude Brown's *Manchild in the Promised Land* explains the phenomenon in black Harlem: "they ain't got no kids in Harlem. I ain't never seen any. I've seen really small people actin' like kids. They were too small to be grown, and they might've looked like kids, but they don't have any kids in Harlem, because nobody has time for childhood" (p. 295). An underlying aspect of the lives of children in poor black communities in all parts of the country is how early in life these young people must learn to protect themselves and to survive in a hostile society. In these environments, relationships between parents and their offspring are often more open, honest, and mature than in traditional middle-class American homes. Poor black children assume greater responsibility for themselves and younger siblings at an early age, and in many cases, the earnings of the very young children are an essential part of the family budget. While these experiences are harsh and cruel, especially in light of the middle-

the Other': Reading Toni Morrison's *Sula* and the Black Female Text," in *Critical Essays on Toni Morrison*, ed. Nellie Y. McKay (Boston: G. K. Hall, 1988), pp. 78–89, for discussions of differences affecting a unified black female identity.

class American cult of childhood, and they offer none of the protective insulation of privileged environments, on the positive side, the children's participation in the creative process that determines who they will eventually become lends itself to the development of strong personalities and gives the young people a greater sense of control over their destinies.[5]

This essay examines how three black women who, as adults, took radical private and public stances against the dehumanizing conditions of black people's lives in America recall their actions and responses in the childhood worlds of their memories. My emphasis is on the relationship between their reconstructions of childhood behaviors and their adult public responses to a hostile social world. From their recollections of their early lives we learn that while they were quite young they became aware of and actively resisted the arbitrarily designated boundaries of race, class, and gender, unconscious of the path toward which they were headed. Thus began their searches for independent black female selfhood. Since the women come from different, but equally important, historical periods for Afro-Americans, their social and economic circumstances offer a view of living conditions over a cross section of the larger black American community; and because they were different ages when they wrote their stories, their texts reflect different stages in individual physical and psychological development.

Harriet Jacobs, whose *Incidents in the Life of a Slave Girl* was published in 1861, was a former slave, already in her middle years when she wrote of her childhood experiences in bondage and her pre–Civil War years as a fugitive. Her narrative is a document that cries out against the institution that permitted black men and women to be treated as less than human, and subordinated black women to the sexual whims of white men. According to Jacobs, who enjoyed greater protection than most slave children, during her early years she did not realize she was a slave. After age twelve, however, she spent her life continuously resisting the forces that dehumanized her and all others of her race. Before the emancipation, although she was not formally connected to the abolitionist movement, she engaged in anti-slavery struggles. After January 1, 1863, when chattel slavery was no longer the issue, she devoted most of her time to work among poor southern black people (Jacobs, pp. 223–25).[6]

Mary Church Terrell's *A Black Woman in a White World* appeared in 1940, when she was almost eighty years old and still actively involved in

---

5. Kenneth Keniston, *Young Radicals: Notes on Committed Youth* (New York: Harcourt, Brace & World, 1968), p. 76; Claude Brown, *Manchild in the Promised Land* (New York: New American Library, 1966), p. 295. See also Joyce A. Ladner, *Tomorrow's Tomorrow: The Black Woman* (New York: Doubleday, 1971), pp. 44–66; and Robert Coles, *Children of Crisis* (New York: Little, Brown, 1964).

6. Harriet Jacobs, *Incidents in the Life of a Slave Girl*, ed. Jean Fagan Yellin (Cambridge: Harvard University Press, 1987). Subsequent references to this book are taken from this text. From Jean Yellin's chronology of Jacobs's life, we learn that in 1863 she distributed clothing and worked as a nurse and teacher among poor blacks in Alexandria, Virginia, and in 1865 she carried relief supplies to Edenton, her hometown as a slave. Yellin's biography of Jacobs is in progress.

civil rights issues. Her story is a reflection on a long and successful life which combined a sense of public responsibility with family duties. As *Benjamin Franklin: The Autobiography* chronicles the growth and development of the Republic in the eighteenth century, Terrell's book combines the black female personal narrative with her vision of the history of black America from Reconstruction to World War II. Unlike Franklin, however, she could not use the social or political values of the country for her personal or group development, so she questioned the hypocrisy of the rhetoric of the nation's most cherished public documents and struggled to assert her humanity. As a member of the first generation of post–Civil War children of ex-slaves, Terrell belonged to a group that used whatever educational advantages and economic good fortune came its way to enable us to see her as one of those who forged the beginnings of a recognizable black middle class. She is well known for her pioneering work and her long and distinguished record on black women's liberation and other civil rights activities.

Anne Moody published her autobiography, *Coming of Age in Mississippi*, before she was thirty years old. This work documents the early life of a young black woman who came of age as an activist in the recent civil rights movement within a family that, almost a hundred years after emancipation, remained crippled at the intersection of race, sex, and poverty. Of the three women in this study, Moody is the only one who not only received no support from family or close friends for her radical activities, but, like Richard Wright earlier in the century, endured open hostility from those who knew her best because of her rebellion against the status quo. Her book is especially important because of its child's-eye view of twentieth-century poor black life in the deep South and her own herculean efforts to resist the victimization of the poverty and dehumanization into which she was born. Moody's contributions to the civil rights struggle of the 1950s and '60s placed her in a position of leadership in the movement. But unlike Jacobs and Terrell, who pursued public political activities all of their lives, Moody has discontinued such actions since the publication of her book in 1968.

Although the lives of these women are very different from each other, their stories reveal that each, in her memory of early self-concept development, identified and resisted aspects of the social expectations of black people in general and of black women in particular. Such actions, taking place at different historical times, in different ways, and in different parts of the country, give us a useful reference point from which to examine separate modes of growth and the development of radical ideologies of race, class, and gender in black women's autobiographies. For my examination, I use a paradigm of development from Carol Pearson's study of archetypes of the hero in Western culture, *The Hero Within*. Although Pearson points to six stages in men's and women's journey patterns toward individuation, my discussion focuses on three: the Innocent, or the

Edenic stage; the Orphan stage, which embodies the fall from innocence and the acquisition of knowledge; and the stage of the Warrior, the time when those who have the courage to fight for themselves can have an effect on their destinies and on events in their larger worlds.[7] Two of the women have experiences that conform to these three stages; for one, the severity of the physical and psychological oppression of her early years left no remembrances of a period of innocence.

Harriet Jacobs spent all of her childhood in slavery in North Carolina. In her narrative, she divided her early life into three parts. In the first, when she lived with and enjoyed the love and security of her immediate family—her mother, father, grandmother, and brother—she was completely unaware of her slave condition. Her parents were mulattoes who were treated as benevolently as the system allowed. Jacobs's father was a skilled, highly valued tradesman; her grandmother, an old and trusted bond servant, reputed for her faithfulness and the quality of her work. The family was more comfortable than many others, and Harriet Jacobs did not experience the oppressiveness of slavery then. This was the Edenic period of her life, the "fortunate" times. The sudden death of her mother when she was six made her an orphan in social terms and propelled her into a psychological fall from innocence. Removal from her parental home to that of her slave mistress revealed her status to her, but since she was still humanely treated, she failed to comprehend its meaning. When Jacobs was twelve, the death of this woman ushered in the third stage of the slave girl's childhood and ended her "happy days." Instead of finding herself free, as her mistress had promised before she died, Jacobs discovered that she was now the property of a five-year-old girl. This time, removed to the home of the child's lecherous father and jealous mother, she learned, firsthand, what slavery had in store for her. This was her second awakening: determined not to be a wholly passive victim, she took actions that foreshadowed her subsequent struggles against strong contending forces.

At the age of twenty-nine, Harriet Jacobs made a dramatic escape from slavery. At age forty-three, when wide expanses of time and place separated her from the events of her early life, she published *Incidents in the Life of a Slave Girl* in the hope of kindling "a flame of compassion" among northern white women for still-enslaved black women. *Incidents*, like the autobiographies of the other women in this essay, focuses on the themes of bondage and freedom within a framework of the writer's consciousness of race, class, and gender oppression from an early age.

In her earliest childhood recollections, Jacobs emphasized her happiness and claimed that until she was six years old she "was so fondly

---

7. Carol Pearson, *The Hero Within* (New York: Harper & Row, 1986). Page references to this work appear in the text.

shielded" that she never "dreamed" she was a slave, "a piece of merchandise, trusted to [her parents] for safekeeping, and liable to be demanded of them at any moment" (Jacobs, p. 5) [9]. These years fit perfectly into Carol Pearson's archetype of the first stage of human development. In every way, Jacobs was "the Innocent [who] lives in an unfallen world, a green Eden where life is sweet and all one's needs are met in an atmosphere of care and love" (Pearson, p. 25). One seldom encounters such terms as "happy childhood" and "fondly shielded" in slave narratives. No doubt other slave children were unaware of their true condition for a part of their young lives, but Harriet Jacobs grew up with familial love and the illusion of parental protection over an extended period of time. Unaware of her class, she identified authority within her family, and thus, in her first six years, was separated from the more common slave child's experiences and gained a greater sense of positive self-worth than many like herself.

According to Pearson, the fall from innocence to orphan state usually causes "political, religious, or personal disappointment and disillusionment" (p. 27). Jacobs's fall and the beginning of her orphan stage occurred when her mother died, an event that initiated her into the realities of slave life. The loss of her mother precipitated great personal grief for her and, as she soon discovered, left her bereft of her imagined familial protection and any illusion of personal freedom. Taken from her home and loved ones to the abode of her mistress, she lost the place of pampered child to that of maid-in-waiting, which epitomized her true condition. Thus, her memories of the period include the child's awareness of her connections to the broader social and historical context: to the meaning of slavery. Knowledge withheld from her for six years came rudely flooding in.

Although she was not treated harshly, she sensed her powerlessness, and that of her father and grandmother, against the system. She realized that her father, as much as he loved her and as much as he was deemed trustworthy by the community, could not keep her with him or influence the course of her life. All his life he suffered the humiliation of having the status of property. Repeatedly, his owners refused to permit him to purchase his children out of slavery. As for Jacobs's grandmother, her five children were sold away from her, and in spite of promises to the contrary, she was never able to redeem them. It was not difficult for the grieving and disillusioned Jacobs to see, at the child's level, that the evil in the system made slavery intolerable and beyond compromise. But worse was yet to come. When she was twelve her mistress died. Having assured Jacobs that in her will she would free the child, from the grave she reneged on the promise. The woman Jacobs recorded that she never forgot the outrage and frustration she felt when she discovered this betrayal. Years later, she wished that she could "blot out" from her memory "that one great wrong" (Jacobs, p. 8) [11].

A sense of the injustices in the slave system dominates Jacobs's re-membrances of the second and third periods of her childhood. Her major complaints were not the hardships of work or the deprivation of material comforts, but the violation of common decencies toward black people by white people. She presents the adults in her family as well as the other slaves as honest, hardworking, trustworthy, moral human beings whose labor was brutally exploited and whose dignity denied. Had they been born to other circumstances, for industry and responsibility the Jacobses would have been the ideal American family, but their hopes for them-selves and their children's freedom were lost to the immorality of slavery. Jacobs's grandmother suffered a worse insult when her owner defrauded her of money she accumulated to purchase her children.

If innocence and ignorance of slavery marked the first years of Jacobs's life, and the second part brought personal knowledge and a political awareness of race and power, then the third added gender to the list and forced her to confront the three issues in respect to the lives of black slave women in America. In this third phase, she is a paradigm of the warrior on a perilous journey toward selfhood and early womanhood. By age twelve, the deaths of her "kind" mistress and her caring and devoted but powerless father changed her world completely—from a benevolent to a hostile place. Alone, and seemingly impotent to affect her circumstances, she seemed to have made a deliberate decision to challenge and resist the system, never doubting that good was on her side and would triumph over evil.

Jacobs knew both the extent of the racial demoralization that all slaves suffered and black women's added vulnerability to sexual abuse by mas-ters and their agents. In addition, the girls/women endured harsh treat-ment at the hands of the outraged wives of the sexual offenders; unable to vent their anger and humiliation at the actions of their men, these women abused the victims of their husbands' lust. Writing on this prob-lem in recalling her fourteenth birthday, Jacobs observed that two years of living with the Flint family (her owners) had given her the knowledge of what it meant to live in the world as a woman and a slave. She be-longed, she said, among those who, because of the place of black women in slave culture, were "prematurely knowing of evil things." In similar terms, Joyce Ladner notes that in twentieth-century urban ghettos girls in early adolescence gain "emotional precocity" that "far exceeds their chronological ages" (p. 52). The knowledge of her sexual vulnerability frightened Jacobs, for she knew that in her master's eyes she was no longer a child and that her slavery meant more than his ability to command her physical labor.

However, fear did not paralyze her: like Anne Moody later, it made her sufficiently angry that she acted. Jacobs's struggles to thwart her master's designs on her, especially between her fourteenth and fifteenth year, have been widely written about and need not be repeated here. In this, "the

war of . . . [her] life" (Jacobs, p. 19) [19], her master had the power of
the slave codes on his side, and she had the determination not to give in.
Given that she had no one to turn to for advice or comfort, her flagrant
open defiance of his sexual advances was astonishing. Strong elements of
self-worth, handed down to her in her religious grandmother's moral
teachings (her grandmother's rigid moral codes precluded the young
girl's confiding her troubles in her) motivated Jacobs to obstinate resistance. Literally, she took power to herself and challenged her master to
kill her first.[8] Her relationship with another white man who brought no
such pressure to bear on her was the climax of her childhood rebellion.
The sexual liaison with the other was a fifteen-year-old child's claim to
full ownership of her body and the dignity of an autonomous self. She
wrote: "there is something akin to freedom in having a lover who has no
control over you, except that which he gains by kindness and attachment" (Jacobs, p. 55) [47].

A year later, before she was sixteen years old, Jacobs left childhood behind as she took on the responsibility of a new, younger life. Her first
child was a boy. Her second, born the following year, was a girl, and that
fact made her "heart . . . heavier than it had ever been before." In a
much-quoted evaluation of the slave woman's plight, she wrote: "slavery
is terrible for men; but it is more terrible for women. Superadded to the
burden common to all, they have wrongs, and sufferings, and the mortifications peculiarly their own" (Jacobs, p. 77) [64]. With this in mind,
Harriet Jacobs schemed and suffered in her efforts to escape from slavery
and to save her children from the kind of childhood she perceived her
own to be. She succeeded. Her determined and courageous resisting of
the sexual advances of her master, when she was yet a girl, led to her imaginative escape and eventually to a life dedicated to the struggle against
black American slavery.

Mary Church Terrell had a very different childhood from Jacobs's, yet
her early life followed similar patterns of development. Born in Memphis, Tennessee, in 1863, of parents freed by the emancipation procla-
mation, she barely escaped slavery. Like the parents of Harriet Jacobs,
hers were industrious mulattoes, and freedom enabled them to turn ingenuity and initiative to economic advantage. Unfortunately, her father
and mother separated while Mary and her younger brother were very
young, but the children did not suffer for love or material comforts. In

8. For detailed discussions of this and other aspects of Jacobs's life, see Andrews, *To Tell a Free
Story*, pp. 239–63; Carby, *Reconstructing Womanhood*, pp. 45–61; Valerie Smith, *Self-Discovery
and Authority in Afro-American Narrative* (Cambridge: Harvard University Press, 1987), pp.
28–43; and Yellin's Introduction to Jacobs, *Incidents in the Life*. See also Frederick Douglass,
The Narrative of the Life of Frederick Douglass, An American Slave, Written by Himself, ed. Benjamin Quarles (Cambridge: Harvard University Press, 1960), pp. 104–5. After successfully
resisting an unfair whipping, Douglass feels transformed from a "brute" into a man who was no
longer "a slave in fact," regardless of the law. Jacobs has a similar psychological response when
she defies her master.

contrast to the confinements of slavery that Jacobs knew, Terrell, one of the first black women to attend and graduate from Oberlin College, had advantages of class privilege that set her apart from the majority of black children of her generation.

Mary Church's arrival in the world caused some distress for her parents, however. For more than a year, she was a completely bald baby. Women's hair had always been a matter of great importance in female image-making in Western culture, and black women's hair has caused anxiety and discomfort for them ever since they arrived in America. Was Mary Church's hairlessness a pre-birth protest forewarning her own great distress over the social expectations of women? Did the absence of hair on this black woman-child indicate that she would focus her attention on issues of more fundamental concern to the human condition? Did she, inside her mother's womb, decide to make a dramatic protest against how women "ought" to look? In childhood, as in later life, Terrell actively resisted the limitations and expectations that others close to her and those outside of her family sought to place on her.

By all standards except race, Mary Church Terrell's early childhood shared many of the earmarks of a childhood in the white middle class. After emancipation, her parents reordered their lives and acquired a new social standing. Robert Church, son of a slave owner, seemed not to have suffered many of the indignities that large numbers of slaves had. His father neglected to educate him, yet gave him the impression that he had value in himself. After 1863 he engaged in a variety of successful money-making activities, including land speculation. His daughter recalled him as generous, reserved, unusually intelligent, with great business ability and a violent temper. He never spoke of his life in slavery.

But Terrell also saw her mother as a model of independence. The older woman had an entrepreneurial spirit and shared her husband's desire to rise out of the ranks of the underclass. She had artistic talents as well, but because she was a pragmatist, she became a business woman. After her separation from her husband, Mrs. Church, one of the first black women in the black beauty-culture profession, became a great success in the hairdressing business, first in Memphis and later in New York City.

The Edenic period of Mary Church's life, like Harriet Jacobs's, lasted for the first six years of her life. In those years, as she recalled them, she had the security of a home life that inspired her with self-confidence. Both of her parents were hardworking and successful, and even through separation and divorce, they seemed in harmony with themselves and the world. Remembering her childhood, Mary Church noted she had no divided loyalties between her parents, only the confidence that they loved her, wanted the best for her, and shared the responsibility of making the decisions affecting her young life. Her father paid for her schooling and daily living; her mother was generous with clothes and other necessities. A grandmother's "brutal," inhumane stories of slavery and a racist incident on a train when she was five years old invaded the perfection of Mary Church's Eden without having an adverse impression on her. She made no connection between herself, her family, and the old woman's tales, nor did she understand why the conductor on a train going North roughly tried to eject her from a reserved-for-whites compartment. This period, as for Jacobs, was one of pure innocence for Mary Church.

Mary Church journeyed beyond Eden and into her orphan stage when, at age six, she went to school in Yellow Springs, Ohio, because her parents wished to protect her from the racially segregated, inferior, Memphis school system.[9] But if they shielded her from poor education, they could not save her from the deep-seated racism of peers and teachers elsewhere. Awakening to the knowledge of her racial identity was difficult for Mary Church, although not the same horror it had been for Jacobs: there were positive buffers between herself and the reality of her place in the world. While Jacobs left home to take up service in the home of her mistress, in Yellow Springs Mary Church lived with family friends, and made a rapid and successful adjustment to her new home. For two years she attended a model school then moved to a regular public school. She reported that, in general, she loved school, learned German from an Antioch College student, and was happy at home and with her friends. In the autobiography she noted the picturesque beauty of the place, and the famous spring that gave a yellow tinge to everything over which it flowed. She named it the "John Brown Spring" in honor of that man's courage in standing up for the humanity of slaves. In those years she also learned to appreciate the majesty of nature.

On the negative side of that experience, Mary Church acquired racial awareness in two particularly painful events in school, a ritual ground for black children's awakening to racism at the hands of white children or grown-ups.[1] The incidents in which she learned of her identity as a black person in a white world and a woman in a society in which gender de-

---

9. See Mary Church Terrell, A Colored Woman in a White World (Washington, D.C.: Ransdell Inc., 1940; rpt. New York: Arno Press, 1980). Subsequent references to this text are taken from this edition.

   It is not unusual for young black children to leave home, sometimes alone, for faraway destinations. Maya Angelou discussed this in I Know Why the Caged Bird Sings, the first volume of her autobiography. At age three she and her brother, Bailey, age four, with tags on their wrists, traveled alone by train from Long Beach, California, to Stamps, Arkansas, to their paternal grandmother. Angelou writes: "I don't remember much of the trip. . . . Negro passengers, who always travelled with loaded lunch boxes, . . . [fed us] with cold fried chicken and potato salad" (p. 4). Angelou further comments that thousands of frightened black children cross the country each year traveling to or from their "newly affluent" northern parents or to grandmothers in the South.

1. In James Weldon Johnson's The Autobiography of An Ex-Colored Man, the protagonist's entire life changes when at age nine he learns from a teacher that he is not white. Maya Angelou also recalls, in I Know Why the Caged Bird Sings, how devastating it was for an entire class of young black elementary school graduates to discover that their education was over at this juncture, while their white counterparts would go on to training that would make them professionals. In contemporary life, the inadequacies of segregated education and white harassment of black children in white schools confirm how much black children learn about their inferior place in the world from white teachers.

fines one's roles mark her real loss of Eden and the beginning of her orphan stage. At age eight, in the model school, fair-skinned Mary Church discovered from her white classmates that she was racially different from them and that her difference made her less attractive and less desirable than they. Here, for the first time, she faced race and gender as negative aspects of her life. The unattractive black girl will become an unattractive woman, and an unattractive black woman has no place in the social world.[2] Previously sheltered and pampered, this child faced difficult realities. More than sixty years later, Terrell recalled that that experience "indelibly impressed" her racial identity on her.

Further loss of innocence and another awakening came to Mary Church in a history class in which she learned that she was intimately connected to the slave heritage. When Jacobs moved to the home of her slave mistress at age six, her recognition of her servitude precipitated her knowledge of her connection to the broader history of her people. Living within the slave community also gave Jacobs another advantage over Mary Church: in her predicament she could identify with her family and loved ones. She could feel grief for herself and the lot of her people without suffering a loss of personal worth. On the other hand, the unprepared Mary Church, surrounded by those racially different from herself, felt only alienation from them and great shame for herself. Of the impact of this knowledge she wrote: "I was stunned. I felt humiliated and disgraced, . . . I had never thought about my connection with slavery at all. But now I knew I belonged to a group of people who had been brutalized, degraded, and sold like animals. This was a rude and terrible shock indeed. . . . I was covered with confusion and shame" (Terrell, p. 21).

For all her shame, like Jacobs, Mary Church did not internalize a sense of worthlessness, even from this shock. Her final encounter with a negative racial incident in school launched her into her third stage of childhood, heralding the beginning of her life as a warrior. In this, again like Jacobs, she took power to herself and moved forward from defensive to offensive action by refusing to take the role of the stereotyped "darky" servant in a school play. This pre-adolescent show of resistance looks toward her college career and her refusal to conform to conventional policies there, and beyond that to her long career in civil rights and feminist activities.

At Oberlin College, Mary Church added gender consciousness to her increasing awareness of racial consciousness, and the battle moved from the private to a more public sphere. As a young child, she knew that women could have independent careers. Since both of her parents approved of her educational ambitions, she took no stock in privileged middle-class views on the subject. Consequently, in college, Mary Church

---

2. For one painful example of the problems of "unattractive" black women, see Wallace Thurman, *The Blacker the Berry* (Macaulay, 1929; rpt. New York: Macmillan, 1970).

ran into difficulties by refusing to enroll in the Literary Course, designed for women, and insisting on taking the more rigorous Classical Course, designed for men. Although her parents supported her decision, many students (including women) did not. Her friends tried to dissuade her and advised her that a too-highly educated woman, especially a black one, would encounter difficulties in finding a husband.[3] Nevertheless, she remained adamant and graduated from the "gentlemen's course" wearing a "wonderful black jet dress," the gift of her mother. The young women who dared to challenge the conventions and chose to take the "gentlemen's course" always "dressed in sombre black" for their graduation.

But the tension over her education did not end with Mary Church's graduation. Although Robert Church fully supported his daughter's wishes in her course of study, he was not prepared for her subsequent decision to take a position as a teacher. Since he was financially able to do so, he encouraged her to travel abroad for as long as she wished, until she was ready to marry. She, on the other hand, wanted a life of "usefulness" and was determined to enter work that "could promote the welfare of [her] race" (Terrell, p. 60). She understood that her father wanted her to be a lady, to take advantage of opportunities for genteel leisure that black women never had and only a few could yet afford. But she was not willing to accept his ideas of her privileged social role. Once she began to define her place in the world as a black person with a sense of autonomy, she linked her role as a woman to that persona, for both were indivisible in the quest for the full black female self. She acted on this principle for the rest of her life.[4]

Anne Moody was born in Mississippi in 1940, the year that Mary Church Terrell published her autobiography. Her mother, father, and later her stepfather, sharecroppers and menial laborers, were so defeated by racism and economic failure that they could not support her optimism or her educational or social ambitions. Thus, her early struggles against the triple oppression of poor black women was a solitary endeavor that took place at home and abroad. The ascendency of the civil rights movement in the South, beginning in the 1950s, parallels her growth and development toward consciousness of the conditions of black life in that region. Her commitment to the movement during the later '50s and the

3. In 1891, in "the most notable event in colored society in years," Mary Church married Robert Terrell, a teacher and lawyer who later received five appointments to a judgeship in the municipal court in Washington, D.C. The Terrells led active political lives which appear to have complemented each other. He died in 1925. She continued her civil rights and women's rights activities until her death in 1954.
4. Mary Church Terrell was one of the founders of the National Association of Colored Women and of the NAACP. She was president of the former from 1892 to 1898. Among her many activities from 1892 to 1953 she addressed the National American Woman Suffrage Association in 1898 and the International Congress of Women in Zurich in 1919, organized voters, and picketed the White House and places of public accommodation in Washington.

early '60s is the ultimate declaration of her rejection of the subordinate position that tradition decreed as her place in the world.

Unlike Jacobs and Terrell, Anne Moody had no consciousness of an Edenic period in her life, only of the physical and psychological fears encumbering her and those around her. In rural Mississippi, subsistence living and fears of racial violence leave no room for black or white innocence. Moody's family, long-time residents of the area, were paralyzed by the despair of the lot they inherited.[5] Moody's four-year-old impressions of her landscape were of how dismal, depressing, and degrading it was for them. For blacks the legacy of slavery, almost a century later, was poverty, fear of whites, and powerlessness within the social system. In place of the Eden of the childhoods of Jacobs and Terrell, Moody recalled a nightmare when she wrote of her earliest childhood memories: "I am still haunted by dreams of [that] time. . . . Lots of Negroes lived on [this] place. We all lived in rotten wood two-room shacks . . . ours . . . looked just like the barn with a chimney and a porch but Mama and Daddy did what they could to make it livable" (Moody, p. 12). Thus, she experienced no fall, no sudden awakening to a knowledge of her condition, no personal or political disillusionment that stripped away her innocence, for she was never innocent.

In the absence of stability or an illusion of parental protection, impermanence, delapidation, and the sense of social impotence are her reality. Moody, eldest of six children, had only a vague memory of a time when her mother seemed beautiful: "slim, tall, and tawny skinned with high cheek bones and long black hair," vivacious and happy in spite of the difficulties (Moody, p. 18). She recalled more poignantly how a husband's desertion, anxieties over poverty, the physical difficulties of field work and the equally back-breaking domestic work in white people's homes, along with frequent pregnancies and the burdens of many children robbed her mother of her charms, her physical attractiveness, and the joy of living. Thus, in her earliest childhood memories, Moody accumulated a storehouse of knowledge regarding the plight of poor black women and their children in rural Mississippi. At age four, poverty and physical abuse were not abstract terms to the child whose staple food was beans or who cowered in the presence of an eight-year-old male caretaker who constantly beat her. Nor was responsibility an incomprehensible concept for the five-year-old charged with taking care of herself and her younger sister all day while her parents worked in the fields. At the age of nine, when millions of pre-adolescent American children received small allowances or

---

5. Anne Moody, *Coming of Age in Mississippi* (New York: Dell, 1968). Subsequent references to this text are taken from this edition. Moody remembered constantly moving from one place to another. By the time she was fourteen years old, and until her mother remarried, the family lived in six different two-room shacks. They slept in one room, cooked and lived in the other. Bedroom walls were usually covered with loose paper held up with thumbtacks. Sometimes they lived with relatives in even more overcrowded quarters. Other times they stayed in places provided by white employers.

did odd jobs at home or in their neighborhoods for small fees, to learn the meaning of money, Moody went to work and realized her earnings were a necessary part of her family's income. Her mother's unhappiness also impressed her. Only twice did she recall the older woman seeming otherwise: once, shortly before her second marriage, and again, immediately following the birth of the first child she bore for her second husband. Moody was a young teenager by then and recorded, from an unobserved place, her mother's aura after the birth: "Her face looked different, I thought—so calm and young. She hadn't looked young for a long time. Maybe it was because she was happy now. She had never before been happy to have a baby. . . . For a long time I stood there looking at her. . . . I wanted to think she would always be that happy, so I never would be unhappy again either. Adeline and Junior [the younger children] were too young to feel the things I felt and know the things I knew about Mama. . . . They had never heard her cry at nights as I had or worked and helped as I had done when we were starving" (Moody, p. 57).

Having no experience with innocence, Anne Moody entered the warrior stage of her development at roughly the age at which Jacobs and Terrell came to their first awareness of themselves as part of a group separate from and unequal to the dominant group. As noted earlier in this essay, Joyce Ladner observes that children exposed to these conditions experience rapid emotional development: they learn to protect themselves from the hostile forces in their environments much earlier than those in more sheltered circumstances; they take responsibility for their futures considerably earlier than others in their peer group. By age seven, having observed the hierarchical differences between white and black people all of her life, an angry Moody began to question the rationale for white superiority and black inferiority. Moody's recollections of black adult reactions to her questions were similar to those Richard Wright, asking the same questions a quarter of a century earlier, received. Out of fear that the children might speak out of turn in racially dangerous situations and thus endanger themselves and the community, frustrated adults refused to discuss these problems with their children.[6] Like Wright before her, Moody responded to the silence with greater anger and more confusion.

By the time she was a young teenager, open violence against blacks by individuals or groups of whites, including the death of Emmett Till in her neighborhood, raised unbridled fury in Anne Moody and marked her as a danger to the frightened black community. Their fears for their lives not only prevented them from supporting her in her activities or mounting opposition to their oppression, but caused them to view her as a pariah. She, in turn, saw the black adults whose lives intersected with hers as cowardly—passive in their acceptance of the injustices they suffered and in

---

6. In *Black Boy* (New York: Harper & Row, 1945), Richard Wright reported several whippings from his mother when as a child he questioned race relations in the South.

their refusal to discuss their condition. She considered them participants in their oppression. In college, away from her hometown, to which she could not return on pain of death, she found the civil rights movement gave her an opportunity for leadership and activity that expressed her outrage at the impotence of black people in the face of the oppression that stripped them of all human dignity.

As a girl growing up in a community beleagured by race, Moody was also conscious of gender roles as an added burden of black women. She knew that white and black women had fewer options for self-determination and more potential for physical and emotional abuse from the men of both races. In the white community, where she worked from age seven, much of her interaction was with women. Some treated her kindly and encouraged her to seek a better life; others made her even more aware that race and gender conspired to lock her into a subordinate position for the rest of her life. Their conscious, overt treatment of her as an inferior, and sometimes as the sexually promiscuous, immoral black woman, made that clear. In this way, Moody learned of the gulf that separated white and black women in much the same way as Harriet Jacobs did. Black women suffered the same economic exploitation as black men, and in addition, they were often the objects of the sexual lust of white men and of the anger and contempt of white women.

Within her family and the black community as a whole, Moody saw another kind of black women's oppression. Most of the women she knew were burdened with too many children and lacked means of providing for them adequately. The men often deserted when the burdens were greatest, leaving the women to raise the children by themselves or to seek the help of other men, which in turn increased the sizes of already too-large families. Uneducated, black women in rural Mississippi were tied to poverty and oppression by race and gender. Moody's recognition of this double oppression of black women created additional conflicts between herself, her mother, and her stepfather. This only increased her anger. In addition, her ambitions to have a life other than that of her mother, particularly her rejection of labor on the land, increased the tensions between mother and daughter. As a result, the closing years of Anne Moody's childhood, the years between twelve and fourteen, were marred by rifts that eventually separated her physically and emotionally from blood kin and the community in which she was raised.

In her early painful realization of the meaning of the black experience, issues of class place Moody's remembrances of childhood closer to those of Harriet Jacobs than to Mary Church Terrell. On the other hand, in the absence of black support and reinforcement for her ideals and her desires to change her situation, her story differs significantly from either woman's.

The backgrounds and times of these women were different, yet they distinguished themselves by breaking out of the boundaries others set for

black females in white America. In reconstructions of childhood, they reveal that resistance to those boundaries began before they were fully
aware of the meaning of their actions. Unimpressed by attempts to protect them from the insults of a hostile world, refusing to conform to familial efforts to define the courses of their lives, the women chose
identities and actions that defied society's expectations. Later, they used
autobiography to explain vital connections between childhood and adult
actions, and to show us why they became who they were.

Refusing to be contained by their race or gender or class, these three
black women enabled themselves and others to act with self-determination, and to take an active role in the development of positive self-con-
cepts. Harriet Jacobs, born a slave, experienced the full impact of that
institution on the lives of black women, yet her sense of herself and her
struggle for freedom belie the slave mentality. To Jacobs goes all the
credit. She made herself. Encouraged even by the grandmother she
deeply respected to accept her position as a slave and trust in Providence
for release from her trials, she disregarded the older woman's advice and
devised her own weapons for survival and self-confirmation. Later, a
sympathetic community rewarded her courage by helping her to escape.
A biography of her, being prepared by Jean Yellin, promises to bring to
light even more remarkable achievements of this remarkable woman.

Mary Church Terrell narrowly escaped a slave's birth, and the economic situation of her family shielded her from the worst assaults of segregation and racism during Reconstruction. Living in the North, with
adequate financial resources, she found life considerably easier than it
would have been in the South. But escape from the racist traumas of that
region meant permanent separation from her parents when she was still
very young. Nothing in her autobiography suggests anxieties on this level,
yet it seems unlikely that the separation did not have psychological effects
on her. In a different way, like poor children in contemporary urban ghettos, she drew on internal resources to gain the confidence to stand up for
herself, even against her father. Independently, she identified herself with
personal achievement and with work for the uplift of those of her race
who were less fortunate than herself.

As a child, Anne Moody experienced some of the worst aspects of the
poverty and powerlessness of black life in America. Early in her life, she
began to question the social structure that defined her as inferior to white
people. Unlike Jacobs, who had no parents to turn to because they were
dead, or Church Terrell, who was separated from hers, Moody sought answers to the knotty problems of race from her mother. Although the answers were either never forthcoming or unsatisfactory when they came,
she persisted in seeking them. She recalled her impatience and anger
with the black community for what she saw as apathy and acceptance of
a subordinate racial and economic position. But unlike Richard Wright,
who turned similar frustrations into alienation from and disparagement

of the black community, she translated her emotions into action in the civil rights movement.

For Terrell and Moody, place and economics were as important to their experiences as time was in their separation from the experiences of Harriet Jacobs. But in spite of time, place, and circumstances, their stories reveal that even as children the three women believed that they had ultimate control over their lives. The question for us might be: What was childhood for them? None enjoyed the luxury of the Western storybook period of life. Their environments forced them to grow up and to learn to take care of themselves by making crucial decisions about their lives when they were very young. We might agree with Claude Brown's friend that many black women and men in America have no childhoods, only periods of young lives marked by degrees of innocence and partial knowledge of the true state of their American existence. All who survive are warriors beginning very early in their development; consciously or unconsciously they are the major architects of their concepts of themselves. Often they are alone on the journey to self.

At the center of each of these black women's autobiographies is a rebel with a moral cause that joins her to a tradition of women resisting and transcending the oppression of race, class, and gender. For Jacobs, Terrell, and Moody, childhood was not a period of parental indulgence, but the training ground on which they discovered themselves as black female persons. In this period we first observe the vision that enabled these girls, in the face of seeming powerlessness, to empower themselves in ways that foreshadowed the women they became.

HARRYETTE MULLEN

Runaway Tongue: Resistant Orality in *Uncle Tom's Cabin, Our Nig, Incidents in the Life of a Slave Girl,* and *Beloved*†

The mainstream appeal of Harriet Beecher Stowe's *Uncle Tom's Cabin* catalyzed literary as well as political activity in the nineteenth century. Leaving aside the numerous attacks, defenses, adaptations, imitations, and parodies the book inspired among white writers, let us note that Stowe, through the unprecedented popularity of her sympathetic black characters, had an impact on black writers so immediate that *Uncle Tom's*

---

† From *The Culture of Sentiment: Race, Gender, and Sentimentality in Nineteenth-Century America*, ed. Shirley Samuels (New York: Oxford UP, 1992), 244–64, 332–35. Copyright © 1992 by Oxford University Press, Inc. Used by permission of Oxford University Press, Inc. Page references to this Norton Critical Edition are given in brackets following Mullen's original citations, with the exception of references to extratext material included in the Yellin edition.

Cabin can be regarded as an important precursor of the African American novel. Through the broad influence of this fictional work, Stowe almost single-handedly turned the interests of black readers and writers to the political, cultural, and economic possibilities of the novel. Recognizing the value of their personal and collective experience, black writers of both fictional and nonfictional works were influenced by Stowe's exploitation of subliterary genres, her provocative combination of sentimental and slave narrative conventions, and her successful production of a text at once popular and ideological.[1]

Certainly Stowe provided an enabling textual model, especially for fledgling writers struggling to represent the subjectivity of black women; yet another way of looking at the response of black women writers in the nineteenth century to *Uncle Tom's Cabin* is to notice the different ways their texts "talk back" to Stowe's novel. Stowe's grafting of the sentimental novel, a literary genre associated with white women and the ideology of female domestication, onto the slave narrative, a genre associated with the literary production of black men and linking literacy with freedom and manhood, is countered by black women writers who produced texts that ask where the black woman finds herself, caught between these two literary models. Stowe uses the slave narrative as a reservoir of fact, experience, and realism, while constructing black characters as objects of sentimentality in order to augment the emotive power and political significance of her text.

Harriet Jacobs, the only black woman author to publish a book-length fugitive slave narrative, and Harriet Wilson, the first published black woman novelist, place the slave narrative and the sentimental genre in dialogue, and often in conflict, in order to suggest the ideological limits of "true womanhood" or bourgeois femininity, while they also call into question Frederick Douglass's paradigmatic equation of literacy, freedom, and manhood in his 1845 *Narrative*. As Harriet Jacobs's text *Incidents in the Life of a Slave Girl* (1861) and numerous dictated narratives of ex-slaves also suggest, slaves countered institutionalized illiteracy with a resistant orality. Not everyone found opportunities to steal literacy or successfully escape slavery as a fugitive, but oral transmission passed on the verbal skills of runaway tongues: the sass, spunk, and infuriating impudence of slaves who individually and collectively refused to know their place.

Nineteenth-century black women writers struggled in their texts to reconcile an oral tradition of resistance with a literary tradition of submission. Jane Tompkins, while arguing in favor of reading sentimental novels for the "cultural work" they accomplished, nevertheless reads them as texts that instruct women to accept their culturally defined roles

---

1. Eric J. Sundquist, ed., *New Essays on Uncle Tom's Cabin* (Cambridge: Cambridge University Press, 1986).

in order to exercise the power available to bourgeois white women operating within the ideological limits of "true womanhood."[2]

Slave narratives, on the other hand, do not advise submission to a higher authority imagined as benign; they celebrate flight from overt oppression. Having neither the incentive of cultural rewards available to some white women nor the mobility available to some male fugitives, slave women in particular and black women more generally would have found both the slave narrative and the sentimental novel deficient representations of their experience as black women. For this reason the texts of nineteenth-century black women writers concentrate not only on reconciling the contradictions of disparate literary conventions, but also on grafting literacy onto orality. Their texts, by focusing on a continuum of resistance to oppression available to the illiterate as well as the literate, tend to stress orality as a presence over illiteracy as an absence. The oral tradition often permitted a directness of expression (particularly within family networks in less Europeanized slave communities) about matters of sex, violence, and sexual violence that literary convention — particularly the indirection and euphemistic language of sentimental fiction in its concern with modesty and decorum — rendered "unspeakable." It is in the oral tradition (itself preserved through transcription), rather than either the sentimental novel or the male-dominated slave narrative genre, that we find the most insistent representations of strong black women resisting oppression and also passing on, through their oral expression to their daughters, a tradition of resistance to physical and sexual abuse from white women and men.

Illiterate slave women operated within a tradition of resistant orality, or verbal self-defense, which included speech acts variously labeled sassy or saucy, impudent, impertinent, or insolent: the speech of slaves who refused to know their place, who contested their assigned social and legal inferiority as slaves and as black women.[3] "Impudence" has a sexual connotation: the impudent woman is an outspoken "shameless hussy" whose sexual materiality (pudenda) is exposed. The impudent woman refuses to be modestly silent. Rather, she speaks the violation and exposure, the sexual, reproductive, and economic exploitation of her body, revealing the implicit contradictions of the sex-gender system which render her paradoxically both vulnerable and threatening. Her speech as well as her sexuality threaten patriarchal order, so that her immodest verbal expression and sexual behavior are continually monitored, controlled, and suppressed. The exposure of the slave woman's body — in the field where she worked, on the auction block, at the public whipping post, along with her sexual vulnera-

---

2. Jane Tompkins, *Sensational Designs: The Cultural Work of American Fiction, 1790–1860* (New York: Oxford University Press, 1985).
3. Joanne Braxton, "Harriet Jacobs' *Incidents in the Life of a Slave Girl:* The Redefinition of the Slave Narrative Genre," *The Massachusetts Review*, Winter 1986.

bility within the master's household—is at odds with the hidden sexuality and corresponding modesty of the respectable bourgeois white
woman, whose body is covered, confined, and sheltered within the
patriarchal household designated as her domestic sphere.

The literary tradition that produces the sentimental novel is concerned
with the white woman's assumption of her proper place, upon her internalization of the values of propriety and decorum, while the African
American oral tradition represents the exposed black woman who uses
impudent speech in order to defend her own body against abuse. In some
instances the stark materiality of their embodied existence gave black
women a clarity of vision about their position as slaves and as women that
could occasionally produce the riveting eloquence of an Isabella Baum-
free, the former slave woman whose chosen name, Sojourner Truth,
encapsulates both her determination to move beyond the static confinement of female existence, and the bold self-authorization of an illiterate
black woman to enter a discourse from which she had automatically been
excluded.

If institutionalized illiteracy was intended to exempt African
Americans from access to or participation in the discursive formations
of bourgeois society, then to the extent that it succeeded, it also left
them outside conventional ideological constructions that played a part
in determining white identities. To the degree that undisguised coer-
cion permeated their lives and invaded the interior of their bodies, the
self-awareness of such black women was unobscured by ideological
constructions of the dominant race and class that shielded the majority of bourgeois white women from sustained consciousness of their
own genteel subjugation. Sojourner Truth, memorialized as a body
with a voice, packs into a concise "immodest" gesture the ability to
shame those who attempt to shame her as a woman. Her power is built
upon the paradox of the black woman's possession of a public voice.
Because she has endured much worse in slavery, the fear of public
humiliation cannot threaten her into silence. She holds up under the
gaze of the heckler intent on shaming her off the lecture platform,
calmly enduring the scrutiny of an audience demanding the exposure
of her body, supposedly to "prove" that she was a woman, but in fact
to punish her for daring to speak in public to a "promiscuous" assembly. Freed from slavery as well as the need to embody the dominant
cultural aesthetic of feminine purity, Sojourner Truth could present
herself as a black woman unabashed by her body's materiality.

Lydia Maria Child's introduction to Jacob's narrative expresses the
concern of white women with a feminine delicacy too easily contaminated by association with the materiality of black women's experience, as
much as it suggests a racial division of labor in which white women bore
the ideological burden of trying to embody pure womanhood, while
black women suffered the harsh materiality of female experience unsoft-

ened by ideology.[4] Child's sponsoring of Jacobs's narrative in order to unveil the "monstrous features" of slavery, especially its component of female sexual slavery, might be read as a response to Stowe's assertion that
the successful artist must "draw a veil" over slavery.[5] Child endorses Jacobs in an attempt to divest the white woman reader of the ideological
veil that separates her from black women's experience. An unusual instance of a black woman publicly stripping a white woman of her clothing, if not her ideology, occurs in the oral account of the slave woman
Cornelia, remembering the spirited resistance of her mother to the physical abuse of a mistress.

> One day my mother's temper ran wild. For some reason Mistress
> Jennings struck her with a stick. Ma struck back and a fight followed.
> Mr. Jennings was not at home and the children became frightened
> and ran upstairs. For half [an] hour they wrestled in the kitchen.
> Mistress, seeing that she could not get the better of ma, ran out in
> the road, with ma right on her heels. In the road, my mother flew
> into her again. The thought seemed to race across my mother's mind
> to tear mistress' clothing off her body. She suddenly began to tear
> Mistress Jennings' clothes off. She caught hold, pulled, ripped and
> tore. Poor mistress was nearly naked when the storekeeper got to
> them and pulled ma off. "Why, Fannie, what do you mean by that?"
> he asked. "Why, I'll kill her, I'll kill her dead if she ever strikes me
> again."[6]

As Sojourner Truth turned the supposed shame of exposing her breasts
back onto her brash male accusers and the ladies who were too abashed
to look at her body, Fannie's runaway temper turns the slave's degradation back onto her mistress with a gesture intended to shame the white
woman who was not too delicate to beat a black woman. The humiliation involved in being publicly stripped seems calculated to deny the
white woman the superior status assigned her in the race-gender hierarchy. Fannie's inspired frenzy leads her to attack the white woman's sense

4. "I am well aware that many will accuse me of indecorum for presenting these pages to the public: for the experiences of this intelligent and much-injured woman belong to a class which some
call delicate subjects, and others indelicate. This peculiar phase of Slavery has generally been
kept veiled; but the public ought to be made acquainted with its monstrous features, and I willingly take the responsibility of presenting them with the veil withdrawn. I do this for the sake of
my sisters in bondage, who are suffering wrongs so foul, that our ears are too delicate to listen to
them." Lydia Maria Child, "Introduction" to Harriet A. Jacobs, *Incidents in the Life of a Slave
Girl*, ed. Jean Fagan Yellin (Cambridge, Mass.: Harvard University Press, 1987), 3–4 [6]. Originally self-published by Child in Boston, 1861.
5. Harriet Beecher Stowe, *The Key to Uncle Tom's Cabin* (1854; Salem, N.H.: Ayer, 1987), 1. "The
writer acknowledges that the book [*Uncle Tom's Cabin*] is a very inadequate representation of
slavery; and it is so, necessarily, for this reason—that slavery, in some of its workings, is too dreadful for the purposes of art. A work which should represent it strictly as it is would be a work which
could not be read; and all works which ever mean to give pleasure must draw a veil somewhere,
or they cannot succeed."
6. Bert James Loewenberg and Ruth Bogin, eds., *Black Women in Nineteenth-Century American
Life* (University Park: Pennsylvania State University Press, 1976), 50.

of modesty and decorum. This behavior, along with the threat to "kill her dead" if she is beaten again, demonstrates how completely she rejects the idea that her mistress is her superior. Fannie's overt resistance and violent temper initiate a chain reaction of dire consequences affecting her entire family, especially her daughter Cornelia, from whom she is separated after this incident and another violent confrontation with white men hired to punish Fannie with a public flogging.

> Pa heard Mr. Jennings say that Fannie would have to be whipped by law. He told ma. Two mornings afterwards, two men came in at the big gate, one with a long lash in his hand. I was in the yard and I hoped they couldn't find ma. To my surprise, I saw her running around the house, straight in the direction of the men. She must have seen them coming. I should have known that she wouldn't hide. She knew what they were coming for, and she intended to meet them halfway. She swooped upon them like a hawk on chickens. I believe they were afraid of her or thought she was crazy. One man had a long beard which she grabbed with one hand, and the lash with the other. Her body was made strong with madness. She was a good match for them. Mr. Jennings came and pulled her away. I don't know what would have happened if he hadn't come at that moment, for one man had already pulled his gun out. Ma did not see the gun until Mr. Jennings came up. On catching sight of it, she said, "Use your gun, use it and blow my brains out if you will."[7]

Fannie's open defiance makes her too dangerous to remain on the small farm, so she is hired out and sent away. Her determined resistance also nearly results in her committing infanticide when her master threatens, in addition, to separate Fannie from her youngest child.

> "Fannie, leave the baby with Aunt Mary," said Mr. Jennings very quietly. At this, ma took the baby by its feet, a foot in each hand, and with the baby's head swinging downward, she vowed to smash its brains out before she'd leave it. Tears were streaming down her face. It was seldom that ma cried, and everyone knew that she meant every word. Ma took her baby with her.[8]

The mother's subjectivity is underscored by her daughter's oral account, dictated to a Fisk University sociologist around 1929. Through this dictation, Cornelia's memory preserves her mother's small triumphs as a slave, even though both had paid the price of a lengthy separation for Fannie's victories. Indeed, it is only in her mother's absence that Cornelia comes to understand:

> Yes, ma had been right. Slavery was chuck full of cruelty and abuse. I was the oldest child. My mother had three other children by the

7. Ibid., 51.
8. Ibid., 52.

time I was about six years old. It was at this age that I remember the almost daily talks of my mother on the cruelty of slavery. I would say nothing to her, but I was thinking all the time that slavery did not seem so cruel. Master and Mistress Jennings were not mean to my mother. It was she who was mean to them.[9]

Their forced separation changes Cornelia's opinions about slavery and about her mother. It also transforms her own personality, as she emulates her mother and becomes a fighter. Only in Fannie's absence does she decide to "follow [her] mother's example," and only then does it occur to her that the madwoman who had threatened to murder her baby, and had challenged white men to "blow my brains out if you will," was "the smartest black woman" in their community. Stressing her mother's bold intention "to meet [her punishers] halfway," Cornelia is alert to the fugitive "thought [that] seemed to race across [her] mother's mind," as Jacobs's narrative endorses the runaway tongue of slaves her master intended to silence. While the slave narratives employ the trope of writing on the body, with the narrator transformed from a body written upon to a body that writes, Cornelia's illiterate mother Fannie relies upon the spoken word to figuratively brand her child in order to give her some defense against the physical and sexual abuse of slaveholders. "The one doctrine of my mother's teaching which was branded upon my senses was that I should never let anyone abuse me. 'I'll kill you, gal, if you don't stand up for yourself,' she would say. 'Fight, and if you can't fight, kick; if you can't kick, then bite.'"[1]

The older woman's language is situated in the violence of slavery, from which she hopes to protect her daughter by instilling in her the spirit to fight back. Cornelia's retrospection also resorts to the violent imagery of branding. Fannie does not threaten to "kill" her daughter in order to teach her docility, but rather to burn her words into her daughter's memory and impress on her the importance of her message. The harsh words of the mother simultaneously teach the daughter what she can expect as a slave and how to resist it. A continuous tradition of resistance also contextualizes the trope of women's bodies and voices as oppositional or supplemental historical texts, motivating the women of Gayl Jones's novel *Corregidora* (1975) to see their bodies as the means to preserve an oral record of atrocities endured in slavery.[2] Within the folk milieu, the African American mother's persistent practice of a labor-intensive oral transmission and her distrust of the labor-saving technologies of writing and print culture are the result of her systematic exclusion from the discourses of educated people, whom she often has reason to count among her oppressors. The reliance on resistant orality results from the place-

9. Ibid., 50.
1. Ibid., 49.
2. Gayl Jones, *Corregidora* (Boston: Beacon Press, 1975).

ment of slaves, blacks, women, and the poor at the coercive interface of literacy and orality, with the institutionalization of illiteracy as a mode of "silencing" populations rendered "voiceless" so long as their words are not written, published, or disseminated within a master discourse. It is this effect of discursive silencing that the ex-slave narratives and other abolitionist writings attempted to overcome, producing black speaking subjects within a counterhegemonic discursive practice. The textualization of African American subjectivity makes black voices discursively audible and black speakers discursively visible.

While Harriet Jacobs's literacy was a tremendous source of empowerment, it also exposed her to an even more concentrated dose of the ideology of domesticity than the training she received while living and working in the homes of white women and observing their behavior. Quoting Frances Smith Foster's observation that, in the minds of white women, the black woman's "ability to survive degradation was her downfall . . . since her submission to repeated violations was not in line with the values of sentimental heroines who died rather than be abused," Hazel Carby stresses the role of nineteenth-century literature as a major transmitter of an ideology of womanhood that polarized black womanhood "against white womanhood in the metaphoric system of female sexuality, particularly through the association of black women with overt sexuality and taboo sexual practices."[3]

However, Jacobs is resourceful, almost visionary, in her use of writing to place in dialogue literary and extraliterary resources. From her "loophole of retreat" in the slaveholding South as well as her attic servant's room in the North, she manipulates the ideology of domesticity through successive recombinations of tropes on the home as woman's shelter and prison. In the text, her various confining positions within the sub- and superinteriors of the white household become loopholes in the patriarchal institutions of property, slavery, and marriage, where she gains insight into domestic ideology, allowing her to question and revise the figure of the woman whose interiority is derived from her confinement in domestic space. Thus she is able to link the bondage of slavery with the bonds of marriage and childbearing. Her creative appropriation of literature, which allowed her the latitude to identify herself with Robinson Crusoe the adventurer at the same time that she identified in her bondage with the slave owner Crusoe's native sidekick Friday, suggests that the racial and social ambiguities informing her life developed in her a self-affirming intelligence, a life-affirming empathy, along with a notable capacity for the imaginative transformation and reconstruction of metaphorical and ideological material.[4] Jacobs extends the oral family

---

3. Hazel Carby, *Reconstructing Womanhood* (New York: Oxford University Press, 1987), 32. Frances Smith Foster, *Witnessing Slavery: The Development of Ante-bellum Slave Narratives* (Westport, Conn.: Greenwood Press, 1979), 131.
4. Jacobs, *Incidents*, 115 [92].

history she knows through the matrilineal heritage of her maternal grandmother and great-grandmother, in contrast to Frederick Douglass, who
constructs himself as the first member of his slave family to acquire a
voice. His darker-skinned family members remain symbolically in the
dark while he, the master's unacknowledged son, becomes enlightened.[5]
Within his text they are narratively silent, while his literacy bestows upon
him the authority of a narrator.

Harriet Jacobs's narrative, which may be seen as ascribing gender to
the generic (male) narrative genre, demonstrates that it is possible to appropriate bourgeois ideology to affirm the humanity of slaves and illiter-
ates — without Douglass's rhetorical conflation of literacy, freedom, and
manhood, which reinforces rather than challenges the symbolic emas-
culation of the male slave and the silencing of the female slave. Because
she associates the slave's humanity with defiant or subversive speech, resistant behavior, and the ethics of reciprocal relationships, as well as with
writing and individual autonomy, Jacobs affirms the humanity of the col-
lectivity of slaves as well as the successful fugitive and literate narrator. Jacobs implicitly regards her own narrative voice as the continuation of
other voices, especially that of her grandmother, whose story she reiter-
ates in the process of telling her own story.

For Jacobs, literacy serves to record for a reading audience a continuity of experience already constructed and preserved within her family
through oral accounts. She credits without question the oral history of her
family that her grandmother supplies, while Douglass uses orally transmitted information cautiously, and is suspicious of any fact not verified
by a written document. While Jacobs reproduces and extends the story of
her family that she had heard all her life from her grandmother, in Douglass's 1845 text the narrator's acquisition of literacy represents a discontinuity, a definite break with the past, signaling the emergence of a new
consciousness. He later states in *My Bondage and My Freedom* that his
mother in fact was literate. Yet for the purposes of his first narrative, she
is represented as holding him in the dark during her occasional night visits before her death. As a slave she is symbolically with him "in the night"
of ignorance and illiteracy.[6] The narrative is the story of a slave son's resistance to the imposed destiny of a slave woman's offspring, his determination *not* to follow the condition of his mother, but to seek mastery
through the instrumental literacy of his father.

In figuring literacy as radical discontinuity, Douglass foregrounds his
own emerging subjectivity within the text against the literal and
metaphorical darkness and silence that envelop other slaves, including
members of his own family, who remain narratively silent in his depic-

5. Frederick Douglass, *Narrative of the Life of Frederick Douglass, an American Slave*, ed. Benjamin Quarles (1845; Cambridge, Mass.: Harvard University Press, Belknap Press, 1979).
6. Ibid., 25.

tion of them. Douglass is perhaps unique in the consistency of this figuration. The bond that he forges between freedom and literacy is managed rhetorically by a narrative silencing of the voices of other slaves; yet this insistent tropology has become, paradoxically, the source of the paradigmatic status of this text within the slave narrative genre. Henry Bibb and William Wells Brown, for instance, are much closer to Jacobs in their acquisition and appreciation of literacy without overvaluing it, and in their use of the narrative voice as an expressive construction of continuity in the face of cultural disruption.[7]

Jacobs's text may be usefully contrasted with Douglass's in her depiction of an instance of the master's punishing a slave. In both cases the slave's punishment may be traced back to a sexual transgression committed by the master. Douglass's Aunt Hester, who has apparently replaced his mother Harriet as the object of the master's lustful desires, is beaten when she defiantly visits her black lover on a neighboring plantation. The master indulges himself in an orgiastic flogging, with the young child Frederick an eyewitness to the "horrible exhibition" of Hester's naked, bleeding body. His harrowing description of the first flogging he ever witnessed employs a balanced rhetoric of repetitions and antitheses as a mimetic device. He flails away at the reader with his language, making the scene disturbingly vivid. The flogging is primarily a visual rather than an aural experience, with Hester's voice unable to affect the master. "No words, no tears, no prayers" move him. All are as ineffective as her "most heart-rendering shrieks." If anything, her voice seems to egg him on: her screams constitute one side of a ghastly, mostly nonverbal, dialogue that Douglass represents as an obscene call and response in which language is debased, and discourse is reduced to "her shrieks and his horrid oaths."[8]

Jacobs serves as "earwitness" to the beating of a man whose wife is among their master's concubines. Jacobs deals more explicitly with the slave woman's sexual subjugation than Douglass, who is always reluctant, in the 1845 *Narrative*, to rely upon information transmitted orally by slaves, which he generally treats as unsubstantiated gossip or "whispered" opinion, inferior to authenticating (written) documents, perhaps anticipating the skepticism of contemporary historians who are reluctant to state that black women were raped in slavery, and who not surprisingly find scarce documentation of sexual abuse in the journals of slaveholders. In addition, Douglass almost silences his Aunt Hester in the stress he lays on the inability of her voice to affect the master who beats her. Hester's speech is not recorded in his narrative. Jacobs concentrates on her own response to the master's violence, rather than on the implacable master, unmoved by the slave's voice and speech.

7. Gilbert Osofsky, *Puttin' on Ole Massa: The Slave Narratives of Henry Bibb, William Wells Brown, and Solomon Northrup* (New York: Harper and Row, 1976).
8. Douglass, *Narrative*, 28–30.

> When I had been in the family [of doctor Flint] a few weeks, one of
> the plantation slaves was brought to town, by order of his master. It
> was near night when he arrived, and Dr. Flint ordered him to be
> taken to the work house, and tied up to the joist, so that his feet
> would just escape the ground. In that situation he was to wait till the
> doctor had taken his tea. I shall never forget that night. Never be-
> fore, in my life, had I heard hundreds of blows fall, in succession, on
> a human being. His piteous groans, and his "O, pray don't, massa,"
> rang in my ears for months afterwards.[9]

Her textual strategy does not involve the mimetic rhetoric Douglass
employs, but a mimesis of quotation and a narrative constructed from collective testimony. Rather than mirror the master's silencing of the slave,
rendering the slave as a silent victim, she represents the slave as a speaker
in the text, a more dialogic practice of writing. Jacobs gives a voice to the
slave specifically to counter the master's attempt to silence the man and
his wife, whose fugitive tongues have "run too far" from his control.

> I went into the work house next morning, and saw the cowhide still
> wet with blood, and the boards all covered with gore. The poor man
> lived, and continued to quarrel with his wife. A few months after-
> wards Dr. Flint handed them both over to a slave-trader. The guilty
> man put their value into his pocket, and had the satisfaction of know-
> ing that they were out of sight and hearing. When the mother was
> delivered into the trader's hands, she said, "You *promised* to treat me
> well." To which he replied, "You have let your tongue run too far,
> damn you!" She had forgotten that it was a crime for a slave to tell
> who was the father of her child.[1]

Although Jacobs does reinforce the aural with visual proof, the result
of her own investigation, she sifts through "conjecture," relying overtly
upon the knowledge and speech of slaves to penetrate beyond the official
story of a slave whipped for "stealing corn." Through sight and sound she
assembles evidence and documents proof of a different crime, which the
guilty slave master tries to cover up by selling the victims "out of sight and
hearing." Even more consistently than Brown, she not only speaks for oppressed slaves, but gives them a voice in her text. Her narrative does not
mimic the silencing of those still in bondage, but endorses the runaway
tongue of the slaveholder's victim. "There were many conjectures as to
the cause of this terrible punishment. Some said master accused him of
stealing corn; others said the slave had quarrelled with his wife, in the
presence of the overseer, and had accused his master of being the father
of her child. They were both black, and the child was very fair."[2]

9. Jacobs, *Incidents*, 13 [15].
1. Ibid., 13 [15–16].
2. Ibid., 13 [15].

Jacobs is aware that she is sheltered not only by the community of slaves and free blacks who do what they can to help her, but also by the white community, which protects her indirectly through the voices of gossip and opinion, fueled by rumors among slaves and the "open-mouthed jealousy of Mrs. Flint." The interconnections between blacks and whites in the community, while often, as in the above instance, resulting in tragedy for the slaves, also potentially empower slaves to influence public opinion about their masters. What slaves say among themselves may be powerful when heard and repeated by influential whites. To protect his reputation in the white community, Flint avoids a public whipping of the domestic servants whose lives are so intimately entwined with his family life.

> [Mrs. Flint] would gladly have had me flogged for my supposed false oath; but . . . the doctor never allowed any one to whip me. The old sinner was politic. The application of the lash might have led to remarks that would have exposed him in the eyes of his children and grandchildren. How often did I rejoice that I lived in a town where all the inhabitants knew each other! If I had been on a remote plantation, or lost among the multitude of a crowded city, I should not be a living woman at this day.[3]

Within the stifling intimacy of the master's home, violence is more a shameful secret than a public spectacle. Both as master and as man he may hide his sins behind closed doors, while the slave woman whose lover has few opportunities to see her and thus must meet her in the street, lives without privacy, with her emotional life, and her sexual behavior and its consequences, all in plain sight. Jacobs contrasts his power to conceal both his brutality and his sexual affairs, against her own exposed vulnerability to his prying eyes and physical abuse. Under the guise of supervising her morality and protecting the value of his property, the master patrols both the public and private behavior of his slave. As a male he moves freely in the public sphere, and as a master and head of his household he controls everyone in sight within the interior of his home. Learning to evade the master's gaze allows her to conduct a secret affair which results in her pregnancy by another white man. The slave girl's attempt to empower herself through an affair with her master's social equal backfires when she discovers how much she values her own reputation. Literacy at first paradoxically increases her sexual vulnerability and desirability as her master begins to conduct a perverse courtship consisting of a one-way correspondence in which he writes lewd propositions to her, slipping the notes into her hands as she performs her chores within the suffocating intimacy of the domestic space. Eventually, as Jacobs grasps the instrumentality of her literacy, the production of an ostensibly private

3. Ibid., 35 [31].

correspondence, with her grandmother, intended to be read by her master, becomes a means for Jacobs to outwit her would-be seducer.

While Douglass stresses the definitively heroic and "manly" acts of physically fighting a master and escaping from slavery to become a fugitive headed north to freedom, both oral and written narratives by women concentrate instead on the oral expression of the fugitive thought and the resistant orality of a runaway tongue. Not everyone could physically fight a slaveholder, although the oral tradition offers many examples of slave women resisting masters, and more often mistresses, with physical self-defense. Nor could everyone physically escape from slavery, particularly given the realities of women's role as childbearers and child-care workers, which made escape more difficult for them.

Literacy, the field of bourgeois knowledge, and the technologies it makes possible, Douglass himself recognized, helped white people to define black people as commodities, while providing the means to disseminate a discourse justifying the institution of slavery. But Douglass's text constructs him as an individual acquiring mastery over knowledge as he interiorizes technologies of literacy, while Jacobs's literacy continues to be associated, even in freedom, with the confinement of women and strictures of bourgeois feminine modesty.[4] As a woman, she is caught in the narrative double bind of using her literacy to expose the consequences of her vulnerable sexuality, rather than to attain the mastery identified in Douglass's text with the achievement of manhood.

As the salutation of a letter to Amy Post suggests—"My Dear friend I steal this moment to scratch you a few lines"—Jacobs's correspondence with Post and her letters to the newspaper, printed under the heading "fugitive," are in one respect—like the narrative itself—pointedly similar to the letters written for a different purpose in her "loophole of retreat."[5] All her writing, even in the free North, falls under the heading of fugitive writing, accomplished in stolen time by a woman who legally remains a fugitive slave until her freedom is purchased by her Northern mistress. In her freedom, the time in which she writes is stolen from her sleep rather than from her master, since her writing occurs in her attic servant's room, after a full day of work for her employers.

Like Harriet Wilson's novel *Our Nig*, Jacobs's writing struggles to overcome the compartmentalization of the bourgeois home, with its parlor, kitchen, servant's quarters, and family living space, which tends to reify the existing relations of domination and exploitation between social classes and genders. As Valerie Smith has suggested, these concrete divisions within the patriarchal household provide the material basis for their

---

4. I have adapted Ong's concept of writing as a technology that restructures consciousness as literacy is "interiorized," along with Lowe's concept of "bourgeois perception," as the dominant mode of subjectivity prevalent in print culture. Walter J. Ong, *Orality and Literacy* (New York: Methuen, 1982). Donald Lowe, *The History of Bourgeois Perception* (Chicago: University of Chicago Press, 1982).

5. Jacobs, *Incidents*, 234.

respective critiques of "true womanhood" and its ideological limits. Linda's "loophole" (which Hortense Spillers calls her "scrawl space") and Frado's "L-chamber" figure the cramped, hidden spaces in which black women's self-expression moved toward literary production.[6] These writers, conscious of the inaccessibility of literacy to the majority of black women, deploy the trope of orality to represent in their texts a "social diversity of speech types" or "heteroglossia."[7] Thus nonstandard dialects may enter the text as something other than literary minstrelsy, even as the authors themselves are required to demonstrate mastery of standard English. Through their practice of dialogic writing, Jacobs and Wilson (following Stowe and the first black novelist, William Wells Brown) exploit as literary resources discursive conventions familiar to a diversity of speakers, readers, and writers. In Wilson's novel the compartmentalization of the house, which confines the colored servant "in her place" under the supervision of a white mistress herself confined to the domestic sphere, produces a compartmentalized language deployed by the white woman, who speaks like an angel in the parlor but like a "she-devil" in the kitchen, where she disciplines "Nig" with a rawhide kept there for the purpose. Wilson exploits both novelistic convention and the resources of oral invective and sassiness through her manipulation of narrative and dialogue. Wilson's acquisition of a literacy sophisticated enough to produce this novel figures critically as an ellipsis somewhere between author and protagonist, between "Nig" and "Frado," between "I" and "she," as autobiographical materials are placed in dialogue with the slave narrative and the sentimental novel and transformed through the textual operations of fiction. The novel's protagonist, Frado, counters the compartmentalized language of the "two-story white house" with a resistant sassiness, while the narrator appropriates the literate, public, and euphemistic language of the sentimental novel and condemns Mrs. Bellmont for the private, abusive speech she uses, as she-devil of the house, to discipline the colored servant confined with her to the domestic sphere. Because Frado's sass challenges the assumption that her body "belongs" in the kitchen rather than the parlor, or elsewhere, it operates very differently from the so-called sauciness of Stowe's Aunt Chloe in *Uncle Tom's Cabin:*

> "Yer mind dat ar great chicken pie I made when we guv de dinner to General Knox? I and Missis, we come pretty near quarrelling about dat ar crust. What does get into ladies sometimes, I don't

6. Valerie Smith, "Loopholes of Retreat: Architecture and Ideology in Harriet Jacobs's *Incidents in the Life of a Slave Girl*," in *Reading Black, Reading Feminist*, ed. Henry Louis Gates, Jr. (New York: Penguin Books/Meridian, 1990), 212–26. Hortense Spillers, "Mama's Baby, Papa's Maybe: An American Grammar Book," *Diacritics* 17 (1987): 65–81.

7. Mikhail Bakhtin, *The Dialogic Imagination,* trans. Caryl Emerson and Michael Holquist, ed. Michael Holquist (Austin: University of Texas Press, 1981), 262–63. See also Mae Gwendolyn Henderson, "Speaking in Tongues: Dialogics, Dialectics, and the Black Woman Writer's Literary Tradition," in *Changing Our Own Words*, ed. Cheryl Wall (New Brunswick, N.J.: Rutgers University Press, 1989).

know; but, sometimes, when a body has de heaviest kind o' 'sponsi-bility on 'em, as ye may say, and is all kinder *'seris'* and taken up, dey takes dat are time to be hangin' round and kinder interferin'! Now, Missis, she wanted me to do dis way, and she wanted me to do dat way; and, finally, I got kinder sarcy, and, says I, 'Now, Missis, do jist look at dem beautiful white hands o' yourn, with long fingers, and all a sparkling with rings, like my white lilies when de dew's on 'em; and look at my great black stumpin hands. Now, don't ye think dat de Lord must have meant *me* to make de pie-crust, and you to stay in de parlor? Dar! I was jist so sarcy, Mas'r George."

"And what did mother say?" said George.

"Say?—why, she kinder larfed in her eyes—dem great handsome eyes o' hern; and, says she, 'Well, Aunt Chloe, I think you are about in the right on 't,' says she; and she went off in de parlor. She oughter cracked me over de head for bein' so sarcy; but dar's whar 't is—I can't do nothin' with ladies in de kitchen!"[8]

Although it can justly be said that the author has depicted an act of "sig-nification," or verbal indirection, Stowe's representation of the black woman's sassiness rings false, since Chloe's speech only confirms that the black woman belongs in the kitchen, just as the mistress in the parlor occupies the proper place of a bourgeois white woman. This rendering of a black woman's speech is not an example of a textual representation of resistant orality, but rather an instance of jocular acquiescence, owing more to the conventions of minstrelsy (whites caricaturing blacks who are mocking/"marking" whites) than to African American women's tradi-tional deployment of sass as verbal self-defense. Although the cook indeed knows how to defend herself from the meddling of a well-intentioned mis-tress, Stowe's evocation of the sassy black woman settles for a comic rep-resentation that refuses to construct a complex subjectivity for the black woman who is "a cook . . . in the very bone and center of her soul."[9]

More serious investigations of sass as a form of signification, or verbal self-defense, may be found within African American oral and literate tra-ditions. These accounts frequently demonstrate the ways black women used speech strategically in potentially violent encounters with white women who sometimes felt anxious about their own authority within the patriarchal household. The possibility of a white woman's whipping a slave is raised in Miss Ophelia's disciplining of Topsy for stealing and lying, although Ophelia never actually whips the child. Stowe suggests that Topsy's "wickedness" is the result of her former master's brutality and must be countered by love. Topsy's habit of responding to any accusation with an automatic lie, and perhaps also the verbal inventiveness that made her a popular comic figure, are cured as she is tamed by a Christ-

8. Harriet Beecher Stowe, *Uncle Tom's Cabin* (1852; New York: Harper & Row/Harper Classics, 1965), 26–27.
9. Ibid., 22.

ian education. Similarly, Chloe's comic sassiness in no way challenges the mistress's decorous role as lady of the house.

Stowe's examples of spunk and sassiness do not explore the relationship of sass and invective to violence between servants and mistresses. Violence between women, a significant fact reported in slave testimony, is precluded because the mistress is a "true woman" and because Chloe knows and accepts her place within the patriarchal household, where the white man is master and the white woman is overseer. In this case Mrs. Shelby is too genteel to exercise her authority by cracking the black woman over the head as she "ought" to have done to punish her sauciness. Marie St. Clair, no exemplar of true womanhood, declines to discipline impertinent slaves out of laziness rather than scruples. When it comes to applying the rawhide, neither laziness, Christian uprightness, nor conformity to the ideals of true womanhood stands in the way of Mrs. Bellmont, in Wilson's novel *Our Nig*. She vows incessantly to "strike or scald, or skin" her servant Frado, because of her "impudence."

> James sought his mother; told her he "would not excuse or palliate Nig's impudence; but she should not be whipped or be punished at all. You have not treated her, mother, so as to gain her love; she is only exhibiting your remissness in this matter."
>
> She only smothered her resentment until a convenient opportunity offered. The first time she was left alone with Nig, she gave her a thorough beating, to bring up arrearages; and threatened, if she ever exposed her to James, she would "cut her tongue out."[1]

Mrs. Bellmont, enraged that her son judges her deficient in the virtues of true womanhood and venting her anger on the most convenient target,[2] seems far closer to the mistress of an actual slave woman, Silvia Dubois, whose dictated narrative appeared in 1883.

> [My mistress] was the very devil himself. Why she'd level me with anything she could get hold of—club, stick of wood, tongs, fire-shovel, knife, ax, hatchet; anything that was handiest; and then she was so damned quick about it, too. I tell you, if I intended [to] sass her, I made sure to be off aways. . . . [O]nce she knocked me till I was so stiff that she thought I was dead; once after that, because I was a little saucy, she leveled me with the fire-shovel and broke my pate. She thought I was dead then, but I wasn't.[3]

In the spiritual tradition of Sojourner Truth and Harriet Tubman, both illiterate women who spoke to God and expected God to hear them, and of Nat Turner, who taught himself to read at an early age, and whose famous slave insurrection was precipitated by Turner's reading of "signs in

1. Harriet E. Wilson, *Our Nig; or Sketches from the Life of a Free Black*, ed. Henry Louis Gates, Jr. (1859; New York: Vintage Books/Random House, 1983), 72.
2. Ibid., 47.
3. Loewenberg and Bogin, *Black Women*, 45.

the heavens," black women preachers demonstrated another way to move out of their assigned place within a racist-sexist hierarchy. Nineteenth-century women who pursued a spiritual vocation as itinerant preachers renounced sass, the verbal self-defense of illiterate slave women, in favor of a visionary literacy based on emotionally charged religious experience that confirms the truth of the Bible and empowers them as speakers and writers. As God's chosen spokespersons, Jarena Lee, Zilpha Elaw, and Julia Foote—through their acquisition of spiritually driven literacy and personal communication with God by means of visionary experience—purify their "impudent" tongues of the "sinful" speech in which, like Wilson's Frado, they had indulged as indentured servant girls, separated from their families and growing up under the discipline of white adults.

The fictional Frado affects a partial conversion to Christianity, remaining ambivalent about a religion professed by her "she-devil" mistress. At first she defiantly pursues spiritual training at least partly because her mistress resents any influence that might loosen her own control over her servant's behavior, or cause that servant, even temporarily, to forget "her place." Just as she wedges Frado's mouth shut with a block of wood, Mrs. Bellmont zealously blocks her access to literacy and to Bible-centered religious teaching, insisting that her own style of obedience training is all the education a black child needs. School and church are precisely the institutions that left lasting impressions on Elaw, Foote, and Lee. Apart from their exuberant embrace of Bible study as an intellectually challenging and pleasurable activity, they all seem to have been propelled into religious experience in part because it supplied channels of expression, and emotional contact with kindred spirits, denied them as young servant girls. Their parents were either dead, or unable to rear and educate them because of extreme poverty. These young girls were disciplined at the discretion of their employers, and relied on their own spunk and sass in conflicts with these powerful adult authorities. When, during her term as an indentured servant, Foote was beaten by her white mistress for a transgression she never committed, the child responded by taking the rawhide whip out of the house and cutting it into small pieces, so that it could never be used again.

To such young children, commonly indentured between ages six and twelve, it must have seemed that the authority of masters and mistresses not only superseded that of their own parents, but also, as they began to be influenced by Christianity, that such authority must be compounded by the power of an omniscient God, usually figured as white and male, who could read their innermost thoughts. Stricken by her conscience after telling her employer a lie, Jarena Lee relates, "God . . . told me I was a wretched sinner."[4] Such women had the opportunity to develop

---

4. William L. Andrews, *Sisters of the Spirit: Three Black Women's Autobiographies of the Nineteenth Century* (Bloomington: Indiana University Press, 1986), 27.

both their profound spirituality and a Bible-based literacy, which enabled them to go beyond exhorting sinners to convert and fellow worshipers to keep the faith. Ultimately some of them also claimed the authority of a preacher to "take a text," even when it meant opposing the Pauline restrictions on women's speech espoused by a male-dominated church hierarchy.[5]

While attending a "solemn love feast," Zilpha Elaw, whose mother had died in childbirth after twenty-two pregnancies, took the opportunity to participate in a free expression of emotion, having found a social space in which she could define herself as an expansive soul rather than a circumscribed body.[6] At an outdoor camp meeting that brought worshipers of different races and classes together for a common purpose, she found herself moved to speak, following a profound spiritual experience which freed her to begin her life with a new leaf; the social inscription of her black, female body was erased as she became a blank (white) page to receive God's Word.

> [M]y heart and soul were rendered completely spotless—as clean as a sheet of white paper, and I felt as if I had never sinned in all my life . . . when the prayer meeting afterwards commenced, the Lord opened my mouth in public prayer; and while I was thus engaged, it seemed as if I heard my God rustling in the tops of the mulberry-trees. Oh how precious was this day to my soul![7]

As they reach higher levels of literacy, the study of scripture liberates their "bridled" tongues for preaching and exhorting; through spiritual activity and chaste behavior they attempt to cleanse and purify the black woman's body of the significations acquired through her association in slavery with abusive sexuality. Julia Foote's spiritual autobiography implicitly constructs such a relation between the physical agony of the enslaved mother's body and her daughter's quest for spiritual autonomy and ecstasy. Glorious "heavenly visitations" in which Christ appears to gently strip her body of clothing and wash her in warm water to the accompaniment of "the sweetest music I had ever heard," are spiritual balm for the child who never forgot the story of how her mother had suffered as a slave. Foote's narrative begins significantly with her mother's sexual vulnerability and the painful consequences of her verbal self-defense:

---

5. Ibid., 1–22.
6. For Elaw the camp meeting functions similarly to the "Clearing" in Toni Morrison's novel *Beloved*. It is a site of spiritual empowerment for black people, and particularly black women. While Elaw exalts the soul above the despised earthly body, Morrison reinscribes the camp meeting as a scene in which a black woman preacher, "Baby Suggs, Holy," a self-called preacher whose voice rings through the Clearing, powerfully exhorts newly emancipated black men, women, and children to reclaim their broken, unloved, and abused bodies. Toni Morrison, *Beloved* (New York: Plume/ New American Library, 1987), 86–89.
7. Andrews, *Sisters of the Spirit*, 67.

My mother was born a slave, in the State of New York. She had one very cruel master and mistress. This man, whom she was obliged to call master, tied her up and whipped her because she refused to submit herself to him, and reported his conduct to her mistress. After the whipping, he himself washed her quivering back with strong salt water. At the expiration of a week she was sent to change her clothing, which stuck fast to her back. Her mistress seeing that she could not remove it, took hold of the rough tow-linen undergarment and pulled it off over her head with a jerk, which took the skin with it, leaving her back all raw and sore.[8]

Seeking a figure that could combine the secular representation of a blissful black body, emancipated from the negative social inscriptions of slavery, racism, and sexual exploitation, with the spiritual empowerment of the African American prophetic tradition, Toni Morrison invents a character in *Beloved*, Baby Suggs, an illiterate black woman preacher whose interest in holiness extends beyond the spirit to the body's wholeness. Her eloquent sermons urge black people to love every part of the bodies that white masters and mistresses abused, overworked, injured, and dehumanized. Implicitly problematizing Douglass's linking of literacy and freedom, *Beloved* and Sherley Anne Williams's novel *Dessa Rose* include a critique of literacy as an instrumentality of white male domination, represented in both texts by educators: a schoolteacher whose curriculum includes racist pseudoscience, and a social-climbing tutor who covets the material wealth of the slavocracy he serves.[9]

Yet each also offers an alternative to the binary opposition of predatory literacy and institutionalized illiteracy: the child who takes dictation from an illiterate mother in *Dessa Rose*, and the African American schoolteacher Lady Jones, who teaches the ex-slave's daughter to read, in *Beloved*. Morrison's slave community's attempt to process unassimilable experience occurs within what is still an oral culture. Sethe, Paul D, and Baby Suggs must orient themselves in a hostile environment without the perceptual apparatus or instrumentalities triumphantly claimed by Douglass. Their individual struggles take place outside the epistemic order of bourgeois society, through processes that Morrison extrapolates by way of her considered appropriation of the African American expressions "disremember" and "rememory," which she employs not as corruptions of the standard English words "remember," "forget," or "memory," but as cultural neologisms invented to refer to ways that African Americans retained specific perceptual habits of their African cultures of origin despite

8. Ibid., 166.
9. My reading is informed by that of Deborah E. McDowell, "Negotiating Between Tenses: Witnessing Slavery after Freedom—*Dessa Rose*," in *Slavery and the Literary Imagination*, ed. Deborah E. McDowell and Arnold Rampersad (Baltimore: The Johns Hopkins University Press, 1989), 144–63.

(or because of) their traumatic encounter with an often brutally applied, certainly exclusionary, instrumental literacy.[1]

The writer's text seeks to undo the amputation or erasure of the ancestor's voice and presence in the irrevocable break from primary African orality to institutionalized illiteracy, and restore dignity to black speakers of stigmatized dialects. The nonstandard speech of slaves expressed different cultural perceptions as much as it reflected and often reinforced the power relations of slavery, which were established and maintained in part by means of a predatory and exclusionary practice of literacy. This exclusive literacy produced a correspondent black illiteracy, or what W. E. B. Du Bois called "compulsory ignorance," as well as "the curiosity born of compulsory ignorance, to know and test the power of the cabalistic letters of the white man, the longing to know."[2] The conflation of folklore with ignorance and the persistent, erroneous identification of literacy as the possession of "the white man" are discursive tropes that black writers have always struggled against in their production of literacy texts that incorporate the subjugated knowledge of black folk.

Being neither white nor men, black women's possession of literacy and mastery of literate discourses has been especially problematic. African American women writers have often used their texts to "talk back" to texts by white men, white women, and black men in which representations of black women are absent or subordinated to other aims. With her decision to portray the silenced, but not speechless, black ancestor in *Beloved* as an illiterate, pregnant slave woman, Morrison insists on a "herstory" that must be intuited through empathy, as well as a history that can be read, remembered, recorded, and reconstructed by the literate descendants of an illiterate ancestress. Within the oral tradition black women have been anything but silent, unless literally beaten, muzzled, starved, or otherwise suppressed to the point of speechlessness. As for black women writers, if anything, their discursive silencing has been itself a by-product of literacy and of their inability to control the sites and conditions of their own textual production, or ensure it an appropriate reception. The literal bit, muzzle, and whip used to silence the slave woman gave way to the repressive social structures, discursive silencing, and literary oblivion that continued to mute her emancipated descendants, prolonging the discursive effect of black women's silencing even when they not only used their voices to speak, but had also thoroughly interiorized the technology of writing.

Scholars and critics today are unearthing and reevaluating the works of a number of African American women writers: texts that have finally become marketable commodities, having lain dormant for a century, disqualified from serious study by presuppositions about the tradition of

1. Morrison, *Beloved,* passim.
2. William E. B. Du Bois, *The Souls of Black Folk,* in *Three Negro Classics,* ed. John Hope Franklin (1903; New York: Discus/Avon Books, 1965), 217.

African American writing derived from the study of male-authored texts that dominated the black canon until the 1980s. Suspicious scholars excluded both Wilson and Jacobs from the African American canon because of their self-conscious appropriation of nineteenth-century fictional conventions, which were familiar especially to women readers. Similarly Morrison's novel, which mines the resources of the slave narrative tradition while placing an African American woman at its center, has been scorned by at least one African American critic as "sentimental" and "melodramatic," the unfortunate result of the writer's loss of control over her materials owing to a "failure of feeling" he associates with sentimentality.[3] Morrison's literate ghost story has as much, or more, in common with the Gothic as the sentimental tradition. Unquestionably her work self-consciously excavates popular fictional genres associated with traditions of women's writing and oral narrative, as well as the slave narrative. Her deployment of historically gendered generic codes might be compared to Ishmael Reed's use of vaudeville patter or Charles Johnson's use of the tall tale.

While Morrison privileges the point of view of the illiterate protagonist, it is through the figurative possibilities of a written form, the novel, that Morrison imaginatively constructs and validates the perceptual field of the illiterate, offering image after image of a spatiotemporality that is not static, but allows a simultaneity of the present and past, a communication between the dead and the living based on interiorizations of the spoken word: the mother telling stories to a ghost that she has never told her living daughter. Sethe's oral transmission of a legacy of struggle and resistance empowers her daughter Denver to overcome a history of silencing and seek instruction from a literate black woman in their community. In the process Sethe also discovers within half-forgotten memory, through the "rememory" of oral narrative, stories from her own childhood of the mother who had killed every child before Sethe, allowing her alone to live, the child not born of rape.

Writing is a literal inscription on the body of Sethe's African mother, the brand on her breast signifying her violent possession through rape and

3. While feminist scholarship has in some instances made possible complex critical readings of sentimental literature as a genre exploited by socially conscious women writers, sentimentality — and for that matter feminism itself — continue to be regarded by both male and female critics as suspect contaminants by which feminized modes of thinking and writing threaten masculine/universalist norms that have long been implicit in standards of literary criticism and value. In a review of *Beloved*, Stanley Crouch seems to conflate sentimentality and melodrama with feminism in order to censure Toni Morrison. He complains that this novel "is designed to placate sentimental feminist ideology, and to make sure that the vision of black women as the most scorned and rebuked of the victims doesn't weaken. . . . *Beloved* reads largely like a melodrama lashed to the structural conceits of the miniseries. . . . Morrison almost always loses control. She can't resist the temptation of the trite or the sentimental. . . . [T]o render slavery with aesthetic control demands not only talent but the courage to face the ambiguities of the human soul, which transcend race. Had Toni Morrison that kind of courage, had she the passion necessary to liberate her work from the failure of feeling that is sentimentality, there is much that she could achieve." Stanley Crouch, "Aunt Medea," *Notes of a Hanging Judge* (New York: Oxford University Press, 1990), 202–9.

enslavement. For Sethe, writing is a commodity acquired through prostitution—the word gained in exchange for a mother's body.[4] The concreteness of this inscription (the word "Beloved"—her name is *not* recorded—engraved on the tombstone of the preverbal baby girl) sets the vengeful spirit loose in the haunted house of memory. The ghost is not just embodied but hyperembodied, as it seduces Sethe's lover and becomes pregnant. Beloved emulates the phallic mother's power, as the written word gives a perverse body to the repressed spirit of an oral tradition in which the pain of the child's death and the mother's terror might otherwise be disremembered. Morrison's representation of an illiterate mother, rather than a literate father, implicity comments on the gaps African American women have discerned, and tried in their own work to bridge, between the male-oriented tradition of the slave narrative genre and the oral folk tradition, which have both been strong influences on the production of African American literature.[5]

The circular, monumental time of primary orality disrupted by slavery and compulsory illiteracy—represented by the ghost in *Beloved*—may be seen on the one hand as covering over all the ruptures and discontinuities that linear historical time, itself a product of writing, is equipped to register. On the other hand, if claims on history implicate the literate slave in the obsessional mastery of linear time, it is through a return to "women's time," which is also "primitive time," that Morrison addresses the power of the pre-Oedipal mother, the power to give or deny life to her child—just as Sherley Anne Williams suggests the power, as mother and as killer, of a woman whose subjectivity is formed outside or at the margins of bourgeois ideological constructions of true womanhood.[6] While slave mothers (as well as their offspring) affirm and stress their life-giving power, Morrison chooses to explore the other aspect of women's power over life by constructing a supernatural character that has access to language, yet mimics the child whose "relation to the pre-oedipal, phallic mother is pre-linguistic, unspoken, and unrepresentable," so as to give an embodied voice to the voiceless maternal semiotic identified here, as in Julia Kristeva's theoretical writing, with both mother and child.[7] For Kristeva, the maternal semiotic comprises the unorganized, presymbolic bodily impulses of the infant's physical interaction with the mother's body.

---

4. African American women novelists Morrison, Sherley Anne Williams, Gloria Naylor, Gayl Jones, Alice Walker, and Octavia Butler have all contemplated the conundrum that the African American literary tradition is, in a sense, founded on the bodies of raped and mutilated ancestors, whose bodies are literally inscribed by the scars of slavery and sexual abuse, or whose illiteracy motivates their offspring to acquire an empowering literacy.
5. The folk tradition itself is sometimes identified primarily with male speech, as in Hurston's novel *Their Eyes Were Watching God*, as opposed to her study of African American folklore, *Mules and Men*, in which women and men participate as equals in the "lying sessions."
6. Julia Kristeva, "Women's Time," in *Feminist Theory*, ed. Nannerl O. Keohane, Michelle Z. Rosaldo, and Barbara C. Gelpi (Chicago: University of Chicago Press, 1982), 33–35. See also Julia Kristeva, *Desire in Language: A Semiotic Approach to Literature and Art* (New York: Columbia University Press, 1980).
7. Elizabeth Grosz, *Sexual Subversions* (London: Allen and Unwin, 1989), 87.

In Jacobs's account, the exchange of breast milk in nursing binds both the white and black child in a reciprocal relationship which is betrayed by the white child's entry into the patriarchal symbolic of law, property, and inheritance. For Morrison, the theft by the dominant class of that which would nourish a subjugated class, ritualized in the custom of wet-nursing, graphically demonstrates the interactive workings of the slave woman's exploitation. Sethe is exploited both as breeder and as worker, her body's labor producing both milk and ink.[8] The black woman's milk is stolen and, through institutionalized illiteracy, so is her ability to control her discursive representation within a print culture. Her self-definition as mother and human, her ability to operate as a speaking subject, is contradicted by a body of writings constituting a pseudoscientific discourse that helped to rationalize her enslavement. In *Beloved* the maternal semiotic not only is the physical interactions of the individual mother-child dyad, but also becomes, figuratively, an analogue of the relationship, within African American tradition, of the problematic historical opposition of orality and literacy at the point of linguistic imperialism. African languages were lost to the descendants of captive Africans as access to interiorized epistemological constructions, leaving little more than paralinguistic traces in the rhythms of speech, song, and dance. English, therefore, is associated with the symbolic order of law and the enunciation of the ego in language. The *collective racial* maternal semiotic of the novel includes a number of associatively related figures: the preliterate African who dies on the slave ship, the non-English-speaking mother with a brand on her breast, as well as the prelinguistic infant. All these "ghosts" are repressed in the formation of the psyche through insertion into a masculine (white male) symbolic. This process is here made analogous to the slave's internalization of English, literacy, and the symbolic order of Western discursive formations. Yet in any language or semiotic system, something always remains unexpressed—or, in Morrison's own words, "blocked, forgotten, hidden"—whether one operates within primary orality, institutionalized illiteracy, or interiorized literacy.

> When Sethe locked the door, the women inside were free at last to be what they liked, see whatever they saw and say whatever was on their minds.
> Almost. Mixed in with the voices surrounding the house, recognizable but undecipherable to Stamp Paid, were the thoughts of the women in 124, unspeakable thoughts, unspoken.[9]

In Morrison's novel the unnamed character variously referred to as a witch, a sexually abused young woman, a "crawling already?" baby girl,

---

8. Anne E. Goldman, "'I Made the Ink': (Literary) Production and Reproduction in *Dessa Rose and Beloved*," *Feminist Studies* 16 (Summer 1990): 313–30.
9. Morrison, *Beloved*, 199.

a dead and buried child, a vengeful ghost, and Sethe's "Beloved," comes to speak not only on the matter and manner of her individual death, but also as ghost/survivor of the harrowing Middle Passage, perverse racial birth canal and mass slaughterhouse. A supernatural and multiplex character—indeed, she operates within the text as a sibyl or medium, emblematic of the fragmentation of the unitary self effected in the multiple personality by extreme abuse, or the ultimate shattering of the ego by death itself—Beloved speaks for "Sixty Million and more" silenced black souls estimated to have died in captivity, including all who lost their lives while trying to escape. The child ghost, whose voice blends and merges with the voices of her living mother and sister, is loosed on the household by the act of inscription and called into embodiment by a challenging male voice. She, Beloved, is made to represent the "disremembered" (repressed, unmentionable, nonexistent) offspring who are voiceless because they either died in infancy, or were never born because African American women who were potential childbearers died while physically resisting slavery, or practiced contraception, abortion, or infanticide to avoid the designated role of breeder. Although the majority of slave women chose to give life, even if it meant that their children would be slaves, Morrison's novel, by stressing the alternative, underscores that motherhood was an active choice, as does Jacobs's narrative.

The slave woman's subjectivity is based upon her self-construction as she who communicates, beyond words, with the dead and the unborn, through her body and through her spiritual commitment to the continuity of generations and the transmission of cultural values. Neither the baby talk of nursing mother to babbling infant, nor the call to and response from a ghost, qualifies as proper discourse within the masculine symbolic order. One is infantile nonsense, a kind of naturalized glossolalia, and the other is evidence of the woman's "hysteria" or the slave's "superstition." The death of the author and the mother's labor in childbirth are conflated in the pregnant child ghost, whose materialization authorizes the collaborative narratives of *Beloved*, in which Morrison puts "his story next to hers."[1] In a writerly yet popular mainstream novel, Morrison merges preoccupations of a Europhallogocentric literary production with the uterocentric tendencies of African American women writers. The exorcism of the malicious ghost set loose by writing is performed by a chorus of black women producing a sound before or beyond words, an indescribable sound to "break the back of words": perhaps moaning, keening, ululating, or panting as in childbirth, when the woman who has chosen to complete a pregnancy is most aware of her human effort to organize and control the rhythmic involuntary contractions of a body in labor.[2] Kristeva's *chora*, a space "anterior to naming,"

---

1. Ibid., 273.
2. It was Molly Hite, in a 1989 discussion sponsored by the Cornell University Society for the Humanities, who first suggested to me that the sounds made by the chorus of women, all mothers,

associated with the maternal semiotic, may bear a relationship to Morrison's chorus of mothers unnaming the unspeakable desire that precedes language.[3] Like the unborn child, which has not yet entered culture, the *chora* is a figure of the prelinguistic, yet should not be equated in any simple way with the woman or mother. While conception, pregnancy, childbirth, and lactation continue to be represented as natural events, Maria Mies stresses their importance as cultural activities contributing to a materialist concept of female humanity which seems particularly appropriate to the slave woman, labeled "breeder," who yet managed to transmit coherent cultural values to her offspring.

> [Women] did not simply breed children like cows, but they appropriated their own generative and productive forces, they analysed and reflected upon their own and former experiences and passed them on to their daughters. This means that they were not helpless victims of their bodies' generative forces, but learned to influence them, including the number of children they wanted to have.[4]

Black women's appropriation of materials from African American oral tradition, as well as their interiorization of writing technologies productive of bourgeois subjectivity, are equally products of analysis and reflection upon their own and antecedent experiences passed from mothers to daughters. They were not helpless victims of predatory literacy any more than they were passive or silent victims of their bodies' generative forces or of the abuse of masters and mistresses. On the contrary, they have frequently insisted upon a dialogic writing practice that operates against the tendency of the literate to view the illiterate and the oppressed as "voiceless." In telling the story of her own life to her dead daughter, Sethe is able to communicate with her living daughter and at the same time to recover a forgotten connection to her own mother, a captive African who spoke little or no English. The unspoken (unconstructed) history that has silenced Denver, the living daughter, comes to light (is constructed) when Sethe speaks to the ghost, just as Denver loses her paralyzing fear of leaving the haunted house upon hearing the voice of her dead grandmother.

The stories Beloved solicits are Morrison's way of imagining an oral,

---

who participate in the exorcism/psychodrama/communal ritual at the conclusion of *Beloved*, might resemble the extralinguistic utterances of a woman in labor. This works well with Barthes's notion of "the grain of the voice," which he describes as "the materiality of the body speaking its mother tongue," the intimate associations among mother, body, tongue, voice, and speech constituting the discursive grain of Morrison's text. Roland Barthes, *Image-Music-Text*, trans. Stephen Health (New York: Hill and Wang, 1977), 182. In their conscious and collaborative manipulation of this collective noise, the women all participate in the unbirthing of Beloved. The ghost child's hysterical pregnancy is terminated as she is spirited back into the unconscious, destined to be forgotten, the memory of her existence repressed by the Christian women who briefly perform the rite of a coven of witches in dispatching her back to the spirit world.

3. Kristeva, *Desire in Language*, 133.
4. Maria Mies, Veronika Bennholdt-Thomsen, and Claudia von Werlhof, *Women, the Last Colony* (London: Zed Books, 1988), 74.

spiritual, intuitive analogue of the written, material, empirical history of slavery. In Morrison's text such stories have been pieced together hopefully, like Baby Suggs's color-hungry quilts. For the occasion of writing this novel, haunting tales inspired by words black women have spoken about their lives have been stitched together as provisional fragments, out of which Morrison constructs stories about a ghost that the text assembles and finally unravels, like Sethe's furtively constructed wedding dress. In such "mammy-made" garments our black foremothers wrapped their human dignity, unable to fit themselves and their histories into the ready-made ideologies of true womanhood. *Beloved* may not be "a story to pass on"—it is neither a folktale nor a text to be lightly dismissed—but Morrison's literate ghost story underlines, through its exploration of opposing, interactive forces of rupture and continuity, how difficult and necessary it is that black women construct and pass on personal and collective "her-stories." Like Wilson and Jacobs before her, Morrison insists that the oral traditions of slaves and the popular genres appropriated by women speak and write a mother tongue of resistance.

MICHELLE BURNHAM

Loopholes of Resistance: Harriet Jacobs' Slave Narrative and the Critique of Agency in Foucault[†]

Located in the exact center of Harriet Jacobs' 1861 slave narrative, *Incidents in the Life of a Slave Girl,* is a chapter entitled "The Loophole of Retreat." The chapter's title refers to the tiny crawlspace above her grandmother's shed, where Jacobs hides for seven years in an effort to escape her master's persecution and the "peculiar institution" of slavery which authorizes that persecution. This chapter's central location, whether the result of accident or design, would seem to suggest its structural significance within Jacobs' narrative. Yet its central location is by no means obvious, for "The Loophole of Retreat" goes just as easily unnoticed in the middle of forty-one unnumbered chapters as it becomes—after careful enumeration—potentially quite prominent, as the hinge which balances twenty chapters on either side. It is almost as though this chapter is hidden in plain sight, much like the body of Harriet Jacobs herself, who finally discovers the safest hiding place to be the most obvious one imaginable: in her own grandmother's house and in the center of her master Dr. Flint's domain.

† From the *Arizona Quarterly* 49.2 (summer 1993): 53–73. Reprinted by permission of the author and the Regents of The University of Arizona. Page references to this Norton Critical Edition are given in brackets following Burnham's original citations.

What Jacobs calls her "loophole of retreat" thus provides a strategic site for concealment even as it masks its own location. This spatial loophole becomes for Jacobs a means for escape from slavery, and her manipulation of textual loopholes in dominant discourse allows her narrative to escape, as well, from the constraints which her culture necessarily imposes on it. It is this tactical operation of the loophole which I intend to explore not only in Jacobs' narrative but, through her text, in the work of Foucault. This loophole operation opens up possibilities for locating and imagining resistance in any discursive structure, including ones which—as Foucault would sometimes have it—effectively exile autonomous agency by producing and then recuperating their own opposition. Critiques of Foucault, including those inspired by Lacanian and pragmatist theory, have all solved this dilemma only by ignoring its very basis: Foucault's important critique of the individual subject as s/he is produced by institutional structures. The figure of the loophole permits a reconfiguration of agency that, unlike the psychoanalytic rescue of agency, accommodates Foucault's critique of the subject and also integrates, rather than elides, the problematic and overlooked category of the structure.

I. Confession and Concealment

Lydia Maria Child introduces Harriet Jacobs' slave narrative with a gesture of unveiling that promises a subsequent revealing. In her editor's introduction, Child confronts the difficulty of offering to the public Jacobs' account of sexual oppression, by claiming that "this peculiar phase of Slavery has generally been kept *veiled*; but the public ought to be made acquainted with its monstrous features, and I willingly take the responsibility of presenting them *with the veil withdrawn*."[1] Child's theatrical, almost voyeuristic, gesture suggests that what will be revealed is not only the body of the desirable female slave, but the truth about that body, and about the Southern institution of slavery that has inscribed it.

A similar language of unveiling proliferates throughout Jacobs' own text, in her recurrent promises "to tell . . . the truth" (53) [46] and to "not try to screen [her]self" from "the painful task of confessing" (54) [46]. Jacobs' larger project is to lift the veil of deception that hangs between the North and the South, and it is therefore for her Northern listeners—even those whose "ears are too delicate to listen to" (4) [6] the details of her story—that Jacobs constructs the personal history which was denied her in the South. By confessing the history of her concealed body, she constructs that body as a text for "the women of the North" (1) [5] who, in this sense, function as confessors for Jacobs. Thus her narrative

---

1. Harriet A. Jacobs, *Incidents in the Life of a Slave Girl*, ed. Lydia Maria Child, ed. and intro. Jean Fagan Yellin (Cambridge: Harvard University Press, 1987) 4 [6]; emphasis added. All citations from Jacobs' narrative, unless otherwise noted, will refer to this edition and will appear within parentheses.

appropriately ends with a statement that suggests on the one hand free-dom, and on the other self-display: "when I rode home in the cars I was no longer afraid to *unveil* my face and look at people as they passed" (200; emphasis added) [155].

Clearly, however, the recurrence of such verbs as screening, veiling, and hiding signifies in her text a process of secrecy as much as it does one of exposure. For all its confessional rhetoric, this narrative seems finally far more concerned with that which is hidden, disguised, or kept secret.[2] Slaves are marked by the lack of a last name and quickly learn to keep the name of the father silent. Slavery is characterized as a con-dition whose "secrets . . . are concealed like those of the Inquisition" (35) [31], and which actively promotes such deception, for Jacobs claims that "so far as my ways have been crooked, I charge them all upon slavery" (165) [130]. Slavery enforces secrecy, makes speaking the truth an impossibility, and consigns one's personal history and geneal-ogy to silence. If the North acts as confessor in Harriet Jacobs' narra-tive, the South plays the role of concealer.

It is perhaps because slavery demands such concealment that slave-owners are so obsessed with what might be kept secret from them. Jacobs first hides from her master when he attempts to visit her during an illness. When he later "demanded to know where I was when he called," Jacobs answers by *confessing the truth*: "I told him I was at home. He flew into a passion, and said he knew better" (61) [52]. Because the truth is bound to appear to her inquirer so unlikely, Jacobs is able to both confess and keep her secret at the same time. Later, when Jacobs' "grandmother was out of the way he searched every room" (81) [67] in a futile effort to find the lover he was convinced that his slave was hiding from him. Such anx-iety and obsessive suspicion belong not only to Dr. Flint; the preacher Mr. Pike delivers a sermon which accuses the slaves of being "hidden away somewhere" "instead of being engaged in worshipping" (69) [58], and the chapter entitled "Fear of Insurrection," which describes the Southern slaveholders' response to the Nat Turner Rebellion, reveals a search for conspirators so frantic that one of the only safe places for a slave to be was already confined and concealed in jail.

Concealment is thus both what slavery demands and what it fears; con-cealment produces a reservoir of secrecy that perpetuates slavery but also unsettles it from within. The central act of concealment contained in this confessional text—Jacobs' seven-year confinement in the crawlspace of her grandmother's shed—reveals the potential of that hidden space to empower. A multitude of smaller but similar acts occur within this text: Jacobs' grandmother "screened herself in the crowd" (21) [21] in order

---

2. Joanne Braxton has pointed to Jacobs' many uses of disguise and concealment, including keep-ing her literacy, her pregnancy, her love for a black man, and the identity of her white lover se-cret, in "Harriet Jacobs' *Incidents in the Life of a Slave Girl*: The Re-Definition of the Slave Narrative Genre," *Massachusetts Review* 27.2 (1986): 379–87.

to see her captured son Benjamin without his knowledge, the slaveholder Mr. Litch "was so effectively screened by his great wealth that he was called to no account for his crimes" (46) [40], and Jacobs narrowly escaped detection in the shed only because she "slunk down behind a barrel, which entirely screened [her]" (152) [120]. Concealment—whether by crowds, wealth, or barrels—continually marks off in this text a protective space from which one might gaze or act, even if it is only to gaze, like Aunt Marthy, at acts of oppression, or to act, like Mr. Litch, in oppressive ways. It is therefore as necessary to discover such spaces as it is to expose them, generating a process that continually encloses even as it exposes.

This interplay between confession and concealment characterizes, of course, all autobiographies.[3] Harriet Jacobs' text, however, goes further than most in its continual demonstration that these two operations are mutually implicated in each other, that hiding is always accompanied by exposure, that enclosure always performs an escape. It is this complex relation between concealment and confession that ultimately enables a black feminist agency to operate in Harriet Jacobs' narrative. That double movement structures both her strategy of a quite literal resistance to the oppressions of slavery and patriarchy, as well as a literary strategy of narration that resists a dominant abolitionist discourse which, as Karen Sánchez-Eppler has shown, was largely appropriated by white feminists for political purposes considerably more self-serving than black emancipation.[4]

II. The Loophole and the Law

If "the loophole of retreat" chapter in Jacobs' *Incidents* marks and conceals its own importance, then the phrase which makes up its title amplifies that significance through a series of intertextual references. The phrase "the loophole of retreat" originates in William Cowper's 1784 poem *The Task*, where it designates a site from which "at a safe distance" the poet can protectively observe the extent of the world's woes:

> 'Tis pleasant through the loop-holes of retreat
> To peep at such a world . . .
>
> . . . .
>
> Thus sitting, and surveying thus at ease
> The globe and its concerns, I seem advanc'd
> To some secure and more than mortal height,
> That lib'rates and exempts me from them all.[5]

3. Elizabeth Fox-Genovese has suggested that this tension "between exhibitionism and secrecy, between self-display and self-concealment" (166) may be especially marked in the autobiographies of African-American women. "To Write My Self: The Autobiographies of Afro-American Women," *Feminist Issues in Literary Scholarship*, ed. Shari Benstock (Bloomington: Indiana University Press, 1987): 161–80.
4. Karen Sanchez-Eppler, "Bodily Bonds: The Intersecting Rhetorics of Feminism and Abolition," *Representations* 24 (1988): 28–59.
5. William Cowper, "The Task," *The Poetical Works of William Cowper*, 3rd ed., ed. H. S. Milford (London: Oxford University Press, 1926) 184.

Cowper's hidden loophole is a specifically domestic site—his poem begins by singing, with whatever mock heroism, the praises of a sofa—and the strategic location of that loophole grants him not only a liberatory escape from the world's injustices, but the power of surveillance over those practices.

Because quotations from Cowper's anti-slavery poems often served as epigraphs to chapters in slave narratives or abolitionist fiction, it is quite possible that Jacobs intends a direct reference to Cowper in her chapter title. Yet it is also possible—especially if Jacobs' editor, Lydia Maria Child, influenced or undertook the naming of chapters—that it refers to Child's own use of the phrase in the preface to her 1826 novel *Hobomok*. Child anonymously writes there in the persona of a reclusive man who "so seldom peep[s] out from the 'loop-holes of retreat' upon a gay and busy world" that he experiences great insecurity about offering his historical novel to the public. Once Child's gender is revealed, as it soon was, the phrase suggests here, too, an explicitly domestic space.[6] Whether Child or Jacobs generated the title, however, and whatever its external references, the word "loophole" alone involves a set of definitions that elucidate the larger textual strategy of Jacobs' narrative.

According to the *Oxford English Dictionary*, the first definition of loophole is "[a] narrow vertical opening, usually widening inwards, cut in a wall or other defence, to allow of the passage of missiles."[7] In addition to describing the crawlspace Harriet Jacobs eventually inhabits, this definition's battle imagery perfectly describes the saga of Jacobs' defense of her body against strategic attacks on it by Dr. Flint. She occupies a position that, like the loophole described here, is simultaneously defensive and offensive. Although Jacobs inhabits the descriptively "female" space of the loophole, she deploys from that space the kind of "male" power that one would ordinarily associate with "the passage of missiles." For Jacobs, however, those weapons are not missiles, but the letters (missals?)[8] addressed

---

6. Lydia Maria Child, *Hobomok and Other Writings on Indians*, ed. Carolyn L. Karcher (New Brunswick: Rutgers University Press, 1986) 4. The domestic space to which both Cowper and Child refer is one with which Harriet Jacobs' white middle-class female readership would have been able to identify.

7. "Loophole," *Oxford English Dictionary*, 1971 ed.

8. A "missal," in addition to a prayer book, is an obsolete variant of "missile" according to the *OED*. In a slight twist on the Derridean postal system in which letters always potentially fail to arrive at their destination, these letters successfully reach their addressee only to utterly misrepresent their origin and sender. Alan Bass' glossary suggests the fascinating possibility of an association between the postal system and the loophole in his analysis of the term *trier*, which

> . . . means "to sort," especially in the postal sense of sorting letters for distribution. . . . The false link between sorting and death is contained in the word *meutrière*, which means both murderess, and *the vertical slot in a fortress wall through which one can project weapons* [that is, a loophole]." (xxviii, emphasis added)

See Alan Bass, "Translator's Introduction: L Before K," *The Post Card: From Socrates to Freud and Beyond*, by Jacques Derrida, trans. Alan Bass (Chicago: University of Chicago Press, 1987) ix–xxx.

to Dr. Flint which she arranges to have postmarked from New York in order to convince him of her escape.

Those letters are one means by which the power relation between master and slave is structurally reversed once Jacobs conceals herself in her "loophole of retreat." Jean Fagan Yellin's claim that Jacobs "uses her garret cell as a war room from which to spy on her enemy and to wage psychological warfare against him" (xxviii) both contains the sense of loophole as fortification and suggests the extent to which power has been redistributed between them. Jacobs' powerlessness as a slave is exemplified by Flint's belief that she "was made for his use, made to obey his command in *every* thing" (18) [18] and "that she was his property; that [she] must be subject to his will in all things" (27) [26]. Whereas Jacobs had formerly been compelled to accept and read the notes with which Dr. Flint persecuted her, from the garret she controls his behavior by compelling him—by way of her letters—to travel North in search of her.

Not only has Jacobs been utterly subject to the command of her master, but she had been the constant object of his gaze as well:

> My master met me at every turn, reminding me that I belonged to him, and swearing by heaven and earth that he would compel me to submit to him. If I went out for a breath of fresh air, after a day of unwearied toil, his footsteps dogged me. If I knelt by my mother's grave, his dark shadow fell on me even there. (28) [27]

Jacobs escapes such surveillance only by going into a captivity that in many ways enacts the condition of slavery on a hyperbolic scale. The absence of freedom, the physical hardships, the separation from children and family, and the secrecy that all mark the slave's condition are repeated and exacerbated by Jacobs' confinement "in her dungeon." Yet that repetition is one with a signal difference, a difference that is concealed within the enormity of hyperbole, for "alone in my cell . . . no eye but God's could see me" (133) [105]. Not only is Jacobs free from Flint's gaze, but she has appropriated the power of surveillance for herself, since through her "peeping-hole" she is able "to watch the passers by," including Dr. Flint, without being seen, and to "hear many conversations not intended to meet my ears" (117) [93–94]. Jacobs becomes an eyewitness to slavery, a position of spectatorial objectivity which William L. Andrews has argued is usually filled by the abolitionist editors of slave narratives, while the ex-slave authors more commonly serve as the subjective and participatory "I-witnesses" to their own experience. These two positions clearly conflate in Jacobs' text, since she is in the very center of the system of slavery at the same time that she is to some degree distantiated from it.[9] Thus, like Cowper, Jacobs is able to survey "at a safe dis-

9. William L. Andrews, *To Tell A Free Story: The First Century of Afro-American Autobiography, 1760–1865* (Urbana: University of Illinois Press, 1986) 65. According to Andrews, abolitionist editors privileged objectivity in order to substantiate a narrative's truth value, which was mea-

tance" the "globe and its concerns," and although her space or confinement is far from being conventionally domestic, one of its most important characteristics is that it allows its occupant to survey her children with a protective and disciplinary maternal gaze.

By inhabiting this spatial loophole, Jacobs inadvertently enacts a second definition of the word as "an outlet or means of escape. Often applied to an ambiguity or omission in a statute, etc., which affords opportunity for evading its intention."[1] This sense of the word generally refers to the law, and particularly to written law, where a loophole is not produced so much as it is discovered, and even then it is typically discovered only by accident. Although such escape routes, once detected, are often closed down, by logic every law—no matter how carefully phrased—contains a loophole, since every law contains the permanent possibility of a loophole. A loophole uniquely allows one to transgress the law without actually breaking it, and thus to elude as well any potential punishment for that transgression. Harriet Jacobs' loophole condition is precisely such a simultaneous inscription and transgression of the law of slavery. She is able to reverse the master-slave power relation and to assume a kind of male power only because that reversal and deployment are concealed and contained within the semblance of black enslavement and female powerlessness. Jacobs' relation to that power shift is neither one of conscious premeditation nor one of unconscious passivity. Her unexpected leverage over her master follows solely from her fortuitous habitation in the loophole. Her resultant access to agency is a circumstance of which Jacobs, it seems, becomes only gradually aware, and which she begins only cautiously to exploit.

Both her physical and textual strategies succeed because they mime[2]—sometimes to the point of hyperbole—those systems or discourses which otherwise oppress her. The ironic force of that mimicry discovers loopholes in the structure that escape detection because they are concealed within what appear to remain dominant hierarchies and power relations. Inhabiting those loopholes can transform them into sites of resistance: it is because Harriet Jacobs inhabits a structural site where the practice of power seems so incredibly unlikely that she is able to get away with her resistance to and manipulation of her master.[3] Thus, by inhabiting a loop-

---

sured by the distance between the "I" and the "eye" (63). It is no doubt because that distance is minimized in *Incidents* that it has taken readers so long to accept its authenticity.

1. "Loophole," *Oxford English Dictionary*, 1971 ed.
2. I am using mime here in the sense which Luce Irigaray gives it as a feminist strategy in which "one must assume the feminine role deliberately. Which means already to convert a form of subordination into an affirmation, and thus to begin to thwart it. . . . To play with mimesis is thus, for a woman, to try to recover the place of her exploitation by discourse, without allowing herself to be simply reduced to it" (76). *This Sex Which Is Not One*, trans. Catherine Porter (Ithaca: Cornell University Press, 1985).
3. This arrangement is roughly analogous to Nancy Armstrong's reading of domestic novels and the Victorian domestic sphere, where female power is able to operate precisely because it is hidden in the home, where its operation is so unlikely. However, the link between such a textual strategy of camouflage and subsequent social empowerment or escape is far more obvious in Ja-

hole in the first, more spatial, sense of the word as a defensive and enclosed space, Harriet Jacobs enacts the second, more textual, definition
of loophole as "a means of escape"; she has discovered and retreated into
a *loophole* in the patriarchal institution of slavery. Although Jacobs' loophole of retreat is the most confining space imaginable, it is finally a space
of escape.

III. Subject and Structure

The operations of concealment and confession that play so critical
a role in Harriet Jacobs' narrative of slavery and escape also form the
subjects of much of Michel Foucault's work. Foucault's analyses in
texts like *Discipline and Punish*, his study of the birth of the prison system and its normalizing practices of confinement and surveillance, and
the first volume of *The History of Sexuality*, which argues that the confession is a truth-producing practice which generates discourse about
sexuality rather than—as psychoanalysis would have it—repressing it,
reveal that confession and concealment combine to form a power relation that produces and exposes. The pastoral or criminal confession
makes hidden thoughts known, while institutional concealment opens
the body and its behavior up to the disciplinary gaze. While Foucault's
confessional economy acknowledges a necessary relation between hiding and revealing, wherein "the obligation to conceal [is] but another
aspect of the duty to admit,"[4] that economy has been repeatedly criticized for too perfectly reproducing (confessing) all that it consumes
(conceals). By the same token, the model of Bentham's panopticon
which Foucault uses to define a new disciplinary architecture, in
which the subject internalizes the power relation which subjugates her,
has been accused of positing a totalizing economy of complete recuperation. New historicist criticism, which has been particularly influenced by Foucault's work on the prison and on sexuality, has in turn
generated much critical debate over its use of such models which, the
argument goes, deny agency to subjects who are inescapably determined by their historical and cultural context, and who therefore
inevitably support and reproduce the dominant power structures they
might have set out to resist and subvert. It is not my aim to reproduce
that debate here, but rather—through Foucault's own critique of the
individualized subject—to shift its terms. Where might one locate the
source of that recuperative movement in Foucault's work? Does the
panoptic eye in fact see everything, or does it have a blind spot? If a
confession is a production of truth, does it produce secrets as well?

cobs' narrative than in any of the domestic novels Armstrong reads, where it is unclear how their
readers' "fantasies of political power" (29) extended beyond their status as fantasies. *Desire and
Domestic Fiction: A Political History of the Novel* (Oxford: Oxford University Press, 1987).
4. Michel Foucault, *The History of Sexuality, Volume I: An Introduction* (New York: Vintage Books,
1980) 61.

While her subject is Foucault's influence on film theory rather than in the new historicism, Joan Copjec's Lacanian critique of the panoptic model insists on the subject's capacity for keeping secrets and concealing thought, and thus locates that blind spot in the panoptic theory's disregard of what she calls "the permanent possibility of deception."[5] Faulting Foucault for denying repression and thus a split subject, Copjec argues that "the orthopsychic relation (unlike the panoptic one) assumes that it is just this objective survey [which the subject performs on itself] that allows thought to become (not wholly visible, but) *secret*; it allows thought to remain *hidden*, even under the most intense scrutiny."[6] Copjec's analysis reveals that because the contents of the unconscious can remain undetectable, the subject can practice deception and thus can always undermine the ideal functioning of the panoptic gaze. Therefore any confession, one assumes, remains incomplete and leaves a residue, forming an imperfect economy with an inevitable degree of waste that is never recuperated. Even as Copjec's solution significantly realizes and includes the possibility of that hidden residue, however, it does not make it at all clear whether or how that might generate a comparable hiding-place for the body, nor how it might enable escape or resistance. Bringing Lacan to the rescue of the Foucauldian panoptic trap springs that trap only to finally re-trap the possibility of agency within the unconscious where it, for all intents and purposes, suffers a kind of paralysis.

That paralysis resembles the very predicament that the psychoanalytic approach set out to solve, a predicament associated with the new historicism and its seemingly irresolvable opposition between independent agency and historical determinism. Anthony Appiah has called that new historicist problematic "structural determinism,"[7] and has further suggested that its grounding opposition is based on the mistaken belief that subject and structure are connected categories and that their terms belong to the same discourse. Appiah argues instead that subject and structure represent "two different discursive economies" whose distinction should be recognized and maintained, since "everything that a theory of structure claims to explain belongs to the language, the discourse, of the structure; to insist on autonomous agency within this discourse is, if I may say so, simply to change the subject."[8] Appiah's pragmatic solution therefore is the institution of a complete separation of discourses. As he himself acknowledges, however, such a separation would continue to dissolve in practice, since the impassable gulf he insists exists between subject/structure is continually crossed. Instead of completely discon-

---

5. Joan Copjec, "The Orthopsychic Subject: Film Theory and the Reception of Lacan," October 49 (1989): 65.
6. Copjec 63.
7. Anthony Appiah, "Tolerable Falsehoods: Agency and the Interests of Theory," in *The Consequences of Theory*, ed. Jonathan Arac and Barbara Johnson (Baltimore: Johns Hopkins University Press, 1990) 66.
8. Appiah 79, 84.

necting these two terms from each other, I propose to shift attention toward the space signified by that slash which already (dis)connects them. It is in that juncture where subject and structure meet, rather than in an independent discourse of the subject, that I wish to locate agency. The problem is not, as Appiah suggests, that the independent categories of subject and structure have been falsely wedded, but that the categories of subject and agency have been so.

Perhaps the most consistent, and consistently overlooked, aim of Foucault's own work is to critique and oppose processes that individualize the subject. Despite the fact that Foucault has claimed, for example, that "the political, ethical, social, philosophical problem of our days is not to try to liberate the individual from the state, and from the state's institutions, but to liberate us both from the state and from the type of individualization which is linked to the state,"[9] the notion of agency in general, and the one employed by Foucault's critics, remains constructed in terms of the (individual) subject. As a result, and as new historicist criticism reminds us, agency necessarily becomes a *form* of subjection even as it struggles *against* subjection. The ongoing critical debate over the problem of agency in Foucault and/or the new historicism therefore often spins in the kind of recuperative circle marked out by this last formulation, and it does so, I am suggesting, because it remains unable to think of agency other than in terms of an autonomous subject working against, rather than within, the structure. The circularity of the subject/structure debate is thus in a sense as much the point of Foucault's work as it is a problem with it. "To change the subject"—to change the meaning of Appiah's phrase—has always been one of the primary aims of Foucault, who has claimed that "we have to promote new forms of subjectivity through the refusal of th[e] kind of individuality which has been imposed on us for several centuries."[1] Why not refuse, then, the individualization of agency and its entrapment in the discourse of the subject, and posit instead an agency that operates within not only the discourse, but the very architecture of the structure? Only by shifting the conceptualization of agency away from the subject and toward the structure might one locate sites that, like loopholes, escape detection and thus enable resistance and agency. This is to argue that, like every law, every structure contains a loophole (since it always contains the possibility of a loophole), regardless of how carefully it is designed—like, for example, a panopticon or slavery—to eliminate the possibility of subversion or escape.[2] Those

9. Michel Foucault, "The Subject and Power," in Hubert L. Dreyfus and Paul Rabinow, *Michel Foucault: Beyond Structuralism and Hermeneutics*, 2nd ed. (Chicago: University of Chicago Press, 1983) 216.
1. Foucault, "The Subject and Power" 216.
2. In fact, and almost as though to prove the point, Bentham's original panopticon design contained its own inadvertent loophole. As Alan Liu has noted, "Bentham's totalitarian vision . . . had a loophole," for "Bentham discovered after drawing up his plans that a blank space had inadvertently been left in the central tower in the area of the chapel" (103). Liu's short and limited discussion of that space focuses on the vision of the tourists with whom Bentham proposed

seemingly monolithic methods of surveillance that ostensibly make escape from detection impossible may finally enable escape by the very fact that they make it seem so impossible.

Discussions among historians about agency within slavery and black culture reveal a problematic tension between oppression and resistance similar to the one associated with Foucault. Slavery has certainly been characterized as an institution with a disciplinary structure so total that resistance to it was ineffective if not impossible. Stanley Elkins, in his influential book on North American slavery, calls it a "closed system" which prevented rebellion because slaves had no access to standards of judgment or modes of behavior outside of the institution that contained them. Critics of Elkins' thesis resist this monolithic construction by insisting that this closed system in fact contained openings where subversion and sometimes escape could occur. These critiques focus for the most part on the existence of a distinct culture within the slave community which enabled resistance through the residual or emergent alternatives it offered to the dominant culture.[3] More recently Clarence E. Walker, who has labelled this approach "the slave community/culturalist paradigm," accuses it of "romanticizing" the notion of community and of overestimating the force of an autonomous culture. Walker urges "black history to rise above the romantic and celebratory" by acknowledging the tensions within any oppressed community and by recognizing the extent to which marginal groups internalize dominant culture.[4] Walker's critique does not specifically address the question of agency, but it is nevertheless an important intervention in a debate which has tended to move in cycles that alternate between foregrounding the psychological and physical damage produced by slavery on the one hand, and the liberating and revisionist potential of black communities within slavery on the other. Walker's project of deromanticization, like Foucault's of deindividualization, explicitly warns against too easily making claims for autonomous resistance and implicitly suggests the need to reformulate conventional constructions of agency.

The example of Jacobs' text opens the possibility of a model for agency that falls between the culturalist paradigm and its critique, a possibility suggested by the fact that it is able to support both positions. Walker, for example, is able to use *Incidents* to illustrate that a slave community often did not devalue dominant taboos like illegitimacy,

---

to fill the space, rather than on the implications that empty space might have for the inmates themselves. See Liu's *Wordsworth: The Sense of History* (Stanford: Stanford University Press, 1989).

3. Stanley M. Elkins, *Slavery: A Problem in American Institutional and Intellectual Life*, 3rd ed., rev. (Chicago: University of Chicago Press, 1976); Ann J. Lane, ed., *The Debate over Slavery: Stanley Elkins and His Critics* (Urbana: University of Illinois Press, 1971).

4. Clarence E. Walker, *Deromanticizing Black History: Critical Essays and Reappraisals* (Knoxville: University of Tennessee Press, 1991) xviii. Walker's larger agenda is to urge a shift away from class-oriented Marxist analyses of race relations in nineteenth-century America and toward a theoretical model that would not conflate race with or reduce it to economic categories.

since the pregnant Jacobs fears the censure of her grandmother as much as that of her readers.[5] At the same time, this narrative clearly serves as an ideal example for those historians intent on asserting the possibility of resistance within slavery. However, Harriet Jacobs' "loophole of retreat" does not so easily fit the culturalist model. Although she enjoys a limited degree of communal support, her hiding place is hardly a space of autonomous culture like the family or religion might be, and it is certainly not a space that can be readily romanticized. Aunt Marthy's garret does not offer a retreat from the oppressive conditions of slavery—as, one might argue, the communal life in Aunt Marthy's house does—so much as it enacts a repetition of them. Because this loophole so resembles that which it opposes, it evades the conceptual opposition between oppression and resistance, as well as the critical opposition between Elkins' "closed system" and the more optimistic emphasis on black community or culture. Harriet Jacobs escapes reigning discourses and structures only in the very process of affirming them. She disobeys social norms of proper motherhood, for example, precisely in order that she might eventually enact those norms.[6]

The example of agency which Harriet Jacobs' slave narrative provides reveals that when Foucault announces the arrival of "a panopticism in which the vigilance of intersecting gazes was soon to render useless both the eagle and the sun,"[7] he fails to consider that panopticism carries within it the inevitable blind spot associated with its predecessors; the loophole, both as hiding-place and as escape route, is that blind spot, and it is in that blind spot that secrets reside and through which bodies may escape. The paralytic circularity of the subject/structure debate can be avoided by relocating agency in the juncture between the structure and the subject, in sites that elude the gaze not because they are outside the structure (or distinct from its culture) but because they are so clearly and centrally a part of it. Harriet Jacobs inhabits such a fissure in the very architecture of the "'patriarchal institution'" (146)—a structure that she has already ironized by means of framing quotation marks—and that fissure eludes Dr. Flint's searching gaze because it is located directly in front of that gaze. The loophole is in this sense akin to the sites of feminist agency posited by Teresa de Lauretis as "the elsewhere of discourse here and now, the blind spots, or the space-off, of its representations. I think of it as spaces in the margins of hegemonic discourses, social spaces carved in

5. Walker xvii.
6. William L. Andrews has similarly argued that the spiritual autobiographies of black women justify their transgression of cultural conventions against women preachers only by invoking and obeying theological conventions such as sanctification. Andrews, ed., Sisters of the Spirit: Three Black Women's Autobiographies of the Nineteenth Century (Bloomington: Indiana University Press, 1986) 16.
7. Michel Foucault, Discipline and Punish: The Birth of the Prison (New York: Vintage Books, 1979) 217.

the interstices of institutions and in the chinks and cracks of the power/knowledge apparati":[8] patriarchy's space-off, Dr. Flint's blind spot, the loophole of retreat. The garret of the shed beside Harriet Jacobs' grandmother's house was the least likely place of escape because it was from the beginning the most likely place of concealment: "it was the last place they thought of. Yet there was no place, where slavery existed, that could have afforded me so good a place of concealment" (117) [94].

IV. Sentimentality and Slavery

In her struggle against slavery and patriarchy, one might claim that Harriet Jacobs practices a kind of camouflage, since she hides by miming the confinement and suffering that characterize those very conditions against which she battles.[9] Jacobs' physical strategy of escape and her narrative strategy of protest are finally quite alike in their inadvertent but fortuitous use of camouflage. While Jacobs' body is inscribed by the law of slavery, through the figure of the loophole she simultaneously transgresses, even as she embodies, that law. I would argue that Jacobs' use of the sentimental discourse prevalent in popular women's novels of nineteenth-century America[1] operates by a similarly double movement. Just as her hyperbolic miming of the condition of slavery produces a rupture that her body can inhabit, and from which a feminist agency can operate, her employment of sentimental discourse, associated especially with the fiction of white feminist-abolitionists, opens loopholes within that discourse that allow her to critique it.[2]

Jacobs clearly employs the strategies and structures of sentimental fiction throughout her narrative in an effort to inspire her Northern female readers to respond emotionally to her story and to translate that emotion into moral behavior. The similarities, for example, between her text and Samuel Richardson's *Pamela* suggest the extent to which Jacobs may

---

8. Teresa de Lauretis, *Technologies of Gender: Essays on Theory, Film, and Fiction* (Bloomington: Indiana University Press, 1987) 25.

9. Lacan makes precisely such a connection between mimicry and camouflage when he writes that "the effect of mimicry is camouflage in the strictly technical sense. It is not a question of harmonizing with the background, but against a mottled background, of becoming mottled—exactly like the technique of camouflage practiced in human warfare" (99). Jacques Lacan, *The Four Fundamental Concepts of Pychoanalysis*, ed. Jacques-Alain Miller, trans. Alan Sheridan (New York: Norton, 1971).

1. Harriet Beecher Stowe, Susan Warner, Maria Cummins, and Catherine Maria Sedgwick are among the best known, and were among the most popular, of these sentimental novelists. Their work makes up what Lauren Berlant has called an "American female culture industry" that had enormous economic success on the print market in nineteenth-century America, as well as a substantial cultural impact on its readership. See Lauren Berlant, "The Female Woman: Fanny Fern and the Form of Sentiment," *American Literary History* 3 (1991): 429–54.

2. Valerie Smith identifies in Jacobs' narrative "linguistic spaces—verbal equivalents analogous to the garret in which she hides" (xxxiii) that are similar in conception to my notion of a textual or discursive loophole. Smith's focus, however, is on Jacobs' *revision* of the male slave narrative and the sentimental novel, while I am emphasizing Jacobs' far more tactical *attack* on the latter. Valerie Smith, "Introduction," *Incidents in the Life of a Slave Girl*, by Harriet Jacobs (New York: Oxford University Press, 1988).

have consciously borrowed from that genre.[3] Conscious borrowing, however, was hardly necessary, since in mid-nineteenth-century America
both women's writing and abolitionist writing were in large part characterized by sentimentality. Such writing appealed to a reader's sympathy
by portraying scenes of often theatrical pathos, and by constructing plots
of familial separation and individual trial. This sympathetic readerly response, often marked by the physical response of tears, ideally translated
into political action, especially in the case of abolitionist fiction. Thus the
aim of such fiction is to convert passivity into activity, to transform the objective response of "being moved by" the text into the subjective action
of "moving."[4]

There are, of course, several places where Jacobs reveals significant disjunctions between standard sentimental plots and the facts of her own
life. Those moments include her decision to take a lover, the birth of her
two children out of wedlock, and the impossibility of her story ending in
marriage—differences that lead Jacobs to suggest that "the slave woman
ought not to be judged by the same standard as others" (56) [48]. William
L. Andrews has argued that interstitial or liminal narrators like Jacobs
were able to fashion new versions of self by virtue of their "betwixt and
between" positions.[5] Thus it is the disjunction between the cultural ideal
embodied in the cult of true womanhood and the impossibility that Jacobs could ever conform to such an ideal that leads her to suggest the
need for an alternate standard for the slave women.

Such revisions of the conventional sentimental narrative, however, signal less significant moments in Jacobs' text than those in which she stages
an outright condemnation of sentimentalism. By far the most bitingly
ironic depiction of sentiment is Mrs. Flint's response to the death of Aunt
Nancy. Jacobs writes that "Mrs. Flint had rendered her poor foster-sister
childless, apparently without compunction; and with cruel selfishness
had ruined her health by years of incessant, unrequited toil, and broken
rest. But now she became very sentimental." The worst effect of such displays like the grand funeral, at which "the mistress dropped a tear, and
returned to her carriage, probably thinking she had performed her duty
nobly," is that

---

3. Valerie Smith notes the similarity between Harriet Jacobs' story and Samuel Richardson's novel
   (xxxi–ii). It is especially striking that Flint, like Mr. B., seems as obsessed with obtaining his servant's consent as he is with achieving her seduction.
4. The definition of sentimentality with which I am working here is one which insists on a certain
   readerly response—that is, sympathy, pity, tears, and the potential transformation of such emotion into political action or social change—achieved through a stylized use of language and of
   a narrative structure based largely on deferred agnition. Therefore it is the affective similarity between such disparate works as *Pamela* and *Uncle Tom's Cabin*, rather than their historical and
   cultural differences, that I emphasize. Such a definition necessarily leaves out those "sentimental" novels whose affective sincerity is erased or undercut by a critical irony—the eighteenth-
   century English novels of Sterne or Goldsmith, for example. Whether the reader's emotional
   response does in fact translate into political action is another, highly debatable, question. The
   tears which respond to scenes of injustice are just as likely to blur those scenes.
5. Andrews, *To Tell a Free Story* 175, 203.

Northern travellers, passing through the place, might have described this tribute of respect to the humble dead as a beautiful feature in the "patriarchal institution"; a touching proof of the
attachment between slaveholders and their servants; and tender-
hearted Mrs. Flint would have confirmed this impression, with
handkerchief at her eyes. (146) [116]

Jacobs' intent, in exposing Mrs. Flint's performance, is therefore to unveil such sentimentality's deception of the North, to reveal that which
sentimentality conceals. She manipulates a similar unveiling, with similar irony, when she includes the highly sentimental letter written by Dr.
Flint to her in New York. Pretending to write as his own son, Flint tells
Jacobs that he "sympathize[s] with you in your unfortunate condition,"
promises to "receive you with open arms and tears of joy" (171) [134], and
describes the death of her aunt as someone who

taught us how to live—and, O, too high the price of knowledge, she
taught us how to die! Could you have seen us round her death bed,
with her mother, all mingling our tears in one common stream, you
would have thought the same heartfelt tie existed between a master
and his servant, as between a mother and her child. (172) [134]

Despite Jacobs' use of sentimental discourse throughout her narrative, in
these two instances Jacobs attacks sentimentality as deceptive, as a discursive technique that hides rather than confesses the truth. Such an offensive against sentimentality from within sentimentality resembles
Harriet Jacobs' strategy of escape from slavery by miming its condition.

The movement of sentimentality in this text is like the movement of
the loophole, which inscribes that which it simultaneously transgresses.
That double action constitutes, I suggest, a fundamental property of sentimental discourse, which employs the very tactics it attempts to argue
against, and whose politics therefore seem to be so easily recuperated.
The politics of sentimentality have always, it seems, been caught in a debate between those who see it as a legitimately liberating discourse that
gives women access to a revisionist economic and political power, and
those who see it as a rationalization of dominant orders that deny women
power.[6] Even those sentimental texts which, like *Uncle Tom's Cabin*,

6. Though the use of sentimentality is by no means limited to female writers and feminocentric
plots, discussions of the politics of sentimentality are generally, and curiously, limited to just such
texts. Karen Sanchez-Eppler, in her essay "Bodily Bonds," convincingly demonstrates that fem-
inist-abolitionist discourse in its sentimental mode appropriates and bleaches the body of the
black slave in its representation of slavery as sexual oppression, thus constructing images and
plots with which white feminist writers and readers could identify. Ann Douglas insists that sentimental fiction supports the developing capitalist system in *The Feminization of American Culture* (New York: Alfred A. Knopf, 1977), while Jane Tompkins and Gillian Brown claim,
respectively, that sentimental fiction stages a critique of traditional economic and domestic orders. See Tompkins' *Sensational Designs: The Cultural Work of American Fiction, 1780–1860*
(New York: Oxford University Press, 1985), and Brown's *Domestic Individualism: Imagining Self
in Nineteenth-Century America* (Berkeley: University of California Press, 1990).

most overtly criticize existing relations are subject to readings that emphasize instead their reactionary effects. As a result of this fundamental political ambiguity, conventional and radical claims are frequently made for the same narrative. The miming strategy that underlies Harriet Jacobs' conflict with a master who oppresses her and with a sentimental discourse that marginalizes her reveals in its double movement the source of that ambiguity. Sentimental fiction is politically subversive, it would seem, only to the extent that it appears to be politically conservative. Such a strategy necessarily generates both reactionary and radical reading effects. It is the action of such a contradiction, however, that uncovers loopholes, loopholes which—as we have seen—can become autonomous feminist, and black feminist, sites of agency. Confession conceals as much as it reveals; it constructs veils in the very gesture of unveiling.

That play between concealing and revealing secrets structures the very functioning of sentimental discourse, which typically claims tears as a mark of its success. Those tears are not, as one might imagine and as the texts themselves suggest, a sign of the catharsis of complete confession, but a sign rather of confession's inevitable incompleteness; it is as though the tears that are secreted (in the sense of produced) substitute for, and serve as a sign of, that which remains secreted (in its other sense as hidden). Perhaps the most pathetic moment in her narrative, for example, is when Harriet Jacobs' son runs, covered with blood from being attacked by a dog, past her hiding-place. Her inability to comfort or even speak to him produces a tearful moment. The reader's sentimental response occurs when Jacobs' desire to confess—to reveal the secret of her location in the "loophole of retreat"—is repressed and she is forced instead, like the reader, to endure the suffering of passive spectatorship. That pathos is generated in the disjunction between what is confessed and what is concealed, and the structural interstices that result from such disjunctions are sites that enable agency.

Harriet Jacobs' immediate political goal of encouraging her readers to resist the Fugitive Slave Law points out a loophole in that law which, too, provides access to agency. Since Northerners were expected to report runaway slaves so that they might be returned to their Southern owners, this law was unusual in that it required rather than forbade action in order to be obeyed. As a result, by simply remaining passive and silent, it was possible to transgress and resist the Fugitive Slave Law without actually breaking it. One might claim that such passivity mimics Northern abolitionists' failure to actively oppose slavery, particularly since the North's capture and execution of the radical anti-slavery activist John Brown occurred not long before the publication of *Incidents*. Given the camouflage effect of mimicry, detection of such resistance by passivity would be virtually impossible.

The absence of Harriet Jacobs' final chapter on the John Brown incident from her published narrative suggests that even Lydia Maria Child's

se of confession and unveiling practices its own conceal-
, in fact, advised Jacobs to excise that last chapter and to add
an internal chapter on the Southern response to the Nat Turner
Rebellion.[7] Though Child's advice may have been artistic or financial—
encouraging greater aesthetic cohesion or better sales—rather than political, its effect is nevertheless to end *Incidents in the Life of a Slave Girl*,
as Jean Fagan Yellin has pointed out, on a personal and sentimental
rather than a public and political note.[8] Thus this text's ending conceals
another one, and the chapter added in its stead suggestively portrays the
obsessive anxiety among Southern whites about what might be concealed
from them. In that added chapter, marauders search through Jacobs'
grandmother's house for secrets. All they uncover, however, are letters
which, Jacobs explains to them, "'are from white people. Some request
me to burn them after they are read, and some I destroy without reading'"
(66) [55]. Lydia Maria Child and Harriet Jacobs present this narrative to
the North as a true and complete confession from an escaped female
slave. Yet that supplementary chapter and its unread letters stand as one
sign, perhaps, of the North's suppression of a different kind of historical
and political consciousness in this text.

NELL IRVIN PAINTER

Three Southern Women and Freud: A Non-Exceptionalist Approach to Race, Class, and Gender in the Slave South[†]

In my work on sexuality in the nineteenth- and twentieth-century
South, my mind returns often to what the late Herbert Gutman used to
say about Marx, but with application to Sigmund Freud: He raises some
very good questions. While I have plenty of feminist company in my turn
toward psychoanalysis, the Freud I am using here is not quite the
Freud who has been making recent appearances.[1] As a historian of the

---

7. For more background on this editorial change see Bruce Mills, "Lydia Maria Child and the Endings to Harriet Jacobs' *Incidents in the Life of a Slave Girl*," *American Literature* 64 (1992): 255–72.
8. Yellin xxii.
† From *Feminists Revision History*, ed. Ann-Louise Shapiro (New Brunswick: Rutgers UP 1994)
195–216. Copyright © 1994 by Rutgers, The State University. Reprinted by permission of Rutgers University Press. Page references to this Norton Critical Edition are given in brackets following Painter's original citations.
1. I am coming to Freud's writing from a direction that is different from that of the literary critics
and most Lacanians. Although Freud's work is the starting place for object relations theory, it,
too, would be more useful to me than certain Lacanians (notably Jane Gallop, whose insights
are valuable here) if object relations analysts were not so relentlessly mid-twentieth-century-mid-
dle class. The family structure that objects relations scholars—such as Nancy Chodorow—en-
vision is strictly nuclear, whereas many nineteenth-century southern families included parental
figures who were not related to children by birth.

nineteenth- and early twentieth-century United States South trained in a
history project grounded in the archives, I find Freud valuable mainly as
an acute observer of nineteenth-century bourgeois society, as an analyst
(no pun intended) who recognized the relationship between sexuality
and identity. His writing permits unusually clear views into the ways in
which social, economic, and ethnic hierarchies affected households and
families, for he was accustomed to dealing with people in households that
encompassed more than one economic class. Such vision enriches southern studies, which is still impoverished by an exceptionalism that cannot
see commonalities between the American South and other hierarchical
societies that were not structured along racial lines and by a tendency to
see race as an opaque barrier to feminist investigation.

My subject is the family relations that affected the richest and the poorest of antebellum southern daughters. The tragically tiny number of
black daughters who would have been actually or nominally free, and the
large cohort of white daughters who would have lived beyond the reach
of the aristocracy, belonged to families who were able to shelter them
from predatory wealthy men and were more likely to escape the fate of
the daughters under discussion here. But whether black or white, if
young women lived in households in which men had access to the poorest and most vulnerable—women who were enslaved—these daughters
ran gendered risks related to sexuality that did not respect barriers of class
and race.

It has been no secret, then or now, that during the slavery era, owners
and slaves lived on terms of physical closeness and often engaged in sexual intimacy. Yet historians have followed the lead of privileged nineteenth-century southerners who, though well aware that sex figured
among the services that masters demanded of slaves, briskly pushed the
matter aside. Even psychoanalysts like Abram Kardiner and Lionel
Ovesey pass quickly over the repercussions of interracial sexuality on
southern white families and hence on southern society generally.[2] Virtually by default, the conclusion in southern history has been that master-
slave sex was a problem for the families of slaves, not the families of the
masters; thus as a social phenomenon, interracial, interclass sexuality has
been relegated solely to African-Americans. This is not the position I
hold. Because intimate relations affected white as well as black families,
I argue that such sexuality and its repercussions belong not to one race or
the other, but must reside squarely in southern history.[3]

One needs only read the work of class- and gender-conscious historians of Great Britain and Europe to recognize the parallels between nine-

2. Abram Kardiner and Lionel Ovesey, *The Mark of Oppression: Explorations in the Personality of
the American Negro* (New York, 1951).
3. I should add that family relations also affect more than women and girls; men and boys deserve—
and will ultimately receive—a far larger place in this piece of work in progress than they currently occupy.

European bourgeois societies and that of the United
... in a similar period.[4] Such usefulness is not limited to his-
... insights. While it is very much in vogue with literary critics,
Freudian psychoanalysis also offers thought-provoking assistance to historians, particularly on the formation of individual identity. Specifically,
Sigmund Freud's "Dora" case history raises fundamental questions about
the dynamics of elite families in a hierarchical society in which the employment of servants—and here I concentrate on female servants—is
routine. This essay addresses the pertinence of three pieces of Freud's
writing to southern society, as reflected in the histories of three southern
women: Gertrude Thomas, "Lily," and "Linda Brent."

Gertrude Thomas (1834–1907) spent much of her life as a plantation
mistress near Augusta, Georgia. Her journal, written over the better part
of forty years, takes a long but self-censoring look into one privileged
white woman's family. Gertrude Thomas was not a fictional character,
but she tried to make the record of her everyday life into a portrait that
fitted her ideals.

Lily is the title character of an 1855 novel by Sue Petigru King (Bowen)
(1824–1875), a daughter of the very respectable Charlestonian Thomas
Petigru. Having been educated in Charleston and New York, she had
returned to South Carolina to pursue her career as a writer. King's protagonist, Lily, is the quintessential young plantation mistress: hyper-
white, wealthy, and beautiful. Much better known today, thanks largely to
the work of Jean Fagan Yellin and others, is Linda Brent, who in contrast
to Lily, is a slave. Brent is both the central character and the pseudonym
under which the Edenton, North Carolina, fugitive slave Harriet Jacobs
(1813–1897) wrote her autobiography, *Incidents in the Life of a Slave
Girl*, originally published with the help of abolitionists in Boston in 1861.[5]

If rich, white, and free Gertrude and Lily stood at the top of the antebellum South's economic and racial hierarchies, then poor, yellow, and
enslaved Linda Brent lived near, but not at the very bottom. Linda, after
all, has some free relations, and her grand-mother, though nominally enslaved, lives in her own house in town. Things could have been much
worse for Linda Brent. Gertrude's, Linda's, and Lily's stories are about
women and sex; taken together with Freud's "Dora" they tell us a great deal
about southern family dynamics in slaveholding households. As all three
of these texts are about race and sexuality, I begin with the phenomenon
of master-slave sex as I discovered it in Gertrude Thomas's journal.

---

4. E.g., Leonore Davidoff, "Class and Gender in Victorian England: The Diaries of Arthur J.
Munby and Hannah Cullwick," *Feminist Studies* 5 (Spring 1979) and Maria Ramas, "Freud's
Dora, Dora's Hysteria," in *Sex and Class in Women's History*, ed. Judith L. Newton, Mary P.
Ryan, and Judith R. Walkowitz (London, 1983).

5. Sue Petigru King Bowen, *Lily* (New York, 1855) and Jean Fagan Yellin, *Incidents in the Life of
a Slave Girl, Written by Herself*, by Harriet A. Jacobs (Cambridge, Mass., 1987). Although I am
aware the controversy surrounding the designation of genre of *Incidents*, I am treating it here as
autobiography.

Gertrude Thomas's Secret

Although historians have not begun to quantify its incidence, we know that sexual relations between male slavemasters and female slaves were exceedingly common in the antebellum South—as in any other slave society, as Orlando Patterson points out.[6] Nineteenth-century fugitive slave narratives, such as those of Frederick Douglass and Moses Roper, and the Fisk and WPA ex-slave narratives from the 1930s, are full of evidence that masters did not hesitate to sleep with their women slaves, despite the marital status of either. Although I have not had an opportunity to pursue this hunch, I suspect that about ten percent of masters also slept or wanted to sleep with their enslaved men and boys; some mistresses may also have regarded their female slaves as objects of desire.[7] On the other side of the class and racial continuums from the Frederick Douglasses and Moses Ropers, nineteenth-century white women—southerners and observers—penned and sometimes published criticisms of the institution of slavery based on what they perceived as the demoralization of white men who engaged in adultery and/or polygyny.

I began to draw my own conclusions as I concentrated on the journal of Ella Gertrude Clanton Thomas, published in 1990 as *The Secret Eye*."[8] Thomas was wealthy, educated, and white, and she began keeping a journal in 1848, when she was fourteen years old, and stopped writing definitively in 1889, when she was fifty-five. Although born into an immensely wealthy, slave-owning family, she married a man who was a poor manager. Her husband, Jefferson Thomas, succeeded financially as a planter before the Civil War, thanks to unpaid labor and continual financial help from Gertrude's father. But her father died in 1864, and their slaves were emancipated in 1865. After the war the Thomases entered a long cycle of debt that sent Gertrude into the paid labor force as a teacher. Her earnings kept the family afloat economically, but poverty imposed great strains. This journal, therefore, chronicles a life of privilege before the Civil War, the trauma of supporting the losing side, the loss of the labor and prestige that slavery had assured, and the chagrin of downward mobility. Thomas joined the Woman's Christian Temperance Union in the 1880s and became a suffragist in the 1890s. She died in Atlanta.

Initially I appreciated this journal for its value as a primary source for the study of the social history of the South, for which Thomas is an excellent witness. Extraordinary as is the historical source, however, the

6. Orlando Patterson, *Slavery and Social Death: A Comparative Study* (Cambridge, Mass., 1982), 50, 229, 230, 261.
7. Hortense Spillers makes some tantalizing observations in this regard in "Mama's Baby, Papa's Maybe: An American Grammar Book," *Diacritics* 17 (Summer 1987).
8. Virginia Burr, ed., *The Secret Eye: The Journal of Ella Gertrude Clanton Thomas, 1848–1889* (Chapel Hill, 1990).

yet another level that is characterized by the keeping of
candor, and self-deception and that psychoanalysis is well-
to explore. What Thomas tried to hide in her journal offers
glimpses into persistent tensions over gender and sexuality in the South
and, ultimately, into the nature of nineteenth-century southern society.

The Thomas journal contains a hidden layer of secrets that is murky,
personal, and highly gendered. There are actually two great secrets in the
journal, one of which, Jefferson's drinking, Gertrude did succeed in hiding. The other proved too painful to suppress entirely. Whereas the surface of this text presents a southerner of a certain class at given historical
junctures, a less straightforward message also emerges, though it is not so
easy to decipher. The veiled text, less bounded chronologically, concerns
families and gender, and it contains and reveals a great secret that is relatively timeless: adultery.

Even when she is strongest and most outspoken, Thomas draws a
veil across certain realities of her life that she shared with large numbers of other plantation mistresses. Like them, she tries not to see. But
unlike the great majority of her peers, Thomas left a huge, magnificent
journal. Her writing hints—through what psychologists call "deception
clues" (cues that something is being withheld) and "leakage" (inadvertent disclosure) of highly-charged material—that some important
truths remain obscured.[9]

Both leakage and deception clues are associated with the phenomenon
of self-deception, the concealment of painful knowledge from the self.
The line between deception of her readers (her children) and self-deception is not entirely clear in the Thomas journal, for Thomas's concept
of her audience varied over the many years that she wrote. At times she
addresses her children, at other times her God. In the later years she
speaks with remarkable candor to her journal as a confidante (herself).
Drawing the line between deception and self-deception may not be an
indispensable task here, for as observers as disparate as the sociologist Erving Goffman and the poet Adrienne Rich point out, the intention to mis-
lead others quickly becomes the misleading of the self.[1]

The most obvious deception clue is one of Thomas's favorite refrains.
Four times between 1852 (the year in which she married) and 1870 she
cites this poem (or alludes to it by quoting the first line) by the Georgia
poet Richard Henry Wilde:

9. Paul Ekman, "Self-Deception and Detection of Misinformation," in *Self-Deception: An Adap-
tive Mechanism?*, ed. Joan S. Lockard and Delroy L. Paulhus, (Englewood Cliffs, 1988),
231–232. Building on Sigmund Freud's observations that individuals provide nonverbal clues
that undermine what they are saying, psychologists have usually looked for deception clues and
leakage in the realm of nonverbal communication, which, of course, is not available in the present case. Thomas, however, provides verbal clues and verbal leakage that undermine conventions that she expresses in her writing.
1. Erving Goffman, *The Presentation of Self in Everyday Life* (Garden City, 1959), 81; and Adrienne Rich, *On Lies, Secrets, and Silence: Selected Prose 1966–1978* (New York, 1979), 188.

There are some thoughts we utter not.
Deep treasured in our inmost heart
Ne'er revealed and ne'er forgot.[2]

In addition, the intensity of portions of the writing manifests Thomas's uneasiness over certain subjects (e.g., competition between women, the dual sexual standard), without going to the heart of her distress. The most important deception clues begin with the entry of 2 June 1855, in which Thomas says:" [T]here are some thoughts we utter not and not even to you my journal . . . yet there are some moments when I must write— must speak or else the pent up emotions of an overcharged heart will *burst* or *break*. . . . With a heart throbbing and an agitated form. How can I write?" Thomas cites "one of the most exciting conversations I have ever held. A conversation which in a moment, in a flash of the eye will change the gay, thoughtless girl into a woman with all a woman's feelings" and the "chilling influence (it may be of disappointment) to wonder at the wild tumultuous throbbings of early womanhood." She says that she is troubled by something.

I have never succeeded in decoding this confusing entry entirely, for the language is more than ambiguous; these phrases lead in two separate directions at once. Thomas's language echoes other women's private descriptions of infatuations at the same time that it represents Thomas's own language of disappointment. When she writes of "all a woman's feelings" elsewhere in the journal, she speaks of chagrin rather than fulfillment. Neither this entry nor those around it provides clues as to the cause(s) of her agitation. But she clearly manifests great anxiety over the contents of a conversation that takes place when her first child is eighteen months old. Moreover in two other entries in the same season, she speaks of the "bitter agony" and the bitterness of "taunts and expressions" that are the lot of married women.

Several years later Thomas begins to explicate her concerns in what I call her leakage entries, in which she inadvertently reveals that certain matters are significant to her. The lengthy, intense entry of 2 January 1859 deplores miscegenation, which she acknowledges as matter "thought best for [white] women to ignore." Thomas castigates white men of uncontrolled, animal passions who buy mulatto slave women for sex. In general, Thomas had a very low opinion of southern white men's morals, but bachelors' fortunes were not uppermost in her mind.[3] Rather, she

2. After writing the entry for 4 November 1852, in which she explained Jefferson's illness that postponed their wedding and quoted the first line of the poem twice in three sentences and added that "there are some emotions too powerful for words. . . ." Thomas did not write again until 8 April 1855.
3. In the 12 May 1856 entry she includes the following cryptic comment on men's morality: "were that faith [in her husband] dissipated by *actual experience* then would be dissolved a dream in which is constituted my hope of happiness upon earth. Of course between a husband and wife, this is (or should be) a forbidden subject but to *you* my journal I would willingly disclose many thoughts did I not think that the prying eye of curiosity might scan these lines."

laments the effect of miscegenation in "our Southern homes." While she
believes that white men are more degraded by slavery (i.e., the miscegenation that accompanies the institution) than blacks, her main preoccupation is with white families.

A young mother worrying over slavery's pernicious effect on children,
Thomas points away from her own nuclear family and toward the setting
in which she was herself a child: her parents' household.[4] She also mentions "others," whom she does not name, who are equally guilty. Thomas
deplores interracial sex as a violation of the racial hierarchy, but she is
aware that the significance of the miscegenation she has in mind exceeds
mere race mixing. It is also sex outside of marriage, so that someone worth
worrying about in her father's household and in the household of "others" had violated one of the Ten Commandments. As a devout Christian
who knew that there was a heaven and a hell and that the sins of the parents were liable to be visited upon the children, she worried "upon whom
shall the accountability of their [the illegitimate children's] future state
depend."

By January 1865 the combined strains of the war, her father's death,
and the impending Confederate defeat brought Thomas's anxieties
closer to the surface. She writes at length about competition between
women. Finally, in 1869, she writes of her son, Turner, a mulatto plow-
boy, and his mother who is only slightly darker than Turner's mother.

With this entry, much of Thomas's impassioned writing falls into
place. Gertrude Thomas worried about competition between women because it was a bothersome part of her own life as a daughter and a wife.
Thus her long, fervent comments on the effect of slavery on white families and on black women's usurpation of the places of white wives now
appear as commentary on her own family's tragedy. She believed that her
father had had children and that her husband had had a child outside
their marriages. It is possible, though far from certain, that whatever unspeakable thing distressed her when her first child was a baby was the discovery that her husband was sleeping with someone else.

Pulling all these leakage entries together, I conclude that the great
secret of Gertrude Thomas's journal is something that she experienced as
adultery. As a devout, nineteenth-century Methodist, she was deeply concerned with matters of moral rectitude and divine retribution. At the same
time, however, she reacted to her husband's sexual relations with a slave

---

4. Thomas writes of her father's "estate," which would indicate a larger place than the Clanton
   household. Virginia Burr, Thomas's great-granddaughter and the editor of the Thomas journal,
   says: "Thomas, in referring to 'so many' mulatto children 'growing up on Pa's estate, as well as
   others,' includes Turner Clanton's entire estate of five plantations and the Clanton household.
   In that context, it is highly probable that resident overseers contributed to the mulatto population. Turner Clanton was, without doubt, guilty of miscegenation to some degree." [Virginia
   Burr to Nell Irvin Painter, 2 April 1989] I believe, however, that Thomas would not have been
   so disturbed had she not suspected her father. Hence I understand "Pa's estate" here to mean the
   Clanton household.

as people have traditionally responded to adultery—with jealousy, anger, and humiliation, not with the placid assurance of racial superiority.

This should come as no surprise, as some of the best known observations about antebellum southern society make more or less the same point. Abolitionists—who are currently out of favor with historians as analysts of southern society—routinely pilloried slaveowners for the sexual abuse of mulatto women.[5] Female visitors to the South criticized slavery for its deleterious effect on white men's morals. In the 1830s Harriet Martineau spoke of the plantation mistress as "the chief slave of the harem." Fredrika Bremer in the 1850s coined a famous phrase about slaves of mixed ancestry—the "white children of slavery"—which Thomas quotes in her journal. And Mary Chesnut wrote of the mulatto children present in every slaveholding household. Gertrude Thomas was far, very far, from alone.[6]

The intense hurt and anger in Thomas's entries on competition between women and sexual relations between slaveowners and slaves indicate that she experienced her husband's action as a breach in her marriage. Yet there may be an alternative and more appropriate definition of the phenomenon that Thomas deplored.

The pattern of slaveowning married men's sexual relations with women to whom they were not legally married was widespread, and these nonlegal relationships sometimes endured—like marriages. Seen another way, Thomas may have been party to a social pattern that she did not recognize and for which anthropologists use the term "polygyny." It may well have been that men like Jefferson Thomas, more than regularly committing adultery, were establishing something like polygynous mar-

---

5. E.g., Harriet Beecher Stowe, *A Key to Uncle Tom's Cabin; Presenting the Original Facts and Documents upon Which the Story Was Founded. Together With Corroborative Statement Verifying the Truth of the Work* (Leipzig, 1853), 63, 142–143, and L. Maria Child, *An Appeal in Favor of Americans Called Africans* (New York, 1836, republished, 1968), 23–24. Historian Ronald G. Walters quotes abolitionists who wrote of the antebellum South as "ONE GREAT SODOM" and of the male slaveowner as one who "totally annihilates the marriage institution." Ronald G. Walters, "The Erotic South: Civilization and Sexuality in American Abolitionism," *American Quarterly* 25, no. 2 (May 1973): 183, 192.

6. Harriet Martineau, *Society in America*, vol. 2 (New York, 1837), 112, 118; Fredrika Bremer, *Homes of the New World; Impressions of America*, vol. 1 (London, 1853), 382; C. Vann Woodward and Elisabeth Muhlenfeld, *The Private Mary Chesnut: The Unpublished Civil War Diaries* (New York, 1984), 42 (18 March 1861).

See also Deborah Gray White, *Ar'n't I a Woman?: Female Slaves in the Plantation South* (New York, 1985), 27–47; Catherine Clinton, *The Plantation Mistress: Woman's World in the Old South* (New York, 1982), 203–204, 210–222; James Hugo Johnston, *Race Relations in Virginia and Miscegenation in the South 1776–1860* (Amherst, 1970), 165–190, 243; Kenneth M. Stampp, *The Peculiar Institution: Slavery in the Ante-Bellum South* (New York, 1956), 350–361; Eugene D. Genovese, *Roll, Jordan, Roll: The World the Slaves Made* (New York, 1974), 413–429; and Bertram Wyatt-Brown, *Southern Honor: Ethics and Behavior in the Old South* (New York, 1982), 307–324; Marli Frances Weiner, "Plantation Mistresses and Female Slaves: Gender, Race, and South Carolina Women," (Ph.D. diss., University of Rochester, 1986), 131–139, 177–190; bell hooks, *Ain't I a Woman: Black Women and Feminism* (Boston, 1981), 26–41; Angela Y. Davis, *Women Race and Class* (New York, 1981), 25–29, 173–177; Elizabeth Fox-Genovese, *Within the Plantation Household: Black and White Women of the Old South* (Chapel Hill, 1988), 325–326.

riages. Gertrude does not say how long Jefferson's relationship with his slave-partner lasted, whether it was a fling or might qualify as a marriage. Evidence from the journal supports at least a suspicion that the relationship may have endured from 1855 to 1870, perhaps even until 1880, but it is far from conclusive.[7] The stresses that Gertrude reports in her marriage—Jefferson's irritability, his refusal to give her moral support, his withdrawal from intimacy—could as easily represent the human cost of financial ruin as an expression of the distance between partners that accompanies extramarital relationships.

There can be no well-founded representation of the circumstances that led to the conception of Jefferson Thomas's outside child, but other cases are clearer. James Henry Hammond, a prominent antebellum South Carolina statesman, for instance, had two slaves who were, in effect, multiple wives. Southern court records are full of litigation over which set of families might inherit from men who had had children by more than one woman.[8]

Thomas's unwillingness to spell out what was taking place in her marriage hints by indirection at her husband's adultery. Her South pretended not to see slave wives, whose existence was a sort of elephant in the living room of family secrets.[9] Secrecy, the very heart and soul of adultery, is much of what makes adultery toxic to marriages, families, and, ultimately, society. Of itself, secrecy stifles intimacy and rigidifies relationships, even when partners are not so deeply religious as Gertrude Thomas.[1]

In the early nineteenth century Harriet Martineau understood that adultery places enormous strains on families, and modern scholarship makes the same point. Adultery breaks the pact of sexual exclusivity in marriage and undermines the betrayed spouse's trust in the other. The consequences of such ruptures could not always be confined to the private sphere. James Henry Hammond believed, with good foundation, that his wife's angry reaction to his taking his second slave wife ruined his political career.[2]

---

7. In December 1870 Thomas draws a parallel between herself, Hester Prynne of *The Scarlet Letter*, and African-American women who bear mixed-race children, and in November 1880 she writes of her cross to bear.
8. Clinton, *The Plantation Mistress*, 213–221.
9. See Ann Taves, "Spiritual Purity and Sexual Shame: Religious Themes in the Writings of Harriet Jacobs," *Church History* 56 (1987): 65–66.
1. Herbert Fingarette, in his classic *Self-Deception* (London, 1969), explains the tactic of not spelling out or hiding uncomfortable truths (especially 43–50). Fingarette's not spelling-out is analogous to Jean Paul Sartre's *mauvaise foi*, which is translated as "bad faith," in the context of self-deception. Jean-Paul Sartre, *Being and Nothingness: An Essay on Phenomenological Ontology*, trans. Hazel E. Barnes, (New York, 1967), 47–56. The terms "toxic," "toxicity," and "spoiled" are Annette Lawson's, in *Adultery: An Analysis of Love and Betrayal* (New York, 1988), 12, 30–31, 53. See also Sissela Bok, *Secrets* (New York, 1982), 25, 59–72. A recent southern autobiography, Sallie Bingham, *Passion and Prejudice: A Family Memoir* (New York, 1989), exemplifies the pernicious effects of not telling the truth within a family.
2. Carol Bleser, ed., *Secret and Sacred: The Diaries of James Henry Hammond, a Southern Slaveholder* (New York, 1988), 170, 134–244, 254–269.

Adultery also subverts the social order by weakening the most fundamental social relationship upon which procreation and socialization depend. Adultery breeds moral and sexual ambivalence in children, who vacillate between the outraged virtue of the betrayed parent and the adulterous parent's indulgence in sin. Ultimately adultery creates chaotic inheritance patterns, which in the antebellum South meant that fathers were liable to own and sell their children. Lillian Smith, a perceptive twentieth-century southern observer of her region, grasped the way that secrets, miscegenation, sin, and guilt combined to endow white southerners with a terrible fear of impending disaster. Smith would have agreed that southern society, riven by so many instances of bad faith, was pathological.[3]

According to the ostensible mores of her society, Gertrude Thomas was the superior of nearly everyone in it. She was a plantation mistress in a society dominated by the 6 percent of white families that qualified as planters by owning twenty or more slaves. She was an educated woman at a time when only elite men could take higher education for granted. And she was white in a profoundly racist culture. Yet neither Gertrude Thomas's economic or educational attributes nor her social status protected her from what she saw as sexual competition from inferior women. From Thomas's point of view, white men saw women—whether slave or free, wealthy or impoverished, cultured or untutored, black or white—as interchangeable sex partners. She and other plantation mistresses failed to elevate themselves sufficiently as women to avoid the pain of sharing their spouses with slaves. The institution of slavery, which assured female slaveowners social prestige, also gave them sexual nightmares. The effects of the victimization of slave women could not be contained, for (otherwise) privileged women like Gertrude Thomas felt that their husbands' adultery intruded into their own as well as their slaves' families.

Some of the most interesting evidence of this pattern comes from fiction, which, considering the subject, should not be surprising. Most respectable nineteenth-century people retreated—or attempted to retreat—behind the veil of privacy, rather than reveal their actual patterns of sexuality, whether in their homes, in their letters, or in their journals. The very ability to conceal the rawer aspects of the human condition, an ability that we sum up in the term privacy, served as a crucial symbol of respectability when the poor had no good place to hide. Nonetheless the topic of interracial sexuality was of enough fascination to reappear in fic-

3. See Lawson, *Adultery*, 10, 35, 56–59, 221, 260; and Philip E. Lampe, ed., *Adultery in the United States: Close Encounters of the Sixth (or Seventh) Kind* (Buffalo, 1987), 3–9, 13. Sue M. Hall and Philip A. Hall, "Law and Adultery," in *Adultery in the United States*, point out that adultery is often cited as a reason for denying child custody. An adulterer appears to be unfit to care for children and unable to serve the child's best interests (73–75). Thomas discusses parents who own or sell their own children on 2 January 1859. Lillian Smith, *Killers of the Dream*, revised ed. (New York, 1961), 83–89, 121–124.

tion under various disguises. Taking my cue from Gertrude Thomas, who was hypersensitive about sexual competition between women, I began to pursue sexuality through the theme of competition. Tracked in that guise, southern fiction reveals some interesting manifestations.

Lily

Sue Petigru King sounded themes that occur in the work of several white southern women writers, such as Caroline Hentz, Grace King, and Willa Cather. For example, Cather's final novel, *Sapphira and the Slave Girl* (1940), is precisely and openly about a white woman's perception of sexual competition between herself and a Negro woman. In its racial candor, *Sapphira* is exceptional. More often the competition between women is not about individuals with different racial identities, but about two white characters who are color-coded in black and white. While I realize that European writers such as Walter Scott and Honoré de Balzac used light (blond) and dark (*la belle juive*) female characters symbolically, Ann Jones, Mary Kelley, and Jane Pease, scholars familiar with southern writers, corroborate my view that nineteenth- and early twentieth-century white southern women writers were singularly fascinated by competition between light and dark women. While most publications by these women followed the usual theme of a young woman's quest for autonomy and her eventual marriage to a good man, they also echo Gertrude Thomas's fixation on female rivalry.

The author Sue Petigru King is no longer very well known, but she loomed large in Gertrude Thomas's literary world and was known in Great Britain. William Thackery, one of Britain's most celebrated authors, visited her on a trip to the United States. In the mid-nineteenth century King published several novels which repeatedly stress themes of jealousy and competition between women, the best-known of which is *Lily*, published in 1855.

Very briefly, *Lily* is the story of Elizabeth Vere, whom her father calls "Lily" because she is "as white as any lily that ever grew." Over the course of the novel's plot, Lily goes from age seven to seventeen. King describes her heroine with words like "white," "pure," "innocent," "simple," and "lovely." The character with whom King pairs Lily is her cousin, Angelica Purvis. Angelica is also a rich white woman, but King focuses on the blackness of her dresses and the intense blackness of her hair. At one point, King contrasts Lily, who "seemed made up of light and purity," with Angelica, who "was dark, designing, distracting." Angelica is exotic; King describes her as an "Eastern princess" and calls her looks "Andalusian." Whereas Lily is pure, Angelica is passionate, evil, voluptuous. Angelica says of her attractiveness to men: "I am original sin . . ."[4] At the

---

4. King (Bowen), *Lily*, 206, 227–228. W. J. Cash also utilizes Spanishness to hint at the blackness within white southerners. See W. J. Cash, *The Mind of the South* (New York, 1941), 25.

age of seventeen, Lily is engaged to her first great love, Clarence Tracy, a childhood friend who is a graduate of Princeton. Despite all her goodness, however, Lily is not rewarded with love, for Clarence is crazy in love with Angelica, who is married.

On the face of it, the most obvious theme in *Lily* is competition between two white women, which the less virtuous is winning. But race hovers in the very near background. First, these ostensibly white competitors are color-coded in black and white. Then, as though to make the point conclusively, King abruptly introduces a new character, Lorenza, at the very end of the novel. Lorenza is Clarence's Negro mistress. On the night before Lily's wedding, a jealous Lorenza murders Lily.

King leaves nothing to guesswork in this novel, and to hammer home her message, she also addresses her readers directly. Her point is the same made by Mary Chesnut in her Civil War diary: that southern planter husbands repaid their wives' faithful virtue with base infidelity. Wealthy southern men married young, pure, rich, white girls like Lily, then left them for mistresses tinged by blackness, whether of descent or intimation. King sums up Mary Chesnut's conviction and Gertrude Thomas's fears: "It is not the woman most worthy to be loved who is the most loved." This conclusion is echoed in the writing of Sigmund Freud.

In 1912 Freud discussed exactly that phenomenon in his second contribution to the *Psychology of Love*: "On the Universal Tendency to Debasement in the Sphere of Love." Freud appraised the practical results of "civilized morality" and the sexual double standard from the standpoint of middle- and upper-class men who were susceptible to psychosomatic impotence with women of their own class. Freud said, making King's point: "Where such men love they have no desire and where they desire they cannot love."[5]

In *Lily*, the pure, young, rich, white daughter is the most dramatic loser in the southern sexual sweepstakes. In this interpretation of southern sexuality, the motif is competition between women and the victims are wealthy white women. Writers from the other side painted a disturbingly similar, yet differently shaded portrait.

Linda Brent

While many exslave narrators discuss master-slave sexuality, the most extended commentary comes from Harriet Jacobs, who, writing under the pseudonym Linda Brent, tells of being harassed by her master for sex

5. King (Bowen) *Lily*, 278. *Sigmund Freud: Collected Papers*, trans. Joan Riviere (New York, 1959), 4, 207. According to Freud, well-brought-up women who have been taught that sex is distasteful and who reject their sexuality tend to be inexperienced, inhibited, and frigid in marriage. This means that their husbands, who also regard the sex act as polluting, relate to their wives more as judges than as joyous physical partners. Hence only love objects who seem to these men to be debased—prostitutes, women of the lower class—can inspire in them full sensual feelings and a high degree of pleasure. This explains why these men keep lower-class mistresses (207, 210–211).

from the time she was thirteen. Her character, Linda, becomes the literal embodiment of the slave as sexual prey in the testimony of slaves.

Harriet Jacobs depicts puberty as a "sad epoch in the life of a slave girl." As Linda Brent becomes nubile, her master begins to whisper "foul words in my ear," which is the kind of act whose consequences Freud comprehended and that we term sexual harassment. Jacobs generalizes from Linda's predicament and says that "whether the slave girl be black as ebony or as fair as her mistress"—she, the slave girl, is sexually vulnerable. This vulnerability robs her of her innocence and purity. Hearing "foul words" from her master and angry and jealous outbreaks from her mistress, the slave girl, in Jacobs's phrase, becomes "prematurely knowing in evil things." The more beautiful she is, the more speedy her despoliation. Beauty, for Linda Brent and young women like her, is no blessing: "If God has bestowed beauty upon her, it will prove her greatest curse."[6]

Incidents in the Life of a Slave Girl is of great interest in this discussion because Jacobs confronts the sexual component of servitude so straightforwardly. She recognizes, too, that slaves and owners interpreted the situation very differently. Jacobs dedicates an entire chapter of *Incidents* to "The Jealous Mistress." Here and elsewhere, Jacobs maintains that mistresses whose husbands betrayed them felt no solidarity whatever with their slaves. Like other exslave narrators, Jacobs could ascertain the view of slaveowning women but emphatically did not share their conclusions. Writing as Linda Brent, Jacobs supplies a key word: "victim," and recognizes that it is a matter of contention between slave and mistress.

White women, black women, and black men all resented deeply white men's access to black women. But the comments from the two sides of the color line are contradictory: where white women saw sexual competition—with connotations of equality—black men and women saw rank exploitation that stemmed from grossly disparate levels of power. Moses Roper, his master's child, relates the story of his near-murder, shortly after his birth, by his father's jealous wife. Frederick Douglass also noted that slaveowning women were distressed by the bodily proof of their husband's adulteries.[7]

For Jacobs as for other exslave narrators the prime victim was the slave woman, not the slaveowning woman, no matter how slaveowning women perceived the situation. So far as slaves were concerned, slaveowners' sexual relations with their women slaves constituted one of several varieties of victimization of slaves by men whose power over their slaves was ab-

6. Harriet A. Jacobs, *Incidents in the Life of a Slave Girl, Written by Herself*, ed. Jean Fagan Yellin (Cambridge, 1987), 27–28, 33 [26, 30].
7. Moses Roper, *A Narrative of the Adventures and Escape of Moses Roper from American Slavery*, 5th ed. (London, 1843), 9–10, quoted in Frances Smith Foster, *Witnessing Slavery: The Development of Antebellum Slave Narratives* (Westport, Conn., 1979), 78; and Frederick Douglass, *Narrative of the Life of Frederick Douglass an American Slave* (Boston, 1845), 4, quoted in Foster, *Witnessing Slavery*, 79.

solute. Slaves of both sexes were oppressed by class and by race, and women slaves suffered a third, additional form of oppression stemming from their gender. Slaves were victims several times over, and extorted sex was part of a larger pattern of oppression embedded in the institution of slavery.

Harriet Jacobs and Gertrude Thomas provide examples of the family dynamics of cross-class adultery. Located in very different places within the complicated families of slavery, each explicates the deleterious effects of adultery within their households. Like Jacobs and Thomas, Sigmund Freud, in his analysis of "Dora," recognized the damage that the father's adultery did to the daughter.

"Dora"

In the "Dora" case, Herr K had made sexual advances toward "Dora," Ida Bauer, who had overheard Herr K's propositioning a servant woman in exactly the same phrases that he used with Bauer. Entangled emotionally with several women, Bauer identified (at the least) with Frau K, who was her father's mistress, and with the servant. She also felt as though she were being made a pawn in an adulterous game between her father and the Ks. When Ida Bauer's father took her to Freud in October 1900, after she had tried to commit suicide, Freud was already anxious to try out his ideas.[8]

Freud had been thinking about hysteria for several years and had worked out his notions in letters to his close friend and regular correspondent, Wilhelm Fliess. These comments are exceedingly helpful to me, particularly in observations that Freud enclosed with a letter dated 2 May 1897. Here Freud notes that children, even very young babies, hear things that later become the raw material for fantasies and neuroses. Accompanying this letter was "Draft L," which includes a paragraph on "The Part Played by Servant Girls."

In Draft L, Freud echoes his society's assumption that the poor young women who worked in bourgeois households were "people of low morals" because they were likely to become sexually involved with the men and boys of the household. Here Freud was echoing the commonest of common knowledge about black people in the South. But whereas Freud identified morals with class, white southerners saw low morals as

---

8. See Jane Gallop, "Keys to Dora," in *The Daughter's Seduction: Feminism and Psychoanalysis* (Ithaca, N.Y., 1982), 137, 141–145, 147; Elisabeth Young-Bruehl, ed., *Freud on Women: A Reader* (New York, 1990); Jim Swan, "*Mater and Nannie: Freud's Two Mothers,*" *America Imago* 31, no. 1 (Spring 1974); Hannah S. Decker, *Freud, Dora, and Vienna 1900* (New York, 1991); Maria Ramas, "Freud's Dora, Dora's Hysteria," in *Sex and Class in Women's History*, eds. Judith L. Newton, Mary P. Ryan, and Judith R. Walkowitz (London, 1983); and Mary Poovey, "The Anathematized Race: The Governess and *Jane Eyre*," in *Uneven Developments: The Ideological Work of Gender in Mid-Victorian England* (Chicago, 1988).

a racial characteristic of African Americans. For my purposes, however, this comment about morals is not the crucial point of Freud's failed analysis of Ida Bauer. For me Freud's most useful observation relates to the critical importance of servants in the psychological and hence social dynamics of the families in which they work. Although Freud thought mainly of the ramifications of the situation on the family of the employers, servants, too, as we saw with Linda Brent, felt the effects of adulterous—should I add incestuous?—family dynamics.

Freud wrote to Fliess that in households in which servant women are sexually intimate with their employers, the children—and here I believe he means the female children—develop an array of hysterical fantasies: fear of being on the street alone, fear of becoming a prostitute, fear of a man hidden under the bed. In sum, says Freud, "There is tragic justice in the circumstance that the family's head's stooping to a maidservant is atoned for by his daughter's self-abasement."[9]

Freud underscores the degree to which women in a household are emotionally intertwined, for he observed that "Dora" identified with the servant whom her would-be lover had tried to seduce. Observing situations in which race was not a factor, Freud understood that the very structure containing class and gender power dynamics is virtually Foucauldian in its leakiness. No class of women remained exempt from a degradation that aimed at the least of them. Just as Gertrude Thomas saw that her adulterous father and husband treated rich and poor and black and white women as interchangeable sexually, Freud saw there was a "part played by servant girls" and an object connection between "Dora" and her father's mistress. A recent Freud scholar, Hannah Decker, put her finger on the phenomenon that poisoned young women's lives in Freud's Vienna and that also characterized the nineteenth-century South: the careless sexual abuse of *das süsse Mädel*—the sweet young thing.[1]

Freud's letters to Fliess, "On the Universal Tendency to Debasement in the Sphere of Love," and especially the "Dora" case analysis, show that "Dora's" predicament is reflected in both *Lily* and *Incidents in the Life of a Slave Girl*, but in somewhat different ways. Linda Brent is more directly comparable with "Dora," for she is the object of unwanted sexual advances, as was young Ida Bauer. The case of Lily Vere is less obvious, for she is the daughter of "Draft L," of "The Part Played by Servant Girls." Lily is the daughter whose affective value is lowered by the existence of the sexually vulnerable servant class and the allure of enticing dark/Negro women like Angelica and Lorenza. While Linda Brent is a clear victim of her society's hierarchies of race and gender, Lily, unloved by her fiancé and murdered by her servant lover, is victimized as well. Her

---

9. Jeffrey Moussaieff Masson, *The Complete Letters of Sigmund Freud to Wilhelm Fliess, 1887–1904* (Cambridge, Mass., 1985), 241.
1. Decker, *Freud, Dora, and Vienna 1900*, 109.

fiancé, Clarence, is the very figure of the Freud patient suffering from psychically-induced impotence.[2]

Conclusion

Listening to these southern women's stories and taking Freud to heart leads to two conclusions: First, that historians of the United States South have sheltered too long in southern exceptionalism and let an intellectual color bar obstruct their grasp of the complexity of gender roles within households that were economically heterogenous. Lily and Linda Brent, two examples of a spoilation of young women that is no respecter of race or class—underscore both the sexual vulnerabilities and the psychological interrelatedness of southern daughters. Second, Freud points the way toward an understanding that families and societies cannot designate and thereby set apart one category of women as victims. The victimization spreads, in different ways and to different degrees. But where historians have been prone to construe southern family relations within watertight racial categories, the stories of Gertrude Thomas, Lily, and Linda Brent pose complicated new questions whose answers do not stop at the color line.

Historians have wanted to reach a single conclusion that would characterize the relationship between slaveowning and slave women in the antebellum South: *Either* slave women were at the bottom of a hierarchical society, as the exslave narrators testify, *or* all southern women were, finally, at the mercy of rich white men. The relationship between black and white women through white men deserves to be named, for slavery often made women of different races and classes into co-mothers and co-wives as well as owners and suppliers of labor. The question is whether there should be one name or, corresponding to the number of races involved, more than one.

So far no historian of southern women has given more than a chapter or its equivalent to interracial sexuality and the gender relations that flowed from it, but the work is coming along. The older, full-length studies of race and gender in the antebellum South by Deborah Gray White, Catherine Clinton, and Elizabeth Fox-Genovese and the newer work that builds upon them all tend toward use of one concept to characterize relations within extended southern households: oppression. Deborah

---

2. See also Freud's "'Civilized' Sexual Morality and Modern Nervous Illness" (1908) and *Civilization and Its Discontents* (1930), in which he surveyed what he saw as the psychosexual dysfunctions associated with civilization. In "'Civilized' Sexual Morality" Freud makes some observations that might be useful in southern history: "In her [the girl's] mental feelings [as she marries] she is still attached to her parents, whose authority has brought about the suppression of her sexuality; and in her physical behaviour she shows herself frigid, which deprives the man of any high degree of sexual enjoyment. I do not know whether the anaesthetic type of woman exists apart from civilized education, though I consider it probable. But in any case, such education actually breeds it. . . . In this way, the preparation for marriage frustrates the aims of marriage itself." In Young-Bruehl, ed., *Freud on Women*, 176.

Gray White, in *Ar'n't I a Woman*, stresses the "helplessness" and "powerlessness" of slave women vis-à-vis slaveowners and in American society in general. Conceding that white women and black men may have envied black women, White nonetheless views black women at the bottom of a malevolent system that disempowered all women, even those who were rich and white. She places slave women at the negative end of a continuum of power, on which white women also occupied positions of relative powerlessness and exploitation.[3]

Viewing matters from the other side of the class/race divide, Catherine Clinton, in *The Plantation Mistress*, also acknowledges a "parallel oppression of women, both white and black." But where Deborah White cites instances of aggression on the part of white women against black, Clinton stresses plantation mistresses' roles as nurturers, mediators, and nurses. Clinton speaks of a patriarchy, in which rich white men possessed slaves of both sexes as they possessed their own wives. In *The Plantation Mistress*, slaveowning women do not appear in hierarchical relationships with slave women. Rather than portray slaveowning women as rulers of their workers. Clinton sees white male masters as the font of all power and all evil.[4]

In *Within the Plantation Household*, Elizabeth Fox-Genovese departs from the view of black and white women's parallel exploitation that White and Clinton evoke. Stressing the spacial and emotional intimacy in which many slave and slaveholding women lived in plantation households, Fox-Genovese softens the domination of the master. She prefers the term "paternalism" to Clinton's "patriarchy," because paternalism carries an air of "legitimate domination," which was how slaveholding men viewed their role. (Let us not quibble about whether slaveowners should be allowed to chose the words we historians use to characterize them a century and a half later.)

Fox-Genovese stiffens the authority of slaveowning women over their female slaves, providing theoretical and empirical arguments for a somewhat ambiguous but clearly hierarchical relationship between women of different races and classes. Rather than see masters as the proximate wielders of power, Fox-Genovese shows that slaveholding women and slave women were cognizant of who held the power between them and who could inflict the greatest violence with impunity. To make her point, Fox-Genovese enumerates instances of violence and minimizes slaveholding women's abolitionist leanings. For her, slaveholding women who saw themselves as victims of the kind of adultery that the slave system allowed were simply mistaken.[5]

Clinton's more recent essays reveal the pathologies of planter families

---

3. Deborah Gray White, *Ar'n't I a Woman*, 15–17, 27–28, 58.
4. Catherine Clinton, *Plantation Mistress*, 6–15, 35, 222.
5. Elizabeth Fox-Genovese, *Within the Plantation Household*, 29–30, 34–35, 43–45, 63–64, 313–315.

in which rape and adultery distorted descent and parental attachment. While "Caught in the Web of the Big House" glimpses the ways in which owner-slave rape affected mistresses, the emphasis still falls mainly on the tragedy of the direct victim of assault: the slave woman. "Southern Dishonor," Clinton's spiked critique of both southern historiography and slavery's brutal system of reproduction, announces themes and works-in-progress in the study of sexuality and slavery. Martha Hodes's 1991 Princeton dissertation and Mary Frances Berry's 1991 presidential address to the Organization of American Historians further enrich the historical literature by revealing the complexities of southern sexuality.[6]

So far, this work, though intriguing, stops short of completing the investigation of the relationship between southern families, society, and history. If feminist history has taught us anything in the last two decades, it is that important private matters become important historical matters. The example of the South Carolina fire-eater, James Henry Hammond—whose emotional turmoil following his wife's deserting him when he took a second slave wife so incapacitated him psychologically that he missed an important secessionist meeting that would have bolstered his sagging political career—makes the point. Hammond's wife serves as a reminder that Gertrude Thomas's preoccupation—competition—needs to reenter the equation, or historians risk missing much of the psychodrama of southern history. Focusing on one part of the picture, even if more compatible with present-day understanding of relations of power, flattens out the inherent complexity of southern history. If historians do not acknowledge that wealthy white women saw themselves as victims, as the losers in a competition with women who though black and poor and powerless seemed somehow more attractive, we miss a vital dimension of southern history that helps explain the thorniness of women's contacts across the color line well into the twentieth century. We must acknowledge the existence of two ways of seeing, even while we keep our eyes on fundamental differentials of power.

What my approach means for southern history is a renunciation of a single "The South" way of thinking. For me there is seldom a "The South," for simple characterizations eliminate the reality of sharp conflicts over just about everything in southern culture, slavery most of all.

6. "Caught in the Web of the Big House: Women and Slavery," in *The Web of Southern Social Relations: Women, Family, and Education*, ed. Walter J. Fraser, Jr., R. Frank Saunders, Jr., and Jon L. Wakelyn, (Athens, Ga., 1985), 19–34: "'Southern Dishonor': Flesh, Blood, Race, and Bondage," in *In Joy and in Sorrow: Women, Family, and Marriage in the Victorian South, 1830–1900*, ed., Carol Bleser (New York, 1991), 52–68; Mary Frances Berry, "Judging Morality: Sexual Behavior and Legal Consequences in the Late Nineteenth-Century South," *Journal of American History* 78 (December 1991): 835–56; Martha Hodes, "Sex Across the Color Line" (Ph.D. diss., Princeton University, 1991); Eugene Genovese, "'Our Family, White and Black': Family and Household in the Southern Slaveholders' World View," in Bleser, ed., *In Joy and in Sorrow*, 69–87, grasps the reality of slaveholders' ideology of the family almost as though to substitute it for reality and without following its significance in family relations.

Saying that "The South" was proslavery (or, later, prosegregation) equates the region with its rulers and annihilates the position of at least one-third of its inhabitants. As a labor historian with a keen sense of the historical importance of all groups of people within a society (not simply the prestigious, published, and politically powerful) I insist on going beyond neglectful characterizations in the singular. Recognizing the complex and self-contradictory nature of southern society, I can rephrase my conclusions about the study of southern history succinctly: Southern history demands the recognition of complexity and contradiction, starting with family life, and therefore requires the use of plurals; and though southern history must take race very seriously, southern history must not stop with race.

FRANCES SMITH FOSTER

Resisting *Incidents*[†]

Particular communicative contexts seem inevitably to trigger resistance. When a writer or narrator is different in race, gender, or class from the implied or actual reader, questions about authority and authenticity multiply. As Susan Lanser points out in *The Narrative Act,* a writer's or a narrator's social identity is never totally irrelevant, but readers automatically assume that the "unmarked" narrator is a literate white male.[1] When the title page, the book jacket, or any other source marks one as not white, not a man, or not to the manor born, different sets of cultural assumptions "determined by the ideological system and the norms of social dominance in a given society" (Lanser, 166) come into play. When the topic or the general development of the text coincides thematically with the readers' assumptions about the writer's or narrator's social identity, status becomes particularly significant to the discursive context. "Social identity and textual behavior," Lanser concludes, "combine to provide the reader with a basis for determining the narrator's mimetic authority" (Lanser, 169).

Lanser uses gender as her primary focus, but her thesis applies as well to other writers whose race or class places them outside the courts of power and privilege. Any attempt by an individual who is not white, male, and at least middle class to be acknowledged as part of the literary or intellectual community is inevitably challenged, even by readers who share

---

[†] From *Harriet Jacobs and* Incidents in the Life of a Slave Girl: *New Critical Essays,* ed. Deborah M. Garfield and Rafia Zafar (New York: Cambridge UP, 1996) 57–75. Reprinted with the permission of Cambridge University Press. Page references to this Norton Critical Edition are given in brackets following Foster's original citations, with the exception of references to extratext material included in the Yellin edition.

1. Susan Lanser, *The Narrative Act: Point of View in Prose Fiction* (Princeton: Princeton University Press, 1981). Subsequent references are found in the text.

their racial, social, or gender status. When a readership is invited into communicative contexts with writers of a race, gender, or class that it assumes to be equal or inferior to its own, questions about authority and authenticity take on an intensity and texture that obscure other aspects of the discourse. Readers tend to assume that cultural landscapes not dominated by written texts are inferior and individuals native to such cultures can hardly be expected to represent the best thoughts of the best minds or to create things of beauty that are joys to behold. When, as they often do, such writers do not replicate that with which readers are already familiar, claims and challenges to authorial prerogatives and to the authenticity of their depictions may become contentious. More readers try to compete with the writers, to rearrange the writers' words, details, and intentions to make them more compatible with the readers' own experiences and expectations. Oppositional intensity varies by time, place, and circumstance, but African Americans inevitably encounter a significant number of obstinate readers. From the publication of *Poems on Various Subjects, Religious and Moral,* the earliest extant volume by an African American, to the present time, the mimetic details, social relevance, and political implications of their texts have been particularly challenged.

Although resistance may be absolutely the right way to read a particular text or a particular author, the fact that literary productions of African American writers, particularly of those who were or had been slaves, are habitually greeted with resistance is provoking and problematic. Consider the case of Phillis Wheatley, the author of the earliest extant volume of poetry by an African American. In order to convince readers to accept Wheatley as the author of *Poems on Various Subjects, Religious and Moral,* before the book was published (1773), it was deemed necessary to include various authenticating documents, including her picture, a biographical sketch from her master that explains how she came to acquire literacy, and an affidavit from eighteen of "the most respectable characters in Boston,"[2] who had examined her and determined that Wheatley was indeed capable of writing the poems.

Once her authorship was established, Wheatley became a celebrity, but the significance of her contributions, even her identification as a poet, were not unequivocally granted. Phillis Wheatley wrote *Poems on* <u>*Various Subjects, Religious and Moral*</u> (emphasis mine), but eighteenth-century readers, especially, were inclined to read her words as those of a former pagan who could testify to acquired piety but could contribute nothing original about theology or morality. Thomas Jefferson spoke for many when he stated, "Religion, indeed, has produced a Phyllis Whately [*sic*]; but it could not produce a poet." In order to bar Wheatley from poetic society, Jefferson had to ignore the consensus of Western aesthetics

---

2. Phillis Wheatley, *Poems on Various Subjects, Religious and Moral,* in *The Poems of Phillis Wheatley,* ed. Julian D. Mason, Jr. (Chapel Hill: University of North Carolina Press, 1989), 48. Subsequent references to Wheatley's poems and letters are from this source and noted in the text.

that *utile and dulce* were essential literary components and that *utile*, especially in the New England colonies, had always meant that the writings serve a religious and moral purpose. To demonstrate that religion may have inspired Wheatley to write but that her writing about religion precluded her acceptability as a poet, Jefferson defined not religion or morality but romantic love as the "peculiar oestrum of the poet." Romantic love, Jefferson then pontificated, could kindle the senses of blacks but not their imaginations.[3]

Whether Phillis Wheatley was surprised by her readers' reactions is a matter of conjecture, but that misreadings and misinterpretations of her work and worth continue to this day should shock more people than it does. Today, Phillis Wheatley is lauded as the first African American and the second woman in colonial America to publish a volume of poetry. Her works are included in virtually every anthology that purports to be "inclusive." Her debts to Greek and Roman mythology, to evangelical Methodist rhetoric, and to neoclassicism are frequently cited as evidence that, when given the opportunity, she—and by implication other blacks—could and did learn as well as or better than whites. But until recently, most readers considered her to be of "the mockingbird school," able to imitate but not to interpret or debate. Until recently, few scholars would entertain the notion that Phillis Wheatley made original contributions to eighteenth-century theology, to the rhetoric of the U.S. Revolution, and to the discourse on race and gender.

The standard interpretation of "On Being Brought from Africa to America," the most anthologized of Phillis Wheatley's poems, demonstrates this. The poem is an eight-line monologue addressed to Christians by an African convert. It has three distinct parts with three increasingly authoritative tones. The poem begins as a hymn of gratitude for the divine mercy that brought the speaker from a "benighted land" to one where she learned to seek and to know spiritual redemption. In line five the narrator switches from grateful testimony and reproves those who believe that the "sable" skins of Africans signify diabolical natures. The last two lines are didactic and ominous: "Remember, *Christians, Negroes*, black as *Cain*, / May be refin'd, and join th' angelic train" (emphasis hers). In this poem, a newly enlightened member does not simply recite catechism but argues theology and warns the entire congregation against presumptions of exclusivity by declaring that the gift of salvation makes all converts joint heirs in Christ. Despite, or perhaps because of, the simple diction and the authority manifest in the tonal changes, readers have historically misinterpreted the text. They have emphasized the first lines and read the poem as Wheatley's disavowal of her African heritage and as evidence of her "pious sentimentalizing about Truth, Salvation, Mercy, and Goodness"[4]

---

3. Thomas Jefferson, *The Writings of Thomas Jefferson*, ed. Albert Ellery Bergh (Washington, D.C., 1907), Vol. 2, 196; quoted in Mason, *The Poems of Phillis Wheatley*, 30, n. 10.
4. Richard Barksdale and Keneth Kinnamon, *Black American Writers* (New York: Macmillan, 1972), 39–40.

while ignoring the changes in tone and focus that begin with line five and saying nothing of the audacity of the last two lines, which claim divine authority to testify for racial equality. Although summaries or interpretations that take into account only part of the text subvert literary convention and violate basic tenets of exposition, it seems easier for readers to ignore half of a poem than to acknowledge that an African slave girl barely out of her teens would be audacious enough not only to write poetry, but also to use it to instruct and to chastise her readers.

For African American women writers, the resistance to the authority of blacks or of slaves was compounded by gender prejudices. Even if the authorship were acknowledged and their accounts were verified, their writings were still perceived through a veil of sexism that obscured their individuality and revealed only the shadowy contours their readers expected to see. As African American women proved their imaginativeness with romantic prose and poetry and their political acumen with logical and incisive analyses, nineteenth-century audiences struggled desperately against the belief that black women could be intelligent and eloquent. The nineteenth-century author and orator Frances Ellen Watkins Harper provides another example of the lengths to which some audiences would go to deny what they saw and heard. By all accounts she was very ladylike in appearance and few contemporary reporters failed to note her "slender and graceful" form and her "soft musical voice" when recounting her public presentations. Harper's writings have often been summarized as sentimental, moral, and chaste. Some of them were. But Frances Harper was also a militant evangelist for equality. She worked with the Underground Railroad, staged sit-ins on public transportation, and supported John Brown's Harper's Ferry attack. During Reconstruction, Frances Harper went around the South lecturing on political and social change. Hers was not a pitiful plea for acceptance. "We are all bound up together in one great bundle of humanity, and society cannot trample on the weakest and feeblest of its members without receiving the curse in its own soul," she argued. Her writings and her speeches explained why the fate of the country rested in its solution to the economic problems of poor whites and blacks, the suffrage demands of women of all races, and a variety of other major issues. For a black woman to speak publicly and aggressively on political, economic, and social issues was so alien to traditional expectation that many simply could not believe their ears or eyes. In a letter to a friend, Harper writes, "I don't know but that you would laugh if you were to hear some of the remarks which my lectures call forth: 'She is a man,' again, 'She is not colored, she is painted.'"[5]

5. Frances E. W. Harper, "Almost Constantly Either Traveling or Speaking," in *A Brighter Coming Day: A Frances Ellen Watkins Harper Reader*, ed. Frances Smith Foster (New York: Feminist Press, 1990), 126–7.

Other African Americans learned from the experiences of writers such as Wheatley and Harper. African Americans who wrote for publication in the eighteenth and nineteenth centuries knew as well as, if not better than, other writers that successful communication required appropriate attention to content and context. They knew that some readers would be unable or unwilling to concede that they legitimately could or would act, think, and write in ways contrary to the ideas with which those readers approach that text. African Americans quickly understood that in order to employ the power of the pen, they had not only to seize it but to wield it with courage, skill, and cunning. Unable to trust their readers to respond to their texts as peers, they developed literary strategies to compensate.

It is beyond the scope of this paper to entertain all the manifestations of resistance or to speculate about their motivations. This discussion will focus upon examples of reader and writer resistance as demonstrated in Harriet Jacobs's *Linda; Or, Incidents in the Life of a Slave Girl*. The case of this author and this text has its own unique aspects, but it is a good representation of the more general situation. Resistance to Jacobs's *Incidents*, like that to Wheatley's *Poems on Various Subjects*, to Harper's lectures, and to other African American writers, stems in large measure not from the text or its author's manifest ability but from the readers' response to both. Resistance to *Incidents* is rooted in a usually unspoken, perhaps unconscious, recognition that the book exposes as fabrications many of the truths which we hold to be self-evident and that the writer expects us to reconsider both the grounds for our perceptions of reality and the limitations of our abilities to accept competing versions.

Resistance characterized both Jacobs's life and the genesis and the renaissance of her autobiography. Both her biographers and her autobiography demonstrate that she was born into a family that refused to accept others' definitions of who they were and how they ought to live. Jacobs's self-esteem was strong enough that she could reject her master's edict that she consider herself his property and submit to his will in both thought and deed. When her resources dwindled and the confrontations seemed unending, she chose confinement in a nine-by-seven-foot attic for more than six years rather than live as her master commanded her. Eventually she did flee to the North. Harriet Jacobs was regularly asked to contribute her story to the antislavery effort, but she withstood those pleas for almost twelve years before she agreed to testify. It was only after the Compromise of 1850 created the Fugitive Slave Law, which made it possible for slave owners to claim individuals as their private property even in states where slavery was illegal, that Jacobs agreed to publicize some of her most personal experiences.

Hers was a particularly difficult decision because Harriet Jacobs valued her privacy and believed that "no one had a right to question" her.[6] She

---

6. Letter from Harriet Jacobs to Amy Post in 1852. Quoted in *Incidents in the Life of a Slave Girl: Written by Herself*, ed. Jean Fagan Yellin (Cambridge, MA: Harvard University Press, 1987),

was proud of her triumphs and her achievements, but she did not consider hers to be "the life of a Heroine with no degradation associated with it" (Jacobs, 232). Although she could justify her actions in her own mind, Jacobs was reluctant to explain them to strangers and unwilling to accept their pity or censure. When she finally decided to reveal some of her personal history, however, Jacobs resolved to "give a true and just account . . . in a Christian spirit" (Jacobs, 242), but not to pander to her audience. As a former slave, she knew that stereotypes about people of her race and class encouraged her audience to expect a certain kind of testimony, yet Jacobs refused to divulge the kinds of things that she thought "the world might believe that a Slave Woman was too willing to pour out" (Jacobs, 242). She decided to use her position as one of a very few antislavery writers who could relate from personal experience incidents in the life of a slave girl to introduce a different perspective on slavery and slave women. Like other antislavery writers, she did not deny the prevalence of rape and seduction. In fact, her text appears to be unprecedented in its use of sexual liaisons and misadventures as a prime example of the perils of slave womanhood. But hers was a story of a slave woman who refused to be victimized. Harriet Jacobs used her own experiences to create a book that would correct and enlist support against prevailing social myths and political ideologies.

Another reason for her original resistance to writing her narrative was that Harriet Jacobs knew that writing a well-crafted autobiography required more time and talent than she had. During an era in which the majority of Americans could barely write their names, Jacobs enjoyed reading, corresponding, and conversing with a coterie of intellectuals, artists, and social activists, and she had enough literary sophistication to know that literacy was but one requirement for authorship. She was well acquainted with many of the attitudes and assumptions of the Anglo-American literary establishment, for not only did she read widely, but she lived in the household of Nathaniel Willis; the editor and writer whose home was a rendezvous for New York literati. She knew also the conventions of abolitionist and African American literature. Jacobs had worked for a year in her brother's Rochester antislavery reading room. Since it was located over the offices of Frederick Douglass, she may have heard the history of the resistance that Douglass had encountered; especially from his most ardent abolitionist friends, when he decided to tell his story his way. Because Jacobs was a live-in domestic worker, stealing the time and marshalling the energy to develop her own writing skills to the level that she judged adequate for her intentions were more complicated for her than for many others. As a fugitive slave, she also knew that friends or employers, who were willing to adhere to the "Don't ask, don't tell" philosophy in her case, might not be supportive if she went public

p. 232. Unless otherwise noted, all quotations from Jacobs's letters and from her book are from this source and noted in the text.

about her status. And if Jacobs had not known about professional jealousy and competition, she soon learned that she had to fight to protect her story and to establish her right to determine what should be told and how to tell it. In the process of getting her story told, she had to defy such opportunists as Harriet Beecher Stowe, who wanted to appropriate her narrative in order to enhance Stowe's own authority.

Harriet Jacobs had ample reason to know the perils that African American writers, especially women, faced, and it would have been very strange indeed had she not carefully considered the rhetorical and narrative strategies that they had used as she outlined her own story. When she stated in the preface that "I want to add my testimony to that of abler pens to convince the people of the Free States what Slavery really is" (Jacobs, 1–2) [5], the words "convince" and "really" were undoubtedly chosen with care. She knew she could not trust her readers to understand or to accept what she would relate. She also knew that there was no literary model to fit her task and her temperament. Nonetheless, Harriet Jacobs chose to record her history as she had lived it, to confront her readers with an alternative truth, and to demand that they not only acknowledge it but act upon it. To that end, Harriet Jacobs created a new literary form, one that challenged her audiences' social and aesthetic assumptions even as it delighted and reaffirmed them.

Jacob's narrative records the struggle of a young girl to resist the sexual advances of a man who was thirty-five years older, better educated, and socially superior. Obviously its story of a young virgin's attempts to defend her chastity against the wiles and assaults of an older, more experienced, and socially privileged male makes it clear kin to Fielding's *Pamela* and other such seduction stories. However, Linda never confuses a threatened loss of chastity with a loss of self-worth or reason for living. Harriet Jacobs colors the plot even further by painting the man—Flint—as driven by more than lust or moral turpitude and the girl—Linda—as resisting from motives only partially shaded by fear of social censure or pregnancy. Perhaps she had learned from fireside stories of Brer Rabbit or from observations within the slave quarters, perhaps it was just common sense, but Linda understood that physical superiority or social status is not necessarily the deciding factor in any contest.

With *Incidents in the Life of a Slave Girl* Harriet Jacobs reconstructs the standard seduction pattern of urbane seducer versus naive maiden. Jacobs expands the peasant or proletariat categories to include the slaves in the United States. Moreover, she makes it clear that the impoverished are not the only oppressed and that slaves are not the only victims. Mrs. Flint is driven to distraction by her husband's infidelity, and the narrator informs us that the seventh is not the only commandment violated in such situations, that young white boys follow the grown men's examples, and so do some white women. Jacobs asserts that slave girls are not the only ones to be prematurely robbed of their innocence. The daughters of slaveholders, she warns, overhear the quarrels between their parents, learn about sexual oppression from slave girls, and sometimes "exercise the same authority over the men slaves" (Jacobs, 52) [45]. While she writes to encourage Northern women to resist slavery, Harriet Jacobs does not allow them to distance themselves too thoroughly. She reminds her readers that they sometimes marry and ofttimes are kin to slaveholders. She explains how the Fugitive Slave Law represents an attack upon the freedom of Northerners. And in noting that Linda technically belonged to Dr. Flint's daughter, who was not able either as a child or as an adult to claim or to direct her inheritance, Jacobs suggests a larger definition of "slave girl." Linda is the heroine who struggles against evil, but Harriet Jacobs identifies other women and men, white and black, Northern and Southern, who are similarly victimized or are potential victims.

Once Harriet Jacobs had completed the narrative of her life in bondage and her struggle for freedom, she spent several years trying to find a publisher. Although publishers, especially those of antislavery leanings, were generally eager to print slave narratives, Jacobs's account was so original and so striking that they required more than the usual endorsements by others. Two prominent friends, one a white woman and the other a black man, had written ten letters of recommendation to be published along with Jacobs's text. But as Jacobs reported in a letter to a friend, the publishers wanted "a Satellite of so great magnitude" as Harriet Beecher Stowe, Nathaniel Willis, or Lydia Maria Child before they would issue her account (Yellin, xxii). With the help of William C. Nell, another African American writer and activist, Jacobs contacted Lydia Maria Child, who agreed to serve as her editor. With Child's support, the firm of Thayer and Eldridge contracted to print two thousand copies. In 1861, nearly a decade after she had decided to write the book, Harriet Jacobs's narrative was finally published. It appeared as the anonymous testimony of "A Slave Girl: Written by Herself." Child was identified as its editor. The publication immediately stirred controversies that have waxed and waned but continue to this day. Despite the testimonies of Jacobs's contemporaries and the meticulous evidence of present-day scholars, a good many readers continue to resist identifying the book as an autobiography by a former slave woman named Harriet Jacobs.

Some antebellum reader caution is understandable. Slave narratives were written to help destroy an institution, swaddled in myth and mystery, and deeply rooted in U.S. culture. Slave narrators, like other purposeful writers, were particularly careful to select incidents and language for maximum persuasive value. Readers of such texts had the privilege and probably the obligation to consider carefully the arguments and the motivations of those whom they read. Especially when faced with direct statements of intention, readers, then as now, should not be expected to squelch their inclinations to contest the validity or the relevance of surprising revelations. Not surprisingly, even the most sympathetic readers wanted then, as they do now, to have certain expectations met and some assumptions confirmed. Moreover, in the mid-1850s, resistance to women writers was decreasing but still pervasive, and Harriet Jacobs presented more than the usual challenge to literary tradition. She was one of those strange, modern, and frightening women who dared to take pen to paper about politics and moral values, to urge resistance to laws and social mores. And, finally, questions of authority and authenticity were not then, as they are not now, intrinsically inappropriate or unimportant to the study of any literature and especially not to the study of autobiographical writings. Such scholars as Albert E. Stone have demonstrated that autobiography is a "mode of storytelling" and that any given autobiography is "simultaneously historical record and literary artifact, psychological case history and spiritual confession, didactic essay and ideological testament."[7]

The modifications in genre that Jacobs made probably did not bother antebellum readers as much as they seem to bother twentieth-century ones, but they certainly must have noticed them. Since she was obviously not an educated white male, the resistance that other writers routinely inspire was certainly augmented by her daring to tamper with traditional literary forms. Jacobs obviously borrowed from the novel of seduction, the criminal confessional, the American jeremiad, the slave narrative, and other popular forms. The melodramatic and feminist elements in *Incidents in the Life of a Slave Girl* were fairly common in antislavery novels. Harriet Beecher Stowe's *Uncle Tom's Cabin* was the most famous, but neither the first nor the last to enlist melodrama in the antislavery cause. Harriet Jacobs began her book at about the same time that William Wells Brown was writing *Clotel* and Harriet E. Wilson was writing *Our Nig*, but by the time *Incidents* was published in 1861, these two writers and others had already introduced the heroic African American woman protagonist. Brown had already demonstrated that an African American female slave might be morally superior to the white man who claimed both social superiority and physical ownership. But Harriet Jacobs claimed more social prestige than did Harriet E. Wilson and Linda is less compromising or compromised than Clotel. Jacobs wrote not to secure money to save her sickly son but to convince readers to heal their ailing society. Dr. Flint's offer of a cottage in the woods and an almost-marriage is comparable to what Brown's heroine accepts, but Linda is not in the least tempted, and the relationship between Linda and Congressman Sands may be read as a deliberately empowered version of the Clotel and Horatio affair. The

7. Albert E. Stone, "Introduction: American Autobiographies as Individual Stories and Cultural Narratives," in *The American Autobiography: A Collection of Critical Essays*, ed. Albert E. Stone (Englewood Cliffs, NJ: Prentice Hall, 1981), 1–2.

struggle between Linda and the father of her children, like that between her and Dr. Flint, is a true contest. Sands, like Flint, had "power and law on his side," but, Linda says, "I had a determined will. There is might in each (Jacobs, 85) [70].

The changes that Harriet Jacobs wrought in the slave narrative genre were even more remarkable. When she agreed to write her personal narrative, Jacobs set out to wrestle with the "serpent of Slavery" and to expose and detoxify its "many and poisonous fangs" (Jacobs, 62) [53]. To accomplish this, she incorporated the basic elements of the slave narrative genre, but modified them to fit the experiences of those who did not resist by fleeing the site of conflict. The antebellum slave narrative featured a protagonist best described as a heroic male fugitive. The usual pattern of the narrative was to demonstrate examples of the cruelty and degradation inherent in the institution of slavery, then to chronicle an individual's discovery that the concept and the condition of slavery were neither inevitable or irrevocable. Following that revelation, the typical slave narrator secretly plotted his escape and, at the opportune time, struck out alone but resolved to follow the North Star to freedom. Slave narratives generally ended when, upon arrival in the free territory, the former slave assumed a new name, obtained a job, married, and began a new happy-ever-after life.

In contrast, Jacobs's female fugitive refuses to abandon her loved ones and spends the first several years of her escape hiding in places provided by family and friends. When her grandmother accidently jeopardizes the security of her retreat, Linda has to fleet to the North. Even then she does not run alone. Instead, she leaves the South on a ship in the company of another fugitive woman, her friend Fanny. Jacobs does not report a name change, and Linda does not marry. And although she does set about the task of creating a new life for herself and for her children, that task is complicated by failing health and persistent pursuit from those who claim her as their property. Jacobs's narrative makes it clear that racial discrimination and the Fugitive Slave Law ensured that the North was not the Promised Land. The passages in which Jacobs chronicles the abuses of slaves are common to antebellum slave narratives, but her personal testimony of will power and peer protection proving stronger than physical might and legal right are unique. She weaves incidents that she experienced or witnessed into a narrative that was common to the "two millions of women at the South, still in bondage, suffering what [she] suffered, and most of them far worse" (Jacobs, 1) [5].

In appropriating the elements of various genres into one more suitable for her intents, Harriet Jacobs was following a convention that African American writers had been using for at least a century before her, and it was this tradition of improvisation and invention that also provided her with the techniques that she could adapt to meet her particular circumstances. Some of these African American rhetorical devices have been described quite aptly by others as "sass,"[8] "signifying,"[9] or "discourse of distrust."[1] I say more about the discourse of distrust later; the focus of this discussion is upon specific ways in which *Incidents* resists and is resisted. Like flies or mosquitoes, many of these incidents of resistance would be obvious but insignificant were they not so numerous, did they not unexpectedly appear in inappropriate places, and did their persistent buzzing not distract our attention from more productive occupations.

One example that gains importance when considered in relation to myriad other small instances is the way in which twentieth-century readers have insisted upon renaming Jacobs's book. In 1861 the work was published and reviewed as *Linda: Or, Incidents in the Life of a Slave Girl* and it was as "Linda" that Harriet Jacobs came to be known by the reading public. She signed autographs, letters, and other publications with that name. Today, however, readers know the text only by its subtitle, *Incidents in the Life of a Slave Girl*, and it is by its subtitle that the book is now reprinted, discussed, and claimed as "a classic slave narrative," "one of the major autobiographies in the Afro-American tradition," or simply as a "classic" of African American literature.[2] Although not unprecedented nor without merit, this renaming is a little odd. Referring to the book as *Incidents in the Life of a Slave Girl* subordinates the individual protagonist to the general type, as its author intended. Rather than use her experiences as representative of others, however, too many scholars and critics have used the experiences of others to invalidate those that Jacobs recounted. Their interest revolves almost exclusively around Harriet Jacobs as both author and subject and around how her victories and her values contrast with prevailing theories and opinions of slave life. Since the author/narrator is of such interest, it is particularly noteworthy that the work is not known by the narrator's name and that Jacobs's authorship is continually questioned. To cite racial prejudice would be an inadequate explanation for this because slave narratives do tend to be known by the names of their authors. Nor is gender bias a satisfactory conclusion, for

---

8. Joanne M. Braxton defines "sass" as "a mode of verbal discourse and as a weapon of self defense." Sass and "the outraged mother" are key to her discussion of *Incidents*. Joanne M. Braxton, *Black Women Writing Autobiography: A Tradition within a Tradition* (Philadelphia: Temple University Press, 1989), 10.

9. The most famous discussion of "signifying" is from that of Henry Louis Gates, Jr., in *The Signifying Monkey: A Theory of Afro-American Literary Criticism* (New York: Oxford University Press, 1988). Gates is building upon the work of several people, but two are particularly helpful: Claudia Mitchell-Kernan, "Signifying as a Form of Verbal Art" in *Mother Wit from the Laughing Barrel: Readings in the Interpretation of Afro-American Folklore*, ed. Alan Dundes (Englewood Cliffs, NJ: Prentice Hall, 1973), 310–28, and Geneva Smitherman, *Talkin and Testifyin: The Language of Black America* (Boston: Houghton Mifflin, 1977).

1. Robert B. Stepto, "Distrust of the Reader in Afro-American Narratives," in *Reconstructing American Literary History*, ed. Sacvan Bercovitch (Cambridge, MA: Harvard University Press, 1986), 305. Subsequent references are from this source and found in the text.

2. Here I am quoting from Henry Louis Gates, Jr., *The Classic Slave Narratives* (New York: New American Library, 1987), xvi. I, too, find it easier to go along with the tide than to swim against it. In this discussion, I too will refer to the text as "*Incidents in the Life of a Slave Girl.*"

the formal and functional similarities of Jacobs's narrative to those of nineteenth-century sentimental fiction is consistently mentioned. Still, unlike *Pamela, Clotel, Ramona,* and others, *"Linda"* is not the name by which Jacobs's tale is known. Harriet Stowe's book is linked in content and context to Harriet Jacobs's and has undergone a similar transformation. Despite the fact that Eliza's escape, Eva's death, and Topsy's devilment all eclipse Uncle Tom's crucifixion, we do not normally refer to Stowe's work by its more appropriate subtitle, *Life Among the Lowly.* We accept *Uncle Tom's Cabin.*

Complicating Jacobs's situation is the fact that even while the narrative no longer carries the title "Linda" and while the authenticity of Jacobs's recitations is questioned, it is with Linda or Harriet that readers are most concerned. Given the extraordinary character of most slave narrators and the uniqueness of many of the incidents they relate, one is not overly surprised when their narratives are treated as documentaries and their self-depictions are taken as fact. But even in the case of one so unique as Frederick Douglass, readers tend to accept their personal narratives as representative of at least one particular kind or group of slaves. In the *Narrative of the Life of Frederick Douglass, an American Slave,* the climactic scene is one in which the slave boy physically resists punishment by his white boss. Douglass introduces the fight between him and Covey as if it were representative by saying, "You have seen how a man was made a slave; you shall see how a slave was made a man."[3] Readers have accepted this unusual rite of passage as archetypal even though almost no other narrator admits to such an experience. Douglass's narrative is considered a "master narrative," a model against which all others should be measured, while in fact, though not unheard of, scenes of physical combat between blacks and whites are rare in the genre.[4] With Harriet Jacobs, however, the concerns and consensus are different. Since it is a common belief that slave women were routinely raped and that slaves generally did not know their ancestry or other details of their personal histories, Jacobs's family pride and self-confidence are considered aberrations. Moreover, Harriet Jacobs has more than once been accused of having omitted or distorted details of her own life in order to enhance her personal reputation or to achieve artistic effect. Historian Elizabeth Fox-Genovese, for example, has declared that Jacobs's "pivotal authentication of self probably rested upon a great factual lie, for it stretches the limits of all credibility that Linda Brent actually eluded her master's sexual advances."[5]

---

3. *Narrative of the Life of Frederick Douglass, an American Slave* (1845; rpt. New York: Doubleday, 1963), 68.
4. Another example is that of Elizabeth Keckley in *Behind the Scenes* (1867; rpt., New York: Oxford University Press, 1988), whose graphic accounts of a series of incidents in which she physically resisted beatings despite the inherent sensationalism of the gender differences has excited virtually no comment.
5. *Within the Plantation Household* (Chapel Hill: University of North Carolina Press, 1988), 392.

Another and more worrisome form of resistance has been the skepticism and concern about authorship that has become more pronounced in the twentieth century. That the book was first published anonymously and its editor was herself a prominent figure would provide some excuse were it not in such contrast to the reception of other anonymously published books, including Richard Hildreth's *Archy Moore; or The White Slave*, Mattie Griffiths's *Autobiography of a Female Slave*, and James Weldon Johnson's *Autobiography of an Ex-Colored Man*. That she consulted with and sometimes accepted the advice of her editor should pose no more serious concerns about authorship for Jacobs's text than it does for D. H. Lawrence's *Sons and Lovers*, certain poems signed by T. S. Eliot, or virtually any book authored by Thomas Wolfe.[6] Neither the decision to publish the book anonymously, the reputation of Lydia Maria Child, nor the generic modifications and innovations such as changing names and creating dialogue in an autobiography account sufficiently for the resistance that *Incidents* continues to encounter.

Arguments presented in recent studies of women's and of African American narrative strategies help clarify the reasons for such reader resistance while offering insight into specific techniques by which writers have combated it. Jeanne Kammer's discussion of the diaphoric imagination and the aesthetic of silence suggests two.[7] Like many of the women poets that Kammer discusses, Jacobs adopts an oratorical model and "depends on the capacity of the voice, not only to invest the words with a persuasive *timbre*, but to sustain the performance over a long enough time to move the listener to the desired conclusions" (Kammer, 159). Harriet Jacobs was writing prose of fact rather than poetry; therefore, she could substitute incidents for images, but she too produces "new meaning by the juxtaposition alone of two (or more) images, each term concrete, their joining unexplained" (Kammer, 157). She too elevates the speaker into a focus of interest in the text. She presents that speaker as "the only available guide through its ambiguities, and the source of its human appeal" (Kammer, 159).

Jacobs's text also provides an opportunity for "the broader look at the historical and literary contexts" that Robyn R. Warhol intends her discussion of the "engaging narrator" to stimulate.[8] Warhol's examination is limited to a pattern of narrative intervention used by three novelists of Ja-

---

6. Scholars have long acknowledged that these writers, like many others, relied heavily upon the advice and sometimes the revisions of their friends and editors. This has not been a major impediment to their reputations as writers or to the acceptance of their work as serious contributions.

7. Jeanne Kammer, "The Art of Silence and the Forms of Women's Poetry," in *Shakespeare's Sisters: Feminist Essays on Women Poets*, ed. Sandra M. Gilbert and Susan Gubar (Bloomington: Indiana University Press, 1979), 153–164. Subsequent references are from this edition and found in the text.

8. Robyn R. Warhol, "Towards a Theory of the Engaging Narrator: Earnest Interventions in Gaskell, Stowe, and Eliot," *PMLA* 101:5 (October 1988): 811–17. Subsequent references are in the text.

cobs's time, but its similarities to this nonfiction text are several and significant. Like Stowe, Gaskell, and Eliot, Jacobs wrote "to inspire belief in the situations their [texts] describe" and "to move actual readers to sympathize with real-life slaves, workers, or ordinary middle-class people" (Warhol, 811). Each writer uses her narrator as a "surrogate" working "to engage 'you' through the substance and, failing that, the stance of their narrative interventions and addresses to 'you' " (Warhol, 813). Such an "engaging narrator" intrudes into the text, and although neither she nor her reader is a participant in the narrative itself, the narrator engages the reader in dialogue and sometimes implies "imperfections in the narratee's ability to comprehend, or sympathize with, the contents of the text, even while expressing confidence that the narratee will rise to the challenge" (Warhol, 814).

Both Kammer and Warhol focus their discussions on texts by white women, but they agree that diaphor, oratory, and narrative engagement are employed, with some variation, by other writers. Race and class are two very salient variables for Harriet Jacobs. That she was African American and a former slave was vital to her message and to her mission. Yet, in emphasizing both of these factors, she was stirring up attitudes that she preferred to ignore. Like other African Americans and former slaves, Harriet Jacobs did not subscribe to the racial and literary stereotypes that formed the collective consciousness of her white readers. There may be exceptions that prove the rule but, as Raymond Hedin explains, "Black writers have never relished the need to take into account the racial assumptions of white readers, but their minority status and their unavoidable awareness of those assumptions have made it all but inevitable that they do so. The notion of black inferiority has become the 'countertext' of black writing."[9] "One constant among the variables," Hedin notes, is "a distinctive continuing tradition of narrative strategy deriving from black writers' continuing awareness that a significant part of their audience, whatever its proportions— or at the very least a significant part of the larger culture they find themselves in—clings to reservations about the full humanity of blacks" (Hedin, 36). The result is "an implicitly argumentative tradition" that manifests in the fact that African American writers "felt [an often vehement] need to confront and alter the white reader's possible racial biases" (Hedin, 37).

Hedin's "implicitly argumentative tradition" is quite similar to what Robert B. Stepto calls a "discourse of distrust," for both approaches are derived from the same speech acts regularly used by blacks in conversation with whites. In a discourse of distrust, Stepto tells us, "distrust is not so much a subject as a basis for specific narrative plottings and

---

9. Raymond Hedin, "The Structuring of Emotion in Black American Fiction," *Novel* 10 (Fall 1982): 36. Subsequent references to Hedin's argument are from this source and noted in the text.

rhetorical strategies . . . the texts are fully 'about' the communicative prospects of Afro-Americans writing for American readers, black and white, given the race rituals which color reading and/or listening" (Stepto, 305). Such writers often try to initiate "creative communication" by getting readers "told" or "told off" in such a way that they do not stop reading but do begin to "hear" the writer. In Jacobs's text the telling off begins with the title and the prefatory material. That aspect of "authority," with its implicit claims to accuracy and reliability, is then supplemented by the characterizations and the reconstructed relations among the characters.

The spines of the original editions of Harriet Jacobs's book are imprinted only with the word "Linda." The title pages carry only the subtitle, *Incidents in the Life of a Slave Girl: Written by Herself.*[1] Together the title and subtitle offer a balance of the exemplar and the example. Without the proper name, the subtitle emphasizes the generic and general over the personal and individual. The subtitle in concert with the title also challenges more explicitly the usual hierarchy of race, class, and gender. "Written by Herself" invests authority in the author/narrator's participant/observer status while simultaneously subordinating that of the readers. *Incidents in the Life* also implies that the narrator is not simply reporting her life history, but she is selecting from a multitude of possibilities those events that she chooses to share. *A Slave Girl* establishes this narrative as one common to or representative of a class. "Girl" is a term rarely applied to slaves in literature; thus, it disrupts the expected discourse by resisting more common epithets such as "pickaninny" or "young slave." There may even be a subtle suggestion about the intelligence of African Americans, since there were even fewer girls than there were women being published at that time. But with "Linda," the subtitle more readily establishes this as a female slave's narrative whose authority is not easily disputed since it is *her* life of which she writes. The unnamed author writes as a mediator, a first-person narrator now more experienced but still sympathetic, who looks back upon her girlhood and selects those experiences that she deems most appropriate for her audience and her literary intentions. Reading the words "Written by Herself" that follow the subtitle and the words "Published for the author" that come at the bottom of that page, a reader confronts not only the exercise of literary prerogative, of claiming authorial responsibility for the text's selection and arrangement, but also an assumption of self-worth, of meaning and interest in her personal experiences that exceed the specific or personal.

---

1. Here I am assuming that if the presentation of the book was not orchestrated by Jacobs, it certainly met her approval. Although it is possible that the cover and the title page were her publisher's or her editor's design, Jean Fagan Yellin's documentation of the relationship between Jacobs and Child suggests that Jacobs was actively concerned with every aspect of the production of her text. Moreover, since the original publisher went bankrupt and Jacobs purchased the plates, she had the opportunity to change the design had it been contrary to her intentions.

The title page carries two epigrams that are compelling when read in light of what Karlyn Kohrs Campbell has termed "'feminine' rhetoric."[2] Such writing, Campbell asserts, is

> usually grounded in personal experience. In most instances, personal experience is tested against the pronouncements of male authorities (who can be used for making accusations and indictments that would be impermissible from a woman) . . . [It] may appeal to biblical authority . . . The tone tends to be personal and somewhat tentative, rather than objective or authoritative . . . tends to plead, to appeal to the sentiments of the audience, to "court" the audience by being "seductive." . . . [to invite] female audiences to act, to draw their own conclusions and make their own decisions, in contrast to a traditionally "Masculine" style that approaches the audience as inferiors to be told what is right or to be led.

What Campbell terms "feminine rhetoric" is comparable to the "discourse of distrust" and certain other rhetorical strategies developed by African Americans. It too strives to thwart the resisting reader's urge to compete with the author for authority and to enlist the reader instead as a collaborator. But for Jacobs, as for other African Americans, not all the strategies of "feminine rhetoric" would work for her purposes. Though she was a woman writing primarily to other women, she was also a black woman writing to white women. Racism exacerbates distrust. Racial stereotypes would make certain conventions, such as the seductive speaker, the tentative tone, and the laissez-faire lecturer, work against her. But the use of quoted authority to state the more accusatory or unflattering conclusions had great potential. And, those "feminine" literary conventions that Jacobs does adopt are adapted to project images more in line with her purposes as a writer and her status as a black woman.

Consider, for example, the ways in which Jacobs employs verification, the process of using quotations from others to state the more accusatory or unflattering conclusions. As Campbell notes, women writers frequently used references from scripture to validate their claims and they often cited the words of others, especially the pronouncements of men, to state directly the accusations or indictments that the women writers were implying Jacobs includes two quotations on her title page. The first declares that "Northerners know nothing at all about SLAVERY . . . They have no conception of the depth of *degradation* involved . . . if they had, they would never cease their efforts until so horrible a system was overthrown."[3] This quotation is

---

2. Karlyn Kohrs Campbell, "Style and Content in the Rhetoric of Early Afro-American Feminists," *Quarterly Journal of Speech* 72 (1986): 434–45. Subsequent references are from this source and found in the text.
3. I am grateful to Elizabeth Spelman for recognizing this quotation as having been published by Angelina Grimké. While it may correct my earlier theory that Jacobs was quoting herself, the fact that I originally read it that way supports the overall concept. Attributing the quote to an

unmistakably patronizing if not actually accusatory or indicting. However, Harriet Jacobs does not attribute these words to a man, but cites, instead, an anonymous "woman of North Carolina." Sophisticated readers of abolitionist literature would recognize these words as those quoted by Angelina E. Grimké in her *Appeal to the Christian Women of the South* in 1836. Such a scholarly reference would enhance the author's claim to learnedness. But in 1861, it is doubtful that many readers would have recognized the source of this quote. Jacobs's decision not to identify the speaker with any more accuracy than that of gender and geography allows a more powerful use of verification even as it demonstrates elements of "sass" and "signifying." Given the assumed inferiority of blacks to whites, this modification would be acceptable to most of her readers. They would assume that a black woman's appeal to authority by citing a white woman was comparable to a white woman's seeking verification from a white man and, given the racism of that time, they would undoubtedly assume that the anonymous woman was in fact white. But, the woman's race is not stated, and although there are at least two Southern white women in *Incidents* who surreptitiously work against slavery, none is as outspokenly antislavery as the black women in Jacobs's narrative or the Northern white women who wrote the authenticating statements that frame Jacobs's narrative. The only women from North Carolina in Harriet Jacobs's text who exhibit the spirit and audacity of the woman quoted on her title page are black. Since Harriet Jacobs was a "woman of North Carolina" and her book is designed to effect the kind of awareness and action referred to in the quotation, it is quite likely that readers, especially those who were African American, might assume that Jacobs is quoting another slave woman or herself. Such a reading would be subtly empowering.

Jacobs's second quotation is Biblical. It too functions as verification, to increase her authority. The words are those of Isaiah 32:6: "Rise up, ye women that are at ease! Hear my voice, ye careless daughters! Give ear unto my speech." The relationship between this command and the theme of *Incidents* is fairly obvious. But the quotation does more than refer to a precedent for women becoming politically active. This quotation comes from the section of Isaiah that warns directly against alliances with Egypt, a word synonymous in the antebellum United States with "slavery." And in this chapter, Isaiah's prophecy is actually a warning. The women "that are at ease," the "careless daughters" who fail to rise up and support the rights of the poor and the oppressed, will find themselves enslaved. Again, Jacobs has revised the "feminine" rhetorical convention,

---

anonymous woman of North Carolina in a text where the most assertive and "real" women are black allows and encourages readers to make such assumptions.

for this citation is more demanding and declarative than it is seductive or suggestive.

The author's preface follows the title page. As is expected in the discourse of distrust, Jacobs's first words "tell off" the reader in ways that she or he must "hear." "Reader, be assured this narrative is no fiction." This statement is neither apology nor request. It is a polite command, soothingly stated but nonetheless an imperative. The next sentence neither explains nor defends: "I am aware that some of my adventures may seem incredible; but they are, nevertheless, strictly true." Instead of elaborating upon her claim to authenticity in the preface, Jacobs requires an even higher level of trust, for she advises her readers that she has not told all that she knows. "I have not exaggerated the wrongs inflicted by Slavery," she writes, "on the contrary, my descriptions fall far short of the facts." With these words, the author claims superior knowledge and plainly privileges her own interpretation over any contrary ideas that the reader may have as to the text's authenticity.

At the conclusion of her narrative, Jacobs's struggle has gained her a conditional freedom. "We are as free from the power of slave holders," she argues, "as are the white people of the north." But she continues, "that, according to my ideas, is not saying a great deal. . . . The dream of my life is not yet realized" (Jacobs, 201) [156]. Ironically, her authorial efforts, as creative and effective as they are, have not achieved an unmitigated success either.

The situation with *Incidents in the Life of a Slave Girl* is an extreme example of that faced by "other" writers. Especially with African American women, reader resistance seems neverending. However, I am convinced that Harriet Jacobs, like many others, anticipated a hostile and incredulous reception to her narrative. And using techniques from her multiple cultures, she created a transcultural[4] text that begged, borrowed, stole, and devised the techniques that would allow her maximum freedom to tell her story in her own way and to her own ends. Jacobs may well have underestimated the persistence of resistance, but she did in fact create a brilliantly innovative autobiography. That the incidents of resistance were not quelled may say more about the perspicaciousness of her readers than about imperfections in the text itself.

---

4. Here I am adapting definitions that Masao Miyoshi posits in his discussion of transnational and multinational corporations. The distinction, he argues, is "problematic" and frequently the terms may be used interchangeably. The differences are "in the degrees of alienation from the countries of origin." Multinational corporations belong to one nation and operate in several. Transnational corporations, on the other hand, are not tied to their nations of origin but are more self-contained and self-serving. Although there may be obvious incompatibilities between the discussion of multicultural and multinational businesses and discourse, Miyoshi's discussion stimulated my own thinking in this matter. See his "A Borderless World? From Colonialism to Transnationalism and the Decline of the Nation-State," *Critical Inquiry* 19 (Summer 1993): 726–51.

SANDRA GUNNING

Reading and Redemption in
Incidents in the Life of a Slave Girl[†]

The post–Civil War version of Olive Gilbert's *Narrative of Sojourner Truth* included a curious letter by Indiana abolitionist William Hayward describing an 1858 confrontation between Truth and proslavery forces: During a rural antislavery meeting, a Dr. T. W. Strain declared "that a doubt existed in the minds of many persons present respecting the sex of the speaker"; according to Strain, Truth should "submit her breast to the inspection of some of the ladies present, that the doubt may be removed by their testimony."[1] When Truth inquired about the basis for his opinion, Strain continued: "'Your voice is not the voice of a woman, it is the voice of a man, and we believe you to be a man'" (*Narrative*, 138).

Facing an unruly crowd, the indefatigable Truth replied

> that her breasts had suckled many a white babe, to the exclusion of her own offspring; that some of those white babies had grown to man's estate; that although they had sucked her colored breasts, they were . . . far more manly than they (her persecutors) appeared to be; and she quietly asked them, as she disrobed her bosom, if they too, wished to suck!

Truth thus uncovers herself before the crowd, "not to her shame . . . but to their shame" (*Narrative*, 139). With Truth's sex verified, Hayward gloats that Strain loses a forty-dollar bet on her masculinity.

Though undoubtedly included by the *Narrative*'s white editors as a testimonial to Truth's courage, Hayward's anecdote speaks ironically to the ways in which the ostensibly opposing elements of abolition and slavery could rely on the same mechanism for self-enhancement: On the one hand Strain set out to discredit anti-slavery activists by the obliteration of Truth's voice through a deliberate misreading of her body, a misreading firmly set within a context of de-sexualization provided by slavery, where male bodies became interchangeable with female, where gender was acknowledged only for the convenience of sexual and reproductive ex-

---

† From *Harriet Jacobs and* Incidents in the Life of a Slave Girl: *New Critical Essays*, ed. Deborah M. Garfield and Rafia Zafar (New York: Cambridge UP, 1996) 131–54. Reprinted with the permission of Cambridge University Press. Page references to this Norton Critical Edition are given in brackets following Gunning's original citations, with the exception of references to extratext material included in the Yellin edition. [My thanks to Keith L. T. Alexander, Barbara Christian, M. Giulia Fabi, and Stephanie Smith for their sensitive commentary on early drafts of this essay (Gunning's acknowledgment).]

1. [Olive Gilbert, ed.], "Book of Life" in *Narrative of Sojourner Truth; A bondswoman of Olden times, With a History of Her Labors and Correspondence Drawn from Her "Book of Life"* (1878; rpt., New York: Oxford University Press, 1991), 138. Cited in text henceforth as *Narrative*, followed by page number.

ploitation.[2] But on the other hand Hayward ignores the assault on Truth's modesty and makes the issue instead Truth's willingness to combat slavery by any means available—even with her body. At the same time, however, Hayward is quick to recognize that a physical examination of an unclothed black body by female audience members is an attack on white female modesty: "a large number of ladies present . . . appeared to be ashamed and indignant at such a proposition" (*Narrative*, 138). When he proudly reports on the proslavery advocate's loss of face through the public revelation of Truth's breasts, he inadvertently confirms that Truth's own credibility as an abolitionist speaker must rest finally not with her testimony as an ex-slave, but on the white reading of her body. Whether the incident ends in favor of the proslavery supporters or the abolitionists, successful political agitation seems destined to occur through the medium of Truth's body, the body of the slave interlocutor.

Although abolitionist objectification appears to win out over proslavery fetishization, there is a crucial dimension to this incident produced by Truth's decision to disrobe publicly. Challenging the objectifying gaze of the hostile Indiana audience (and with the publication of Hayward's letter, future generations of white readers also), Truth reunites the ex-slave's body with its voice through an articulation of bodily secrets that confirm white links with black physicality. Truth appropriates the linguistic moment by reinterpreting her breasts not as markers of biological identity, but as signifiers of the long American history of exploitative sexual and maternal contact between black and white bodies. As the crowd insists on their moral obligation to know the truth of her body, Truth's invitation to suckle the crowd recontextualizes that white desire for knowledge as pruriently sexual, as exploitative of her maternity. Thus under Truth's bodily language of critique the distinction between the North and South as ideological opposites in their attention to the slave begins to blur as the black abolitionist resembles the denuded slave woman on a Northern auction block, and the false ideal of slavery as the patriarchal institution merges with and consequently begins to falsify white middle-class idealization of domesticity and maternity.[3]

If we move from this narrated incident in the life of Sojourner Truth to the self-authored narrative of Harriet Jacobs in *Incidents in the Life of a Slave Girl* (1861), we find Jacobs confronting, through the voice of her alter ego Linda Brent, the very similar challenge of a white audience intent on replacing her interpreting voice with her already overinterpreted black body. However, as I argue in this essay, if for Truth the ability to assert herself as a social critic rests on the capacity to interpret the black fe-

2. See Hortense J. Spillers's "Mama's Baby, Papa's Maybe: An American Grammar Book," *Diacritics* 17 (Summer 1987): 65–81, for an excellent discussion of the popular construction of black women.
3. Truth had been a slave in New York state before the abolition of slavery in that region. She escaped in 1827.

male body's history as a narrative about masked relations, a similar strategy is employed by Jacobs to highlight and to challenge her audience's unwillingness to accept the authority of a slave speaker. Like Truth, Harriet Jacobs uses the story of her body's exploitation in slavery as a critical moment to call into question the supposed distances between black and white bodies, and especially the Northerners' (especially Northern white women's) conception of themselves as ideologically distinguished from their Southern neighbors on the subject of slavery. Working to make visible the seemingly invisible, disembodied white reader through the medium of the physically exploited Linda Brent, Jacobs achieves a critique of Northern models of white female domestic activism that in the end establishes hers as the true voice of reform, to which all whites must attend if they are concerned about moral salvation.[4]

Ironically, Jacobs's credibility as a social commentator is compromised not by doubts about her sex, but by the fact of her identity and experience as a female ex-slave. According to the narrative, as a young woman in Edentton, North Carolina, Jacobs (represented through Linda Brent in the story) chooses to escape a lascivious master by encouraging the affections of a sympathetic white admirer.[5] Eventually, in an effort to secure the freedom of their resulting two children, as well as in a final bid to put a stop to her master's continued sexual advances, Jacobs confines herself to an attic hiding place. Only after spending almost seven years in hiding does Jacobs finally escape to the North.

But as Jacobs and some of her supporters well knew, Northern white readers of the narrative would ignore her analysis of slavery's criminality and instead fix upon her "immoral" black body and her apparently willful complicity in sexual relations with a white man. Indeed, the problem was that instead of defining Jacobs as she defined herself, that is, as a mother who has led her children out of slavery and who now seeks to create a subjective role as an abolitionist writer and social critic, her white audience would construct her as the contaminated product of slavery's moral decadence—an object of white scrutiny, of white contempt for her violation of moral codes of female conduct, but certainly not an authoritative commentator on slavery, much less Northern morality.

Like Truth, Harriet Jacobs aims, as she enters the political arena, to become the interpreter of her own body's experience of slavery. But in Ja-

---

4. In her book *The Word in Black and White: Reading "Race" in American Literature, 1638–1867* (New York: Oxford University Press, 1992), Dana D. Nelson also addresses Jacobs's critique of traditional notions of racial difference, and the complacency of readers. Although she and I arrive at what I feel are complementary conclusions, Nelson focuses more on the notion of how "sympathy" mediates Jacobs's critique of the reader: "The text repeatedly appeals to the sympathy of its readers, but at the same time it warns them to be careful about the motives and critical of the results of that sympathetic identification" (142).

5. Recalling her "deliberate calculation" to choose a sexual partner in order to maintain control over her life, Jacobs remarks through Linda Brent's narration that "it seemed less degrading to give one's self, than to submit to compulsion"; in Harriet Jacobs, *Incidents in the Life of a Slave Girl, Written by Herself* (1861; rpt., Cambridge: Harvard University Press, 1987), 54, 55 [46, 47]. Cited in this essay henceforth as *I* followed by page number.

cobs's case, the female ex-slave is determined to provide readings of her
sexual conduct that compete with the already established white middle-
class patterns of judging correct female behavior. As virtually all modern
readers of *Incidents* have noted, Jacobs's commentaries are strategically
embedded within Linda Brent's language of domesticity, a language im-
ported into the text to highlight the black female slave as mother, all in
an effort to make her acceptable to a Northern audience. Indeed "it is not
surprising," Jean Fagan Yellin suggests, "that Jacobs presents Linda Brent
in terms of motherhood, the most valued 'feminine' role" of the antebellum period, given the need to enlist white sympathy for a story which
many might find outrageous.[6] As an escaped slave Jacobs confronts an
American cultural setting that defines black femininity as everything
white womanhood was not: publicly exposed, sexualized, unable or unwilling to create a domestic space of its own.

Jacobs's presentation of the black woman as mother is not simply an
attempt to embrace a white cultural icon of respectability. Within the narrative Jacobs appears to fall into line behind such women as Harriet
Beecher Stowe and Lydia Maria Child in using the language of domesticity to build a platform from which to agitate for social justice. Yet the
text's political aims are continually at odds with the format of the domestic novel, which precludes discussions of sexual exploitation and miscegenation as subjects unmentionable in a white familial setting, despite
their importance to any discussion of slavery. Instead of submission to silence, however, *Incidents in the Life of a Slave Girl* uses the continual
conflict between form and content to problematize the position of white
readers with respect to their role as private spectators to the public story
of Linda Brent and her exploitation as a slave, and, as a result, their political identity as Northern, supposedly antislavery advocates.[7] In the end,

6. Jean Fagan Yellin, "Introduction," *Incidents in the Life of a Slave Girl, Written by Herself* (Cambridge: Harvard University Press, 1987), xxvi. See also Bruce Mills, "Lydia Maria Child and the
Endings of Harriet Jacobs's *Incidents in the Life of a Slave Girl*," *American Literature* 64:2 (June
1992): 255–72. Standard discussions of the cultural binary constructions of black and white
womanhood include Barbara Christian, *Black Women Novelists: The Development of a Tradition, 1892–1976* (Westport, CT: Greenwood, 1980), specifically 7–14; Paula Giddings, *When
and Where I Enter: The Impact of Black Women on Race and Sex in America* (Bantam, 1985),
47–55; Hazel Carby, *Reconstructing Womanhood: The Emergence of the Afro-American Woman
Novelist* (New York: Oxford University Press, 1987), chapter 2.
7. According to Karen Sanchez-Eppler, "the acceptability [of stories from slavery] . . . depends
upon their adherence to a feminine and domestic demeanor that softens the cruelty they describe and makes their political goals more palatable to a less politicized readership." See "Bodily Bonds: The Intersecting Rhetorics of Feminism and Abolition," *Representations* 24 (Fall
1988): 35. For other discussions of Harriet Jacobs, Linda Brent, and their relationship to the narrative's audience, see Carby, *Reconstructing Womanhood*, 45–61; Valerie Smith, "'Loopholes of
Retreat': Architecture and Ideology in Harriet Jacobs's *Incidents in the Life of a Slave Girl*," in
Reading Black, Reading Feminist: A Critical Anthology, ed. Henry Louis Gates, Jr. (New York:
Meridian, 1990): 212–26; P. Gabrielle Foreman, "The Spoken and the Silenced in *Incidents in
the Life of a Slave Girl* and *Our Nig*," *Callaloo* 13 (Spring 1990): 313–24; Beth Maclay Doriani,
"Black Womanhood in Nineteenth-Century America: Subversion and Self-Construction in Two
Women's Autobiographies," *American Quarterly* 43 (June 1991): 199–222; Fanny Nudelman,
"Harriet Jacobs and the Sentimental Politics of Female Suffering," *ELH* (59) 1992: 939–64; Har-
ryette Mullen, "Runaway Tongue: Resistant Orality in *Uncle Tom's Cabin, Our Nig, Incidents*

Incidents in the Life of a Slave Girl gives special meaning to a black woman's physical flight from slavery to freedom and a home by contextualizing such experiences within a continuum of moral corruption where racism, wrongful persecution, and sexual exploitation flourish. This pattern of suffering begins in North Carolina but, as the narrative works to emphasize, it extends even to Northern cities, despite the strong presence of abolitionists. In the narrative, the same terrible hardships that Jacobs and her children must endure regardless of whether they live in the North or the South suggest that the regions might be similar in their moral and indeed their political treatment of black slaves.

And yet *Incidents* does not merely set out to condemn Northern white readers; rather, it is a critique of the traditional practices of reading blackness as a severed relationship between voice and body, as the epitome of powerless victimization. And if Jacobs's text calls into question the patterns of representation for blackness, then it does so for representations of whiteness as well: On what foundation is white privacy based within the context of race? What is the basis of white political self-constructions with regard to liberty and slavery? Why is agency racialized as white with regard to abolitionists? These are some of the questions Jacobs addresses in her narrative, and they are designed to lead readers beyond inane stereotyping of black victimization or black culpability, beyond deluding self-constructions, toward a sense of Northern white moral and political self-scrutiny.

I

Jacobs's project of re-reading posed a challenge to mid-nineteenth-century literary and social ideologies that fetishized the black female body. White women agitating for suffrage employed the image of the chained, denuded, helpless black female slave as a metaphor to describe their own perceived position as patriarchal wards without the social and political power to control their economic and physical lives.[8] Although these representations also epitomized Southern slavery, visions of chained black women did not necessarily encourage white women to empathize with the material condition of female slaves. For example, even though Harriet Beecher Stowe set out in *Uncle Tom's Cabin* (1851) and the 1853 *Key* to the novel to demonstrate black exploitation during slavery, her own

---

in the Life of a Slave Girl, and Beloved" in *The Culture of Sentiment: Race, Gender, and Sentimentality in Nineteenth-Century America*, ed. Shirley Samuels (New York: Oxford University Press, 1992): 244–64, 332–5.

8. See Yellin's *Woman and Sisters: The Antislavery Feminists in American Culture* (New Haven: Yale University Press, 1989). Also, Ronald G. Walters, "The Erotic South: Civilization and Sexuality in American Abolitionism," *American Quarterly* 25 (May 1973): 177–201. For a useful look at the rhetoric of white feminist abolitionists and its relationship to the bodies of male and female slaves see Sanchez-Eppler, "Bodily Bonds," and William Andrews, *To Tell a Free Story: The First Century of Afro-American Autobiography, 1760–1865* (Urbana: University of Illinois Press, 1988), 241–7.

dealings with real black women (and Jacobs in particular) suggests that Stowe was not always inclined toward sensitivity, or antiracist feelings.[9]

For most Northerners, black enslavement (as opposed to the figurative "slavery" of marriage) was made vivid through the numerous descriptions of public slave auctions, the violation of black families, beatings, and allusions to rape and incest within the pages of popular male-authored slave narratives and antislavery fiction by white abolitionists.[1] Such scenes of moral chaos no doubt provided a comforting contrast for Northern whites between their life and the life of the degraded South, a contrast abolitionists capitalized on by presenting slavery as a national threat to traditional concepts of family and personal liberty; indeed slavery marked "the outer limits of disorder and debauchery," and if left unchecked it might spread moral pollution even to the North.[2] Certainly although whites in the North were not necessarily hostile to slaves, blackness and black women in particular signified victimization (hence, as Jean Fagan Yellin and Karen Sánchez-Eppler have shown, the need to act on behalf of the slave, especially the slave-mother), but also the threat of racial pollution (hence the need to keep the de facto miscegenation practices of the South out of the North).[3]

When Lydia Maria Child (who served as the narrative's editor) and Jacobs's white friend Amy Post composed the literary addresses that frame *Incidents*, their presentations of the ex-slave as Linda Brent were clearly shaped by dual Northern attitudes to black women as pariahs and victims.[4] Lydia Maria Child recognized the problem of audience reception, no doubt from her own experience as an abolitionist writer shunned for the publication of her controversial *An Appeal in Favor of That Class of Americans Called Africans* (1833).[5] In the "Editor's Introduction" to *Incidents* Child instructs white readers to look beyond the ex-slave's narration of offending horrors and interpret *Incidents* so as to focus on the injustice of slavery. Indeed, in her role as editor Child reorganized certain aspects of the narrative as part of a strategy against audience alien-

---

9. See Stowe's rebuff of Jacobs over the publication of the latter's story in the *Key to Uncle Tom's Cabin* in Yellin, "Introduction," xviii–xix. Jacobs's letters to Amy Post also reveal her anger and distrust for Stowe. They are reprinted in *Incidents*, 233–37.
1. See Frances Foster's "'In Respect to Females . . . ': Differences in the Portrayals of Women by Male and Female Narrators," *Black American Literature Forum* 15:2 (Summer 1981): 66–70.
2. Walters, "Erotic South," 189. According to Carolyn L. Karcher, one of the many challenges faced by white abolitionist writers was the problem of even discussing the occurrences of rape, torture, incest, or murder under slavery, since any representation of these issues would have been insulting to the sensibilities of American white women of the North. See her "Rape, Murder and Revenge in 'Slavery's Pleasant Homes': Lydia Maria Child's Antislavery Fiction and the Limits of Genre," *Women's Studies International Forum* 9:4 (1986): 323.
3. See Yellin, *Women and Sisters*, and Sánchez-Eppler, "Bodily Bonds."
4. Whereas Child and Post see Harriet Jacobs and Linda Brent as the same person, I would argue that to some extent Jacobs is fictionalizing her life experiences through the character of Brent, or, according to P. Gabrielle Foreman, at least shielding herself through the narrator. See Foreman's "The Spoken and the Silenced."
5. See Carolyn L. Karcher's discussion in "Censorship, American Style: the Case of Lydia Maria Child," *Studies in the American Renaissance, 1986*; ed. Joel Myerson (Charlottesville: University Press of Virginia, 1986), 283–303.

ation, putting "savage cruelties into one chapter . . . in order that those who shrink from 'supping upon horrors' might omit them, without interrupting the thread of the story."[6]

Nevertheless, as her own introduction suggests, Child recognizes that even with the "savage cruelties" pruned, the story of Linda Brent might itself be offensive:

> I am well aware that many will accuse me of indecorum for presenting these pages to the public; for the experiences of this intelligent and much-injured woman belong to a class which some call delicate subjects, and others indelicate. . . . [B]ut the public ought to be made acquainted with . . . [slavery's] monstrous features, and I willingly take the responsibility of presenting them with the veil withdrawn. (*I*, 3–4) [6]

In her effort to protect Jacobs and justify the publication of *Incidents*, Child bypasses Jacobs's authorship—and therefore the notion of Jacobs as a self-conscious critic of an American political and social system—altogether, thereby constructing Linda Brent as an anonymous woman defined not by her role as speaker, but by her (presumed) bodily "experiences" in slavery.[7] These are the real issues of the narrative, according to Child. By focusing on the problem of audience reception (the problem of indecorousness), Child draws attention not to the slave narrator's authority to determine the meaning of her slavery, but to the privatized privilege of the white reader to interpret and pass judgment on Brent's life and—if we follow the gist of Child's metaphor of the unveiling—on Brent's body as well.[8] The white reader's authority (especially that of the white female reader) is constructed through the metaphoric presentation of the unveiled slave woman: Her location within the public realm signifies female contamination, racialized in this context as black, while their location within the realm of shielding domesticity signifies spirituality and moral purity.[9]

At the same time, if Child unveils the "monstrous features" of slavery made visible upon the body of a slave woman, this woman is both an object of charity and a pariah, as her life story vacillates between the "deli-

6. Quoted in Yellin, "Introduction," xxii. Karcher also discusses this practice in the context of antislavery fiction in "Rape, Murder and Revenge," 330. Bruce Mill's "Lydia Maria Child and the Endings to Harriet Jacobs's *Incidents*" is the most recent discussion of Child's role as editor.

7. For other readings of Child's introduction, see Valerie Smith, "Loopholes of Retreat," 218–23, and Foreman, "The Spoken and the Silenced," 316–17.

8. Child is acting the part of the conscientious editor, given the traditional expectations of white readers. According to William Andrews, "nineteenth century whites read slave narratives more to get a firsthand look at the institution of slavery than to become acquainted with an individual slave." Indeed, a "reliable slave narrative would be one that seemed purely mimetic, in which the self is on the periphery instead of at the center of attention, . . . transcribing rather than interpreting a set of objective facts" (*To Tell a Free Story*, 5–6).

9. Though he fails to underscore the importance of race in the determination of privacy, Richard H. Brodhead nevertheless offers an important discussion on the subject of (un)veiled presentations in "Veiled Ladies: Towards a History of Antebellum Entertainment," *American Literary History* 1 (Summer 1989): 273–94.

cate" and the "indelicate"—categories that move the white audience either to protect the vicitimized Brent or to protect their own sensibilities from her offending presence. The problem here is Child's appeal to the conscience of the white reader and her or his interpretation of the narrative; the success of the narrative rests not on Brent's telling, but on how the white reader chooses to read the meaning of the narrative, in effect the meaning of Brent's body as it is exposed in the text.

Child's strategy of mediation becomes clear when she phrases her final appeal to the audience as a celebration of the power of Northern whites to effect correct moral judgments:

> I do this for the sake of my sisters in bondage, who are suffering wrongs so foul, that our ears are too delicate to listen to them. I do it with the hope of arousing conscientious and reflecting women at the North to a sense of their duty in the exertion of moral influence on the question of Slavery, on all possible occasions.(*I*, 4) [6]

Child's final proposal for the proper response to her "unveiling" of Brent identifies the "indelicate" (the offensiveness of Jacobs's story) with the slave testimony ("our ears are too delicate to listen to them"), since the pronoun "them" refers both to the black speakers and to the atrocities committed under slavery. At the same time, since Child has described the readers' proposed encounter with stories of slavery through the visual metaphor of gazing at unveiled images, the suggestion then is that within *Incidents* the mere sight of Brent's enslaved body, unadorned with commentary, will be less offensive than hearing about it from Brent herself. What is indelicate, then, is the black eye-witness interpretation of slavery, the notion of the authoritative voice of the slave narrator.[1]

Only when Brent is silenced can she become the object of charity. Her situation can be perceived as "delicate" (and therefore worthy of sensitivity) only when thoughtful white women readers are allowed to contemplate safely the transparent text of Brent's life for themselves, and in so doing assign what whites would consider to be proper meaning to the ex-slave's experience. In other words, the public body of the slave woman, the site of the grossly physical, becomes the site of intervention and mystification for the disembodied white female reader to "exert" protective moral influence.

If in her "Introduction" Child attempts to win audience support by validating the white right to assign correct meaning to the "monstrous features" of slavery through the construction of a silenced Brent as literally a physical specimen for sympathetic white consideration, Amy Post tries

---

1. In a letter to the *National Anti-Slavery Standard*, one reader of *Incidents* objected to the existence of slave commentary: "A few sentences in which the moral is rather oppressively displayed, might have been omitted with advantage. These, it is to be wished, Mrs. Child had felt herself authorized to expunge. They are the strongest witnesses who leave the summing up to the judge, and the verdict to the jury" (quoted in Yellin, "Introduction," xxiv–xxv).

a seemingly different tactic in her appendix. In a statement of support for the slave narrator that attempts to remain faithful to Jacobs's directives from an 1857 letter, Post seems at first to destabilize the terms of Child's introduction by completely submerging the notion of Brent's physicality.[2] Referring directly to Jacobs through the pseudonym of Linda Brent, Post stresses the slave narrator's perfect assimilation into the private world of Northern middle-class white true womanhood.

As "a beloved inmate" of Post's house, Brent's physical characteristics are referred to in passing as "prepossessing," but in large part the testimonial constructs Brent as a spiritual creature with "remarkable delicacy of feeling and purity of thought" whose body responds to the more acceptable somatic sensations of grief and modesty, rather than to sexual exploitation (*I*, 203) [157]. But whereas the evidence of slavery is concealed in the suppression of bodily knowledge, such suppression seems to have rendered Brent inarticulate and even mute—this after the "incidents" themselves have just been delivered in the ex-slave's own words: "she passed through a baptism of suffering . . . in private confidential conversations"; "even in talking with me, she wept so much, and seemed to suffer such mental agony, that I felt her story was too sacred to be drawn from her by inquisitive questions" (*I*, 203–4) [157].[3] Even though she is ethereal, Brent is being read for what is unsaid about her body. Indeed, her tears and shrinking modesty, even as they signify her rightful place in a white domestic setting, might also betray incriminating secrets. After all, though she is accepted into Post's female community, Brent's claim to true womanhood is always mediated by her race.

Brent's body seems to have been recouped by Post's narrative strategy, yet the slave narrator's interpreting voice is still depicted as nonexistent, since the political foresight to write and publish the narrative is unmistakably stressed as Post's rather than Brent's. In the end, though Brent performs the manual labor of tracing "secretly and wearily . . . a truthful record of her eventful life" (204) [157], Post takes the credit by constantly harping on "the [moral] duty of publishing" *Incidents*. As such, though Brent occupies the favored place of adopted white daughter, though she displays the necessary spiritual grace of white women, she still lacks the moral strength that defines the ideal of white domestic feminism. Thus

---

2. In her letter to Post, Jacobs writes: "I think it would be best for you to begin with our acquaintance and the length of time I was in your family   your advice about giving the history of my life in Slavery   mention that I lived at service all the while that I was striving to get the Book out . . . —my kind friend I do not restrict you in anything for you know far better than I do what to say" (reprinted in *I*, 242).

3. In an earlier letter to Post in 1852, which mentions Post's "proposal" that Jacobs make her story public, the latter says: "dear Amy if it was the life of a Heroine with no degradation associated with it   far better to have been one of the starving poor of Ireland whose bones had to bleach on the highways than to have been a slave with the curse of slavery stamped upon yourself and Children" (reprinted in *I*, 232). Is Jacobs just ashamed of her experience under slavery, as Post's appendix seems to imply, or is she instead trustful of the Northern reading public?

Post's appendix suggests that Brent may be the daughter, but it is the white mother who leads her toward political action.[4]

Despite the disturbing implications of their testimonials, Child and Post offer their respective construction of the slave narrator from a genuine commitment to assisting Jacobs with the publication of her text. Jacobs was no doubt grateful to both women for their encouragement and assistance in helping her with *Incidents*, and she describes them affectionately as "whole souled."[5] However, her own discussion of the writing of the narrative and her implied instructions to the audience about what, who, or how to "read" with regard to her autobiography contradict the interpretive practices employed by Child and Post, and also clearly foreground her awareness of the problems of writing for a Northern audience not likely to grant her respect as a competent social commentator.

Through the persona of Linda Brent in the "Author's Preface," Jacobs's terse description of her past and present condition suggests a woman who has survived physically and intellectually the hardships of drudgery and denial imposed by life in both the North and the South:

> I was born and reared in Slavery. . . . Since I have been at the North, it has been necessary for me to work diligently for my own support, and the education of my children. This has not left me much leisure to make up for the loss of early opportunities to improve myself; and it has compelled me to write these pages at irregular intervals, whenever I could snatch an hour from household duties. (*I*, 1) [5]

In describing her confinement to domestic service Jacobs does not focus on physical tortures, but instead makes clear her dedication to political action ("I want to add my testimony to that of abler pens to convince the people of the Free States what Slavery really is"), and her desire to claim for herself the role of the moral and intellectual authority who will lead the audience to a proper understanding of the complex issue contained within the narrative: "I do earnestly desire to arouse the women of the North to a realizing sense of the condition of two millions of women at the South, still in bondage" (*I*, 1–2) [5].

In an 1857 letter to Amy Post, Jacobs describes the persona she has created for herself in *Incidents* as "a poor Slave Mother [who comes] not to tell you what I have heard but what I have seen—and what I have suf-

---

4. Although Post did urge Jacobs to write the narrative, Jacobs had never doubted the need for her own political activism: "My conscience approved it but my stubborn pride would not yield I have tried for the past two years to conquer it and I feel that God has helped me or I never would consent to give my past life to any one but I would not do it without giving the whole truth if it could help save another from my fate it would be selfish and unchristian in me to keep it back" (reprinted in *I*, 232). One of the chief causes she lists for not writing is her situation on the household staff of proslavery Nathaniel P. Willis.
5. Harriet Jacobs's 1860 letter to Amy Post, reprinted in *I*, 247.

fered" (*I*, 243). The oxymoronic appellation Slave/Mother ironically ges-
tures toward the two entities split in Child's introduction and racialized
as opposites: the sexually degraded, commercialized body that Child
would unveil, and the intuitive, disembodied nurturing image of female
moral force.[6] In the public body of the narrator Linda Brent, both mother
and slave will be united as witness and participant. And it is precisely Jacobs's experience as a participant (the same experience which might re-
pulse the audience) that her preface argues is the premiere qualification
for assigning her the role of judge: "Only by experience can any one realize how deep, and dark, and foul is that pit of abominations" (*I*, 2) [5].
Clearly, what Child sees as the point of danger for white women becomes
a source of authority for Jacobs.

II

In her effort to problematize the authority of a white audience that
deems itself empowered by the privatized moral force of domestic feminism, the narrator Linda Brent situates both the Southern and Northern
portions of *Incidents* within the interior spaces of the home. Her tactic
here is to highlight that setting as the special context of black female exploitation. Representational patterns begin shifting from the very opening of the text, when Brent's first owner turns out to be a godly woman
having more in common with the mothers among the audience than
with slaveholders like Simon Legree. In her introduction Lydia Maria
Child identifies her as Brent's first benefactor who, along with many
white Northerners, provides the slave with "opportunities for self-improvement" by teaching her to read and educating her in "the precepts
of God's Word" after the death of Brent's parents (*I*, 3, 8) [6, 11].

But Brent herself is quick to discuss the full extent of her "opportunities" when as a surrogate daughter within the white family unit she is bequeathed to the white woman's niece, the infant daughter of the
infamous Dr. Flint. Unlike Brent's former mistress, who is ultimately dis-
appointing in her actions because she appears to be falsely the ideal white
mother, Flint and his wife take on demonic proportions from the start:
the doctor tries to sell Brent's grandmother after her mistress's death, even
though both blacks and whites know that the mistress had intended to
free Aunt Martha. A fitting consort to Dr. Flint, Mrs. Flint has no
"strength to superintend her household affairs," but she is strong enough

6. While acknowledging for a moment the critical explanation that Brent/Jacobs embraces maternity within her narrative as a strategy to engage Northern sympathies, we need to recognize that
maternity itself is a highly problematic category in *Incidents*. Although she has been acting in
the capacity of a mother since the birth of her children during slavery, Brent is not officially allowed to accept the status of mother until the final pages of the narrative when, as a free woman,
she can own herself and so own her children. The category of the slave-mother embodied by the
character Linda Brent functions not just as a category for her presentation to American readers,
but also as a metaphor for instability to describe Brent's lifelong struggle against social processes
that govern her identity.

to "sit in her easy chair and see a woman whipped, till the blood trickled from every stroke of the lash" (*I*, 12) [14].

Brent's description of life in the Flint household lifts Child's metaphoric veil of decency to reveal not just brutalized slave bodies, but the nature of the victimization process developed and sustained as part of the means of constructing white privacy. Her first discussion of Dr. Flint's sexual misconduct in the slave quarters makes clear this connection. After only a short time in the Flint household, she witnesses the torture of a male slave:

> There were many conjectures as to the cause of this terrible punishment. Some said master accused him of stealing corn; others said the slave had quarreled with his wife, in presence of the overseer, and had accused his master of being the father of her child. They were both black, and the child was very fair. (*I*, 13) [15]

Eventually Flint sells both husband and wife:

> The guilty man put their value into his pocket, and had the satisfaction of knowing that they were out of sight and hearing. When the mother was delivered into the trader's hands, she said, "you *promised* to treat me well." To which he replied, "You have let your tongue run too far; damn you!" (*I*, 13) [15–16]

Flint conceals his indiscretion by prohibiting the woman from speaking of the crime, so that even the slave community must whisper and conjecture about what has really occurred. Under this system of reversals the pregnant slave bears the guilt of sexual misconduct. Indeed the protection of Flint's private life as father and husband is predicated on the exposure and punishment of black female bodies; they become criminalized, while white paternity is replaced by irresponsible, immoral black maternity. However, Brent's narration works to undermine the careful protection Flint has constructed for himself by moving the narrative beyond the public exhibition of the slaves (the man who is beaten, the woman who is sold), an exhibition that, in its reliance on stereotypical images of victimization, suppresses rather than facilitates truth. Her vocalization finally allows the lost story of the slave couple to surface, despite Flint's prohibition. Brent's motive for speaking out in the case of the slave couple becomes the context for the telling of her own experiences: clearly, as in the case of the slave woman who is sold away, for Brent *not* to reveal the details of her relationship with Flint would be to allow her (potential) bodily corruption to stand as a means of shielding his moral degradation.

Though regional and political differences seem to separate the degenerate Flints from the apparently purer communities of Northern white readers, Brent's emphasis throughout her narrative on Flint's obsession with the silencing of black (especially black female) speech about sexual exploitation suggests frightening parallels in the Northern white readers' own resistance to *hearing* about the horrifying details of slavery as they read the narrative within a familial setting. Indeed, if they resist Brent's authority as narrator, the morally righteous audience addressed by Child's introduction, who are appealed to as saviors but whose ears will be contaminated by slave accounts of oppression under slavery, ironically risk appearing in collusion with Flint, the evil slavemaster so often vilified in abolitionist literature.

This implication has important consequences with respect to how white readers supportive of familial harmony can claim to be innocent spectators to the perversion of their ideals in the Southern patriarchal "family" of slavery. Brent's narrative continually seeks to implicate them in a racial conspiracy against black female modesty that undermines the notion of white sectional difference. She begins by appropriating the concept of delicacy and assigning it to black femininity. Then she depicts this delicacy under assault by the white master "father" who seeks to suppress the detailed discussion of sexual—and therefore incestuous—exploitation of a surrogate daughter: "My master began to *whisper* foul words in *my ear*. . . . He tried his utmost to corrupt the pure principles my grandmother had instilled" (emphasis added; *I*, 27) [26]:

> I saw a man forty years my senior daily violating the most sacred commandments of nature. He told me I was his property; that I must be subject to his will in all things. . . . But where could I turn for protection? No matter whether the slave girl be as black as ebony or as fair as her mistress. In either case, there is no shadow of law to protect her from insult, from violence, or even from death. . . . The degradation, the wrongs, the vices, that grow of slavery, are more than I can describe. They are greater than you would willingly believe. (*I*, 27–8) [26]

The penultimate sentence of this passage re-echoes Flint's own silencing of his victim: "Dr. Flint swore he would kill me, if I was not as silent as the grave" (*I*, 28) [27].[7] And since decency, or more precisely "delicacy," is the same watchword mediating between the audience/slave master and the slave narrator (neither wants their home contaminated by Brent's story), then in the North as well as the South discretion rather than justice remains the better part of valor. Thus, white readers, who shy away from full disclosures from the mouth of the slave narrator, could well be accused of an identical acceptance of a hypocritical standard of public morality.

With regard to Brent's reticence concerning the details of Flint's at-

---

7. For an illuminating recent discussion of Southern etiquette around miscegenation and the rape of slave women by white men, see Catherine Clinton, "'Southern Dishonor': Flesh, Blood, Race, and Bondage," in *In Joy and in Sorrow: Women, Family, and Marriage in the Victorian South, 1830–1900*, ed. Carol Bleser (New York: Oxford University Press, 1991): 52–68, 281–84.

tempted seduction, her silence cannot be attributed solely to her desire to avoid reliving a distressing situation.[8] Precisely because Flint's prohibition occurs within the context of white middle-class privacy, which is dependent on the annihilation of the slave family and the poisoning of black female morality, Brent seems compelled to speak. Her silence is therefore dramatized as an imposed one — in the past by Flint, in the present moment of *Incidents in the Life of a Slave Girl* by the antislavery audience itself: "The degradation, the wrongs, the vices that grow out of slavery, are more than I can describe. They are greater than you would willingly believe."

In many ways Brent's compelled silence forces her to be the guardian of the white reader's morality, since she keeps to herself all the unpleasant, unseemly details that insult a pure sensibility. Consequently, the exploited slave girl is transformed into the physical receptacle of slavery's contamination, standing as the victim abolitionists want to rescue, the pariah they feel compelled to keep at arm's length.[9] But it is precisely in dramatizing how the protection of both Northern and Southern white morality is constructed through the particular usage of the slave body in tandem with the silencing of the slave's voice that Brent resurrects herself as social critic. This point is made clearer when we read the rest of her comments to a disbelieving audience:

> Surely, if you credited one half the truths that are told you concerning the helpless millions suffering in this cruel bondage, you at the north would not help to tighten the yoke. You surely would refuse to do for the master, on your own soil, the mean and cruel work which trained bloodhounds and the lowest class of whites do for him at the south. (*I*, 28) [26]

Thus Brent, artless, reticent, bowed down by shame, uses the apparently limiting construction of herself as mute victim to reveal her binary opposite, the depraved tyrant whose "monstrous features" depict not just Flint, but also the moral citizens of the North who tolerate the Fugitive Slave Law. So when Brent describes Flint as a fiend, Northerners, because of their own hypocrisy and their refusal to listen to "truths," are likewise constructed as the monstrous bloodhounds and uncivilized slave-catchers in antislavery territory.

This refiguration of the well-meaning readers is particularly devastating with respect to its implication for white women. Their participation, as readers, in the silencing of Brent sanctions her sexual exploitation by Flint; the identification of their need for silence with his recontextualizes

---

8. Certainly the descriptions of Flint's initial attempts to corrupt Brent are marked with what other readers have called "omissions and circumlocution" designed to give some modicum of protection to the narrator — who seems unwilling to relive the details of the event — or to encourage the potential voyeurism of the white reader regarding Brent's experience of a distressing situation. See Yellin, "Introduction," xxi, and especially Foreman, "The Spoken and the Silenced," 317.
9. I am grateful to M. Giulia Fabi for helping me develop this idea.

these women's popular representation as saviors. They have, in fact, joined the ranks of Brent's male tormentors, a shift that threatens to de-feminize them. So, clearly, Brent's appeal is not solely for the protection of the slave victim: What is at risk also is the very notion of femininity and true womanhood white Americans have hitherto idealized.

Since Brent wants to arrest the attention of her audience without alien-ating it, she provides a vivid but distanced dramatization of white female collusion in a half-sarcastic, half-regretful description of Mrs. Flint as the failed maternal figure who might protect her from the doctor's torments. When her husband's sexual designs on Brent become too obvious, Mrs. Flint's anger is aroused. Up to this point Brent has represented Flint's sex-ual harassment as incestuous, a violation of the codes of familial decency. He demands to have his four-year-old daughter sleep in his chamber, as an excuse for Brent to remain in the room; here one wonders if Flint ex-pects the child to be present while he tries to rape her nurse. The narra-tive thus creates the need for a response from Mrs. Flint, the family's moral guardian, not just to save Linda, but indeed to save the white fam-ily as well.

Brent has already painted Mrs. Flint as the stereotypically lethargic but cruel slave mistress; here she urges the need to understand the secrets of slavery and to act against the institution as a necessary self-protective mea-sure. Mrs. Flint's (and the white female reader's) salvation as the moral center of the family will depend on her ability to uncover the master's se-crets, despite his subterfuge. If she depends on her own abilities of dis-cernment, she will fail: Mrs. Flint "watched her husband with unceasing vigilance; but he was well practiced in means to evade it" (*I*, 31) [28]. Her only hope of comprehending the problem and shifting her position from accommodating ignorance to effecting change is to allow herself to heed the words of the slave narrator.

Significantly, in the same chapter in which Brent teaches herself to write (and thus begins her journey to the present white audience as au-thor/commentator), Mrs. Flint finally allows a painful interview with Brent that lays bare the details of her husband's debauchery. Brent's words also suggest their commonality as virtuous females who have been violated by exposure to a slaveholder's conduct:

> As I went on with my account her color changed frequently, she wept, and sometimes groaned. She spoke in tones so sad, that I was touched by her grief. The tears came to my eyes. . . . She felt that her marriage vows were desecrated, her dignity insulted. (*I*, 33) [30]

But because Mrs. Flint is a model of white female ineptitude, she is un-able to grasp the connection between herself and Brent: "She pitied her-self as a martyr; but she was incapable of feeling for the condition of shame and misery in which her unfortunate, helpless slave was placed" (*I*, 33) [30].

Rather than trust the testimony of a slave who has raised the first blow against the master's evasions by disobeying the order of silence, an angry Mrs. Flint becomes obsessed with observing Brent's body, a move that links her unmistakably with the readers addressed in Child's introduction. Mimicking her husband's construction of the slave woman as the object of (sexual) desire, Mrs. Flint situates Brent "in a room adjoining her own," keeping a constant watch on the slave victim, rather than on her husband. Enacting an "especial care" of Brent, Mrs. Flint scrutinizes Brent's body in hopes of a more comforting version of events that will somehow contradict what she has already heard. And when her attention parallels Flint's own lascivious obsession with Brent ("Sometimes I woke up, and found her bending over me"), Mrs. Flint is transformed into the corrupting seducer intent on tricking Brent into becoming the site of sexual contamination (*I*, 34) [31].[1]

But in a clever repositioning of herself as the reader of Mrs. Flint's body, Brent carefully describes the slave mistress's self-seduction by the details of her own falsely constructed narrative of sexual misconduct. Working under the delusion that Brent is the corrupter of Dr. Flint, the slave mistress attempts to elicit unconscious responses from her (at night "she whispered in my ear, as though it was her husband who was speaking to me, and listened to hear what I would answer"), responses that will confirm her "truth" that Brent is the real threat to the sanctity of her marriage and home (*I*, 34) [31]. But when Brent is represented as the seducer, Dr. Flint is shielded once more by an "audience's" refusal to listen to slave testimony. With the unwitting Mrs. Flint working hard to support her husband's deceptive practices, Brent becomes the only resister holding out for a true account of the events.

Brent's narrative suggests that, as an ideal method of misreading, Mrs. Flint's self-consoling validation of white interpretive powers through an invalidation of the black voice reinforces white visions of racial superiority, but it has little to do with the freeing of slaves or with national moral reform. The story of Mrs. Flint's failure stands as a textual lesson for Brent's readers about how Northern domestic morality can quickly become ineffective (indeed self-annihilating) when whites fail to recognize the folly of designating the victim's, rather than the slaveholder's, testimony as the source of offense. At moments such as these the text forces a confrontation between the dual myths of a manifestly present white authority and a manifestly absent black authority to interpret the meaning of slave speech. The interview between Mrs. Flint and Brent provides the Northern audience with two choices: either they participate in the exploitation of the slave body and remain deaf to the only credible interpreter available (Brent herself), in which case they are identified with the

---

1. Though Hortense Spillers gives a different but related reading of Mrs. Flint's role as seducer, I am indebted to her discussion for the formulation of my own.

duped and demonic slave mistress, or they admit to the necessity of allowing Brent not just to speak to but to guide them, as part of the initial
step toward abolition.

If we are indeed meant to read this failed interview between Mrs.
Flint and Brent as a representation of the reader's rejection of the black
female slave narrator, what is at stake finally is not Mrs. Flint's (and
the Northern audience's) misplaced obsession with the artificial
dichotomy of white spiritual morality versus black bodily immorality,
but rather the hope that there might exist a national moral landscape
where respect and protection for white ideals will translate into respect
and protection for the black victim. I am not suggesting here that
Incidents in the Life of a Slave Girl is voicing a simplistic call to interracial unity. Rather, I am suggesting that the text questions the character of a white nation that establishes its moral ideals on a victimiz-
ing construction of blackness.

Earlier, in describing her plight as an unprotected slave girl, Brent
has evoked the traditional contrasts between the sexually exploited
female slave and her supposedly more fortunate white counterpart:
The black slave accepts "the cup of sin, and shame, and misery,"
whereas the white child becomes "a still fairer woman" whose life is
"blooming with flowers, and overarched by a sunny sky" up until the
moment of her marriage (*I*, 29) [28]. But although the ideal of the
white true womanhood depends on the perceived existence of its opposite, the sexualized black female, how ideal an image is sanctified, privatized white ladyhood, and thus domesticity, if it has to be safeguard-
ed through the silencing of slave discourse on rape and sexual terror,
and a tolerance of slavery?

The notion that white ladyhood will have no real value in any community supporting slavery is made clear by Brent when she analyzes the
implication of Flint's attempt to bribe her with promises of fair treatment:
"'Have I ever treated you like a negro? . . . I would cherish you. I would
make a lady of you.'" (*I*, 35) [32]. Brent suggests that Flint's offer of a falsified female respectability is not that of the pampered quadroon mistress
but that of white femininity itself. At this point Brent drops the personifi-
cation of corrupted white womanhood as exclusively Southern by referring directly to Northerners supportive of slavery through acceptance of
the Fugitive Slave Law. They willingly jeopardize the sensibilities of their
own women when they "proud[ly] . . . give their daughters in marriage
to slaveholders" (*I*, 36) [32]. Lulled into ignorance by "romantic notions"
about Southern life, these woman (again note the connection with Mrs.
Flint) enter brothellike settings: "The young wife soon learns that the
husband in whose hands she has placed her happiness pays no regard to
his marriage vows. Children of every shade and complexion play with her
own fair babies. . . . Jealousy and hatred enter the flowery home, and
it is *ravaged* of its loveliness" (*I*, 36) [32]; emphasis added). Brent's choice

of words unmistakably implies that through white moral neglect, the rape of the slave woman will translate into the rape of the Northern/Southern home.

III

In recounting her life with the Flints, Brent demonstrates the futility of white analyses that address neither the sexual politics of slavery nor the right of slaves to speak. Such avoidance cannot lead whites to effective agency in the abolition of slavery and, in the face of the audience's failure to act its part (as exemplified by Mrs. Flint), *Incidents in the Life of a Slave Girl* suggests that without white sympathy Brent is not only compelled to enact her own strategy for emancipation; she must succeed on the very terms of what whites perceive to be black female moral failure. In contrast to those who interpret black bodies as merely metaphors for slavery, Linda Brent works to achieve her own liberation by dictating a radical resignification of black physicality against the fundamentally linked expectations of both Dr. Flint and Northern white readers. Though the moral vacuum created by Mrs. Flint's retreat forces Brent to take a white lover to save herself from Flint, this moment of the female slave's apparent physical self-abasement is transformed by the narrative into an articulation of staunch resistance: "I knew nothing would enrage Dr. Flint so much as to know that I favored another; and it was something to triumph over my tyrant even in that small way" (*I*, 55) [47].

To authorize her appropriation of the white power to liberate, Brent enacts a second moment of confrontation when she addresses offended readers who, like Mrs. Flint, come across distasteful information (her decision to submit to Sands's overtures). Will the readers blame Linda for sexual promiscuity, or will they accept her pronouncement that "the slave woman ought not to be judged by the same standards as others" (*I*, 56) [48] in the struggle for her freedom? At this point the narrative exhibits an oft-noted schizophrenic quality, retreating back and forth between a very matter-of-fact, dispassionate detailing of a material strategy of manipulation and admissions of guilt and emotional appeals for the audience's forgiveness:

> I thought he [Dr. Flint] would revenge himself by selling me, and I was sure my friend, Mr. Sands, would buy me. . . . Pity me, and pardon me, O virtuous reader! . . . I know I did wrong. No one can feel it more sensibly than I do. (*I*, 55) [47–48][2]

2. Contemporary scholars have long been fascinated by Brent's discussion of her affair with Mr. Sands, because it seems to be a curious mixture of shame, regret, defiance, and "deliberate calculation" (*I*, 24) [46]. For illuminating discussions of Brent's description of her affair with Sands in the context of a domestic narrative that shuns any discussion of sexuality, see Yellin, "Introduction," xxix–xxxi; Foreman, "The Spoken and the Silenced," 322–3; Valerie Smith, "Loopholes of Retreat," 222; Andrews, *To Tell a Free Story*, 254–6. See also Laura E. Tanner, "Self-Conscious Representation in The Slave Narrative," *Black American Literature Forum* 21:4 (Winter 1987): 415–24.

But does such a duality signify regret for mistaken action and a desire to be seen as a truthful, virtuous witness, or does it dramatize the conflict between, on the one hand, Brent's desire to record in her own words the transformation from victim to actor on the very terms of the slave woman's oppression (that is, her sexuality), and, on the other, her white audience's determination to reject that transformation and its implied transference of agency from the abolitionist to the slave? *Incidents* is patterned after novels of domesticity but, as Carolyn Karcher has shown, Brent's literary tradition is the domestic novel specifically politicized as antislavery fiction.[3] Thus, although Brent's problematic apologies would seem to refer to the indelicacy of her sexual choices, they stress that such acts of self-liberation are unacceptable only within the context of antislavery fiction that would value the passivity rather than the resistance of the exploited female slave.

Up to this moment, Brent's role as victim is crucial to effect the construction of the white savior. Up to this moment, the fairly traditional presentation of Brent as the silent, shamefaced slave girl whose ordeal remains inoffensive as long as it is discreetly unvoiced has exemplified, at least superficially, Child's promised history of bodily horrors presented in the slave's silence. But Brent's body becomes offensive in the text precisely when the narrative begins to articulate a different system of bodily representation, one that jeopardizes the political role of the reader. Thus what is now offensive in Brent's account is her claim to agency: the move toward self-ownership that transforms her body from an emblem for white self-construction to the enabling tool for black action. Again, the implied sense of the Northern reader's affront to, condemnation of, and even anger at Brent is also shared by Dr. Flint, revealing that even as Brent appears to pay homage to pure Northern sensibilities, she questions those sensibilities by aligning them with a designated foe of domestic morality. Such an alignment also implies that anger at her action must come from the same basic source: a resentment for her defiance of white power over the slave.

After the narrative's indictment of the reader's authority to comprehend Brent's situation or to act on her behalf, the slave suggests an alternative audience and agent of salvation: female slaves themselves. If Mrs. Flint is a failed reader, Aunt Martha is cautiously styled as her opposite — cautiously, because even though she receives Brent's story of sexual manipulation with "an understanding and compassion readers are meant to share," she does not grant Brent her forgiveness.[4] Nevertheless Aunt Martha's acceptance of Brent's narrative (which has a cathartic effect for Brent) signals the potential for a transformed relationship between

3. See her "Rape, Murder and Revenge," esp. 330.
4. Mills, "Lydia Marie Child . . . ," 259.

speaker and reader and provides the next step in Brent's achievement of physical freedom from the Flint household.

Once she acknowledges the conditions from which Brent has emerged, Aunt Martha—along with other women in her community— offers her shelter as Brent enacts a scheme to free her two children by Sands. In her effort to disappear from sight and thereby convince Flint he has nothing to gain by refusing to sell her children, Brent retreats to an attic crawl space of Aunt Martha's house. What is important here is the fact that Brent removes her body from the relations between herself and Flint, so that the master's power is now diminished precisely because the material basis for his role has vanished. In a narrative dramatizing the struggle to tell a supposedly sympathetic audience about the need to abolish slavery, Brent demonstrates the power of her voice as Flint is forced to follow the directives of her discourse via letters sent from various Northern locations by the "escaped" slave Linda. When her manipulations eventually lead a frustrated Flint to sell the children to Mr. Sands, Brent emerges as the true liberator in the narrative.

It is important that as a mother herself, Brent achieves her children's freedom by both enacting and critiquing the central metaphor of maternity which describes the abolitionist platform for social reform. From her hiding place Brent watches over her children, appears mysteriously to urge their father to take them north, and visits them at night as if she were an apparition. As the "disembodied" matron who must literally watch her children from above, Brent ridicules Northern white metaphoric self-construction (abolitionists supposedly watch over the slaves) as "maternal" saviors. In describing herself as the ethereal mother within the relative privacy of her grandmother's home, Brent continually indicates the white impediments to safeguarding that privacy, as Aunt Martha's domestic peace is regularly violated by Dr. Flint and other enforcers of white law. Brent's self-construction here registers a warning against an idealization of the spirit of maternity that severs it from the material conditions of the body. Lest we romanticize her role as maternal figure in the "Loophole of Retreat," Brent continually reminds us that she is actually cut off from her children and that she also suffers a confinement of the body that is tortuous: enduring sickness, painful insect bites, extremes of heat and cold, and frostbite, she has to accept that her limbs might never recover from their imprisonment (I, 114) [91].

Her articulation of bodily torture in the performance of maternal duty becomes a plea for a new construction of maternal power that includes black women; idealized maternity, like idealized womanhood, cannot function for black women if it celebrates moral action but denigrates attempts at physical survival. Brent acts like a mother while she is hiding, but she achieves liberating motherhood for her children only when she is reunited with them. Otherwise Brent is destined to imitate in part the life of her deceased Aunt Nancy, whose physical connection to motherhood has been stolen by slavery until she is "stricken with paralysis" (*I*, 144) [114], and finally dies without the ability to speak.

The text stresses the need to attend to the slave woman's body, as well as her soul, when Brent's position is juxtaposed with that of the dead Nancy: she calls herself "a poor, blighted young creature, shut up in a living grave for years" (*I*, 147) [116]. Although some readers have recently argued that Brent's confinement can be read partially as a metaphor of birth in that Aunt Martha has provided "a protective womb for Linda's birth to freedom," or that Brent "manages to convert that tomb into a womb" by reaffirming ties with her family, by remaining in the attic she risks a still-birth into inertia, rather than physical freedom or active motherhood.[5] Eventually, when Brent goes north, her escape from slavery is framed within the specific context of the need to address the alienated black body. Indeed, the freedom signified by the North can be tangible only if it signals a reclamation, a reversal of that alienation.

Brent goes north in 1842, after her daughter has been sent to New York to live with relatives of Mr. Sands, where she is later joined by her son. Yet what will become of her ultimate search in the North for "a home and freedom," a material situation first promised by Dr. Flint when he tried to bribe Brent into sexual submission (*I*, 83) [69]? Her search for the genuine article beyond the South is constantly frustrated by Northern conditions that duplicate almost exactly those survived by Brent and her family in North Carolina. Even before the passing of the Fugitive Slave Law in 1850, these conditions of "free" life included fear of physical capture, constant confinement, subterfuge, racism, and—for Brent's daughter Ellen—direct enslavement and even the threat of sexual harassment from white relatives. When Brent obtains a post as nursemaid in the Bruce household (the same post she occupied with the Flints), she must accept the position of surrogate mother. Such characterizations of Brent's experiences as essentially repetitions of slave life, despite the shift in region, demonstrate the narrative's active critique of the "freedom" offered to blacks by the North.

An important variation within the text's repetitive moments is Ellen's shift into Brent's former role, and Brent's into that of her grandmother. While Brent's own position improves (she has a kind employer), Ellen's condition worsens. Evoking a tangle of blood, capital, and control that characterized Brent's position in the Flint household, Mr. Sands's relative Mrs. Hobbs echoes Flint in her insistence on a tie of ownership between her family and their cousin Ellen: "I suppose you know that . . . Mr. Sands, has *given* her to my eldest daughter. She will make a nice waiting maid for her when she grows up" (*I*, 166) [131]. In addition, to hide

---

5. Ibid.; see also Stephanie A. Smith, "Conceived in Liberty: Maternal Iconography and American Literature, 1830–1900" (Ph.D. dissertation, University of California, Berkeley, 1990), 179.

their own alcoholism, Mr. Hobbs and his Southern brother-in-law Mr. Thorne employ Ellen to fetch their liquor, so much so that "she felt ashamed to ask for it so often" (*I*, 179) [139]. Though she suppresses this information so as not to burden her mother, Ellen is distressed by such concealment. This situation recalls Brent's own discomfort about, and concealment of, similar experiences during her girlhood: "I did not discover till years afterwards that Mr. Thorne's intemperance was not the only annoyance she suffered from him. . . . He had poured vile language into the ears" of the young girl (*I*, 179) [139].

Brent's metaphoric description of the exchange between Thorne and Ellen exactly mirrors those she used earlier in describing Dr. Flint's attempts to seduce her. Such reoccurrences challenge the notion of regional and political differences (Brent will soon call New York under the Fugitive Slave Law "the City of Iniquity"), since the use of the silenced black "slave" Ellen as a shield for white sins provides a parallel between the domestic life of slavery in the South and the domestic life of "freedom" in the North.

This pattern of duplicated suffering occurs in the vacuum created by white inaction, a vacuum that again demands that Brent emerge as the liberator. When it is discovered that Mr. Thorne has betrayed her location to Dr. Flint, Brent goes into hiding, but this time she takes Ellen with her. This rescue of another "slave girl" is achieved through "a mother's observing eye" (*I*, 178) [138], since Brent has read distress on Ellen's face: Replaying both the failed role of Mrs. Flint and the problematic role of Aunt Martha, Brent again defines the ideal of liberating maternity as one that must be informed by a willingness to come to terms with the physical nature of black female exploitation. Because of her own experience in slavery, she alone can claim the power of bodily interpretation. Also, Brent's recognition of Ellen's pain is mirrored by the daughter's own attempt to quiet her mother's silent fears about revealing the circumstance of her birth: "I know all about it mother. . . . All my love is for you" (*I*, 189) [146]. Thus the acknowledged suffering of mother and daughter enables isolating silences to be replaced with mutual understanding and comfort. In a sense Ellen and her mother do not need to speak of their experiences: the nature of their slavery—and Brent's ability to understand the terms of black female exploitation and to use them as the basis for a successful rescue of herself and her family—has already been voiced by the narrative's account of their reunion.

Long before Brent obtains her legal freedom, then, she articulates a particular kind of salvation that reunites the voice with the body of the slave, celebrates black actions against slavery, and finally appropriates the domestic discourse of maternity in order to reform it for the use of black women. But if Brent is now the successful mother, the successful speaker, and the successful abolitionist (at least in the sense of obtaining a relative

freedom for herself and her children), what role then does the Northerner play? Although *Incidents* suggests that Northern whites might actually represents a negative social force against the abolition of the slave's
condition, the text does not finally accept rigid binaries as the only
ground for black–white interaction. Throughout Brent has been helped
in small ways by Southern slave mistresses, slave traders, and others who
empathize with the slave's plight. But for Brent effective white empathy
must be accompanied with an activism that acknowledges a connection
rather than a dislocation between black and white bodies.

After the death of his English wife, Mr. Bruce remarries, and Brent's
new American mistress serves as the narrative's closing model for the
ideal white abolitionist. When Brent is forced into hiding to escape the
Flint family, the new Mrs. Bruce, like her Southern counterpart, is called
upon to offer protection. However, unlike Mrs. Flint, who recoiled from
any connection to Brent, Mrs. Bruce embraces a strategy of redemption
that causes her to risk her own domestic peace for the sake of resisting the
North's moral ineptitude.

Mrs. Bruce allows her own child to accompany Brent into hiding as a
scheme to force the slave-catchers to alert the white mother should the
slave be caught. For Brent this is not a paternalistic act, but one of self-
sacrifice: "How few mothers would have consented to have one of their
own babes become a fugitive, for the sake of a poor, hunted nurse, on
whom the legislators of the country had let loose the bloodhounds" (*I*,
194) [150]. Mrs. Bruce's temporary abandonment of her child for the
sake of a slave's freedom redefines the possibility of domestic feminism's
role in abolition, because it forces Mrs. Bruce, even in a limited way, to
experience the same sense of maternal loss that Brent experienced when
she left her children in pursuit of their freedom. By breaking the Fugitive Slave Law, Mrs. Bruce invites imprisonment and financial penalties,
and in doing so she demonstrates a willingness to endure a kind of physical suffering that does not duplicate slavery, but comes close to it: "I will
go to the state's prison, rather than have any poor victim torn from *my*
house, to be carried back to slavery" (*I*, 194) [150–51].[6] Yet, although
Brent's representation of Mrs. Bruce's active sympathy suggests that
whites can help through a more sincere and deliberate sharing of risks,
the fact that the slave's freedom can be secured only by a bill of sale between her benefactress and the Flint family still indicts the North: "the
bill of sale is on record, and future generations will learn from it that

6. Interestingly, Jacobs originally ended her narrative with a chapter on John Brown, the white militant abolitionist executed for his attack on Harper's Ferry. In a letter to Jacobs, Child said she
thought it "had better be omitted," adding that "Nothing could be so appropriate to end with, as
the death of your grandmother" (reprinted in *I*, 244). [Reprinted on pp. 193–94 of this Norton
Critical Edition (*Editor*).] Arguing for the appeasement of the audience through an appeal to
their sympathies, Child wanted to steer Jacobs away from discussions about direct political action by encouraging her to end with "tender memories of my good old grandmother, like light
fleecy clouds floating over a dark and troubled sea" (*I*, 201) [156]. For a discussion of Child's reaction to John Brown see Mills, "Lydia Marie Child . . . ," 255–72.

women were articles of traffic in New York, late in the nineteenth century of the Christian religion" (*I*, 200) [155].[7]

In concluding her critique, Brent refuses to validate the freedom offered to her in the North, but instead problematizes this freedom almost to the last sentence: "We are as free from the power of slaveholders as are the white people of the north; and though that . . . is not saying a great deal, it is a vast improvement in *my* condition" (*I*, 201) [156]. Brent's ambivalence arises from the fact that "the dream of my life is not yet realized. I do not sit with my children in a home of my own" (*I*, 201) [156]. These bitter reflections (Is the North really free of slavery? Do homelessness and the struggle to overcome poverty in the North represent a major improvement?) challenge naive notions of freedom and as such affirm the black critiques Jacobs has been working to uncover through the narrative of Linda Brent. Revering the memory of Aunt Martha, and fully aware of the new struggles that await her on the "dark and troubled sea" signified by Northern black life, Brent ends the narrative by validating herself as a survivor and an active critic of both the North's and the South's peculiar forms of social injustice.

ELIZABETH V. SPELMAN

The Heady Political Life of Compassion[†]

One important function of slave narratives and other critical depictions of North American slavery was to generate compassion in their audiences, provoke the kind of feeling that would incline readers to help relieve suffering and oppose evil. In *Incidents in the Life of a Slave Girl, Written by Herself*, the ex-slave Harriet Jacobs, writing under the pseudonym Linda Brent, expresses hope that she can "kindle a flame of compassion in your hearts for my sisters who are still in bondage, suffering as I once suffered." Having been so moved, perhaps readers will cease being silent and join others "laboring to advance the cause of humanity."[1]

---

7. Echoing William Andrews, Dana D. Nelson argues that Mrs. Bruce is still a slaveholder and that for Brent, "serving, whether under compulsion or privilege, remains servitude: the structure of this sympathetic identification is one of hierarchy, not equality." However, although Brent articulates an unmistakable resentment by the narrative's end, her anger is directed not at Mrs. Bruce herself, as some critics have suggested, but at the contradictory legal and social "circumstances" allowed to develop in the North, so that Mrs. Bruce's genuine act against the slaveholders is itself compromised by its resemblance to slavery. For Nelson's comments, see *The Word in Black and White*, 141. See also Andrews, *To Tell a Free Story*, 260–2.

† From *Fruits of Sorrow: Framing Our Attention to Suffering* (Boston: Beacon Press, 1997) 59–89, 184–89. Copyright © 1997 by Elizabeth V. Spelman. Reprinted by permission of Beacon Press, Boston. Page references to this Norton Critical Edition are given in brackets following Spelman's original citations.

1. *Incidents in the Life of a Slave Girl, Written by Herself* [1861], ed. Jean Fagan Yellin (Cambridge: Harvard University Press, 1987), 29–30 [27–28].

But as Harriet Jacobs herself well understood, far from tending to undermine the master-slave relation, kindly feelings of various sorts may simply reflect and reinforce it. For example, the white abolitionist Angelina Grimké exposed the political logic of certain emotions when she rightly read the "pity" and "generosity" of certain whites as indicative of their "regard[ing] the colored man as an *unfortunate inferior,* rather than as an *outraged and insulted equal.*"[2] Frances Ellen Watkins Harper found it necessary to insist, in an 1891 speech to the National Council of Women of the United States, that she came "to present the negro, not as a mere dependent asking for Northern sympathy or Southern compassion, but as a member of the body politic who has a claim upon the nation for justice, simple justice."[3]

So while Harriet Jacobs was in part hoping to arouse compassion and concern in an apathetic and neglectful white audience, like Grimké and Harper she was aware that appeals for compassion could be politically problematic. *Incidents* is a political text not simply because it is meant to get its audience to challenge existing institutions but also because it constitutes an ex-slave's struggle against readings of her experiences of slavery that would reflect and reinforce the master-slave relationship. Indeed, we cannot adequately understand the plea for compassion in *Incidents in the Life of a Slave Girl* unless we look at Jacobs's ongoing attempts throughout the text to assert and maintain authority over the meaning of her suffering. As Mary Helen Washington has pointed out, narratives such as Jacobs's exhibit slave women as "active agents rather than objects of pity."[4] Jacobs wants her audience's compassion, but she wants that compassion to be well informed. She needs to have the members of her audience understand that she and others are suffering, but she is highly attuned to the power that their knowledge of her suffering can give them, and so she simultaneously instructs them how to feel. She insists on her right to have an authoritative—though not unchallengeable—take on the meaning of her suffering.

Jacobs is aware of the debates going on over her suffering. She knows that something is at stake in the determination of the nature of her pain, its causes, its consequences, its relative weight, its moral, religious, and social significance. And if there is such an explicit or implicit struggle, the meaning of her pain is not a given. Competing interpretations are

---

2. Angelina Grimké, letter 17 to Catharine Beecher, in *The Public Years of Sarah and Angeline Grimké: Selected Writings 1835–1839,* ed. Larry Ceplain (New York: Columbia University Press, 1989), 171. Emphasis in the original.
3. Frances Ellen Watkins Harper, address, "Duty to Dependent Races," National Council of Women of the United States, *Transactions* (Philadelphia, 1891), 86. As quoted in *Black Women in Nineteenth-Century American Life,* ed. Bert James Loewenberg and Ruth Bogin (University Park: Pennsylvania State University Press, 1976), 247.
4. "Introduction: Meditations on History: The Slave Woman's Voice," in *Invented Lives: Narratives of Black Women 1860–1960,* ed. Mary Helen Washington (Garden City, N.Y.: Doubleday-Anchor, 1987), 8.

possible, and something important hangs on which interpretation or interpretations prevail.

For the meaning of someone's pain to be debatable in these ways is to give it a place in what Hannah Arendt referred to as the "public realm," that is, for the pain to be a topic about which different people may well have different views, and thus for it to be among the items consituting a common, public world for these people not despite the fact but precisely because of the fact that their separateness is thereby revealed. Like Harriet Jacobs, though in another context a century later, Hannah Arendt was deeply interested in the relationship between compassion and political action. But in Arendt's account the kind of debate over the meaning of suffering which I have described as a crucial context of *Incidents* cannot even take place, for the kind of pain to which compassion is an appropriate response is not something over which varying perspectives are even possible. Moreover, according to Arendt public professions of concern about the suffering of others are by their very nature bound to degenerate into pity, which accentuates the distance and inequality between those in pain and those exhibiting feeling for them. By Arendt's lights, Harriet Jacobs's invocation of the compassion of northern white women runs the serious risk of simply reinforcing the very forms of inequality Jacobs hoped her plea would begin to undermine. * * *

* * *

Harriet Jacobs published *Incidents in the Life of a Slave Girl, Written by Herself,* in 1861.[5] Jacobs had by this time been living in the North almost twenty years, having escaped from North Carolina in 1842. At the suggestion of the white abolitionist Amy Post, Jacobs, using the pseudonym Linda Brent, began writing about her life in 1853. *Incidents* covers major events in Brent's[6] life during her years as a slave in the South and a fugitive in the North, including her attempts to rebuff and put an end to the incessant sexual advances of her de facto owner, Dr. Flint, as well as to avoid the emotional and physical cruelty of Dr. Flint's jealous wife; it also details her struggles to free her two children. The text ends in what Brent considers the self-contradictory moment at which her freedom is purchased by the northern white woman by whom she was employed.[7]

Incidents is explicitly addressed to northern whites, particularly north-

---

5. *Incidents.* Page references in this section are to this text.
6. Harriet Jacobs used the pseudonym Linda Brent no doubt for a variety of reasons, among them the desire to preserve the anonymity of Blacks and whites who had helped her. I shall refer to the main character of *Incidents* just as Jacobs did—as Linda Brent.
7. Though of course greatly relieved finally to be free, Brent rankles at the thought that her own freedom had to be *purchased:* "being sold from one owner to another seemed too much like slavery" (199) [155].

ern white Christian women.[8] And it is in many ways quite self-conscious about its aims: as mentioned earlier, Brent explicitly says that she hopes to "kindle a flame of compassion in [northern] hearts for my sisters who are still in bondage, suffering as I once suffered," in such a way that readers will join those "laboring to advance the cause of humanity" (29–30) [27–28], that is, join the abolitionist movement.[9] Well aware that most northerners were ignorant, misinformed, or simply complacent about the meaning of slavery for slaves themselves, Brent wanted to provide the kind of information that would generate the sort of feeling likely to lead to action on behalf of slaves.

Linda Brent's anxiety about the extent of the members of her audience's knowledge of events in her life, and the accuracy of their interpretation of her experience, is expressed throughout the text. Sometimes she worries that they can't possibly know what slavery is like ("You never knew what it is to be a slave" [55; see also 141, 173 (47; 111, 135)]).[1] At other times she insists that surely the mothers in particular in her audience can know what it is like to have their children torn from them (16, 23) [17, 23]. *Incidents* is a sustained attempt to give shape to and control the meaning of the compassion of its white audience. Brent wishes to contribute to determinations of what the actual harms of slavery are and what, in considerable detail, ought to be the response to such harms. In this way she is hoping to highlight the insidious political dynamics of caring for the downtrodden about which Grimké, Harper, Arendt, and others were so concerned: feeling for others in their suffering can simply be a way of asserting authority over them to the extent that such feeling leaves no room for them to have a view about what their suffering means, or what the most appropriate response to it is.

Brent, then, was keenly aware of the risks she was taking in pleading for compassion. Her recognition of these risks, and the lengths she went

8. "I do earnestly desire to arouse the women of the North to a realizing sense of the condition of two millions of women at the South, still in bondage, suffering what I suffered, and most of them far worse" (1) [5]. The rest of *Incidents* makes clear that it was to their virtues as Christian women, particularly Christian mothers, that Brent especially appealed. As Frances Smith Foster has pointed out to me, Jacobs's work dates from a time in her life when she was nominally free and actively engaged in abolitionist activity not only with whites but with other free Blacks (for example, she and her brother ran an abolitionist reading room in Rochester, New York). She knew her work was likely to be read by other ex-slaves, who were an implicit if not explicit audience.

9. There were, of course, different abolitionist camps, but distinguishing among them is not a major concern of Brent here.

1. Linda Brent indicates in a variety of ways the limitations on the slaves' knowledge of their own and other slaves' experiences. In the context of commenting on to what extent the brutality of slavery blunted slaves' awareness of "the humiliation of their position," she includes herself among those who, precisely because they were so aware of what they went through, "cannot tell how much" they actually suffered nor how much they are "still pained by the retrospect" (28) [26–27]. So while she insists that she has a much better idea than her audience of what slavery means, she does not hold that her claims to knowledge are themselves complete or unblemished. She also points out that though slaves went through many similar experiences, there is much one slave may not know about the trials of another. For example, Linda Brent rhetorically asks, in connection with another female slave from her hometown: "How could she realize my feelings?" Not having had children herself, Linda implies, Betty couldn't really understand why Linda's attachment to her children made such a difference to her (102; cf. 157) [83; 124].

to to counteract them, tell us a lot about the moral and political dangers of becoming the object of compassion. In many ways *Incidents* is a lesson in how to assert your status as moral agent, and maintain authorship of your experiences, even as you urge your audience to focus on the devastating suffering to which you have been subjected against your will. Brent is well aware that in the process of getting her audience to feel for her and other slaves as crushed victims of an evil institution supported by cruel people, she may simply provoke hostile disapproval of her actions and character, or an anemic kindliness, mistakenly understood by those who feel it to be proof of their Christian virtue. So she takes great care *instructing* her audience about what they are to think and feel: she alerts the members of her audience to the kinds of misreadings and misunderstandings to which they are likely to be subject; she tries to establish herself as a moral agent and political commentator and not simply a victim; and she encourages her audience to feel not only compassion but outrage in response to slavery.

First, Brent distinguishes the response she is looking for from other responses with which it had been or could be easily confused, especially in the social and political climate of the United States in the mid-nineteenth century. She has only scorn for those alleged forms of affection and generosity not uncommonly exhibited by slave owners for their chattel—for example, treacly memories of "faithful slaves" (7) [11] and yearly gifts of hateful clothing (11) [13]. Slaves are so often deceived by whites, Jacobs says, that they have no reason to trust that "kind words" have anything but some "selfish purpose" (169; cf. 158) [132; 125]. She sees right through Dr. Flint, whose dealings with her centered around his incessant sexual harassment, and she ridicules his offer of kindly feelings toward her as proof of his forbearance from using all the powers of violence at his disposal. She refuses to regard such feelings as something for which she ought to feel gratitude (59, 61) [50–51, 52].

In her commentary on the meaning of all these varieties of "kindly feeling," Linda Brent puts her audience on notice: she does not wish to be understood to be asking for feelings in whites that are simply weapons demonstrating their cruel power. She makes clear that the kind of response she is hoping for from northern whites is entirely different from what passes as kindly Christian feeling in the South (12, 31, 124) [14–15, 28, 98–99]. Even when expressions of charity are not laced with condescension, being the object of charity is hardly to be compared with being the subject of freedom (89, 201) [73, 156].

She does provide instructive examples of the type of feeling she *does* value. She singles out for readers' attention unnamed abolitionists who in the process of inquiring about her life and her escape from slavery indicated recognition of her full membership in the human community by careful concern not to "wound [her] feelings" (161) [127]. In expressing admiration and gratitude for the response she got from the abolitionists

Amy and Isaac Post, Brent makes no reference to how they feel but rather to how they judged: "They measured a man's worth by his character, not by his complexion" (189) [147].

Indeed, in many ways Brent is much less interested in how friendly people may feel about her and her story than in whether their actions reveal that they take her seriously as a moral agent. I don't say this because I think we ought to dismiss her plea for compassion. There is no doubt that however stylized it was—however much it was the expected and proper mode of politely if urgently drawing attention to her plight—she was dismayed and appalled not only by the absence of such feeling but by the presence of cruelty (see 28) [26] and so certainly welcomed what she sometimes called "womanly sympathy" (162) [128] or deeds of "Christian womanhood" (100) [82]. But Brent was not to be satisfied with the simple invocation of the right feeling, and there is much to suggest that Brent herself was well aware of the ironic uses to which such stock images as "[the one] who pities my oppressed people" (201) [156] or "the poor, trembling fugitive" (111) [90] could be put even if she did not always uses them ironically.[2] Brent was aware of the need to employ wooden, stereotypical images of the helper and the helped, the savior and the sufferer, even as she did much to complicate and revise the impoverished ideas they invoked.[3]

But going beyond stock imagery was risky, too, for to talk about the particularities of her experience as a slave was to reveal facts about her that she had good reason to believe would not induce compassion, but harsh judgment. Among the horrors and great difficulties of being a slave was engaging in behavior that you might only not like but that you found immoral, that you felt bad about doing even while rightly reckoning that you had little or no control over whether you did it or not. Many if not most slave girls and women were raped or otherwise sexually assaulted or harassed by white boys and men; there was an unwritten law among white and Blacks that this was not to be talked about (28).[4] But as Linda Brent makes clear, it was also painful and risky for slave women to talk about such experiences to white women they implored for help, on account of that cruel logic according to which being subject to sexual assault is first and foremost an indication of the victim's immorality. (Indeed, Brent was reluctant to talk to her own dear grandmother about Dr. Flint, saying she

---

2. For example, on 201 [156] she does use these images ironically; on 111 [90], she doesn't.
3. Jean Fagan Yellin comments on the variety of ways in which Jacobs uses the "conventions of polite letters" in the "genteel manner of the period" while driving home an unconventional message. See her "Text and Contexts of Harriet Jacobs' Incidents in the Life of a Slave Girl: Written by Herself," in *The Slave's Narrative*, ed. Charles T. Davis and Henry Louis Gates, Jr. (Oxford: Oxford University Press, 1985), especially 267–274. Yellin also points out, in her introduction to *Incidents*, that Jacobs battled against the stereotype of the "tragic mulatto," whose inevitable demise could satisfy the emotions of those whites who prefer their Blacks to come to sad ends rather than achieve freedom (xxx).
4. Though Brent refers to criminal charges against slaves who reveal the names of white men who were fathers of their children (13) [16].

"felt shamefaced about telling her such impure things" [29] (27).) At the same time, part of the case she wishes to make to her white Christian audience about the evils of slavery is that it not only sanctioned and encouraged sexual encounters between white men and Black women but in many ways depended upon them for the continued creation of slave bodies.[5]

Having decided to put herself and other slave women forward as in need of the compassion of white northerners, Brent faced what we might call the dilemma of compassion: she could keep to a minimum the information necessary to invoke compassion, relying on stock images of trembling fugitives and kindly rescuers, and hence risk playing into the master-slave relationship she deplored; or she could reveal herself much further, in hopes of presenting herself as more than a mere victim, but at the risk of incurring hard questions about her behavior. That is, on the one hand she could try to invoke the aid of others without providing much contextual information. But this invites people to think of you only in terms of how you have suffered or been victimized; it risks forfeiting the possibility of establishing other facts about yourself that you don't want your audience to lose sight of, such as how you are not a victim but a moral agent. It obscures your right to question and critically appraise your would-be helper as a moral equal. The extent to which one person imploring the help of another does not dare to criticize the helper is a measure of the extent to which the sufferer is at the mercy of the savior.

In order to avoid the narrow roles of sufferer-savior, you can leap to the other horn of the dilemma and provide the kind of information about your state that will not only adequately inform your helper about important details but also will preclude the helper from seeing you simply as someone to whom horrible things have happened. By presenting yourself as not only in need of great help, but also as someone who makes decisions and judgments, you open up the possibility to your helper that despite your being in great need you are still capable of and insist on the right to make judgments about her even as she helps you. However, this course has serious risks, too: you cannot assume the benefits of being considered such an agent without also being subject to its burdens. The more you reveal about yourself and the more you establish yourself as other than a victim, the more likely you are to be the object of others' harsh judgments—especially if you are a nineteenth-century Black female slave alluding to sexual liaisons.

Linda Brent refers fairly directly to this dilemma when she reports to her white audience about an exchange she had with a particularly helpful abolitionist: Brent "frankly told him some of the most important events of my life. It was painful for me to do it; but I would not deceive

5. Slave women "are considered of no value, unless they continually increase their owner's stock. They are put on a par with animals" (49) [43].

him. If he was desirous of being my friend, I thought he ought to know how far I was worthy of it." The gentleman warned her: "Your straightforward answers do you credit; but don't answer every body so openly. It might give some heartless people a pretext for treating you with contempt" (160) [126–27].

This is a spectacular move by Brent. While it's true that earlier in the text she lets the members of her audience know that what she has to say may disturb them, here she instructs them about how any decent person would regard her revelations: only heartless people would have contempt for such honesty, would fail to see that Brent must provide authentic information if her would-be helpers are really to understand her situation.[6]

Brent, then, instructs her audience members in what they are to feel by distinguishing the reactions she hopes for from ones that she distrusts, by talking about exemplary responses, and by indicating her recognition of the risks she takes in providing the kind of information that she does.

Second, Brent insists on expressing her status as a moral agent. She sometimes speaks as if much of what slaves do they have to do, they are compelled to do. For example, early in the text, as she subtly introduces her audience to the "foul" (27) [26] and "impure" (29) [27] things white masters talk about or did to their Black female slaves, she says "she drank the cup of sin, and shame, and misery, whereof her persecuted race are compelled to drink" (29) [28]; so powerful are the forces allied against slaves that "resistance is hopeless" (51; cf. 100) [44; 81]. And yet *Incidents* celebrates her and other slaves' resistance,[7] even as Brent acknowledges that often in resisting she did things that she regards as "wrong" (55) [48] and for which she cannot and does not wish to "screen [my]self behind the plea of compulsion" (54) [46]. In particular she is "haunted" by the "painful and humiliating memory" of entering into a sexual relationship with another white man, in order to get Dr. Flint off her back. But she uses the occasion of bringing up this fact about her life to carve out a moral position somewhere between excusing herself, on the one hand, and presenting herself as unqualifiedly deserving of blame, on the other. She suggests to her audience that there are indeed standards by which she ought to be judged, but perhaps they are *not* those by which free people, free women, are to be judged (56) [48]. She takes pains to make clear that she has standards by which she appraises her own actions, even those toward whites: she takes pride in never "wronging" or ever wishing to wrong her cruel mistress Mrs. Flint (32) [29]; she worries about the harm that may come to those helping her escape, and insists that being caught would be better than "causing an innocent person to suffer kindness to me" (98) [80].

6. Sometimes (180) [140] Linda Brent worries that telling her whole story—"impurities" and all— would risk losing sympathy and the good opinion of someone (in this case Mrs. Bruce).
7. In this connection see Hazel Carby, *Reconstructing Womanhood: The Emergence of the Afro-American Woman Novelist* (New York: Oxford University Press, 1987), 22 and passim.

We may be inclined to regard some of this as evidence of her height-ened awareness of the need to convince her audience of her moral stature. But that is the point: she doesn't want her plea for help to erase her status as someone who nevertheless has difficult moral dilemmas about which she has had to make painful decisions for which she bears responsibility. For example, she takes responsibility for having made the extremely difficult decision to separate herself from her children in order to try to save them (85, 91, 141) [70, 75, 111]. She puts herself forward as a person with moral standards, who wishes to live under conditions in which she can be "a useful woman and a good mother" (133) [105]. She is ready to rebuke herself for selfishness (135) [106]. If she doesn't want her call for help to erase or exclude her status as someone who has moral standards to live up to, neither does she want it to render her ineligible as a moral critic of whites, southern or northern. For example, she does not hesitate to make sarcastic remarks about Mrs. Flint, her mistress, who prides herself on her Christian charity but enjoys inflicting mental and physical pain on Brent and other slaves (12, 13, 124, 136) [14–15,16, 98–99, 107–8], even while pretending to be moved by their sorrows (124, 146) [98, 115]. Mrs. Flint well knows her husband's ways, but instead of helping her female slaves respond to them, she simply inflicts her rage on the women (31) [28]. Like many other slave owners' wives, Mrs. Flint uses cruelty toward slaves to establish authority over them (92) [75].

And yet just as she has wondered aloud about the extent to which slav-ery forces slaves into morally compromising dilemmas, so Brent has an eye for the moral damage slavery does to whites (52) [45]: "slavery is a curse to the whites as well as to the blacks. It makes the white fathers cruel and sensual; the sons violent and licentious; it contaminates the daugh-ters, and makes the wives wretched. . . . Yet few slaveholders seem to be aware of the widespread moral ruin occasioned by this wicked system. Their talk is of blighted cotton crops — not of the blight on their children's souls." (52) [45]

In remarking that "cruelty is contagious in uncivilized communities" (47; cf. 198, 200) [41; 154, 155], Brent wonders just how "civilized" slave-owning society can be. Slavery "pervert[s] all the natural feelings of the human heart" (142) [112]. The power it affords poor whites prevents them from seeing how it in fact keeps them in "poverty, ignorance, and moral degradation" (64) [54].

Brent thus establishes herself in the moral community in a variety of ways. She expresses worry about what she takes to be immoral acts that slavery pushed slaves to commit. She presents herself as subject to moral standards. But she also exercises the right to contribute to an examination of what those standards ought to be, not only by introducing the possi-bility that people living under slavery ought not to be held to *all* the same standards as free people, but also by frequently offering biting critiques of the character and actions of southern and northern whites.

Third, while there is no doubt that Linda Brent values and hopes to succeed in prompting compassion from her audience, she also frequently suggests, directly or indirectly, that outrage would be an appropriate response to the conditions under which slaves (and fugitives) live. For example, early in the text she describes a scene that at first might strike the reader as a somewhat stylized attempt to pull the heartstrings, particularly those of the mothers in her audience: "Could you have seen that mother clinging to her child, when they fastened the irons upon his wrists; could you have heard her heart-rending groans, and seen her blood-shot eyes wander wildly from face to face, vainly pleading for mercy" (23) [23]. "Could you have seen this . . . ," then what? You would have been moved to tears? You would have felt for the mother, and stretched out a helping hand? That is not what Brent says: "could you have witnessed that scene as I saw it, you would exclaim, *Slavery is damnable!*" (23 [23]; emphasis in original).

Brent does not hesitate to express scorn for white northerners—especially "doctors of divinity" who make quick trips to the South, allow themselves to be hoodwinked, wined, dined, and flattered by their slaveholding hosts, and return North to chastise abolitionists. About such a "revered gentleman" she comments: "What does *he* know of the half-starved wretches toiling from dawn till dark on the plantations? of mothers shrieking for their children, torn from their arms by slave traders? of young girls dragged down into moral filth? of pools of blood around the whipping post? of hounds trained to tear human flesh? of men screwed into cotton gins to die? The slaveholder showed him none of these things, and the slaves dared not tell of them if he had asked them" (74 [62]; emphasis in original). Such a description does not seem intended so much to promote compassion for slaves as to evoke outrage at slave owners and the northerners who are duped by them. Brent's tone here is much different than when she refers to a slave mother wringing her hands in anguish (16) [17], or describes herself as "one of God's most powerless creatures" (19) [19], or expresses her fervent desire that her daughter "might never feel the weight of slavery's chain" (79) [66]. While these latter phrases leave room for, indeed seem to encourage a kind of weepy sadness (shades of *Uncle Tom's Cabin*), the former refer to conditions too horrible, too mean, too painful, too degrading, to be met with feelings as tender as compassion. Even more to the point, compassion in this context would direct us to slaves, while anger and outrage direct us to the slave owners and those who abet them.

In a passage somewhat similar to the above, Brent compares her own situation to that of most other slaves: "I was never cruelly over-worked; I was never lacerated with the whip from head to foot; I was never so beaten and bruised that I could not turn from one side to the other; I never had my heel-strings cut to prevent my running away; I was never chained to a log and forced to drag it about, while I toiled in the fields from morn-

ing till night; I was never branded with hot iron, or torn by bloodhounds"
(114–115) [92]. While it is true that she concludes this description with
the comment "God pity the woman who is compelled to lead such a life!"
(115) [92] this inventory of slavery's wrongs is calculated, I suggest,
to evoke much more than pity or compassion.[8] These are unspeakable
horrors, and hearing about them in this way directs attention not so much
to those who had to endure them as to the people and the institutions that
are responsible for them.

These renderings of the conditions of slavery, geared more to the generation of outrage than compassion, are of a piece with Brent's searing
critique of white society. So, even when her description of slavery is not
painfully lurid, it is clear that she is not so much concerned about her audience's response to slaves as its response to those who sustain slavery:
"Yet that intelligent, enterprising and noble-hearted man was a chattel,
liable, by the laws of a country that calls itself civilized, to be sold with
horses and pigs!" (156; see also 184, 191) [123; 142–43, 148].

In assuming the task of providing information about slavery to her audience that will instill outrage and sustained indignation about such
things taking place in their country, Brent is further instructing her
audience about how it ought to feel. Here she seems to be resisting (self-
consciously or not) two fairly strong forces current in the society. (1) Although appealing to the compassion of white northern women played to
a virtue that, according to a powerful stereotype for women of their class,
religion, and "race,"[9] they were supposed to have and cultivate, appealing to their sense of outrage did not (for example, Angelina Grimké battled with Catharine Beecher over white women's proper role in ending
slavery, and their differences in turn reflected a larger battle within abolitionist circles and between abolitionists and non- or anti-abolitionists
about the shape and goal of antislavery action).[1] (2) Slave narratives and
other abolitionist literature had a very wide readership, but at least some
of those readers seemed to find pleasure in the kinds of depictions of cruelty and pain of which we've just seen examples. For such readers some
of the narratives were what Robin Winks has referred to as "pious pornog-
raphy."[2] Lydia Maria Child, who edited *Incidents*, perhaps was referring

8. This is not to suggest that pity and compassion are the same.
9. The quotation marks around "race" are meant as a reminder that while the concept has had and
   continues to have a place in the way we think about ourselves and our histories, there is no good
   reason to think that the kinds of deep distinctions exist among human beings which the concept
   typically has been supposed to refer to. An idea doesn't have to be coherent or scientifically well
   founded in order for it to have profound effects on relationships among human beings. See, for
   example, Howard Winant and Michael Omi, *Racial Formation in the United States* (New York:
   Routledge & Kegan Paul, 1986).
1. See Angelina Grimké, letter 7 to Catherine Beecher, in *The Public Years of Sarah and Angelina
   Grimké: Selected Writings 1835–1839*, ed. Larry Ceplain (New York: Columbia University Press,
   1989), passim.
2. Robin Winks, ed., *Four Fugitive Slave Narratives* (Reading, Mass.: Addison-Wesley, 1969), vi. As
   quoted in Frances Smith Foster, *Witnessing Slavery: The Development of the Ante-Bellum Slave
   Narratives* (Westport, Conn.: Greenwood Press, 1979), 20.

to such tastes in her comment on rearranging some of Jacobs's manu-script: "I put the savage cruelties into one chapter . . . in order that those who shrink from 'supping upon horrors' might omit them, without interrupting the thread of the story."[3]

Describing slave experience in such a way as to provoke outrage thus could expand some readers' emotional responses even as it checked those of others. Those comfortable in their role as agents of care and compas-sion might think about whether reluctance to become angry or indignant was keeping them from some kinds of political action. Those finding de-light in the revelation of cruelty might find obstacles to their pleasure in hearing moral outrage, not simple pleas for mercy, in the voices of those on whom the cruelty is inflicted.

Linda Brent was highly attuned to the political logic of the variety of emotions her account of slavery was likely to stir up. Knowing the risks she was taking, at every turn she did what she could to minimize the dan-gers, instructing her readers about the differences among "kindly" re-sponses and about the special moral burdens slavery placed on both slave and slave owner. Instead of allowing her plea for compassion to become an invitation to her audience to take price in its good feelings, or to de-mean her as a helpless victim, she uses it as an occasion to exhibit the sig-nificance of the slave as moral agent and social critic. And yet she never for a moment suggests that she and other slaves do not need (though they should not "make capital out of"[4]) the good feelings of the very audience receiving lessons from her about what those feelings ought to be.

* * *

Compassion, like so many of our other complex emotions, has a heady political life. Invoking compassion is an important means of trying to di-rect social, political, and economic resources in one's direction (indeed, compassion is one of those resources). Existing inequalities between per-sons may be exacerbated rather than reduced through the expression of compassion. Interpretive battles over the significance of a person's or a group's suffering reflect larger political battles over the right to legislate meaning. The political stakes in the definition, evaluation, and distribu-tion of compassion are very high.[5]

---

3. As quoted by Jean Fagan Yellin in her introduction to *Incidents*, xxii.
4. *Incidents*, 190 [147]. At this point in the narrative Linda Brent is describing the importance to her daughter Ellen that her northern school classmates didn't know her slave history: Ellen "had no desire to make capital out of their sympathy."
5. In its various incarnations, this chapter has prompted probing questions and helpful suggestions from Molly Shanley, Uma Narayan, Martha Minow, and patient audiences at Williams College, Miami University, Hartwick College, the Institute fur die Wissenschaften vom Menschen in Vi-enna, and the University of California at Santa Cruz.

CHRISTINA ACCOMANDO

"The laws were laid down to me anew": Harriet Jacobs and the Reframing of Legal Fictions[†]

The narrative of Harriet Jacobs's life in slavery and eventual escape, published the year the Civil War began, poses a political argument that both condemns the laws of slavery and critiques dominant standards of (white) womanhood. As a literary text, *Incidents in the Life of a Slave Girl* has helped to reshape the genre of the slave narrative, previously discussed and defined primarily through male-authored texts.[1] In gaining recognition and prominence, both in critical studies and in course syllabi, Jacobs in many ways has come to represent "the" female slave narrator. This focus has been useful to emphasize family, constructions of womanhood, sexuality, female community, and other issues often de-emphasized or treated differently by male narrators. At the same time, there is a risk of reductiveness, of using Jacobs's multifaceted text only to discuss supposedly "female" concerns.[2] In addition to and intersecting with such issues is Jacobs's sustained *legal* critique, articulated on literal and figurative levels throughout her narrative. In the crucial years before the outbreak of civil war, Harriet Jacobs engaged in the legal debates over human enslavement. In *Incidents*, she reframes and rearticulates legal and cultural discourses of slavery and womanhood to uncover their fictive construction. Jacobs does not merely replace fiction with truth; instead, she calls on her readers to pay attention to framing (legal and otherwise) and to put into the frame erased perspectives.

As a multiply disfranchised subject, Jacobs writes against the dominant voices of Southern slave law and of the law itself. Antebellum legal scholars, like her contemporary Thomas Cobb (a Georgian who wrote the fundamental Southern treatise on slave law), framed their defenses of slavery in the falsely neutral and universal terms of legal rationality and precedent, while discrediting or omitting slave voices.[3] In numerous and var-

---

[†] From *African American Review* 32.2 (1998): 229–44. Reprinted by permission of the author. Page references to this Norton Critical Edition are given in brackets following Accomando's original citations.

1. See for example Braxton's article on *Incidents* as a redefinition of the slave narrative genre. Stepto takes male narrators and especially Douglass's 1845 book as his starting point in his influential study of African American narrative. Starling's pioneering work *The Slave Narrative* asserts that it is Douglass's book that "stands for the entire genre" (xvii). Foster's groundbreaking study *Witnessing Slavery* by her own account "seriously slights slave women's narratives" (xxii), although Foster would later focus on Jacobs and other women writers in *Written by Herself*.

2. Some readings concentrate on one element at the cost of reducing the complexity of Jacobs's approach. In a book that centers on constructions of the body in feminist and abolitionist rhetorics, Sanchez-Eppler emphasizes Jacobs's focus on sexual experience, arguing that sexuality and childbirth "are" this slave narrative (84). While interesting and provocative, her reading also de-emphasizes other concerns in Jacobs's book.

3. The erasing of slave voices persists well into the twentieth century. A 1991 Congressional briefing paper defends two Harvard professors accused of offering an imbalanced presentation of slav-

ied ways, the laws of slavery attempted to erase and silence African Americans, to deny their subjectivity, to say they did not exist as individuals. Laws governing legal testimony, racial identity, literacy, miscegenation, rape, and reproduction defined slaves and African Americans in specific yet contradictory ways—as nonhuman, with dangerous sexuality and nonexistent subjectivity. These legal and political fictions were just that—constructed fictions—but they have had tremendous power. Analyzing legal, political, and literary discourses of slavery can help deconstruct these fictions and their power (which did not vanish with emancipation). This article examines nineteenth-century statutes and Thomas Cobb's 1858 legal treatise alongside Harriet Jacobs's critique of slave law in order to probe contradictions in discourses of slavery and to demystify legal fictions more broadly.

Part of the power of legal discourse is its pretense at objectivity, neutrality, and rationality. The legal system attempts to make its workings and maneuvers invisible. Exposing instabilities and slippages, as Harriet Jacobs does in her narrative, helps to demystify these workings, not just in slave law but in its descendants as well. Legal scholar Angela Harris argues that introducing multiple voices and shifting perspectives as a theoretical approach to both law and literature can help dislodge this appearance of neutrality. In "Race and Essentialism in Feminist Legal Theory," Harris argues for "multiple consciousness" as an antidote to disciplinary restrictions in the voices of law and literature. It is crucial, she argues, not to let either possible extreme—the single "neutral" voice of law or the lack of context of literature—narrow the scope. While law and literature often are seen as occupying completely different spaces, challenging these boundaries can illuminate the study of both disciplines. Harris discusses literary and legal scholars who "struggle against their discipline's grain,"[4] and she argues for the need "to understand both legal and literary discourse as the complex struggle and unending dialogue between these voices." She seeks not a "static equilibrium between two extremes, but rather a process in which propositions are constantly put forth, challenged, and subverted" (237). I want to use her approach to destabilize the seemingly neutral language of law and policy by critiquing these discourses and eventually shifting discussion to other narratives as well. "In order to energize legal theory," argues Harris, "we need to subvert it with narratives and stories, accounts of the particular, the different, and the hitherto silenced" (255). I want to subvert the falsely "neutral"

---

ery by asserting that slaves failed to leave behind their own records: Stephan Thernstrom and Bernard Bailyn "were accused of racial insensitivity for . . . reading from the diary of a southern plantation owner without giving equal time to the recollections of a slave (of which none exist)" (Hyde 6). The brief and unsupported parenthetical erases what Starling estimates to be over 6,000 extant slave narratives (337).

4. Harris cites Henry Louis Gates, Jr., Gayatri Spivak, and Abdul JanMohamed, who read texts against codes of power, and Mari Matsuda, Patricia Williams, and Derrick Bell, who juxtapose legal theoretical voices with marginalized voices (237).

categories of slave law with narratives from Harriet Jacobs's book and with resistant readings of the laws themselves. Jacobs herself takes such an approach by subverting the dominant discourses with multiple voices and accounts of the silenced.

Such a project is important not only to understand a past moment in history, but also to contribute to an understanding of racism and legal discourse in the present. The current political climate in the U.S. is marked by both retrenchments in civil rights law and claims of progress and "color-blindness." From the Supreme Court's dilution of voting rights to the UC Board of Regents' elimination of affirmation action, attacks on the gains of the last three decades are cloaked in the language of neutrality and fairness. Judge and legal scholar A. Leon Higginbotham provides strategies for decoding such language through his examination of both slave law in U.S. history and racism in current law. Arguing that Americans must pay attention to the *legal* roots of slavery, he exposes various ways the seemingly neutral law sought to deny personhood to slaves and to African Americans more generally. "However tightly woven into the history of their country is the legalization of black suppression," he writes, "many Americans still find it too traumatic to study the true story of racism as it has existed under their 'rule of law'" (11). This "true story" is difficult to come by through a passive reading of law. Since "the language of the law shields one's consciousness from direct involvement with the stark plight of its victims," Higginbotham argues for a "skeptical reading" of legal discourse. Slave narratives can provide some of the material for such a reading of antebellum law. While Higginbotham focuses on historical analysis, he also points to modern legacies: "The poisonous legacy of legalized oppression based upon the matter of color can never be adequately purged from our society if we act as if slave laws had never existed" (391). By examining legal tellings of slavery in the mid-nineteenth century, from apologist Thomas Cobb to abolitionist Harriet Jacobs, we can confront that existence of slave law in an historical moment when debate over the legality of slavery was especially fierce. In the midst of modern-day claims of color-blindness and race neutrality,[5] it is particularly crucial to confront our history of *legalized* racial oppression.

"I have diligently sought for Truth": Thomas Cobb and the Rhetoric of Objectivity

Harriet Jacobs wrote her book during the 1850s, after Congress had further federalized slavery by passing the Fugitive Slave Act and after celebrated abolitionist author Harriet Beecher Stowe, whose literary help

---

5. One key example is California's Proposition 209, passed in 1996, which sought to dismantle civil rights policy throughout the state but ironically (and strategically) called itself "The California Civil Rights Initiative" and deployed the misleading language of evenhandedness, neutrality, and *anti*-discrimination.

had been sought, questioned Jacobs's authenticity and suggested incorporating Jacobs's story in her own upcoming book.[6] Both of these events helped to persuade Jacobs of the importance of publishing her own account of slavery. She completed her manuscript in 1858, the same year that Thomas Cobb published *An Inquiry into the Law of Negro Slavery in the United States of America: To Which is Prefixed, An Historical Sketch of Slavery*. In these years before the secession of the South, legal debates over slavery had taken on particular currency. A Georgia attorney, highly respected legal scholar, and later a framer of the Confederate Constitution, Cobb produced the only comprehensive Southern treatise on slave law.[7] Cobb would play a key role in articulating and interpreting Southern law, producing several legal works used by lawyers, law students, and judges, in his home state and elsewhere.[8] His articulation of slaveholding ideology expressed the dominant legal fictions that Jacobs counters in her narrative.[9] Cobb's treatise uses the rhetoric of legal "objectivity," positioning itself as neutrally based on law and precedent, while making an argument. Without stating his position as a position, Cobb supports the institution of slavery and constructs an argument about human enslavement as a positive good. Significantly, Cobb is not an extremist or even much of a partisan in his time; he is comfortably inside the dominant conversation—civilized, scientific, legal, rational.

That Cobb connects the law to eternal truths is made clear in the prospectus for the law school Cobb co-founded with his father-in-law Judge Joseph Lumpkin (who wrote key rulings on slave law).[1] The founders declare their intention "to teach law, not as a collection of arbi-

---

6. Stowe was working on *A Key to Uncle Tom's Cabin*, a nonfiction response to critics of her novel who claimed that its events were fabricated. Jacobs asked that Stowe not use any of her story in the book, stating, "I wished it to be a history of my life entirely by itself which would do more good and it needed no romance" (235).

7. In addition to his own credentials, Cobb was well-connected in Georgia. His brother, Howell Cobb, served as governor, member of Congress, and cabinet member under President Buchanan. Cobb's father-in-law Joseph Lumpkin was a Georgia Supreme Court justice. Cobb served nearly a decade as the reporter for the Georgia high court and co-founded with Lumpkin the first law school in Athens, Georgia.

8. In addition to his treatise on slave law, Cobb published *The Supreme Court Manual* (1849), *A Digest of the Statute Laws of the State of Georgia* (1851), fifteen volumes of Georgia Supreme Court decisions, and, most importantly, *The Code of the State of Georgia* (1861).

9. Cobb was respected and mainstream. "We can honestly recommend Mr. Cobb's Treatise as an able, liberal, and intelligent exposition of the views now held by the leading statesmen and lawyers of the South," stated the Philadelphia-based *American Law Register*. The *Register's* Northern editor praised Cobb for his reliance on the law: "Many vexed questions are examined, but always in a temperate spirit, and with reference solely to legal principles and established precedents" (qtd. in McCash 173).

1. Lumpkin's judicial rhetoric reveals the blurred lines between legal and other discourses. In an 1853 ruling on the limited rights of freed African Americans, for example, he concluded that "the social and civil degradation, resulting from the taint of blood, adheres to the descendants of Ham in this country, like the poisoned tunic of Nessus; that nothing but an Act of the Assembly can purify, by the salt of its grace, the bitter fountain—the 'darkling sea'" (*Bryan v. Walton* 185). In the midst of legal precedents, he also invokes the biblical son of Noah and the mythological centaur Nessus (whose bloody tunic adhered to Hercules, setting his skin on fire and killing him) to demonstrate the ancientness and permanence of blackness (set in contrast to the purity of legislation).

trary rules, but as a connected logical system, founded on principles which appeal for their sanction to eternal truth" (qtd. in McCash 125). The preface to his slavery treatise asserts objectivity: "My book has no political, no sectional purpose." Quickly noting and dismissing his likely bias as a Southerner, he affirms, "I have diligently sought for Truth, and have written nothing which I did not recognize as bearing her image" (x). With "Truth" as his goal, declarations of "fact" permeate the book. His assertions, though questionable, are frequently preceded with "in fact" or "it being admitted by all" or followed by "are indisputable facts." He rarely tries to persuade on the surface level: He merely recites "facts" and invokes "reason." Cobb sets zeal against reason and puts abolitionists in the camp of zealots. He indicts the "infatuated zeal of many fanatics." "In fact," he states, putting us in the realm of reason, "the history of abolitionism in the United States has been the history of fanaticism everywhere. . . ." He repeats that "in fact" any obstacles such extremists meet only "feed the flame of zeal, and more effectually dethrone the reason" (ccix–ccx). Cobb asserts that questions about the federal role in stopping slavery—questions that at this moment were setting the stage for civil war—are mere trivialities: "That these questions may be allowed here to rest, and be no longer used as hobbies by interested demagogues to excite sectional strifes for personal advancement, should be the sincere wish of every true American citizen" (ccxi). While Cobb asserts and reasserts his objectivity and claims to be on the side of "true" Americanism, anyone supporting national abolition is characterized as "interested."

"We could have told them a different story": Placing Frames at the Center

Harriet Jacobs and Thomas Cobb both claim the truth, but they have very different views of truth-telling, objectivity, and evidence. Jacobs frames her own text—an autobiographical narrative told by "Linda Brent," a constructed first-person narrator—with an awareness of framing and with attention to multiple perspectives. Jacobs knows that context matters and that narratives frequently are contested. The first line of the preface promises truth: "Reader, be assured, this narrative is no fiction" (1) [5]. Unlike Cobb, however, Jacobs does not pretend to lack purpose or agenda. Jacobs not only crafts her text with great power and purpose, but she also calls attention to craft in various ways. She often presents two different versions of something to reveal the differences between versions depending on the framer and her or his agenda. This approach reminds her reader to question sources and pay attention to who is telling the story.

For example, when Linda Brent is hiding in her grandmother's attic (her refuge for seven years while she plans her escape to the North), she writes a letter to try to fool her owner, Dr. Flint, into thinking that she is already in the North. Jacobs includes both the summary of Brent's staged letter to her grandmother as well as the text of a falsified letter with which Flint replaces it. Jacobs includes Flint's counterfeit letter in direct quotes and indented, so it looks real, but she precedes it with a discrediting introduction: "The old villain! He had suppressed the letter I wrote to grandmother, and prepared a substitute of his own" (130) [102]. So the letter appears genuine, but we know it is fake. Jacobs is fully aware of the many layers of representation here. Flint invents a manipulative and phony version of the letter, and the hidden Brent—along with the reader—is in the privileged position of knowing that he is lying. The "original" letter, however, also is a construction and a manipulation, as Brent, hiding in North Carolina, pretends to write from New York. In fact, the narrator obtains the data for the false letter by lifting street names from a *proslavery* newspaper: "It was a piece of the New York Herald," she writes, "and, for once, the paper that systematically abuses the colored people, was made to render them a service" (128) [101]. Jacobs uses the *Herald* subversively, reminding us that texts are *used*—that they can be employed, deployed, reframed, and revised for various purposes, good and bad.

By juxtaposing different framings, Jacobs dislodges the speaking authority of those who are complicit in slavery. While status might otherwise validate these voices, Jacobs urges us to question the source. The narrator reports a white version of her brother William's escape before she recounts William's own version, for example. Mr. Sands, the white father of Linda Brent's children (and a member of Congress), purchases Brent's brother, supposedly with plans to free him, and takes him to the North. Once there, the brother flees, and Brent hears two different tellings of the escape. In this pairing of stories, Jacobs first includes the white slaveholder's rendition without comment, presented as Sands's direct words. Then she immediately follows that version with another, in the narrator's voice, opening with: "I afterwards heard an account of the affair from William himself" (136) [107]. The direct quotes around the white man's story do not lend it validity. In fact, quoting the story without interruption, like quoting and indenting Flint's fictitious letter, highlights its constructedness. Jacobs's text clearly forces us to notice sources and speakers and to take into account agendas and points of view. In particular, anyone implicated in the institution of slavery, including the seemingly well-meaning Sands (who also neglects to free Brent's children), is to be viewed with special skepticism. The conditions and events of slavery, Jacobs contends, are best conveyed by the voices of slaves themselves.

Jacobs demonstrates a subtler contrast with the difference between a constructed white telling of Aunt Nancy's funeral and an implied slave perspective. She provides pages of context and history, describing Mrs. Flint's cruelty and hypocrisy toward Nancy in life and death, and then observes:

Northern travellers, passing through the place, might have described this tribute of respect to the humble dead as a beautiful feature in the "patriarchal institution"; a touching proof of the attachment between slaveholders and their servants; and tender-hearted Mrs. Flint would have confirmed this impression, with handkerchief at her eyes. *We* could have told them a different story. (146–47) [116]

Jacobs argues for multiple representations by and for African Americans—the italicized "*We*" who "could have" offered an alternative narrative. The dominant narrative is represented by the quoted and discredited phrase "patriarchal institution." She cautions against believing interpretations that fail to take into account multiple perspectives and silenced voices. Neither story actually is told here: Whites "might have described" those images; slaves "could have told" them something different. Different, contested framings exist even when they have not yet been uttered. Jacobs demands an active reader who will focus on the "different story" that normally remains untold or unheard, from sources likely to be unauthorized or silenced.

As Jacobs was well aware, various laws existed in the nineteenth century to silence slaves, to attempt to deny them a legal, political, or literary voice. They could not testify against a white person or serve on a jury. They could not vote, run for office, or petition the government. They generally were barred from learning, teaching, or practicing reading and writing.[2] Free blacks were denied many of these rights as well. While slavery's defenders asserted that the enslaved were happy, they also were determined not to let these happy slaves say a public word, whether in a courtroom, ballot box, or novel. The official line on slavery declared that slaves had no subjectivity to speak of, yet there was tremendous anxiety that there be no public arena where such a subjectivity might somehow speak. This central contradiction helps reveal the fictions underlying legal constructions of slavery.

The official story suggested that slaves had no will, and no real arena in which to express any such will. As it turns out, the official story was not the true story. Slaves and ex-slaves—like Lucy Delaney's mother and Sojourner Truth, for example, who both sued for their children's freedom—found their way into courtrooms.[3] Numerous slaves learned to read and write, and taught others to do the same, and many used their literacy in the fight against slavery, from the well-known cases of Frederick Douglass and Harriet Jacobs to individuals like the Louisiana woman who taught hundreds of fellow slaves to read in her clandestine "midnight school"

2. State laws varied, but these basic restrictions on slave subjectivity and voice held true throughout the South.

3. In addition to petitioning Congress, Truth initiated three successful lawsuits. The first freed her son, who had been illegally sold into Southern slavery. For an analysis of legal questions in Delaney's story, see Barrett.

(Davis 22). Such gaps between legal fictions and actual experiences occurred in various forms, and exploring these gaps reminds present-day
scholars not to rely upon "official" discourses alone. Especially interesting here is the anxiety-ridden attention to detail in the official discourses
designed to suppress the subjectivity that slaveholders claimed did not
exist in the first place.

"His mouth being closed as a witness":
Bans on Slave Testimony

Those who escaped from slavery were particularly aware of the power
of testifying against the institution they had left behind. In her preface,
Harriet Jacobs declares: "I want to add my testimony to that of abler pens
to convince the people of the Free States what Slavery really is" (1–2) [5].
The idea of "testifying" or "witnessing" is a powerful trope in nineteenth-
century African American literature. Frances Smith Foster, in her essay
"Testing and Testifying: The Word, the Other, and African American
Women Writers," states that, in revising American literary tradition,
African American women "were testifying to the fact of their existence
and insisting that others acknowledge their existence and their testimonies" (2). Jacobs's act of publishing her story directly confronts the
context of states' outlawing slave testimony against whites. While not
naming individual slaveholders, Jacobs is testifying against all slaveholders and the institution of slavery. She is bearing witness, and her book is
entered as evidence. This language of testimony, which also has religious
connotations, is metaphoric. At the same time, Jacobs quite literally is
giving evidence of crimes—wrongs that cannot be prosecuted legally,
since witnessed by and committed against slaves. Denied a legal voice,
Jacobs prosecutes the perpetrators through her literary voice. Her book
becomes a symbolic courtroom—a lawsuit for her own freedom and a
criminal trial against slaveholders and complicit Northerners. Whatever
the law says, once someone reads Jacobs's book, her testimony has been
presented and she becomes both a witness and a subject, a position slave
law tries to deny.

In testimony restrictions, as in many slave laws of the period, the language used to identify who was affected frequently addressed an individual's condition and the degree of that individual's blackness. Virginia's
law, for example, stated that "any negro or mulatto, bond or free, shall be
a good witness in pleas of the commonwealth for or against negroes or mulattoes, bond or free, or in civil pleas where free negroes or mulattoes shall
alone be parties, *and in no other cases whatsoever.*"[4] By listing all the cir-

---

4. 1 Rev. VA Code 422, qtd. in Stroud 44. Stroud, in his 1856 legal work, acknowledges his *anti-
slavery* position but distances himself from *abolitionism*. Stroud cites Cobb's 1851 *Digest* in his
critique of Georgia law. Cobb cites Stroud to discredit him as an abolitionist instead of an objective legal scholar.

cumstances under which an African American may speak in court, the phrasing makes it sound as if the act *creates* a right, whereas it actually *restricts* a right by silencing such a witness in any case involving whites. The number of categories invoked—negro, mulatto, bond, free—reveals anxiety about the complications of slave society. The law attempts to include every possible permutation to make sure the presence of African blood (which seems to be the real fear here, not simply the *status* of being a slave) absolutely bars testimony against whites. Thomas Cobb cites such restrictions as proper and justified by both condition and race. The fact that many states, including some free states, extended the ban to free blacks is evidence for Cobb that race rightfully is the disqualifier. Cobb argues that the ban "is founded not only upon the servile condition of the negro, but also upon his known disposition to disregard the truth" (226). "That the negro, as a general rule, is mendacious, is a fact too well established to require the production of proof, either from history, travels, or craniology" (233). Here Cobb invokes a variety of disciplines—history, anthropology, science—to authorize his unsupported assertion, named as fact.

"Mental instruction in a secret or confined place": Literacy Restrictions on Slaves

Under the legal fictions of slavery, slaves could not read or write or teach others to do so. Many slaves, of course, did read and write and teach. But denying blacks legal access to literacy served the purposes of a slave society, since literacy was a marker for reason and reason a marker for humanity. This circular proposition naturalized what was a legal constraint, and it functioned as a convenient, self-fulfilling prophecy.[5] Cobb briefly addresses the writings of slaves, in a skeptical summary of a published abolitionist collection of black achievements. He reinterprets this "testimony" for his own purposes:

> . . . in poetry we have Phillis Wheatley, whose productions Mr. Jefferson pronounced to be "beneath criticism." In composition, is Gustavus Vasa, whose only work was a narrative of himself (by whom written, or revised we know not), which would hardly give credit to a schoolboy in his teens. (45)

Cobb mocks the "meagreness" and the quality of this work, then observes that the majority of writers cited are former slaves, concluding, "The inference would seem irresistible, from the testimony of this volume, that the most successful engine for the development of negro intellect is slavery" (46). Cobb wants it both ways: Slavery is justified because slaves are

5. For a discussion of constructions of race and Enlightenment arguments about literacy and reason, see for example Gates. Douglass in his 1852 speech "What to the Slave is the Fourth of July?" cites anti-literacy laws as *proof* of the slave's humanity and manhood: "When you can point to any such laws in reference to the beasts of the fields, then I may consent to argue the manhood of the slave" (286).

ignorant, and if one is found who is not, then that only proves the beneficial effects of slavery.

For all his citations, Cobb never quotes African Americans, supporting his claim that they have no literate voice. He does not mention that slave literacy was generally outlawed. In the effort to enact the self-fulfilling prophecy of slave ignorance, anti-literacy laws placed slaves in physical danger if they pursued learning. Harriet Jacobs tells the story of breaking the law to teach an old man to read the Bible.[6] The narrator tells "Uncle Fred" (and the reader) the legal implications of their act: "I asked him if he didn't know it was contrary to law; and that slaves were whipped and imprisoned for teaching each other to read. This brought tears into his eyes" (72) [61]. The risk of whipping is framed by descriptions of Fred's earnest religious faith. The extremity of the punishment is in stark contrast to the gentleness of this criminal accomplice. In their state of North Carolina, the law specified different penalties depending upon the race and condition of the lawbreaker:

> Any free person who shall teach any slave to *read* or *write* upon conviction shall if a *white* man or woman, be fined not less than *100* dollars, nor more than *200* dollars, or *imprisoned*; and if a free person of colour, shall be *fined, imprisoned* or *whipped*, not exceeding 39 lashes, nor less than 20. And for a similar offense, a slave shall receive 39 lashes on his or her *bare* back. (34 Rev. Statutes of NC 74: 209; cited in Stroud 61, emphasis his)

As with so many other laws under slavery, there is a specific breakdown along lines of color and condition. Status determines how much money the offender would lose, but race determines whether physical integrity could also be violated. A free black could be treated as harshly as a white (subject to fine or imprisonment) *and* as harshly as a slave (up to thirty-nine lashes). Only a slave, however, has the bodily details so specified: Unlike the amount of the fine, the number of lashes and the bareness of the back are not left to the court's discretion. The specificity reveals not only the brutality of the punishment, but also the public nature of the slave body, according to law.

"The want of chastity in the female slaves": Lascivious Slaves and Honorable Statutes

The slave body also is regulated by laws involving sex, reproduction, and family. Such laws also deny subjectivity and reveal inconsistencies

---

6. Stepto and others cite as a prominent feature of the slave narratives the quest for literacy and power. Some critics have noted that female slave narrators sometimes see literacy as not only powerful but also potentially treacherous. Brent's owner tries to use her literacy against her, for example, forcing her to read sexually threatening notes. Sanchez-Eppler's analysis of what she terms "Jacobs's anxiety over literacy" here is useful, but it also downplays the narrator's active deployment of literacy (she writes manipulative letters from her place of confinement, for example) and Jacobs's power over language and awareness of the power of discourse.

and instabilities. Interracial sex, for instance, is banned, whereas interracial rape is not.[7] Permitting slave marriage or prohibiting rape might suggest the humanity of slaves and could challenge the fictions upholding slavery. Southern law generally failed to protect slave women from rape committed by fellow slaves as well. The rape of white women, however, was punishable by death if the man convicted of the act was a slave.

Thomas Cobb's treatment of rape is simultaneously to deny its existence and to blame slave women for interracial sex. Rather than naming the rape of female slaves, he shifts the causal relationship so that the lechery of slave women is defined as the problem. "An evil attributed to slavery, and frequently alluded to," writes Cobb in the historical preface to his legal treatise, "is the want of chastity in the female slaves, and a corresponding immorality in the white males" (ccxix). Slave women become the cause and white immorality merely the *correspondence*. Cobb uses qualifiers and indefinite references, which cloud how he is removing white responsibility: ". . . to the extent that the slave is under the control and subject to the order of the master, the condition of slavery is responsible." The "condition," not the men, may be responsible, "to the extent" that slavery gives power to the master. Having nearly blamed slavery, Cobb readjusts quickly by invoking what he considers another well-known fact: "Every well-informed person at the South, however, knows that the exercise of such power for such a purpose is almost unknown. The prevalence of the evil is attributable to other causes. The most prominent of these is the natural lewdness of the negro. It is not the consequence of slavery. The free negro . . . exhibits the same disposition. . . ." He must blame race, not the institution, so the flaw becomes "natural." This immorality results not only from female lust, this legal scholar asserts, but also from female cunning: ". . . the negress knows that the offspring of such intercourse, the mulatto, having greater intelligence, and being indeed a superior race, has a better opportunity of enjoying the privileges of domestics; in other words, *is elevated* by the mixture of blood" (ccxix–ccxx). He makes mulattoes a separate and "superior race," permitting an additional layer of hierarchy. He makes absolutist declarations about the characteristics of the races, yet race itself is not absolute, by his own admission.[8]

7. Unless the accused rapist is black and the accuser is white. As with other areas of slave law, regulations of sexuality varied over time and from state to state. These characterizations give a general picture.
8. Such slippages persist in twentieth-century legislation, such as anti-miscegenation laws, which attempt to draw firm lines while also revealing anxiety about the ambiguity of these divisions. Virginia's 1924 Preservation of Racial Integrity Act banned interracial marriage and defined "white" as one with "no trace whatsoever of any blood other than Caucasian," while it permitted in the category white "one-sixteenth American Indian blood" to protect descendants of Pocahontas and John Rolfe. There were multiple contradictions in the law, revealing that racial mixing did occur even as its effects were being denied: "The racial boundary was drawn differently for white/Indian and white/Negro mixtures, it changed over time for both, and all of the 'pure' racial categories defined by the law—white, Indian, and Negro—included in their definitions mixed-race individuals. Yet the myth of natural categories was maintained, with all the

In the course of his legal analysis, Cobb eventually acknowledges that the failure to address the rape of slaves is a "defect in our legislation," but he asserts that this is a theoretical defect only. Such "occurrence is almost unheard of," he remarks, and to the extent it does occur, there is the factor of "the known lasciviousness of the negro." Finally, Cobb suggests a change in the law not for the honor of black women but "for the honor of the statute-book" (99–100). The brief slippage of acknowledging the rape of black women, previously constructed as essentially un-rapeable, is quickly covered up. Placed at the center is the chastity of the statute book. Cobb's legal treatise constructs personhood and subjectivity not in the slaves but in the law and the text of the law. The slippage also reveals the contradiction of constructing slaves without subjectivity but with dangerous sexuality—black women are not subjects, under this configuration, but they can be dangerous agents against white men.

Case law erased not only the rape of slaves by white men, but also the rape of female slaves by fellow slaves. The lawyer in the 1859 Mississippi case *George v. State* argued, successfully, that the rape of a black female was essentially not rape:

> The crime of rape does not exist in this State between African slaves. Our laws recognize no marital rights as between slaves; their sexual intercourse is left to be regulated by their owners. The regulations of law, as to the white race, on the subject of sexual intercourse, do not and cannot, for obvious reasons, apply to slaves; their intercourse is promiscuous, and the violation of a female slave by a male slave would be a mere assault and battery. (*George v. State* 317; see discussion in Burnham)

The female slave in this case was under ten. Mississippi Supreme Court Justice William Harris relied on prior cases as well as ancient Roman law and multiple references to Cobb's *Law of Slavery* to decide against recognizing the crime of rape against a slave. Exceptions to such precedent Harris dismissed as "founded mainly upon the unmeaning twaddle, in which some humane judges and law writers have indulged, as to the influence of the 'natural law,' 'civilization and Christian enlightenment.' . . . From a careful examination of our legislation . . . , we are satisfied that there is no act which embraces either the attempted or actual commission of a rape by a slave on a female slave" (320). The power of legal precedent makes it easy to erase the specifics of the case. The unevenness of precedent is itself erased by dismissing exceptions as "unmeaning twaddle" and mere "humane" indulgence.

In an 1852 Georgia case where the minor was white, the legal result was different. While the slave is constructed as inherently promiscuous—even at the age of nine—the white female is constructed as inherently vir-

---

moral force that the idea of a 'natural order' could confer on such a categorization" (Higginbotham and Kopytoff 1982). The law remained in effect for forty-three years.

tuous. The opinion in *Stephen v. State* was delivered by Judge Lumpkin and reported by Cobb. Lumpkin declared that he would try to be dispassionate, even though "the crime, from the very nature of it, is calculated to excite indignation in every heart; and when perpetrated on a free white female of immature mind and body, that indignation becomes greater, and is more difficult to repress" (230). As he moves through evidence and legal precedents he concludes in increasingly first-person terms: "I would, were I in the Jury-Box, seize upon the slightest proof of resistance . . . even the usual struggles of a modest maiden, young and inexperienced in such mysteries, to find . . . that the act was against her will, and that the presumption of law was so strong, as to amount to proof of force" (239). The indignation arises not from the crime of rape, but from the idea of rape against "free white" females. Lumpkin's emotional language—"excite," "heart," "seize"—combined with the romanticized image of white seduction—"struggles of a modest maiden . . . inexperienced in such mysteries"—suggest not sensitivity to the vulnerability of women to male power but rather outrage at black male access to a white maiden. No such indignation appeared in the Mississippi case where the young girl was black.[9]

"Do not judge": Rewriting Legal Fictions of Womanhood

Harriet Jacobs counters this idea of the "want of chastity" in slave women and specifically revises the premise of white women's inherent virtue versus black women's inherent corruption. She rewrites virtue as a legal construction, as opposed to a racialized, naturalized fact. Viewed in the social context of ideologies of "true" womanhood and the literary context of women's domestic fiction, Jacobs radically subverts convention as she calls for revised standards that account for the experiences of black women.[1] She admits breaking certain rules of womanhood *and* declares that these rules ought not apply to slave women; she invokes bonds between black and white women *and* points out the legal differences. She critiques absolute and unvarying standards, and her style of shifting perspectives—and of calling attention to whose perspective is authorized—helps to convey this critique.

Jacobs breaks down the division between white and black women partly through her direct appeals to a constructed audience, designed to evoke "womanly" sympathy and to call for political action. " . . . I do

9. While the Mississippi defendant was discharged. Lumpkin's ruling resulted in the execution of Stephen: "He must be left to abide the penalty of that awful sentence, which adjudges him to be unworthy to have a place longer among the living." The law makes it clear that capital punishment applies in this case based on the race of both accused and accuser, for "rape, and an attempt to commit a rape, by a slave or free person of color, upon a free white female, are both capitally punished by the laws of this state" (241–42).

1. See Carby for a discussion of the implications of the ideology of true womanhood for women of color.

earnestly desire to arouse the women of the North," Jacobs announces in her preface, "to a realizing sense of the condition of two millions of women at the South, still in bondage, suffering what I suffered, and most of them far worse" (1) [5]. She both claims unity and emphasizes difference in these appeals. The audience she invokes is the stereotypical construct of the virtuous "true (white) woman," morally bound to feel sympathy for her suffering sisters. Whether or not members of her audience live up to this fiction is secondary to playing the constructions off each other. According to Jacobs, the "virtue" of slave women is different from that of free Northern women not because of nature or essence but because of legal status. White women have the protection of the law, while laws—and the men who make them—conspire against slave women. Black women might be just as virtuous, but they face laws that prevent their exercise of virtue. White women might be less virtuous, but they have laws protecting their virtue and their homes (constructed as the repositories of white female virtue). In both cases, but for the law, their virtue might be otherwise.

Emotional appeals of identification to her white sisters at the north are sometimes followed by stark declarations of how the narrator's situation is different. The narrator seeks sympathy from her "virtuous reader" and simultaneously tells her, "You never knew what it is to be a slave." Her poetic appeal is immediately followed by the calm conclusion: "Still, in looking back, calmly, on the events of my life, I feel that the slave woman ought not to be judged by the same standard as others" (56) [47–48]. Jacobs uses techniques of sentimental fiction while subversively undercutting some of the expectations of this genre. Jacobs makes sentimental appeals to her reader, and at times turns the appeal into an indictment. She moves between personal statements ("my life") and more generalized, generic declarations ("a slave," "the slave girl") to make her argument personal *and* political. Differences result from categories of race and condition, not individual choices or shortcomings on her part. The bond she seeks goes beyond personal sympathy (though that is the avenue) and becomes political union as well. On the verge of confessing her sexual transgression, for example, the narrator interrupts herself:

> But, O, ye happy women, whose purity has been sheltered from childhood, who have been free to choose the objects of your affection, whose homes are protected by law, do not judge the poor desolate slave girl too severely! If slavery had been abolished, I, also, . . . could have had a home shielded by laws; and I should have been spared the painful task of confessing what I am now about to relate. . . . (54) [46]

If white women possess the "true womanhood" characteristics of virtue and domesticity, it is because laws create and protect these elements. Their "purity" is not inherent but "has been sheltered"; their "homes" are not automatically intact but "are protected by law." Jacobs uses a legal model for her appeal and subverts it. The language of confession, judgment, and pardon suggests that the narrator might be setting herself up as supplicant or criminal and the white women as judge. While offering to confess, however, Jacobs's narrator simultaneously commands that her audience "not judge"—she undercuts the reader's authority to render judgment even as she sets the reader up as judge.

"A *hearthstone of my own*": Familial Fictions

Slavery advocates construct another central contradiction: Families do not matter to slaves, *and* slave families are preserved.[2] Cobb treats separation as an unfortunate possibility that, like rape, never really happens: "That the marriage relation between slaves is not recognized or protected by the law, is another evil. . . . In practice, public opinion protects the relation. The unfeeling separation of husband and wife, is a rare occurrence. It never happens when both belong to the same master" (ccxxi). Protecting slave relations, he cautions, is a dilemma "of exceeding nicety and difficulty." On the one hand,

> the unnecessary and wanton separation of persons standing in the relation of husband and wife, though it may rarely, if ever, occur in actual practice, is an event which, if possible, should be guarded against by the law. And yet . . . to fasten upon a master of a female slave, a vicious, corrupting negro, sowing discord, and dissatisfaction among all his slaves; or else a thief, or a cut-throat, and to provide no relief against such a nuisance, would be to make the holding of slaves a curse to the master. It would be well for the law, at least, to provide against such separations of families by the officers of the law. . . . How much farther the lawgiver may go, requires for its solution all the deliberation and wisdom of the Senator, guided and enlightened by Christian philanthropy. (245–46)

The owner is to be protected from being helpless before the marital rights of slaves. The most important actor is "the Senator," whose Christian charity shall decide the fate of slave families. In addition to denying the separation of spouses, Cobb also denies the prevalence of separating children from a parent: "The young child is seldom removed from the parent's protection, and beyond doubt, the institution prevents the separation of families, to an extent unknown among the laboring poor of the

2. The paradox many slave narrators tried to demonstrate was that slavery hindered families, *and* families endured. Exact numbers of separations under slavery are impossible to ascertain, since slave families had no legal standing, and official records did not mark their existence directly. Slave narratives are rife with examples, such as Douglass's descriptions of separation from his mother. Gutman generates some numerical data: For example, records in Mississippi and Louisiana during and after the Civil War show that more than twenty percent of partners in slave marriages registered by the Army and Freedman's Bureau had previously been married elsewhere, in unions dissolved by slave sales or moving (126–30).

world" (ccxviii). The institution is not merely humane to families, it is also superior to systems of white labor. Evidence is cited through one personal example in a footnote: "On my father's plantation, an aged negro woman could call together more than one hundred of her lineal descendants. I saw this old negro dance at the wedding of her great granddaughter." Cobb invokes as proof a familiar stereotype of the happy, dancing slave.[3]

Jacobs shows that, despite the legal erasure of slave families, family survives, though often in a redefined form. The redefinition of family is part of her redefinition of womanhood and is linked to her reformulation of the domestic novel. She subverts the marriage plot of domestic fiction, the expectation that the story will end with male-female domestic union. Family is privileged, but husband is not; motherhood is valued, but marriage specifically is omitted. While the last chapter of *Jane Eyre* opens with "Reader, I married him," Jacobs offers no such hope of domestic closure. "Reader," opens her penultimate paragraph, "my story ends with freedom; not in the usual way, with marriage" (201) [156]. She dethrones marriage as the goal, replacing it with legal and physical freedom and family outside of marriage, and she even questions the compromised nature of this freedom. The climax of this chapter is not a marriage contract but a bill of sale.[4] This legal record of Brent's freedom yields not personal triumph but political outrage:

> "The bill of sale!" Those words struck me like a blow. So I was *sold* at last! A human being *sold* in the free city of New York! The bill of sale is on record, and future generations will learn from it that women were articles of traffic in New York, late in the nineteenth century of the Christian religion. (200) [155]

The chapter titled "Free at Last" climaxes with the revelation that she instead is "*sold* at last." Jacobs locates the geographic, religious, and temporal moment of this outrage to direct possibilities for political action. Instead of celebrating the happy personal resolution, she forces her readers to redirect anger at the still existing political situation. Brent still lives with racism and class division. She still lives in a position of servitude, even if constructed as grateful service to the woman who purchased her. Laws of slavery no longer directly bind her, but God as well as "love, duty, gratitude, also bind me to her side." Hers is a lesser version of slavery (she

3. Cobb elsewhere uses the image of dancing slaves. Citing ancient Egyptian monuments to prove that slaves always have been black, he declares: "It is, moreover, well agreed from these monuments, that many of these domestic slaves were of pure negro blood" (xliv). His footnote explains: "That they were the same happy negroes of this day is proven by their being represented in a dance 1300 years before Christ." Dancing is a stereotype that proves both "negro" identity and happiness.

4. This rhetorical move recalls Fanny Fern's inclusion of her character's stock certificate in the closing pages of *Ruth Hall* (1855). While the context is very different, Fern also displaces marriage as the culmination of a woman's life. Economic freedom and professional success, along with motherhood apart from marriage, are the rewards at the end of this largely autobiographical novel.

is bound because paid for) and an altered version of marriage (she is bound for love, duty, and a bill of sale). Because of this economic status, the final image of her life is one of domesticity denied: "I do not sit with my children in a home of my own. I still long for a hearthstone of my own, however humble. I wish it for my children's sake far more than for my own" (201) [156]. Domestic motherhood more than marriage is the goal, and that goal is both achieved and frustrated.

Marriage is mentioned—and dismissed—fairly early in the book, and its denial is the result of legal not romantic factors. The narrator halts the story of her romance with a freeborn carpenter with a reminder of her legal status: "But when I reflected that I was a slave, and that the laws gave no sanction to the marriage of such, my heart sank within me" (37) [33]. She opens this chapter, "The Lover," with sentimental language of "the tendrils of the heart" but ends with stark delineations of her lack of options under the law: "Even if he could have obtained permission to marry me while I was a slave, the marriage would give him no power to protect me from my master. . . . And then, if we had children, I knew they must 'follow the condition of the mother'" (42) [37]. She quotes directly the law that guarantees slaveholders ownership of children produced by slave women, through voluntary or involuntary unions, with enslaved or free men.[5] Jacobs exposes in no uncertain terms the motivation of such a regulation when Brent later does have children. Even though the father is white and free, Brent cannot ignore Flint's threat to sell her child: "I knew the law gave him power to fulfil it; for slaveholders have been cunning enough to enact that 'the child shall follow the condition of the *mother,*' not of the *father,* thus taking care that licentiousness shall not interfere with avarice" (76) [64]. Her succinct analysis names the law for what it is—an intersection of gender, sex, race, and economics. Her reframing exposes the legal fiction. Cold, legalistic language is followed by her naming the real motivation: the desires of licentious and avaricious slaveholders. Jacobs quotes the law a third time, in the chapter on the Fugitive Slave Act, pointing out the complications of this irrational federal law, newly passed and intersecting with existing irrational state laws, for residents of a so-called free state: ". . . many a husband discovered that his wife had fled from slavery years ago, and as 'the child follows the condition of its mother,' the children of his love were liable to be seized and carried into slavery" (191) [148]. She articulates the contradiction that slave law powerfully stands in the way of family and that some version of family *does* powerfully endure.

---

5. State statutes varied, but by the nineteenth century it was a fairly uniform principle in U.S. slave law that the child's status was determined by the mother's. The rule derives from the ancient Roman principle: *partus sequitur ventrem.* In a rare translation, Cobb puts in his own words the ancient justification: "From principles of justice, the offspring, the increase of the womb, belongs to the master of the womb." (69).

"Regulations of robbers": Exposing Ironies of Legal Fictions

While Cobb worries about the "honor" of the statutes, Jacobs constructs the law as dishonorable. Jacobs often plays with the definition of crime to point to the ironies of slave law. While the law constructs white women as chaste, slave law obliges slave women to obey their masters at any cost. The narrator describes a slave's struggle to preserve her "pride of character"—a trait marked as feminine for white society. But because she is a slave, virtue is criminalized: "It is deemed a crime in her to wish to be virtuous." Indeed, such a life is worse than the life of the criminal, as Jacobs's imagery makes clear: "The felon's home in a penitentiary is preferable" (31) [28]. The chapter "Still in Prison" uses similar imagery and addresses the irony of Brent's freedom as a prisoner in her grandmother's garret. She could wish Flint no worse punishment, "yet the laws allowed *him* to be out in the free air, while I, guiltless of crime, was pent up here, as the only means of avoiding the cruelties the laws allowed him to inflict upon me!" (121) [96]. The law endorses cruelties against black women and outlaws opposition to these cruelties. Thus, Brent's every action against Flint's rape attempts can be deemed criminal by Flint. The narrator, following her child's birth, describes one of Flint's outbursts in legal terminology: "Then he launched out upon his usual themes,—my crimes against him, and my ingratitude for his forbearance. The laws were laid down to me anew, and I was dismissed" (61) [52]. These particular laws are metaphoric, but the literal law is clearly on Flint's side as well. The larger irony here is that it is Jacobs who ultimately lays down the law anew by deconstructing legal fictions in the course of her narrative, which long outlives Flint and his real-life counterparts. She recodes the law as criminal to undercut the legitimacy of legal practices in the South and North. When Flint is pursuing Brent in the North, she evaluates her legal standing and then reframes these legal fictions: "I knew the law would decide that I was his property, and would probably still give his daughter a claim to my children; but I regarded such laws as the regulations of robbers, who had no rights that I was bound to respect" (187) [145]. The keepers of the laws become the outlaws, and her allegiance is to some higher law, not made by white men.[6]

Part of Jacobs's purpose in emphasizing law is to shift the focus to the *institution* of slavery, as it was designed and supported, as opposed to mere exceptions or excesses. Focusing at times on *national* law also helps reveal Northern complicity in Southern slavery. Through measures like the Fugitive Slave Act, she reframes the practice of slavery from a South-

---

6. The narrator often contrasts Flint's construction of criminality to a higher law. ". . . though you have been criminal towards me," Flint declares, "I feel for you, and I can pardon you if you obey my wishes. . . . If you deceive me, you shall feel the fires of hell" (58) [50]. Legal imagery often becomes Christian imagery, a link Jacobs refuses. Brent ignores the legal reference and rejects the Christian claim: "I have sinned against God and myself, . . . but not against you." She invokes a higher law, and she insists on her definition of that higher law.

ern tradition to a federal problem. This shift also serves her call for activism, especially from Northern white women. She also wishes to indict the North for its own legal manifestations of racism. Brent rides in segregated trains and boats, stays in segregated hotels, and describes racist work rules and work places. When she thinks she can buy a better seat on a Northern train, her Northern friends explain: "O, no. . . . They don't allow colored people to go in the first-class cars" (162) [128]. The narrator compares this affront to Southern treatment: "Colored people were allowed to ride in a filthy box, behind white people, at the south, but they were not required to pay for the privilege. It made me sad to find how the north aped the customs of slavery" (162–63) [128]. Even when Brent is immune from a particular policy of segregation (in the following case because she was serving as nurse to a white woman), Jacobs uses that very exemption to condemn the practice:

> Being in servitude to the Anglo-Saxon race, I was not put into a "Jim Crow car," . . . neither was I invited to ride through the streets on top of trunks in a truck; but every where I found the same manifestations of that cruel prejudice, which so discourages the feelings, and represses the energies of the colored people. (176) [137]

Her description makes the exception she benefited from sound little different from slavery. Her conclusion makes a connection between external laws and practices and internal reactions. Her proposals for action generally address whites in the North, calling on them to take action against slavery for their black sisters. At the close of this chapter, Jacobs also calls for action among fellow African Americans, having first warned against the repression of their energies. After describing her persistence in the face of racist treatment at a Northern hotel, she reveals her triumph in quiet, general terms: "Finding I was resolved to stand up for my rights, they concluded to treat me well." She does not stop at example, however, going on to declare: "Let every colored man and woman do this, and eventually we shall cease to be trampled under foot by our oppressors" (177) [138]. Everyone who might read her book—black or white, Northern or Southern—is given avenues for action. She seeks in her testimony not only to inform and educate, but also to enrage and activate.

While not always read as legal critique, Harriet Jacobs's narrative certainly issues a call to activism—a demand to reframe the law and redefine standards of womanhood. Since Thomas Cobb argues through the law, he always claims rationality and objectivity, not the "zealous interest" of abolitionist tracts. Part of Cobb's power is his pretense at disinterest and political neutrality. Part of the power of racism is its ability (in ever-static *and* everchanging ways) to appear rational, objective, invisible. Jacobs, on the other hand, exposes that lie of neutrality as she challenges the legal fictions of black subjectivity created by the laws that Cobb itemizes.

The contradictions of slavery run deep and have a long history in this nation. While the pilgrims were stepping on Plymouth Rock to escape European oppression, European ships were bringing kidnaped Africans to the American continent.[7] While the founding fathers were writing about "life, liberty and the pursuit of happiness," many of them also were fathering slaves. In the same breath as they spoke of equality and morality, nineteenth-century legal scholars and judges also would speak of African Americans as aliens and animals. Examining Jacobs's analysis, Cobb's rhetoric, and laws around slave subjectivity and sexuality helps expose the erasures and instabilities of such legal fictions that present themselves as fact. Such an exploration also reminds us to interrogate the seeming rationality and neutrality of modern legal discourse that also may obfuscate racism and sexism today.

WORKS CITED

Barrett, Lindon. "Self-Knowledge, Law, and African American Autobiography: Lucy A. Delaney's 'From the Darkness Cometh the Light.'" *The Culture of Autobiography: Constructions of Self Representation.* Ed. Robert Folkenflik. Stanford: Stanford UP, 1993. 104–24.

Braxton, Joanne. "Harriet Jacobs' *Incidents in the Life of a Slave Girl:* The Redefinition of the Slave Narrative Genre." *Massachusetts Review* 27 (1986): 379–87.

Bryan v. Walton. 14 Ga. 185. Ga. S. Ct. 1853.

Burnham, Margaret. "An Impossible Marriage: Slave Law and Family Law." *Law and Inequality: A Journal of Theory and Practice* 5 (1987): 187–225.

Carby, Hazel. *Reconstructing Womanhood: The Emergence of the Afro-American Woman Novelist.* New York: Oxford UP, 1987.

Cobb, Thomas R. R. *An Inquiry Into the Law of Negro Slavery in the United States of America.* 1858. New York: Negro UP, 1968.

Davis, Angela Y. *Women, Race and Class.* New York: Vintage, 1983.

Douglass, Frederick. "What to the Slave is the Fourth of July?" *My Bondage and My Freedom.* 1855. Chicago: U of Illinois P, 1987. 284–88.

Foster, Frances Smith. *Witnessing Slavery: The Development of Ante-bellum Slave Narratives.* 1979. Madison: U of Wisconsin P, 1994.

———. *Written by Herself: Literary Production by African American Women, 1746–1892.* Bloomington: Indiana UP, 1993.

Gates, Henry Louis, Jr. "Writing 'Race' and the Difference it Makes." *"Race," Writing and Difference.* Chicago: U of Chicago P, 1985. 1–20.

George (a Slave) v. State. 37 Miss. 316–320. Miss. S. Ct. 1859.

Gutman, Herbert. *Slavery and the Numbers Game: A Critique of Time on the Cross.* Chicago: U of Illinois P, 1975.

Harris, Angela P. "Race and Essentialism in Feminist Legal Theory." *Feminist Legal Theory: Readings in Law and Gender.* Ed. Katharine Bartlett and Rosanne Kennedy. San Francisco: Westview, 1991. 235–62.

Higginbotham, A. Leon, Jr. *In the Matter of Color: Race and the American Legal Process, The Colonial Period.* New York: Oxford UP, 1978.

———, and Barbara K. Kopytoff. "Racial Purity and Interracial Sex in the Law of Colonial and Antebellum Virginia." *Georgetown Law Journal* 77 (1989): 1967–2029.

Hyde, Henry. *The Collegiate Speech Protection Act Briefing Paper.* Washington, 1991.

Jacobs, Harriet A. *Incidents in the Life of a Slave Girl, Written by Herself.* 1861. Ed. Jean Fagan Yellin. Cambridge: Harvard UP, 1987.

McCash, William. *Thomas R. R. Cobb: The Making of a Southern Nationalist.* Macon: Mercer UP, 1983.

Sanchez-Eppler, Karen. *Touching Liberty: Abolition, Feminism, and the Politics of the Body.* Berkeley: U of California P, 1993.

7. A Dutch ship brought twenty kidnaped Africans to Jamestown in 1619, the same year the House of Burgesses met and a year before the Mayflower landed at Plymouth. Notions of representative government and religious freedom in the "New World" emerge along with practices of human enslavement.

Starling, Marion Wilson. *The Slave Narrative: Its Place in American History*. 1981. Washington: Howard UP, 1988.

Stephen (a Slave) v. State. 11 Ga. 225–242. Ga. S. Ct. 1852.

Stepto, Robert. *From Behind the Veil: A Study of Afro-American Narrative*. Urbana: U of Illinois P, 1979.

Stroud, George M. *A Sketch of the Laws Relating to Slavery*. 1856. New York: Negro UP, 1968.

Harriet Jacobs:
A Chronology

1813	Born in Edenton, North Carolina, daughter of Delilah Horniblow and Daniel Jacobs.
c. 1819	Mother dies.
1825	Mistress (Margaret Horniblow) dies. Jacobs becomes property of three-year-old daughter of Dr. James Norcom.
c. 1826	Father dies.
c. 1829	Begins sexual relationship with Samuel Tredwell Sawyer, a white attorney and, from 1837 to 1839, U.S. congressman. Their son, Joseph, born.
1833	Louisa Matilda, daughter of Sawyer and Jacobs, born.
1835	Runs away from plantation.
1842	Escapes to New York City and finds work as a domestic in the family of Mary Stace and Nathaniel Parker Willis.
1845	Travels to England as nurse for Imogene Willis.
1849	Moves to Rochester, New York, to live with her brother, John S. Jacobs. Her social circle includes several prominent abolitionists, including Frederick Douglass and Amy Post.
1850	Returns to New York City and works as domestic servant for Nathaniel Parker and his second wife, Cornelia Grinnell Willis.
1852	Cornelia Grinnell Willis purchases Jacobs and her children.
1853	Publishes "Letter from a Fugitive Slave" and "Cruelty to Slaves" in the *New York Tribune*. Begins writing *Incidents*.
1858	Travels to England in search of a publisher for *Incidents*.
1861	Publishes *Incidents in the Life of a Slave Girl*.
1862	Publishes "Life among the Contrabands" in the *Liberator*. *Incidents* published in England as *The Deeper Wrong*.
1863	Establishes the Jacobs Free School in Alexandria, Virginia.
1866	Moves to Savannah, Georgia.
1868	Travels to London, England, to raise money for an orphanage.
c. 1870	Fleeing increased terrorism against blacks, Jacobs moves to Cambridge, Massachusetts, where she runs a boarding house.

c. 1880   Moves to Washington, D.C.
1897   Dies in Washington, D.C. Buried in Mount Auburn Cemetery in Cambridge, Massachusetts.

Selected Bibliography

• indicates works included or excerpted in this Norton Critical Edition.

• Accomando, Christina. " 'The laws were laid down to me anew': Harriet Jacobs and the Reframing of Legal Fictions." *African American Review* 32.2 (1998): 229–44.

Andrews, William L. "Culmination of a Century: The Autobiographies of J. D. Green, Frederick Douglass, and Harriet Jacobs" and "Free at Last: From Disclosure to Dialogue in the Novelized Autobiography." *To Tell a Free Story: The First Century of Afro-American Autobiography, 1760–1865.* Urbana: U of Illinois P, 1986. 239–75, 320–31.

Bartholomaus, Craig. " 'What Would You Be?' Racial Myths and Cultural Sameness in *Incidents in the Life of a Slave Girl.*" *College Language Association Journal* 39.2 (December 1995): 179–94.

Braxton, Joanne M., and Sharon Zuber. "Silences in Harriet 'Linda Brent' Jacobs's *Incidents in the Life of a Slave Girl.*" *Listening to Silences: New Essays in Feminist Criticism.* Ed. Elaine Hedges and Shelley Fisher Fishkin. New York: Oxford UP, 1994. 146–55.

• Burnham, Michelle. "Loopholes of Resistance: Harriet Jacobs' Slave Narrative and the Critique of Agency in Foucault." *Arizona Quarterly* 49.2 (summer 1993): 53–73.

Carby, Hazel V. "Hear My Voice: Ye Careless Daughters." *Reconstructing Womanhood: The Emergence of the Afro-American Woman Novelist.* New York: Oxford UP, 1987. 45–61, 183–85.

Cutter, Martha J. "Dismantling 'The Master's House': Critical Literacy in Harriet Jacobs' *Incidents in the Life of a Slave Girl.*" *Callaloo* 19.1 (1996): 209–25.

Daniel, Janice B. "A New Kind of Hero: Harriet Jacobs's 'Incidents.'" *Southern Quarterly: A Journal of the Arts in the South* 35.3 (spring 1997): 7–12.

Davie, Sharon. " 'Reader, my story ends with freedom': Harriet Jacobs's *Incidents in the Life of a Slave Girl.*" *Famous Last Words: Changes in Gender and Narrative Closure.* Ed. Alison Booth. Charlottesville: UP of Virginia, 1993. 86–109.

Doriani, Beth Maclay. "Black Womanhood in Nineteenth Century America: Subversion and Self-Construction in Two Women's Autobiographies." *American Quarterly* 43.2 (June 1991): 199–222.

Foster, Frances Smith. "Writing across the Color Line: Harriet Jacobs and *Incidents in the Life of a Slave Girl.*" *Written by Herself: Literary Production by African American Women, 1746–1892.* Bloomington: Indiana UP, 1993. 95–116.

Garfield, Deborah M. "Speech, Listening, and Female Sexuality in *Incidents in the Life of a Slave Girl.*" *Arizona Quarterly* 50.2 (summer 1994): 19–49.

• Garfield, Deborah M., and Rafia Zafar, eds. *Harriet Jacobs* and Incidents in the Life of a Slave Girl: New Critical Essays. New York: Cambridge UP, 1996.

• Gates, Henry L., Jr., and K. A. Appiah, eds. *Harriet Jacobs: Critical Perspectives Past and Present.* New York: Amistad, 1997.

Haselstein, Ulla. "Giving Her Self: Harriet Jacobs' *Incidents in the Life of a Slave Girl* and the Problem of Authenticity." *(Trans)Formations of Cultural Identity in the English-Speaking World.* Ed. Jochen Achilles and Carmen Birkle. Heidelberg: Universitatsverlag C., 1988. 125–39.

Humphreys, Debra. "Power and Resistance in Harriet Jacobs' *Incidents in the Life of a Slave Girl.*" *Anxious Power: Reading, Writing and Ambivalence in Narratives by Women.* Ed. Carol J. Singley and Susan Elizabeth Sweeney. Albany: State U of New York P, 1993. 143–55.

Jones, Anne Goodwyn. "Engendered in the South: Blood and Irony in Douglass and Jacobs." *Haunted Bodies: Gender and Southern Text.* Ed. Anne Goodwyn Jones and Susan V. Donaldson. Charlottesville: UP of Virginia, 1997. 201–19.

Kaplan, Carla. "Recuperating Agents: Narrative Contracts, Emancipatory Readers, and *Incidents in the Life of a Slave Girl.*" *Provoking Agents: Gender and Agency in Theory and Practice.* Ed. Judith Kegan Gardiner. Urbana: U of Illinois P, 1995. 280–301.

• McKay, Nellie Y. "The Girls Who Became the Women: Childhood Memories in the Autobiographies of Harriet Jacobs, Mary Church Terrell, and Anne Moody." *Tradition and the Talents of Women.* Ed. Florence Howe. Urbana and Chicago: U of Illinois P, 1991. 106–24.

• Mullen, Harryette. "Runaway Tongue: Resistant Orality in *Uncle Tom's Cabin, Our Nig, Incidents in the Life of a Slave Girl,* and *Beloved.*" *The Culture of Sentiment.* Ed. Shirley Samuels. New York: Oxford UP, 1992. 244–64, 332–35.

Nudelman, Franny. "Harriet Jacobs and the Sentimental Politics of Female Suffering." *ELH* 59 (winter 1992): 939–64.

• Painter, Nell Irvin. "Three Southern Women and Freud: A Non-Exceptionalist Approach to Race, Class, and Gender in the Slave South." *Feminist Revision History*. Ed. Ann-Louise Shapiro. New Brunswick: Rutgers UP, 1994. 195–216.

Sale, Maggie. "Critiques from Within: Antebellum Projects of Resistance." *American Literature* 64.4 (December 1992): 695–718.

Sánchez-Eppler, Karen. "Righting Slavery and Writing Sex: The Erotics of Narration in Harriet Jacobs's *Incidents*." *Touching Liberty: Abolition, Feminism, and the Politics of the Body*. Berkeley: U of California P, 1993. 83–104.

Smith, Valerie. "Form and Ideology in Three Slave Narratives." *Self-Discovery and Authority in Afro-American Narrative*. Cambridge: Harvard UP, 1987. 9–43.

——. " 'Loopholes of Retreat': Architecture and Ideology in Harriet Jacobs's *Incidents in the Life of a Slave Girl*." *Reading Black, Reading Feminist: A Critical Anthology*. Ed. Henry Louis Gates, Jr. New York: Meridian, 1990. 212–26.

• Spelman, Elizabeth V. *Fruits of Sorrow: Framing Our Attention to Suffering*. Boston: Beacon Press, 1997.

• Taves, Ann. "Spiritual Purity and Sexual Shame: Religious Themes in the Writings of Harriet Jacobs." *Church History* (March 1987): 59–72.

Vermillion, Mary. "Reembodying the Self: Representations of Rape in *Incidents in the Life of a Slave Girl* and *I Know Why the Caged Bird Sings*." *Biography* 15.3 (summer 1992): 243–60.

Warhol, Robyn R. " 'Reader, Can You Imagine? No, You Cannot': The Narratee as Other in Harriet Jacobs's Text." *Narrative* 3.1 (1995): 57–72.

Warner, Anne Bradford. "Harriet Jacobs's Modest Proposals: Revising Southern Hospitality." *Southern Quarterly: A Journal of the Arts in the South* 30.2–3 (winter–spring 1992): 22–28.

——. "Santa Claus Ain't a Real Man: Incidents and Gender." *Haunted Bodies: Gender and Southern Text*. Ed. Anne Goodwyn Jones and Susan V. Donaldson. Charlottesville: UP of Virginia, 1997. 185–200.

Yellin, Jean Fagan. "*Incidents* in the Life of Harriet Jacobs." *The Seductions of Biography*. Ed. Mary Rhiel and David Suchoff. New York: Routledge, 1996. 137–47.

——. "Texts and Contexts of Harriet Jacobs' *Incidents in the Life of a Slave Girl*." *The Slave's Narrative*. Ed. Charles T. Davis and Henry Louis Gates, Jr. New York: Oxford UP, 1985. 262–82.

• ——. "Written by Herself: Harriet Jacobs' Slave Narrative." *American Literature* 53.3 (November 1981): 379–486.